The Priestess and the Magus
Book Two: We the People

by the same author

BOOKS
Fiction

The Lineage of the Codes of Light

The Brotherhood of the Magi

The Priestess and the Magus
Book One: The Gift

Non-Fiction

Awakening and Healing the Rainbow Body

Awakening and Healing the Rainbow Body
Companion Guide to Self-Mastery

AUDIO

Deep Trance Shamanic Journeys

Volume One: Pachamama's Child

Volume Two: Right Relationships

Volume Three: Reclaiming Power

The Priestess and the Magus
Book Two: We the People

Jessie Ayani

Heart of the Sun
2013

First Edition 2013
Ayani, Jessie E.
The Priestess and the Magus, Book Two: We the People/ Jessie E. Ayani – 1st Heart of the Sun Edition
ISBN# 978-0-9648763-9-2

Cover Art:
"Beloved" – by Autumn Skye Morrison
www.autumnskyemorrison.com

Cover Design:
Silverlining Designs, Leanne Zinkand
www.silverlining-designs.com

Published by
Heart of the Sun
www.heartofthesun.com
info@heartofthesun.com

Dedicated to

We the People

In Gratitude ...

In the middle of this trilogy ... an unexpected twist.

I wish to thank Leah, my intrepid heroine, whose passion to know and understand the truth has led to 'our' bold but thoughtful interpretation of the referenced spiritual-scientific, clairvoyant work of Rudolf Steiner. In doing this, 'we' feel the consequent probability of error (of shallow comprehension) is offset by Steiner's wish that we take his gifts of wisdom and truth into our souls, make them our own, and direct our expression of them toward humanity's future. I, personally, hope that their inclusion in this story makes his legacy a bit more accessible. At whatever depth we understand his spoken and written work, we can be assured that it springs from the good and true.

Dr. Steiner's lifelong dedication to the development of his own clairvoyance, and its application to scientifically researching spirituality, has provided us with a written legacy (his books and transcribed lectures) of profound wisdom and truth. It must be said that he is difficult to read. That, I feel, is because he speaks to our souls. He challenges us not 'to be', but 'to become' – to evolve. It is in that self-evolution, that we find our soul's fulfillment, as well as our own opportunity for selfless service to humanity. I stand in awe of his.

jea
Mount Shasta, CA
July 2013

contents

"I remembered the Pearl,
for which I was sent down to Egypt.
And I began to charm him,
the terrible loud-breathing serpent."

... The Acts of Thomas*

[* From the Hymn of the Pearl
Translated in GRS Mead's Fragments of a Faith Forgotten]

part one: raising the bar

chapter 1: samhain

Leah lay on the well-trod path through the *Lacy Phacelia*, anticipating dawn. There had been a hard freeze during the wee hours of this first day of November 2011, and she wanted to be there when the frozen plants finally bowed to the sun's warmth. The bees favored these flowers above all others. Though they would be out of their hives on warm days looking for water, the bees would be without nectar until the spring blossoms of willow and dandelion appeared. They would otherwise remain in torpid clusters, slowly eating their honey stores and caring for their queens. Leah, her community, and the bees were at important turning points in the seasons of life.

While face up on that path to the apiary, surrounded by the tardy hand of winter, Leah recapitulated the impossibly rich passages of the previous four days. On Friday, the *New Avalon* Community had hosted a visit from Ali Cat and his rapper friends who'd brought with them a lot of enjoyment for the community, and funding to launch the first Restorative Justice Project. There were plenty of hurdles yet standing in its way, but funding wasn't going to be one of them. *Praise Be.*

The highlight of Saturday had been the passing over of her dear friend and neighbor, Henry Brenner. He'd asked Leah to lead him through the initial stages of his after-death journey. It had been an honor and a privilege to gift him in that way. Mr. Brenner had been amazingly generous with the community, having gifted his farm for their second village the week before his passage. She'd become the new mistress of his deceased wife's magnificent horse, Holly-Go-Lightly, as well as the bewildered recipient of a Remington UMC .44 caliber rifle, crafted with beautiful cherry wood. The men in the community, especially her husband, Chris, were smitten with the collector's firearm, placing its value in the thousands of dollars. She admitted a real attraction to the look and feel of the cherry wood.

Everything about the story of Mr. Brenner was directly connected to a part of her personality, named Alice, who had engaged service to the nature spirits, the little group of girls in the homeschool, and Holly, trying to find her pathway to higher consciousness. She'd found that portal through facilitating Mr. Brenner's passage but Alice's ascension step wasn't fully integrated until the next day, whilst meditating on a rise overlooking the peaceful valley that embraced *New Avalon*, their ever-expanding community. A prolonged grooming of Holly-Go-Lightly had sealed the deal. Alice found herself in the higher consciousness of Leah's soul, where she would learn how to use the resources available through higher self. Amongst those gifts would be those that had accompanied Alice's stream of personality in this life. After Alice's arrival in consciousness soul, the only part of Leah's personality remaining bound to the cultural mind received both a gift and a blow.

The gift given to Dragon Lady had been the removal of a patriarchal implant by Demetri Malkodina, a wild Greek–Cypriot of the Order of the Ruby, whom she knew and trusted. The blow had come in the form of 30 lashing welts across her back in vivid, visceral memory of the day the implant entered her astral body during a life 200 years previous to the present one. Though greatly diminished from their initially inflamed state, she could feel those welts, at that moment, making contact with the frosted path through the *Lacy Phacelia*. The visceral memory of the lashing had put a damper on the celebration of the implant's release — an understatement. Chris had cared for her with great kindness and compassion. They both thought it odd that the actual experience had bled through to this time and place.

There was still much to be sorted out about Sunday. It colored Monday in many unexpected hues. Monday, just yesterday, had been *Samhain*, the celebration of final harvest and an honoring of the ancestors — the traditional day of the dead. Leah had proposed the day's festivities well ahead of her time-travel lashing, and rose to the occasion in spite of lingering pain and a very unattractive back. Chris had applied healing ointment and she'd protected the greatly reduced welts with a winter–weight singlet.

The festivities began with the preparation of harvest gift baskets for their close friends outside the community. The rest of the community's women had come together in the morning to do this while Leah put time in at the studio towards that week's *Light in the Crisis* show. It had been blessedly quiet at the studio giving her a good jump on a show topic she was passionately invested in — the homeless. She'd looked over the baskets in the back of Will's truck — ready to be delivered to their friend's homes and farms. They were filled with love, produce and farm products for the winter. Will and Sonia had volunteered to drop off the surprise, back-at-you, trick-or-treat gifts, and they'd stopped on the way home, in Yreka, to purchase a bottle of eucalyptus oil for the initiation of the sauna, a welcomed new feature within the village.

On Monday afternoon, the festivities began in two locations. Most of the women, with Demetri, who loved to cook, were at the warehouse kitchen, preparing the feast planned by Shelley and Jenny. The men spent the morning finishing the sauna, giving pony rides to the children, and building the big fire, for the evening, in a clearing where the farm road met the commons. Georgia supervised games and apple bobs for the children and everyone managed to find time to prepare offerings for the fire to honor their ancestors.

Leah assembled two offerings. One, for her mother, was made joyfully, whilst recounting their beautiful friendship in life. However, it also held a request for forgiveness on behalf of her formerly miscreant subpersonality, the Bee Mistress, who'd caused her mother pain. The Bee Mistress was now anchored in consciousness soul, where she was celebrating the arrival of Alice.

Her second offering had been meant to fire the transformation of Dragon Lady by honoring one of her past lives, as a slave, during which she'd picked up the baggage of the 30 lashes and the patriarchal implant. The intent built into the offering included reconciliation with the slaveholder, whom she greatly admired as an historical figure and wished to work with clairvoyantly. Dragon Lady had everything to gain with an ascent of consciousness to soul awareness, and nothing to lose — except a boatload of opinions and judgments about the dreadful state of affairs in the world at present, along with an overly-romantic picture of America's founding era.

Their dinner had been magnificent. That night, community members faced more gourmet choices than any of them could remember. Leah opted for Tilapia *ceviche* from their fish farm, butternut squash soup with sage, lemongrass chicken and a bit of lamb shoulder Greek-style, kale salad, snap–peas, broiled tomatoes and garlic mash potatoes. She'd limited herself to a third of the menu choices and very small portions at that, leaving just enough room for Spence's famous carrot cake. There were no leftovers, making clean up an easy task for the men. When the fire was blazing, and with more giggles than chills, Chris and Nick had told scary stories to the children before they went off to bed. Those two brew-masters had also come up with a first rate beer for the event and would make it their standard recipe owing to the enthusiastic reaction of the *New Avalon* Rangers.

The older boys, Rob, Mike and Alex, their Chilean WWOOFer, had taken the children home to bed, sitting with them while their parents entered the space of ritual at the fire. Tommy had slipped off before the storytelling to build and begin stoking the inaugural fire in the sauna wood stove. By the time the men gathered to initiate the new sauna it was deemed 'bloody hot' by the lot of them. Nick had been asked to lead them through a Native American sweat lodge ritual. Each of four rounds of sweating, with offerings of specific herbs burned on the stove as gifts, had been followed by four dips in the ice-cold river. Tommy had designed and built the sauna to accommodate steam or dry heat. The men decided to splash eucalyptus water on the top of the stove to turn it into a steam bath, while they drank a tea of wild Bergamot.

While the men had their sauna, the women drummed and danced around the bonfire, in the middle of the farm road running between the two guesthouses. Beautiful offerings had been made by all of the women from the dried plants, seedpods, cedar fronds and other gifts of the land. Accompanied by the loud 'pops' of bursting seedpods, sparks rose heavenward with every addition to the fire, sending the intent to all of their mothers, living and dead. Leah had come last to the fire. After consciously connecting with the intent of her mother's gift she'd placed it gently in the fire, her arms engulfed in flames. The fire was friendly. She felt no heat.

After gifting the offering on behalf of her Dragon Lady subpersonality to the fire, she removed her heavy cardigan and stood before the fire in the black dress that had been Dragon Lady's uniform for every single *Light on the Crisis* show until fairly recently — always with a string of pearls. With the serendipitous background yelps of the men plunging into the river, she shocked her sisters by pulling the dress over her head to gently offer it to the fire. Natalie, Georgia and Leslie screamed in unison, and began slapping each other, laughing, because they'd all hated the dress — or, more precisely, the idea of a 'uniform'. They helped her put her sweater on over her singlet and panties, and fetched a blanket from the nearby lawn to wrap her up. The women built up the fire for the men before saying goodnight to Katia, whose doctor, Leah, had advised her to avoid saunas and hot tubs during her pregnancy.

Georgia had led the sweat lodge ritual for the women after they and the men had switched bonfire for sauna. Though retaining her singlet until she was in the sauna, Leah joined the women in stripping and clambering into the 'bloody hot' sauna amidst the linger scent of male sweat. They added their own sweat to it, completing the sauna initiation with the complement of differences. After three rounds of sweating and river plunges, they'd hunkered down for the last round feeling more than a little out-of-body.

Leah had taken a position in the back corner of the sauna, resting her shoulders against the two sides to protect the welts on her back. As she lay in the *Lacy Phacelia*, she remembered having drifted off into meditation when the women had started sharing about the astounding changes in their sexual life with their men. That had pulled her right back into the sauna to pay closer attention. Age seemed not to be a factor in this upgrade of pleasure. They were all smitten with a new consciousness that honored woman and respected their needs, including sharing housework on a more equal basis. Leah remembered slamming her hand over her mouth to suppress the giggles. They'd gone on to talk about kundalini, opening the chakra gates, their men's attempts and successes at withholding their orgasms, and the miraculous generation of their own as a result. It seemed that the men were capable of directing their kundalini in such a way that it became mutual. Wow! Mind you, it was experimental at this stage, but very exciting.

Leah had felt privileged with invisibility, whilst holding space in the corner … *so precious*. It had taken until the fourth round to open the floodgates of the spirited discussion in the sauna that night but it wouldn't stop there. Leah vowed to take them into circle once again. They were all ready to engage the next level of consciousness. And what perfect timing as the whole community was on the verge of stepping out in service to humanity. As they'd walked home together, Natalie asked her why she was so quiet during the discussion. Her best friend had noticed. Of course, it was her horse-whispering magus of a cowboy, Chris, who was leading the New Avalon Rangers into the euphoric land of cosmic love. She'd come away with a much better understanding of the sudden need for bi-weekly meetings of the Rangers and had discreetly saved her giggles for the shower.

But the giggles persisted — every time she thought about it. Right there, in the Lacy Phacelia, she burst into joyous laughter again. And then the sun rose over the crest of the eastern ridge to strike her face, as well as the sturdy native flowers that had fed the bees, through succession seedings, for an entire summer and fall. Their heavy fronds of purple blossoms, mostly spent and heavy with seed, slowly bowed to the sun. As the sun rose higher in the sky, the entire mass of phacelia, on both sides of the path, collapsed on their hollow stems. They would self-seed the new life of springtime but, for now, it was time for them to imprint themselves within the soil of the earth to guide the germination and growth of the seeds they would so generously scatter. Leah was flat-out in awe of Lacy Phacelia.

She arrived back at the house in time for a late breakfast with Chris. He'd been out until midnight the night before, with Tommy and Will, making sure the fire was out, and she'd been up early to do yoga before her visit to the Lacy Phacelia. They actually hadn't caught up with each other since the feast at the community center before the bonfire. He was cooking scrambled eggs and baby sausages with a side of French toast — the latter his excuse to use maple syrup on the lot. Having grown up in the presence of abundant maple syrup, Leah didn't need an excuse to pour it on.

"Aye, lass. Where've you been? Off with the bees?" he asked, coming to give her a cuddle while being careful of her back.

"We finally had a freeze last night, cowboy. I'd a strong impulse to witness the finale of the Lacy Phacelia. It was awesome. How'd the sauna and fire go for you blokes ... if I might ask?"

He sped back to the fry pan and dished up breakfast to plates set out on the counter. "It was all good, lass. The sauna's a powerful experience, especially when the Indian rituals are applied — a good bonding for us. How about the women?"

"Profound," she replied, dreamily, sitting at the table. He served her breakfast with a fresh pot of tea. "Dragon Lady got a butt kick from the rest of me, my mother got all she deserved, and the sauna was a real revelation."

"How so?" he asked, pouring a nice puddle of syrup in the center of his French toast.

"My sisters are reaping the benefits of their husband's 'joy of sex' lessons; I presume at the bi-weekly meetings of the Rangers?" she giggled, whilst raising her brows in question.

"You reckon?" he grinned.

"It's all good, cowboy. You're talents are endless ... or so it would seem."

"Aye, a man shouldn't *have* a wife if he doesn't recognize the divine and honor the divine within her. That's my philosophy. We've beautiful women in this community, every one of them worth our best efforts to raise the bar," he stated, whilst dragging a sausage slowly through the syrup puddle.

"Hmmm, I agree. I can't wait until you fellows sit in circle with the homeless men. I reckon you'll start a revolution. As long as the patriarchs are transitioning to co-creation, they might as well transform the controlling of others into the controlling of their own kundalini. And, how fitting that the epicenter of that revolution is smack dab in the middle of the reddest district in Northern California. I'd be willing to do a show on it when you men are ready."

He gave up pretending to be serious and grabbed her ticklish knees under the table. "Truce, Dragon Lady?" he pleaded. Leah jumped up from the table laughing to get away from him. "How's your back, lass? I'm ready to bungee jump when you are," he grinned.

She sat back down to finish breakfast. "Pretty good. I'd love for you to look at it before I get ready for the studio. I can sense it but it's not getting me down. I've got Paula starting today so nothing could get me down."

"I forgot about that. How many staffers are coming on board this morning?"

"Besides Paula, we've Jennifer Lane starting in the lobby to become Leslie's right hand gal, and Matt Duffy will be the first to join Stu's film crew. He's our new web master but can also sub as a cameraman and is really keen to learn the computer programs for filmmaking along with Rob. He'll be busy. I'll need to stick with Paula the first day to lead her through the routine. There's a great new progressive website up for getting money out of politics and lobbyists out of Washington. I want her to add that to the news review ritual. The good news is; we've the newsroom set up so she can stay in the studio to work. You can join me for Joel's show there."

"Is her partner going to help Tommy out?" he asked.

"That was the plan but Will is under so much pressure right now, I think Sam will have to, at least, split his time between Tommy and Will. Tommy has a lot of local labor to choose from and Will hasn't. So, we're having a big day at the studio today. What's on your plate, cowboy?"

"I've got a bit to do on the musical, so about half the day I'll be in the community center at the piano, then lunch with my sweet lass, followed by afternoon in the stable. Thunder needs to start higher education and Mike is coming over to work with Lucy. I'll take a ride down to Mr. Brenner's to check fences and make sure the animals are fed and watered."

"Good idea. What's Demetri up to?" she asked.

"He's messing around in the fish farm halftime these days. I find that an odd fascination for him, though the *ceviche* was bloody brilliant. He's otherwise helping Greg here and over on the *Harmony Valley* land."

Leah rose, picking up the dishes to wash them, but Chris stopped her. "I can do that, lass. Let's take care of your back instead. I'm in no rush to leave this morning but you do need to show up early."

She felt Dragon Lady's urge to protest, thought better of it, and sank into his lap for a little cuddle. "Thank you, darling, for breakfast, for the cleanup, and for filling my life with joy. I so appreciate you. I have to keep pinching myself to make sure I haven't dreamed you into my life again."

He gave her a remarkably flavorful maple syrup kiss then they promised themselves a quiet evening together. It had been nonstop for four days, and now it was time to slow the pace and refresh the spirit. Cosmic love, bungee jumping style, was an option on the table.

Chris had a look at her back when she dressed for work and applied a very light coat of pawpaw ointment to several of the welts. The rest of them were fading away. Leah found a clean, winter-weight singlet in her drawer to keep the ointment off her clothes, and opted for a loose sweater and pants to assure a comfortable day. She asked Chris to fill out the warehouse order (*New Avalon*-style grocery shopping) and get it into Jenny before noon. Then she picked up a few files from the counter, kissed him goodbye, and walked around the commons and up the hill to the studio, which was part of the *New Avalon* courtyard complex.

Leah was at her desk, mapping out her strategy for the Saturday show when Natalie breezed by her door on the way to her office, which was kitty-corner across the hall. Natalie's Bichon, Harry, trotted along behind her. He came right in to jump up in Leah's lap for their routine morning cuddle. Natalie hung up her jacket and came across the hall to have a chat. She liked to pull a chair up along side of Leah's desk to engage her best buddy.

"Hey, girlfriend," Natalie began, with a smile, "I was sure proud of you at the fire last night," — a reference to the dress-burning ritual.

"One small step for Dragon Lady, Nat. It was a wonderful day, from start to finish. I don't think I'd time to tell you that Joel and I had our Skype session, a good one, and that it ended with a discussion of his wife's interest in starting a community in the Virginia foothills as well as a homeless community in DC or Baltimore. Kim and her friends are already looking at purchasing land and want to start the work with you soon."

"Fabulous. Wow! How good would that be to get the word out on the east coast?"

"I reckon. I invited Joel and his family to visit soon. We'll see what they come up with for a date. Meanwhile, what a nice way for you and Chuck to have a little extra time together, eh?"

"Well, yes. That would be a bonus, wouldn't it? I wonder if things would be different for us on his work turf?" she pondered. "Geez, listen to me? That can be worried about later — or not at all."

"Good idea. It's best if we give in to the divine plan," Leah suggested.

"Speaking of which … what is going on in those bloke meetings? Chuck just went to the last one and was keen to try some new ideas in bed. The charmed newness of relationship hasn't faded yet but, goodness me, it was nice upgrade."

Leah laughed, heartily. "Chris is on mission. I have no details for you and don't want them, but suffice to say, he knows what he's doing."

"I have to admit that you've positively bloomed since he arrived back on the scene, girlfriend. So, I believe you, — no questions asked," she giggled.

I do have one question for you, Nat. I don't want to overstep your work at facilitating the rainbow body work but I sat in the corner of the sauna last night wondering what we women could do to better receive what our men are learning to give us."

"That's not my territory at all, doll, so go ahead. I'm rapt to hear your thoughts."

"Well I didn't come up with anything until I was laying in the *Lacy Phacelia* this morning witnessing their surrender to the hard freeze. As you know, I've a connection to our sisterhood and the brotherhood in lifetimes past but what's really coming to the fore here is a connection to a profound lineage of powerful bee mistresses. What would you think of the community women meeting twice a month, instead of once, for our fun in the kitchen, candle-making, craft and all of that, but at the same time in a circle committed to even higher consciousness?"

"I would adore it, likely all of us would. We don't have to keep bees, do we?" she asked, looking a little worried.

"Not at all. Historically, the Order has, but the passion here is for selfless service to the community and humanity — what we're intending to do as a matter of course in *New Avalon*. This way, we'll be organized and actively engaging the higher work in sisterhood. It feels the right time for us."

"We've a night coming up. Why not propose it then? I, for one, will appreciate it. It's easy to put the spiritual work aside to get the work in the world done, but then they're really one big picture."

"Exactly. As for the bees, I'm happy to tend them myself, as maintenance is periodic and not difficult. I'll find the next bee mistress from our community of young girls, I reckon, and that will be growing with *New Avalon II*."

"What are the women in this sisterhood of the bees called, historically?" Natalie asked.

"The Melissae," Leah responded. "The Bee Mistress and the Melissae. She was in service to them and they in service to community. In those days I think it was a fulltime job being the Bee Mistress. Nowadays, it'll have to be multi-tasking," she laughed. "We're all in service to mission."

"It sounds sweet and soulful. And, really, we're already doing it."

"Good. I'll mention it when we get together. Are you ready for the Outreach board meeting this afternoon?" she asked.

"It'll be nothing like last time, but I've a few things to prepare. We're going to propose my assistant job and another tech staffer for Stu — one who already knows the film manufacturing process. Have you worked up the apprenticeship program yet?"

"I started but need to dedicate my afternoon to it. I'll get Paula settled in first. She can get to know everyone today, get organized in her office and the newsroom, then tackle the evening news at the end of the day."

"Is there anything else for the board?" she asked.

"Of course. We need to have a preliminary discussion about our second community on Mr. Brenner's farmland, whether Will needs more staff besides Sam, what to do about Tommy, and the prison program."

"Full plate is becoming the norm," Natalie laughed. "What about Tommy?"

"He's basically running a multi-project architectural and engineering business out of his woodworking shop, their kitchen table, and, I'd imagine, his truck. I think it's time to talk realistically about a proper office, properly staffed."

"I *guess*. How does he do it?"

"He's the most tolerant, easy going man I've ever met, and I thought Chris was top dog in that department – no offense Harry," she added with a kiss to the top of his head. "Chris asks for what he needs. Tommy waits for the divine plan to give it to him. I admire his humility but also need to act on behalf of the divine plan here since he won't. Will's over there in the credit union buried in donations, contracts, land transfers and big money. He's too competent to ask for help so we need to step in there as well, before these two fellows lose the fun and joy in their work."

"This should be interesting since they're both on the board."

"It will be. We'll approach it with humor," she laughed. "They'll be fine as long as someone else has seen the need and proposed it."

Just then, Paula appeared in the doorway — live and in person. She was even more impressive than Skype was able to convey.

"Welcome Paula!" they sang out in unison, standing up to give her a hug.

"Thank you, Leah. I recognize you from the show. And are you Natalie, the producer?" she asked Natalie.

"Yes, I am. It's a pleasure to welcome you on board, Paula."

Paula was excited to be there but professional in every way. "I can see why you wouldn't want to be in the city. This place is gorgeous. I love the setting at The Lodge. We were hiking and fishing already yesterday," she exclaimed. "We met Jen and Matt yesterday too, when they moved in."

"We're glad you like The Lodge and the surroundings," Leah said, speaking for the community. "Maybe you, Sam, Jen and Matt could take a walking tour of the community with Leslie this afternoon while we're in a meeting. I think you'll be surprised at what's here. I do want to meet Sam today, too, when it works out."

"Me too," Natalie added. "Right now, I'll leave you two to sort out Paula's day and make some calls for the Saturday show. I'll see you often, Paula. It's nice to have you here," she said, returning to her office with Harry trailing behind.

"Thanks, Natalie," she smiled, watching Harry trot out of the room.

"And that's Harry, Paula. He spends most of his day here, but often meanders over to the stable looking for my husband, Chris."

"You have horses! Oh my God, I so miss my horses," she said, on the verge of tears.

"I reckon Chris can fix you up with a horse, darling. You just need to ask when you want to go out and take care of tack and grooming."

No problem there. I know the ropes. I did a lot of riding in Montana. Now, how do I begin?"

Paula was a beautiful young woman and a good match for the studio staff and community. Leah was pleased with her choice and so ready for her help.

Leah and Paula stepped out of her office to have a quick tour of the studio. They found Leslie in the front lobby, just arriving from homeschool drop-off, and Jennifer who would begin taking over Leslie's reception/secretarial duties, including reviewing the comments on twitter, facebook and email about the show and/or Outreach. Leah introduced Paula and met Jennifer, another bright, energetic millennial who had moved in next door to Paula and Sam at the staff quarters in The Lodge Annex.

They had a chat about the usual Monday morning review of the show, which would now include Paula and Jen in addition to Leah, Natalie, and Leslie. The Monday meeting would take place after Paula was done with her news review at nine o'clock. Stu, Leslie's partner, who was putting the tech side of the studio together and running it all, would often join them. A regular full-staff meeting was being planned and would include the entire staff and Will Martin, the community banker/attorney, who presented a brief financial review on the show.

The four women embarked on the studio tour walking down the hallway where Leah and Natalie had their offices. On the right side of the hall, beyond Natalie's office, in what was formerly a storeroom, there was now an office for Paula and Natalie's future assistant to share. Each desk had a new slim laptop sitting on it and all necessary office furnishings and supplies were stocked. Pleased with the arrangement, Paula dropped her backpack on a chair and they continued down the hall.

The next room on the right was the new newsroom, formerly Stu's office. Now there was a bank of four large computer screens with pull out keyboards down one long wall. Each station had a pullout side worktable and a decent ergonomic chair. The lighting was LED spots aimed at workstations, tables and equipment. There was also a reference library, a large worktable, and a wall of low storage and file cabinets with a beautiful framed collection of Tommy's four perspective drawings of *Harmony Valley* on the wall above. On top of the cabinets were the printer–scanner–fax machine, and a mobile phone charging station. The hard drives, wireless broadband router, and battery back up systems were above the computers on a sturdy shelf to avoid heat buildup under the stations. Each computer was equipped with high quality speakers, noise canceling headphones and a Skype video camera and microphone. The room had a good exhaust fan and a cooling system. If Paula needed anything else, she was to fill out a requisition and give it to Stu.

After pointing out a short hall across the way with the restrooms, they went on to the makeup room on the left side of the hall. Then they met up with Stu, Rob and Matt in the new addition, the door to which was the last on the left of the long hallway just past the makeup room and before the studio doors.

In the new addition, there were more introductions and sharing, then Stu gave them all a tour of the fledgling film department. Leah's head was swimming with technical terms, specs, and astounding capabilities by the time they left Stu and company to look at the Studio and the soundproof 'green room' for waiting guests. There was an entrance to the studio control room from the 'film department', where they were shown the new equipment for controlling an upgraded lighting system, including remote color and lens control, and angle adjustments made from the control room. There were now state of the art cameras on dollies and tripods and two shoulder cameras.

The set had been redesigned for group discussion and the backdrop had been reworked in aqua, blue and blue-violet colors with the show marquis in luminous eggshell white. There were built-in video screens for transmissions via Skype, broadband or graphic presentations. They could be automatically covered with colored panels when not in use. Stu had spent the better part of a week submerged in the learning curve that accompanied all he'd materialization for the studio. He'd shown up at the *Samhain* feast looking pleased, but exhausted.

The tour moved onto the 'green room', where guests or presenters could hang out before being called to their positions on the set. This soundproof room had been redone with light pink interior walls to soften the effect of the rammed earth exterior wall, and with the addition of amenities, comfy leather sofas, and a screen for viewing the show. On the walls, Stu had begun creating a Rogue's Gallery of some of their most beloved guests.

Light on the Crisis had just produced their first 90-minute show, which Paula had missed whilst driving two-plus days up from Austin to *New Avalon*. She would give it a good look on YouTube today when time permitted. They exited the studio through windowed double doors and entered the main hall to the lobby. Above the soundproof doors was an 'On the Air' light, like the one in the studio above the control room window and in the 'green room', to warn people that a show was in session. However the doors would be locked from the inside to prevent entry when they were on the air, transmitting video, or taping.

Leah and Paula went into the newsroom to boot up a computer. She'd made Paula a list of the news programs she typically scanned as videos, including conservative news, network news and CNN, along with NPR's Morning Edition and All Things Considered audio or article transcripts. She'd a second list of Internet news websites that she favored, including the newest one, *unitedrepublic.org*. Paula could add others but needed to let Leah check them out for truthful reporting.

Leah let her know that she would come in and check out some of her summarized news herself, especially if it was breaking news or of great interest to her. She also suggested that Paula watch *Joel Robertson Live*, either with she and Chris, at home, or on YouTube the next morning to keep up with him. She explained their collaboration, which was obvious to Paula, who had seen the last show whilst still in Texas. She let her know their filming schedule with Joel and that she would be locked up in her office Skyping with him three times a week for an hour. Their collaboration was having a profound affect on their viewer numbers and non-profit donations. Paula was happy with the arrangement. His show was positioned at the top of her list, so no worries there.

Leah left her to the news review, expecting that she would do a great job. She'd plenty of experience doing the same in Austin and she'd been watching *Light on the Crisis* since shortly after its inception. Returning to her office, she sat quietly, trying to integrate the extent of the studio upgrade and 'film department', as the tour content had been a bit staggering. Stu had done a fantastic job with all of it and needed to be honored for his work. She would pay attention to guidance for that and expected he would sum up the whole transition at the board meeting to clear her head of details. Her live interview for Joel's show on Thursday would be the maiden voyage for the studio upgrade but she was sure Stu would run plenty of equipment tests with Rob and Matt ahead of it.

She checked her phone to find a text from Willow Pearce, her and Joel's Occupy Wall Street (OWS) girl-on-the-ground. She was letting Leah and Joel know that she'd submitted an accounting of her October expenses by email. When Leah finally got around to checking emails, it was there, along with one from Joel suggesting that he and his family spend Thanksgiving at *New Avalon*. The beauty of it, for him, was that he typically shut his studio down for the long holiday weekend. He would have his favorite sub sit in for him on the Wednesday before and Monday after the holiday weekend. This visit was genuinely important to Kim, and he was keen to meet everyone in person.

"Yes!" she squealed, loud enough to motivate Natalie to come knocking on her door. "Come on in, Nat," she urged, but, as soon as Natalie opened the door, Leah asked her to turn around and get the guestroom and lodge reservation books first. While Natalie was doing that, Leah looked at her show schedule for Thanksgiving Saturday. They planned to do a live show, the theme of which was 'single-payer health care'.

Natalie returned with the guest books and pulled up her chair. Harry had crashed over in her office. "What's up, sister? You sound excited."

"Joel and family want to come for Thanksgiving. Do we have space for them?" she asked.

Natalie looked over the roster. "Well, we have Sonia's parents and her daughter who wanted to be in The Lodge. Will's folks are coming too, so they'll be having a big family weekend at The Lodge. Ellia's son and his family are coming into the guesthouse on our side of the commons. Shelley's mother, sister and niece are reserved in The Lodge, along with the sister's boyfriend. That's it. We'll be booked up at Christmas but Thanksgiving has family space in the East Commons guesthouse."

"How about the show guests? How far along are you nailing them down?" Leah asked.

"We have Christina, of course. Then I have asked Michelle Markum to return for that one since she's very invested in the health care system. Chuck will be here and would love to get in on the discussion. That's it so far. We're still looking for a progressive health care administrator. Do you think Joel would take a seat at the table?" she asked.

"I'll make him," Leah laughed. "He would be great *and* we could forgo his 15-minute interview and make the discussion an hour in length. I would like to have someone in hospital administration. Michelle and I can give the doctor perspective. See you who can rustle up – a progressive hospital CEO, perhaps?"

"Seriously? That sounds like an oxymoron, " she mumbled. "Okay, we'll start asking around. So do you want me to book Joel and his family into the guesthouse and put Michelle over at The Lodge?"

"Good idea – along with the CEO. Thanks, Nat. I'll answer his email and ask what his kids are interested in, their ages and all that. Kim will want to pick your brain and we should give her a lot of space to see how community works. It'd be fun to tape a couple of interviews with Joel in person for coming shows while he's here, so I'll get to work on our topics. What a great opportunity for them and for our community," she exclaimed excitedly.

"You two certainly have something special going on," Natalie said. "Have you any idea what that's all about? Is it past life? Or some connection with the brotherhood?" she asked.

""We do. I think it will include Chris as well. He feels quite an affinity with Joel. It's interesting that Demetri is here now, too. But I can't get a fix on it over Skype other than the obvious 'wavelength' resonance. He may be brotherhood. For sure we're soul-contracted from past lives and the present. I've a feeling the sisterhood will be kindled in Kim, if it isn't already. Don't you feel the stirrings of an uprising there?" she asked.

"I do," Natalie replied. "In fact, it occurs to me that all these solutions we're putting out there will become foci for the unification of the sisterhood and brotherhood. We're all looking to serve, especially in currencies of love and gift. It's a gratifying way to look at this mission, sister. We're serving the servers as well as those who need the service."

"That's a brilliant observation, Nat. Why don't you speak about that at the community meeting next week?"

""I'll give that some thought. Meanwhile, I'll let you email Joel and get on the homeless discussion for Saturday," she smiled, setting her chair back against the wall.

"I've a good leg already, I just need to prepare some things for the Outreach board this afternoon and integrate Paula's analysis into my news summary."

Leah focused on the board meeting. She had a few hours before lunch to get her proposals in order. The rest of the day was booked. She wanted to discuss Mr. Brenner's gift of his farm and how to proceed with their second village. It was as urgent as all the other projects budding from Outreach, since the existing community could not be tapped for teaching and training position with Outreach whilst shouldering all of the food production and other specializations at *New Avalon*. Not wishing to create a breaking point for Will or Tommy, she would engage them in solutions to this dilemma and ask them to help reframe it for the community the following week. They made decision by consensus. For Outreach that meant the board began the process and the community finished it.

Natalie would ask to hire an assistant as her area of expertise was being stretched as well. Then Leah would bring up a preliminary review of the Restorative Justice model for which they had start-up funding and the land, but needed state participation. California's Assembly was in recess until early December but she thought, possibly, that Senator Buxley (Chuck) could run the model by the governor during a winter senate recess. He and the governor were close political allies and friends. Then there was the apprenticeship program, which was where she applied herself to the keyboard of her laptop for a good 90 minutes, allowing the fullness of the idea to flow out of her into print. She made copies for herself and Natalie, asking her to take a critical look at it before the meeting while Leah, or, rather, Alice, was reading stories to the children at their Waldorf homeschool.

She found Paula working at news analysis, making notes into her staff laptop, which was positioned on the computer desk's pullout shelf. She'd spent a fair amount of time book-marking sites as she'd scanned the news and had a thorough read of *unitedrepublic.org*, since it was a new website. Paula would be back at it for the evening news at four o'clock and somehow work in the tour of *New Avalon*.

Leah left at noon, taking the apprenticeship proposal home with her but stopping first at the clinic to chat with Nick to see if everyone was okay. Her skills as a family practice physician were rarely called up in the community but she checked in with him regularly, regardless. Nick handled the alternative medical modalities. They were a good team though Nick was about her son's age. He was making notes behind the entry desk when she walked in.

"Hey Nick. Are we all still healthy?" she asked.

He sighed. "Our little Billy has a goose-egg on his head but he's on the mend already. I'll take him out riding with me this afternoon. That should fix him up nicely," he laughed.

"If he can stay on the horse," she offered. "I've seen you ride, Nick. You don't mess around on a horse."

"We'll take it easy. That's how I learned. I was stuffed between my uncle's legs and told to hang onto the mane — all bareback, Indian-style," he laughed. "It worked."

"It sure did. I've never seen anyone as comfortable on a horse as you are."

"Thanks, doc. Are you reading to the kids today?"

"Of course. It's the fastest, most absorbing, hour of my week. I wouldn't miss it for the world. What've we got planned for a follow-up with Demetri?"

"He's due in here at the end of the week for a check up. Just keep Friday noon open, after you rehearse the show. Alice Wilson called just to let you know she figured the hard freeze did in the bee venom therapy 'til spring."

"That's correct. We'd talked about that very high probability at soccer on Sunday."

24

"Yesterday was really nice, Leah. Thanks for that," Nick said, sincerely.

"You can thank my mother, Nick," she smiled. "She inspired the idea of the fire and offering. We were really lucky you fellows finished the community sauna in time, and the gifting, well, that's natural for us."

"I know all that. We all know that and we all know that things like that happened because you put it out there. So, thanks," he repeated with finality.

Leah laughed. "Okay, Nick. You're most welcome."

She kissed him on the cheek, told him she'd see him at the board meeting, and then took off for home to have lunch with her cowboy. She stopped in the community center to see if he'd finished his work on the piano and found him playing Mozart. *Good grief! What doesn't this man know how to do – perfectly,* she thought. She sat quietly, listening but also feeling the music move through her as balm to her soul. It turned her so deeply within that she found herself, back in time, in Thomas Jefferson's parlor hearing the same piece played on the harpsichord by his dear friend, Dolley Madison. She and John Madison had been the most frequent guests at Monticello, and Mozart, who would have been a contemporary of these guests, had he lived past 35 years, was a consistent favorite.

Leah took the opportunity to search out Jefferson, himself, and found him in his cabinet speaking with Madison. She waited patiently for them to finish. Jefferson told Madison he would join them soon in the parlor, and then turned his attention to some papers on his desk. Leah watched him from a chair opposite his desk. It was placed along a short bit of wall next to the passageway to his sunroom and library. She reckoned she'd been freed by then, from her life of slavery there, since he looked older than her first clairvoyant encounter with that lifetime. She began focusing her intent upon him. He looked up several times as if he'd heard something unusual but as hard as she tried, she couldn't make contact. Then she noticed a luminosity emanating from his heart and moved from the chair to take a closer look. It was the white heart of the Ruby Order reaching out to meet her own. Making that heart connection was enough for Leah, for the moment. She began to picture herself in her present life to bring her soul back through her etheric body to settle in again.

She opened her eyes to find Chris pulled up in a chair in front of her, his arms resting on his knees, and his eyes soft and loving. "Where've you been, lass?" he asked.

She took a deep breath and blinked her eyes. "You sent me packing, cowboy," she sighed, "back to Monticello again. Dolley Madison was playing the same Mozart piece you were."

"Aye, I love that one. So what happened?" he asked, eager to know if she'd made soul contact with Jefferson.

"I would say a little progress, maybe. I did see his white heart, Chris. He showed me his deepest secret, and he felt mine, even if he didn't see it. Don't you think?"

"It would have to be, lass. At soul level, he would know you were there. Had he already freed you?"

"I think so. He was much older and so was Madison, so maybe around 1818-1820. I wasn't intentionally trying to reach him. I got a big hit from Joel this morning and then you with the music. So are we talking Broadway, Carnegie Hall or the Philharmonic with you, cowboy? Your talent staggers me."

"Likewise, lass. Shall we be off to lunch, my Bee Mistress?" he laughed.

"Sure," she agreed, acquiescing to his humility. "I've the kids at two o'clock remember, and then the Outreach board meeting."

As they were walking home, Leah kept turning Chris' playing over in her mind. Finally, she stopped and grabbed his arm. "Cowboy, I need you to tell me something, to fill me in."

"As you wish. What would you like to know, lass?" he grinned.

"For me, there's this big gap in your life that I know nothing about. I know you went to university, got a doctorate in Anthropology, for some reason, had a position teaching there, connected with the indigenous people, got awakened … and then what? Did you stay at university researching? When did you find out you were Order of the Ruby or even brotherhood? A lot of years passed in there and then there's this thread back to Nan and Pops and song and dance — and I'm really confused, but suddenly intensely interested in knowing this story."

"It's curious you've never thought to ask," he mused. "On the other hand, I've a few gaps in your life story that you could fill in for me, lass. I reckon this would be good tonight with a glass of Zinfandel. What do you think?"

"You're right. I'll have much less on my mind then. I won't let you off the hook, though."

"No worries. I'm happy to tell you the story. It seems to be a gathering force within me wanting expression anyway. So you, as you do, just picked up on it."

"We've a date then, and maybe bungee jumping," she laughed.

"How's your back?" he asked.

"I'd forgotten all about it. We'll have you take a look before lunch."

When they got home, Leah pulled off her sweater and Chris lifted the singlet to look at the lash marks and welts. Every single one had vanished.

"Gone? Seriously, darling, they're gone?" she asked, incredulously.

"You may want to go back and think about those white hearts, lass. I suspect mutual love and forgiveness," he suggested, reaching around to caress her breast. Her kundalini rose rapidly, leaving her breathless and giggling. "Bungee jumping it is tonight?" he asked, whispering in her ear.

"What've we got to lose?" she laughed — then added, soberly, "all forgiven, Mr. Jefferson."

Lunch was filled with the expectation of Joel's visit. They were both keen to meet Joel and his family. Then, homing in on the present, they made final plans for Mr. Brenner's service and burial the next morning and discussed the immediate agenda at the Outreach board meeting. They left home together, she walking back to the community center to read to her group of little girls, and he to the stable to step up the training of his newly civilized stallion, Thunder. Leah warned him that a horse-starved gal, named Paula, would be showing up while touring the village.

Leah finished a lovely hour with the children, reading *The Story of the Snow Children*, and then walked to the studio to pick up her file for the board meeting, and Natalie and Stu, who were also on the board of the Outreach arm of their non-profit. She found Paula's news summary printed out on her desk. It warmed her heart. Paula was well organized, articulate and on the right track. Leah would let a few summaries pile up out of necessity, what with the meeting and the funeral the next day, but find time to go over them with her on Thursday morning. Ideally, it would be nice to see if Paula could write the summary for the Saturday show as well. She would ask her to try that on her own while Leah continued to do it herself. At some point they were bound to merge.

She grabbed her Outreach file and met Natalie and Stu in the lobby. A tentative agenda had been sent out that was meant to spark their imaginations to bring in the future. The board would be ready for anything. The three of them were arranging the tables at the community center when Will and Nick arrived to pitch in, freeing Leah and Natalie to assemble everyone's preferred liquid refreshment from the community kitchen. That would be five *kombuchas* and two pear ciders. When they returned to the group, Tommy and Greg were there to complete the board. It was Nick's turn to raise the gavel, tap the table, and call the meeting to order. They joined hands in a moment of silence then met the first agenda item head-on.

Since they favored handling simple matters first, the hiring of new staff was discussed. Natalie put her request for an assistant on the table, the need for whom was contingent upon board and community approval of expansion into apprenticeship that would be discussed further on in the meeting. There was an easy consensus for a hiring if apprenticeship was approved, and even if it wasn't Natalie needed help with her workload. Then Leah proposed an assistant for Will at the Credit Union in addition to Sam who had just started in. She felt one of these two assistants should become fully capable of running the credit union in Will's absence and that should include looking ahead at *Harmony Valley* and even the San Francisco Inner City Project to ascertain whether these banks should be under the same umbrella or distinct non-profit co-operatives.

That led to a lengthy discussion, the facilitating of which she turned over to Will, who couldn't deny the overwhelming amount of work before him. He felt a real kinship with Sam and could imagine him as the credit union administrator, while Will took more of a CEO position overseeing *New Avalon I* and *II* as well as *Harmony Valley* banking. A staffer to manage the NAD transactions and day-to-day operation of the credit union would be a nice compliment to Sam's skills at accounting, taxes, and the US dollar part of the banking. He felt *Harmony Valley* could easily run on NADs — or their version of them — as they were quite close by. He couldn't wrap his head around San

Francisco at all, but would try to include that in the Inner City project profile he was creating. Both Sam and a second staffer, at appropriate salaries to their workload, were given consensus approval with few questions asked. Will was a fantastic banker and attorney as well as the Inner City project manager and a budding TV star. Day-to-day operations could easily be delegated.

With that in place, Leah bolding suggested that Tommy ought to re-imagine his position into something that was humanly possible. She suggested the discussion of a staff and workspace more in line with the ever-increasing number of projects on his plate. Tommy had a stake in everyone's projects because he was the builder, engineer, and architect of all physical structures, power installations and infrastructure in general. *Harmony Valley* had come into this reality on Leah's kitchen table but it was on Tommy's drafting table that it magically came to its fullness. And it would be under his guidance that it would spring from the earth not far from *New Avalon*. He needed project managers, draftsmen, engineers and craftsmen. Ordinarily, he worked out contracts with local businesses, like the Wilson's excavating company, and laborers, which he managed. But, the fact was he couldn't be cloned and was spread too thin for the good of it all. He did admit to that.

From the discussion, it was agreed that he would propose to the community the building of an engineering and architectural office alongside his woodworking shop. It was also agreed that the office should be staffed with actual employees from *New Avalon II, Harmony Valley*, and the greater community, in that order. Additionally, he really needed reliable project managers on a payroll for *Harmony Valley*. Will would set that up for him and take care of payroll as he was currently managing the contracts. On second thought, but more precisely on account of the way Leah looked at him when he proposed doing that, Will decided he would ask Sam to take care of it all. Whew! Natalie and Leah were hard pressed not to laugh at these two dedicated, much loved men.

Leah gave an updated report on the Restorative Justice model. That took a minute or two because it had really just come into the realm of possibilities on Friday when Ali Cat and company had shown up with the intent to help finance the first prison. Right now it was being written up as a proposal by Christina to present to the Assembly in Sacramento in December when they reconvened. She would, however, engage the committee chair on prisons well ahead of that to have it before his committee without delay.

That brought them to Mr. Brenner's kind gift of his farm for *New Avalon II* and begged the question of what they would put before the community the next week to get the ball rolling? For the moment, it was agreed that Leah and Natalie would look into the waiting list for the new community. They would need to go through the same process that Ashland had just completed making it important to get that training under way. The community would be asked if additional family members were interested and ready, then Natalie and Leah could look at people they'd guided spiritually as potential community members and, possibly their interested friends. If that didn't give them numbers, they would start with less than a full house. Katia and Mitch had, successfully, come on board later in the present community. Greg suggested that they speak with their neighbors. Gayle and Jim Taylor, who were coming around to embrace New Avalon by the back door. Leah had 'seen' Jim running the farming end of *New Avalon II*. She and Greg could have a chat with them. It might be good to wait until after the holidays to make any decisions since a few of the family members who were interested would be visiting.

It was conceded that little of a concrete nature could be proposed to community beyond the continued conversion of Mr. Brenner's land from inorganic chemical fertilizer (luckily no pesticides or herbicides had ever been applied) getting buffalo on the land, as Mr. Brenner had suggested — a great idea — and integrating Mr. Brenner's ewe's into their flock. Maud, his sister, would have the two steer butchered for her freezer but would leave the chickens to *New Avalon*. Ellia, who managed the poultry, was already seeing to the new additions. They would ask the community for ideas about additional community facilities, businesses, services and food production for the farmland and village that would soon be built there.

Tommy wasn't into radically changing what was already successful, so the housing would be a carbon copy of their village. However, the commercial area, the equivalent of their courtyard, could bring forth a good many new ideas and look completely different. The farms would best be managed separately until such time as the Taylor's entered community. There were questions about what to do with the remaining old farmhouses on the mid-valley farm and Jim Taylor's place should they choose to be in community. Those would sit on the back burner for the moment.

Greg gave them an update about farm preparations at *Harmony Valley*, which were proceeding nicely. He was ready for barn building and further fencing, since the land had been sprayed with the BD 500 prep, spread with compost and seeded with winter cover crops that would be ready for spring grazing. He would get that all ready to put to the community but the whole project had already been approved making it a formality rather than a requirement to get consensus. Tommy followed with a project update that was very hopeful as well. The weather was on their side to keep on with infrastructure and hotel remodeling as planned. They'd found good well water at 100 feet and completed drilling three wells for the town, the production gardens and the farm. Rainwater catchments would offset the well water as much as possible, along with grey water, for the farm and gardens but the wells would be there for backup. It was a good-sized aquifer, essentially in Shasta's interior, and the water was as nice as spring water with a five out of ten rating on hardness, with minimal iron. The biomass plant was underway along with wind-power installations and the first phase of the solar farm. *Harmony Valley* was coming along.

They would soon be searching for the Phase I of the homeless participants, with backgrounds in farming and gardening, to begin taking on those operations. They'd be lodged in the remodeled hotel. Phase II, already plotted out, included homeless participants with construction experience, who would help complete the first neighborhood and the downtown businesses.

Construction would begin in the early spring or late winter if the weather continued to be mild and dry. Tommy would prepare a good report for the community meeting and only needed consensus on the previously discussed office staff and new office facility proposal, which he would draw up. Leah didn't need to give him 'the look'. He was relieved, grateful ... and it showed.

That brought them up to the last item on the agenda, apprenticeships. This was a totally new idea to put before the board but one that Natalie and Leah had been discussing for weeks. Natalie, who was the director of the Outreach Community Program, passed each board member a handout for her part of the presentation.

"Alright team, here is what is happening with the community program. Ashland has finished the preparatory work. We've a group of six couples in the Founder's Circle; four of these couples are empty-nest parents, while two have teen- and college-age children at home. Two of the empty-nest couples are retired. Then we've six couples in the second wave circle, all with children of various ages. I've talked to them about spending time down here apprenticing the different key positions that make a community work. Tommy, they're going to be contacting you for the architecture and engineering, but will get local builders to do that work up there. You may have to consult for them about the power and infrastructure elements."

Tommy was taking notes and appreciating the heads up. This gave further impetus to getting an office up and running as soon as possible.

Natalie continued. "Will, in addition to being a key player with whom to apprentice, you'll likely be called upon as a consultant to get their credit union up and running. They're getting their non-profit set up over the winter, but will need help with the credit union part of the umbrella. I know you're working on the overall scheme of community banking for the Inner City projects and imagine it applies to community projects in the same way?" she asked.

"The physical aspects of it do, yes, but when you get into backing currency, keeping clear distinctions between currencies and within divisions held under the umbrella, it will vary considerably. But that's not a problem, Natalie. We do need to define the banking for every initiative in a unique way. I expected that," Will assured her.

"Yours is one position that should be apprenticed by someone with financial and, if possible, legal skills. One of the retirees in the Ashland founders group has qualifications and would like to work with you on that."

"Great! How will it work?" Will asked.

"He could be down here five days a week working at your side. This is the idea with the apprenticeship. Ideally it would be full-time residential for up to a year. The folks in Ashland can get back there in an hour and we could work out a schedule for them to visit but the idea is immersion in the community, using the NADs, and eating what they grow or receive from the farm livestock. *New Avalon* is the model, so this is where we all need to step up to the plate and actively serve, but at the same time we've an apprentice or two to help out for a year. It's kind of a WWOOFer program for communities."

The board loved the idea. It was the perfect way for people to prepare to do it on their own. "So what do you consider the key positions?" Nick asked.

"Well, some of our people are specialized to the extent that they make *New Avalon* unique. You don't want to open a natural medicine school, and someone with your skill knows what to do without apprenticing because that will have been part of their training. Spence would be a great baker to apprentice with if they don't have someone with the skill or a local baker they prefer. A lot depends on the focus of their community. However, a financial person, the farmers, the community garden managers, the landscape manager, the poultry managers, the power grid and infrastructure people and the warehouse manager need to apprentice, unless they have worked in those areas before, and, even if they have, it would be the best of all worlds to work in a successful system. Greg, you and Sonia will want to pass on the biodynamic skills and may be called up to consult in that regard, as time goes on. They may have someone interested in making cheese, or essential oils, or brewing beer and smoking meat. Those are more peripheral skills, but we can offer that as a short-term apprenticeship.

"I'll continue in a monthly one-day circle with them to see them through the establishment of their community. That brings up the next level of apprenticeship, which will be training others to do what I do. I'm not available for cloning, either," she laughed, winking at Tommy. "At the same time it's not recommended that someone in a particular community do what I do. We're lucky here because most everyone worked with Leah, who holds a good space for me to carry on for her, without hierarchy. That won't be the case in these communities. So from amongst *us* and perhaps our second village, we need a few more of me to teach these circles to police themselves for conflict, adherence to the rules of sexuality, unhappiness and depression, and feelings of unfulfilled dreams, to name a few. The aim would be an egalitarian group that can come together and lay their concerns on the table freely and with full support. They could maybe take over after a year of training — so another type of apprenticeship. The apprenticeship program trains an entire community to pass it on — pay it forward, so this idea is for the preliminary and ongoing spiritual aspect of community, which provides the core values."

"Natalie, can you lay out the immediate future with respect to this apprenticeship idea?" Greg asked.

"Sure can, Greg. The folks in Ashland are ready to commit to apprenticing the major skills. There's one man with small farm experience and three or four couples with chickens at home now, loads of gardeners, two of whom have worked commercially, two women interested in baking, the financial fellow for the banking, and they do have a doctor, a naturopath/herbalist and two nurses amongst the expanded group. The founders, especially, have worked very hard on their own consciousness. If we've skills they need, we can assign them on a short-term basis, say for seasonal skills. It doesn't look like they'll have a big dairy–cow operation, but maybe goats, which Katia can apprentice handily and benefit from their help. Shelley might pass on her cheese-making skills if they're interested. We'll still have our WWOOFers but may be able to assign some of them to *Harmony Valley* to help the farmers there. There's a huge amount to work out with all of this, including the balance between what we charge them for the training, food, housing and what they work off as apprentices. The Community Program is not charitably-funded like *Harmony Valley* and they wouldn't expect charity.

"There're two gardeners interested in the fish farm greenhouse model, the herbalist would like to establish a school and pharmacy with products for local stores, and, then there's a music teacher and a primary school teacher in the second wave who could get a homeschool program up and running. They would work with local homeschool education support. So that's where Ashland stands right now.

"The Ukiah group is coming in this weekend for their first intensive. We'll be sorting them out over 2012. Because of the incredible response to all of our programs through *Light on the Crisis'* surge in the ratings, we've a long list of those wishing to get community going. I'm working on an online program to engage them — sort them out — then will go out for a long weekend to initiate the process before we bring them in here. Leah can speak to how interest is growing better than I can. I get a little overwhelmed," she concluded, looking to Leah to take over.

"Thanks, Nat. That was a great overview. Look, my beloveds, we've done too good a job at *New Avalon*. Everyone wants what we have," she laughed. "We really do have a long list and it feels, as we take these folks on, that we need an innovative approach or they'll still be on our wait list after we've all passed over." That was timely comic relief, since they were all looking exhausted and overextended before they'd even voted on the program. "Where I suggest we look is 'the gift'. We can't possibly take all of this on, and hope to change America in the many ways coming out of *New Avalon*, without help. With the documentaries and the video set for the Outreach Community Project, I feel those who go through an apprenticeship here, with further assistance as they set up their own communities, should be able to do the same for others. We can field requests to become satellite communities living *New Avalon* principles in higher consciousness. The same is true for the Inner City Community Project and, potentially, for the Restorative Justice Community and the Homeless Community Project. When we engage these projects we need to be passing it on in the process, as well as documenting it. We've a growing list for both projects, from all over the country. Many already have startup funding and can apply for more. After they've proved themselves, Federal and State funds should become readily available for these highly functional models.

"That's all good. In fact it's fantastic and exactly how our mission is meant to unfold. We just need to step up to meet the challenge. We're fully capable in the video department. Stu, here, and his crew, are on a steep learning curve, but it won't be long before they've mastered it. Stu can speak to that when I wrap this up. To me, this looks like multi-level marketing of 'the gift'. I want to call it the 'gift pyramid'. In our pyramid, beneath *New Avalon* we will have Ashland, Ukiah and, it looks like, Virginia. One becomes three. Each of those can spawn three more who will learn from them and on we go to take care of everyone wanting this lifestyle. We will have the documentaries and filmed modules, and apprenticeship, to back up the tiers as they're added. This will be true for the Inner City Project, as well. Hypothetically, because this is Will's domain, when Will initiates the San Francisco project, it will be the model, just like we are. A roadmap needs to be established and we'll need to pitch in and help out with training, here and on their turf, I expect. I think we'll be lucky that *Harmony Valley* is in our neighborhood for the homeless and, conceivably, the prison model apprenticing, but the Inner City Outreach Project will best be worked out in San Francisco.

"For each of these models the personal work is the same but the approaches will be different. We won't be able to go into the Inner City community the way we approached Ashland. The same is true for *Harmony Valley*. It won't work. Will, you'll need to look at that and work on it with Natalie and me. The prisons are a whole different ballgame. We're stretching, growing, and testing the limits, if there are any, of where we can take this. The Marin community of Elliot's is yet another interesting and unique model. On top of all that we have big plans in *Harmony Valley* for the addition of a Camphill Community, a retirement village model and more, yet to come through. We'll have the second community here to give us the time to do this right and train others to pay it forward. Your take?" she asked, looking around the table.

"You know me," Stu responded. "Bring it on. The bigger the pile the more energy and ideas I seem to have. I've a good crew already and another staffer to hire and we'll be steamin' in the film department. I feel, absolutely, that this is what I was born to do." He got an unexpected round of applause. "It has also been suggested that the studio have a dedicated webmaster/IT staffer to manage the computer systems and keep the websites up-to-date and visually inviting."

"Ask me in six months," Will said, soberly, when check-in came around to him. "My plate is full and taxes are coming on too. I know the Inner City Project is part of my life work and with the new help maybe I can get the time to sit down thoughtfully to map it out. It's all go, we've the funds and the city is helping with the land purchases and will help find the neighbors too. We need to work on the farm part of the project and might share it with Oakland and maybe Sacramento, which are on our tentative list with Los Angeles. Ali Cat is spearheading LA. I just can't believe how fast this is all happening. I guess we've Leah and Joel Robertson to thank for that," he laughed.

"You can thank Joel in person over Thanksgiving, Will. He's bringing his family out for the holiday," Leah offered.

"Why am I not surprised," Will smiled.

"I can't wait to meet them," Tommy began. "Look, it's all good from my perspective. Now that I see the big picture a little better, I might break ground on that office the day after the community meeting," he laughed. "I love a challenge as long as I still have time to keep abreast of the latest in my fields and to guide Mike and Rob, a bit still. Shelley loves being busy and would surely be keen to teach cheese-making and meat-smoking. I feel best about inspecting each site first, and then providing the plans to their own contractors who can consult with me. I'll help you, personally, in San Francisco though, Will. You can count on that," he concluded, giving his mate a roughing up.

Greg was deep in thought. "Where are you going to put these apprentices, ladies?" he asked.

"I had a little vision, Greg," Leah started. "I saw where we will have the homeless project apprentices and WWOOFers housed over in *Harmony Valley* between the town and where we would put the prison. It looked like a courtyard hacienda arrangement, FYI, Tommy," she laughed. "For those apprenticing with us over here, I reckon we'd lodge them in the old farmhouse for starters. In time, I see that central valley area becoming a hub for apprenticing, our own Waldorf School, part of the farming operation and more."

"Should we be informing Jim and Gayle that they'll be moving," he laughed.

"I think we'll let spirit take care of it, Greg," Leah grinned. "My guess is that if we keep them informed about the new community at valley end, the wheels will start turning. I'm guessing they're as strapped as the rest of the small farmers in America. Say, why don't we start inviting them to community events?"

"Good idea," Greg agreed. He'll become biodynamic at the same time as Mr. B's property. It'll be an easy fit. *You* just ask spirit to time it right so they can get into Natalie's training program on time," he laughed.

"I'd be happy to work on that, Greg," she smiled, "but no guarantee."

That left Nick for comments and the voting procedure. "You folks are awesome. I feel like a slacker what with no patients to speak of and Chris stepping in to bring the beer up to snuff. I'll be looking for an opening to commit to more, especially as Billy gets old enough for a whole day with Georgia at school. We're going to let Katia and Mitch have the babies from now on. We've a full house as it is. So, shall we tackle the vote?"

"Yeah!" they all agreed.

The only exemption from consensus vote, on all that the board discussed that day, was the visionary part of community that involved Jim Taylor's property — for obvious reasons. For the time being, their vacant farmhouse and spare rooms in the WWOOFer Village and The Lodge Annex would have to do for apprentice lodging … and probably would for the Ashland group. Each presenter assured the board that they would prepare well for the community vote on the following Tuesday. The meeting was adjourned, with Nick's rap of the gavel.

chapter 2: amazing grace

Chris was already in the newsroom waiting to watch *Joel Robertson Live* with Leah, when she returned from the board meeting. He'd met Paula and Sam at the stable, gave them a tour of the building and introduced them to some potential riding partners for the weekend. She and Sam both rode and wanted to explore the valley, if that was okay? Chris arranged to be there for their first outing and asked them to check it out with him whenever they wanted to ride. Nice young couple, he reckoned.

Joel had cycled around to *Citizen's United* again, calling it the lynchpin of civic revolution. OWS was just the beginning, in his opinion. If the unelected conservative majority of kings sitting on the Supreme Court thought they could establish the laws of the land, and persisted in rolling out decisions that favored corporate money over *We the People*, they could be in for a battle with those very people. Even conservative Americans understood that their elected representatives are meant to make the laws. This was about the power elite owning the court majority and a dandy time for conservatives to file suits hoping to take them to the high court for right-sided decisions.

He was urging people to think past the re-election of the president to make sure the House of Representatives regained a progressive-leaning majority and that the Senate's democratic majority was boosted to eliminate filibuster on democratic sponsored bills and blocked appointments. Further, looking at the majority of state governorships in the red camp gave him the jitters. It went hand in hand with the conservative 'small government' mantra that favored transferring power to the states. Oh yea, they'd be ready in those state capitols, all right. Hadn't we already learned that it does little good to elect a so-called progressive leader if the lawmakers are corporate owned? Shift the majority and we could talk impeachment of court members and give the court and country back to the people. We could also pass the legislation already in the house to amend the constitution – corporations are not people and money isn't free speech. He actually referenced Leah's *Social Threefolding* show about the separation of the economic, cultural and legal/government spheres and had a clip with Elliot Davis who had delivered the enlightened idea to the public via *Light in the Crisis* on October first.

Willow Pierce, their young reporter on the ground at the OWS encampment in New York City, was also a shining light of hope on Joel's show that night. Leah and Chris walked home discussing Joel's closing remarks about the need for local economies, the resurgence of 'Main Street' values, *now*. Leah felt Joel could help mobilize people to communicate with each other and begin networking within their communities if they hadn't already. Chris suggested she do a show on some communities who were getting it together. She could take Joel up on the challenge by demonstrating change at the local level. Now there was an idea whose time had come, she agreed, before giving him a big hug on their front porch.

While preparing their dinner, Leah's mind was turning around Joel's warning of an uprising. Yes, she agreed that *Citizen's United* was a lynchpin but lynchpins needed some one to release them. There were statistics out now confirming the trend for people all over the world to look for real news on the Internet rather than network news. The days of infotainment would soon be over, save for the morning and late night talk shows that people seemed to have social contracts with in the living rooms. That trend was hopeful but, then, there were plenty of radical right websites, and those devoted to any number of conspiracy theories, along with the liberal and more balanced news shows. It was the same trend that had crushed the printed newspapers. Now, most had online free and subscription versions of their papers in hopes of mitigating losses from the tech migration.

Chris had stoked the boiler out back for theirs and Natalie's home heating, and was rehearsing *Oklahoma!* in the shower, while she finished the salad. He was reminding her that their first small group rehearsal for his Christmas production was the next night. She'd best have a look at her lines at some point during that busy day. She and Joel would Skype early, at eight o'clock, to accommodate the community's attendance and participation in Mr. Brenner's funeral service and burial in Etna. They'd all be heading out at nine-thirty for that, leaving *New Avalon* in the care of their new staffers and those WWOOFers who had over-wintered. Of course, she and Will would have their phones on vibration, in case there were problems, and the bank would be closed with Sam locked inside.

After they'd eaten and cleaned up the kitchen, they finally sat down across from each other in the living room with Harry, who was over for a visit, snuggled up next to Chris. Chris had been fully briefed about the board meeting proposals that had been approved whilst eating dinner. He'd informed her that Mr. Brenner's farm was all in order, animals fed, fences checked and fine, and that Maud had vacated the premises leaving a tin of chocolate chip cookies for whoever came to check on things first. There was just no stopping the nurturing thoughtfulness of that woman. Chris would save them to pass out at the rehearsal, *after* the singing parts had been rehearsed.

Leah had brought in their glasses of Zinfandel, setting them on the coasters laid out on the end table they shared. After taking a sip, she addressed the question she'd asked him before lunch. "The way I see it, cowboy, you accounted, fairly well, for your childhood, sketchily for your time at University, and thoroughly for years spent with the indigenous people, when we met in Peru. Recently, you've added a good bit of your life story occurring after our work in Peru. The part that I know, of the years intervening between your indigenous experience and our meeting, includes Aikido mastery and teaching occasional workshops bridging the indigenous teachings to the present culture in Australia. Of course, somewhere in there you would have received the call to service with the Order of the Ruby. Then, you get here, and out comes all of this talent — broad, brilliant talent — as we really get to know each other here in *New Avalon*. What are we looking at here — 20 to 30 years of your life in the realm of mystery?" she asked, with her most engaging smile.

"Somewhere in that neighborhood, I reckon," he said, with that irresistible grin of his stealing over his face.

"Well, come on," she laughed. "You have my undivided, *eager*, attention."

"Aye, lass. This community is bringing forth a part of me I reckoned I'd never see again in this life. So to catch you up and review just a bit, I was born in 1944 in Perth - about as remote as a city could be, and still is," he began.

"Stop right there, cowboy. I don't even know your birthday," she laughed.

"Aye, well that would be June 12, for your records, lass. You know the boyhood parts from stories in Peru and those about Nan and Pops that I've recently shared. He was a talented man, Pops. He saw a spark in me, and likely some natural abilities coming down the bloodlines. My time living with them was a treasure — my fondest memories through my teenage years. I was lucky in that respect, when my dad left and Mum was too overwhelmed to deal with me. It was a gift. But, she re-engaged to take control when it came to university because that was *her* gig. She was the perfect professor archetype and quite overbearing as a single parent. I sought haven with Nan and Pops every chance I could get, but they lived up in Kalamunda, so that was mostly weekends and holidays.

"Yeah look, I did university in engineering and a graduate degree in Anthropology so that I, too, could be a professor — which I was. Then, during that tenure, I had the experiences with the Aboriginal people and the Maori in New Zealand. I was getting more and more incompatible with my position at the university. So, that takes us up to the early 70's when I began branching out. I still taught to get that paycheck and buy the house in Kalamunda but my interests had nothing to do with my work. Mind you, I had, all along, done

37

summer-stock theater and loved it. So here is where the missing pieces get picked up for you, my curious wife."

"Yippee! Do tell," she laughed.

"Pops had a heart attack and died in 1971," he sighed. "He was pushing 90 so that wasn't a surprise but I reckon he just went out there into the astral and made it his full-time project to straighten me out. I followed the lead and took serious voice lessons and began favoring the musicals in summer stock and always got the parts I wanted. I also worked with a dance company and polished what Pops had taught me with a number of great dancers and their teachers. That broadened my choices of roles in the musicals, which you could call my genre, at the time. A number of us formed a company and had our own summer-stock theater up in Kalamunda, and then it became more than Summer Stock. We were soon performing all over the country. I quit the university, with no love lost, and worked in theater full-time — broke my poor mother's heart. I'd found my joy and rode with it free of stress or conflict, within or without. It was a great time in my life to come into the fullness of a lot of gifts.

"Well, as the story goes on, I began taking parts in television dramas and eventually in the Australian movie industry, which was growing steadily in those days. Our theater troupe stayed together though, and we had a ball doing Summer Stock all over Australia and, frankly, had real magic performing together. In 1979 we wound up at the Sydney Opera House performing in a *West Side Story* revival with a great supporting cast. What happened next was remarkable.

"The recognition for our work became Australia-wide and a lot of talented young people wanted to do what we were doing. They wanted to learn what we could teach them. We went back to Perth and started a school of performing arts that's still around today. We coerced some of the best teachers in theater, film, dance and voice to be our teachers and our colleagues at this school. It was incredibly rewarding both in the way it enhanced what skills I already had, and in the way young people came into the program and left for careers in the performing arts. Some of Australia's best have gone through that school."

"I've heard of it. So what happened to you? Obviously you left the school. Was that when the brotherhood moved in?"

"No. I left with a nice studio contract for films in Sydney."

"You were a film star?" she asked, incredulously.

"I was. It was a good experience. As you can tell, I have a lot of fun performing and organizing others to do the same. In a way, Pops was smiling down on me having a vicarious acting career. When you think about that, he was doing exactly what my mother did, but from the safety of the astral," he laughed. "But he knew I was in joy and a lot of fulfillment. One thing film did teach me was that I much preferred live theater. I stuck with the contract, made the films, which was good for my resume, and went back to live theater in Sydney, getting into directing as well. Before I could make it to Broadway," he smiled, "the brotherhood got me. And that was that."

"What do you mean, that was that. Did you have to quit and go on mission, just like that? And when was that?" she asked.

"I'd a good 10 years in theater after the school in Perth was founded. I also took up Aikido to balance the dance and calm my mind. And, I began meditating. In '92, when I got the call from the Order, I was asked to finish up what I was doing — a directing job — and show up in Italy for training. A part of me wasn't surprised by the summons. I'd felt for a long time that I was living a treasured life on borrowed time. So, I went. That was the beginning of my picking up foreign languages as well," he laughed, "starting with an immersion in Italian."

"Wow. What happened next, darling? Can you tell me?"

"Giorgio Stravali was the Lord of the Ruby at that time and he was preparing to leave the planet. He'd navigated the World Wars for the brotherhood and the Order, was in his 80's, and fresh blood was needed to prepare for the new millennia. As you know, that was yours truly. He hung in there for five years polishing me up for the job and sent me out on countless missions, including the mastery of my double. He was an incredible master and I had to let go of everything else in my life to absorb what he had to give. Though it was challenging, a part of me loved every minute of it. I'd gone from acting and directing to the live role of warrior and magician. Oddly, the previous career was a great help, especially when theatrics were called for," he laughed.

"So all of that was to bring you to Peru, the first meeting of the Order in the flesh, and the beginning of your mission?" she asked, putting the pieces together.

"You have it, lass. After Giorgio died, I did have a few years to roam Europe and go back home. That was when you would have heard about the workshops I taught to keep myself busy, the Aikido to keep my warrior skills sharp, and, I had the good fortune to work with a master swordsman at the school in Perth — for future roles in swashbuckling films — or reality."

He had Leah laughing, remembering his excellent form with the Sword of the Master in Peru. "So, cowboy, your mission has been completed. Do I get the impression that you are going to return to theater to recapture your joy in those gifts of yours?"

"Would you mind?" he asked, with the grin of his.

"I would *love* it. You bring me so much joy just being here, how could I not want to share that with others?"

My lass has embedded 'the gift' in her soul, he silently mused — heart swelling. "I reckon we don't have to go anywhere to make magic happen. I'd a long meditation in Mr. B's barn today — nice and clean as it is," he laughed, "and Thunder and I had a wander up the road from the highway that cuts down between ours and the next valley. Is it as easy to access as the road into our courtyard?" he asked.

"Easier. What do you have in mind, my lad?" she asked, excitedly.

He leaned forward, eager to share his idea. "Let's start the school again, right here," he suggested passionately. "The barn can be converted to a theater quite easily. We can start with Summer Stock in a regional way, but I'd like to teach again and convert the smaller side of the barn into music, voice and acting classrooms. Stu is already setting us up for film and could, when his life calms down, teach filmmaking. What do you think?"

"You're bringing tears to my eyes, cowboy. Mr. Brenner's barn will be used and preserved and the community will grow and participate in yet another important aspect of the cultural sphere. Please work this up for the community meeting, Chris. I think you should get going on it right away. Build it and people will come, as they say."

"I think you're right, lass. It could be the first 'business enterprise' of the second village and with the easy access at valley end, the students don't need to live on the premises, though we could establish a dorm like the WWOOFer Village to accommodate that if it were needed. I'll draw it up and present it. I've got this second chance with life. I'd like to leave a gift behind."

"One amongst many, my love. No wonder you are so good at all of it. Where did you pick up the classical piano?" she asked.

"I learned piano from Nan, initially, then at university, doing a minor in music, and I kept up training after I was free of the university. As it turned out Giorgio, Lord of the Ruby, was a concert pianist who was happy to coach me in return for my taking over the position of his personal winemaker."

Leah was once again shocked. "So your also a winemaker? How do the Cummings' rate with the Zinfandel, aficionado?" she asked.

"They do quite well," he smiled. "It's my first encounter with Zinfandel, not a popular wine in Oz, but I recall its roots are in Italy — maybe *Tempranillo*. I reckon we'll do even better," he grinned.

"Did you share this with Sonia?" he asked.

"Not yet. The vines are young. I'll keep an eye on them and propose a collaboration when the time comes."

"Would you like another glass, cowboy?" she laughed.

"I would. We still have to hear the missing parts of your story," he reminded her.

"That won't take long and will be relatively dull compared to yours. Are there old films of yours we can watch online?" she asked.

"I hope not," was all he had to say about that.

"Awe, spoilsport. I'll bet you were a gorgeous, sexy, young lad. None of that has changed with maturity, I assure you."

"Okay lass. Fill the glasses and take your turn," he laughed, changing the subject.

He walked Harry home, while Leah poured another half-glass of wine into each glass. She reflected on his story, and how the performer part of him persisted both in the expression of his art but in small things like the meticulous way he groomed himself. Leah had often thought that Chris had the most beautiful hands she'd ever seen on a man. He manicured his nails carefully and took excellent care of his skin. He never left the house without a soft pair of leather gloves hanging out of his back pocket. He'd a spare pair at the stable and had bought a pair for her work with Holly as well. Of course, she was the beneficiary of his soft touch in more ways than she could count.

amazing grace

She settled into her chair, curious to know what he felt was missing from her story, though she'd a suspicion. When he'd settled in again, she asked him what he wanted to know.

"I reckon we should start with your birthday, lass," he laughed.

"Easy. I'm a Libran, finding comfort in the quest for balance. I was born October 10, 1945. What else?"

"I have to say that the Bee Mistress has filled in a great deal of the missing pieces for me." This was a reference to the clearing work she'd just completed for this mischief-making part of herself. "Where you never seem to go is your life with your son, Nathan. I know next to nothing about this special man's place in your life. Why so private about Nathan?" he asked.

"Ah-h, that," she began. "Well, I do recall telling you that I'd sent him to a good private school when he was five. I was already a single mom with good support from his dad so that wasn't a hardship. But, then I woke up, suddenly and traumatically — well, you remember the Casey William's story," she said, to his raised eyebrow. "Anyway, I realized Nathan wasn't at all suited for the strict, disciplined kind of school he was in and moved him into a Waldorf School instead. How I did that without getting to know Rudolf Steiner is something to ponder. I was a busy working mom.

"Nathan adapted well to the change and fit right into his class. He had a wonderful experience, but when he got out of the high school, at 18, to go on to college, he accused me of not properly preparing him for the rigors of that world. He had a point, but I realized he was also belatedly making the separation from family to enter the world. He was a wonderfully agreeable adolescent. He floundered around trying to find himself and decided to go to work instead. To make a long story short, it was through his job at a publishing company that he found his purpose — writing. He'd been a wonderful storyteller in school and dug out his old work to go over it one Saturday afternoon. I remember it well — the look on his face as it dawned on him.

"Then he did decide to do the coursework in writing but not at a college. He found a school of creative writing in the Bay Area with well-published authors as the teachers and continued to work while attending night classes there. The foundation of Waldorf education was the best he could have had and he admitted it years later. He and I established a new relationship as friends and housemates, rather than mother and son. I gave him considerable space to find himself and develop his talents, and he did. When he met his wife, Julie, at the publishing company, we shifted again. Initially, Julie was afraid she couldn't compete with me for Nathan. I know, that's a self-esteem issue, but I wasn't going to take on a potential daughter-in-law for the spiritual work. So I detached to give them the space for their love, marriage, family and life together. They have done really well together and she and I are good friends."

"What do you mean by detached, lass?" Chris asked.

"Oh, I don't mean that I didn't communicate, or attend their wedding — I put it on at the old house, actually. What I mean is that I refrained from

41

advising, hovering, and financially supporting – like that, as egos were fragile in the beginning. We're fine now. I adore my grandkids, David and Mandy, and had a great time living with them when I lost the house and had to move into their guest room. They have since moved to Boulder where their kids are attending one of the best Waldorf Schools in the USA. It was after their marriage that I got going on my first big project – waking up the sisterhood. It's all been good. Nathan and I talk, email or text once a week to stay in touch and they'll be in one of the guesthouses for Christmas. I'm really excited that they'll get a change to know how you have filled up my heart, and my life, so completely. That's the story of Nathan."

"And ... what does he write?" Chris asked, curious about his genre.

"Oh, I guess you haven't made it through the whole bookcase here," she said, getting up to open one of the cases behind the sofa. "This whole shelf belongs to Nathan, cowboy. He writes the most incredible stories for adolescents. He's a magician with words. There are three series here and then the rest of the books are individual novels. He's pretty popular with the kids."

"Mind if I take them to the stable to read when I have free time there?" he asked, coming to look them over. "Please do. I'm hoping the two of you find a groove together. Like Nick, he never did have that 'dad' kind of influence in his life – no Pops to fill in the gaps."

"I'm sure Nathan and I will find common ground, lass," he assured her, placing the first book of the first series on top of the bookcase. He drew her into his arms, instantly activating her kundalini. "How about a massage on that 'good as new' back of yours?" he asked drawing her into one of his full-body passionate hugs.

"Alice has been so looking forward to this particular rabbit hole," she giggled, as he picked her up for transport to the bedroom.

Leah woke up early Wednesday morning, dreaming about the Federal Reserve Bank. *Good grief.* This, in stark contrast to the blissful way she'd tumbled out of this reality into the astral world of sleep. Ah, well. There was an odd triangulation playing out amongst the national debt, which was now around $15 trillion dollars; interest rates, which were being held unimaginably low; and the printing of currency, which was occurring at record levels in order to monetize the debt through bond purchases. This felt like something she could pass on to Joel. Getting worked up over the 'banksters', corruption in the government and economic sectors, and fears of survival had been sorted out of her mission in favor of solutions.

Which begged the question: What were the solutions? For the people caught in the aftermath of economic sorcery the answer was community – strong community. A good many pieces of that picture were coming into being through Outreach and many grassroots movements around the country. Perhaps it was time to call in the missing pieces in that picture, and begin looking at the kind of government and economic sectors needed to build from the ashes for *We the People.* She would speak with Joel about it during their

Skype session and make sure they'd time during his visit to go deep into both crisis and solution. What she really wanted to access was the early 19th century brain of Thomas Jefferson, who'd seen it all coming.

In the moment, it was time to look at their most extensive model, *Harmony Valley*, and fill in more of the missing pieces — not that the project was very far along. Leah left her cowboy, deep in sleep, and plodded out to the kitchen to make a pot of tea. She moved through yoga and meditation, asking for inspiration, and was dressing for Mr. Brenner's funeral when Chris came back to life. Having thrown her only black dress into the *Samhain* fire to butt-kick Dragon Lady, Leah was wrapping herself up in a navy and white print, which was quite becoming with her slim figure and fair features. He motioned her over to the bed, with that grin of his, for a morning cuddle and a great bubbling up of temptation. He'd no answers for the fragile economy but he did have a lot of talent in the kundalini department. She allowed herself a five-minute indulgence — quite satisfying, to say the least — and was back on track with the bliss that had become her dominant *modus operandi* since he'd arrived back in her life.

Chris hopped out of bed to start a quick breakfast, knowing she had an eight o'clock date with Joel. He would stoke the fire after she was off to work and was keen to sit down at the kitchen table and plot the path to the performing arts school at valley end — an investment in the future of the cultural sphere. She left for work reminding him to pay attention to the time, while he was imaginatively soaring into the future. The van and car were leaving for the funeral at nine-thirty sharp and *he* was the scheduled entertainment. They would meet at the front door of the courtyard.

She gave him a kiss and a hug before walking off to the studio to boot up her laptop for the Skype session. Paula was already scanning the networks when she stepped into the newsroom to get her charging phone. Between the funeral and her duties in the greenhouse with Sonia and Ellia that afternoon, she'd probably be reading over the reports while Chris cooked dinner that evening.

Joel was cheery and looking good that morning. He couldn't argue about the three wobbles she brought up to him from her dream. He felt all of them were waiting in the wings, had no idea in what order they would play out but did suspect the timing to be right on. There would be bubbles bursting faster than the sleeping media could report them, he reckoned. He also felt a student loan crisis coming that would be a bubble of sorts. The millennials out on the pavement in New York and all over America were facing massive debt for an education that had skyrocketed in cost at the same time it had plunged in quality. It looked, for all the world, like another Ponzi scheme. The kids faced continued unemployment and the loans had no underwriting — déjà vu the sub-prime mortgage crisis that had trigger the housing collapse.

The elusive aspects of the situation had to do with the players who were bringing the country down, and why. Corporate power grabbing and mongering were obvious. Yes, they were sociopaths — no doubt about that. Corporate money had corrupted congress and, it was suspected, the high court. The power brokers had been plotting and working on this project for a lot longer than anyone could imagine. It didn't help that most of America had been lulled to sleep with easy money and worry–free debt that now had them painfully handcuffed — to say nothing of worried sick. Were we arm-wrestling China with the threat of a devalued dollar? What did the power brokers want — a nation of slaves or just all of the natural resources? Or both? Why couldn't the *country* print its own money and boot the Federal Reserve bankers out? When did economic advisers and cabinet members start coming from the banking world instead of the academic world of applied economics? She and Joel didn't solve the problems of the world that morning but he did take it on. She didn't speak to the Ahrimanic nature of the step-wise collapse. They both agreed that cycles of collapse were part and parcel of the bigger cycles of civilization, and that it was imminent.

When the session ended, Leah wondered if she'd really had the dream for Joel. He did lift the load off her shoulders and promised a good thrashing-out of it all while visiting — and it was his pleasure to be on a single-payer health care show the weekend he visited as well. She noted that she hadn't felt anxiety about what she'd confronted ... or anger. Dragon Lady was sorting it out, and that was a good sign.

The *New Avalon* community, Gayle and Jim Taylor, and Mr. Brenner's sister Maud with her children and their families nearly filled the little church in Etna. The minister had lovely stories to tell about Henry and Gert's marriage in that church —'twas before his time, but written in the archives. Members of the congregation stood up and bore witness to his life, as did a good many of the community. Leah could see Mr. Brenner and Gert in their youthful bodies, hovering over the casket, pleased with the turnout, and the stories. When the service was over, the men of *New Avalon* acted as the pallbearers, carrying the casket to the prepared gravesite in the churchyard. Final goodbyes were said and the minister added the last prayers. As the casket was slowly lowered into the earth, Chris, at Mr. Brenner's request, sang *Oh What A Beautiful Mornin'*. There were a good many tears then, and, again, when Maud picked up the spade to throw on the traditional first shovel of the dirt to which we all return — well, in our physicality, at least.

They all took a turn with the shovel, and their personal goodbyes, then joined the congregation for coffee, tea and home-baked pastries in the church hall. Spence had brought along a basket of his cheese Danish to contribute to the social gathering. Gert and Henry attended the social as well and took their leave just ahead of the community. They would all miss Mr. B at the community events but the gift of his farm was a living memory and they would honor his name, giving it to the new community center, which he'd seen replacing his little house to overlook valley end.

Leah had a lengthy chat with Gayle Taylor who, surprisingly, had the heart of a political activist. She'd been watching *Light in the Crisis* since its inception — another shocker — and was currently working her way into the democratic leadership in their precinct. She'd taken Leah's and Joel's (since she watched both shows) advice seriously and was intending to be the precinct committeewoman for the next election caucus. Leah asked her how she felt about being surrounded by their growing community. Gayle thought it was a blessing. She'd sooner be part of it than in the middle of it but Jim got funny about the spiritual work. Asking Greg about the BD preps had been a big step for him but the difference in the farming was obvious. They'd been farming organically since they bought the farm ten years previously. They'd wanted to be self-sufficient but she saw the handwriting on the wall. They were underwater on their mortgage, due to falling home prices and recent farm loans, and feared losing the farm.

Leah didn't offer an invitation or suggest that they should be part of the second village but let Gayle's feelings and words sink into her soul for further contemplation. They would make wonderful community members because they were great neighbors. Jim's reticence was normal – all things in time but only if it was win–win. She would suggest to Chris that the Rangers think about including Jim Taylor in a meeting or two to test the spiritual waters. He'd already collaborated with them on security issues and was, in her estimation, more than curious. Chris or Greg could extend the invitation if the Rangers were agreeable.

It was a garden work afternoon for Leah that day. She checked in with Paula at the studio where all had been quiet and productive. There was now a pile of news reviews on her desk. She added them to her file to take home, certain the Chris would help her squeeze them in before their rehearsal at eight. Leah thanked Paula for the great job and went over her Thursday schedule with her, expecting them to afford the time for a good discussion when she submitted her morning news report. Thursday afternoon revolved around the videotaping with Joel and Willow, which she wanted Paula to observe. Leah would be back after gardening to watch *Joel* with Chris at six, while Paula was opting to watch him over dinner with Sam at their place. Fair enough.

Leah went home to change into her gardening duds and pack a picnic lunch to share with Chris who had already changed and gone off to the stable – with Nathan's book, she noticed. When she got to the stable, she set down her basket and went out searching for Holly to tell her all about the funeral and having seen Gert, her former mistress, as a young vibrant woman. Holly trotted up to the back pasture fence to greet her with a hearty blow and received a nice facial massage from Leah. They made a date to ride after her videotaping the next day since Paula was on news duty these days. Holly was excited to hear about that since Leah had pledged to become a better horsewoman with Paula's arrival. She would ask Chris and Thunder to go with them to see Mr. Brenner's barn and hear all about his vision for it.

Ellia joined Leah and Chris for a nice catch-up before the women went to assist Sonia in the community gardens. After hours transplanting starts to their place in the warm, rich earth of the greenhouse, whilst observing Demetri, who was working with the fish farm, Leah walked back to the studio with her basket to meet Chris for Joel's show. He would have been practicing Aikido with Will across the way in the yoga center. He was already there, with the computer booted up, checking his emails. She pulled up a chair beside him while he switched over to *Joel Robertson Live.*

"How were the seedlings?" he asked, giving her a compelling kiss and caress.

"Rambunctious. They were getting anxious roots but are now happily at home for the duration," she laughed. "Demetri also looked like he needed transplanting but I didn't quite know how to approach that. You may want to have a chat with him, cowboy."

"Thanks for teeing me up, lass. By the way, I've been thinking about the absurdity of owning property in Kalamunda and have initiated the sale of it to the folks who've been renting for the last 10 years."

"Good for you. What's your plan then?" she asked.

"I've been looking at flats overlooking the ocean on the Northern Beaches," he smiled.

"Do tell! What a great idea, and arguably the most gorgeous of the populated beaches in your beach-filled homeland."

"Aye. I'll keep looking. We'll need to go over at some point for that and a few other loose ends. It would be close to Sydney for the airport," he added, giving her back a rub, "and the surf is first-rate."

Then Joel appeared on the big screen and was off and running on the financial crisis brewing in Europe. The UK was already sunk, in his opinion. It was a great show centered on the theme of economic uncertainties in the western world, spending cuts and austerity as a lifestyle. There was a good clip from Willow in New York and a reminder that Leah would be on the show Thursday with some solutions for the ever-increasing plight of the homeless.

That was also the theme on her Saturday show where she would use a 15-minute taped interview with Joel to set the stage for a discussion about the crisis and the *Harmony Valley* model of community for the homeless. Outreach would be putting the call out for homeless farmers and gardeners to begin populating the community soon, both over the airways and through the Northern California and Oregon social services networks.

Joel had interviewed three different economic experts in the studio and via Skype to round out his own presentation of the economic crises. One felt we were out of the woods and on the mend, another felt certain that a second recession was imminent and the third couldn't find an ending to the story other than collapse and restructuring of the very concept of economy. Leah and Chris chatted about economic stability in *New Avalon,* with a great deal of relief that it would be unaffected by collapse aside from the loss of a few non-essential extras. They would have to push productivity on Mr. B's farm to take on ten to twelve more families but that was doable. *Harmony Valley* would need to reach sustainability soon as well. Whether or not the larger *Harmony Valley* model was achievable before collapse was a good, but unanswerable, question.

Chris took a quick shower and managed dinner so she could review Paula's reports. They had to be back at the community center for play rehearsal at eight o'clock. She admitted having had no time to even look at her script, which he, uncharacteristically, tried hard to turn into a crisis before truthfully stating that it wouldn't matter a great deal. She could read them. She had to admit he was a convincing actor. With that reprieve she started making notes on Paula's reports.

At *Oklahoma!* play rehearsal that night, the focus was on the opening scene of the first act, which involved only Leah, Chris, and Jenny, with Ellia on the piano. Chris hardly needed to practice *Oh What A Beautiful Mornin'* but he sang it anyway to set the stage, whilst wandering into Laurey's yard. Leah had a copy of the script and was relieved that the only two songs were his. Jenny, as Laurey's Aunt Eller, had an onlooker part for most of the scene. They went through the teasing interplay between Laurey and Curly, his wish to take her to the picnic and her refusal — her way of paying him back for waiting so long to ask her. That brought in *The Surrey With The Fringe On Top* song without the props but with playful interactions between Curly, Laurey and Aunt Eller. At the end of the scene, she teased him again about the surrey being just a fantasy. He tells her it was just a story he'd made up to get even with her. She walks off, nose in the air, not knowing that he really had rented a surrey much like the one he'd coaxed her into imagining in the song.

Leah had the teasing bit well under control. They loved teasing each other, which made it look almost too natural to Jenny. Leah hammed it up a bit more for the sake of dramatic amplification. Chris, of course, was going to pull the show off with his voice, even if they all blew the rest of it. Ellia was wonderful on the piano, which would be sufficient accompaniment for most of the songs. The evening was a lot of fun. They would meet again on Saturday afternoon with the rest of the cast to work on the second scene. Chris and Leah would get their interactions down at home before then. They walked home, arm in arm, looking forward to a good night's sleep. Chris was scheduled to help Greg over at *Harmony Valley* the next morning and would make certain Demetri came along. It had been awhile since they'd had a good talk about his spiritual and emotional health.

After a good cuddle with her husband in bed the next morning, then a shower rehearsing their lines together, Leah moved through her yoga and breakfast to be out the door by eight. She needed her morning to finish the news reviews, have a good chat with Paula, and pull the Saturday show together before an afternoon in front of the camera. Will would take a break from banking around eleven o'clock to go over *Harmony Valley* progress with her, since that was the topic of Joel's live interview with her at three-fifteen. A Saturday show was planned for the Inner City project two weeks hence, with this interview a key way to introduce the model to the larger viewing audience.

By nine o'clock she'd concluded that Paula was a gift from the cosmos. She missed nothing, highlighted the lies and drama spins, sought out the values and truth and managed to come up with a distillate that fit Leah to a tee. When confronted with that evaluation, Paula laughed and reminded Leah she'd been critically watching her show for several years. They had a wonderful discussion over a list of questions that had come up for Paula, including some big picture inquiries about the overall aims of Outreach. She wanted to know about solutions, and problems that didn't have solutions yet. She wanted to actively engage her creative mind.

After Paula went back to work, Leah applied herself to the news summary and discussion outline for the show. She was nearly two days behind due to *Samhain* and the funeral, but Paula had just sliced hours of work off her week. She would one day reflect back on that first discussion with Paula as the moment she stepped into the role of understudy.

For her part, Paula was secretly relieved that Leah was so easy to get along with — so not on a pedestal like others she'd worked for in her role. And yet, Paula adored Leah and wanted to know what she knew, think like she thought, love like she loved, and serve like she served. She hadn't just found herself a good job. She'd found herself a new life and a mentor to go with it. It helped that Sam really admired Will too, and he felt professionally useful for the first time *ever*. Leah followed an intuition and invited them both to the community meeting to see how the consensus process worked.

Leah and Chris would meet at the stable after she'd finished in front of the camera. That gave her a bit of time over lunch to visit the apiary. It was a sunny day with bees out for air and water from feeders she'd put close to the hives. It gave her a lot of joy to pull out her meditation bench from behind Sophia's hive and sit with them. She'd locked herself into the apiary since there had been a series of poaching incidents in the valley and then a fire at Jim Taylor's sheep shed. Leah had been locked in the apiary when the menacing thieves had tried to attack her. Though the valley had been quiet since they were apprehended, Chris preferred that she be secure when meditating since she often went very deep with the bees. She agreed. The confrontation had been traumatic.

After honoring her four queens, Leah brought forth the clairvoyant Bee Mistress part of her personality on a quest for vision without agenda. Her IMAX screen popped up in her inner visual field with an amazing aerial view of what had to be *Harmony Valley* (see Appendix A p. 448). She scanned the scene and found a few familiar landmarks like the hotel, to confirm the location. There were people milling around everywhere, going about their business, working, chatting with friends, walking toddlers in strollers and sitting on park benches downtown and in small neighborhood green spaces. Leah became a little teary with feeling all the love that Tommy had put into the layout and design of everything in the valley. He'd really got a chunk of his mission under his belt with this one.

She went to town center — the intersection that included the hotel passed on to them by Burt and Alice Wilson along with all the farmland surrounding the town. It looked like everything w,as flourishing and people seemed happy with the community that had grown up from the homeless project. Not clear as to why this vision had come to her, she moved out over the adjunct facilities spawned from the original homeless project and found the Camphill Community for developmentally disabled adults, Alice's retirement village and an Aged Care Facility. Leah noted that the latter wasn't in the plan in its current form. She liked that idea as it completed the cycle of life within the community.

The northern end of the valley had the solar farm and wind farm for the power supply, which she observed as having been doubled over its present size. The farming operation was headquartered at the north end of the town but spread out to surround it and to surround the adjunct facilities she'd observed on the west side of the valley. Moving further down the valley to the south, past the commercial growing operations with packing and shipping depots, she came, after a good many fenced pastures, some with horses, to a small village. The signage in the front gardens of the complex indicated it was a WWOOFer and *Harmony Valley* Apprenticeship Village. The village had a lot of green space and its own veggie gardens. Here also was a horse stable a lot bigger than the one at *New Avalon*. It was close to the road, with a sign reading *'Harmony Valley Stable'* inviting the whole population to try riding. She could feel Chris' hand in that operation.

Across the way, not far from the end of the Retirement Village, she saw a large complex of beautiful buildings. For the whole valley, Tommy had used the inviting style of California Mission, honoring the early influence of Mexico in the architecture. The building exteriors were either of stucco on frame construction, straw bale or adobe brick with mud wash. The valley had the feel of community, warmth and cooperation. There were flowers everywhere, especially in the front of this complex. She took her vision over there to read the signage in the 'lawn' of native groundcover. It read *Harmony Valley Community Medical Center* and beneath that *A Non-Profit Cooperative*. Her heart swelled to see that such a concept wasn't only possible; it was done. She didn't need to see how it operated right then, as her mind was already racing with those possibilities and questions about health care insurance and costs.

Noting fields of crops where the prison of their Restorative Justice Model had been planned at the southeast end of the valley, Leah took her 'sight' back into the *Harmony Valley* community to look at the businesses in the small downtown area. She found the busy clinic with its alternative medicine branch and a counseling/educational center. These, she'd seen before, but next to the clinic she found a health insurance cooperative. She'd all of the puzzle pieces but none of the details. The completing of the vision would be hers to workout in present time. She rose up for a last, gratifying, view of the whole valley, and collapsed the IMAX screen in her inner visual field to re-enter her body in the apiary. She opened her eyes to see, really close up, a bee resting on her nose. She thanked the little worker–girl for holding such a beautiful space of vision on the Path of the Golden Queen.

The video taping session with Willow, who was transmitting live from Joel's New York Studio, was a summation of the week's activities in the OWS movement. She'd sent video clips in to Stu of in depth interviews with

raising the bar

Occupiers involved in the day-to-day organization in New York. They were in possession of half a million dollars in donations and were trying to decide how to manage it. Those who had been arrested previously when the protestors marched across the Brooklyn Bridge were beginning their appearances in court. Willow had a November 2nd film clip of a march past the New York Stock Exchange by veterans coming to join the *Occupiers,* and of a march in Washington, DC that had effectively stopped traffic. The movement was in support of *Occupiers* worldwide and particularly in Oakland, CA and Atlanta, GA, where police had used pepper spray to break up peaceful protests. Stu felt he could make a nice 15-minute segment for Saturday's show from all that Willow had delivered, including her vivacious, articulate interview with Leah. Joel was picking up on the violation of constitutional rights to free speech and assemblage, while Leah homed in on the heart of the *Occupy Movement,* tracking a bigger picture of where it was headed.

Stu and crew were ready for her live interview on Joel's show at three-fifteen – another flawless bit of magic establishing the homeless crisis as a priority in the minds of his viewers. Their love and compassion for those who had lost their jobs, homes and self-worth through the economic crisis was palpable. They both indicated a personal commitment in their areas to solving the problem and he urged his viewers to watch *Light in the Crisis* on Saturday for an in depth discussion of possible solutions.

Natalie and Leslie were both out of the studio, preparing the guesthouses for the show's guests and making sure the local crew, assembled to assist with their first use of The Lodge, were cleaning, making beds, stocking food, and cleaning up the grounds for the Ukiah group's intensive. A smaller hired crew would sleep in The Lodge's caretaking rooms and help with food prep and housekeeping. The Ukiah group would cook and cleanup after meals together, as a group, since they were meant to have an experience of community.

Chris was home when Leah arrived there to change for horseback riding. Exhausted from the combination of farming and analyzing Demetri's eccentric behavior – well, behavior more eccentric than normal – he'd snatched a nap on the sofa with Harry. Leah wanted to have a deeper discussion of that very topic in the evening, since she and Nick would see Demetri in the clinic the next day. For the moment, they agreed to have a joyful ride down to Mr. B's barn where Chris would share his vision for the performing arts.

On their return, after grooming Thunder and Holly, they walked back to the studio to watch Joel's show, including his Thursday interview with Leah. Chris thoroughly enjoyed the way they communicated with each other on the air, and was looking forward to having a bit of that in the midst of *New Avalon* soon. While cooking dinner together, Chris filled her in about the progress over at *Harmony Valley,* with the barn raising and hotel restoration well underway. Greg was baling hay to be stored in that barn, seeing to fences, and irrigating orchards and vines that Sonia and the WWOOFers had planted. She'd designed and installed long, wide hoop houses for the production market gardens. These hoop houses were on sliding tracks to rotate crops through the seasons, whilst allowing interaction with the cosmic forces and weather for half the year. They'd the land to pull that off in *Harmony Valley*. She and Greg had been enriching the soil with biodynamic manure mix and compost – feeling lucky that the land had rested for years, restoring its mineral wealth. The plan was to leave the hoop houses uncovered for the winter to allow the weather time to work the treatments into the soil.

They were maybe a month away from interviews with homeless folks having farm and garden experience. The first crew would probably get started in mid-February, while initially being housed in the hotel. There were seeds to plant, animals to acquire and care for, chicks to be raise, a fish farm to get up and running, and an opportunity for Tommy to test the infrastructure while beginning to build the downtown and first neighborhood. As soon as the Mission design theme had been agreed upon, he'd redrawn the center of town with a traditional Latin American plaza, but without the noisy and polluting vehicles of present day Latin cities. Copies of these four perspective drawings, each a look down a different street from town center, had been framed for the newsroom at the studio. They were very inviting. She would be using them for the Saturday show on homelessness and Natalie would take copies to post when she interviewed the homeless people for participation in the *Harmony Valley* Homeless Project.

Leah and Chris took their expansive conversation to the dinner table and on, through kitchen cleanup to the living room with a pot of tea. There, she shared the Bee Mistress' apiary vision of the medical center at *Harmony Valley* with her cowboy, who was both pleased and amazed that the future community could support such a center. He also liked the part of the vision about the stable and was sure the downtown would have a theater as well.

"No doubt, you'll see to that, cowboy," she laughed. "It was amazing to see the valley teaming with life and sharing the gift. I'm so hopeful about this project and can't let myself get bogged down by the trashing of the economy. It would be easy to stall progress waiting to see what happens. I'm glad we're moving so quickly even if it seems like a small beginning with the first group coming in."

"It could seem that way, lass, but it's wise to take smalls steps. I reckon you'll need to attend to the apprenticeship and WWOOFer housing before you get too far along with neighborhoods."

"You're right. The homeless people coming in are going to need a lot of support. They'll need to rebuild their health in body, mind and spirit at the same time they honor their part of the contract. One of the many important aspects of healing to establish with them is the spiritual core of the incoming community. Therein lies the needed resiliency. Trust and hope might be big hills for them to climb. In the material world, the challenge will be the currency system but once on to it, I think they'll eagerly embrace a new kind of prosperity. We'll fill the hotel with farmer's and gardeners, and hopefully someone with some experience in finance."

"Long shot, lass," he said, furrowing his brow. "Most of that lot are still profiting from the losses of the 99%."

"You never know, Chris. There were a good many small banks put out of business and a large regional bank out of Seattle where the banksters moved in, some say the CEOs had it prearranged, and a lot of the local folks lost their jobs when it was swallowed up. I have one of them on the show this week. Now there are five or six mega-banks running the country and the world. I have a feeling we can find homeless financial people to come into *Harmony Valley* and the Inner City projects to run the credit unions. Whether they could get in the spirit of the gift and local currency/equal pay is a good question, though."

"Quite right," he concluded. "How do you suppose you're going to staff your medical center?"

"An even better question," she admitted. "I'll have to revisit the vision a good many times to see what's going on there. It was a cooperative non-profit, which was interesting, in and of itself. There was a cooperative style health insurance, perhaps like what we have here. I'll have a chat with Will to get some ideas going in his head. It would be easy enough to establish a single-payer health care system there by taking a portion of the earnings in local currency to cover medical expenses, education and so forth – like a tax, similar to how we roll-over our unspent NADs into the community fund for expenses like our insurance. He could invest that externally, or we could invest it in more *Harmony Valley* projects to put the local currency to work. It could be backed by the US dollar income from the many business projects that will spring up," she suggested.

"Or you may be able to keep the US dollars out of the equation, seeing as how they'll be worthless anyway, and get your medical staff to work for local currency as well."

"You reckon they'll do that?" she asked.

"You do," he countered. "I think you might be surprised at the shift coming on us. Yes, the medical system is flourishing right now. More people are getting sick than every before, but, not here. If people get the lifestyle bit down, the doctors can implement preventative medicine in a more productive way. I think it's a great opportunity to attract medical professionals who believe in our inherent good health. I reckon most of them will be young millennials. I love this generation of game-changers."

"I do too, and you may be right," she agreed. "It's exciting in another way to me. It'll be our closest hospital – no more reliance on the old system. Hey, cowboy, it's another solution. I'll have to give this a really good think before we do the single payer show on Thanksgiving weekend. That may be only a part of it. I'll put the Bee Mistress on task to get more information about the new medical model," she said, excitedly.

"It's a great project for you, lass. Between the two of us, we'd better get a large pad of checkered drawing paper and a bigger kitchen table," he mused.

"So true," she beamed, joining in the mirth. Then, observing a cloud casting a shadow over her beloved cowboy, she added, soberly, "I guess we need to talk about Demetri before we get too carried away?"

"We do," he sighed. "He's not right. You saw that yesterday. Why don't you summarize what you know about his condition for me?"

"I'll know more about the physical tomorrow but can tell you he looks much improved. I expect he'll need to stay on the anti-viral herbs for six weeks minimum, since the CMV titer was pretty high. He's put on good weight and muscle but I'm troubled by two observations of imbalance; his lungs and the diminshment of his light, which may be related to the way his etheric body seems to be gripping him, like ... for all it's worth. The lungs feel like unresolved grief to me. If he'd an infection it would've materialized by this time or backed off. There's just this heaviness. It's hard to explain, darling."

"Aye but you've done well, lass. Thank you. And you're right to assume the physical symptoms will clear. And, he does look a lot healthier than he did when he arrived. Unless he's had a serious loss that he's not told me about, I can't figure out the grief. I'll ask though. What concerns me is the lack of light and the pathology in his etheric body. You remember that mine had been loose enough to be life-threatening?"

"Of course, I remember. He couldn't contemplate going after his double in his present condition, right?"

"Right. In fact, the opposite is true. His double's coming after him."

She sighed. "I recall having read something about extreme tightness indicating a kind of possession? Is it possible to implode? Is that demonic?"

"If you consider Ahriman a demon. I don't. He's much more powerful than the demons."

"Possession by Ahriman? How's that different than his being the double in our etheric body for our whole lives, unless we master the double and cast him out?" she asked. "I know this in theory but, without on-the-ground experience, I could use some visuals."

"Aye. When our etheric body is too loose, we tend towards emotionally distraught or hysterical disorders. The etheric over–identifies with the astral because its earthly ties are weakening. This affords an opportunity for the Luciferic beings to dig deeper, forcing their corrupt egos into humanity, and the astral is their territory; so it's going to look like emotional or mental imbalance. In the process, they'll pull the etheric body's astral interface further into the astral than normal. But they've no hope of occupying the etheric body itself — it's not their territory. Remember the fallen ones' greatest desire is to be human so we give them that opportunity when the etheric is greatly loosened. When we master the astral, those beings are cast out and the beneficial angels remain until we're able to take over fully."

"That's step one in mastery," she added.

"Aye. Now on the other end of the spectrum, there are the Ahrimanic Beings. They're not considered fallen angels, although they were varied rebel beings, who turned away from the evolution of their particular hierarchy to join Ahriman. When Lucifer and his legions caused *The Fall*, it was necessary to create a balancing force that brought the material world into existence. We would, otherwise, have been trapped in a reality of Lucifer's making without a path home. The light forces of the sun provide unending creative energy but are incapable of materialization without an opposing force and that's the Ahrimanic — the darkness."

"That makes it sound like the Ahrimanic beings are on mission," Leah remarked.

"They are. It's said that *The Fall* of humanity by Lucifer's actions is Ahriman's karma. The Ahrimanic Beings are bound to the task of materializing this world until we have mastered our etheric bodies, have cast them out, and can live without the need for them. It's the evolutionary story ongoing, because Lucifer caused this perturbation. So here we are, as a result of these two opposing forces, imagining that the maya of their creation is reality."

"Okay. So how is this cosmic saga playing out in our brother, Demetri?" she asked.

"What these two opposing forces are doing within us reflects that balance required for materialization between the Sun — the light-bearing Luciferic — and the Darkness — the Ahrimanic. We wouldn't exist, physically, without them and that's true of the entire material world. If our own balance between these forces is perturbed, the Ahrimanic will instinctively move further into the material world — they deeply desire control of humanity. As you know they inhabit the etheric body from birth until just before the moment of death, and this move to further embody the physical, if not stopped, causes the gripping. You and Demetri will both wobble during etheric mastery because the etheric body does loosen in the process. All of humanity will be moving through this in the future. We all must. If he'd experienced a loosening through his process of astral mastery, or perhaps through our trauma in Iran, and the emotional imbalance you pick up as grief came on him, it could have been enough to allow Ahriman to seize his physical body. Demetri is unable to process whatever is troubling him because his etheric-astral connection has been weaken by the etheric body's pull towards the physical."

"How is this supposed to be managed then, in the process of etheric mastery?" she asked.

"I remember you asking if there was a stage of initiation where we work with the light and the dark?" he reminded.

"R-r-right," she drawled. "That's a real comfort to me, cowboy."

"It's a bugger, I can tell you that," he laughed. "But, back to our brother who's in serious trouble, in this regard. I'm not exactly sure how to intervene. I expect getting to the bottom of the grief will be part of it. He may also be at the threshold of astral mastery, needing a good boot in the bum to catapult some part of him to the bridge. I reckon the two are intimately intertwined."

"What shall we do, cowboy. I don't want anyone getting hurt here, or even the idea of astral mastery to be feared," she gently pleaded.

"That coming from someone recently served up with 30 lashes from the past?" he grinned.

"That *was* a shocker. But I have to admit, it's opened a door for Dragon Lady," she smiled.

"Aye, lass, and good luck with that," he conceded. "Let's be open to a dreamscape with Master Mukda tonight. It feels like he's anxious to share his skills on Demetri's behalf. How does that sound?" he asked, with a slight grin, since they always woke up making otherworldly love.

"Like a plan," she laughed. "I shall look forward to it. That settled, how are you going with your Performing Arts Center proposal?" she asked.

"I've a lot in my head and little on paper — as yet. Can I walk you to work tomorrow and pick up some checkered paper?" he asked.

"Sure can. I have the news summary on my plate first thing in the morning and I want to have a good talk with Will to catch up on the Inner City project and see what he knows about health care cooperatives and local currency. I also need to have the show down, rehearse and see Demetri in the clinic. It's full-on Friday, the day after Super Pac Thursday," she laughed.

"How about I give you time to look Paula's summaries over now, while I get a leg on organizing my proposal," he suggested.

"That's a great idea. There's nothing more we can do about Demetri tonight. By the way, the women are getting together tomorrow night to begin making Christmas gifts for the children. You can get a good bit done with your checkered paper while I'm with them, and then getting into pre-show ritual."

In an hour's time spent with Paula's reports, Leah was prepared to get the news summary going on her laptop in the morning. Chris had an umbrella-like flow chart of all that a Center for the Performing Arts ought to provide. He'd separate sheets of paper for each subheading, detailing the organization, aim, and end product of each. His plan was organized around the *New Avalon* communities but brought in young talent from the outside on work-study programs. They would contribute to community and their NADs would go for their tuition. He would think up a catchy name like the WWOOFer program. Proceeds from public performances would offset the costs of the school. He was interested in talent, not money. He felt it might be nice to search out homeless people with music, dance and acting talent as well as set design, costume making, etc., to form a bridge with *Harmony Valley* and get additional teachers into the school — and to keep the NADs circulating.

When Leah looked it over, she was impressed. He could have all the checkered paper he wanted from her secret stash. One thing she did want to talk to Will about was the currency. *Harmony Valley* was looking monstrous in her clairvoyant visual field, and she wondered whether they should have their own currency that was interchangeable with NADs. Chris felt she had a point but he'd no interest in currency. Along with his instigation of security, he was obviously on to filling in another oversight of the original founder's vision. He'd the talent and energy to pull it off too, and to send a lot of spiritually attuned young people out to offer it to others. When she thought about it, his proposal for the arts and hers for the medical center covered two important missing parts of the cultural sphere.

They set their intent to find each other in a mutual dreamscape in Master Mukda's ashram. After mission completion, Mukda had been the one directing Ramandi to re-establish Chris's etheric–physical body connection and would likely have the proper procedure for the reverse situation. Chris gifted Leah a charge of calming energy to the back of her neck, assuring a deep, undisturbed sleep.

They met in the ashram's garden, coming from different directions to embrace near a reflecting pool. Typically they might have found themselves sparring in the training room for martial arts, but they both recollected that Master Mukda had moved to a new level himself and this was likely a different ashram altogether. A monk approached them. They followed the man inside the ashram to a meditation room where they would have an audience with Master Mukda. He was waiting for them, in his simple orange and maroon monk's robes, seated upon a stack of ornate cushions set on a raised platform. He smiled broadly at the sight of them, his dark eyes twinkling in the light of many butter lamps, and motioned them to the cushions placed before him on the main floor.

"Dear ones, it's so good to see you, again," he said in greeting.

"Likewise, Master Mukda," they replied, in unison.

'I know you've come to me in an effort to help our brother, Demetri. What have you been able to determine about his condition?" he asked.

"We could call it an impulse to over materialize, perhaps," Chris offered. "He seems to have been sabotaged by a personal experience of unfortunate timing."

Leah found that an interesting, almost obtuse, way to put it, but Master Mukda understood perfectly.

"That's true. Demetri calls his mentor's dwelling in Cyprus his home but, as you know, his family is in Athens, where Demetri was born. Eventually, he'll be able to share the details of his loss with you but suffice to say that his family has lost what wealth they had in the collapse of the Greek economy. His older brother suffered enormous losses on investments and through his business. Direct your query to the situation in his family and you will find the way to release him."

"Thank you, Master Mukda," Leah replied, a little teary-eyed. "I'll follow your lead in the clinic situation tomorrow to see if he'll open the door."

"With your signature bedside manner, my dear," the Master smiled.

Jane had her clue, and the heart to pull off the healing of trauma. Chris was satisfied that Master Mukda, who'd provided a dose of resiliency and courage along with the clue, was taking the right tact with Leah – allowing her to use her own gifts on Demetri's behalf. Chris pressed Master Mukda for insight regarding the stage of Demetri's initiatory journey when the trauma occurred.

"What was the destabilizing factor within Demetri's soul … if I might ask?" Chris queried. "Was he quite close to a breakthrough with the gathering of his personality in consciousness soul? And what role did our experience with the dark forces in Iran play in this drama?"

Leah perked up to hear the answer to Chris' inquiry, knowing she would find herself in a similar soul situation when Dragon Lady finally claimed her space at the bridge.

"All good questions, Chris," Master Mukda replied. "You've guessed correctly that he was close to initiating integration and thus in a more vulnerable place with his etheric body. When we get that close, the Luciferic forces put up a fierce offensive — a kind of wrestling match with the last part of the "I" to free itself from the culture. So there was that" he chuckled. "As for your experience in Iran; that was the catalyst for this part of him to arrive at the bridge. He gave himself in service to your life, Chris. That's the mark of a spiritual hero. It did destabilize him for its sheer intensity, but that can be looked upon as a gift. The family situation, on the other hand, pulled that newly arrived part of him right back down into the cultural mind and into a very Ahrimanic place. It didn't help that he was also ill and greatly weakened. A challenging position compared to his usual robust health."

"How can we help him, Master Mukda?" Leah asked, feeling Demetri's losses in her own soul.

"It requires a kind of exorcism, my dear," he replied.

She looked at Chris, who was visibly affected by the suggestion. "Shall we get a priest to help us?" she asked.

"Why? You have more power than they do, my dear."

"Me? You must be joking, Master Mukda," she exclaimed, shocked at the suggestion.

"I recall a recent incident when some drugged vagrants tried to assault you, my dear. The part of you that came forth to command the bees is capable of commanding Ahriman's retreat from your brother's physicality."

Leah silently absorbed the truth of Master Mukda's suggestion. Chris reached over to touch her back, behind her heart. "Your Bee Mistress is one hell of a butt-kicker, lass."

Master Mukda laughed. "Quite true," he affirmed. "Now, what you need to know to motivate this Bee Mistress, my dear, is that if she succeeds in commanding Ahriman's retreat, she'll open herself to a higher level of clairvoyant skill and memory. This could be quite useful in your mission at present. It's my duty to point out to you that you are having difficulty remembering your own wedding. At the same time you are trying to make contact with a Ruby Brother who's life was lived 230 years ago, give or take."

Leah's jaw dropped, while Chris burst into laughter. "Aye, lass. Master Mukda has a point. What are the consequences if we fail?" he asked.

"We'll have to recall Demetri. It's already being considered. He cannot act impeccably on behalf of the Mission in his present condition, which *is* worsening, by the way. There *is* urgency in this regard. If you consider the circumstances unfolding, Leah, you will agree that Demetri used a great deal of his power, impeccably, to remove an implant from your astral body. This is an opportunity to reciprocate — one of the hard and fast rules of the Ruby Order."

Chris continued to rub her back as she replied. "I do understand that, Master Mukda. I've a great love for Demetri and feel that need to gift him in kind. But, what must be done, exactly. My Bee Mistress is short on experience in this life, especially with exorcism."

"Chris will help. You'll need him to hold the space as he did for you and Demetri when the implant was removed. I suggest that you ask the bees," he said, eyes twinkling. "The only way to confront Ahriman is with the balance of Christ Consciousness — even better would be the triangulation of Christ, Lucifer and Ahriman. You have four *biens* in cluster right now, holding a lot of power to reinforce your own deep connection to Christ."

"We'll work this out, Master Mukda," Chris offered. "We've taken enough of your time. Have you any other questions, lass?" he asked.

"No, I don't. I'm stunned by this proposal, but will begin to work with it and with Demetri. Is there anything else I need to know, Master Mukda?" she asked.

"Know that you have done this before, Leah. Now I'll go. I love you both very much. I feel good about Demetri's future."

"Thank you, Master Mukda," they both called out to him, as the vision faded.

They found themselves back in the garden where Chris took Leah gently into his arms to comfort her. He bent down to kiss her inviting lips as they both began to fall back down into the waking state in the bliss of tender lovemaking. When they had these encounters that bridged the worlds, they were both brimming with the sun's energy. They lay back on their pillows, hands joined, basking in the sun's creative light. Leah had full memory of the encounter with Master Mukda though the integration of its profound nature would not be completed until Demetri appeared in the clinic for his appointment.

She and Chris went over the dream before getting up to start their day. Mindful yoga and meditation was helpful, discussing the fine points over breakfast essential, and feeling the depth of Chris' support paramount in Leah's quest to bring the task before her soul into this reality. She would work to understand the whole of it, before visiting the apiary right after the Saturday production of *Light on the Crisis*.

When they arrived at the studio, she fixed Chris up with grid-paper and colored markers for his performing arts project. Before going home, he was going to stop at the community center to go through his songs for the musical with the piano, reminding Leah of rehearsal Saturday afternoon. Her lines were coming along slowly, but coming. She completed organizing the discussion part of the show and, together with Paula, composed the news summary that would be edited the next morning with breaking stories relevant to their big picture view of the week. Then they would download the final version into the teleprompter program and send it to Stu. Leah always had a print out at the news desk as well. All of the new staff was there for rehearsal along with Georgia who was directing, Natalie producing, and Stu on camera with Rob assisting. Will was there to run through his financial analysis of the week as well. They began with the 15-minute news summary, which included Will's analysis, then the videotapes — 15-minutes each — of Willow and Joel's interviews with Leah. Stu included the station identification, and show and Outreach promotion segments, which would appear at each of six 15-minute network breaks, for the benefit of the new staff.

Then the cameras were shifted to simulate the typical, though fairly new, discussion format with Leah and her guests. There were four guests for Saturday's show on the homeless crisis. One was an articulate homeless man who'd lost his job, then home, then family through the past few years of financial hardship. He'd been referred by one of the nurses in the Ashland community group. A second guest was a homeless woman who had worked for the bank in Seattle that had been gobbled up by the 'too big to fail' bank out of New York. She'd been on the streets for three years with significant health problems and was found in Portland by Social Services in Yreka. And there was the administrator of that local homeless program for Social Services on the panel as well as a mental health professional that specialized in assisting the homeless. There was no need for high-powered guests as homelessness was a local crisis that had swept across the whole of America. It was a crisis best solved by a return to local economies and embracing communities.

Leslie was seeing to the arriving members of the Ukiah community group at The Lodge and also saw to the housing and feeding of the homeless guests from Ashland in The Lodge Annex. Natalie would be working with the Ukiah group, as would various members of the community in their specialties, through Tuesday, but she would be there Saturday to produce the show. Stu had rigged up the LCD TV screen in The Lodge's study to pick up the *freedomofspeech.org TV* live stream of the show, since Natalie had made it part of the Outreach Community program. They were all regular viewers of *Light on the Crisis* and appreciated Stu's efforts on their behalf.

After the rehearsal, and a group discussion with the news staff, Leah went across to the credit union to speak with Will. Sam was busy in a back office setting up a tax deadline strategy to make the process easier for the community. The Non-profit filing date of May 15 would, hopefully, lose its menace status with Sam at the helm of the tax department. Will was sitting at his desk, which was piled high with files and research materials. He was on his laptop, working on *Harmony Valley,* when Leah arrived.

"Hey, Will. Have you got a minute?" she asked, all smiles.

"Hi, Light Beam. For you, I have the whole day," he laughed.

"Yeah, it looks like you've nothing to do, brother!" she exclaimed. "I won't take long. I've got clinic this afternoon and a little intro talk with the group over at The Lodge."

"Ukiah, right?" he asked.

"Yeah. They're getting settled in now," she said. "So, I have to report that my vision of *Harmony Valley* is becoming immense, Will. I was given another big piece yesterday morning — a good-sized medical center that was down the valley and across from the proposed site of the Apprentice and WWOOFer Village. The sign told me it was non-profit and a cooperative, which I find interesting."

"The whole idea is interesting, considering how no one ever gets sick here. I guess with the Retirement and Camphill Villages, you may see a little more action in that area, huh?"

"For certain. I also saw a facility for Aged Care in between those two villages, and that will require medical staff. It looks like we're going to fill the valley up in due time."

"Is this your master plan for turning the county blue at the polls?" he laughed.

"That wasn't in my vision but it surely might turn out that way," she chuckled. "I want to go further into the vision and see what sort of facility this medical center is. It could have a research division for preventative medicine and I would love to see a spiritual research center devoted to understanding the etheric and higher bodies. But all of that's not what I want to lay on you, my friend. I'm wondering if we should initiate *Harmony Valley*'s independence from New Avalon, as its own non-profit umbrella and with its own currency, interchangeable with ours?"

"Done," he smiled. "It *is* actually independent of *New Avalon's* non-profit organization. I know it's become quite complicated as we've taken on Outreach projects, but Outreach, which encompasses the show, the Community programs, the Inner City program, Restorative Justice and *Harmony Valley* is a big umbrella. Separating *New Avalon* keeps it simple since *New Avalon* doesn't run on donations and its only risk to survival is crop failure, which is unlikely under our circumstances. The courtyard is *New Avalon's* but the show is Outreach's. The credit union is *New Avalon's* but it processes the funds for both New Avalon and Outreach. We are really just talking accounting, doll. The show pays rent to New Avalon for studio space from its donations, for example."

"Does New Avalon have the equity to build the second community?" she asked.

"We do. We have the liquidated gold, then all of the work Greg, Chris, Sonia, Tommy and Demetri are doing over in *Harmony Valley*, for example, brings income to New Avalon from the Outreach donation fund. People will be contributing to the new village for their homes which is how we'll build them and be able to offer some loan's like Mitch and Katia's. We should plan to go over the waiting list at the community meeting, by the way."

"Natalie and I will work on that and get confirmations that people are still ready to commit. She'll need to get them into the Outreach Community Training Program, which will have to be conducted here since they are from all over the country and Canada. So, does *Harmony Valley* have its own currency?"

"It does. We can call them HADs for now, or ever more," he laughed. "And it has its own credit union. It's the umbrella for your big valley-filled vision, Light Beam. We'll form a temporary board of directors soon. It's my feeling that all of the Inner City projects should be under their own umbrella and have an established currency that's interchangeable with NADs, HADs, and city to city. I have to check interstate commerce laws with that, but it should work locally, say Sacramento, San Francisco and Oakland. In this case it also makes sense to have one big farm servicing all three communities. How do you like that idea?"

"I love it, especially if the farm were centrally located to the three cities."

"It's right pricy farmland anywhere around there but we're looking for donors, estates that can write it off, like that. I want to be prepared for the Inner City show we're doing in two weeks. The banks and city are transferring the San Francisco parcels to Outreach at the moment. That makes it likely we can get going on the project soon."

"I'd better tip Natalie off on that. She'll need to customize an Outreach Inner City Community Program to prepare the founders and other residents with the spiritual work. You'll also need to have a group with the savvy to carry on when Outreach, inevitably, pulls out. Have you got someone working on a selection process?"

"I do. Elliot has been very helpful, as has the City Council. People displaced by job loss and foreclosure have moved in with relatives while others have wound up in homeless shelters and public housing. I think we can run them through the whole program down there, since we're so well supported."

"Great. And, how are *you* doing with your subpersonalities?" she asked.

"I seemed to be spending a lot of time in my multi-tasking businessman," he admitted, with a little frustration.

"That's just the part of you pushed into service first. You also have your TV star in play for five minutes a week," she laughed.

"Five minutes is more than enough for TV but even that has financial content. I do have a different role to play with the Rangers, and with Chris and the horses, and with Demetri though I couldn't tell you what role that is or whether I've been very helpful."

"I'll be seeing to his checkup today. Anything I should know about?"

"He's very withdrawn. I see him for meals, and then he retreats to his room or bundles up and sits on the front porch. It's as if he's being deliberately, maybe even painfully, anti-social."

"Hmm. Thanks for that, Will. It's all part of the big picture. He's keen on the fish farm, I've noticed."

"Sonia's happy for the help with the fish since they're not particularly her bag, but she worries that he's relating more to the fish than the community. I hope he comes through this in good shape. He's a powerful and loveable brother."

"That he is, Will. Well, I'd best get home for lunch so I can come back for that clinic appointment on time. I was going to get into the idea of a cooperative hospital with you, but that can wait. Maybe you can give it some thought in your 'spare' time," she laughed. "Thanks for who you are, my brother. Your service reflects the core of this community to the world. You have all of my support and love."

"Back at 'ya, Light Beam," he laughed jumping up to get a hug from her before she left. Then he went back to his credit union logistical plan for the *Harmony Valley* non-profit umbrella.

Chris had saved them one end of the kitchen table for lunch and had taken the time to make a tasty chicken and veggie soup with salad, accompanied by a fresh loaf of sourdough French bread he'd picked up at the coffee shop. He'd be off to the stable after lunch and meet up with her again for *Joel* at the studio following Aikido with Will. Leah was cleaning up after lunch, worrying a bit about Demetri's appointment when Chris wandered over to seduce her. It was amazing how quickly she could switch into her Bee Mistress to take advantage of these surprise attacks. Left breathless and blissful, she was unable to pick up that worrisome train of thought she'd had and left the house for the clinic higher than a kite — a better way to approach Demetri to Chris' way of thinking. He didn't mind charging the Bee Mistress' batteries ... at all.

Nick was waiting for Leah at the clinic check-in desk. Demetri hadn't arrived yet, giving them a chance to divvy up responsibilities for the appointment. While Nick was running through the naturopathic and homeopathic questions, she could step aside and get a good look at his astral and etheric bodies and observe body language, emotional and mental responses and overall light. She'd no strategy for reclaiming his etheric balance, leaving that to the bees and the Bee Mistress. Jane was present, practicing medicine from consciousness soul, with compassion being her strong suit. Nick would take him into his clinic for chiropractic adjustments when they were finished with the higher frequency version of mainstream medicine. Demetri had benefited enormously from the adjustments at his first appointment two weeks previous to this follow-up. In fact, they'd likely dislodged the stuck emotions presently gripping him.

As expected, Demetri had obviously gained weight, lost most of the jaundiced coloring in his sclera and skin, and was gradually building muscle, through the farm work mostly, and a little bit on the bakery gym set. Leah got him talking about the fish, and soon concluded he was the right man for the job. They brought him peace of mind and he brought forth a greater understanding of their nutritional needs, which translated to good health and better fish on the dinner plate. It was a meager connection to the Mediterranean Sea, but good enough for the moment.

As Nick went through a list of questions relevant to organ health, Leah stepped back under the guise of writing notes in his medical records, but, instead, studied his higher bodies — visible using her clairvoyance. Typically the nadis of the etheric body sat down on the nerve trunks with about three inches of flexible energetic tendril to connect the two bodies. Demetri had an inch of taut tendril, if that, and the nadis were flaring energy. The etheric-astral interface/overlap was much smaller than normal, which, she guessed, would make it a tad more difficult to bring the expressions of the soul into this reality. *Perhaps that was the way Ahriman liked it — cutting off the soul and its angelic guardian.*

When Nick finished, she came back, wanting to listen to his heart and lungs. And then she asked him about burnout or low energy, feeling alone or abandoned by inner guidance, and whether he often awoke between three and five o'clock in the morning with or without difficulty breathing. He admitted feeling drained, especially on arising in the morning. Interestingly, he felt the need to withdraw and even shut himself down from all the mumblings, and even shouting, in his head. He did wake up, usually around three-thirty and wanted to know why.

Leah told him it was the lung meridian time for the circuit of Qi in his body and she'd some feeling about his lungs that she couldn't nail down. She applied a tourniquet to his upper arm then fastened a blood pressure band below it, pumped it, released the tourniquet and noted the readings. They were within the normal range but she was inspired to pump it up again while asking him what he'd heard from home since the government looked to be on the verge of collapse? She deflated the band when his complexion reddened and sweat appeared on his forehead. A chord had been struck. Nick took the cue and excused himself to set up the chiropractic table.

Leah followed the chord, looking for the open door. "Demetri, my heart and your lungs tell me that you've suffered somehow, a loss, perhaps. Would you care to talk about it with me, with Chris or with both of us? It makes my heart heavy to see you in distress. You're my Ruby Brother and I love you, unconditionally," she assured him, resting her hand on his.

A few tears rolled out of his eyes. "Maybe my guardian angel has abandoned me," he said, sadly. "I feel disconnected from my soul, Leah. It feels very strange and threatening to me."

"How would this happen to a Ruby Brother, I ask myself?" Leah questioned. "Chris did share with me the trauma you both experienced in the heart of darkness. Did that set you up for this soul disconnect?" she prodded further.

"It may have, though I felt good in Cyprus and was feeling that my service in Iran had somehow completed my elevation to consciousness soul. I felt the Luciferic loosen its grip on my soul and was very uplifted. To be sure, I wasn't eating well, and my apprentice was driving me crazy," he said, lightening, momentarily, "but I made my plans to come over here with Chris, in the highest of spirits."

"And then, you traveled to your brothers, right?" she asked.

"I did. The situation in Greece is volatile and in Athens there's a lot of violence, anger and despair. It's an emotional hotbed and very unstable. I haven't much interest in the financial markets, but my brothers do. Our father worked very hard to establish his import business and my brothers have stepped in to take care of it since his passing. The business is bankrupt. People cannot afford imports. People cannot find enough to eat. My younger brother had a second career in radiology. The loss of the family company did not affect him as much as my older brother, who was devastated and, like many, despaired that he could not even feed his family let alone face the mountain of debt he'd taken on during the time of easy credit," he shared, and then the tears came.

Leah gave him her shoulder to cry on and he sobbed, barely able to breathe. Eventually he could get breath, and then more and more breath as the grief lifted out of his lungs. She held him until he'd no more tears, then asked if his brother had taken his own life, as so many had.

"He did," he said, flatly. "I'm ashamed for my family, but very worried for his soul."

"This happened while you were there?" she queried.

"It did. We had dinner together with his family then he walked out into the back garden and shot himself in the head. His wife will never recover. She has faced his brains in her flower garden. I needed to take charge of the situation, call the police and ambulance. I was numb for days, even after I arrived over here."

"Thank you, for sharing your story, Demetri. My heart embraces your courage and faith to go on with your mission."

"But I feel I have lost my mission, my reason for coming here, my place in the Ruby Order. I don't know what happened and I don't know who I am any more."

"Demetri, it was less than a week ago that you removed a devilish implant from yours truly," she smiled. "Might I try to repay the debt I owe to you, my brother?"

"What is it you suggest, Leah?" he asked.

"I have the 'sight', Demetri. Would you like me to tell you what I can see within your rainbow body?"

"I would. Can you tell my why I feel lost?" he asked, anxious to have any information. Even though Demetri had some 'sight', she knew for a fact that it was impossible to see your own pathologies, though you might be able to diagnose yourself from feeling or intuiting them.

"Ordinarily the etheric body bridges the physical and the astral or soul body in a balanced way. You know that. It has many other functions besides, but this bridge is vital to living in the fullness of soul — thinking, feeling and willing in this reality. I reckon, when you arrived in Athens, you had just connected with your true "I" in consciousness soul — manifested with a great deal of vulnerability. It would seem to me a time to be within rather than without, quiet rather than boisterous, peaceful rather than agitated. Yes?"

"Quite true," he agreed.

"I believe that the Luciferic Beings would be relinquishing the task of steering your life at that point, leaving your astral body to the angels of the third hierarchy including your personal guardian. Does that sound right?"

"It does, when you are stabilized in consciousness soul. Please go on, Leah," he said.

"I reckon, when you were traumatized by your brother's death, that Ahriman grabbed at your physical body because the usual resistance offered by the Luciferic Beings had not been fully assumed by the Angels for the interim period of your own mastery. It is, obviously, a transition that takes some time to complete. I see that your etheric body is too close to the nerves of the physical body, too deeply into the physical body, and that your etheric body isn't far enough into the astral to build a good bridge. Does that make any sense?"

"It does make sense. And you can see this?" he asked.

"I can see it," she admitted. "I can't tell if that last piece of you to ascend to consciousness soul came crashing back down into the cultural "I", but it's a possibility. I reckon Chris could probably help us figure that out."

"What can be done for me? Anything?" he asked.

"It's complicated, Demetri, but we've taken the first step of grief release. You must complete this through articulation, emotional release, and ceremony, perhaps — whatever it takes, with plenty of forgiveness. You will need to let your brother go, knowing that his soul's journey is his own, but that you can connect on the astral plane with him. You must remove his filaments from your rainbow body, and yours from his. Then we can make an attempt to rebalance your etheric body's relationship to your physical and astral bodies. Your soul needs to reorganize itself to be able to receive the etheric body again, and reestablish the bridge from this world to your soul, my dear friend. You're living with two beautiful souls in Will and Sonia, and Chris and I are two doors away. I leave this to you. When you're ready, the bees and I will engage Ahriman while Chris holds the space, in the apiary. How does that sound?" she asked, eyebrows raised.

"At least as enjoyable as your implant excision," he laughed.

"It's so good to hear you laugh, Demetri. We'll be good. You do your part and the bees and I will prepare for ours," she concluded.

"Now, you and Nick have a date on the chiropractic table. He can discuss organ-cleansing steps with you. For my part, I'll ask you to stay on the anti-viral herbs and off alcohol and coffee for another month, then we'll test your blood again."

Demetri slid out of her examination chair and gave her a long, grateful hug. When they had his new weight for the records, he left to see Nick. Leah sunk into a puddle of empathic tears at her desk, processing a good bit of Demetri's grief for him. She sent a prayer of gratitude to Master Mukda. He'd given her the jailer's key to the cell of Demetri's imprisoned soul.

Amazing Grace.

chapter 3: the church of tango

Natalie came by the clinic to accompany Leah to The Lodge, where she would speak to the Ukiah group, and found her best friend in her puddle of tears. Passing them off to a sad story, she cleaned up the clinic space, filed Demetri's records and splashed cold water on her face at the sink.

"You'll be okay by the time we get there, sister," Natalie assured her.

"Not too blotchy?" she asked.

"Leah you've looked brilliant every day of your life, and that without a stitch of makeup. I doubt anyone will notice," Natalie laughed. "Crank up that inner sunshine of yours and you'll be fine — terrific in fact."

"You ought to be my agent, Nat, but I'm grateful you're my best mate," Leah replied with a hug. "Is everyone comfortable at The Lodge?"

"They all want to move here, if that's any indication. It's such an inviting place. We've a fire roaring in the great hearth, cold cider, coffee and tea, and the hors d'oeuvres plate circulating at the moment. You'll be well received. They're an amiable, extremely progressive, group of people."

She *was* very well received. Leah met a group of bright people who'd known each other a long time but had been unable to figure out how to build their friendship into community. Natalie had taken them on a spiritual journey together, which they were attentive to as a consciousness exercise in the school of life. Leah aimed her talk at the journey's high road, selfless service to humanity, and the whole purpose of a spiritual community. They would find their group mission in the process of materializing their community and embrace it one step at a time. She likened the community to the *bien*, nature's premier superorganism, which operates at a higher consciousness through the selfless service of each individual to the whole. It isn't so much that we lose our identity to the community but, rather, that we're compelled to give it the 'best of the best' of who we are.

In ending the talk, which was little more than 30-minutes, she invited them to Sunday's community dinner and was sure that Natalie and company had written a tour of *New Avalon* into their schedule. She hoped they would stop by the studio to meet all the people behind the show, tour the studio and new documentary film department, and then, perhaps, have a group photo shoot on the set. They were all keen.

Returning to *New Avalon* with an hour to spare before Joel's show, Leah sat at her desk writing about the experience with Demetri. Truly, it was heart wrenching to pull grief out a grown male magician. However, there was something else there — a gift. She was charting unknown waters using clairvoyant vision for medical diagnosis, and expected treatments would be equally unconventional. It made her think of the medical center and the possibilities for the future of medicine — supersensible medicine. It was positively inspiring to think futuristically but it did actually come crashing back to the fact that she'd no clue how to get Ahriman to loosen his grip on Demetri. Recollecting the Bee Mistress' handling of imminent danger in the apiary, not all that long ago, she realized that the Bee Mistress would know what to do. She needed to practice getting the rest of her self out of the way. That worked well in the kitchen with sexual play but in the apiary she'd gone AWOL when face-to-face with the use of raw power. *Sigh.*

She'd turned to practicing her lines for the musical when Chris showed up. He booted up the computer to check his email then called her down the hall when Joel's show theme began. He slipped an arm around her, and although curious about the outcome of Demetri's appointment, gave her the time and space to disclose what she could, when she could. Chris had impeccable boundaries, especially with processes of the soul, and Leah had an extraordinary gift for holding her own space. He'd be giving her the full rundown on horse activities over dinner, which always pleased her, and had the performing arts project as a conversation backup.

When the women got together for craft night, Leah chose to start making a precious doll for her granddaughter, Mandy, who would be coming for Christmas. Georgia called them Waldorf dolls for the imaginative invitation they extended to the child. There were impressions of cheeks, nose, chin and forehead but only the eyes and lips were defined with subtle colored sewing yarn. The doll's hair could be quite creative with an assortment of textured yarns. It reminded her to take up her knitting again, as she was only halfway along with a cardigan for Mandy's older brother, David.

The women were into lively discussion that night, much like they'd been in the sauna at *Samhain*. They were even more enthusiastic about their partner's sudden interest in acquiring steady state levels of bliss through more tantric sexual practices. This was Chris' doing, of course. First he'd organized the blokes club into the *New Avalon* Rangers to provide security for the community

— and proved its usefulness. Then he'd magnetized them into a brotherhood circle, sharing esoteric teaching and, as Leah imagined but never confirmed, moved them into a genuine appreciation of the feminine. She gave him the same impeccable boundaries that he afforded her with respect to his work with the men and his inward process, though he was personally, for her, a fairly open book. Chris was authentic and a realized man. His beliefs about partnership heralded a new era of co-creativity and joy. In his quiet, charismatic way, he was giving the men purpose and values that effectively undermined ingrained patriarchal behavior without marginalizing their manhood.

After half an hour of discussion on this topic, while crafting away, the comments turned to serious questions about their role in the profound awakening of their men. Natalie seized the moment, suggesting that Leah had been contemplating some advanced spiritual work for them. One by one, the women set down their projects and looked expectantly at Leah. They'd had no formal circle work with her since the inception of community, and Katia and Shelley had never experienced it. Natalie had passed on the teachings impeccably and all of them had worked hard on themselves to be able to live in harmony with others. They were anxious to hear what Leah had to say about spiritual advancement.

"I had an idea," Leah began, gently laying Mandy's doll in her lap. "It was the morning after *Samhain* when I was awaiting the sun in the frozen *Lacy Phacelia*, so you know this is going to be about bees," she laughed. "It occurs to me that this community is ready to take a next step. It's time to take people in to train them, as apprentices, in our skills. And, it's time to journey out to train others, on site, where they are establishing community. We'll talk about our second community and apprentices at the meeting Tuesday night, but let's assume that we'll be very busy passing on our gifts to others." They all agreed it was time, and that they were ready.

"That's great. We've a strong sisterhood here, and now we're materializing a strong brotherhood. I'd like to take our sisterhood a step further, down a path that I'm daily defining, as it's new to me in this life, but old within my soul. It's the path of the Golden Queen, the path of the Melissae and the Bee Mistress. There's this 'Bee Mistress' part of me, who's shocked me with her power at the same time she's appalled me with her foul contributions to my story. When I was young, she contributed nothing but grief, whilst dancing around with the darker side of life. Fortunately, that's turned around and she's recently taken on the responsibility of this honorable path. Not that she doesn't have fun, mind you," she laughed. "I confess that Chris playfully brings out the best in her."

This received a communal "Ah-ha."

"Let me tell you about this relationship between the Bee Mistress and the Melissae, then you can decide if you'd like to pursue the path. It doesn't necessarily have anything to do with the bees in this reality, for those of you hesitant to work with the bees. I feel there will be one of the young girls meant to be the next Bee Mistress in this lineage. I'm not asking you to do more than you're already doing, but I will ask you to be more than you've been, and perhaps more than you thought you could be. The Melissae serve the community, and our community is vast. The Bee Mistress serves the Melissae.

"On the path of the Golden Queen, as opposed to the Dark Queen's path of sorcery, our level of consciousness must be the upper astral, consciousness soul. It's been my experience that this ascension step can be attained through the constant step-wise expansion of consciousness that allows us to gradually begin living soulful lives. Our service to others is the best preparation for life in consciousness soul. At that level of consciousness, the ego separates from the culture's con and becomes the servant of higher self. For each subpersonality, this transformation is concomitant with the opening of our gifts. Selfless service comes with the gifts that give it power in the world. Our entry to consciousness soul often requires novel, even heroic acts of selfless service — quite extraordinary life experiences that provoke leaps into the unknown. However this momentous step materializes for you, I would promise to be there to assist you."

"Leah, you're a model of selfless service. In that way you're already our Bee Mistress. What more can we expect of you should we agree to engage this path? Do you have more to give? Or should I say you're a hard act to follow at best?" Sonia passionately asked.

Leah accepted Sonia's pleas. "I do understand how you feel, all of you. You witness my attempt at service to humanity and rightly count yourselves human, as we all are, but I feel called to apply that level of service to you personally, my sisters. I want all of you to access your highest potential as well as your gifts to serve in the same capacity.

"On a practical level we can sit here and speak of the incredible changes in the men, their attentiveness and strivings to honor the feminine. Or, we can learn to open ourselves to receive from them in a way that takes partnership into the realms of the sacred, into spirit — in a way that nurtures their growth as well as our own. If their efforts are met soley with our enjoyment and appreciation, and not with our own mastery of the energy being shared with us, we'll have missed an opportunity to experience the higher worlds together. These skills are both energetic and practical. It's important to be working simultaneously on our subpersonalities through our service work, which is so obviously and rapidly expanding into the greater community."

"I was kind of wondering what to do with the building energy of orgasm I'm experiencing," Shelley offered, shyly.

"My mind gets right in the way of that!" Sonia exclaimed. "Okay, I get the point. What do you think girls?" she asked.

"Oh, yeah, bring it on," they all agreed.

Leah picked up Mandy's doll again, her heart alive with love for her friends. She wanted each of them to experience bliss as a way of life. "Here's what we could do. We've this Christmas project to help us set ourselves up for twice-monthly gatherings. We can stay on task with the projects while we engage the path. I think it wise that we not share what we're doing with the men, but let it sneak up on them. This tactic seems to have worked well on us.

It would be a big help for me if we changed our meeting night, though. I need to be focused on the Saturday's show most Fridays."

They agreed to meet on Tuesday nights starting in two weeks. She asked them to start a private notebook and begin by reviewing each of their subpersonalities — where each of them was on the path currently and what contributions each had made to their beliefs about sexuality. To stimulate this remembrance, she asked that they identify the erotic images they used to bring on sexual arousal or orgasm, either with a partner or on their own. Furthermore, they were to identify the subpersonality attached to each image filed away in their soul.

They were stunned.

She just smiled and whispered, "We have to start by clearing landmines, sweet Melissae. Our partners are learning to be present for and with us — to be authentic. Sacred Union demands it of us. Anything less chains us to the realms of the Fallen Ones in our cultural "I". These images are crutches that inhibit our freedom of expression — our natural bliss. Yes?"

"Have you done this work?" Natalie asked.

"It's all too fresh in my mind, Nat. Two weeks from Tuesday, when we meet again, I will give you the clearing technique and hold the space for you while you try using it. I'd wager that each of you has a sexual priestess of some sort amongst your subpersonalities or you wouldn't have wound up in this community. Intend awareness of these images lodged in your soul's memory bank. Identify their origin and how they colored your beliefs. Do the basic work around that on your own, or maybe call a circle with Nat, to go over the work together. When we meet on the 22nd we'll take care of the landmines."

"Maybe we should end our meetings with a sauna?" Shelley suggested. "It felt really cleansing on *Samhain*. I'm sure Tommy and Rob would fire it up for us."

There was easy agreement on that suggestion, exempting Katia, with her pregnancy. They spent another hour working on their projects in quiet contemplation. The community pot had definitely been stirred.

On arriving home, she found Chris connecting the dots on his project, defining the multiple interactions within the community as well as those within the proposed center. He showed her some sample sketches of the theater and some structural changes to accommodate two stories of conservatory classrooms for voice and music. Acting and dance could be taught on the stage. She was sure he would have an ally in Tommy whose boys were well versed in music, and likely held talents yet to emerge before the community. They were both expected to show up for play rehearsal on Saturday afternoon.

After suggesting that he show his plan to Tommy to see if he could do some quick watercolor sketches, Leah went off to find her expedition sleeping bag for her pre-show, cosmic download on the timber table in the back garden. That, followed by a nice bubble bath, was the Friday evening part of her ritual to prepare for the show. A good breakfast, after a long slow yoga workout on Saturday morning, brought ritual to completion.

Chris had a hands-off policy after the download and during the night's sleep, whilst it was being integrated into Leah's blue diamond heart. She looked positively angelic in sleep on Friday nights, and he had incredible dreams sleeping alongside his angel. Everything changed the next morning when she would cook his favorite breakfast — pancakes, sausages and scrambled eggs with maple syrup. He would find her pouring the batter on the griddle when he emerged from voice rehearsal in the shower. She'd be in her loosely tied blue robe, naked, and seductive. It was the only meal of the week the Bee Mistress cooked. For his part, Chris was interested in arousing the maximal amount of neuropeptide release to assist her work before the camera — this week on behalf of the homeless people — without burning the pancakes. The Bee Mistress was in 'hog heaven'.

That Saturday, Leah was ready to talk about the show *and* Demetri at lunch. She'd held back tears during the stories of the homeless guests. She hoped the show would help the plight of the homeless around the country. They were going to start hunting down their homeless farmers and gardeners and a cook or two in the coming weeks and include their two homeless guests in that search. As soon as the hotel was finished, Natalie would bring them in to begin the work of community building. At the same time, they could start working with their skills on the land. Greg was watching the auctions for stock prices but didn't want to invest until the rains and snow came to green up the pastures, perhaps March or April; rain was really late this year. There was much to be done in preparation, crop plans, tractor purchasing and so forth. Sonia was prepared to get greenhouse and hoop house crops in right away with a crew of gardeners, but Leah was bereft that she couldn't just snap her fingers and provide for all the homeless people in the country.

Chris asked about Demetri, plucking her out of the stream she was about to drown in.

"Well, there we had a small success, and he's given me permission to share it with you, cowboy. I managed to pick the right moment and say the right words to melt his armor. He shared the story to which Master Mukda had eluded. It happened right before he came over here. His older brother lost the family business and all of his wealth in the Greek financial meltdown. Demetri was there when his brother committed suicide — shot himself in the head — and had to take care of the aftermath for the family." Chris winced, feeling his brother's pain as Leah continued. "He cried, a lot, which was a good start at grief release. I took on as much of his grief as I could process, wanting to open the door wider for him. I encouraged him to do a lot more; specifically, he's to begin pulling his filaments back to release his brother with forgiveness and non-judgment. When he's complete with that, we can look at the Ahrimanic grip, which, by the way, is severe."

"How do you propose to look at that … if I might ask?" he smiled.

"I'll meditate with the bees after lunch, cowboy. The Bee Mistress seems to take things into her own hands in spite of me so I expect some spontaneity. For starters I see the *biens* holding Christ Consciousness and you doing the same right across from them with Archangel Michael above. That'll create a high energy field for the healing. Demetri and the Bee Mistress will have to be opposite one another, I guess, though I feel something or someone is missing from that picture. And, somehow Ahriman will be induced to loosen his grip. It's all a bit sketchy at the moment."

"All that, in a perfect world," he added.

"Fair enough, but I've this funny feeling that what happened to Demetri was due to his vulnerability — an accident."

"Explain?"

The picture I get is that his work saving your life in Iran was the ticket to consciousness soul for his last lower-astral subpersonality. It was high service and he felt in a truly uplifted state before he flew to Athens. Now, and correct me if I'm wrong, wouldn't that mean the Luciferic Beings would have lost their influence over him?"

"That's true. He would've separated from the cultural "I" in the lower astral where they have the liberty to influence."

"Well, then who dominates the lower astral when we move fully into consciousness soul?" she asked. "The good angels of the third hierarchy?"

"They do. And as we continue to build the bridge there can be Archangelic influence. Eventually, with the work of mastering the upper astral, we take on a good bit of that duty ourselves."

"Okay, so I get this picture that he was in consciousness soul but the newly ascended part of him slipped back down to the lower astral when the suicide occurred. I think this part of his personality was caught between those worlds and that he'd no angels to assist him. Does that make any sense?"

"It could be true, lass. That might be why he seemed so alienated, although you'd expect his guardian angel to be of some service in the lower astral. That angel might be overwhelmed by the Ahrimanic play."

"That, and he reported a lot of shouting and mumbling going on in his head. This could be the result of an opened portal between one of his lower astral bodies and the collective astral plane. This subpersonality is now stuck in his lower astral and his consciousness is stuck in the subpersonality — in a kind of a bubble apart from the rest of him that he can't access. Sorry, cowboy, this is quite complex."

"No worries, lass. I hear what you're saying. It's quite possibly true, and a brilliant diagnosis on your part if it is."

" I'm floundering, darling, but learning. Would it be insane to suggest that the Bee Mistress will need to call on Lucifer for help?" she asked, eyes wide.

Chris considered that while staring at his leftover chicken soup. "Spot on, lass. He's the Bearer of Light, and strikes the balance between Christ and Ahriman. What's happened here, by the way, is exactly what can go wrong with the ascension process. There's risk navigating in the culture before stabilizing the personality. That's why tradition places the initiate in a monastery or ashram. Demetri will have to elevate this fallen subpersonality again. Fortunately, he's here now, and can be supported. What do you think the Bee Mistress is going to do?" he asked, with that grin of his.

"Not pass out, for one thing," she laughed. "I have no idea, cowboy, but when I do know you'll be the first to hear about it," she promised, getting up from the table to cleanup the kitchen.

He watched her, and the ruby red dress she'd worn for the show, move together to the sink. "Do we have any tango music?" he asked, absently.

"Tango? What's going on, cowboy?" she asked, turning to look at him — unable to stop a round of giggles.

"Can you tango?" he asked, perfectly poker-faced.

"I like the music but I don't know the steps," she admitted, still giggling. "You are so-o-o outrageous!"

""They aren't steps, my lass. They're seductions. Where can we get some music? I'm certain the Bee Mistress is ready to dance with me. Jane and Alice are going to give her a chance, I just know it," he teased.

"Does she have to wear high heels with this red clingy dress?" she laughed, knowing perfectly well the source of his motivation.

"Later. We can start barefoot in our robes. Our floors are warm. Music?" he asked again.

"Ask Sonia," she suggested. "She's got the blood for it. Otherwise you can look on the Internet and download a few tunes to your phone."

"I'm on it, lass. We're lucky, you're such a quick study," he laughed.

"It sounds like there's a deadline."

"There is — tonight. It's time to tango. We're going to have great fun."

"You're always fun. I give you the fullness of my approval in that department, cowboy. I do need to consult with the bees, though. So, I'll leave the music to you and catch up with you at the community center for rehearsal," she announced, taking chicken thighs out of the freezer. "I'm leaning towards a coconut curry tonight but we could as easily do butter chicken, if you'd rather. Ponder that while your chasing up the tango."

"No worries, I'm off to see the neighbors. See you at rehearsal, and don't forget your script."

After putting the red dress away, with another round of giggles, she changed into jeans and a long-sleeved Henley with a cream-colored heavy cardigan sweater. While walking to the apiary, she turned Demetri's odd journey through the dimensions over in her mind. She was especially intrigued by the way it forced her to bring her clairvoyance into a diagnostic process for the etheric body. Could it be that she was tapping into a completely independent complimentary medicine. What if? What if a group of doctors and nurses in the future medical center in *Harmony Valley* had clairvoyant faculties?

Taking a step back in her mental process, she asked how conventional medicine would have diagnosed Demetri. Depression? Schizophrenia? Bi-Polar Disorder? Maybe all of the above would have been considered but none of them were really correct — at best they were manifested indicators of soul imbalance. They'd have been right about CMV and perhaps a therapist might have suspected grief and shame, but after how many appointments? Worse still, none of those were the core dysfunction. In the meantime, the Ahrimanic was tightening its grip and Demetri was in danger of being taken out or, had he not been a Ruby Brother subject to that mandate, of losing his mind — psychosis, according to the books. By the time she reached the apiary, she was convinced that a new medicine was waiting to be birthed. The tricky part would be approaching medical professionals to develop their clairvoyant gifts. She needed the perfect guinea pig ... *Nick!* He would be eager to try *and* he'd the sensitivity for it.

Leah pulled out her meditation stool, set it down next to Sophia's hive, and then called in the Bee Mistress to inquire of the *biens* the proper procedure for restoring Demetri's etheric body to its proper tension and distribution. The Bee Mistress took over, feeling the request a bit scientific for the *biens*. She tagged on the need for the restoration of his soul and his "I". *Well done*, Jane conceded.

The Bee Mistress asked to 'see' the way to proceed, causing the IMAX screen to pop up before her inner sight. She was taken back into lifetimes wherein the Bee Mistresses of her lineage had exercised their power balancing the Luciferic and the Ahrimanic polarities. She became completely engrossed in the visions, to the point of embodying the women; feeling their struggle, sharing their victories or defeats, knowing their inner thoughts and how those thoughts affected the outcome.

The Bee Mistress observed strategies that worked well against the Ahrimanic that would not have phased the Luciferic, and vice-versa. In this way, she learned the weaknesses and strengths of her opponents. Since she'd little experience in this lifetime, she gained a great deal of insight into the extraordinary power — much of it magical — wielded by the women of her lineage. Although she hadn't encounter a situation exactly like the one she currently faced with Demetri, the vision anchored the Bee Mistress in the power of her calling. Her work with Demetri would, unquestionably, be a profound learning experience.

Leah collapsed the IMAX screen, gave her dried *Melissa* offerings to the *biens*, secured the apiary and walked back to the house to get her script. Her thoughts were bouncing between the urgency of Demetri's condition and the lack of details in the Bee Mistress' vision. She knew enough to accept the latter, guessing that if she'd a detailed plan, Ahriman would be aware of it. Whatever was to occur would have to be spontaneous — so fitting for an impetuous brother like Demetri.

Chris was organizing the cast for the second scene from Act I when Leah arrived at the community center. She was needed for the first bit of that scene wherein Jud Fry, the very disturbed farm hand, asks Laurey to the upcoming dance. Wanting to get even with Curly for seemingly kidding her about the surrey, she accepts, despite the fact that Jud scares her. Mitch had agreed to play Jud because he'd had enough acting experience in summer stock to muster up a disturbed and menacing appearance. Greg, who'd the body type for the part, couldn't manage the characterization, so was playing the judge instead.

Leah had to work up fear for the most tenderhearted guy in the community — the dairy farmer — *he who fosters the docile bovines, for heaven's sake*. She imagined Mitch hunting, which was plausible since he did hunt. She was the deer. It seemed to work — especially to give Laurey an aura of suspicion with respect to Jud. As a backup strategy, she imagined him the head of the NRA. That worked even better. The next part of the scene had Will Parker returning from a trip to *Kansas City*. This was the first musical number in the scene with Will as Will, and Jenny joining in the song as Aunt Eller along with the men's chorus. Will and Chris had been working the song up, *acappella*, at the stable, so he had to give it a few goes with Jenny, the chorus and Ellia at the piano, but it was good. Will had a good voice, admitting that he'd sung in gospel choir through high school. Chris looked very pleased with the song and shifted his attention to directing the rest of the cast during the number.

Will brags of having won $50 in the city, which prompts Ado Annie's father, Andrew (played by Bernie), to remind him of the $50 dowry he would need to marry his daughter. He'd spent all the money on gifts for Ado Annie (Sonia) and had even brought back a gift for her dad — a 'Little Wonder' tube for looking at pictures. Unbeknownst to Will, there was a knife hidden within it.

Later in the scene Ado Annie confesses that she'd been spending time with Ali Hakim (Nick), a Persian peddler, while he was away. Laurey (Leah) steps in to reprimand Ado Annie, telling her she would have to choose between the two men. This prompts Ado Annie's key number, *I Cain't Say No*, in which she admits to loving them both. Sonia, a great singer, pulled this one off with aplomb, and got a well-deserved round of applause from the cast.

The women begin to prepare for the Social, while in the background Gertie Cummings (Shelley) flirts with Curly — her high-pitched laughter curdling Laurey's blood. Laurey assures her friends that she really doesn't care for Curly, which brings on Leah's first number with the women's chorus, *Many a New Day*. They went through it several times, with Ellia's accompaniment, while Chris introduced them to some simple choreography.

That was as far as they were going in this rehearsal, so Chris backed it all up to the beginning, assembling his little orchestra for the overture and opening number. He had Ellia at the piano with Mitch on fiddle, Rob and Mike on their cellos, Tommy on harmonica, and Leslie on her flute. They ran through the overture several times and would get together to rehearse on their own, as they could. They stayed together to accompany Chris' solo of the opening number *Oh What A Beautiful Mornin'*, while Leah and Jenny took their places in front of Aunt Eller's little house (a couple of chairs, for the moment). Leah and Jenny had their lines and playful acting down for this part of the scene, which included Chris' rendition of *Surrey With the Fringe On the Top*.

He'd prepared them to take that opening part of the scene right into the bit they'd just rehearsed for the first time, and something extraordinary happened. The way he sang that opening number caused everyone to raise the bar on the individual performances. At the same time, it also provoked cohesiveness amongst the actors and musicians that amazed them all. Everyone suddenly acted together, played together, and felt the essence of the story together.

When Leah and the women were finished with the last song, Sonia could no longer be contained. "What the 'Sam Hill' is going on here, Chris?" she laughed. "That was unbelievable for a first rehearsal."

"It was *Oh What A Beautiful Mornin'*, wasn't it?" Ellia wisely suggested.

"Aye," he admitted, with that grin of his. "That song was written to carry the whole show in its embrace — if it's sung correctly. It has to big and round, filled with the sun at daybreak, rising up with enthusiasm, playfulness and hope, then coming to its finish with reverence and innocence."

"Amazing," Sonia sighed. "This was amazing. It sets the whole stage. Thank you, Chris."

"Thank Rogers and Hammerstein, Sonia. I didn't make up the magic. I 'got ' their intent. You were all brilliant," he replied. "Now, on Wednesday night, we'll add on the third scene in Act I, up to and including Jud's *Lonely Room* number. Men, we'll practice *It's A Scandal! It's An Outrage!* after the community dinner, if Ellia will stay on with us?"

"I'll be looking forward to it," Ellia laughed. "This was great, everyone. You're all wonderful."

Stu had a big smile on his face whilst patting his mobile movie camera. He'd had a lapel mike on Chris and two boom mikes over the set. The play was going to provide great documentary footage. The cast clustered around the musicians giving and receiving hugs and helping the boys pack up their cellos. As the West Commons Lane villagers walked home together, imaginations were running wild about which musical they could perform next. Chris fielded suggestions and was enthusiastic about all of them. He so loved a good musical.

For dinner, he and Leah cooked up a luscious butter chicken recipe with fresh steamed spinach, rice and a salad. Over their meal, they recapped the day, which, for Chris, had started with a Bee Mistress breakie, followed by trail clearing, horse training, and riding school. After a nice lunch and seduction with his wife, he'd been super-pleased with their second play rehearsal. It didn't get any better than that, in his opinion.

Leah had hosted an eye-opener of a show on the homeless crisis, lunched with her seductive husband, witnessed the Bee Mistress' vision of a historic drama with the dark side, and thoroughly enjoyed the *Oklahoma!* rehearsal. The latter had cast away any doubts she might have had about pulling it off for Christmas. Moreover, she felt Chris' plan for the Performing Arts Center would be met with great community enthusiasm. He was *so* coming into his own within the community.

They were in the midst of reading Rudolf Steiner's *The Temple Legend* book to each other every evening, typically with their glasses of Zinfandel and with Leah curled up on the sofa next to Chris. However, on this night, she was in her favorite chair tending to her knitting project for her grandson, David. The book was both interesting and deep, requiring Chris to fill in here and there for her lack of formal Mystery School training. She thoroughly enjoyed it, especially the running theme about Adam and Eve, and Cain, Abel and Seth, which was most enlightening. When he'd finished reading the chapter to her, Chris set the book down, emptied his glass and waited to catch her eyes. When she looked up from her knitting to see what he was doing, it was to find him studying her.

"Yes, cowboy?" she asked, expectantly.

"It's time to tango, lass," he grinned.

"Oh, my God," she burst out laughing. "I'd forgotten all about that. Did you find music?"

"Si, Señora," he grinned. "It'll do for beginning lessons, at any rate."

"Let me finish this row, Señor vaquero (cowboy). I have a feeling this is going to end up in bed," she giggled.

He didn't disagree.

After trading their clothes for dressing robes, Chris loaded Sonia's CD in the player, forwarded to her recommended song and put it on repeat. When Leah came to meet him, he reached out his hand for hers and bowed to kiss it. She was on the verge of getting really silly when he clicked on the music and pulled her, suddenly, into his arms. The first lesson was how to glue your body to your partner's, primarily at the pelvis as you move across the dance floor. The music took it from there — the Priestess and the Magus, and the tango — in uninhibited, lusty splendor.

In the end, the truth of the tango was that it glued them to each other via profuse, mutual sweat. They were, thus, compelled to take their passion into the shower before making hilariously crazy love together.

The next morning, after hours in bed with tea, chatting and cuddling, and with nothing scheduled until afternoon soccer, Chris lit a fire in the hearth for her cozy comfort, stoked the boiler and started breakfast, while Leah cruised through her yoga, feeling giddily titillated throughout. The Bee Mistress was a convert to the Church of Tango, a true devotee-in-the-making.

They decided on a creative morning; he working on the performing arts project at the kitchen table and she imagining the medical center, whilst knitting in her chair before the hearth. At eleven o'clock or thereabouts, they would get dressed for riding then take Thunder and Holly on a good romp with a picnic lunch.

That turned into a foursome with Will and Sonia joining them. Natalie was working with the Ukiah group, along with Georgia, Ellia and Jenny, or she would have come along. Leah ran up to the studio to call Alice and Burt Wilson, letting them know that soccer was on, and that they would be greatly missed if they failed to show up. Then, she was suddenly inspired to call Gayle and Jim Taylor, inviting them to the community potluck dinner. The Ukiah group would be there as well, making it an easy way to experience the whole community without feeling like the only outsiders.

The ride was invigorating for riders and horses alike. Chris wanted to take them up the forestry road on the opposite side of the river, which was accessed in the next valley. In the process, the proximity of the paved road coming down from the main county road to Mr. B's barn was made evident. That valley's road crossed a narrow bridge at the head of the valley to run along the west side of the river. It connected all of farms in that valley with the road down from the highway and with *New Avalon's* dirt road. Indeed, there was far better access for commercial undertakings at the future *New Avalon II's* south end of the valley than there was through their courtyard complex entrance at the north end.

At the top of the forestry road running along the west ridge of their valley, Chris introduced them to an old, but sturdy, fire tower. They climbed the tower to see an amazing view of their land. Visualizing the second village was easier from this height. Mr. B's house looked small, indeed. They could see the falls at the south end of his property, where they were headed for their picnic, and to the north the view included Jim and Gayle Taylor's farm and the second half of *New Avalon* from the bend in the valley near the pig farm to its south end at the Taylor's pasture fence. Leah was very appreciative of the opportunity to see the lay of the land they would begin to develop in the spring. She stood on the fire tower for a long time, wrapped in Chris' arms, feeling full to the brim with happiness.

It was a peerless late autumn day. Their picnic, with their two good friends, was deliciously intimate. Will and Sonia naturally looked to Chris and Leah as their mentors — a fact never discussed and never implied. Sheltered from the prevailing wind by a stand of brilliant mature sugar maples and open to the south for the sun's warmth, the clearing at the falls was a good place for food and conversation. The horses grazed the lush grass and drank from the clear water, occasionally blowing and nickering to each other. *How could the world be such a mess when life had all the makings of perfection?* Leah wondered. Instead of making a list of everything that needed fixing 'out there', a place she could easily have accessed, she decided to savor the moment. Happiness wasn't tangible. It was an in-the-moment expression of the soul.

And, they all enjoyed grooming their horses together at the stable at the end of their ride. Holly had been hankering for her attention (so said, cowboy) and appeared to tune into Leah's soul-filled happiness herself.

The Wilson's showed up for soccer, rosy-cheeked and full of good cheer. Burt went to talk to Nick about the teams. He fancied himself the referee, having learned to deal with their loose rules of true play. Alice caught up with the 'grandmothers' who spread their blankets under the sugar maples on the commons. She'd a fondness for Georgia and Nick's little Billy who often napped in her lap. She wanted an update on *Harmony Valley*, sharing the community's excitement at nearing completion of the hotel remodel and the establishment of the farm and gardens. Leah didn't overwhelm her with the medical center addition to the overall plan, though Alice would have been thrilled with it.

The Ukiah group and the Taylor's enjoyed being drawn into the weekly pot luck at the community center and everyone, except the *New Avalon* mum's with young children, lingered to hear the men practice their chorus songs for the Christmas musical. Chris reminded everyone that Christmas choir practices began every Monday and Thursday evenings starting the next evening at eight o'clock.

On Tuesday night, *New Avalon's* adults gathered for their monthly meeting in the community center. Stu, prepared to film, had set up a lectern with microphone for those presenting, and had a boom microphone for recording the circle discussions that he was filming. Paula and Sam were there to observe how the community managed itself and arrived at consensus. It was Ellia's turn to facilitate the meeting. She called it to order with a smack of the gavel on the lectern. They held hands in a moment of silence, connecting with each other energetically and arriving at a place of calm receptivity.

As was typical, she called those making announcements then those with small projects or requests to the lectern first as consensus, if needed, could often be arrived at with a question or two instead of a longer discussion. Jenny Hellmann, who did the ordering for the warehouse, stepped up first.

"Good evening, everyone," she began. "This is an announcement to let you know you'll be receiving a questionnaire from the warehouse along with your usual Friday email order form. I've talked to Will about a trend I'm seeing in wholesale costs — namely inflation — and some of it's shocking. His assessment was that it's here to stay and this is just the beginning. Of course, we knew this would occur and, frankly, it's been creeping up steadily throughout the two-plus-years of this community. In the survey, I'm asking you to sort out all of the items that we order from the outside using our notations of both a two-year and a 3-month inflation index for each product. Bernie and I worked together on the questionnaire, hoping to arrive at a list of things we can begin eliminating from the outside. This will also give us a list of the most useful, needed or appreciated items for further discussion about possibly producing them ourselves or inspiring Outreach with *Harmony Valley* commerce.

"At present, ninety-percent of our items are manufactured or grown within 200 miles. Problematic 10% categories are green cleaning and paper products, some citrus, avocadoes and other Southern California fruits, sugar, and free trade chocolate, cocoa, coffee and tea. So, if you will, individually, fill-out and return the survey rating your need or desire for each non-local food item, we can then have a follow-up discussion at our December meeting. Thanks, everyone."

Ellia then called Sonia up for a garden report. "Hey, everybody. The over-winter gardening is coming along without a hitch. We'll have an abundance of fresh greens, celery, bunching onions, peas, and early brassicas like kale, broccoli, kohlrabi, radishes and baby turnips from the cool houses and tomatoes, cucumbers, peppers, basil and so forth from the hot house. The fish are doing splendidly with Demetri's vigilance and we've an abundance of potatoes, carrots, parsnips, turnips, rutabagas, cabbages, and onions stored away, or earthed up, to get us through to the next harvest. In the outside gardens we're just coming into Brussel sprout season and have plenty of kale, lettuce, onions, leeks, broccoli and kohlrabi that survived the freeze.

"I'm up here to make a suggestion. I think that, with some supplemental solar power, we could grow citrus, avocados, and pomegranates, maybe down at *New Avalon II*, in tall-sided greenhouses that can be exposed to the climate by degrees. That means we can roll up the sides to any height and even roll up to the peak of the roof in the heat of summer. Citrus is pesky to grow indoors but there are organic and biodynamic methods that can be used periodically to prevent the common pests, plus raising sides on mild days can work wonders for prevention. We'll have to design and build this greenhouse ourselves – maybe two of them to isolate the citrus – and could take this on to *Harmony Valley*, which will have a good population in the future.

"If we could pull this off, we could cross those fruits off Jenny's list of inflated food from outside our growing region. So think about this, and keep it in mind for the discussions about *New Avalon II*, if you will. Thanks, y'all."

As usual, Sonia got a round of applause for always being one step ahead of the game with her gardening and farming approach. Ellia called Natalie up next to make her case for an assistant. An immediate consensus was reached. Her plate was full and getting fuller, and everyone knew it. Stu was ready to start looking for a last staff member as well, now that they were all set up and functioning for TV and documentary production. He gave a good report on the present crew, Rob and Matt Duffy, but needed a third person to work exclusively on documentary filming, editing and production and possibly a fourth with webmaster skills as well as an interest in film. Both he and Natalie had the Outreach board's consensus already, making his request another easy vote.

Will had asked for a consensus at the Sunday night community dinner for the hiring of Sam, who was rapidly making himself indispensable. He was now putting in a request, which the board had approved, for a second staff member to take over the everyday bank transactions and both NAD and USD accounts for the credit union's shareholders. He explained his own position as becoming more like a circus master with shows in all the rings. His time would be divided between the addition of their second village, *Harmony Valley* and the Outreach Inner City Model and its first tier of the gift pyramid, with San Francisco nearly ready to be initiated. He was also given the go-ahead to hire a bank employee who, at his suggestion, would be asked to work a split day between *Harmony Valley* and *New Avalon* once the credit union opened during phase II of *Harmony Valley*.

Leah was next up to initiate some preliminary projects for *New Avalon II*. At the top of the list was the review of their waiting list, selection of community members and initiation of the Outreach Community Training Program that Natalie would supervise. When they began getting requests for membership in the second village they'd agreed that family members would have priority, followed by long-term students of Leah and Natalie, people already well connected with members of the first village in other ways, and thereafter by the date of their request.

She read from the list, accordingly. Ellia and Greg's son, Peter, and his wife, Lisa, and their family were on the top of the list and had been for nearly two years. Peter had been market gardening in Santa Barbara for eight years, Lisa was a professional musician who also taught all the stringed instruments, and their children were Mitzy, age eight, and Mark, age three.

Second on the list were Georgia's parents. Adele Parrish, her Cherokee mother, was a retired teacher who was studying the Waldorf curriculum to get herself ready to assist with a growing school at *New Avalon*. Georgia's dad, George, the African-American half of Georgia's mixed blood, was a skilled horseman, a hunter and a former Forestry Specialist and Ranger for the Cherokee Nation. He was currently apprenticing as a butcher to be able to help out in community with a needed skill. They were both keen to be close to their daughter's family. Community was a given since they'd been on reservation all of their adult lives.

Third on the list were Jerry and Betsy Northrup. Betsy was Christina McMillan's sister. They lived in Marin with their daughter, Stacy, who was ten. Jerry was a high school science teacher and Betsy administrated a health care insurance company. They'd been to *New Avalon* for a good many visits and were well known to the community.

Fourth on the list were Kazmir and Suzie Novakova, Katia's younger brother and sister-in-law, who were living on the family farm in Iowa. They'd been to visit once, and that was enough. They were dairy farmers on a large scale and ready to sell out to their partner's, Katia and Kaz's brother and his wife, and scale down to something manageable, biodynamic/organic, and close to Katia and Mitch. Community, and what *New Avalon* stood for, had been the big motivators to get on the list and established in community before raising a family.

"I have personally contacted all of these family members we've just reviewed to confirm that they're still interested. In fact, they're eager to get moving on the training process, and are willing to travel here for the program to work with Natalie and the community. That brings me to suggest that we not fill this list until after the holidays when many family members will be visiting. In other words, we'll still hold family priority at the top of the list, while we consider folks to fill in the other five to seven homes. We do need to discuss the need for guesthouses in the villages now that we have The Lodge. It seems logical to identify a Founder's Group from the larger group and build in two stages, but I leave that to Natalie and Tommy, who are better qualified to address those efforts when needed."

Leah asked if anyone had relatives who were contemplating the community before she went on. Shelley's sister, who would be coming for Christmas, was interested. She was a single parent with a teenage daughter who was in Waldorf High School in Sebastopol. She would graduate before the village was finished and likely be off to college. Her sister's boyfriend was the question mark in the equation and would check the community out over the holidays. They were both medical professionals. No one else had anyone to add, presently.

Then Leah consulted her list again. "Fifth on the list is Canadian Liu Chow, who was in Peru with myself, Natalie, Ellia, Sonia, Georgia and Chris. She's now married to Tip Richards, an American, who is a financial planner and investor. They're living in Vancouver, BC but, with duel citizenship, are good to join the community. This has been a dream of Liu's since I sent out the call for *our* Founder's Circle. They have a four-year-old boy named Jasper.

"And, finally, sixth, we've Ollie and Patty Osterholm who worked with Natalie for years in New York. They have two children, Max, who is 14, and Pepper (a girl) who is 12. The children have been homeschooled on their small farm where they specialize in organic stone fruit.

"I've spoken with Liu and Patty who confirm that they are interested. Ollie and Patty would have to sell their farm to be able to move to *New Avalon* but they feel the buyers are there for a good business. We've an interesting list here that brings needed assistance in food production, finance, education, and health care. Though we'd have a good Founder's Circle here to begin the process, it would be nice to have the entire community involved with the spiritual work from the get-go."

Leah paused, looking up from the list. "Those are the folks who've been on the list for a year or more. I suggest we save a place here for Jim and Gayle Taylor. I know that Gayle is more than ready to take the leap, and Jim is giving it considerable thought. We need to consider all that they'd bring to community with the farming and their position as the cream in the *New Avalon* sandwich cookie. After a little subdued laughter, she continued.

"Recently, I had a request from Blake Cary and his family. As most of you know, he's CEO of his own software company and Patricia is a Waldorf School Administrator. Emily, their 16-year-old is quite smitten with *New Avalon*. He asked if we might consider them. He's young, but was successful at a young age and would like to turn the CEO job over to someone else and create something new. I thought of *Harmony Valley*'s light industry projects, when he told me that. As you know, they are a beautiful family." Leah looked up to see a broad grin on her husband's face. He and Emily had a great time singing together, and he'd fixed Emily and Rob up horseback riding when the family had visited recently. Emily left determined to come back WWOOFing in the summer and was, obviously, a very persuasive and much loved young lady.

"I'll let it rest until our discussion, unless anyone has someone to suggest from our greater community. Paula very shyly raised her hand. "Paula, what's on you mind?" Leah asked, trying to hold back a smile.

"Is it inappropriate for us to comment?" she asked.

"We aren't to the discussion or voting yet, Paula, and I did invite you, so I would say, go ahead with your comment? Everyone?" The group was fine with Paula's comment though some hadn't even met her yet.

"Could we ask you to save a house for us while we try to measure up to being part of this community?" she asked, with palpable sincerity.

Leah was pleasantly surprised. "We'll discuss that Paula — and Sam. You two have managed to make yourselves indispensable in eight short days and we're giving family until after the holidays. Ellia, can we put that down for a discussion tonight?"

"Already down," Ellia noted.

Thank you," Paula responded. "We'll leave before you discuss it. We'd need to have some help financing but have good jobs here and are hard workers, plus, we've been saving for a few years and would have some family help."

"Alright then. Anyone else?" Leah asked. When no one responded, she suggest they briefly discuss the list and plan to consider putting a call out through their network of former students, communities, and friends before opening the last few spaces to the public. She took her seat next to Chris, giving his hand a squeeze on behalf of Emily.

Ellia called Tommy up to the lectern. His request was simple. "It's been pointed out to me that I need help. In fact, having looked rationally at what's on my plate, I agree with that observation, and with the suggestion by the board that I build an office onto the woodworking shop and hire a draftsman, engineer or two and a project manager for each project I'm planning and overseeing. That would be *New Avalon II*, the San Francisco Inner City project, and *Harmony Valley*, which is an octopus project. We have sufficient funds for all of the projects and the help. Outreach funding isn't likely to slack off as long as we keep producing viable solutions.

"I also want to suggest that we put out a call for building trades labor from the homeless population who could inhabit the first neighborhoods that they'll help to build. To do that, with good planning, I suggest we build the WWOOFer and Apprenticeship Village soon to temporarily accommodate them. We'll be hearing from Natalie about the Apprentice Program, but I just wanted to put that out there. I've facts and figures for the discussion so won't bore you with it now. Thanks."

Next up to the microphone was Natalie who had beefed up and polished the Apprenticeship Program she'd presented at the board meeting. It made perfect sense to a community of hard working people. How were they to get *Harmony Valley* off the ground with the responsibilities they had at *New Avalon*, for example? She like Tommy's idea of building the WWOOFer and Apprentice Village at *Harmony Valley* soon, since they'd a growing list of communities ready to initiate their own projects for the homeless, and it was advisable for them to apprentice *Harmony Valley* from as close to the beginning as possible.

Natalie was asking for approval of the apprenticeship program for all of the Outreach models. That would include key people coming in early for the second village at *New Avalon*. She suggested they discuss using The Lodge Annex, the two existing guesthouses and the spare farmhouse to accommodate them. She'd a well-organized discussion planned before the vote, including the second stage of apprenticeship, which empowered those who had apprenticed with Outreach to gift it forward on their own by apprenticing other's through their own projects.

That left Chris who had been his usual secretive self during the planning stage of his proposal. For some reason, everyone in the *Oklahoma!* cast was suddenly sitting on the edge of his/her seat. His presentation was more like a one-man show, which pleased Stu no-end, and had the community in continual laughter. Somehow he managed to move through a very complex plan for Mr. B's barn, which included the theater, teaching rooms, rest rooms, and an espresso, wine and homebrew bar for the theater goers. He was determined to bring culture, entertainment, and a great love for the performing arts to the community and to the region.

He proposed a work-study program, to be called HOOFers — for their fancy dance steps (a pause for hilarity). Then, if the community thought this might be a good idea, he suggested that they initiate the theater with the production of *Carousel*, Rodgers and Hammerstein's follow-up to *Oklahoma!* However, he felt an original production written by present or incoming members of the community, both uplifting and transformative, would be forthcoming. He did, more or less, fess up to his years in theater and the movie industry as qualifications for pulling this off. Along with the vote to fix up the barn and provide a HOOFer village soon — to put them to work on the second village gardens and farm — he suggested they be thinking of a name for the Thespians and simply call the barn *The New Avalon Center for the Performing Arts*.

The performances would be public events, generating donation income for *New Avalon*, and helping to hire a few excellent teachers to fill in the gaps with the community's artists. The school, or academy as he preferred to call it, would recruit students and teachers from the two villages, from Outreach communities and projects far and wide, and the general public. There would be tuition, with a talent-based scholarship program, to cover their curriculum and work-study to cover room and board. He was after raw talent in need of nurturance at the same time he believed that everyone could learn to sing, dance and act as part of community. He hoped the center could send well-trained artists out into the world to share the infectious joy of their art and the qualities gained though community living — the gift. As an afterthought, he wondered aloud whether they ought to consider establishing a center for fine arts, perhaps associated with the Waldorf School? That was a good cultural point to put on the community agenda.

The community was speechless. Leah could see Henry and Gert Brenner listening in with great pleasure, and imagined how pleased Emily would have been, since the whole notion took hold in Chris while singing *Oh, What a Beautiful Mornin'* with her as they'd cleaned up Mr. B's barn. Chris was fairly well fired up with passion about his project and everyone was ready and willing to let him have at it. He managed a consensus vote without a discussion. That was probably the reason why they got home at eleven o'clock instead of one in the morning. Everything else was approved with a lot of good discussion and a few modifications.

The waiting list for the new village was discussed in a non-committal way as much hinged on the holidays and ultimately on a gathering of the whole new tribe to start their community program with Natalie. She'd conceded needing not only the hired assistant, but also commitments from Georgia, Ellia, and Sonia to become program facilitators to occasionally share the load. She also requested that other community members who'd been at their personal work for some years begin sitting in on the trainings to be able to help out the four of them.

There was some skepticism of Paula and Sam's intention, given their short time in employment at the bank and studio. Leah could only say that Paula was more than she could have hoped for as a news analyst. Will stepped in to support Sam who had just taken on a quarter of the bank work and all of the taxes without a blink. Layering on *Harmony Valley* in all its complexity didn't seem to faze Sam, either. It was agreed that there was plenty of time to save a space for these two vivacious young people and the spiritual work would enhance their lives and job performance regardless of their acceptance as community members.

On the way home, the West Commons half of the community chatted about the potential new community's diversity in age, talents, and how many children would be added. Surely it would be time for a formal school teaching the Waldorf curriculum. Everyone was keen to add their talents and help materialize the Performing Arts Center, with Sonia and Shelley questioning Chris about his film career. He pointed out that until recently one could be well known in Australian theater and never be heard of outside Oz. That was all they were going to get from him.

Chris and Leah found themselves scheduling time with each other, what with women's and men's groups, rehearsals, choir practice for Chris, and Leah's Friday night ritual. They were left with every other Tuesdays from three o'clock onward, Saturday evening from the end of rehearsal onward, Sunday day, and an abbreviated evening after the community dinner. On the nights Chris had choir practice, Leah found time to work on her knitting and doll projects, to read the Steiner books that Elliot Davis and Chris had given her, to contemplate the medical model and to keep the house clean, though Chris help out with that chore. On Saturday evenings the Bee Mistress and Chris attended the Church of the Tango, which carried over well into Sunday morning, Every other Tuesday evening was Jane's night for cosmic love. Alice rode Holly-Go-Lightly on Tuesday later in the afternoon and Sunday over lunch, with picnic and partner. Dragon Lady went to work and had her fun with Joel Robertson.

Leah kept in touch with Joel by Skype, three times a week, their regular filmed interviews with each other, and text messaging when in a hurry. Life sped by through two great Saturday shows. The first was on the foreclosure crisis and the second on the Inner City solution to the foreclosure crisis — or any withering neighborhood. Will and Tommy came on the air with Leah for that one and the emails, facebook entries and tweaks surged. One mention of the homeless building trade search efforts gave Tommy a pool of over 40 applicants (most just out of work) within a 300-mile radius of *Harmony Valley*. They were all willing to engage their spiritual work. Natalie would make sure they were added to her interview lists by their various social service agencies. How the homeless had been informed remained a mystery until Tommy heard that some homeless centers were showing the YouTube videos of their relevant shows to the residents and transients passing through. The network was forming itself. He started the office addition to his woodworking shop and he, Will, Natalie and Stu put the word out for staff. By the first of the year, Outreach planned to be a functioning force of change in the world, able to accommodate legitimate requests using their gift pyramid model.

The first official meeting of the Melissae was extraordinary. They decided to do their circle work first, while working on their Christmas projects, and then end with the sauna (minus Katia) to release all that they'd brought up and out. Rather than the circle work being agonizing and guilt-ridden, the women brought their sexual image crutches to the table for a great discussion, a myriad of ah-has, and a truly remarkable amount of good humor. They loved the paint gun technique and couldn't wait to get at it. Everyone agreed they'd not hit the bottom of the barrel, but it was a great start. It was amazing how many of the images were shared — mostly from movies — and most of them big hits. All of them saw how the images kept them from truly being present and authentic with their partners. The timing was perfect, as their partners were working that angle in their own way with Chris.

Leah suggested they pursue the paint gun with great fervor, whilst taking notes about the experience, the memories that arose (for she'd had a good many missing pieces show themselves during the exercises), and other images that emerged. All of that should come to their next meeting, along with aspects of their shifting relationships with their partners that were troubling, frustrating, incomprehensible, and fantastic. At the next meeting, she would introduce the kundalini experience and how to make the most of it.

Spence and Bernie were tending the sauna fire and, with Mitch and Will, had taken a sauna while the women were in circle. The thermometer indicated 140 degrees Fahrenheit inside the sauna ('bloody hot' acceptable) and the river was close to ice. It was a perfect night for detoxing body and soul.

In what seemed a wink of time, Thanksgiving was upon them, with family coming in for some community members, a feast to prepare, turkeys to be butchered for that feast, and a much-anticipated visit from Joel and his family. Kim, his wife, was keen to see and experience *New Avalon I and II* since they would begin working with Natalie preparing spiritually for community in 2012, ending in an apprenticeship for their group in 2013, while their community was being built in the Virginia countryside. Leah, Will and Tommy would work with her group, and another group she'd formed, to put together a Baltimore version of the homeless project, and they were talking to Will about an Inner City project for DC as well. Kim, both socially and politically active, was exceedingly well connected in the greater Washington area community.

Joel had a good sub for himself on his show — his version of Paula but with live TV commentator experience. He needed a sub occasionally when asked to speak at conferences, rallies, and as a guest on other shows. Leah and Chris had both given Gavin Thompson high marks when he was filling in for Joel.

Leah had applied herself diligently preparing for the Thanksgiving Saturday show, which would feature Joel, Chuck, Christina, Michelle Markum, and Michelle's friend, Amy Donnelly, the CEO of a non-profit hospital in the bay area. Leah would also share her views on single-payer health care for California and the nation, and on health care cooperatives. She left the news to Paula, though promptly read the daily reports she submitted, and decided to ask her to give the written summary a try as well. Leah would put it all together on Friday morning while reveling in the degree of freedom that Paula's assistance gave her.

The arrival of Joel and his family in *New Avalon* coincided with the Wednesday night play rehearsal. Natalie, who was playing a dispensable bit-part to avoid overload, saw to greeting them and settling them into the guesthouse on East Commons Lane. A dinner, prepared for them by Jenny and Katia, was waiting in a warm oven. Other family members had already arrived in The Lodge and the second guesthouse, and Natalie was expecting Chuck later that evening. *New Avalon* had no vacancies, although they could have squeezed a few more people into the WWOOFer dorm and The Lodge Annex, if it had come to that.

Natalie met Joel and family in the courtyard, pointing out the studio and the Community Center should they care to walk back and check out the rehearsal after settling in. She suggested they hop back in his car and bring it around to unload luggage at the back of the guesthouse, and then Joel could return it to the lot when they were all moved in. After a short tour of the house, ending with the manifestation of their dinner, she returned to join the women's chorus. They were rehearsing the last scene in the first act of the play, intent on running through the whole act that night. This scene begins with Laurey's confused feelings for Curly and her mounting fear of Jud. She asks Ali Hakim for a potion to help her know her true love. Ali, true to his snake-oil peddler role in life, sells her smelling salts containing laudanum. She (Leah) sings *Out of My Dreams* before falling into a drugged sleep.

This begins the dream sequence in the musical with Mitch and Katia playing the dream figures of Laurey and Curly, in a ballet number, with all the musicians accompanying them in an instrumental version of *Out of My Dreams*. They'd studied the choreography on their own and took good direction from Chris to arrive at an ethereal and tender performance that needed work, but was excellent at its core. Laurey awakens knowing Curly is the man for her ... but it's too late. She's agreed to go to the box social with Jud, and he comes for her. The fourth scene and first act end.

As they took a short break to prepare for the rehearsal of the entire first act, Joel stepped out of the shadows. Leah and Chris, who were discussing her sleeping position, turned to look when Ellia, in her typical, timely humor, started playing the theme from Joel's show. Everyone came forward to greet Joel, except for Chris and Leah, who stood their stunned at the sight of him. They were both entranced by the presence of a faint White Heart, indicative of the Ruby Order, which was centered near to his physical heart but within his etheric body.

Leah gripped Chris' arm, then looked up at him as shock turned to recognition and that grin of his appeared. "Ruby Order, lass," he whispered. "No wonder you two are so tuned in to each other."

"How can it be?" she asked in a whisper. "If Sean has stepped in for Don Eduardo, whom is Joel coming forth to replace?"

"It didn't sound like Master Mukda intends descending back into the material world," he answered as the crowd parted for them to greet Joel. They each had a huge hug for him, which served to fire his white heart completely. In person, Joel was just over six feet tall, sandy-haired with a fair amount of grey, blue-eyed, fair-skinned, good looking to be sure, and thin but athletic – kind of a cyclist's body to Leah's eye. He was dressed in blue jeans, a chocolate brown pullover sweatshirt with a cream-colored 'Occupy DC' on the front, loafers, and a really beautiful, naturally charismatic smile. He'd momentarily teared-up with the hugs, but was then quick to encourage them to continue with their rehearsal, as he was eager to watch.

He took a seat as the players found their positions, instruments, and props to begin the show. That beginning, of course, was the overture followed by Curly's gradual entrance, singing *Oh, What a Beautiful Mornin'*. As it always did, the song set the cast and musicians into the magical world of theater, forgetting that anyone was watching, or that anything else mattered in that measure of time. In spite of the fact that they'd no sets as yet, the story was easily imagined, if not in memory, and Joel was completely captivated by it. He was frankly astounded at Chris' voice whereas the community was gradually accepting the huge talent in their midst and working hard at being the best they could be for the production.

When they'd finished, Chris gave them assignments for the next rehearsal on Saturday afternoon when they would move into Act Two's first scene, which started with some solid choreography and fun music for the square dance. He cancelled the Thursday night choir practice due to Thanksgiving but reminded the men of the Rangers' meeting Friday evening, and the need to show up at the stable to exercise the horses. Leah had taken a seat next to Joel for the wrap-up and was chatting with him about his trip west when Chris joined them.

Joel had no preconceived ideas about Chris. Leah had been quite surreptitious when speaking of him to Joel, who admitted to being floored by the entire package. Chris assured him he'd get over it, especially after he'd been through the Ranger's initiation on Friday night. *Surprise!*

Like his family, Joel was looking to retire early given that it was well after midnight in Washington, DC. Leah and Chris made plans to come by for all of them at eight o'clock the next morning for a walking tour of *New Avalon*. It would give them time to get to know each other better and familiarize them with life in community. They walked Joel home and continued around the commons to find Chuck just arriving at Natalie's house. He was eager to see and spend some time with his sweetheart. That made for hasty greetings and a promise to see them in the morning, which provided Chris and Leah the time for a catch up with each other before bed. Leah hopped on her knitting (an arm) while Chris took care of a half-glass of Zinfandel for each of them. Joel's White Heart was a discussion topic priority for both of them.

"Don't you find it interesting that one-third of the Order of the Ruby is at *New Avalon* right now?" Leah asked.

"Aye, lass, I do. However, Joel has no idea who he is and Demetri is teetering on the brink. That diminishes the power of the gathering somewhat."

"Maybe Joel is meant to help us with Demetri?" she suggested.

"In what capacity?" he mused.

"No clue. Maybe I'll have another look at Demetri's etheric body, cowboy. I'd just as soon avoid an emergency situation. His nadis were beginning to fire on Friday, which could bring on restitution. We don't want to lose him waiting for some sort of sign from above."

"It's your call, Bee Mistress. If you've a plan, what are you waiting for?" he queried, curious about her strategy.

"A sign from above," she laughed. "Unfortunately, we do need a kind of crisis. My greatest ally is surprise. I'm not convinced that Ahriman wants to take him out completely. He may be intending to use Demetri to further his own cause, instead."

"I would've thought Lucifer to be your greatest ally, lass. Not so?"

"Lucifer will not assist until the Christ Consciousness presence is established. Dualistic encounters evoke battles — winners and losers, whereas the triangulation of these forces evokes balance. Christ stands in the center holding that ground. On my IMAX, I watched a good many disputes over an individual's etheric body between Lucifer and Ahriman with dismal outcomes. When the Christ Consciousness was present — truly strong in Its presence — the outcome was beneficial."

"Aye. So you need the triangulation of the three forces to support your Bee Mistress' power to intervene, and you need a trigger as an organizing principle. Eh?"

"So it seems. How do you plan to align Joel with his Ruby family?" she asked.

"I reckon I'll wait for a sign from above," he teased.

"I knew you would say that, cowboy," she laughed. "It all feels imminent. So, here's to a Thanksgiving weekend of Divine Providence," she winked, touching her glass to his in toast.

"Aye. I have much to be grateful for, my sweet lass. To the ongoing pleasure of being with you, add your manifestation of a Ruby Brother and the breaking of bread with a community I never dreamed I'd be part of, and you have Divine Providence at its very best. Cheers!"

"Don't forget your horse, cowboy!" she laughed, raising her glass.

What better way to start the holiday than pancakes, scrambled eggs, sausage and sensuality? By the time they left to meet Joel and family, Leah was flushed and high on the gift walking beside her. An undercurrent of fallen angel mischief was temporarily replaced by the hope and gratitude this day always brought to America. Truth was, for many, the momentary dropping of differences brought families together in the ritual breaking bread in Thanksgiving. It was, in that sense, a holiday of peace as well as gratitude.

Kim came to the guesthouse door to greet them. Leah and Chris stepped into the entry for proper introductions to the whole family. Kim was Joel's college sweetheart. She'd her mother's prematurely silver hair and deep hazel-green eyes, set in a heart-shaped face that held a lot of joy. Overall, she'd the strikingly beautiful features, and body, of a film star. They later learned that she'd spent her pre-parenting days as a fashion model in New York City. The children had been late arrivers to the marriage, after careers had been enjoyed, in Kim's case, and anchored, in Joel's. Dark-haired Candice, who looked to be the clone of her mother, was 16, and Perry, at 14, was not that far off from a 'Joel double' though still awaiting that final growth spurt typical of boys his age.

Joel was finishing a cup of coffee during the introductions, then, after hugs from Chris and Leah, donned his cap and jacket for their tour. They started with the community gardens, which were right behind the house, and worked their way down the farm road visiting the bakery, warehouse, dairy, main barn, with its view of the valley, and poultry yard before starting back towards the village past the WWOOFer housing and arriving at the stable. Candice and Perry were nuts about horses — one reason Kim wanted to get them out of the city soon. Most of the horses were out on pasture, but, as Alex explained, Holly and Magic were in their stalls all saddle-up for a morning ride with Chuck and Natalie, who were back at her house putting a picnic together. Holly made a very big impression on Candice who was in dressage training at their local horse-riding academy.

Chris was open to taking the kids out for a ride that afternoon, maybe with Will, Rob and Mike. They both made their reservations on the spot. Joel was surprised to meet US Senator Charles Buxley, alias Chuck, when he and Natalie arrived at the *New Avalon* stable, as their group was leaving. He was even more surprised to learn that they'd be on *Light on the Crisis* together Saturday morning. They made a date to chat while the kids were out riding.

Kim was keen to help with the feast preparations, which were already underway when they toured the warehouse kitchen. She loved to cook for a crowd, though 67 people for Thanksgiving dinner would be a first.

The tour continued to the brewery and smokehouse, the west side of the gardens with the heated greenhouse and fish farm, and then down West Common Lane — Leah and Chris' side of the commons — including a little tour of their house, which was much like the guesthouse but with only one bedroom. It gave them the large and small versions of community housing. They finished at the courtyard, which was closed, but Leah opened up the shop, clinic and studio for them to look at the more interesting parts of the commercial end of *New Avalon*. They would be in the community center for dinner at four o'clock, so bypassed it on the tour. Leah promised to take them down valley and over to *Harmony Valley* during their stay.

Leah, Joel and Kim stayed at the studio to talk about their community efforts, while Chris took Candice and Perry off to find Rob and Mike to set up a riding time for their little group. The boys let him know that Megan and Ellie Prescott, who were coming to dinner along with their parents, were coming over early to ride Sparkles and Major, the horses they'd given to *New Avalon*. Alex would be taking them all out and Candice and Perry could come along with them. Alex had enough experience to manage what they'd planned, a picnic lunch at the falls, leaving Chris to other tasks. He would get Joel's kids fixed up with their horses, meeting them all at the stable at eleven-thirty.

Leaving the young people to work out their day, Chris stopped by Sonia and Will's to ask after Demetri and found Will and Tommy planning a trip to San Francisco to survey the Inner City Community project site, inspect and sketch existing houses, and locate infrastructure before Tommy got going on the architectural and engineering plans. Will would be looking into finances and recruitment of community members. Natalie had given him some open dates to work with though she was planning to co-facilitate the community program with Ellia and Georgia, who would begin apprenticing Natalie's role. The men were flying down for Monday and Tuesday and promised to be back for rehearsal on Wednesday. When Tommy asked Chris what he was up to, Will suggested he saddle up Myrtle and maybe ask Sam to take her along on the picnic, since Paula was helping in the kitchen. That struck Chris as a bloody good idea. Sam had far more maturity than Alex, the Chilean stable WWOOFer, whose principle interest was Megan, and Sam was very capable in the saddle. All of the young people rode regularly making the whole affair a great independent outing for their age group, though Chris would help them all saddle up and, with Alex, guide the grooming of their horses after the outing.

Chris asked after Demetri and was told he'd just gone over to check on the fish farm and was otherwise laying low. That felt like a non-problematic activity to Chris, so he went back to the studio to share the new plan with Joel and Kim and have Leah call Sam to come along. He then went on home to stoke the boiler, put on a load of wash, and clean the back entry/laundry. Packing a sandwich, an apple and kombucha for lunch, he left for the stable ahead of the kids with a couple of Nathan's books tucked under his arm. Nearly finished with the first series, he was discovering that he'd a very talented writer for a stepson. Privately, he was looking forward to Christmas in a way he hadn't since Nan and Pops were alive.

Until he and Chuck met in the guesthouse at three o'clock, Joel was going to covet some alone time and maybe catch the news in the tech room he'd toured with Leah and Kim. That left the two women to catch lunch with the cooking crew at the warehouse kitchen. Leah was pre-assigned the making of cranberry relish, and pumpkin and eggnog pies. Kim felt those good projects to help out with, and an opportunity to get to know Leah without Joel around. There magnetism for each other was non-threatening to Kim. She was excited for Joel to have such a soul connection with a kindred spirit. On the other hand, it was a bit overwhelming, especially when discussing lobbyists wasn't your highest priority.

Leah and Kim had a thoroughly enjoyable time together. Their finished pies made Stu's day when he got around to filming the finishing of the meal preparation. He'd thus far documented the mob of young people taking off on their horses, Spence with Chris in the bakery, and the little kids' nature tour with Bernie and Nick. He would head over to The Lodge to pick up some nice atmosphere there with their guests, and then take a break before filming the dinner.

Spence was baking his famous carrot cake and fresh country-crust sourdough seed bread at the bakery. Shelley and Katia had reserved extra fresh and well-aged cow and goat cheeses for the starter buffet. Some were to be served with Spence's whole-grain seed crackers but goat *chevré* was to be rolled, sliced thin, dredged in crushed Wasabi peas and baked in a very hot oven to melt the cheese inside the pea crust. These were a particular favorite of the men. There would also be sunflower seed and yogurt dips with garden-fresh, raw cauliflower, carrots, and celery. That, along with heaps of Spence's buttery cheddar cheese crisps, which he baked especially for the children, took care of starters.

Jenny and Sonia had readied the turkeys with Georgia's special stuffing, while Shelley, Natalie, Ellia, Christina and Gayle Taylor organized beef, pork, chicken and vegetarian alternatives to the two huge turkeys that Bernie and Mitch had butchered the day before. Paula, Jennifer (Shelley's niece), and Lisa (Ellia's daughter-in-law) pitched in with everyone else in the preparation of butternut squash, mashed potatoes, Brussels sprouts, broccoli, and roasted roots like carrots, parsnips, beets and sweet potatoes, after they'd prepared three different salads — arugula (rocket) with snap peas and pear slices, cabbage slaw, and lettuce salad with tomatoes, cucumbers, and so forth.

Nick, and Chris had seen to a big batch of beer well ahead of the holiday. That with fresh and hard apple cider, pear cider and *kombucha* were already on hand in the community room cooler with a nice cold Chardonnay and slightly chilled Zinfandel from the Cummings' vineyard. Those children who weren't cider fans had raw cow or goat milk, honey-sweetened raw eggnog and apple juice for drink choices. There would be an adult version of eggnog, with a splash of non-local rum, as well.

Nick and Bernie took the younger children on a nature hike with a picnic lunch while their mothers were preparing the dinner. They were going to track wild animals and identify birds in the forest as well. Peter was out farming with his dad, Greg, and over at The Lodge, Will and Sonia's parents, and Shelley's mother were into a deep discussion about education in front of a cozy fire in the great room. Shelley's sister and her boyfriend were off on a hike. Sam had come by to ask if the two girls - Sonia's daughter Rosita, who was 20, and Shelley's niece, Jennifer, who was 17, wanted to ride with them. Jennifer had already gone over to help in the kitchen with her Aunt and mother, but Rosita was more than keen to ride.

When the mob was saddled up and on their way, Chris stood their absently rubbing his neck under the steady gaze of Thunder, who, along with Lucy, were the only horses left in New Avalon. Had an additional eager, young rider shown up he'd have been faced with the inevitable decision of letting someone else ride Thunder. Realizing he'd been holding his breath, he let it go, with a deep sigh. Unbeknownst to him, it was his luck that Jennifer had gone ahead to help the women because Thunder, an unpredictably spirited stallion who'd just been broken, was not ready for inexperienced riders. They had a long talk, he and Thunder, discussing the possibility of letting Nick and/or Will have a go at riding him — for starters.

Thunder liked both Will and Nick, they concluded — no harm in trying. Anything beyond that was out of Chris' comfort zone, and especially not Leah, whose horse, Holly, was doing most of the work in their riding forays. Chuck had her out strutting her stuff that morning and returned just in time for Holly to turn around and trot off with Candice on her back.

Chris settled down on his favorite bale of straw to have his lunch and read the penultimate book in Nathan's first series. They were perfectly marvelous mysteries with an overtone of magic for adolescents past puberty. The story line had captured Chris right away, perhaps because Nathan's youth in the care of his mother, Leah, seeped through almost imperceptibly throughout. How could it not? After an hour or so, he put the book down and saddled up Thunder for a ride down river to Mr. B's barn. Thunder, who'd thought he'd been completely left out of any fun that day, began romping around his stall kicking the walls and blowing when Chris came with the saddle. A rambunctious adolescent himself, Thunder had a hard time containing his enthusiasm.

It was an awesome day to be out riding, though Chris was well-aware that Greg had begun irrigating the winter wheat and oats for lack of rain, and felt the Rangers might have to help him out there if it kept up so dry. Greg's son, Pete, was helping him for the weekend. They were hard at work when Chris and Thunder rode down river.

The barn visit proved to be quite inspiring as he was able to make a decent drawing of the backstage, stage and audience area of the south end of the barn. He was considering the hayloft for balcony overflow from the middle of the main theater back, since they would need to remove the loft from that point onward for lighting and curtain space, and back stage scaffolding, rigs and sets. And who knows what else. If they produced Peter Pan they'd have to fly!

Thunder let out a whinny when he saw the young riders coming up the road from the falls, on the backs of his stable mates. Chris wrapped up his reverie, neatly tucking his folded drawing into his back pocket, then shut up the barn and mounted Thunder to overtake the kids. Half the mob cantered up the road with him, while the rest took their time at a nice-paced trot. It was a high time in the stable with all of them teaming up together on the grooming. Alex organized those who were unfamiliar with the stable and the whole job was completed by three o'clock. That gave everyone time to shower and dress for Thanksgiving dinner. When all of the horses were out to pasture and the young ones on their way, Chris stashed his books in a special box he kept in the tack room for valuables and stopped into the bakery to see if Spence needed help. In fact, he did, and the two men finished off the bread baking and packed it up with bricks, hot from the wood oven, to keep it warm for dinner. Spence took the whole load, including the carrot cakes, cheese crisps, seed crackers and bread up to the community center on one of the pushbike delivery carts for the veggie boxes. Chris went on home after looking in on the brewery and was in the shower when Leah arrived home. He was working on his songs for the second act, prompting her to shed her clothes and jump in with him for the reprise of their duet, *People Will Say We're in Love.*

You reckon!?

part two: the woodland folk

chapter 4: to fool a fallen angel

With a Thanksgiving gathering this large, the cooks carved the meat in the warehouse kitchen and all of the food was taken to the community center to be kept warm in a long row of candlelit chafing dishes. Drinks were available at the bar, though the children's beverages were on a shorter table where they would all be eating together. Three round tables with the starters were dotted amongst the larger round tables set for the adults, with an autumn theme of dried leaves and gourds at their centers and thoughtfully placed name signs in front of each place. Sonia rang a bell calling everyone together, hands joined, in a huge circle, around the buffet table. There were several minutes of silence followed by a sweet little song of thanks to the earth by Georgia's school children, and then a group proclamation — *Blessings on the food, blessings on the land, blessings on the cooks, and blessings on us all!*

The children were brought through the line first with parent's serving up the little ones. The guests of the community were next, followed by the WWOOFers and new staff members, and then the community members with the founders coming at the end of the line, along with Harry, Natalie's amiable, always hungry Bijon. Leah and Chris brought up the rear, he at his first American Thanksgiving and she at her favorite traditional holiday. More than any celebration, this one put her in touch with her mother's ancestors who had arrived from England in Connecticut by ship in 1637. Her commitment to her country had deep colonial roots.

Dinner lasted for hours. There were seconds for many and thirds for some. The younger children dispersed to play in their classroom and the older ones dashed out on the commons to kick the soccer ball around, until called back for dessert, which was accompanied by coffee, tea, or a glass of milk. The pumpkin pies were given a generous plop of whipped cream, fresh from Sally, the queen of their Jersey dairy herd, and conversation became subdued while everyone enjoyed their dessert choice(s).

They all pitched in to clean up after the meal and judiciously split up the leftovers amongst The Lodge guests and the community. Chris was wondering at his luck while toting home a slice of pumpkin pie with whipped cream in one hand and a container of sliced turkey breast, stuffing and gravy with roasted roots in the other. Leah had a bowl of slaw and carrot cake to add to Friday's lunch. Harry, opting to come home with them for a Chris cuddle, had a full tummy of leftovers. They'd made plans with Joel for a nightcap in their living room as he felt his tribe would crash early again that night.

Leah heard the horse report and viewed the barn drawings while they put the food away. She was gob-smacked by the sparkling clean laundry when she went to find a bottle of Zinfandel — having noticed Joel's preference at dinner. Chris and Harry stepped out to stoke the boiler for the night while she took care of three glasses of red. It had been some time since she'd put a coaster on the other living room table, she noted. It was good to have Joel here. It would never have entered her head to ask him to come until the moment she had. Life had certainly hopped on Stu's high-speed train!

Chris lit a fire in the hearth and sat down to catch up with Leah about Demetri before Joel arrived. While knitting away on David's sweater arm, she shared that she'd had a good close look at his etheric body at dinner. He wasn't even trying to be sociable, which actually made it easier to view him sitting against the wall by himself. Leah was worried. His nadis were firing more intensely. Of course, the closer they were to the fire of restitution, the easier her work would be, but she felt the unease of heading into her two most intense days of the week with little time to spare.

Chris volunteered to keep Demetri in close tow until Sunday when they'd plenty of time to engage him in ritual. He also prepared her for Joel's impending knock on the door by warning her that Joel would know who he was by the time he went home.

"Have you been meditating on that topic, cowboy?" she asked, needles clicking.

"Long and hard, lass. We could leave him in the dark and be responsible for putting his life in peril. His white heart is open now. He's visible to the dark brotherhood."

"Shivers! I hadn't thought of that," she exclaimed, a look of horror flashing across her face. "Was it a destiny play to ask him out here, … I hope? I'm responsible for having invited him."

"Like Demetri, Joel's time's come, lass. Don't worry about that. He'll need to be more vigilant. At the same time he needs training."

"There's no one near him to do that, Chris. Can you work with him in the dreamscape for starters?"

"Will do, lass," he replied, tipping his glass to her and giving Harry a good rub. "Don't count yourself out on his training. We triangulate comfortably. There's written work I can secure for him as well. We'll need some time together, but not necessarily any time soon," he said, absently messing up his hair — a sure sign of his deep concern for both of their Ruby Brothers.

Leah saw Joel coming to their gate and reached the door to open it just as he raised his clenched fist to knock. They had a good laugh over their impeccable timing as Joel settled into the second winged-back chair adjacent to the far end of the sofa. They shared a toast to lasting friendship. Then Joel opened the conversation, asking Chris to explain his reference to the Ranger initiation.

"Yeah, look, Joel," he began, glancing at Leah, who looked to be seriously knitting but was, in fact, dropping a good many stitches, "we have a bloke's club called the Rangers, due, in part, to the fact that we have taken on security in the valley on horseback, but in large part because my fine wife dubbed us so."

"Are you fellows armed," he asked.

What was it with men and guns? Leah silently pondered — needles clicking away.

"We are. Though our intent is non-violent, uncertainty prevails when you're faced with the unknown coming out of the forest."

"I can see that. So I'm meant to come to this Ranger meeting tomorrow night? I'm not a community member," Joel reminded Chris.

"We make exceptions for real quality," Chris grinned. "Chuck will be there too, as well as our neighbor, Jim Taylor, who is contemplating community. He admits to being at a loss to manage security on his farm without help. That could be his path into community," he said, looking at Leah.

"You can be certain it won't be the fact that they're dangerously close to losing the farm," she offered.

"No. But it's good to know that," Chris agreed. "So back to the Ranger meeting, Joel. We're starting it off at the sauna, and then we'll move to the community center."

"And, I assume we're not going to discuss initiation in front of Leah?"

"Aye, that's correct — top secret," he grinned, again. In fact he was holding back a good deal of laughter, to Leah's intuitive eyes and ears.

"What do you think of *New Avalon*, Joel?" Leah interjected, deliberately veering them off their present course. "You had told me that Kim was more the community person in your marriage."

"She is, but what's not to love about *New Avalon*? If we can pull this off in Virginia, I'll start my own bloke's club," he laughed. "You folks have a great model here and Stu tells me it's to be the first documentary you're putting out."

"It is. He'll film through the holidays, get some winter scenes with the kids and the sleigh, their sledding hill going full bore, and the peaceful winter scenery in the forest and valley. Then he'll pick the camera up again for spring planting and the early harvests, which will give him the big push into the growing season and, hopefully, the advent of our first apprentices. I think he and Will are putting together a separate documentary on the currency, which will include New Avalon, *Harmony Valley*, and the Inner City projects."

Joel went into a space of thoughtful contemplation, which Leah and Chris held with silent knowing. He was focused on his wine glass but they were observing the pulsations of his White Heart. At length, he spoke in serious tone. "Can I ask the two of you something?"

"Of course," they chimed together. Then Leah added, "Anything, Joel."

"Well," he began, "it occurs to me that you two are more than you seem. Leah, I've known that about you from our interviews and Skype sessions together. And, granted, there are clairvoyant people a-plenty. However, there's a certain power you possess that I'm both in awe of and most curious about. Let's call it the clear light of day vision as opposed to garbled, so-called channeling. That said; you, Chris, are more dumbfounding than anyone I have ever met!" This did elicit the hint of his engaging grin. But the two of them remained silent while Joel continued.

"Your talent is staggering, I'm told you're equally adept with the horses and likely anything you attempt in life. But, I suspect, though it's all fun for you, it's some sort of masquerade to hide your true power, which, I expect, is immense. Would you two care to share about that and about what the hell happened to me when you hugged me last night?" With that he drew a long sip of wine. His hosts were looking at each other, getting a telepathic priority list in place for their response. It was decided that Leah would begin and Chris would polish it off. She stilled her needles, laying the half-finished sleeve (now in need of stitch repair) in her knitting basket.

"You're quite a good observer, Joel," she began, with a smile. "That's no surprise to me. If I were to go back and track our conversations from your first call, I would conclude two things; firstly, you were genuinely appreciative of what I could offer you clairvoyantly. This created and intimacy that might not have occurred otherwise. I'll always be grateful for that, and the forum it provided to share my gift with you, because what you do in your life and work really matters to the future of humanity.

"I'll let Chris explain the hugs, because the second thing I sensed, from the beginning of our friendship, was the need for you and Chris to work together … somehow. Are you at all familiar with the White Brotherhood and the mystery schools they've kept alive?"

"Kim is an avid reader and does pass quite a bit on to me. I'm typically immersed in the global political, social and economic picture — from all angles, but not from that one."

"Hmm," she nodded. "Kim will be running across references reading Rudolf Steiner, and I understand your priorities. And yet, you're a deeply spiritual man, Joel. I've known that watching your show for many years. Underlying all that you present to the public are a set of morals; let's say a very high standard that you set for yourself as a human being. Right?"

Joel laughed. "You're a good observer, too. I do have a spiritual side. My parents made sure we all had a moral basis for making choices in life. I can, and do, thank them for that. Then, in college, I'd a philosophy professor who opened a larger world to me with the writings of Eastern religions, Gurdjieff, Ouspensky, and a good many others."

"It shows. I mention Steiner because he was more than what people saw on the outside. As deep and important as his contemporary written and spoken message was, there was another side to him that upheld the mystery school truths, which had come down from ancient times on the earth. He did so with impeccability and integrity. During those ancient times, we were just developing our brains and Higher Beings came to teach and guide us. They can no longer come to earth from the ascended state as we're meant to integrate the "I" on our own. Steiner revealed a good many of the mysteries, in the face of great opposition, for the times we're living through now. We can approach that opposition later but what seems important to me, right now, is that you understand that the White Brotherhood, and the 'nested boxes' of brotherhoods within it, does exist, and that we're part of it. And, when I say we, I'm including you. I'm going to turn this over to Chris now," she said, with a tender smile, while re-engaging her knitting — this time with a crochet hook to pick up the recently dropped stitches.

Joel looked sufficiently confused. He took another drink of wine, set the glass back down on its coaster and leaned back in his chair waiting for Chris to continue.

Chris rose to add a log to the fire. He stood in front of the fire for a moment, making a full connection with the off-planet masters of the Ruby Order. When he felt the three of them fully connected to the greater circle, he strolled around the room to lean on the back of the sofa. After making full and intense eye contact with Joel, who seemed mesmerized by his gaze, he launched into his explanation.

"Joel, this White Brotherhood is a large soul group dedicated to the evolution of humanity. Many of us are further dedicated to the Christ Consciousness initiative on earth as the most viable stream within which to pull this mission forward. Others of the brotherhood are engaged in bringing forth variations in this stream and many are engaged off the earth, either in the astral world or on other planets and in other solar systems in forms indigenous to those worlds."

Chris paused, allowing that much to sink into Joel's soul for recognition. "Within that large brotherhood, there exist many brotherhoods that have specific ways in which they approach their missions when incarnate on the earth. We, for example, are part of the Brotherhood of the Magi, the magicians, who master the art of moving energy. We have a master, who has fully ascended from the earth realm, leading our earthly efforts. To have fully ascended, as all humans eventually will, he'll have mastered his astral, etheric, and physical bodies. Which, he did. He is the Master Saint Germain. He is committed especially to overseeing the Magi Brotherhoods' efforts in America."

Joel nodded, giving recognition to Chris' description of the Master, but he didn't speak. He waited.

Chris moved to lean on the back of Leah's chair, grasping the hand she extended towards him as she lay her knitting in her lap. He went on. "Joel, we have all spent many lifetimes of service with the Magi. Within the Brotherhood of the Magi, there exists another nested box called the Order of the Ruby.

Someone making a sci-fi film would call them an elite-fighting force for the truth and light. That's seems a glorification, but it's actually the truth of our mission. There are only twelve of these brothers activated on the planet at one time. If they falter, in any way, through a lack of impeccability or deliberate alliance with dark forces, for there are just as many dark brotherhoods as light, their lives are terminated. However, their returning souls are welcomed back into the brotherhood's Upper Astral Ashram. That statement speaks both to the impeccability required of us on mission and the recognition of the actual odds of success."

Joel had transited through subtle reactions as Chris spoke, but his last statement brought on raised eyebrows from Joel, as well as a nearly imperceptible gulp.

Chris continued. "I say this to you to emphasize the seriousness of our work on behalf of humanity's evolution. I also say it to explain the urgency of another situation that we can discuss momentarily. Obviously, it's often the case that one of our twelve incarnates as a woman." The White Brotherhood exists in soul, without gender. With that he leaned over to kiss Leah on the forehead, then took his seat on the sofa again.

"Leah also represents a huge sisterhood within the physical world who are working on the same Christ Consciousness mission as our brotherhood. All of our souls exist within the Great White Brotherhood. The soul group is one. We can be brotherhood or sisterhood. The Ruby Order has maintained its present soul group 'pool', if you will, since late Lemurian times when more female than male embodiments were the norm. Characteristic of the members of the Ruby Order, when incarnate, is the presence of a filamentous white heart within their etheric body. At first, it's a potential. Then, with maturity and the engagement of soul-directed streams of the unfolding life, it typically takes shape, but remains invisible to the eye of seers outside the Order — until the individual meets and is activated by another of the twelve incarnates of the Ruby Order. Your white heart was activated by both of us, almost simultaneously." Joel's mouth fell open, ever so slightly.

"Leah and I recognized its pre-activated form, its shape, when we first saw you at the rehearsal. And, we've spent time conversing about the magical way in which you've appeared in our lives, the nature of your work for humanity, and the fact that one of our twelve brothers has recently ascended from earthly life. The other, a wise elder in Peru, left the planet around this time last year after completing a major piece of work for the Order. Now, we've two relatively new active members, yourself and a Scotsman name, Sean McNeil, with whom I've worked closely with over the last 10 years. It's, therefore, our duty and pleasure to welcome you as an active brother of the Order of the Ruby, and to advise you that it's also our duty and pleasure to see to your training as a *master of energy*."

Joel was stunned. His White Heart grew very bright and distinct to their eyes, and Leah watched a kind of expansion and involution of Joel's astral body take place. She sensed the need for grounding and slipped out to the kitchen to put on the kettle for some *Melissa* tea. She also prepared several small plates of cheese, crackers, and apples slices since their big dinner was beginning to wear off. Leah could hear Joel and Chris having a quiet conversation as she stepped out back to pick the herbs off the drying rack in the garden shed. She felt a growing sense of warmth in her heart and anticipatory tingling all over. *How fitting for Thanksgiving Day.*

When she re-joined them with the plates of food, Joel looked flushed, balanced, and serene, while Chris' grin had taken on a slightly impish quality. Apparently Harry had opted out, having been let out the front door to wander home. Leah set the plates on the end tables and moved her mother's tea table from its nested home beneath the end table she and Chris shared. As the men began to munch on the cheese and crackers, she returned to the kitchen to bring in the brewed tea and a tea towel (also her mother's) to cover the table. On her last trip she gather up the teacups and saucers. After pouring their brewed tea, Leah started to return to her favorite chair, but Chris reached out and gently pulled her down on the sofa next to him.

She curled into his warmth, noticing her tingle morph into an uprising of kundalini. His sexual energy was palpable and greatly excited her. Chris, aware of her reaction, gave her a gentle squeeze and re-initiated conversation.

"What have we got on the agenda tomorrow, lass?" he asked, lifting his teacup to his nose to take in the lemon-mint of the *Melissa.*

Leah had become aware of Joel's blazing lightbody as she'd soften her gaze and relaxed. It took a minute for her to shift into the mundane world. She set her tea down on the tea table and rested a hand on Chris' knee. "Would you two care to share with me what you've been up to these last fifteen minutes or so, first?" she asked.

"Aye, Joel's had a little third eye activation," Chris offered.

"I'll say," she affirmed, looking up at her magus. When no further comments were forthcoming, she laughed and answered his question. "Well, in addition to the usual preparations for the show on Saturday with rehearsal, I need to have a short chat with Joel, Chuck, Christina, Michelle Markum and Amy Donnelly to get their personal takes on single payer health care.

"After lunch, with Paula's help, I think I can accompany anyone who wants to visit *Harmony Valley* for a tour. I know Kim wants to see it. I would also love to ride Holly with my cowboy, here, when Chuck isn't riding her, and wonder if Joel and Kim would be interested in coming down to valley end with us on horseback? Kim already informed me that we'll be at your table for dinner tomorrow night, Joel, along with Natalie and Chuck, and your children. After dinner, the Rangers meet and I'll need to pull back to get ready for the show. That's my take on Friday."

"I'm not a great rider but I would like to come on both outings," Joel replied. "Kim can handle a horse and I'm guessing the kids have plans with the other young ones. They don't often get plunked down on a kid-filled farm, surrounded by forest, with a river to boot."

"They're sure to have a great time," Chris agreed. "I'll be off in the morning to workout and then take care of the horses. Chuck wants to ride while Natalie is working so I'll just ask him to be back by three o'clock. Remember, I'll have

Demetri in tow but he'll not mind riding. I might leave him to commune with the fish in the morning and ask him to come to the stable when he's done with them. After lunch, he and I can help Greg take the last of the lambs to the abattoir and be back in time for a ride to valley end. Sound good?" he asked.

"Sounds great," Leah, agreed. "Please remind Greg to have all of the pelts tanned and sent back to us by the tannery."

"Will do. You're piling up a lot of sheepskin pelts. What's the plan?" he asked.

"We use them for the children at the school and there are a lot of kids on the second village list. Also, Katia will need one for their bubby, and I just have a feeling we should tan and keep them for the future. Call it a hunch," she laughed.

"Fair enough," he said, raising his cup.

"Have you said anything to Joel about Demetri?" she asked Chris.

"I haven't, lass. Why don't I speak to his affiliation and leave the medical business to you?" he suggested.

"Carry on, cowboy," she replied, pouring a little more tea for herself and Joel, who reached forward with his cup.

"You will have met Demetri at dinner tonight, Joel. He is visiting from Cyprus and though his English is excellent, his Greek heritage is unmistakable."

"Yes, Natalie introduced to me to Demetri. I hope I didn't disturb him by speaking of the news from Athens with him. He was unaware of George Papandreou's, the Greek Prime Minister's, resignation and replacement with a former vice-president of the European Central Bank, Lucas Papademos. It looks like the same thing is going to happen in Italy. We're looking at the complete breakdown of democracy with non-elected technocrats as heads of state."

"Ouch! No wonder he was huddle against the wall. You wouldn't have known about his delicate energetic state, Joel, and it may act as the catalyst we need to help him," Leah replied.

"Who is he?" Joel asked, grateful for Leah's deft backhanded release from self-judgment and blame.

"Aye, Joel, he's a Ruby Brother. I referred to him earlier as having been on mission with me for ten years but he's in a bit of a jam right now. The incarnate Ruby Order met for the first time on the planet in Peru, during the planetary alignment in 2000. That's where Leah and I met — at least in this reality — and where both of us met Demetri and the other brothers. It was organized by Don Eduardo, whose photo is in the alcove over yonder," he said, nodding his head towards the back wall of the dining area. "We can go into the details of that reunion as they come up, but suffice to say, the energy of mission started moving on the planet at that meeting. In the wake of 9/11, four of us were sent on the last mission, the content of which will have to wait as well. We were assisted on mission by additional members of the Order — both on and off the planet. Don Eduardo passed over near the end of the mission and, subsequently, our Master Mukda has ascended. You're his replacement." Joel sat contemplating the shoes he was to fill as Chris went on.

"The four of us directly involved in the decade long mission were myself, Sean McNeil, who became Don Eduardo's replacement, Peter Wilshire, who is Welsh, and Demetri. Demetri gained tremendously in light and honor on the mission. In truth, I owe him my life. I'm here because of Demetri and a bit of leniency on the part of the Ruby Order. My agreement with them is to be in ongoing service in reciprocity for the blessed continuation of my life," he said, giving Leah a good cuddle. "Suffice to say, we were all wasted and wanting in body, soul and spirit at missions' end. Demetri doesn't live in an environment that could properly nurture his recovery. In fact it was quite agitating. So, I asked the community if he could come here for restoration. On his way over here, he visited his brothers in Athens and one of them, feeling the enormous pressure of economic ruin, took his own life during a dinner party with Demetri in attendance. Our brother is psychically damaged from that incident and now close to a moment of crisis — hence, his deteriorating behavior. I say this to you in confidentiality; on behalf of the role you will play in his healing. It wouldn't serve for you to be in the dark about the circumstances of his energetic state." After a moment of introspective silence, Chris wrapped it up. "Aye, mate. That's my bit. Leah can pick up her end of the story now."

"Thanks, darling," she said, with a kiss to his cheek. Then she directed her attention to Joel, who was refilling his teacup. "I had a look at him in the clinic with Nick, Joel. We've done what was needed for his physical body, besides the ongoing intake of good food, exercise and rest. However, on the level of his etheric body, we have the makings of a real crisis. He and Chris took a dive into the center of darkness on the planet. What they experienced was akin to PTSD, even though they had powerful help in stabilizing their rainbow bodies. Chris was guided to come here as soon as he could, but Demetri went home in an elevated consciousness to encounter agitation in the mundane world. I feel this kept his rainbow body in a vulnerable place. When his brother committed suicide, he lost his footing again, and since then has been in an etheric struggle with the dark forces. He's on the verge of losing, and won't be able to turn that around without intervention."

"Shit!" Joel mumbled under his breath. "What the hell can be done about it? Why does this sort of thing happen?"

"We'll get to all that eventually, mate," Chris assured him.

"Look, Joel," Leah continued, "there are a couple of important points for you to glean from this right now. One is that being a Ruby Brother doesn't make you invincible. The other is that it can also make you a target. Chris can carry on about all of that with you, but I want to assure you that a plan is unfolding to pull Demetri back. Our etheric bodies are dependent on their association with forces emanating from the hierarchies as what we would call the dark forces. We need these forces to stabilize the etheric within the physical. Their downside is their ability to form a shadow side of us — an ugly conglomeration of our weaknesses and less than honorable deeds and thoughts, if you will.

the woodland folk

"At the same time the Luciferic beings stabilize the higher aspects of the etheric in the astral body, thus creating the etheric bridge between the physical world and the soul world. Demetri's dive was concomitant with a kind of ascension that he experienced saving Chris. As I understand it, when the elevation of the "I" occurs, the Lucifer beings must relinquish their hold on the etheric body and the good Angels take on the responsibility for the integrity of the bridge — the interface between the etheric and astral bodies — for us until, in full mastery of the astral, we can do it ourselves, with their guardianship. This might be a very gradual process. It speaks to the fact that we're still in a process of being created. What I feel certain about is that this transition is accompanied by vulnerability and a need for a quiet, introspective lifestyle until it stabilizes. It's my feeling that this transition was incomplete when Demetri's brother committed suicide, and the dark forces were able to extend their control over his etheric body. He now finds himself in a skewed struggle — the dark forces, which we call the Ahrimanic, are winning. It happens to be a poor moment to try to intervene but I'm looking for that to shift very soon. That's really all I can offer as medical explanation," she sighed.

"It seems I have stepped into a higher rendition of my self, and a major crisis at about the same moment," Joel mused.

"We can't disregard that, Joel," Chris pointed out. "Leah has the ability to save Demetri given the right timing. What she needs from us is the holding of space. I believe you are meant to participate in this healing ritual, or you would not be here with your big, radiant, white heart," he smiled.

"I wouldn't have agreed at six o'clock, but I do now," Leah added.

"How shall I prepare?" Joel asked.

In this case," Leah explained, "spontaneity rules to day. Just try to be present in every moment, Joel. Since we need the bees to hold a particularly high space of Christ Consciousness, the healing will likely take place in the apiary. I'm hoping for Sunday afternoon but beggars can't be choosers — we'll do it when it needs to be done and rearrange life to suit. Guidance tells me we'll get through the show on Saturday. By the way, Stu wants to record our future interviews after the show and before a luncheon Leslie and Natalie have planned for the guests and staff, if that works for you. Then we're done with our studio work together."

"That suits me just fine. What are the topics? I haven't even glanced at the email my staff printed out about it," he admitted.

"The first interview theme is 'your home town'. We'll be bringing in two key people from Sebastopol, CA to represent a Transition Town approach to local living, and two more from Bellingham, WA to talk about the Local Living Economy approach. We'll be covering local legislative actions to counter corporate personhood and power, taking money out of politics and more. The second weekend theme is 'canaries in the coalmines', which focuses on waking up to the warning signs of climate change, chemical-laden food and crops, the vanishing of the bees, the failure of education, and the unrealized dream of democracy, to name a few. If we can get those two on tape, we'll need one more interview session to cover us through the first week in January."

"'I'll give that some thought. I like both topics," Joel said, stifling a yawn. "My plate is overflowing and jetlag's setting in. Can we continue this brotherhood discussion tomorrow? And am I able to speak to Kim about this?" he asked.

"Absolutely, Joel. Go home and have a good rest," Chris suggested, "Kim should know about your affiliation, but you might not want anyone else to know. I would keep it quiet as a service to the Order."

"Some people in this community were with us at the gathering of the Order in Peru, Joel," Leah added, "but it never comes up. However, if knowledge of the Order and our affiliation with it were to get out into the wider world, it could be problematic."

"It's only Kim with whom I would share it and try to understand it. She's my tried and true sounding board. She'd never divulge the information — especially if it might jeopardize our safety. Well, fat chance I'll get any sleep with all of this to process," he laughed, standing to go.

Leah looked up at Chris, "You'll fix him up for sleep, eh, cowboy?" she requested.

"No worries, lass," he assured her. Leah gave Joel a big hug and Chris walked him to the door, pausing to pulse his magical sleep energy into the back of Joel's neck. Their newest Ruby Brother walked down the path to the gate a tad off the ground.

Chris took the tea table to the kitchen while Leah gathered up the wine glasses and empty plates. As she dried and put away what Chris washed, she spoke to him about the catalytic role the Greek political crisis might play in Demetri's own crisis. It was a boldface autocratic breech of the necessary separation between the state and the economic sector. She was astounded at the audacity of the power elites and felt a stepping up of their not-so-hidden agenda to seize power, wealth (both individual and sovereign), and the commons from one country after another. Italy, Spain and Portugal were in equally precarious economic situations.

Chris assured her he'd look after Demetri and try to converse with him about the work he was meant to do releasing his brother from his field. They discussed Joel's need for training at some point, the love they both had for him, and the odd timing of the divine plan. Chris had gifted Joel *shaktipat*, to begin the awakening process within his soul. Joel had a deep connection to spirit, was extremely aware, but hadn't been guided to open supersensory vision. When Leah playfully asked him why he'd not done that for her in Peru, he wrapped her up in one of his full body possession hugs and informed her he'd delivered it all right, just not to her third eye.

R-r-right.

They practiced their lines with each other in bed and drifted off in a tender cuddle. The Bee Mistress was saving herself for Saturday morning's pancake seduction and the night's tango lesson ... *affectations.*

On Friday morning, the studio was abuzz. Leah and Paula worked together on the news summary, Will came in to go over the economic report — mostly about Greece — then Stu and Rob taped Willow's weekly report to Leah with film clips from the Thanksgiving dinner for 2000 people in Zucotti Park. Leah had brief chats with Chuck (before he took Holly out riding), Christina, and Joel about their single-payer health care views, and would catch up with Michelle and Amy after they arrived from the bay area. Georgia came by to run through the show with Leah, Natalie, Leslie and Stu. Paula covered more than usual to free up Leah's afternoon. After a brief stop at the clinic to see Nick, she made it home in time for lunch with Chris.

Demetri was parked on the front porch with Harry, who, to Leah's 'sight', was actively engaged in stabilizing him. *What a little trooper you are, Harry.* Leah gave Demetri a kiss on the cheek and asked how he was feeling.

"I'm not feeling much, Leah, but I'm having periods of darkness, like the lights go out and I don't know where I am," he admitted.

"Have you been able to release your brother?" she asked.

"I've tried. Yet, it doesn't feel complete. I'm not sure what else to do about that. My own power seems lost to me, right now," he said, sadly.

"I can understand that, my brother. Perhaps the final connection can be released when we attempt to restore your etheric body. I'd like to do that on Sunday afternoon but I realize it isn't something we can schedule. Chris may have told you that Joel is also Ruby Order and can give me that much more stabilization for what must be done."

"He did. I guess it's lucky he's here, though I'm in no place to be with him as a brother. I do appreciate that he'll help. What exactly are you going to do?"

"I've no idea, Demetri. We'll know in the moment and take guidance from spirit and the hierarchies," she replied.

"I trust you, Leah. I think I can hold out until Sunday. It was a Sunday when I removed your implant wasn't it? It seems the right day for such work," he smiled weakly.

"I reckon it is. I'm most anxious to assist you. I love you very much, Demetri," she said, squeezing his hand. "You boys come in for some lunch when you're ready. We're going over to see *Harmony Valley* at two o'clock with Joel and Kim. Would you care to come along?"

"I'd rather stay here and catch a nap, maybe check on the fish again," he said, sinking back down into the porch chair with Harry.

Harmony Valley was happening! Tommy had the infrastructure in place, the streets brought up to his specifications, the power installation nearly completed, and had broken ground on the Apprentice and WWOOFer Village outside the town. The barn was being built, fields were fenced into pastures around the town, and the production gardens looked ready for planting and hoop house installations. They drove towards the center of town, and parked in a lot behind the hotel because the walking-only town plaza had been paved two blocks out in each direction from where the two main streets crossed at the hotel. Businesses would be serviced from the rear. The crossroads was now a beautiful round plaza with a center fountain, and many benches for conversation on the artistically paved surface. Whereas the *New Avalon* courtyard had pavers configured in a great compass, this plaza reflected the mission style with inset gardens and grass. Mission–style post lights completed a charming picture. Though the fountain wasn't yet running, they all gathered around it, excited about what was coming together in what used to be decrepit, deserted Felix.

Leah had her drawings with her and described what would be fanning off town–center in each direction. Chris was frankly amazed at the manifestation of what they'd put to paper about eight weeks prior. He asked to look at the drawings himself while he turned from street to street.

"What's happening next?" he asked Leah.

"That would be completion of the hotel, which will house the farm and garden team, the power installation help, and a cook or two. The barn and outbuildings construction is nearly finished. We want a supportive operation in place — we called it phase I — before there's a true influx of people. Like your community group, Kim, everyone will go through the same spiritual training for community that Natalie has developed. It's quite likely we'll bring in the phase II group here, with phase I, if we can house them temporarily in the Apprentice and Woofer Village to the south of town. These will be trades people who'll get busy building the first two neighborhoods, which will, when done, house the phase I and II participants. That will free up the hotel to bring in phase III participants who will start filling in the cultural and economic spheres and the third neighborhood, followed by the fourth to house them. These will be shopkeepers, teachers, warehouse employees, and so forth. This is the maiden voyage for the homeless model. We're expecting to learn plenty."

Chris and Joel wandered over to the hotel, while Leah and Kim lingered a moment at the fountain. Chris was keen to see what Tommy had done with the surprisingly beautiful staircase banister. It had been the subject of an ongoing joke before Burt and Alice Wilson had generously given Outreach the hotel and the whole valley. He came over to *Harmony Valley* often to help Greg with the farming and Tommy with the power installations, but had not been back to the hotel for some time.

The women talked about the project in Baltimore and their community in Virginia. Kim was especially interested to know how much help they could count on with the engineering and logistics and their own need to pass it on through the gift pyramid. Leah laid out the gift pyramid plan, assuring her that Outreach would help in every way to find the three communities and homeless initiatives to fill in their pyramid of gifting. She also shared the Outreach intention to begin an apprenticeship program specifically for training leaders to guide apprenticeship within projects. These were tasks fulfilled by Tommy, Natalie, Greg and Sonia in *Harmony Valley. New Avalon* community members were joining Natalie's teaching efforts and would be available to run the community programs around the country. The aim was self-sufficiency with a leader who'd been through the proposed leadership program in *New Avalon.*

Leah assured her that, in addition to their apprenticeship training on the ground in *New Avalon and Harmony Valley*, Tommy and Natalie's help would be ongoing in terms of problem solving and troubleshooting, as well as structural engineering designs, etc. In response to Kim's suggestion that their community participate in the leadership program, Leah admitted that she and Natalie had hoped as much and that they would become a partner center on the eastern seaboard for all the programs. Finally, Kim asked about the economic infrastructure for charging and gifting within the programs.

"Big question, Kim — and, a good one for Will. I'll make sure you two have some quality time here before you leave. From my perspective, Outreach is the hub. So, you may want to consider your non-profit an umbrella for the different initiatives you are going to pursue. As you know, we charge your group members for the community training work with Natalie. She partly earns her NADs that way. Those prices include her expenses to come to you and those to cover lodging and food when you come for an intensive here. The bank disperses her pay and expense reimbursement when she travels, and funnels portions of the balance into Outreach accounts for The Lodge, the warehouse, etc. Tommy will charge you consulting fees for his work out of which he and his staff will be paid, and part will go to rent for his building, supplies, his travel, etc. Most of it circulates in our community and contributes to the coffers for Outreach and community.

Apprenticeship will be handled differently, and you will want to follow this model as you set up your organization. Apprentices are getting on–the–job training at 20 NADs an hour and will have to use that to pay for lodging and food. What they don't use will cycle back into the program. So, the program is self-sustaining and the community experience is full on. When we bring in WWOOFers, they get room and board in trade for their work and don't enter the currency system. If they want something other than food and supplied beverages from the store, like toothpaste, for example, they need to come up with USD to buy it. That's in keeping with their WWOOFer program."

They started walking towards the hotel to catch up with the fellows. "I get that," Kim replied. "But here's a theoretical question for you that I'm sure we'll hear from our pyramid members. Aside from paying for what you've detailed, what about profits to enrich your community, in return for the incredible ideas and modeling you've provided?" she asked.

"Ah, well, then it wouldn't be 'the gift' would it? We're not after profits in *New Avalon* and that will have to be a stipulation of all those engaging these models. What we do earn, as we increase Outreach, will enrich community — to help us build Chris's theater, for example. The same is true for *Harmony Valley* initiatives. The charges for lodging and food will go back into the coffers to help them build their own theater, or workout gym, or increase the gardens. One of the agreements will be that inflated overhead, skimming profits and other economic gain not in the original protocol will disqualify the participants from the programs. There will be oversight."

"Great. I was hoping to hear that. I love the spirit of generosity and the way in which currency is mobilized continually on behalf of the communities and their charitable initiatives."

"We can do this, Kim, because generous people have donated to make sure it happens. If we were to dishonor that spirit of 'gift', the flow of our inspiration and thus our ability to help humanity would cease or be badly obstructed. You'll learn about 'gift' in the community training, and find it's an investment with a high rate of return — in happiness and quality of life. The same will happen for your non-profit once your pyramid is activated."

Kim stopped Leah in front of the hotel and gave her a huge hug. "Thank you for that, Leah — and thank you and Chris for recognizing and activating Joel. He was seriously in need of a spiritual handhold. What he got was far more than that but, of course, the timing was impeccable." Kim, an outwardly beautiful woman, was deeply in love with her husband. She proved to Leah that her inward beauty far outweighed the superficial. She would serve humanity with the ease and grace of a great soul, while holding a space for the mission of her newly awakened magus.

They entered the hotel in the warmhearted space of sisterhood to find the men admiring the staircase banister. Leah couldn't help laughing. The banister would be the magnetic epicenter of *Harmony Valley* — at least for admirers of woodworking, which most men were. She was keen to see how the restaurant grade kitchen was coming along, as well as the remodeled rooms. Everything that had been dark and dingy when they'd originally looked at the hotel was bright and airy now. The parlor, barely in her memory, looked huge and filled with sunlight from its tall south windows reflecting light off the restored plank floors. It would hold a good many people, game tables, sofas and so forth.

They walked through a sunny dining area big enough for two huge timber tables. The counter along the back wall had a filtered water service and a boiling water tap at a bar sink and coolers for drinks at a sidebar next to the door leading into the kitchen, which had been quite a dump in Leah's memory. Tommy had turned it into a first class, very efficient, chef's kitchen with walk–in freezer and refrigerator rooms adjacent to the main room. The back wall was rigged up for dishwashing but also had a two-door sliding refrigerator and an ice machine. There were ample shelves for staples and dishes and, under a big exhaust hood, a grill and commercial gas cook stove with eight burners and a large griddle. In the center of the room Tommy had built a food prep area with warming lights on the end by the dining room, and warming drawers and storage below. There was a washroom off the kitchen, all built to code, storerooms for bulk items, and a janitor's closet by the back delivery entrance.

It was awesome. Leah stood there gob-smacked. If Tommy had been there she'd have smothered him in kisses and hugs. A lot of food would have to be prepared in this kitchen during the process of settlement and, when the project was complete, this hotel would be used for functions, eating out, and guest lodging, morphing back into its originally intended purpose. She wanted to be there the day Burt and Alice Wilson saw the remodel. She'd bring smelling salts!

Off the east side of the kitchen they opened a door into a bedroom for the cooking crew. There were two bunk bed sets with dressers, an adequate folding–door closet, and a bath with the toilet in a separate room — Aussie style and perfect for group living. A second door opened to the lobby hallway, which had two public toilets and a clothes closet under the main staircase. Leah and Chris had not explored that area of the hotel when they'd originally seen it on their multi-tasking wedding day. It was a pleasant surprise.

They looked at a few bedrooms upstairs, which had shared baths and a communal laundry on each floor. Noting a back staircase for emergency exit use, they clambered up the main stairs to the roof, to get the lay of the land. It was windy and cold, though the sun was shining. Tommy liked to point out that *Harmony Valley* was the perfect spot for mid-sized wind turbines. And, so it was. A lot of power was being generated. They took a quick look at the aerial view of town center, the windmills at the north end of the valley and the solar farm's first phase to the northwest, with the power station between the two sources of electricity. There was no getting around the sense of isolation with nothing else in the valley but that would be changing as the many offshoots of the homeless project took shape.

Gathering around the fountain again, Leah briefly described the Camphill Village, Retirement Village and the Aged Care Facility to be built to the west of town. They left *Harmony Valley* down the south dirt road to observe the construction crews at the Apprentice and Woofer Village. Leah stopped the van there for a minute to explain the still-to-be-filled-in vision she'd had of the nonprofit, cooperative Medical Center across the road. Then driving further down to connect with the paved county road, she pointed to land in that area on the east side of the road as the possible site of the first Restorative Justice Transition Community.

"Not bad for a county with more cows than people, eh?" Chris grinned.

"Your red here, right?" Joel asked.

"Has been forever, Joel," Leah offered, "but soon it will be purple and eventually blue. We need to fill *Harmony Valley* with happy, progressive people who get *the gift*, because cows can't vote," she laughed. "If they could, I'm sure they'd be progressive."

When Leah was dropping her passengers off at the *New Avalon* courtyard, Chris, who was opening the van door for Kim and Joel, had a suggestion. "How about we stop at our coffeehouse before horseback riding? The wind over in *Harmony Valley* can be bone-chilling."

Everyone was agreeable to that suggestion, and to sampling some of Spence's baked goods with their drinks. Leah asked her cowboy to order her a chai latte while she parked Stu's van in the underground parking garage. She knew he'd be giving Joel and Kim a lesson from Local Currency 101. Chris was especially taken with the way *New Avalon* circulated goods and services with their NADs.

The horseback ride to Mr. B's farm at valley end was a turning point for Kim. Her group was looking at a similar farm site in Virginia and Leah was able to relate the formation of the first *New Avalon* village to its original farms while explaining Tommy's vision for the village and community center in the second village. The theme here would be different since they wouldn't have the studio and Outreach as the focus of service. This community would serve the first community in many ways, expand the overall farming and food production capabilities of both communities and have a theme meant to fill in the gaps of the cultural sphere. Leah turned the visioning over to Chris who shared his plan for the performing arts. Eyes lit up as he gave the vision his best magical polish. He'd brought his sketches of the barn–turned–theater and tickled everyone with his HOOFer program.

In keeping with Mr. B's requests, his house would be replaced by the community center bearing his name, and Greg already had a line on buffalo herd stock to begin reclaiming and healing the land. The community would be settling on the new members early in 2012 and start their training program. They would be apprentices in residence, since Tommy was hoping to have both *Harmony Valley* and *New Avalon II* under construction simultaneously.

They went on to visit the falls where Joel brought up something he'd been churning around in his mind. In the presence of three fellow members of the Ruby Order and his wife, Kim, who knew of his affiliation and need for training, he proposed that they spend the apprentice year for their community group living in *New Avalon* as a family. He felt he could easily broadcast his show from the studio while maintaining his staff back in DC to do his legwork. By then, he figured their two shows would be back-to-back daily. Kim would have people on the ground in Virginia to oversee the building of their community and could travel back as needed. This way, he could get started on his Ruby Order training with Chris and Leah and be a part of the community as well.

Leah and Chris loved the idea. She saw Kim as a perfect candidate for their future training to pass on apprenticeship, and was open to their community in Virginia being the East Coast arm of Outreach. Big ideas were tossed around at the falls that afternoon and, to Leah's amazement, she felt the strong presence of Mr. Jefferson listening in.

Their discussion about the communities continued through dinner with Chuck and Natalie joining them. The children were open to the experience of *New Avalon* and a year of home schooling Waldorf style. They'd become fast friends with Rob and Mike. Kids at their school back home regularly took off a year for study overseas. They shared their adventures from the day together, including, interestingly enough, an encounter with some people in the forest. Chris immediately perked up but didn't interrogate Candice and Perry, figuring Tommy would have a reliable report from his boys and bring it to the Ranger's meeting after dinner.

Joel, Chuck and Chris went off to the sauna for the start of their meeting, while Natalie and Leah helped Kim with the dishes, then walked home together with Harry, who'd been an uninvited, but much cuddled guest. Leah put a few clothes away from their fast-paced day of outfit changing, started a load of wash, and eased into her pre-show ritual with a cup of *Melissa* tea.

The stars were glorious from her sleeping bag on the timber table and the blue diamond download? — A whopper. *Of course! Joel was right here.*

She never felt Chris slip into bed beside her but had a good cuddle with him before she got up at dawn — in spite of the fact that he was sound asleep. She was into their ritual Saturday breakfast when he turned on the shower and launched into *Pore Jud is Daid.* She wasn't inspired to sing along with that one so hummed *Out of My Dreams* instead. Studying lines and practicing songs had taken a backseat to Joel and family's visit but they would pull it together for rehearsal that afternoon, and have a lot of fun in the process. After their deliciously sensuous greeting to each other they indulged in their favorite breakfast and a much-anticipated catch-up.

Most anxious to hear about the older children's encounter in the forest, Leah, eyes twinkling, dove right into the recapitulation of their Friday. "So, cowboy, not to pry into the blokes secret initiations and all of that, can you share what Tommy had to say about the kids' adventure yesterday?"

"Sure can. I can also report that Joel passed muster with the Rangers. He's in like Flynn," he assured her, matter-of-factly. "As for the kids, it's not so much worrisome as curious. I suggest we get the four of them with their parents together with us before Joel and Kim leave on Monday. They've discovered some interesting children in the forest - quite friendly, but their English is rudimentary at best."

"Seriously, cowboy?" she asked, astounded.

"Aye, lass. Rob was able to speak with them in German, which is the traditional second language the Waldorf children take on. Tommy is fluent, and taught the boys."

"I remember that about Tommy. Well, this *is* interesting. I would very much like to hear about this adventure. Let's assume we can do this tomorrow afternoon, after rehearsal and before dinner, which we're hosting, by the way. Could you put it together, cowboy?"

"No worries, lass. They're very keen to tell us all about it."

"Great. I'll wait for the details with some anticipation and feel it important that the children tell their own story."

"Agreed."

She was packed up and out the door for the studio, having wrapped herself up in another closely guarded timeless dress from the past — this one the color of her eyes. Around her neck she wore a Mother-of-Pearl Maori carving of their friendship symbol on a white-gold chain, and in her ears, creamy pearls. She'd seen Chris eying her as she put on her coat, gave him a wink, and raised her left hand to assure him her wedding ring was onboard. *Joy of joys!* Her heart exclaimed. Tonight they would be attending the Church of Tango.

Leah took a deep breath of crisp air on the doorstep after closing the front door and before starting around the commons to the studio. Chris would be trail clearing with the Rangers before heading over to the stable to work with Thunder, Mike and Lucy on higher equine education. She would meet up with him at play rehearsal at the community center where she, her guests and staff would be having a celebratory luncheon after the show. That would be followed by her taped interviews with Joel.

The 'single-payer health care' show was going to rival *Social Threefolding* in a number of ways. She could feel it right in the midst of the discussion. As the panelists explained their takes on it, the idea began to blossom into a mandate. It wasn't a new idea, but it was an idea whose time had finally come. At the very end of the discussion, and consequently the show, Christina reviewed the three bills for *Medicare for All* single-payer health care, which had come before the state legislature. Twice before in 2006 and 2008 the assembly and senate passed legislation for single-payer health care in California but the Republican governor vetoed both of them. A third attempt was withdrawn at the end of 2010 and shelved to be resubmitted during the new Democratic governors' tenure. He was agreeable to the bill. So when it came up for vote earlier this year with all of that going for it, it was defeated because four democrats failed to show up to cast their votes, shorting by two votes the majority needed to pass it.

Stu posted the names of the four moderate Democrats who failed to cast their votes on the LCD screen along with the tally of campaign contributions they'd received from health care corporations. Two of the men had voted for it in the past, perhaps wishing to look good but with the assurance that the previous governor would veto it. Christina advised the audience that the bill would once again be brought up for a vote as a 2016 allowable state option to The Affordable Care Act. "If one of those four men was elected from your district," Christina advised, "there's no time like the present to contact him about your preference for single-payer. A full third of the state's general fund goes to health care and related expenditures. Costs are increasing at five times the rate of the inflation upon which the funds were allocated. Something has to be done, and there's no time like the present for this solution to manifest."

After a final word from each of the five panelists, Leah wrapped up the show, graciously thanking each of them for caring enough about the health and well being of the American people to contribute their thoughts to this timely topic. CEOs and middlemen skimming off huge profits, and corporate sponsored lobbying to defeat progressive legislation had no place in health care, which should be soley in the domain of the cultural commons. Profiting from sickness was immoral. It couldn't help but lead to corruption at every level. And so it had.

She and Joel taped two thoughtful interviews on 'local living' and 'canaries in coalmines'. He'd got up inspired that morning, in a good many ways that included these two topics. They moved on to the luncheon to be inspired by the other guests who'd been conversing with each other over appetizers and cold drinks, while they'd been recording. Leah, with Michelle and Natalie listening in, picked Amy Donnelly's brain about non-profit hospital administration. Hers was a mainstream hospital with alternative medical integration and emphasis on lifestyle change to avoid recurrence. When Leah proposed that the medical center she had in mind would also be a cooperative, worker-owned, Amy registered mild shock but great interest. She offered her consulting services as a gift to Outreach just to be involved with such an innovative concept. Leah didn't press her luck attempting to explain how they'd all get paid fictitious money. Some things were better left unsaid.

Joel and Chuck were head-to-head, discussing a whole raft of Washington issues with all of the young staff gathered around them. Christina, embraced in their conversation, was, at the same time, gaining much from listening. Paula was taking notes and Stu, ever ready with his camera, was filming the luncheon for his documentary archives. Leslie saw to the smooth flow of food (poached wild salmon, Tuscan kale, sautéed in butter with mushrooms and red onion, and garden salad), which Shelley and Jenny had prepared at the warehouse kitchen.

The group was still conversing when a good many of the community showed up for play rehearsal. At this point, the luncheon ended and the staff and guests opted to leave, or stay to watch the rehearsal. Kim and the kids slipped in to join Joel, having been snatched off the commons in front of their guesthouse by the director. Since Rob and Mike were part of the production, Candice and Perry were keen to see them play cello and perform in the group scenes — and they would be right there to discuss their encounter the previous day with Chris and Leah. All of the relatives staying in the guesthouse and The Lodge were tipped off to wander in for the run–through of the first five scenes.

Act II, scene one, to be rehearsed first, opened with the arrival of everyone at the social. During a lively square dance to the song *The Farmer and the Cowman*, arguments erupt between the farmers and cowboys over water rights. Aunt Eller intervenes by firing a gun. Though she is responsible for having snubbed Curly, Laurey is jealous of Gertie (played by Shelley), whom he's brought to the social. Next, there's the auction of the picnic baskets with two unfolding dramas of triangulation. The first, of a lighter nature, involved Ado Annie, Ali Hakim, who's trying to dump her, and Will Parker, who wants to marry her, but has spent her dowry money on gifts for her and her father in Kansas City. Sonia fully embodied the role of Ado Annie, much to everyone's delight, and Nick and Will played off each other beautifully as the two men in her life.

The second drama, more serious in its nature, begins with the bidding on Laurey's basket. Jud has saved all of his money to win her. The other men bid him up to try to save her from that fate, but Jud outbids them all. Then Curly puts all that he has in life — all that defines him as a cowman — horse, saddle and gun, into the bidding to win Laurey's basket. The bidding gets ugly but Curly prevails. He then realizes he no longer has what he needs be a cowboy and must become a farmer. While the dancing continues, Jud discretely tries to kill Curly but fortunately Aunt Eller is watching and quickly intervenes by asking Curly to dance. The scene closes later that night, with Will and Ado Annie coming to an agreement about relationship during their song *All Er Nothin'* — Will and Sonia at their best. Everyone, including the relatives who'd trickled in, applauded the end of the scene.

Chris was holding things together fairly well considering the complexity of this scene. He went over some fine points with the cast, had a few great suggestions for the musicians, and declared it a good idea to work the play through to this point again at the Wednesday night rehearsal before moving on to scene six. He wanted to work on music and choreography for the dance scene, and the emotional undertones of the basket biddings. They broke for refreshments before running through the play thus far. And, when they did run through it, their very first audience was thoroughly gob-smacked. That was a good sign, even if they were friends and family. The cast and musicians were enthusiastic and beaming as they received hugs from all of the onlookers and each other.

Chris, Leah, Tommy, Shelley, Joel and Kim sat on the floor in circle with Rob, Mike, Candice and Perry in the homeschool classroom to hear the story of their adventure in the forest. Rob, the spokesman for the group, began by explaining the group's plan, when they set out on their adventure. Their aim was to embody the role of the explorers who first came into these Indian lands, likely trying to find a way west to the coast. This would have been well before the gold rush. All they carried was a pocketknife, a compass, string, a drinking cup, an apple and a Spence-style power bar, which would make do as the modern equivalent of *pemmican*. The adults glanced at each other in wonder though this was no surprise to Tommy who'd taught the boys all their survival skills — nor was it to Shelley who held firm the Waldorf curriculum of living history. They did allow that they had Dad's two-way radio with Mom tuned in at home.

The kids started out at ten o'clock in the morning walking down the dirt road towards the south. When they found an easy path up to the cleared horse trail, they climbed up to join it and followed it south to the big spring waterfall that fed the pond in the barnyard. There they made the decision to climb up following the spring to its source, as any explorer might. It would be a good place to rest and get a drink of water and maybe build their survival shelters nearby. Tommy knew the source of that spring well enough to follow them along in his minds eye, nodding for Rob to continue.

They did make it to the source of the spring and were having their drink of water from its gushing fountain, when Candice saw movement in the forest. They hadn't considered confrontations with mountain lions or bears on their adventure and became scared enough to begin packing up to run. Rob turned the storyline over to Candice at this point since she'd noticed the movement. She described it as being shadowy and subtle, moving behind the trees. Her feeling wasn't that of a large predator, but something spookier, like an unnamed force.

Chris offered an affirming *hmmm* … in solidarity with Candice's flare for drama, while Leah was having an empathic, visceral journey into their group fear. Candice then disclosed that a little boy shyly peeked out from behind a tree. He was maybe the size of Paul, Georgia and Nick's nine-year-old. Their group saw the boy and quit packing up in favor of focusing on what he would do next. He hid himself behind the tree again. They waited very patiently for him to peek out again, but he didn't. Then Mike saw him peek out of a tree well above them. How that could have happened was anyone's guess. Mike called out "Hello, boy," not knowing what else to do.

Rob gave Mike his part of the story, and then took it up again at the point when the little boy called out to them. They couldn't understand him and called back and forth until Rob's ears caught something he and Tommy had listened to once in German lessons. They'd been learning about the subsets of the German language through folk stories. Rob's ear caught a word of Low German, from the area of Austria and Bavaria. It had been called Tyrolean but was now called Corinthian German. He vaguely remembered that people called the Hutterites had come to the new world from a previous migration to Russia in the mid-to-late 1800s. They migrated to Canada and in America all the way to Washington State. That was little help to their communication difficulties but Rob knew a good many German words that crossed the lines of dialect and the boy responded.

It was then that an older girl appeared next to him. She was grasping a basket filled with the fruits of the forest. The four children beckoned the boy and girl down to the rocks by the spring source offering them two of their shiny apples. All six children lost their fear and found friendship in sharing their food. The New Avalon children ate blackberries picked dried and shriveled on the bush that burst with flavor in their mouths. The forest children ate sweet-tart Cortland apples and laughed as the juice rolled down their faces. They saved the apple seeds in their baskets to take back to their home. Before parting company, they exchanged names (theirs were Jürgen and Zenzi) and agreed to meet again at the spring source around the same time after two more sleeps. That would be Sunday late morning by Chris' reckoning.

"How were the children dressed?" Leah asked.

"I remember," Perry offered, eagerly. "They wore heavy sweaters with designs in the natural colors of sheep's wool, and matching knit hats. The boy had pants of a heavy material and the girl's dress was similar. It didn't look like wool but they did look quite warm. They had funny boots on. Zenzi had long blonde braids and big blue eyes. Jürgen's hair was under his hat but seemed a little darker. His eyes were also blue but not as big as Zenzi's."

His father's clone, Leah laughed to herself while catching the humor in Joel's expression. Perry doesn't miss much, and neither does his dad.

Rob was keen to research the language with Tommy to improve his rudimentary communications and teach it to Mike. The children called them the *Woodland Folk,* never giving a thought as to where they lived or if they had family. Candace and Perry wanted to go find more blackberries. "Wow, they were awesome!"

"Perry, did you see what all they had in their basket, besides the blackberries," Leah asked, with a big smile.

"I did," he replied. "I saw a lot of greens, acorns that were different from ours in Virginia, and the berries."

"Well, they sound like lovely children," Leah affirmed to the group of youngsters. "What do you plan to do when you meet tomorrow? Any ideas?"

"We still want to build our survival shelter and think they might want to help us," Rob put in.

"It could be a kind of clubhouse for us and our new friends," Mike added, though that was obviously a long shot with a working brother and the other two children returning home on Monday. "I'd like them to teach me how they moved around the forest without us seeing."

"I'd like to help you with your clubhouse, Mike," Chris suggested. "I reckon this friendship is worth pursuing. We can go at odd times and build a sturdy clubhouse for your meetings. Maybe we can take Paul and Mark along since they would be about Jürgen's age."

"Oh Wow, would you?" Mike exclaimed. "We need Rob to come though because of the German. I don't know many of the crossover words."

"I'm keen for Rob to be there when he isn't working," Chris agreed. "Let me work with Rob and your Dad on the crossovers. I know German fairly well. Then we could make it a German-speaking clubhouse project so all you boys can learn the words. We'll have to ask Nick and Spence, but I think it a worthy plan. In fact, Nick might like to help out. How do you feel about it, Mom and Dad?" Chris asked Shelley and Tommy.

"It does sound like a ready-made homeschool project," Tommy laughed. "I think it's a great idea. Shel, how about you?" he asked.

"As long as they have the radio and don't go over the ridge and out of radio range without an adult, I'm fine with it. You've given them good skills in the wilderness, Tommy. It might be time to test them."

"Maybe we can make our meetings on the weekend," Rob suggested. "Then I could be there to learn more about these people. I'd like to research the Hutterites in America and write a paper on it."

"A great idea, Rob," his mother said, agreeably, knowing Rob would want to protect the boys *and* not miss anything. His transition to adulthood called for conscious parenting with tender hearts.

"Well, Candice and Perry, you will have one more meeting and some stories to take home with you," Leah commented, drawing them back to circle.

"It's already a good story, Leah," Candice replied, "but I would like to know more about how they survive in these mountains. And, I want Rob to show us how to build the lean-to shelter. I hope Rob and Mike can continue the story with us?"

"I have an email now," Rob announced. "I'll be sure to let you know Candice."

It was agreed that Candice and Perry would join the Wiesner's for dinner that night and that Joel and Kim would have an adult dinner at Chris and Leah's. This inadvertently opened the door for more brotherhood discussions with Joel and the mapping out of a plan for Kim's Outreach projects. They agreed on seven o'clock for dinner and a simple menu, which turned out to be coconut beef curry. Chris got the boiler stoked for the night while Leah tidied the house and made a batch of Anzac bikkies for her favorite Aussie. According to Chris, she'd raised the bar on your average Anzac bikkie, though he couldn't exactly nail down how. She wasn't telling and neither was Sally, who provided all that butter, bur the real secret was a splash of maple syrup. When it dawned on Chris that their maple syrup was shipped from Wisconsin — perhaps with Jenny and Bernie's forthcoming list of escalating imports — Leah was sure he'd be down at the falls drilling holes in Mr. Brenner's sugar maple trees for a spring tapping. She'd let the divine plan work that one out.

While they prepared the meal together, both of their minds were meandering through the children's story. It was certainly the last sort of encounter Chris had expected in the forest.

"How do you reckon the children's family found their way to these mountains?" he asked her.

"I doubt it was deliberate, cowboy. Maybe they got lost from their colony. Or people died out leaving them behind. We don't know that they're alone but I imagine forestry would be aware of them if there was a community."

"You'd think. As far as I can tell, there's nothing over that ridge but more and higher ridges and a whole lot of trees. Most of the trees are mid-sized so the forest has been clear-cut, maybe 50 years ago, but there could be some protected pockets."

"So what are you really up to — building a cubby with the boys, cowboy?" she asked, looking him in the eye with humor.

"Aye, lass, you're on to me. You've the radar of a bat, you know?" he laughed.

"A bat, now? I'll accept that as a compliment ... but I still want to hear your plan, Ranger Rick."

He braced himself against the counter for a moment, having a good laugh. "I'll get even with you during our tango lesson, rest assured. I do have a plan, as you've guessed. I'd like Nick to come along to do a little scouting while the boys and I are putting the cubby together. We'll make a safe fire circle by the water and maybe an A-frame to keep them warm. When I was their age, I was out in the bush as much as possible and Pops helped my friends and me build our cubbies. This is all good boy play, lass. We'll see what Nick picks up on. He and I might take the horses over the ridge at some point to have a look around the next valley."

"That actually sounds like a logical plan. What are you going to do if you find a homestead?"

"If they're Hutterites they'll be sworn to non-violence, so we'll not be brandishing any serious weapons and can approach them peacefully. I reckon we'll load up Gert's saddlebags with apples, carrots and potatoes," he posited.

"Splendid idea. It sounds as if they live partially off the wild food in the forest and would appreciate some farm food," she suggested. "I can't imagine living as isolated as they must. What about communications?"

"I'm sure I can make something happen in the way of Low German. When apprenticing with Giorgio, I'd some interesting experiences in the Alps and did travel through Bavaria and the Tyrol. Though not common, Low German is still spoken there in pockets — privately. We'll see what Rob comes up with in his research paper. I reckon their migration from Tyrol to Russia to America would be quite a good study for him."

"It's nice, cowboy, the way you've taken the boys on, and to include Paul and Mark would be really swell. I'm thinking David will want to get in on this exploration when he's here — unless we're buried in snow."

"I could see Nathan coming up with a whole new series," he laughed. "I'm really enjoying his stories."

"This is exactly what he missed in his childhood and adolescence for lack of a male role model," she sighed.

"Aye, but he's more than making up for it in his books, lass. Age, time and place have little to do with meaningful experience, vicarious or otherwise," he said, nuzzling the back of her neck.

That warmed her heart so much she had to stop slicing red peppers to give him a bear hug.

The evening was fluid, relaxed and truly enjoyable. Leah reckoned inviting Joel and family to *New Avalon* was maybe her best idea *ever*. The discussions were light-hearted, often funny, since the evening before had changed the playing field — for Joel especially. There was naught to be done about his White Heart and warrior training in the next day and a half, so getting to know each other more intimately made a lot more sense. Joel suggested that Chris and Leah travel out east to make the same sort of connection at their end of the rainbow. She could do her show from his studio one Saturday and have the time around that weekend to explore, meet the community and even take the train up to New York to connect with Willow in person.

It was as tempting as caramel crunch ice cream to Leah's palate. Her mind took off on a side trip to Monticello with Joel, Chris and, who else? — Jacques de Villey, a Ruby Brother to whom she was distantly related. Surely they could get Jacques to come over the pond to meet a new brother! Imagine what he could remember of Monticello and Mr. Jefferson himself. She got goose bumps all over.

They ended the night with a run through of Sunday, which would be their family's last day and night in *New Avalon*. The children were off to the forest to meet the *Woodland Folk* in the morning and Kim, Leah and Tommy were getting together to go over her projects. Tommy had been spending his evenings compiling logistics, schedules, costs, and projected completion time periods for community and homeless projects in general. He also had copies of his drawings of *New Avalon* and *Harmony Valley* that she could take home. That with Stu's documentaries, module DVDs, and her 'in person' experience would put her in good stead with her group back home for planning and execution. He would come out to work with them and consult with the local 'living architect' of their choosing, as well as engineers and contractors.

After that, Kim was scheduled to work with Natalie on the organization and scheduling of the training programs. Joel and Leah planned to have a political powwow at the studio, with Paula as a laptop, note-taking witness. She'd asked to be part of any discussions on current events ... if they didn't mind.

As that discussion materialized the next morning, Paula was most welcome and seemed to hold a nice space for Joel and Leah to dig deeper into issues than he normally could on the air. He was after her spiritual input and her clairvoyant illumination. For her part, she realized that she'd done nothing with her gift in terms of researching the past, and needed to get on it without further ado. The discussion, dubbed 'Joel meets Dragon Lady', was thoroughly enjoyable, even uplifting. Joel was a bona fide catalyst for Dragon Lady's journey to higher consciousness.

Chris was happily tending the horses that Sunday morning while Demetri communed with the fish. He'd taken along his performing arts plans and had Nathan's books on hand. He also had a wander over to the barn to chat with Greg about sheep. He'd been thinking about Leah's intuitive need to have all the lambskins tanned for the school and new babies. It occurred to him, if not to her, that it would take a monumental population explosion in *New Avalon* to make use of all the lambskins. This conundrum had ushered in the vision of a cottage industry for *Harmony Valley*. He'd remembered (how could one forget) the tourist store in the Sydney airport filled with wool and sheepskin items — all very pricy — and wished he'd picked up a drover's jacket for the unanticipated winter in the California mountains. Sure, synthetic materials were warm enough. He'd been layered up that way in the mountains of Pakistan and in Peru, but there was a natural attraction to the natural. That was a fact. He thought it might be interesting for the community to make up a list of personal items just as Jenny and Bernie had for the food. He reckoned polar fleece wasn't made in America, but didn't know for sure. Sheepskin was sustainable.

Greg felt their flocks of sheep would triple with the additional pasture space at *New Avalon* and that *Harmony Valley* would have at least as many sheep as they did. Sheep mingled well with buffalo, goats and alpacas. He was even giving thought to a sheep's milk dairy. There were some fine cheeses and yogurts to be made from sheep's milk. Chris was well aware of that from the groceries in Kalamunda. Sheep yogurt and feta cheese were readily available in Oz — and delicious. *New Avalon II* would bring them two additional dairy farmers, who might take on something unconventional, for community only.

He meandered back from the barn thinking about the numerous by-products of farming that could provide economic stability for *Harmony Valley*. There would be a serious amount of leather, from the cattle, that could be tanned and worked with by artisans. That had been a major local industry in Giorgio's village in Italy. He had a little chuckle at himself coming into 'community mind'. *Well, about time.* He knew it wasn't his project, but would bring it up with Will and Tommy at the community dinner that night, and suggest it to Leah, but after they'd attempted Demetri's healing. Soccer had been voted 'over the top' for Thanksgiving weekend, allowing all afternoon for the healing work. On examining Demetri's etheric body before going off to meet Joel, Leah declared the time for action to be fast approaching.

Joel, Chris, Demetri and Leah met in the apiary at two o'clock. The sun was on its low winter arc but happened to flood the apiary mid-afternoon before sinking behind the forested hills. They locked the apiary gate and, as a precaution, turned on the electric fence. Leah asked Chris to hold a position directly across from her, facing west. She would stand within the gentle arch of the beehives, facing east. Joel was to face south from a position north of center and Demetri would be in the south facing Joel. They were each about five strides from a center point indicated by a sizeable amethyst generator crystal that she'd borrowed from Ellia. The men were free to hold their space whilst seated on low camp seats. Demetri was encouraged to lay supine upon a camping mattress, while Leah remained standing, anticipating the need for mobility.

Chris was to represent the Christ Consciousness — as it might inhabit our etheric bodies. Since that was already partially the case with Chris, it seemed a logical place to begin. Joel was representing Lucifer, which alarmed him until Leah explained that they were working a necessary triangulation between three forces, one of them being the Luciferic. Furthermore, Lucifer was the Light Bearer — our ally in many ways, but especially for the part of our after death journey through the higher realms. It was best to befriend him in right relationship — not in ignorance or fantasy. Joel easily accepted that explanation. Demetri was, as they all knew, in possession of Ahriman and vice versa. And, it wasn't like they were exorcizing Ahriman from Demetri. They were striving for balance and the normal habitation of the double that was true of all people exclusive of energy masters. In balance with these forces, Demetri would regain his chance to cast Ahriman from his double as part of his path of self-mastery.

The *biens* held Christ Consciousness as well, but they would be holding it at the archangelic or fifth dimensional consciousness — the natural consciousness state of the *bien*. Thus, the group held back-to-back triangles with the astral realm (the joined triangle bases) being the playing field between Demetri and Joel — and Ahriman and Lucifer. Leah lit the beeswax candles in hurricane lamps positioned atop the flat ridge of each hive. She and Chris had brought them down earlier, along with Ellia's crystal. While lighting them, she invoked Archangel Michael to protect them and hold the apiary in his warrior's valor, as well as his archangelic benevolent grace. Stepping fully into the Bee Mistress, she invoked Beloved St. Germain, the head of the Brotherhood of the Magi and the Amethystine Order. Suddenly and magically, the Maxine Flame sprang forth from the generator crystal. This caused a perceptible stirring within Demetri as Ahriman began to fear the gathering of his powerful spiritual adversaries. Joel's eyes widened as the flame came forth — his first encounter with the receptacle of the combined seven rays of light.

Standing before Demetri, the Bee Mistress invoked vision to pierce through all layers of Demetri's rainbow body, rapidly sorting through the imbalances that might distract or sabotage his healing. He had plenty of help in the higher realms, distractions aplenty in the mental layer of his astral body, but a great deal of unresolved emotional issues in the lower astral including the disincarnate brother he was meant to have released. Leah quickly dispersed the distractions and, calling him loudly by name (hitherto unknown to her), asked his brother to be off on his own soul journey — with haste. He would no longer be permitted to interfere with Demetri's soul journey. He would, otherwise, be liable to further injure his own soul. Chris watched her sever all of the filaments entangling Demetri and his brother, causing the brother to float out of his field.

She stood back and invoked Lord Sananda with all the power she could muster, which, for the Bee Mistress, was substantial. She asked him to strike the first blow in the battle to reclaim Demetri's rainbow body. To Leah's astonishment, that brought forth the fires of restitution — the initiation of the death process. Quick to see that Jane had stepped in, she moved solidly back into the Bee Mistress, knowing that Sananda had provided the key element of surprise needed to fully arouse Ahriman. They'd now engaged the riskiest game on earth. Lord Sananda had not appeared. He had moved through Leah to light the fires. She turned around to see Lucifer hovering over Joel in the north, and then back to see the Angel of Death approaching Demetri from the south.

Turning back to Lucifer, she commanded him to grasp Demetri's etheric body, pulling it more fully into the astral as was normal. Lucifer refused … refused, that is, without a bargain.

"What is your bargain, Bearer of Light?" the Bee Mistress boomed.

"I shall retake control of his astral body," Lucifer demanded.

"You shall not — completely," she declared, establishing the lines of negotiation. "He has rightfully stabilized the greater part of his "I" in higher consciousness. You were banished with the ascension of the last personality aspect, which has now fallen back into your realm. You cannot possess more than that," she demanded. Chris felt Sananda speaking through her and could see Lucifer retract from their combined power.

Leah quickly looked back at Demetri who was limp and losing consciousness. The Angel of Death was at hand and Ahriman, a shadow, was gathering his presence to leave. Ahriman must not experience human death. This law, she knew, was written in his karma. Then re-engaging Lucifer, she raged, "You will have nothing of him Light Bearer should restitution proceed."

"I'll take what you offer," he conceded, raising his torch. Lucifer was well aware of the Christ presence and no stranger to compromise within this cosmic triangulation.

"Then grasp the etheric bridge quickly, Light Bearer, and stabilize it in his astral body. She moved quickly to stand between the Angel of Death and Demetri. As Lucifer commanded his end of the etheric bridge and began to draw it into the astral, nadis began to release. Ahriman had abandoned Demetri's etheric body; now his etheric body was abandoning the physical. The Bee Mistress let out a heart-breaking shriek. It was as if Mother Earth was keening. She quickly gathered the forces of nature around her and sent in the undines to quell the fires of restitution. Then, right behind them she sent the sylphs to cool and calm the nadis. Demetri did not respond, nor did he look alive — to Chris.

What more could be done? The Bee Mistress summoned the Holy Messengers of Spirit. Ten from each hive flew through the higher dimensions impervious to the winter wind — single-minded in their service. The luminous bees of the Golden Queen restored the connections of the nadis to Demetri's nerve trunks, and then held a space for Archangel Michael to pierce Demetri with his sword, enlivening his etheric body once more. However, the fight had just begun, for Ahriman re-entered as well. That's also written in his karma. And he and Lucifer struggled to gain control of Demetri's etheric-astral body bridge.

Demetri not only came around, he was greatly agitated by the struggle, and stood up looking exactly like the wild Cypriot who'd arrived in the Andes to join his Ruby Brothers in receiving their mission. The Bee Mistress called the Golden Queen's bees around her and commanded Demetri to fight for his own life. She withdrew to her position in front of the hives in a whirl of nature spirits and luminous bees. Archangel Michael hovered above her as Demetri regained his power, rebalanced his etheric body, agreed to the bargain the Bee Mistress had made on his behalf with Lucifer, then turned to confront Ahriman with a firm set of boundaries for the remainder of this earthly life. Furthermore, he vowed to defeat him in his quest for mastery.

When the calming cloak of balance settled down upon the apiary, the Bee Mistress bowed her head, holding back the torrent of tears that sought to flood the playing field. At the same time, she felt a surge of energy enliven her soul. A luminous golden queen bee flew out of Sophia's hive to alight on the Bee Mistress' third eye. The forty luminous workers swarmed around her as the Golden Queen delivered her cosmic sting. Then she and her luminous workers flew back into the hives.

The Bee Mistress relaxed her shoulders with a deep sigh of relief and looked across at her cowboy's pulsing White Heart. He was watching a glowing light retreat into the heavens. When she'd returned to the hives in the swirl of nature spirits, Archangel Michael had thrust his sword into her astral body. Like her etheric body, it was now in a honeycomb arrangement of golden filaments of light.

She looked to Joel, who was slumped over weeping, to see Lucifer gift light from his torch to their new brother before disappearing into the heavens. Ahriman was back on duty within Demetri's etheric body. According to Chris the Angel of Death and flown off, eager to retreat from the conflict. Chris had experienced the healing on new levels of conscious 'sight', as had the Bee Mistress. It was an amazing learning experience, but that was shared in retrospect. In the moment, Leah was energetically exhausted and in a mild state of shock. It had been a very big rabbit hole for Alice, all things considered. She'd thought to bring rescue remedy with her, and after dosing herself, knelt before Joel, who gratefully received a dropper full, and a strong hand from Chris to pull him up into a brotherly hug.

Demetri was somewhat confused, but had regained what he'd lost in his brother's garden. He'd not been able to completely sever the emotional ties to his brother. Both unresolved grief and the burden of his brother's remorse had steadily led him to the brink. He hugged Leah fiercely, then Joel, and finally Chris. He turned to Leah and asked if she thought it might be okay for him to have a beer with his Ruby Brothers and sister?

"Have two, my brother, " she laughed, happy to have the old Demetri back. "I'll give you mine. I need to stay a few minutes with the bees. Mind the hot fence, boys."

Chris took her in his arms, charging her heart chakra with his own White Heart and kissing her deeply. "Thank you, lass," he whispered in her ear. "We'll wait for you before discussing the healing. Shall I take the crystal back to Ellia?"

"Please, cowboy. And maybe you, Joel and Demetri could carry a lamp each?"

They left her with one lit candle on top of Sophia's hive and the warm glow of Chris' love to keep her warm. She entered a prayerful meditation with the Golden Queen who laid before her the tasks awaiting the Bee Mistress' ever-developing skills. Well, that was the first task — to develop those skills. She was to begin by reviewing Demetri's healing down to the smallest detail. What she'd been able to facilitate was well beyond her previous level of skill, which had been, basically, to see the abnormalities in the etheric body and sense the aberrations in the astral or soul body. She learned that the skills had developmental steps that could be tracked, anticipated, and invoked.

Her second task was the application of these skills to founding of a new medicine that administered to the higher bodies in such a way as to heal the entire rainbow body — Exhibit A: Demetri. Clairvoyant vision could be opened by anyone willing to work at it. However, in the heart of every doctor, of any modality, who was truly engaging medicine as a vocation, there was a courageous healer who could access a developed third eye to support this new medicine. Until that time people would take their soul pain to an eager, though often ungrounded, group of spiritual healers who always hoped for the best, but had no higher world credentials to guide them. She was to start a medical school for professional medical administration to the higher bodies. She was beginning to see inside the Medical Center at *Harmony Valley*.

Her third task was to give herself fully to her Melissae, weaving the luminous golden filaments of this illumined path within the group and out into the world through their service. *They're the sweet nectar of sisterhood,* the Golden Queen assured her. She also promised that her apprentice would come forth in due time.

Her fourth task was to use her newly acquired skills to anchor her entire personality in consciousness soul in the fullest service to mankind. In fact, she would begin working on the medical skills immediately, but taking it out into the world would require the participation of Yoda, not Dragon Lady. Leah asked if Joel was key to Dragon Lady's ascent? The Golden Queen agreed but pointed out the sacred geometric importance of the triangle — a fact Leah surely must have noticed in the healing just completed. She thought about that for a few minutes, and then asked if Mr. Jefferson would be amenable to the project? The Golden Queen charmed her with a loud buzz before ending the meditation with a sharp blast of winter wind.

Leah found the men scattered around the kitchen table enjoying their beers with cheese and crackers. Demetri jumped up to hug her and pull out a chair for her, while Chris fetched a kombucha from the fridge. It was as if Demetri had just arrived. In fact, he had.

They'd waited for her to recapitulate the healing and the profound affect it had on each of them. Chris had regained the astral level of 'sight'. He'd seen and heard Lucifer and the Angel of Death. He had also seen Demetri's brother attached to his astral body and the work with the filaments the Bee Mistress had done to release his soul. Joel had seen none of that but had heard Lord Sananda speak through Leah and had seen the Maxine Flame burning from the generator crystal. His cup was full. Demetri's story was similar to a near-death experience until he returned, shaking violently, to reengage his physical body. At that point he could see Lucifer and feel the power of Ahriman within him and the over-arching presence of Archangel Michael.

The sight of Michael, the nature spirits and the luminous bees with their beloved queen were for the Bee Mistress' eyes alone. Her ability to see into Demetri's emotional and mental astral bodies was indicative of heightened clairvoyance not unfamiliar to her but far more precise. Her view into the world of spirit was a gift. Chris said nothing of the honeycomb filaments of her astral body, saving that for a bedtime story.

At the community dinner, Chris and Leah heard the next chapter of the *Woodland Folk's* story from the children, who'd already shared it with their parents. Jürgen and Zenzi had returned with an older sister named Sissi, who spoke a little bit of English. She asked many question, which Rob was sure originated with their parents. In fact, she asked a lot more questions than he did. So the family will have found out quite a bit about *New Avalon* as seen through the children's eyes, and *New Avalon* found out that the children were all alone in the wilderness with their parents, lived in a cabin by a small lake with some fish, and they had chickens and a small number of sheep and goats. They grew some vegetables and wheat from seeds their parents had brought with them and continued to save every year. There was a great deal of food to be found in the wilderness as well, and it was their job to forage for it. Their cabin was beyond the next valley and ridge to the east. The children didn't know where they'd come from specifically, but assumed there'd been a whole tribe of people at one time because their parents talked about them. All of the children had been born in the cabin and Sissi looked to be fourteen.

When Rob asked if they ever went out into the towns to get supplies, Sissi had emphatically replied, "nein." They did remember a few times coming down into the valley to pick up windfall apples and pears at Mr. B's house. He was very kind and didn't ask them where they lived or anything like that. While the group of new friends shared food with each other, the *New Avalon* children found out that the *Woodland Folk* father and mother were named Zacker and Trynel, and that their last name was Truetlen.

They'd good fun building a lean-to and huddling inside (a real squeeze) to share their food. Rob had explained that Candice and Perry were visiting and returning home in the morning, but that two other boys might come next time. They made a date for seven sleeps from today, next Sunday, at around the same time if there wasn't deep snow. They were each to bring something unique from their village or homestead.

Rob thought to ask Sissi how she knew any English. She told him that a lost hunter had come by their cabin, nearly starved, several years before and had stayed until he was strong. She learned what she knew from him to communicate between the hunter and her father. The hunter had left before the snow came that year, hopefully to make it home safely. Sissi was another pretty blue-eyed girl with long blonde braids but with a different shaped face than the younger children. She wore an apron over her skirt and happily took several apples for her parents.

Leah and Chris exchanged knowing glances, prompting Chris to make plans with Mike, Paul and Mark to start on the cubby after school on Wednesday. Then, on Friday morning, he and Nick would have a little meander on horseback with Billie.

Joel and Kim graciously thanked all of the community for the wonderful time they'd had at *New Avalon*. Kim promised to be back with or without Joel to apprentice community and would send apprentices for the homeless model. In the meantime they'd arranged to have Natalie come out to Virginia to start their community program. Their last hours before an early bedtime were spent with Chris and Leah in the guesthouse living room within the intimate zone of comfort they'd found together, discussing the possibilities of a visit to the east, including an extended, off-hours, private visit to Monticello that Joel felt he could arrange. The two committed Skype-sters would work out the details.

"Now, about that 208-year-old (more-or-less) French brother of ours, Jacques de Villey?" Joel asked. "Do you suppose he'd agree to an interview?"

chapter 5: medicine for the soul

Because there'd been no time for a decent catch-up together, nor would there be that night with Chris' choir practice, Leah suggested they have the afternoon together to get back in their groove and learn what they could from the last four days. They were up early to send Joel and family and Will and Tommy to the Medford airport for their separate journeys to the east and down to San Francisco.

Leah had been looking forward to the coming Saturday's show, on 'your hometown', and had a pile of notes ready to help her organize the flow of the discussion. When she reached, the studio she found Paula tracking the news and Natalie bent over some paperwork at her desk. She'd parted with Chuck before the community dinner for his all-night journey back to Washington. He had to be there on Monday morning, in committee, though, admittedly, most everyone would be functioning in slow motion.

When Natalie pulled up her chair to have a chat with Leah, they'd already been through a blazingly good staff report of show feedback, which ended with Paula's comical lobbying effort on behalf of their millennial staffers to be made eligible for choir. Leah declared the situation a dreadful oversight on her part, and advised them to show up at eight 'o'clock that night, in the community center, with their jingle bells. Chris would be overjoyed.

Natalie wanted to talk about teaching in Virginia. She felt Kim was as steady as they come for steering a founder's group and she liked the idea of an eventual Outreach East centered in their community. They'd arranged for their first large circle of community, the introductory session, to be the weekend of February 18th. Their first intensive would follow in April, the shake out weekend in June, and the second Intensive in September in *New*

Avalon. To conclude the series, the two circles, one of founders and the other of the second wave group, would occur in November. They would be on track to begin building in the fall and spend their year in apprenticeship at *New Avalon* beginning January 2013.

Leah marked all of the dates on her calendar, pleased that Kim's group would follow in the footsteps of the Ashland group and alongside the Ukiah group with their apprenticeship and building efforts. That gave her a time frame in which to manifest the housing facilities for the apprentices and the necessary studio adjustments to facilitate Joel's show as a bi-locale production. Personally, she needed a strategy to get what she felt was an advantageous triangulation in place for her ascent to Yoda-hood. She was certain that this should precede Kim and Joel's apprenticeship period. Admittedly, that fantasy was open to the whims, and good sense, of the divine plan. Dragon Lady's ties to the cultural mind were inextricably linked to a similar subpersonality belonging to Joel. They'd be undergoing their own versions of *collapse.*

Kim would also be spearheading the first homeless project outside of *Harmony Valley* with a second group of benefactors, who were forming the non-profit presently. Theirs would be the first apprenticeship at *Harmony Valley.* Although, Will indicated keen interest in a homeless project in Sacramento as well. Kim 'got' the gift pyramid and wanted to make sure her group was in on *Harmony Valley* before Phase II began in the spring. All in all it was quite a productive four days on the Outreach front, and Will and Tommy were off in the third direction, the Inner City project. To Leah, it felt like these initiatives had lives of their own and that *New Avalon II* would be the chick tucked under the wing of its mother hen. She would stay intimately involved in each and watch the progress on the Restorative Justice front as it took off in 2012, but her main focus would be on the future of medicine and innovative systems for the government and economic spheres. She kept this to herself to avoid rocking boats that were just finding their stability in the unpredictable waters of the unraveling.

Chris was filling out the warehouse box order when she got home for lunch. He loved ordering the food and not having to fetch it, and she was happy to be free from thinking about it. She set her notebook on the table and crawled into his lap. He began singing *Just the Two of Us,* which made her giggle — mostly from fatigue.

"My sentiments exactly, though I loved every minute of it," she sighed.

"What next, lass?" he asked, in an open-ended way.

"Well, the Bee Mistress has a few mind-boggling assignments to work on should I get a free moment, but we're pretty well booked through New Years' day ... delightfully so. I can use your choir nights to work on her suggested work, finish up the kid's gifts, and catch up on my Steiner reading. We adults don't do Christmas gifts, by the way. It's all about the children — but simple and heartfelt. I think you are giving the boys a great gift with the cubby project. That fits the *New Avalon* model of Christmas to a tee."

"Suits me. What can I do for you right now? I'm amazed you could get out of bed this morning after Demetri's healing, followed by a community dinner, followed by a social get-together."

"All with my favorite progressive talk show host in tow," she laughed. "That was a pleasure. I have much to learn from the work with Demetri — part of my assignment — but it didn't cause a meltdown, which was good for a change."

"The Bee Mistress is a formidable force for the good and true, lass. You've done well with her."

"Think about it, cowboy. She's managed to win you away from Jane for tango night, and that after her outrageous Saturday breakfasts. And she intends to marry you at the end of *Oklahoma!* Life is truly going well for the Bee Mistress," she sighed, kissing him playfully.

"Marriage number four?" he teased.

"One for each of my subpersonalities. You married Jane in Peru, the Dragon Lady in Yreka on the horse pickup day, and Alice when you returned from San Francisco with my beautiful ring," she recounted. "This last one will be a real production, which suits the Bee Mistress ... to be honest."

"We'll have to conjure up a fifth wedding when you get these characters integrated and I get to marry your higher self."

"Don't hold your breath, cowboy. It won't be tomorrow."

"No worries, lass. I'm enjoying today. How about a massage before lunch? Would that suit the Bee Mistress as my gift of gratitude for restoring a good man's life?"

Oh, if you insist," she teased, knowing perfectly well where a massage would end up. She was happy to receive the gift.

While Chris put lunch together, Leah, feeling loosened up and well loved, began the painstaking task of detailing Demetri's healing. She'd taken careful notes of her Ruby Brothers' observations, correlating them to steps or levels of clairvoyance. Chris was the most open and helpful in that regard — and handy, as her good fortune would have it. But, the bulk of the data was to be extracted from her clairvoyant memory. The Golden Queen's directions were to track, anticipate and invoke the skills she'd used. Defining the skills might be a good start, as well as targeting their effectiveness to a particular layer or layers of the rainbow body.

She'd little more than a strategy outline when lunch arrived at the table, along with life's most welcomed distraction. Whereas she was floundering for details, Chris was into the overviews of the healing. She allowed him that and pulled from it a larger framework within which to see the details. Neither of them could see Ahriman, which was no surprise as he was a very high being amongst the hierarchies. She'd sensed his withdrawal ahead of the etheric and had seen a kind of shadow as she had with Mr. B, when he'd passed over. They concluded that the sight of Ahriman would have sent anyone of them, including the Bee Mistress, into a major meltdown. So *God Bless* on that one.

"You know, cowboy, I'm reminded of that beautiful poem, *The Pearl*, from the Gospel of Thomas. The poem that Sheik Fakoum and I shared in Peru. In reflection, I see clearly that snatching the pearl from the dragon or serpent is the story of mastering the double, the etheric body. The pearl, the etheric body, is the mirror of Ahriman and our own shadow when they're present within it, or the mirror of Christ when he is present within it. Do you agree?"

"Brilliant, lass. You have it in concept and, one day, in your hand — a pearl of great price."

"It's too bad that Demetri has to regain astral mastery but kind of nice to have a buddy on the journey with me."

"You're forgetting that I'm in a similar place."

"R-r-right," she drawled, rolling her eyes. "Spoken like a true slave of the culture," she teased. "You've banished him, cowboy. You just have to grab back your etheric body — piece of cake, I reckon," she smiled.

"R-r-right," he drawled back at her, with a grin. "You never really banish the Ahrimanic, by the way, so long as you are in physicality. He and Lucifer provide the two poles that allow us to be physical. He can be banished with ascension beyond the physical incarnation — mastery of the physical body."

"Then what is the object of this quest Demetri and I are embarking upon?" she queried.

"That neither he nor Lucifer have free reign with your souls. The strengthening of the soul lifts the veil, revealing them both. Then we can be consciously using the best that they provide whilst avoiding their darker impulses. Now, lass, we've had no time to talk about your meditation with the Golden Queen and I've a proposal for the community that I've not had time to share. Do you have a preference?"

"Let's take Harry for a wander and end up at the stable to see how Holly and Thunder are going. For some reason I feel like what I need to bring into my awareness requires movement and fresh air, maybe to lift the complexity of the last four days from my mind. Does that work for you?" she asked, picking up the dishes for washing.

"Perfect, lass. My proposal is stable-suitable for sure," he agreed.

They began their walk talking about Joel's visit, its timing, the intimacy and the amazing blooming of this brother they both loved so much. And Kim? What was left to say about their brother's choice of a life partner? She was golden. The year spent in residence at *New Avalon* would be much anticipated as would their own trip to the east, likely in the spring, when Washington and Monticello's fruit trees would be blooming and *New Avalon* would still be in late winter. Chris, who'd been meaning to email Jacques, would remember to do so the next time he was in the tech room. As they meandered down river, taking the back way to the stable with Harry in tow, Leah began to lay down the Golden Queen's message.

"Cowboy, my soul is sorting out a myriad of feelings about the big item on her list. The other's are easier to comprehend, like nurturing our beautiful women, understanding the skills the Bee Mistress used in Demetri's healing — like tools in her medicine bag — and even the Dragon Lady-to-Yoda transformation, though she did indicate I'd benefit from the favorable use of triangulation as was demonstrated in the healing."

"Do tell?" he queried.

"Well there's Joel, of course. We're continually working towards our mutual transformation in our work. Dragon Lady gets it. Step one. Secondly, there's my very strong affinity for Thomas Jefferson and desire to communicate with him regarding new systems for government and even economics."

"I'm certain the Bee Mistress is on the verge of a breakthrough," he said, encouragingly. "And, is there a catalyst?" he asked.

"Jacques, of course!" she smiled. "He was visiting at Monticello my first time traveling back there. He would remember, and I think he holds a key that connects all the dots between our slave lives, Jefferson, the Ruby Order and the brotherhood — which is to say, Saint Germain."

"Might as well think big, lass. It suits you," he grinned.

"Well it kind of makes sense. So that's all somehow tied into Dragon Lady since she is the one who carried the implant from the slave life, remember?"

"Right you are. Go on, then ... with the Golden Queen," he encouraged as they stooped to climb through the split-rail pasture fence behind the stable.

"So the last bit is huge. Obviously my clairvoyance was heightened in the healing, opening to certain pathologies in the lower astral body that weren't your typical stuck emotions and thought form obsessions, but precisely managed interferences of the angelic realm. I have to wonder how much disease we typically assign to physicality has its origin in such interference."

"What are you meant to do with this?" he asked, genuinely curious.

"I'm meant to develop a new kind of medicine that accounts for the whole rainbow body, cowboy. It's a bit staggering, to be honest."

""Aye, so that's why you became a doctor," he laughed. "I'd not figured that out. You're a good one, to be sure, but why the Ruby Order presence in medicine, at this time, has puzzled me. Good for you, lass," he said, giving her a good squeeze.

"It makes as much sense to me as 'why the Ruby Order in slavery 200 years ago?' cowboy. Which is very little. At any rate, that's the task. With this in mind, I can go forward in vision to the Medical Center with a better understanding of its purpose. I doubted it was for conventional medicine, though I surely see current medicine needing to be a model more in service to people than to economic gain. There is, apparently, a protocol or methodology to be worked out for each layer of the rainbow body."

That's all very exciting and promising for humanity, lass," he said, as Holly came trotting up to greet them. "We can regard it as a sign that it will one day be regarded as the medicine of choice, though we'd best not expect that in our lifetimes."

"No kidding!" she laughed, as she walked Holly into the stable to curry her while Chris shared his proposal with her. Thunder seemed content to be in pasture with Cinnamon since Chris had greatly challenged his capacity for higher education that morning. She kept Holly out in the stable passageway where the light was better, loosely fastening her by lead to a hook near her stall door. Chris got his notes from the tack room then sat on a bale of straw leaning against Lucy's stall.

"Yeah, look, I want to present this to the community next Tuesday at our meeting. Mind you, they're just ideas, not projects I'm looking to initiate, or oversee. I thought we might start having a discussion about them. I have enough on my plate with the barn renovation and so forth."

She'd started currying Holly, who always showed her appreciation of a good grooming with equally good manners. "Okay, cowboy, I'm all ears."

"Good, because you were the one who inspired this first idea," he winked.

"Glad to be of service," she laughed.

"You do remember telling me to have the abattoir send your lamb pelts to the tannery for the school children and Mitch and Katia's bubba?" he asked.

"Of course! You told him, didn't you?"

"No worries. Greg beat me to it. But it got me to thinking about how many sheep we have. We have a lot of sheep, lass. With Mr. B's land, Jim and Gayle Taylor's — and I'm reasonably certain you'll be hearing from him soon — and add to that *Harmony Valley*, we're talking an Aussie level of sheep in our custody."

"It certainly sounds like it," she replied, seriously, whilst stifling an inner giggle. "Did you check with Greg about the plans for flocks?" she asked.

"Yeah. We're talking a lot of sheep — endless sheep, in fact. Which brings to mind all the pelts from the lambs that go to market to say nothing of the wool that comes off this mob every spring."

"Right," she said, thoughtfully. "What do we do with them?" she asked, "Usually?"

"Greg sells the wool to the shearers for market price to be rid of it, and, if we don't have the pelts tanned, they get sold too, for a fraction of their worth. We've no need for them."

"But you *do*?" she prodded.

"*We* do, lass," he said, referring to his notes with a tapping index finger. "Think about cottage industries in *Harmony Valley*. Wool has a good many uses, including your yarn for sweater knitting, blankets, shirts, felting, doonas, and so forth — even insulation. The sheepskins can be used to make coats, boots, gloves, slippers, hats, you name it — and it's all out there, costing a fortune, in the tourist stores, like in the airports of OZ. I saw a good many women in Aussie shearling boots in San Francisco. They're inexplicably trendy, according to Will. Why can't we make high quality products from our animal by-products? Why can't we tan the cowhide for leather goods, including the slipper soles? There's heaps of tallow for soaps. In the past people would never have wasted a scrap of what the animal had given them.

"I could see the prison having a tannery, for instance. Then they sell that to the village leather artisans, who make handbags, boots, shoes, and coats — the lot. This is small village Italy at its best and it used to be Outback Australia at its best. Now it's global–corporate. We could take a step back in time here and create quality goods. It's doubtful the ships are going to be coming from China when the oil runs out. We could prepare now and enjoy better, more natural products in the process and support our initiatives at the same time. I've been wishing I'd picked up a shearling jacket for winter on my way over, and then you brought up those pelts. Well, I'm rambling, but do you get my drift?" He looked up from his notes to see Leah, Holly and Harry gaping at him.

"Chris, that's brilliant! Of course, it has likely hurt some part of Greg to let the wool and pelts go but there's just so much a man can do. We have people coming into *Harmony Valley* who can be taught to do these things if they don't have skills already. Tommy is planning a trade school. Maybe we can find homeless people who already have some of the needed skills for these industries. They could be trained to shear the sheep. I love it! Let's make it a wish — that you'll have your coat for next winter — perhaps, made right here."

"Well that's the deal, lass. I'd like that jacket, but I've no mind to make this happen."

"But that's the beauty of community, cowboy. Someone will see this as a good cottage industry plan for *Harmony Valley* and away we go! We already have the sheep, as you have insightfully noted. We'd need to look into the toxicity of tanning. I think it's pretty toxic. If so we could send them out or use the Indian methods of tanning which, if I recollect, used the animals' brains for the alkaline solution. We'd have as many brains as pelts, I reckon," she conjectured.

"Nick would know about that. He might actually be keen on this as a project, at least partly. I do need him on the medicine front though. Hisbrewing skills can be passed on to any number of people through short-term apprenticeship. Can you put something together for the Outreach Board meeting on Thursday?"

"I've not the time or mind to research this tanning business but can certainly propose what I just ran by you."

"Great. You'll get some immediate feedback before the community meets on Tuesday. I'll let the board know you'll be there — four o'clock, after I'm finished on Joel's show."

"Thanks, lass. I don't feel quite so burdened by it now. I'll get back on task with the performing arts project once I organize these ideas."

They continued their walk, circling the village, to have a look at the footers for Tommy's office addition to his woodworking shop. Then they tracked back to the studio for Joel's show. The show was just as good without Joel, a credit to his non-aggrandizing ego and his articulate producer's broad range of talent and political savvy. The show was well done and focused on the ongoing deadly uprising in Syria where journalists were in grave peril at all times. Gavin ended by plugging Saturday's *Light on the Crisis* both because Joel had been a principal guest but also because the theme of 'single-payer health care' at the state level was likely the most viable route to having it for the nation one day.

Leah picked up the news summary Paula had laid on her desk and they finished walking the circle back home for the choirmaster's quick dinner. She'd let him be surprised by the influx of young voices. *Joy to the World!*

While Chris was off singing Christmas songs with the majority of the community, Leah curled up in her chair with a pot of herbal tea and her notebook. The task, at hand, was to detail the healing with Demetri using her quickly scribed, 'big picture' notes as a guide. She'd drawn a diagram of their positions equidistant from Ellia's crystal — the four corners of a square. The *biens* had *shielded her back* in the soft semi-circle of their candlelit hives — like the first sliver of moon after its passage through darkness. Chris held Christ Consciousness at the etheric level with the clarity of a master, connecting with her and the *biens* to create the first beam of the cross. Demetri, in the throws of Ahrimanic possession, was positioned at the south end of the square, and Joel, holding a space for Lucifer, was opposite Demetri connected through the second beam of what looked like ... the Templar Cross.

She remembered invoking Archangel Michael as she lit the candles on the hives. His enormous presence came in to overshadow the *biens*, strengthening the fifth–dimensional pole of the Christ Consciousness beam. In the center of the cross, the amethyst crystal held the space of the Amethystine Order and the Brotherhood of the Magi. When she'd invoked the presence of the Ascended Master, St. Germain, leader of those orders, he brought forth the Maxine Flame through the crystal, setting the stage for higher world intervention. Looking at her drawing from a different perspective, she remembered feeling like the space in the center, on a plane between Demetri and Joel, was in the astral world.

At the side of the drawing she wrote a summary: *The Bee Mistress established solid connections to five dimensions and energetic connections to even higher worlds by virtue of the gift of the Maxine Flame. She seemed comfortable navigating in five dimensions. Ahriman wasn't aroused until the Maxine Flame appeared. Can we assume his hierarchical origin is beyond the fifth dimension?*

Leah pondered that, while pouring a cup of honey-sweetened, well-steeped, chamomile tea. The next passage in the healing brought her before Demetri with heightened vision. A sip of the calming tea drew her back into that moment. *How much of the rainbow body had been visible to the Bee Mistress?* she asked. She'd seen his consciousness soul bridge to spirit, and had looked across it. Rather than 'seeing' anyone or anything, she 'felt' a benevolent energy emanating from his spirit-self. His spirit was protected, just as Chris' had been with the loss of his double. The Bee Mistress was unwilling to cross his bridge and seemed unable to use her own bridge to meet an adversary in spirit world for him. Chris might have been able to do this, had it been necessary. He did rescue Jane when she'd fled the trauma in the apiary back in October.

The Bee Mistress had clear vision of Demetri's astral body — all three layers and the two bridges. As expected, his upper astral had been perturbed by the sudden withdrawal, and descent, of the recently ascended part of his personality. The turmoil was in the lower astral, where she clearly saw his brother's filamentous hold on Demetri, and Demetri's reciprocation of the bond. She'd somehow known his brother's name, though Demetri had never uttered it in her presence. The way in which the Bee Mistress had severed the filaments and released the brother to his astral journey had been swift and decisive — absolutely *no nonsense*. After reliving this part of the healing, Leah drained the cup of tea and added a summary to the side of her recollections: *The Bee Mistress has a comfortable and impeccable connection to power in the astral world for the good and true. How different this picture would have looked without her hard work to release herself from self-absorption and her ascent to the bridge.*

Recalling the next sequence in the healing gave her chills. She got up to put another piece of wood on the fire Chris had lit for her. Leah paced around the living room with this recollection, which contained the heart of the healing. She relived it, in trance, while staring at the photo of their wedding day in Peru that sat atop the secretaire. She'd spontaneously invoked Lord Sananda, asking him to initiate the healing in keeping with Demetri's highest good. His presence roared in like a cyclone to possess her, at the same time the fires of restitution were lit within Demetri's nadis. She was clear that she would not have had the courage to do that on her own — didn't know if it was possible — doubted it would have been. But, it certainly did bring the situation to a head. She could see the shadowy presence of Ahriman rise up to leave Demetri and the approach of the Angel of Death, whose form was quite distinct — and no comfort.

Breaking the trance-state, she sat back down with her notebook to add the details of this critical juncture of the healing, including her feelings, the clarity of sight, the thoughts that ran through her mind, and Lord Sananda's will forces acting through the Bee Mistress — including a powerful voice that wasn't her own. On the side of her notes, in summary, she wrote: *How is it that I was able to embody Lord Sananda? Or, should I be asking how he was able to commandeer the use of my senses? A puzzle unsolved. Moving on to the healing ... as she'd predicted, surprise was the key element. Ahriman is too clever for less. Lord Sananda has some command over Ahriman, but aren't the Kumaras Archangelic? Has he ascended beyond? Or does his commanding force come from the power of his love? To light the fires of restitution, risks death. Was Demetri's death impending? Such a huge risk! Nonetheless, it was the correct choice for the situation. The Bee Mistress, already aware of the etheric body and the nadis, can now distinguish the shadow of Ahriman within it and see the bridge from the etheric to astral world. That bridge was close to collapsing into the etheric — so little of it remained in the astral.*

At that moment, she'd turned to look at Joel with Lucifer looming above him, while, at the same time, Demetri collapsed. She clearly remembered the negotiation with Lucifer and the bargain Sananda offered through her, giving Lucifer jurisdiction over Demetri's fallen ego aspect. She'd looked back to see the Angel of Death coming to grasp Demetri's soul, and then recalled the way in which Sananda forced Lucifer to accept his bargain. Again, she added margin notes: *How interesting that the hierarchies compromise with each other, and with our rainbow bodies. Sananda was still fully within the Bee Mistress, carrying on this negotiation. The Bee Mistress — distinct to me in feeling — was holding a solid* space but feeling the urgency as Demetri's life force diminished. She'd been unable to see the Angel of Death when Mr. Brenner passed over.

And then, the nadis started releasing, separating from the physical nerves. She'd moved instinctively and swiftly to ward off the Angel of Death as Lucifer began energetically pulling on Demetri's etheric body to bring it to the point of balance. She didn't remember the commanding shriek the Bee Mistress had used to summon the nature spirits, but Chris and Joel said it was a heartbreaking cry of grief. The undines put out the fires at the nadis, and then the sylphs calmed and cooled them. She could see that many nadi filaments were detached, flying around aimlessly — distorting Demetri's etheric body. She had to stop the recounting to go within again in an effort to understand it. The margin notes that followed were: *Sananda has departed. The Bee Mistress is, once again, in charge of Demetri's life — or death. She calls on her power with the nature spirits as she did in the bloody mongrel incident. This seems (twice now) to be accompanied by ear-splitting sound, accompanied by profound feelings — this time grief. Demetri looked, for all the world, to be dead.*

In the next of the sequences of this event, the Bee Mistress summoned a new ally, the Golden Queen, who sent her luminous worker bees to reconnect the nadis. They held that space while Archangel Michael re-enlivened Demetri's etheric body. None of her witnesses had seen these bees or the nature spirits. Ahriman re-entered Demetri's etheric body and the real battle between Ahriman and Lucifer began, with Demetri staggered to his feet, to defend himself. She'd retreated with the transcendent bees and nature spirits to her post in front of the *biens*. Notes: *I had previously seen the nature spirits, am learning to distinguish them and what power they have to intervene for those that can work with them. The luminous bees were a brilliant surprise. The thought of them makes my soul soar. The Golden Queen is a magician of the highest order for these bees were sixth dimensional beings. And, it was absolutely awesome to see them! The Bee Mistress instinctively called the Golden Queen into the healing.*

With Demetri (a powerful magician in his own right) taking command, the Bee Mistress held a space of balance in the west. And, when the balance was achieved within Demetri's rainbow body, The Bee Mistress was ceremoniously stung on her third eye by the Golden Queen. She felt the sting, and the wave of the venom's etheric force flow out through her rainbow body. Her vision expanded, much as it had when she'd taken San Pedro one time in Peru, to reveal the many layers of her rainbow body's geometric scaffolding — including the virgin honeycomb layer of the etheric body that Chris had seen when she'd integrated a dramatic energetic change. At the same time, she saw the coloring up of the entire rainbow body — as a rainbow of scaffolding layers. And, then the vision faded. Chris had told her that a light had entered her, and he'd seen her astral body take on the geometry of the honeycomb.

This was complex in the extreme. Her margin notes reflected this: *I had been told that the Bee Mistress' clairvoyant vision would be enhanced as a result of my work with Demetri. Am I to guess that this takes her vision to the level of the heart fully, as that's the gift of San Pedro? I have no idea. What does it mean that my rainbow body is turning into a bien? I must ask the Golden Queen if this is characteristic of walking this path to mastery ... and Archangel Michael? What a gift, and why? More questions than answers here! My God, we are beautiful beings of light!*

After that astral body shift, her awareness had turned to Chris whose White Heart was pulsating within his etheric body. When they'd compared notes privately, he admitted regaining more of his 'sight', and being able see to the Angel of Death and Lucifer, as well as Demetri's brother. He was clear about the presence of light above the Bee Mistress, which he took to be Archangel Michael. She was assuming he'd used his sword to enliven her astral body because she'd actually seen him re-enliven Demetri's etheric body using it. Chris had not seen Michael but he'd seen the re-enlivening energy enter his brother and he'd seen at least the lower layers of her new honeycomb astral body scaffold. So what have we here: *I have seen Archangel Michael, not in meditation but with expanded vision in the physical world. He has intervened on behalf of mission whenever I have invoked him — and God knows how many times when I haven't. He seems intimately connected to the Christ Consciousness Initiative on earth. He seems also to be connected to the luminous bees and the Golden Queen of high magic. She and her workers are likely sixth dimensional, or have built that bridge. If the bien is fifth dimensional sitting right in the apiary in the midst of the third dimension, these magicians are likely ascended from the biens into sixth. This is the magic of the Path of the Golden Queen — now, to the hard work of learning to access it for the good and true.*

Lastly, she gave her attention to Joel, who'd been visibly shaken by the healing, but also gifted enormously by Lucifer, the Bearer of Light. Joel was clearly on the initiate's path of the Order of the Ruby. It was no mistake that he was in *New Avalon* to assist with Demetri's healing. As Chris had predicted, he would know who he was on Thanksgiving evening, and now he knew firsthand the power and capabilities that come with service in the Ruby Order. He'd not seen more than the physical world, into which the Maxine Flame had been materialized. However he'd *felt* both the battle and the gift within his astral body. Notes: *A-Ho, brother!*

As a last effort to bring what she'd experienced into alignment with the Golden Queen's first task, she focused on the margin notes and imagined herself trying to convince a group of eager, spiritually inclined, medical professionals of the importance of heightened awareness or supersensory awareness, in making accurate medical assessments and the most beneficial treatment choices for each patient. Add to that the caveat that some treatments would be 'out of this world'.

From her first set of notes, she concluded that some knowledge of sacred geometry would be necessary, as well as a clear understanding of the rainbow body. As an aside, she noted that Ahriman was a very high being.

From her second set of notes, she concluded that her medical professionals would need to have done some high-level work on themselves, in order to be able to observe the souls of their patients. This could come in time, with expanded vision, but, realistically, required that they be well on their way to impeccable selfless service — egos in the process of gathering at the bridge. Without filling this tall order, sorcery remained an option.

The third set of notes confounded her. Yes, the masters can, and will, intervene when conditions merit it, but she felt this was extraordinary. Her ability to hold Sananda's commanding presence baffled her and merited a lot of investigation — a thorough interrogation of her husband, for starters. She frankly felt this was an intervention to preserve Demetri's mission and would likely not come up often, if at all, in patient relations. Thus, it wasn't going to come into play with her medical professionals. It did, however, give her some diagnostic guidelines for possession by Ahriman, which might be suspect when specific organic and mental health symptoms were present. This was an area in which data through observation of mentally ill patients might be compiled.

From her fourth set of notes, she concluded that ego existed in the higher realms, just as it did in this realm, and that, when dealing with the indwelling spiritual being, negotiating skills can serve you well. Also, it was important to acknowledge — but separate yourself from — your feelings when holding space for beings of the higher realms.

The fifth set of notes held two separate truths. Sound is useful, perhaps mandatory, in the summoning of assistance from the natural world, whereas impeccable intent seems to have more power with the higher worlds. That did not preclude the use of sound in healing in general, as it could have profound affects on the astral and etheric bodies. Her own (Jane's) experience of the world of spirit beyond the bridge was accompanied, in memory, by the sound of a heavenly choir. The second truth was the importance of the nature spirits to the Golden Queen's path of mastery. This would be more helpful to the Melissae, at some point, than to her medical professionals. She considered these spirits to be second dimensional beings within the Earth's etheric/ elemental field, a sight few people cultivated since the focus of clairvoyant vision was, typically, on the astral world.

She felt the sixth set of notes spoke to territory reserved for the Bee Mistress. Her own excitement at having discovered, summoned and seen the luminous bees and the Golden Queen was palpable. She would eagerly pursue greater knowledge of the Path of the Golden Queen. One day, she would be called upon to consciously pass on the lineage. That provoked a query in her mind – *who had passed it on to me?*

The last two sets of notes brought up a good many esoteric questions. They weren't really medically related, but would spur on her personal research, both clairvoyantly, in meditation, and in reading the books of Rudolf Steiner.

How, then, to proceed? She asked. For those medical professionals interested in expanded awareness healing, two imperatives were obvious, to educate them about the rainbow body and to guide them through their own rainbow body healing. Stage-specific, progressive, clairvoyant exercises could be integrated into that work, facilitating a real opening to vision when the candidate began tapping into the upper astral world of selfless service. These would be exceptional healers with little interest in modern medicine's focus on monetary gain.

Leah started a new section of her notebook, separate from the professional education aspect of the project. This she headed: 'Clairvoyant Diagnostic and Treatment Research'. Here she felt like an explorer without a compass. And, yet, this was the heart of the matter. She could probably write something here about the etheric body pathologies that resulted in the poles of possession and mania, but thought both of those conditions to be extreme. What was the average person's experience on the etheric body level in illness? Traditional Chinese Medicine (TCM) had done much to relate etheric pathology to the physical body. TCM also conceded that most illness began in the emotional body, or the lower astral, as she would have put it. The astral world of the soul was the place to take clairvoyant vision and possibly link the findings with the TCM pathologies in the etheric body, as it worked its way into the physical.

Plan of action: 1) Talk to Nick about some experiments with homeopathic and flower essence treatments; 2) Find some study participants who'd allow her to clairvoyantly view the effects of various preparations on their rainbow bodies; 3) Read Steiner's books on Anthroposophical Medicine looking at the theories and conclusions that he would have used clairvoyance and spiritual-scientific theory to define; 4) Research into actual disease patterning in the astral. Angelic interference or intervention was, obviously, going to require some unhealthy study participants.

She could hear Chris saying goodnight to Natalie, Ellia and Greg as they all reached their homes. He opened the door, full of good cheer and 'chestnuts roasting on an open fire'. It was a brisk night, though not a bit like a typical December. He was keen for hot chocolate, a sofa cuddle and a summary of her reflections.

While in the midst of holding warrior pose during her Tuesday morning yoga workout, Leah was led on a journey back in time by Little Alice. Little Alice's love for the bees had provoked a need to know where the bees that came to her mother's *Spirea* lived. Her mother, always open to the magic of childhood, took her for a walk down their country lane to a sweet little cottage surrounded by old-fashioned flower gardens. Mrs. Morrison was a friend of her mother's. The women greeted each other with a hug, and kiss on the cheek. Little Alice was given a hug and kiss too, which made her feel very grown-up and neighborly. They all went around to Mrs. Morrison's back garden for lemonade, after which Mrs. Morrison took Little Alice to the back of her garden to see her beehives.

"This is where the bees live, Leah," she kindly explained. "These hives are full of honey made from the nectar they've gathered from the flowers in the garden, the fruit trees in the orchard, and many other places, including your mother's beautiful *Spirea*."

Mrs. Morrison invited her to come back when she was working in the hives to harvest honey but also to wander down anytime to see the bee's house and have some lemonade. And she had ... often. The warrior's pose wobbled and she collapsed to the mat in tears of catharsis. Sometimes the very best of life's memories were swept under the carpet by life itself. Whereas the dark side of the Bee Mistress had been born hanging upside down on the monkey bars, the path of the Golden Queen had been initiated in Mrs. Morrison's backyard, by an elderly Bee Mistress who had every confidence that Leah would one day wake up to know her destiny. *And Mother! Thank you, Mother, for always being open to magic.*

Chris came out, after his shower, to find her in the bottom drawer of the secretaire searching through her box of photos, certain that her mother had saved one of Mrs. Morrison. She found several — both early, high-quality small color photos. One photo caught Mrs. Morrison in her bee hat, tending to the hives and the other showed Leah and Mrs. Morrison, close up, watching one of her bees drawing nectar from (*would you believe it?*) *Lacy Phacelia*. The second picture was amazing because the sun bounced off Mrs. Morrison's gray hair and Leah's white-blonde curls to create a halo of light around them.

"Good tears?" he asked, squatting down to give her a hug while noting her blotched face and broad smile.

"Yes, cowboy. Another puzzle piece has plunked into place as well. Meet Mrs. Morrison. I'm pretty sure her first name was Betty. Here we are in her *Lacy Phacelia* with one of her bees. She was a neighbor and good friend of my mother's, and now I can truthfully say, she was also a Bee Mistress who recognized the lineage in me. This was all before the dark clouds came in to obscure the good and true of my Bee Mistress. It was only the dark side that emerged with Eric. She was already there and activated when I was this little. I'd forgotten all of this until this morning."

"What provoked the memory, lass?" he asked, studying the luminous photo.

"Reviewing Demetri's healing. It's not been lost to me that I need to pass this power on to the next Bee Mistress but I'd no memory of having received it. Now, the Golden Queen and Little Alice have provided me with that knowledge through clear-sighted memory. And Mother, in her knowingness, had the intuition to take, and *save*, these photos for me."

"That's pretty high magic. I think you ought to frame these pictures, don't you?" he asked, standing up with them, as she closed her photo box and pushed in the drawer.

"Absolutely. I'll put them in a double frame, right next to mother's photo on the bookcase. And, after lunch, before I go to read to the children, I'll visit the apiary in recognition of this gift and Betty Morrison." She gratefully sank into his leather and sage maleness, for a warm morning cuddle.

Saturday's show was going to be great fun. Natalie had booked in a founding board member of the Sebastopol Transition Town, who was bringing along a visiting leader in the movement from the UK, where it had begun. From Bellingham, she'd book a top administrator for BALLE (Business Alliance of Local Living Economies), an entrepreneurial coalition for locally owned businesses, Main Street-style, with hometown jobs and local goods and services. There would also be a representative from the Evergreen cooperative in Cleveland — a non-profit coalition of worker-owned businesses creating sustainable, local jobs. She decided to expand the anchor's desk and have Will join her in facilitating the discussion.

Leah and Will had carved out sacred time together on Thursday morning after he returned from the Bay area, to work up the discussion flow. She already had her taped interview with Joel on the topic, Paula was working on the news summary, and Willow was prepared to talk about the OWS plans for over-wintering the movement.

Finding herself with a few hours of coveted free time, Leah wandered over to the clinic to talk to Nick. He was at the front desk reading his chiropractic journal, keeping up to date with his practice.

"Hey, Nick. Is this not a good time to chat about the future?" she asked, leaning over the front desk.

"It's always a good time to talk about the future. I'm actually trying to decide on some CEU coursework to keep my license current. What's on your mind, doc?" he smiled.

She took a seat in their waiting area and motioned for him to join her. "I want to share with you this vision I've been receiving for a medical center at *Harmony Valley* — down the road."

"Okay, Doc. What's the purpose of the medical center? It's not like we don't have plenty of them already. It'd have to have an interesting twist to have captured your imagination."

"It does. The sign in front of the sprawling place indicated it was non-profit and a cooperative. That's a bit innovative to begin with, but I also see a marriage of modalities, kindness overall, and a research facility devoted to the higher bodies."

With eyebrows raised expectantly, Nick urged her on. "Now, that really does sound interesting. What've you got to back that up?"

"Not heaps, which is why I'm here discussing this with you, darling," she smiled. "I've my own clairvoyant vision to use as a tool, some experience — although it would be considered extraordinary — but no data. I want to propose a number of things to you. Let me know your interest level and degree to which you might participate, okay?" she asked.

"Go for it. Jazz up my otherwise boring life here in the clinic."

"I expect that's going to change with *Harmony Valley*, Nick. We're going to have to deal with illness there, including mental illness, life rehabilitation, conflict resolution, self-empowerment, and much more. From here on out, including *Harmony Valley*, I'd like to do what we did with Demetri, as a matter of course. We would intake together using allopathic and alternative diagnostics and concur on treatment strategies. I'd also like to be able to stand aside during your part of the session and assess the health of the higher bodies. We might ask patients to enter a spiritual medicine study to help us correlate my findings with the physical, etheric and emotional body aberrations. In this way we can define a spiritual correlate to disease."

"So far so good — exciting, in fact," he replied, leaning forward in his chair.

"That's one arm of the project. Another arm would be observing the changes in the higher bodies with treatments, especially homeopathic remedies and essences. I'm certain Steiner did a lot of work in this regard. Both of us should commit to reading and discussing his books on medicine that Tommy has in his library, and ongoing studies by Anthroposophical doctors since then, as well as current findings."

"Maybe I should see if I can get some CEU coursework in Anthroposophical Medicine," he added.

"You might be able to, Nick. I could for sure with my MD. We can look into that and begin a library of spiritual medicine here in the clinic — a good proposal for the board meeting. So those are two arms of my vision. The third arm is more complex. I'm being urged, through vision, to establish a medical school for the whole body at this complex, and we're talking the first six layers of the rainbow body. That would require that our doctors establish their own consciousness in the sixth body, consciousness soul, meaning they'll be preparing for initiation on the path."

"How are you going to do that, Doc?" he asked, truly curious.

"I'm going to start with you, Nick," she proposed, with humor.

"You're making me feel stupid, doc," he laughed. "I'm no where near that level of consciousness."

"That might be the first criteria for admission to our school. Forget all you've learned in order to see it quite differently. You stand a better chance than an allopath since your modalities are already touching higher bodies, consciously. You also have a heritage that honors vision and soul-level medicine."

"That's true. But I can't *see* a damn thing," he protested.

"Neither can most doctors. However, you know, very well, that many chiropractors are opening to see the etheric body. That's a start, if insufficient, to understand the whole picture. Perhaps I can tease you by sharing that Demetri's healing took place on the level of the hierarchies — both opportunistic and welcomed, who are still creating our astral, etheric and physical bodies. Intervention came from spirit world through the masters and archangels, as well. Mental illnesses cannot be properly diagnosed without mental and emotional body input. So we aim to see the whole big picture of health — and in doing that, get to glimpse the future of our evolution. We might also look at clairaudience and clairsentience as equally valuable gifts to foster. Not everyone will have the 'sight'."

"Yeah, okay, you hooked me, Doc," he laughed. "How do we go about this?"

"One thing we could do is get baseline data on fairly normal, healthy folks, by asking our community to participate in a study. We're constantly doing spiritual work on ourselves wherein higher body changes could be observed. When Alice and I resume her apitherapy treatments, we can observe her higher bodies responding to the bee stings. Bee venom has life-giving forces, so this idea fascinates me. If I can get you to apply the stings, I can stand back and observe her on those levels. I know she would agree to this study. She's as fascinated by the results as I am.

"In our work here we'll expand our assessments to include the higher bodies. That's one way you will begin to make correlations in your mind and expand your medical consciousness to accommodate something new. You can put your research thinking cap on and decide on some vibrational support to open your own clairvoyance. We can try it and I'll make observations during your treatment sessions while you make observations in your meditation time. In addition, I'll put you through a protocol that we'll need to develop to train doctors in the future at the center. There should be a graduated opening of the third-eye. Furthermore, we'll need to establish criteria for acceptance into the program — a measure of readiness and probability of success, if you will."

"I'm the guinea pig?" he asked, with a smile.

"*Who else?*" she laughed, looking around.

"I've no experience in psychotherapy?" he countered, mentally rifling through his shortcomings.

"Excellent!" she exclaimed. "Truth *loves* a clean slate."

And so, it was agreed that they would work together to bring the three arms of the project to fruition. Nick would also ask Chris for his input on the path of self-realization and the three of them would form an open working triangulation to guide him toward consciousness soul and vision. Nick felt a surge of energy move through him. When Leah left to return to the studio, he went back to the Internet looking for entirely different CEU options, wondering if they'd be offering them to doctors at the medical center one day. Leah stopped in the center of the courtyard compass and looked back at the clinic with a joyful heart.

Back at her desk, she downloaded it all into her notebook, fully conscious of the fact that she'd had no strategic plan before the conversation — for Nick or the medical center. Now she had three arms — another triangulation — to more thoroughly develop. She'd no concern about their work being accepted on a larger scale. *Harmony Valley* would validate it or not.

Another niggling issue came forward to land in her notebook that day — the application of *Social Threefolding* to *Harmony Valley*, from the get-go. With the Outreach board meeting on Thursday, the community meeting on the following Tuesday and interviews with *Harmony Valley* resident applicants planned for early January, she reckoned it was vitally important to hash out the societal infrastructure now. Another item was added to the list for board approval. This called for a committee of community members representing the three divisions — the economic, the social and the judicial — to brainstorm the concept. They could bring in Elliot Davis as a consultant and whoever else was knowledgeable on the topic. *Social Threefolding* was essential for all the efforts of Outreach, including community programs in the varying stages of completion. If they could come up with an overarching model of *Social Threefolding* the educational aspect of implementation could more easily be streamlined to the individual projects.

As an afterthought, she wrote some notes reminding her to review her subpersonality work again, asking a few questions relevant to the guidance of others. What role did conscious connection with mission play in the ascent of each subpersonality — and, later on, with integration? How did that compare to ascent with belated conscious connection to mission? Was it a motivating factor or a deterrent — or did knowing and engaging it not matter? She realized she had the Melissae, Will and now Nick ripe for guidance. She and Chris would collaborate helping these men while his influence on the women would come through the work he was doing with the Rangers.

Checking email, she found a lovely thank you from Kim. Joel had to dive right into studio work but was looking forward to his Wednesday Skype lunch with Leah. He'd a growing list of esoteric questions for her— not exactly Dragon Lady's forte. The old warrior might be running out of distractions to spiritual growth. It occurred to Leah that she could educate this recalcitrant aspect of herself by forcing her to pass on the wisdom the rest of her held to Joel — like an in-house channeling. That idea deserved a line in her notebook, suggesting applied contemplation.

Chris had accompanied Greg to pick up two pregnant buffalo cows and their still nursing female calves to launch the future herd in *New Avalon* and heal Mr. B's land of any leftover family drama. It also fulfilled the community's promise to Mr. B to see that buffalo grazed that particular land along the river instead of cattle. Chris had taken a lunch with him and left with the promise to return in time for her riding lesson with Holly, which entailed a ride down to Mr. B's farm.

Leah had a quick lunch and hiked down to visit the apiary before reading to the children, and then moving on to her riding lesson. Tuesdays were like a variety show flipping from one beloved activity to another and culminating in a night of cosmic love with her magical cowboy. Joel's show had been excellent, he looked renewed and, to Chris and Leah, a tad more luminous than he had previously. He was talking Main Street economics versus classical Keynesian and the Ayn Rand brand toted by the Tea Partiers in congress. He staged a great debate and then interviewed several excellent progressive economists, a Rand economist, and one hard-line conservative.

On this particular Tuesday night, the evening was free for a leisurely catch up and discussion after dinner. Chris built a fire while Leah cleaned up the kitchen and poured them each a glass of Zinfandel. When they settled in — she with her notebook and knitting, and he with Harry, who'd come over to checkout the leftovers — it was with candle and firelight and welcomed relaxation. He'd shared the story of his first buffalo round up, and futile attempt to come up with some buffalo nonsense, over dinner. There'd be a learning curve with that, for sure. She'd recounted the meeting with Nick and enlisted his support for the development of Nick's extra-sensory gifts. He was convinced this was exactly the intended path of Nick' soul and would do all he could to support this younger man who looked up to him as a father. Come to think of it, Nick might actually know something about the buffalo to help him with his nonsense block. He'd talk to him in the morning.

"What's on your mind tonight, lass?" he asked, as she straightened out her knitting needles and yarn to complete the second sleeve of David's cardigan.

"Well, at the community meeting, I'm proposing that we form three committees, to represent the cultural, judicial and economic spheres for *Harmony Valley*."

"What's the purpose of each committee? How will the residents interact with the committees?" he asked, motioning for her to give him more information.

"We can't expect these homeless people to come in and jump on the organization of a vast project. We could, in decent time, have a larger population elect a council to oversee the commons, and a court to interpret the law — but what law? We need to establish guidelines just as we did here, and consequences for those who chose to follow the beat of their own drum over the set boundaries. We need to have microcosmic *Threefolding* in place for them to step into, not for them to establish. They'll be learning new jobs, settling into new living situations, and getting used to the feel of good food in their bellies as well as a safe pillow on which to rest their weary and wary heads.

"I reckon it's a given that an infrastructure be in place before they arrive, even though they are the infrastructure. The credit union and local currency will help the economic sphere circulate goods and services. This will be made crystal clear to applicants before they agree to be a resident. Guidelines need to be in place from the get-go, whereas the complete judicial system can establish itself over time. The commons can be turned over to them first, but not until the full population is settle in and a democratic council election can be held."

"Aye, you need community members, representing the three spheres, to establish, in theory, each sphere as the *Threefolding* model defines it, and as it applies to this particular situation of rebooting the homeless, in both a balanced and comprehensive way."

"Maybe you can present it, cowboy. That was nicely put."

"I've been turning it around in my mind. We have a chance to implement new models without old systems in place. They may be imprinted in memory, theirs and ours, but without the physical structures, which can be powerful anchors of the status quo."

"True — all of it. And we get to rub the spheres up against each other, testing their autonomy as well as their effectiveness. Everything we learn can be shared with those starting their own communities and with the Inner City model — even the prison when it's in transition."

"What do you hear from Tommy and Will?" he asked, giving Harry a nice tummy rub.

"Tommy's been spending all of his time with city engineers, local contractors, and building inspectors. He said the big picture plan was filling in with details. The physical neighborhood they've chosen for the project has potential for further development. In fact he mentioned the idea of a homeless project in the same area of the city, which could be economically connected to Will's project. They're waiting to see what we put together in *Harmony Valley*.

Will is giving some talks, with discussions, to the potential residents, sorting out those who could live in a non-profit community for the sake of community. It means giving up the *American Dream,* which turned out to be a pipedream for them anyway, and choosing a dream with a higher happiness quotient and real security. And, he's talked to the council again, giving them a progress report. They both met with Elliot to discuss *Threefolding* on the scale of a self-sustaining neighborhood that's part of a city. That's about it. They've been busy and will wrap it up before noon tomorrow to get home for dinner and rehearsal."

"Anything else on your plate, lass?" he asked, feeling certain she was spawning some new venture for *New Avalon.*

"Joel's got a list of esoteric questions for our Skype session tomorrow. I thought I'd force Dragon Lady to channel the answers so she could open to new possibilities," she laughed.

"A long shot, but worth a try," he smiled. "She seems a minor player right now — to me, anyway. Have you been tracking her since the implant removal and healing of her 30 lashes?"

"I have actually had to invite her in a few times. She's standing back, observing, not eager to reconnect with Jefferson, but did have a swell time discussing issues with Joel on Sunday. It's funny … I was feeling the gears shifting back to normal life in *New Avalon* after Joel and family left. As a kid I can remember it being a letdown after the big high of excitement and play with my cousins over the holidays. Instead of going back there, this perfect opportunity presented itself with Nick, I got some clarity about societal infrastructure for *Harmony Valley,* and then I went down to the apiary to talk to the Golden Queen," she recollected, wistfully.

"I see what happens when I skip lunch," he smiled, certain that he was waiting to hear about the apiary visit. "How else could you have worked that into the day?"

"True enough, cowboy, though I do have a preference for lunch with you. Back to the apiary … something you said awhile back has been niggling at the back of my mind."

"Aye, let's hear it. You know I love the Bee Mistress."

"I do know that. You had mentioned that she went all the way back to the Lemurian Temples. And so, I assume she transited through a good many of them and on into the Atlantean temples and right up through the mystery schools of the post-Atlantean epoch."

"I think you can safely assume that *and,* I would add, as both female and male embodiments. There's a tremendously rich and powerful gift given to our spirit self when a tendency follows a path through the ages."

"She does feel like the old soul within me," she sighed, tucking her knitting away in its basket. She took a sip of wine and continued on with the flow of her thoughts. "My idea is to use my clairvoyant gift systematically, and historically, to research the evolution of the temple mysteries as humanity evolved."

"Bloody brilliant!" he grinned. "What's the catalyst here for the Bee Mistress?"

"Well, there was that bit you mentioned, and the memory I experienced in your eyes when you first took Jane out cosmic loving," she smiled. "And then, there was Steiner's *Fifth Gospel*, which I finished reading this afternoon — time well spent, I assure you."

"Did he research these temples?" he asked, continually amazed at the man's breadth and clairvoyant ability.

"I'm not sure. According to Elliot, I need to read another of his books, *Cosmic Memory*, to put those pieces together with his expanded visionary version of the Theosophical history of those ancient times. What has quickened my pulse is a passage in the *Fifth Gospel* about the life in spirit of this entity who came to earth only once to be born as the Jesus who would embody the Christ. He wasn't really human, but came to have a human life with the perfected components of the rainbow body the hierarchies had created for us, before we were corrupted by Lucifer at *The Fall*. This is referenced as the *pre-Fall* Adam body (both physical and etheric) and soul. He seems to me more angelic — perhaps similar to how we might be after we master all of our bodies, and yet ... not like us. And not like the Ascended Masters, because this entity had never experienced being human, had no karma, and no need for death and reincarnation. For me, the beautiful miracle of Christ Jesus has been expanded to unimaginable proportions. I'm grappling with that, at the same time I'm alive with a passion to know the extent of our redemption through his inconceivable love for humanity."

Chris had been listening with his White Heart. It glowed ruby red to her inquiring eyes. "You are speaking of the most sacred mysteries, my love. It must have cost Steiner some black brotherhood retaliation in this reality to make this information public. I agree with him that this truth was needed to navigate through his *future*, which is our *now*. You could imagine humanity in a great triangular sea — the very triangle you established in the apiary for Demetri's healing. Humanity's boat is being tossed violently around in the center of that triangle by the opposing agendas of Lucifer and Ahriman. If people knew the truth of the Christ Mission, they would be drawn towards that third point in the triangle, and find the clarity and calm in the storm."

"You know of this entity and the three sacrifices made for us before the sacrifice of Christ Jesus on Golgotha?" she asked, knowing she'd likely never tap the depths of his soul's journey and the reservoir of truth he held.

"I do. And, so do you. You know that I support you in every way imaginable, lass, but I cannot reveal the truth your soul is meant to discover on its own. You'd lose me if I were to step across that line."

"The Ruby Order would recall you? For that?" she asked in disbelief.

"The breaching of a soul contract related to the mission of the Order is *not* impeccable."

"You're telling me that this revelation is very high play."

"The highest of play in terms of the evolution of human consciousness. I encourage you to pursue the clairvoyant research and put the pieces of this puzzle together for yourself. I'll gladly provide peripheral information, allowable guidance, and steady, unending love," he offered.

"Well, that's substantial, in my book," she smiled. "So let me ask a question. I regard this being who demonstrated unconditional love for humanity in his life as Jesus, as the Ascended Master Sananda. Is that not true? And isn't he a Kumara? What does that mean? With this puzzle piece, I must say I don't consider him an Ascended Master in the same way I do, say, St. Germain."

"I can understand the confusion. As Steiner likely pointed out, he isn't human in origin in the sense that we're human, and yet he did incarnate and experience a life and a death in pure love and sacrifice for our evolution. In that sense we can consider him an Ascended Master, someone to look to for guidance in our mastery. On the other hand, he did not ascend up the stages of mastery as we must, and as St. Germain is, for example. You just said he came in with the perfected bodies created for us before *The Fall*. I don't believe they were corrupted by his life because the mystery of his death was to deliver that potential to us — the perfected phantom of the physical body especially, which was badly corrupted at *The Fall*. The hierarchies withheld these perfected human templates, so called Adam and Eve, until we were evolved enough to receive the "I". Remember that temple in the Himalayas where they were sequestered? The possibility of their re-acquisition was one major purpose of the life and death of Christ Jesus. We're now able to find our way home on our own. Literally, we've been redeemed."

"Steiner did mention that Jesus' birth mother, Mary, had the *pre-Fall* body of Eve. So, another of these templates came to earth? This, he said, was the meaning of 'virgin birth'," Leah offered.

"Exactly. And you can imagine the fragility of these bodies in the midst of the human drama."

"And *pre-Fall*, those bodies would've been accompanied by an astral body but not an "I" since that creative effort has entered man more recently. *Oh, my God!* And, then *He* came, as Steiner said, to correct a disordered "I"." Leah grabbed her notebook, opening to a tabbed page. "All the corruptions we experienced were due to Luciferic and Ahrimanic tampering. Looking back on the history of sacrifices, in spirit world, this entity made, on our behalf, over our evolution, I can equate them to course corrections of the astral body in late Atlantean times, the etheric body in earlier Atlantean times, and the physical body in Lemurian times. We would not have evolved at all without *His* intervention!"

"Righty-o," Chris agreed ... his grin betraying his joy at her illumination.

"In Peru, we spoke of the Kumaras. You admitted to me that you were a Kumara, Chris. I have some recollection of being given a name in that lineage at some point — a blur connected with the ruby red dress in the Valley of the Blue Moon. Who are the Kumaras? Again, please — if you've already told me."

"You've much to discover on your own in this regard, lass, but I'll remind you that they're the Planet Tamers from Venus who came in to assist the Elder Race by working directly with humanity during the early stages of earth evolution. It was in a long and revered time during *pre-Fall* earth evolution when humanity was sequestered with the angels, free from the influences of those who had already turned their backs on their own evolution — the fallen angels we now call Luciferic. This was part of the Kumara mission uniquely associated with the Christ mission in this solar system."

"How is it that you, and even more outlandishly, I, could be Kumara? Sorry, darling, it just smacks of New Age fantasy to me. I have an over-active red flag for Luciferic distractions."

"It serves you well. I honor that. You also have amazing radar for the truth. I can just hint at the fact that we're not Kumara in the same sense as Jesus and those great Kumara beings who helped to steer humanity into earth evolution. However, those were ancient times of instability on the Earth. Humanity's relationship with the sun was drastically changed and although humans weren't in physicality, it affected their astral and especially their etheric bodies, which are linked to an ancient sun past. You'll learn about the Elohim's role in planetary changes that created the circumstances of *The Fall* into physicality. We talked a bit about this in Peru, but the actual fall of the angels had occurred well before humans fell into form. It was a perfect example of cause and affect — the workings of karma, as we know it now. This point of *The Fall*, brought about by the circumstance to which I eluded, removed the protection that had sequestered humanity with the angels. As a consequence, the Kumaras had to leave earth and humanity to return to Venus."

"I'd better order that book, cowboy. I suddenly have a puzzle with a million missing pieces. It's exciting, though. So what is this connection that we have with these beings?"

"This is really going to sound fantastic, until you are well-versed in the mysteries," he warned.

"I have to gain a toehold somewhere. Just give me a taste of the truth, impeccably, of course," she grinned.

"Okay. As you know, the Elohim are part of the Powers hierarchy, who were and are managing the evolution of earth in solid, physical form — as earth. They allowed the Kumaras, also of the Powers, to bud-off soul material, creating lineages of *self* that could incarnate on earth. It isn't any different than the way all human souls came to be, but they had a specific agenda, as you can imagine, and that was to continue the work they'd begun *pre-Fall*. These have budded further to the point that 12 soul aspects evolved to be able to bud 12 more aspects of soul, thus giving us up to 144 aspects for any Kumara."

"Wait a minute, I've got to bring Alice in here for the math," she said, hastily.

"No need, lass. You'll make no sense of it. hese beings are beyond mathematics. You could have a 12-soul level incarnate along with 10 of its 12 aspects. When Jesus — the only complete Kumara to incarnate on earth — was alive, he was accompanied by all twelve of his aspects, and all of their 12 aspects simultaneously — all 144 human souls incarnate at once with his totality. This was important. They were meant to be in body to experience his incarnation and directly receive the potential for redemption he offered humankind. Remember they'd experienced many incarnations, had their karmas, died human deaths, and were every bit as human as everyone else, except that they had an achievable archangelic capacity for illumination that the rest of humanity is in the process of acquiring — fifth dimensional consciousness. Of course, they continue to grow in their own souls but, all together, they comprise the vital core of the Christ Consciousness Mission on earth."

"Interesting," Leah mused. "I recollect being somewhat confused about this in Peru."

"Understandable, lass," he offered, reaching for his glass.

"From talking to Elliot and reading Steiner on education, it's clear to me that the Waldorf curriculum is meant to embrace and foster that potential intelligence in the maturation of the child. Child development studies would now correlate the curriculum with fostering the great transition into the prefrontal lobes, which the culture systematically inhibits. I equate that with consciousness soul, so imagine the archangelic intelligence to be in our spirit world, in the *manas*. In physicality, I'd imagine the touchstone to be the heart, as our fifth brain. If I recall correctly, we used to have the odd priest, mystery school master and teacher of old with this capacity, up until the collapse of Atlantis. Do you think those were references to some of these Kumara aspects coming to guide humanity?"

"That and to the few human individuals who acquired their "I" and became illumined well ahead of human evolution. The bell curve has been around since the get-go, lass. Advanced humans were guided in the mystery schools. I suppose Steiner's access to the mysteries and his clairvoyant ability to research historically allowed him to see the great flaw in the education that accompanied the industrial revolution. He seemed undaunted, no matter in which direction he turned to transform social institutions," Chris concluded, amazed.

"Okay, cowboy," she said, finishing off her last sentence of notes. "My cup is full for the moment. The Bee Mistress wants to quit her job to research this, but then she'd be abandoning mission — not the best idea," she sighed.

"Correct. On the other hand if this newscaster of yours managed to log into her archangelic capabilities, the world would be a brighter place than it is right now," he countered.

"R-r-right," she drawled, closing her notebook. She emptied her wine glass and sat for a moment studying him. "So, was it by intention or luck that you were packaged into a deliciously seductive human form with a personality that tickles my soul?"

He declined to answer that question, as she knew he would, but chose instead to study *her*. "How would Jane like to go to the far side of Venus, tonight?" he asked.

"I'll polish my halo, and be right with you, cowboy" she sang. "I can't wait!"

chapter 6: over the ridge

The aftermath of the dark side of Venus was reintegration of their rainbow bodies over chamomile tea and homemade Anzac bikkies in bed — in bite-size pieces for crumb-free sleeping. In the hour it took them to ground themselves, a lot of territory was covered in conversation. Amongst all of the truth to take in whilst reading *The Fifth Gospel*, Leah had come away with a better understanding of her experience with Mr. Brenner's passage. She told Chris that the release of the etheric body, a sight of great magnificence, creates a kind of firmament of a lifetime spread out in the heavens. In addition to, or concomitant with, the life review, the dead have the soul's sympathies and antipathies spread above them. She expected this to be more evident beyond Mr. B's tunnel and not in the intermediary space that she'd shared with him. In the three days it actually takes for the dead to disconnect the etheric body — for the fires of restitution are just the instigation — they feel the future death of the earth, for earth will go through a physical death in her own ascension process. But, if the dead are Christ aware, they also feel the germinal spirit of her next stage of consciousness in that firmament above them, which, she assumed, was merged with the etheric body of the earth and the presence of the Christ within it — and this gives them hope.

"This gift of hope and light," she shared, "is a fairly new addition to the death experience, which would otherwise be depressing. In fact, it feels redemptive, in and of itself. When Mr. B showed up at his funeral with Maud, four days after his death, he would have been completely free of his etheric body." Chris corroborated these truths, for Alice especially, and went on to ask her what approach she was going to take with the Bee Mistress' ancient temple investigation.

"No clue, cowboy. It'd be nice if it were as easy as getting back to Monticello, with your magical accompaniment on the piano. How do *you* think I ought to start? That's always the most difficult step to take."

"I reckon your insight about the four sacrifices, correlating to course corrections for the layers of the rainbow body, is your ticket to ride."

"Yeah? Steiner would call the rainbow body the fourfold man — the physical, etheric, astral and "I". That covers body, soul and the bridge to spirit."

"Go for it, lass. You've a remarkable gift for investigation."

Leah would dream of temples on a vastly different earth that night, and then awaken in the midst of a condensed review of brain evolution. It was a gift akin to 'the pearl of great price'. The door had opened, and she was eager to pursue the story with the clues at hand — the rainbow body, the evolving brain, and the four sacrifices on humanity's behalf. She would begin with the first sacrifice, the stabilization of sensory experience, drawing together a correlation with the brain and the physical layer of the rainbow body. When she felt something coming together, moving towards insight, she would take it to the Golden Queen for correction and embellishment, and then schedule an evening discussion with the Lord of the Ruby. Leah got a zingy little feeling in her heart when she thought of the Melissae. Surely there was a gift for the women in this timely research project. She'd be vigilant, to grasp those pearls for her beloved girlfriends.

When she and Joel connected via Skype that morning, Leah was actually grateful to talk esoterics rather than politics and economics. It didn't take long for her to realize she'd lined up her third male seeker of higher consciousness — and one with a good shot at it in the near future. Joel wasn't a spiritual neophyte. He'd done a great deal of work on what Leah would call his lower astral relationship with the culture, but had no experience with the ascent of the personality — except to have put it in a good place for Leah to step in with the subpersonality work. He got it straightaway, recognizing his rendition of her Dragon Lady, which made for some timely humor. She was able to guide him in the self-observation and identification of his subpersonalities — the launching pad for the ascent.

"So, Leah, when Kim talks about 'lightbody', what's she referring to, in your spiritual rhetoric?" he asked.

"Lightbody is a term some teachers use in reference to the soul, which is the astral body. 'Mastering Lightbody' would find your consciousness in the upper astral or consciousness soul with your higher self, your true "I", at the helm. You will have mastered yourself to the point of abandoning the cultural "I". In terms of the personality, it means that you've mastered and ascended all sub-personality aspects and engaged them in an integrated state within consciousness soul. As you might expect, there're a lot of stages to actual 'lightbody' mastery along the way, many of them within consciousness soul. At that stage of mastery you'd be fully soul–conscious and able to begin building a bridge to spirit to bring in fifth dimensional awareness. Many lifetimes are dedicated to walking this path. Usually we walk a little further each life but sometimes, we have setbacks."

"Is that awareness what some people call Christ Consciousness — like the space Chris held at Demetri's healing?" he queried further.

"Yes. But, from what I understand, attaining consciousness soul and accessing spirit are two different things. Bringing higher thought over that bridge from spirit into soul is the beginning of another ascent into spirit, the mastery of which is Christ Consciousness. I think you'd be the first to agree that spirit-filled thought is sorely needed on the planet, Joel. I suggest you go for it," she teased.

"Well, for starters, I'll start mopping up my lower astral. I feel blessed to know the truth when I see, hear or feel it. I'll use that as my touchstone."

"I expect that's a Ruby Order gift, well-hone over those many lifetimes, my friend. We're on to the 'canaries in coalmines' show next week. By the time the canary stops singing, it's nearly too late for the coalminers. The truth lies in the revelation of 'coalmining'. What is obvious truth is veiled by the power brokers' influence over humanity — right now through big-money sponsored media — turning truth into deceit, either through outright lies, misinformation or no information at all. Under their influence no one stands a chance at hearing the canary singing let alone bearing witness to its silence."

"There we have the crux of our work, sister. How can *we* wake up the vast majority of our citizenry to take back the country they've lost?"

Leah proceeded to share with Joel, the idea of the rising of the Phoenix from the ashes, and the golden moment when change can be magically implemented. It wasn't unfamiliar to him. If they were to work together, helping people to begin building the constructs of those new systems in their minds, the work of materializing them in this reality would be greatly assisted. After all, imagination was the architect of reality.

Chris barely made it to Joel's show on time that night and caught up with her briefly during the breaks. He and Nick had been up to the springs with the boys, Mark, Paul, and Mike, to start building an A-frame cubby for their meetings with the *Woodland Folk* children. They'd loaded up Cinnamon with scrap boards (from a pile Mike and Tommy had sorted at the woodworking shop), a handsaw, hammer and nails. The floor of a simple shelter had been completed. Nick had quietly wandered off to do some scouting and was holding on to his report until after rehearsal for the play that night.

Joel had a lineup of economists and politicians expressing their personal views on banking regulation. The economists had their varied ideologies at the core of their arguments and opinions, while the politicians wobbled between party platforms, lobbyists' agendas, and those of their 1% and corporate campaign contributors. For the most part, they'd bartered morals, if they had them, to retain the power of their positions.

Leah concluded that the institution of politics, which had served well enough — considering human nature — for most of American history, was so mired in corruption as to be teetering on the brink of self-destruction. It brought to her mind Judas Iscariot, whose betrayal for silver set the stage for humanity's redemption, but cost his soul dearly at the hands of Ahriman. Corrupt politicians were the pawns of the power elite who were, in turn, the pawns of Ahriman. One could argue which stakes were higher (she wouldn't) but it did make her wonder if this wholesale betrayal of the 99% would have a redemptive outcome, possibly a purer, higher-minded form of democracy, in collapse. Joel supported his ending arguments with film clips from the *Light on the Crisis* shows on 'social threefolding' and 'money and media in politics', and Joel's previous interview with Elliot Davis. *Gotta love you, Joel.*

Tommy and Will were back in *New Avalon* for the rehearsal of *Oklahoma!* Leah would get the up close and personal review of their trip from Will as they walked home and the official version at the board meeting the next the afternoon. They were rehearsing Act II, scene one for the second time since it was multifaceted, involved everyone, and had no one's full attention on Thanksgiving Saturday with guests and staff present. In retrospect, Chris wished he'd had two days for each of the rehearsed scenes as he was able to do a fair amount of educating, upping the bar on performance — both individual and interactive. He was sure to have many opportunities as December unfolded, but would spirit the observation away in his burgeoning director's memory bank.

Leah had taken the time to watch the movie on her laptop. She'd seen it a good many times when she was a young teen. Reflecting back to that time in her life, she remembered the anticipation of each new movie musical — South Pacific, The King and I, Carousel, and on and on. It was a perfectly wonderful time in American theater and film just prior to the 'bust it open' social change of the 60s, when sex and violence came storming in to stay. Though she had her dramas, Shirley Jones looked innocent when compared with present-day film actresses. Leah could manage that in her role as Laurey, but there was no way she could replicate Shirley's voice — a soprano, she was not. She would do her best, though. The second scene, coming up on Saturday afternoon, was high drama for Laurey, who rejects Jud's advance and fires him as her farmhand, screaming at him to leave her property. She couldn't remember the last time she'd screamed — except, justifiably, for Will and Tommy, when the bloody mongrels tried to attack her in the apiary. That assessment didn't include some of the very strange sounds the Bee Mistress had spontaneously sent forth whilst bringing through her power.

In this scene, Jud threatens her and she turns to Curly for support and safety. He proposes marriage and they get to sing the reprise of *People Will Say We're In Love* before it dawns on him that he must now become a farmer to care for their land. Besides this drama between Laurey, Jud and Curly, there would be a closing piece with Ali Hakim (Nick) leaving Ado Annie (Sonia), suggesting she find her love with Will (Will).

While transplanting seedlings in the greenhouse that afternoon, Leah vowed to buckle down practicing her lines with Chris, who could play both

Jud and Curly for her. He seemed to have the musical in his cellular memory though, in fact, he might have been over in the stable, right then, practicing with Thunder. Leslie and Jenny had approached her about how she wanted her dress to look for the wedding scene. All of the women would be wearing long frocks of ginghams, floral patterns, and solids colors with a lot of white lace trim and petticoats — the typical dresses of the time. They'd even fashioned matching bonnets for the fun of it. However, the wedding scene would take Laurey out of context at the same time it wouldn't have been an overly fancy dress, since it was Oklahoma Territory 1906. She'd have a think about it.

After rehearsal, Will was spilling over with the progress in San Francisco. He was ready for Natalie to help him sort out the community applicants and get their circle going. The city was ready to go ahead with infrastructure, which Tommy had plotted out, as engineers do. They would be on city water and sewage. Power would be, as in *New Avalon,* both bought from and sold to the power company. Tommy had proposed one neighborhood of restored homes to keep the local flavor in the least decrepit area of the project. He presented the city council with the plans for three more neighborhoods of new construction using classical 'Pacific Heights' architecture on a practical scale, as well as plans for the commercial operations that would need infrastructure.

An estimated date of March 1, 2012 had been determined for the commencement of new construction but home restoration and the remodeling of an existing commercial building into the community center would be underway after the first of the year. A lot more details would be presented at the board meeting and a distillate at the community meeting the following Tuesday. Both he and Tommy were excited about the project. While they were in the bay area, Will had heard from Ali Cat, who gave him a date with the LA city council to present a similar plan for their approval — that with very convincing support in San Francisco to back him up. He'd also had an inquiry from Oakland and wanted to know whether Leah thought he ought to approach Sacramento or wait until they approached him. Her intuitive response envisioned Sacramento with a Homeless Community model for starters, but she'd take it a little deeper for the board meeting.

While getting ready for bed, Chris started filling her in on Nick's scouting report. She had an inner giggle trying to remember what she'd done for entertainment prior to the re-entry of Chris in her life. *Oh yes, those weighty tomes on economics!* She hadn't opened one since August 20th — coming up on four months living the life she'd thought she'd missed.

"Are you listening?" Chris asked his unresponsive wife, who was brushing the enamel off her teeth whilst in some other reality.

He hung up his towel then passed his hand between her face and the mirror. That clicked, She looked at him in the mirror. "Oops, did I miss something, cowboy," she laughed, spitting out the toothpaste and rinsing.

"No worries, lass," he replied, gathering her up in his arms. He planted a zinger of a kiss on her forehead and promised he'd start the story over in bed.

Laying her blue robe over the chair, she slipped in beside him for a warm-up cuddle and heard about the presence of a well-trod trail up on the ridge. Nick felt the trail was used primarily by deer coming for water, but he could tell the children had used it as well from the way the soil was packed and a discarded apple core that, amazingly, no animal had polished off, although the seeds had been taken by child or squirrel. He'd walked the trail to the top of the ridge to find that it continued, and assessed whether or not they could use horses to explore further. They'd made Friday afternoon plans to take Thunder and Myrtle for a little ride over the ridge, after checking that out with Will. He was keen to have Myrtle exercised and they were eager to have her agility, should the going get rough. Chris felt confident that he and Thunder could manage most anything, since little Billie would be riding with his dad.

Leah drifted off to sleep in the arms of her cowboy, imagining a sweet little cabin over the ridge, where happy children and honest, hard-working parents had created a slice of heaven for themselves. She awoke feeling an urgency to meet with the Golden Queen that day — a day already fully booked. As it turned out, Chris suggested, at breakfast, that they forgo her riding lesson, giving him time to organize his *Harmony Valley* cottage industry presentation to the board that afternoon. Instead, they would take Holly and Thunder for a picnic outing on Sunday. *Brilliant.*

Superpac Thursdays were no more. Mr. B no longer needed her and having Paula on the news review made her day more manageable with spare time to apply her gifts to their many Outreach projects. That morning, with the show material looking quite solid, she meandered across the courtyard to speak with her favorite banker.

Leah settled into her favorite chair while he sent an email into cyberspace. That finished, he gave her his full attention. "What's on your mind, Light Beam?" he asked, with a huge smile.

"Corruption in politics, little brother," she replied.

"You've come to the wrong banker, sister," he laughed. "What do you want *me* to do about that? You and Joel can handle it, no?"

"I'm not giving it to you as a project, darling. I want it to be foremost in our minds as we work out *Social Threefolding* in *Harmony Valley*. I'm going to bring this up at the board meeting. We need to come up with a process that any community can use to arrive at the appropriate establishment of boundaries for the cultural, economic and judicial spheres. That would necessarily include firm guidelines on the order of a community constitution. I'm providing you with a six-hour heads–up for the economic and judicial spheres, since you're our standard bearer for both. In *Harmony Valley* residents will not have assets and will likely be traumatized. Inner City residents will have few, if any, assets, and most community initiatives, like ours, will have assets that are not equally held by community members. Thinking bigger than that, Will, how could we apply *Social Threefolding* to small town America in transition – our topic for

Saturday's show. You do remember being my co-host?" she smiled.

"Gotcha, Light Beam," he laughed. "Where does your political corruption theme come in?"

"You tell me," she challenged.

"So I get six hours to figure this out?" he queried, with a grin.

"No more, no less," she stated, with mock seriousness. "We would all love to know the answer to that question — and the sooner the better. Do we rely on the spiritual work to keep everyone honest and forthright, or do we build safeguards into our infrastructure for the future, to prevent the deterioration of democracy — keeping in mind the obvious and subtle blurring of the spheres that seems to accompany this, or any, system collapse?"

"Good question. Do we need to create a moral infrastructure along with the power stations, water and sewage?" he asked.

"You tell me, boss, in six hours."

They stood, leaning over his desk for a kiss on the cheek, and then Leah left to wander over to the clinic. *No time to warn Nick,* Will laughed to himself, while bringing up the *Light on the Crisis* website to watch the archived show on *'money and media in politics',* for starters.

Nick had signed himself up for an advanced cranial-sacral therapy course to fulfill his CEUs. He was also compiling a list of books for the clinic library proposal. She wasn't there to give him a butt-kick — just wanted to let him know she was flaking out on their usual noon meeting in order to visit the bees.

"Chris told me I need to work with the bees for vision, Leah," he offered.

"R-r-right," she drawled, accepting her husband's volley of Nick into her court. "Do you like bees, Nick?" she asked.

"I've no idea. I'm curious about apitherapy. Alice Wilson's arthritis seems much better."

"It is. I reckon you could get into the formic acid/venom aspect of that. I'm going to bring you a book about bees, my friend, with lectures given by Rudolf Steiner. We'll see what you make of that and take it from there. I could use some help with the swarms, come spring, and that's a wonderful energy in which to approach the spirit of the *bien* — and soon enough for you to seek vision from the bees. Do you have shamanic or visionary ancestry?"

"Way back, as the stories go, but nothing to go on besides the blood."

"Thicker than water, Nick. I wouldn't discount it, or the idea that you would likely find your vision in nature."

"Sounds like a plan," he grinned. "Did Chris tell you about the trail?"

"Indeed. What do you make of our distant neighbors?" she asked.

"They don't frequent our ridge but the kids will, now that they've met friends. I can't imagine being that isolated, and Chris and I are both curious to see how they're surviving. We have to be their closest neighbors."

"I'll be waiting to hear all about it when you get back tomorrow. Are you taking one of the radios?"

"Of course. We'll be hooked up to Tommy. Chris is super-careful. You know that from your riding lessons. I tend to have a reckless streak — yeah, huge rebel subpersonality there — but he tempers it with amazing calm, and respect for all of life. He'd make a good original Native American ... probably was, eh?"

"No doubt. Are you going back to the res in the near future, Nick?" she asked.

"I was thinking of taking Paul to Sundance next summer — just to watch. Are you thinking Chris might like to come? That'd be awesome." ·

"Ask him, brother. I agree with you. Now, I'd best get myself back to work. See you at the board meeting, Nick."

"Yeah. See ya, Doc," he replied, lost in a deluge of thoughts and ... *visions!*

Back at her desk, Leah realized what was actually happening with these little pot-stirring tours of duty to Will and Nick — beyond the obvious mentoring. Dragon Lady was delegating the sort of projects she would have absolutely relished not so long ago. She had to admit that the application of *Social Threefolding* was an appropriate task for Dragon Lady — and she would happily oversee it — but her tenure as the lifeblood and glue of *New Avalon* had run its course. The old girl was really paying attention.

To test that the trend wasn't just discernment, gained from the patriarchal implant extraction, or a lack-luster outlook on life, Leah put Dragon Lady to the task of outlining a strategy for the research of the Bee Mistress' interest in sacrifice and redemption, beginning with a mission statement. Dragon Lady took it up with passion, consulting frequently with Jane, her moral sounding board, and the Bee Mistress, who actually held the soul memory of the ancient times on earth when course corrections were imperatives. *Wow, she can do team now!*

A four-part aim was arrived at in no time at all — written neatly in another new section of her trusty notebook. Firstly, she wished to understand human behavior before and after each of the Christ redemptions, especially as it correlated to the layer of the rainbow body, or fourfold man, she felt was being redeemed. Secondly, she wanted to explore a correlation between the dysfunction needing correction and the stage of man's brain and overall development at that time in evolution. Thirdly, she wished to see the bigger picture of esoteric initiation, and even the after-death journey. Lastly, she asked for a greater understanding of the Kumaras, their earthly mission, the relationship between the entity who became Jesus and the Master she knew as Sananda, and further illumination about incarnate aspects of this Being, who was, presumably, from Venus.

Beyond these aims, she knew in her heart she would be looking for applications of these pivotal moments in human evolution to the initiatory path of her Melissae and a greater understanding of the history of the lineage of Bee Mistresses and Masters. A commitment was made to share every aspect of her research with Chris, who could fill in the blanks and round out the rough patches as he could — impeccably. He'd also be encouraged to incorporate their mutual findings into his work with the Rangers.

Which ever way she looked at it, the most suitable way to begin the investigation was to take her aims and lay them, respectfully, at the wings of the Golden Queen. And, there was no time like the present. Leah donned her warm outerwear and knit hat. She received Paula's news summary as she was exiting her office and, tucking it in her notebook under her arm, walked down the service road behind the houses of West Commons Lane with determination — the only walk Dragon Lady knew. She stopped briefly in her garden shed to stash her notebook and retrieve some dried *Melissa*, and then headed up through the circle of oaks, and the fallen *Lacy Phacelia*, to stand on top of the hill overlooking the apiary — right next to her Henry E. Brenner memorial *Spirea*.

The archangelic dome was lowered over the apiary, no doubt because a hefty black bear was trying to pick the lock — the only piece of metal that wouldn't have zapped it. She probably could have let out a sound that would have sent the bear running, but for how long? Making the 'better part of valor' choice, Leah executed an about-face, to go back for Chris, and found him standing right behind her. He slammed his hand over her mouth before she screamed from the fright he'd caused her. Then, he took her into his arms until she calmed down. He then point out the other two bears, a big one at the river and a cub under the old apple tree favored by her swarms.

"Oh, my God!" she breathed. "I was coming for you, cowboy. How did you know?"

He was leading her backwards through the *Lacy Phacelia* until they were on the backside of the crest. "I came out to see who was raiding the garden shed, lass," he whispered. "You were already halfway to the oak grove before I could grab a jacket to follow. I had a strong apprehension."

"I didn't," she whispered back to him. "But then Dragon Lady was hell-bent on following through with her investigation strategy." *In that regard she hasn't changed a bit*, she thought.

They fell silent, quickly walking home and latching the back gate before speaking again. After they'd hung up their jackets in the laundry, Leah gave Chris a fierce hug of gratitude for following his intuition.

"You were walking like a woman on mission, lass. Is it important that you get into the apiary soon?" he asked, giving her a zing on the forehead.

"Not really. I was determined, but in retrospect it had more to do with Dragon Lady's re-entry into my consciousness and my ... well, probably *her* need to control this bit of research I'm intending. I'd been to see Will this morning, delegating some great stuff that was right up Dragon Lady's alley. She must have felt a little incensed at having been bypassed, so took the job I did give her a little too seriously. Goodness, I'm going to have to handle her with kid gloves if I want her back in the flow."

"Hypervigilance, I'd say. And the research project?" he queried.

"Well, there you go. I thought I'd ask the Golden Queen to help out and come away with some big revelations on the temple mysteries all on my own.

That was *so* Dragon Lady", she moaned, sinking into a chair at the table. Then she started to laugh uncontrollably. It was a cathartic moment for certain but it was also hysterically funny *in* the moment — wishing to secret away a story that he likely knew in its totality.

He fetched the tissues and waited patiently for her to finish laughing, blowing her nose, and finally wiping the tears from her eyes. "Thank you, cowboy. That feels better. What the hell are we going to do about those bears?"

"Naught," he replied, definitively. Her eyes widened. "I'm assuming the idea is for them to experience partial electrocution as one of life's poignant learning experiences. If that's the case, they'll be foraging elsewhere soon. The real question is ... what are we going to do about you?" he grinned.

She took a deep breath and looked at the clock. "Well, I reckon we're going to sit down and discuss this project of mine, have some lunch, then I'll go back to work to prepare for Joel's interview."

"That's right ... it's Thursday. So the board meeting is after your live interview?"

"Correct."

"Well, clue me in on your strategy then, lass. We've plenty of time," he grinned, pulling out a chair across from her. His own work was neatly piled at the end of the table.

Leah contemplated the events of the last several hours, then replied, hesitantly. "I guess I was feeling the limitation of my research strategy, which is a good one, but, understandably, rich in science and esoteric source and weak in my own confidence to research clairvoyantly that far back in history — even that far back in my own soul life. I know the value of the IMAX for keeping my present self out of the picture and was on my way to ask the Golden Queen if that could be arranged. I had a huge agenda for the research, and three bears standing in the way."

"Could be a whole new childhood story, Goldilocks," Chris laughed.

"R-r-right, cowboy," she drawled, stifling her inner giggle. It sure had looked like a mama, papa, and baby bear down at the apiary. "I'm not going to share my porridge, much less my bed, with those naughty bears."

"Aye, lass, that does back you up against a wall in some respects. I wonder if some structured exercises to open your clairvoyant gift further might be helpful."

"Truly. This gift sprang into my consciousness without any formal training. What do you have in mind?"

"Well, if you'd had formal training, you would have first accessed your etheric body, as a part of you separate from the sensory world and the astral world, where you have some comfort with your clairvoyance. It occurs to me that you came into this gift because mission required that of you — all well and good, but maybe not as richly rewarding for you as it could be."

"But, how could that happen, cowboy? Are there two ways to get there?" she asked.

"There are many ways to get there, lass, but only one path that's without the possibility of error," he said, gravely.

"Good grief!" she exclaimed. "Here, again, we have the Golden and the Dark Queen. I suppose that's a given?"

"Indeed. Carrying such a gift within your rainbow body can present an immense temptation for those who seek to manipulate mankind, especially when it has been opened in non-traditional ways — and that happens more often than not. The will must be strong and the intent impeccable to be of service, selflessly, to evolution. You've no problem in that area though you won't likely forget your own dance with the darkness in the apiary," he smiled.

"Fat chance. I feel this is really important, darling. I can launch into the intellectual areas of research while getting better footing with my gift. Is that what you suggest I do? And will you assist me with this journey into etheric consciousness?"

"Aye, it sounds like a good plan. Maybe we can get the Golden Queen's take on this before plunging into the etheric body exploration. The intellectual work can be shared in evening discussions. I'd enjoy that."

"Okay then, shall I ask the Rangers to surround the apiary, while I consult with the Golden Queen?"

"I don't see why you have to talk to her *in* the apiary, lass? She's everywhere. Have you thought of creating a space for her here? We've Tara and Buddha holding down the hearth, surely there's room for the Golden Queen in the house or back garden."

"Well, *that's* an idea. I have Betty Morrison's picture to start with, beeswax candles, honey ..."

"And a pile of gold," he added, finishing her sentence for her.

"True, and a vial of *Melissa* essential oil. I'll try it but she's so easy to contact at the hives, and I love cycling the energy of the *bien*. I *so* love the bees."

"I think you'd be safe doing that occasionally, lass. I can go there with you, when they're down in the valley foraging, but to sit there, in meditation, with your IMAX? I wouldn't recommend it."

"Fair enough, cowboy. There's no harm in trying to connect with her here. This does bring up another potentially risky endeavor."

"In a day's journey riddled with landmines," he laughed. "Care to share?"

"I wouldn't have mentioned it otherwise," she admitted, with a smile. "One of the mandates issued by the Golden Queen was the education of medical professionals in the care and healing of the entire rainbow body."

"I recall your having mentioned that. Given the mindset of most medical professionals I could see that being exasperating, as a given. Nurse Jane Fuzzy Wuzzy excluded, of course," he added with a wink.

"I have faith in the young, cowboy. I doubt we'd be training anyone satisfied with their practices and their lifestyle, but many young doctors are dissatisfied professionally and are looking for more hands-on medicine — fewer tests and more compassion. However, the care and healing of the entire rainbow body will, in my opinion, require clairvoyant vision to make proper diagnosis. Not all doctors would need this skill personally but they'll need someone in their group, clinic, or hospital with this skill, at least on a consulting basis."

"I'm, as usual, gob-smacked at your courage," he conceded. "But, how are you going to pull that off, lass?"

"There will be those so gifted, Chris, but after what we've just discussed about the right and wrong way to approach the gift of clairvoyance, this proposal is suddenly caring added weight and grave consequences."

"Correct."

"Correct? Period?"

"Do you like the idea of doctors practicing acupuncture after taking a one-weekend crash course?"

Leah sighed. "Gotcha. And, you are right. What to do then? I can't fulfill the Golden Queen's request in a way that isn't impeccable, but I haven't taken the impeccable path myself," she concluded, a bit chagrined.

"I reckon she'll allow you the time to do that, Goldilocks."

She reached out for his hand and gave it a squeeze. "Good. Nick has agreed to be my clairvoyance guinea pig. He'd be happy to forgo a plunge, and mosey into the role instead."

"At least you picked someone with potential," he grinned.

"I reckoned you'd agree, cowboy," she replied, with a wink.

Joel's live interview with Leah was focused on his experience of community at *New Avalon*. He began by admitting his reticence about living in community and ended by admitting to his participation in forming one. He engaged Leah in a discussion of three good reasons to consider community: Local sustainable living; exclusion from system collapse; and the high happiness quotient of residents. The last reason, understandably, varied with core values and the level of spiritual awareness within the community — especially the community's founders, who were counted on to hold those variables impeccably. Having a common purpose and shared core values greatly enhanced all three. With all of the usual plugs for her weekend show and website of archived videos, they signed off with a snapshot slide show of *New Avalon* — thanks to Kim's artful photography.

It was a quick shift from make-up removal to the board meeting. Natalie had been industriously applying herself to the homeless application process, the requests for new community and homeless project initiatives, the Marin community training (with Elliot's guidance), the fledgling apprenticeship program, the hiring of an assistant, booking in guests for the show, and her long-distance relationship. Now she could add the Inner City roster selection to her list. Leah had seen very little of Natalie over that last week and felt for her work load — reminding her of her own recent past, by bringing piles of work home. However, she was bright and cheery as she stepped out of her office to join Stu and Leah, who were heading over to the board meeting. The two women made a date for a good catch-up over lunch after Saturday's show.

With Jennifer in the front office, data was continually streaming in about viewers, donors, and YouTube views. In fact everything had shifted at the studio — from a folksy group of four community members to a bustling center for mission control. The staff was in step with their supervisors, and with each other. Though Natalie was working overtime because she hadn't hired yet, everyone else felt supported such that creativity was surging. The board meeting felt like a download opportunity before the next push forward.

After they were all assembled, including Chris with his proposed cottage industry plan, Stu called the meeting to order with a silent holding of hands in circle. Chris had asked to go first, then to be excused to go back to work at the stable. He was quick to point out that what he was proposing wasn't anything he'd be able to handle but some ideas up front of selecting homeless participants that could bring in some light industry and be implemented into coursework at a technical education school.

The ideas were all well received. Greg scratched his head wondering why he hadn't thought of the sheepskin idea himself, and then admitted he'd no spare time to be thinking such thoughts. He was quick to validate the expansion of the flocks to support the industry. Nick offered to find out more about brain-tanning on a large scale, though it sounded perfectly disgusting to him. They asked Chris to present it, just as he had, to the community on Tuesday night, certain that a lively discussion would ensue.

After he left, Will and Tommy gave a report on the San Francisco Inner City project that got everyone very excited about the future of that Outreach stream. With *Harmony Valley* progressing under a good team of project managers, and his office expansion in Ed Driscoll's care, Tommy planned to live in their Marin home during construction of the neighborhoods and commercial enterprises starting after the first of the year. He would time his visits to *New Avalon* to coincide with board meetings, community meetings and *Harmony Valley* project leadership needs. Shelley and the boys would drive down there one weekend a month to be with him.

Will then discussed the Gift Pyramid aspect of the project, indicating that Tommy would be working hand in hand with project managers from LA, Oakland, and one other city, who could then each take on three other project managers from different cities as their own projects materialized. Sacramento had, finally, put their hat in for a homeless project since that immediate need was more pressing. He was looking at the possibilities of San Jose, San Diego, and Seattle, though favoring San Jose or a second Oakland neighborhood to implement what Leah had suggested to him — sharing a common farm amongst three communities. He'd a few leads on the farm but nothing firm. Leah offer that starting the farm with two communities and adding the Sacramento homeless community as a farm share might work out for the best.

When questioned about the role of Outreach in the expanding tree of projects, Will submitted that his job would be one of oversight — helping each project maintain the core values of the first project, San Francisco. It was the model and, for that reason, needed his, Natalie's, and Tommy's best efforts from the get–go. Natalie could explain her end of it, but suffice to say that the apprenticing of her teaching role would be from *New Avalon* community members until the apprenticeship program had solidly expanded. She'd agreed, with Ellia and Georgia's assistance, to take the first four pyramid communities through an Inner City Community Training Program, which she was working hard to develop.

All in all, the project in San Francisco was on schedule and had amazing support from the city, the banks, and the cadre of combined social services, which was rounding up the misplaced or foreclosed–on residents. Tommy wanted to add a fun aspect to the projects, which was researching the historic architectural styles to restore a sense of the city's history into the projects. He was interviewing job applicants with drafting, surveying, engineering and management skills and felt like hiring someone to hire everyone else. It was a bit of a drag but he was the one who knew what he needed.

Leah suggested that Will get the farm search posted on the Outreach website with a link to it on the show's website. She also suggested that he mention it several times during the Saturday show on 'your home town'. Everyone agreed. It felt like the right time to move forward on the rural arm of the Inner City model. Greg's work in *Harmony Valley* had stabilized and it was a good time of year to get a new operation going in a slightly warmer clime, leaving routine chores to the incoming residents with WWOOFer and apprentice assistance and his periodic oversight and consultations by phone.

Tommy, Will and Greg gave the update on *Harmony Valley*, with Greg, handily, covering Sonia's end of the project for her. The hotel would be finished before the end of the month. Its front room would become the hub of activity when residents arrived, including a temporary bank at the front desk, spiritual circles with Natalie and Ellia on a twice–weekly basis, and a weekly clinic treating minor problems and referring complex situations to *New Avalon*. Nick was going to oversee that, and collaborate with Leah in the *New Avalon* clinic.

Greg had his plan in place for livestock but was holding off for moisture. As soon as rainy season started and grass greened-up, he would bring in the sheep and follow with cattle after the pastures could handle them. He added a buffalo acquisition report and upgrade of the land at Mr. B's end of the valley. Buffalo, it seemed, had little respect for fences and were massive enough to destroy them. This new twist — your own animals are now 'pasture poachers' — called for the immediate installation of heavy–duty, bear-level, electric fencing. He was keen to get on with the 2012 WWOOFer selections — a discussion he would lead at the community meeting. All their meat lamb had gone to slaughter and was now being cut, packed and frozen at the warehouse, thanks to their butcher friend and his apprentice — Bernie. There had been no signs of poaching since the mongrels had been incarcerated.

Will reported that the *Harmony Valley* Credit Union had been approved and the system, much like *New Avalon's*, was ready to roll. He was working out community health insurance when Leah 'gifted' him six hours to come up with an overview of *Social Threefolding* as it applied to *Harmony Valley* — that with a playful wink her way. He proposed that they divide the *New Avalon* community members into three groups to represent the three spheres of society — perhaps by association with their gifts and work. At the community meeting, they could initiate an ongoing debate, maybe in the form of creative drama at some point, to work out the boundaries of the spheres. The intent would be to create an infrastructure or model to apply to all of the projects, assuring balance and protective boundaries in the three spheres right here at home and in every project Outreach undertook. Since *New Avalon II* would, more-or-less, double their numbers, they would need it as much as any project they sponsored.

Natalie felt it ought to be integrated into the programs and that Stu might film the dramas and presentations as perfect examples of what might come up in community. A lively discussion ensued, getting everyone back into *Threefolding* mode with their observers on duty to come up with some sample dramas for the Community Meeting. Their budding thespians could create a separate DVD on conflict resolution between the spheres. It sounded both cosmic and nitty-gritty.

Natalie went on with her lengthy report, mostly organizational and program planning, to handle the spiritual education end of the Outreach initiatives. She and Will would set up some dates for San Francisco but it might as well wait until the third project was on board and she could meet with the project managers about the resident preparation. Her program was coming together, based on the work they'd done at *New Avalon* (originally brought to them by Leah), but with adjustments made to accommodate varying amounts of previous spiritual work.

On one hand, the consequences of homelessness placed everyone at ground zero — literally zero. Foreclosure and job loss in center city could be that harsh but often meant combined families, return to parents, and multi-family living situations, and not a tent city or homeless shelter situation. True, there was a tent city subculture to recognize and deal with in the homeless, but they were all in the same boat, and for most, the boat was sinking. Outreach was offering them a buoyant alternative. She didn't expect applicants in either situation to have medical insurance or any assets. What she was looking for was adventurous spirit, hope, and the willingness to work hard giving something novel a try. What she'd put together thus far was touchingly sensitive and solidly spiritual. She'd had a great deal of input from, and maintained an open line of communication with, the counseling organizations in Southern Oregon and Northern California who worked with homeless people. She was ready to interview Inner City applicants and the homeless to arrive at core groups for each pilot project.

The only one needing a vote was Nick, who had put together a modest proposal for a medical library in the clinic based on Leah's suggestion that they might actually get some interesting cases in *Harmony Valley* to begin studying disease and treatment on a consciousness soul level. He asked Leah to expand on the visionary idea she'd received, which she did with brevity and clarity. They would propose, to the *New Avalon* community, participation in a baseline study of their higher bodies. The medical library request was approved as an

Outreach project and would be put before the community on Tuesday evening. That vote was followed by a brief discussion of the community's readiness to actively engage these models as part of their mission.

It was Leah's night to barely make it to Joel's show on time. The theme song was playing as she dropped her notes on her desk and dashed down the hall to cuddle up with Chris. The rest of the staff had adopted the group ritual of viewing the Thursday show in the theater, with buttered popcorn, leaving Chris and Leah to their own devices. Everybody loved the show and gave a big 'thumbs up' to Kim's photography. *New Avalon* had its sneak preview to the public, who would get the documentary version, by Stu's reckoning, in June.

While she was at the board meeting, Chris had finished up in the stable, showered, and put a meatloaf in the oven and a salad in the fridge, for a quick dinner. They walked in the door to that aroma and set about steaming some spinach to complete the meal. Leah couldn't begin to explain all that had been presented at the board meeting and he would hear most of it on Tuesday. Instead, she wanted to chat about Nick's higher body education.

"Yeah, look, lass, I know you see the doctor side of Nick, and he's a good one, but I see the magician. In a sense, we're suited as father and son, he being the only one thus far with those gifts. He's unaware, by the way," he added. "Those are my personal observations."

"I see that, cowboy. Do you think he's meant to replace you one day?" she asked.

"Perhaps as a magus. He's brotherhood, but not Ruby Order."

"I see. Maybe we're not meant to know who will replace us?" she offered.

"I doubt that. I was tucked under the wing of Giorgio for those years in full consciousness of the duty I was assuming. I reckon I'd need to do the same for my successor. I'd imagine the same would be true for the Bee Mistress, if not your Ruby Order membership."

"Well, yes, that does feel a certainty. I'm in no hurry. I'm on a fantastic mission, having the time of my life with you. Personally, I'm hoping Jacques brings us both a vial of his rejuvenation elixir when we meet up with him at Monticello. Does that smack of bad protocol — to ask?" she grinned.

"It's at least as tacky as Joel's suggesting an interview," he laughed.

She got lost in a round of giggles, remembering Joel's unanticipated question, while Chris took his dishes to the sink and got organized for choir.

"What are you going to do with yourself tonight, lass?" he asked, coming to kiss her goodbye.

"I'm sewing David's sweater pieces together and will need to steam it. And then there's Mandy's doll to work on and the book you gave me on Archangel Michael to begin. Alternatively, I could spend a chunk of the evening trying to sort through a huge day. I'm saving the creation of the Golden Queen's altar for ritual time tomorrow."

"I'll be back by 10:30. There's a hearth fire ready if you want it," he added kissing the back of her neck.

"Have a lovely time singing, cowboy," she whispered in his ear, having stood up to give him a proper send off.

Chris and Nick saddled up Thunder and Myrtle the next morning, packing up Gert's old saddlebags with apples, root crops and several loaves of bread for gifting, should they make contact with the *Woodland Folk*. Nick took a backpack with their lunches and an empty water bottle to fill at the spring. Their intention was to observe — making sure they were doing well enough to leave them alone.

Leah had sent Chris off with a big hug and kiss, along with all the usual cautions, including rattlesnakes. He thanked her kindly for that prickly reminder. She was satisfied that he wouldn't be going alone, had the radio, although with no guarantee it would work, and was, after all, a pretty clever magician. For his part, he'd had a few Low German sessions with Rob, Tommy and their tapes — enough to imagine he was back in Tyrol. She would be in the final stages of show prep with rehearsal. The men doubted they'd be home much before three.

Leah was, therefore, completely unhinged by the sight of Chris suddenly appearing in her office doorway just before rehearsal. He was breathing hard, with beads of sweat on his forehead. She immediately panicked with worry for Nick or Billie, who Nick had taken along.

"Chris, what's wrong?" she cried, jumping up from her desk.

"You've got to come, lass," he said, breathing hard. He'd run all the way from the barn. "Alex is getting Holly saddled up for you," he added, catching his breath.

"Is it Nick or Billie, what's happened, cowboy? Just tell me. I don't know how to respond," she cried.

"They're fine. I just dropped Billie in Jennifer's lap. She'll take him to the school. It's the mum, Trynel, lass. She's got a nasty fracture. I can tell you about it on the way. Do you have an emergency medical bag ready?"

"I do. Which bone, cowboy?" she asked, grabbing her jacket to head over to the clinic.

"It's her lower leg. I'm not sure which bone. It's sticking out of her skin though," he added, hastily.

"When?" she asked.

"Several days out, lass."

"*Oh, my God!* Please take the time to find Nat or Leslie and let then know we'll postpone the rehearsal. It might have to be tonight. I'll assemble what I might need and meet you in the courtyard."

Leah ran to the clinic, unlocked the door, turned off the alarm, and grabbed the black doctor's bag that always sat at the desk for emergencies. In her storeroom she added several different antiseptics, anesthetics, narcotics, topical and oral antibiotics, bottles of alcohol and hydrogen peroxide, casting materials and a selection of sterile surgical instruments wrapped in a soft cloth then a plastic bag. She happened to have an adjustable leg brace, which was clumsy but might come in handy. Her bag had the essentials for bandaging and emergency medicine, homeopathics, and common meds with current dates. She raided Nick's apothecary for horsetail, arnica and comfrey, set the alarm, and ran into Chris outside the door. He took the bag and cumbersome brace from her, agreeing to meet her at the stable. He advised boots and jeans along with a warm sweater, her jacket and hat. She could grab her soft gloves at the stable.

Leah took off, at a jog, down the path behind their houses while Chris circled East Commons Lane to the stable. When she got there, a sack lunch in hand, he had everything packed up and Holly waiting at the stable door with Thunder. It wasn't until they were winding their way up to the springs that he could begin to tell her about their experience. He could have radioed Tommy from the top of the second ridge but didn't want Leah making the trip on her own and wanted to get Billie back to his mum. The path hadn't been that easy to follow. They had a good many shoed hoof prints to lead them back now.

When he and Nick had finally crested the second ridge, they spotted the farm near a small pond in a clearing maybe halfway down into the valley and to the North. Their descent was through forest with no clear view of the settlement but it was, at that point, a path well–trod by human feet. They'd followed a northerly split in the path and came into the clearing roughly an hour's journey from the springs. Sheep and goats grazed in a small paddock with little grass and a crudely patched split rail fence. Chickens and ducks were scattered about, but the family wasn't out on the land.

On instinct, he and Nick had ridden the horses right up to the sagging front gate of a rickety fence. When Chris called out a greeting in Low German, a teenage girl dashed out of the cabin onto the porch, greatly alarmed to hear a human voice, let alone in Low German. It was Sissi, who had come with the children on their second visit to the springs. Chris and Nick stayed mounted so as not to alarm her — a good move as her father soon joined her with a shotgun. Chris had his pistol and Nick a rifle in case they'd had an encounter with a big predator or snake. With Billie between his legs, Nick pulled his rifle out, holding it above his head to indicate a peaceful encounter — at least in his tradition. Chris' pistol was strapped under his jacket, so he didn't bother to show it. Instead, he called to them, announcing that they were from the village of Rob and Mike and that they wanted to make sure they were good with winter stores. Fortunately, he'd established a few language landmarks for first encounters in his mind.

Zacker, the dad, indicated that they should dismount. Nick slid his rifle back in its sling on Myrtle and they approached the gate. Sissi, who'd been the girl with a little English, started to cry with relief and overrode her father to ask if they could help her mother. She ordered her father to put his gun away and accept the help of these good people — more-or-less, as Chris could interpret her German. He lowered his gun and Sissi invited Nick and Chris inside to have a look at her mother's leg.

"What can I say, lass. It didn't look good. Trynel was delirious, laid out in bed with her head propped up and her grisly lower leg uncovered. Jürgen and Zenzi had been sent out foraging for the day to quiet the house for Trynel. Sissi asked us: *What, by the grace of God, brought you over the ridge to find our home?* I told her concern for their welfare with the coming of winter. It seemed a hard life to be alone in the wilderness.

"She agreed, in the moment. I let them know that Nick was a homeopath and herbalist, ready to help if he could, but that my wife was a doctor with bone setting experience, although, to be honest, that was an assumption."

"Quiet true, though. It's common in family practice and the ER, especially with children," Leah offered; glad to be communicating instead of imagining the extent of the break. "What did they say to that?"

"Sissi asked if you would come. Nick had felt Trynel's pulse, then her forehead. She was burning up and the pulse was rapid and full. He told me to take Billie and come get you, to tell you that, and to not waste any time doing it. He would do what he could to stabilize her.

"I excused myself, immediately but engaged Sissi on the way back to Thunder asking how the accident had happened. She said that her mother had been helping her father chopping wood for winter when a huge log roll down the hill crushing her. Zacker had rolled it off and carried her to the house, and hadn't left her side since. They'd little in the way of medicine and Trynel, who knew the herbs, wasn't conscious to direct the use of them. Sissi had been praying hard for two days for help to come. Being the answer to her prayers, lass, we have her full support. I gave her the saddle bags to store the food and got on my way with Billie."

"I understand Zacker's fear, cowboy. You and Nick are the last thing he'd ever expect to come out of the wilderness. However, I *am* surprised that he didn't send the children all the way to *New Avalon* after help."

"Beliefs, I reckon. He looked like a fairly stubborn bloke. That may get in your way treating her too, but Sissi has a lot of influence over her dad for a young lass."

As they were coming down the hill on the last leg of the trip Leah felt a rising dread within. "What did the wound look like, cowboy?" she asked, quietly. *What would Zacker do to her or all of them, if she failed?* Her instincts didn't trust him.

"You know me, lass, I started getting nauseous and faint at the site of the jagged bone. Nick wasn't as troubled as I was, though I'm sure that sort of thing wasn't part of his training."

"More likely his upbringing. It's rough on the res. For such a brave lad, you do go to pieces at the sight of blood," she remarked.

"I'll leave that to you and have a look at the broken paddock fence, if you don't mind."

"Lucky I've got Nick and Sissi to help," she mumbled. "Maybe you can get Zacker out of the way, too. I imagine I'll have to administer morphine and open the leg."

"I'd be happy to try."

Glad to see Myrtle, Holly and Thunder let out a few blows with their arrival. Leah was so unnerved, she would get home and not even remember what the farm looked like as they road up to the gate. Nick had Sissi tending a boiling pot of water on the hearth should they need it, but without antiseptic of any kind, they could do little except hold Trynel's hand and apply a cool cloth to her forehead. He was damn good at that though, Chris noted. She'd settled down quite a bit. Leah nodded to Zacker and conferred with Nick at the bedside. The wound was gruesome. The tibia was jaggedly broken, with the distal part of the break having sliced the lower leg open. It was protruding upward with a fair amount of infection surrounding the gash. Though the surrounding tissue was swollen and inflamed, she saw no typical signs of tetanus, but safely assumed both anaerobic and aerobic bacteria. Leah had seen fractures like this from industrial and motorcycle accidents but not two days after the fact. This wasn't going to be a clean job — or easy.

She asked Chris to tell Zacker that she would try to help Trynel, but could not yet surmise the condition of the second bone. She assumed it to be crushed or similarly broken since it was a much more delicate bone. While doing her very best under the conditions there was no way to tell if Trynel would walk again, at least normally, but she would be better able to predict that after surgery. Chris look visibly distressed when the word surgery had to come out of his mouth.

What surgery? Zacker wanted to know. She explained that she couldn't possibly get the bone pieces back together without opening the wound further — so a simple surgery through the skin to allow proper placement of the bone. She'd all the instruments with her and natural medicine (morphine did come from opium, which did come from a poppy plant) to put Trynel, — who could surely use the rest — to sleep while she did it. It was the best she could do.

Well, that was a lie to give her some wiggle room. As soon as Chris got Zacker out of the house on a tour and fence repairing distraction, she had Nick hold space while she went into a visionary trance. Her 'sight' had to suffice for X-rays and worked well enough to visualize the other half of the tibia and its position within the leg, and from the opposite side of the bed, the fibula, which *was* crushed. She administered morphine by hypodermic while Nick sterilized the surgical instruments. Sissi assisted Leah while she cleaned the outer wound much as she had Chris's wounded leg. Leah brought clean cloths to place under Trynel's leg to absorb the hydrogen peroxide, and then a few more for surgical fluids. For the moment the low winter sun was shining through the window by the bed, giving Leah good light.

Nick set up the surgical tools atop the nightstand on their soft wrapping cloth, covering them with squares of sterile gauze. He would hand them to Leah as needed. When the morphine had taken affect, they scrubbed their hands and gloved up. She centered herself and, in her mind, invoked Archangel Raphael, the healer, to guide her hands and instruments and Archangel Michael as well as Trynel's higher self and guardian angel to hold her steady and fill her patient with healing etheric energy. She felt the need for Sananda as well and asked for his guidance overall. Nick called in Great Spirit, and left it at that.

When they were both ready, she cleaned the site of incision with a disinfectant pad, placed a stack of sterile gauze pads nearby and took up the scalpel.

In a hospital surgery they would likely have pinned the bone fragments together. She would have to rely on near-perfect positioning, stability, and the curative powers of the herbs she'd brought from Nick's pharmacy. For the fibula, there was nothing humanly possible that she could do, so she assigned that to the divine beings gathered above the bed, for herbs alone would not restore that bone. Her aim was to get the fracture and wound site as sterile as possible. Then she would have Nick hold the fracture together from the other side of the leg while she sutured the surgical wound and the jagged wound caused by the break.

In the end, after pouring hydrogen peroxide on the sutured leg, drying it with gauze and following that with a lavish amount antibiotic ointment, she dressed the fracture site with a sterile poultice of comfrey leaf that Nick had put together while prepping the instruments. Then she began wrapping it firmly to hold the bones together without inhibiting blood flow.

Miraculously, her leg muscles were intact and blood loss was significant but not critical. She and Nick agreed that it should not be cast until infection was gone, the surgical wound was mending, and the bones had begun to knit. She used her 'sight' again to witness the fracture as he'd let go of the bones — okay in the moment, but she was sedated. They worked together to stabilize the leg with a lot of padding and secured the leg brace around it. Then it was cleanup, instructions to Sissi for medications, absolutely no movement of the leg, and recipes for horsetail and comfrey teas along with their timing intervals. She was able to get through to her that she wasn't to allow either of her parents to skip the antibiotics (two different ones) because it was a matter of life and death. If her mother made it through the next two days, it was then a matter of her mother having a leg or not. She 'got' it and would keep them hidden in her apron pocket along with the painkillers. The teas would not be a problem.

Leah had a small biological waste bag stuffed with blood and peroxide-soaked gauze, cotton, used surgical disinfectant and alcohol wipes and their envelopes, and suture scraps. She'd capped the hypodermic needle and slipped it into a plastic bag for separate disposal at the clinic. Nick packed all of that into one empty saddlebag and put the surgical instruments wrapped in another waste bag in the other saddlebag. When they returned to the bedside to check on Trynel, Leah was stunned to see Archangel Michael hovering over the bed and piercing Trynel's leg with his sword. Her guardian angel held space at the head of the bed. It lifted Leah's heart into a space of hope. The leg had been a real mess and her surgery skills, though excellent, had been little used in the last few years.

Sissi, who was standing right behind Leah, gasped. "Engeln," she whispered.

Leah was very fatigued, but not so tired as to have missed that. She turned to Sissi and asked. "Did you see the angels, Sissi?"

"Ja, Leah," she admitted, "eins mit schwert von licht."

Nick and Leah looked at each other, wide-eyed. This girl had the 'sight' in no small way. Nick of course hadn't seen anything, but would admit to having felt energy move. Leah gave Sissi a motherly hug — a hug sincerely returned, with much gratitude. Her prayers had been answered and this angel of a woman had come all the way from the green valley to help her mother.

Nick and Leah took the saddlebags outside and sat on the front porch with their lunches and the spring water. Sissi joined them after checking on her mother again and brought a *New Avalon* apple to eat with them. She wanted to know when Leah and Nick would return. Nick volunteered to come the next day to check on Trynel. If Leah was needed he would let her know by radio but otherwise she would come with him on Sunday when she was free and, after checking the wound, they would possibly put her mother's leg in a plaster cast to keep the bone from moving. For the next two days, her mother was to keep it still. The brace would help her remember that. She would clarify that again when Chris returned to translate.

When they finished their sandwiches, Sissi wanted to show them something important. She took Leah's hand and the three of them hiked up a rise behind the house to a flat patch of meadow. Sissi took them to the far side of the meadow to introduce them to her brothers and sisters. There were five graves with markers — two stillbirths, two newborn babies, and one four-year-old — of what sounded like meningitis. Leah shed tears for Trynel, whose life had been no bed of roses.

Sissi took them to a sixth grave, unmarked, her own baby — stillborn. Leah tried to remain calm. She asked Sissi her age ... fifteen years. A stranger? By force? It was none of her business, she knew, but Leah's heart was bound to the heart of this girl, perhaps melded by the sword of Michael. No. And no, were her answers. Leah felt her blood begin to boil. It was a good thing Dragon Lady didn't have Gert's rifle or know how to use one. What of this child's future stuck out in the wilderness with no way out, and an incestuous father to give her a row of unmarked graves? Nick reached out, wrapping an arm around Leah to calm her. He knew perfectly well where Leah was headed because he felt similarly. Nick wanted to stuff Sissi in a saddlebag and take her home ... but not now. She was her mother's only hope.

As they were coming back down the rise, the little children came home with their forage baskets. They were delighted to see strangers, and to find out they were friends of Rob and Mike's was even better. Leah's 'Grandmother Jane' leapt to the fore with good cuddles on the porch steps while they waited for Chris and Zacker. The little ones got Sissi to ask Leah and Nick questions about the other children in *New Avalon* and especially Mark and Paul who they would meet on Sunday. Perhaps here instead of the springs, she suggested to Nick, who told them all about Paul, who was his son.

Chris and Zacker returned a short time later. Of course, the two children glommed onto Chris as all kids did. He took them to meet the horses while Zacker went in to see his wife, sleeping peacefully with her mended, immobilized leg. Sissi explained the rules and the plan for return visits with the kind of authority gained from consensual abuse — consensual only in the sense that she was powerless to do anything about it.

They weren't homeward bound until four o'clock, needing to push it a bit to arrive home before the sun set. Nick did try to reach Tommy from the top of the first ridge and was successful with a fair amount of crackling. That was good to know. Leah rode home in silence, a chunk of her heart left behind with Sissi.

Later, after a simple omelet and salad dinner with Spence's seed bread, she was back at the studio for a late rehearsal. Their guests were comfortably settled in at The Lodge and Georgia, glad to have Nick back fathering, was getting her weekly dose of sisterhood. Natalie had done another sterling job putting the panel together and Paula, back for the rehearsal, handed her a polished first-rate newscast. They would update in the morning but Leah could go over it in rehearsal and take it home to read through a few more times.

She and Natalie firmed up their lunch date, for Saturday post-show at the coffee shop, as they walked home together. Natalie was certain that Leah was caring a heavy load in her heart but thought better than to tap it before their lunch date. Leah was a processing pro and her best friend respected her timing. They hugged at Natalie's gate and Leah returned home to a hearth fire and a pair of sympathetic arms. She'd a cathartic unloading of the tedious surgery (without the gory details), the good pieces with the angels, and the heartbreak with Sissi. Chris had picked up on the incest while still on Thunder that morning. Sissi was more the wife than Trynel, who, frankly, might have been relieved to find a way out of the exhausting situation she'd called life.

He and Zacker had not talked proper husbanding and fathering, but rather the struggle of sustaining life in the wilderness versus the benefits of being in a pristine environment. The farm was a bloody wreck, in Chris' opinion. They weren't going to make it much longer and he made that clear to Zacker, who concurred. They'd depleted the soil without enough animal manure to build it back up. Though Greg could assess it more fully, it was obvious. The stored vegetables were small and lacked flavor. With his only adult farmhand down, Zacker was an odd combination of depressed, angry and fearful of winter — a shit load of unhelpful emotions.

"Did you ask where they'd come from and how they got so isolated, cowboy?" she asked, curled up in his arms on the sofa.

"I did. And I had to read between the lines of Low Germain to get the picture, which is, I reckon, that they were banished from their community somewhere up north because he'd claimed Trynel, against her parents wishes, and likely her own, through rape and pregnancy. Apparently, they judge the woman to be as guilty as the man, regardless of the circumstances. They wandered south as a couple, she pregnant, for months, doing odd jobs, seasonal farm help, getting charity here and there, spending what little they had of money, hunting and trapping as he could, and learning to forage from nature. It seems there's a lot to eat out there at certain times of the year. They ended up finding our valley, fully occupied, of course, but found it so attractive that they followed water up just like our boys did, and explored the valleys beyond until they found their homestead.

"Surely they didn't drag animals with them?" she queried.

"No. He says that they used the rest of their funds, after buying seeds and tools for building, to buy a pair of lambs from Mr. Brenner and carried them around their necks to the first paddock they'd built. The water attracted birds and feeding wild ducks kept them around. The chooks were gifts from Gert and Henry as were a lot of windfall apples. They used to visit our valley often when they were younger and still building their little farm and family."

"What a road to tow," she sighed. "What do you reckon we can do for them?" she asked.

"You've done plenty, believe me. I can't imagine dealing with something like that in an isolated place myself. Beyond that, I see a good project for the Rangers repairing out buildings and fencing. We can chainsaw, split and stack wood for winter. We can scythe and stack some hay, though it's not likely very nutritious this time of year, and we can bring them food stores, especially fresh veggies, and lamb and beef for the short term to rebuild health. It looks like they could use warm blankets and simple household goods. They've got fish in the pond. I reckon Zacker is feeling worn out and lackluster about the future, more so after the accident. I honestly think that Trynel, at least, would not have survived the winter regardless of the injury. In fact it may be a blessing in disguise to give her much needed rest."

"What will be their reciprocity, cowboy? We can't treat them like charity without damaging a potentially fruitful relationship with them, and especially with the children."

"I've been thinking of proposing an unusual exchange," he suggested.

"Do tell, my magus," she urged.

"We can call it the Wee-Woofer program," he laughed. "I would propose that their children come to live in *New Avalon* for four to five days a week, helping out with foraging, farm work, and odd jobs. They'll be *forced* to go to school, drink raw milk and eat heartily, then go back to their home on the weekends to help out. This will give Zacker and Trynel time to work out their relationship, Sissi will be spared her father's abuse five days out of a week and learn to be a teenager rather than a wife. The little ones will grow up with Waldorf education and likely leave home to join the rest of the world. What do you think?" he grinned.

"A real bargain, cowboy," she laughed, sitting up to look him in the eyes. "How do you expect to pull this off? "

"Easy. The kids will come home bearing produce and morals. It has to rub off. And Zacker, being a good German, will see the sense in the exchange. They're otherwise going to die out. Their survival depends on letting their children go, like a foster program, with the benefits of seeing and using them two days a week. It's like boarding school, lass. When Trynel is recovered, and I'm banking on Archangel Michael, my good wife and Nick on that one, she could be employed to exchange sustenance for handcrafts made of wool."

"Where are you going to put these kids? They don't speak English. And what about winter?" she asked, her practical Alice coming forth.

"Good questions. I do have an idea there. It would be far easier for Zacker and Trynel to make it through the winter with good stores and without three extra mouths to feed. Her healing and that of their marriage should be a priority and chores minimal with snow on the ground. So I would suggest the kids stay here all winter and adopt the new system in the spring. I have a friend, a certain Greek Cypriot, who feels ready to abandon Will and Sonia to live on his own. I say he's more than ready. I'd like to put him up in the spare farmhouse with the kids. If they can walk over two ridges to get here they can walk up the road to *New Avalon* to go to school. What do you think?" he asked, rubbing her back.

"If you can pull this off with Zacker, I'll consider it high magic, cowboy," she laughed. "I love the idea. They can eat Greek and become sorcerer's apprentices! It wouldn't bother Demetri, if they didn't understand him and vice versa."

"I figure Rob and Mike could tutor English after school and when Rob is finished with work. We'll have to speak with Georgia about school. It could overwhelm her and the other kids."

"Not likely. She is an all-encompassing woman. I expect she'll be excited about the language challenge and welcome their unusual skills. Children pick up second languages easily."

"And look, it's three-way healing, lass. You and Nick can fix up Trynel. She and Zacker can heal each other. Demetri and the children will become a tight little family and a safe haven for Sissi. You can leave Zacker to me. It's time for you to focus on the show tomorrow, eh?"

Chris had totally lifted her spirits. Leah went off to get her expedition sleeping bag for the download. The altar of the Golden Queen could be worked into Saturday afternoon. Chris was off to rally the Rangers, door-to-door, proposing a spontaneous meeting to discuss the situation after Saturday's trail clearing.

What with the longer show and her much-savored lunch with Natalie, and the play rehearsal in the afternoon, Leah didn't catch up with Chris again until late Saturday afternoon. She was putting the finishing touches on the Golden Queen's altar in Don Eduardo's niche. Don Eduardo had moved to the bookcase, where he could provide auxiliary support during their discussions. In the niche, with Betty Morrison, was a small jar of raw *Lacy Phacelia* honey, nearly the color of molasses, and a beeswax candle she'd made last Candlemas Day with a small amount of wax from the hives. It was molded in the shape of a fir cone. There was another squat pillar beeswax candle on a candle stand, which she'd lit, and a shiny 100-gram gold bullion bar stamped *Pamp Suisse*. On a little dish to the side was a frond of drying *Lacy Phacelia* flowers and *Melissa* leaves on top of a small spray of fresh incense cedar.

Chris wanted to add something to the altar. She was smitten with the idea of having his energy in and on the altar. He produced a stone from the bottom of his jean pocket. She'd seen it often on the dresser top when he was sleeping. He explained that it was a piece of lapis lazuli from Madagascar, holding a pure, late Lemurian energy. Perfect!

They caught up with each other while preparing dinner together. Leah shared that the show had been excellent. It was an opportune time for Will to co-host since she wasn't fully free of her concern for Trynel. Will was also interested in new community models for the Inner City projects. She followed her discussion flow and he came in with a whole new range of questions, a good many of them off-the-wall. Joel's segment, taped with her during his visit, set the stage again with the concept of Main Street versus Wall Street and all that that encompassed.

People were doing it — going local — and they were succeeding. Willow's segment had been rich. OWS was planning to *Occupy* foreclosures in bank hands for needy families and defend those who were threatened with eviction in over 40 cities starting December 6th. There was also a surprise visit to *Occupy* with a concert, from Jackson Browne on Friday, which she got on film and sent to Stu. Overall, Leah felt the show would have left viewers in a positive frame of mind — better able to get something like Transition Town going in their communities. The guests were keenly interested in each other's topics and went back to The Lodge for a closing luncheon with Will to discuss it all.

Her lunch with Nat had been a lot of fun but also spiritually uplifting. Her longtime girlfriend finally felt like she'd hit mission and was keen to get on with the elevation of her ego. That seemed to be an infectious condition spreading around *New Avalon*. It would certainly put her in a good place for partnership with Chuck, who was planning his next working trip to visit with his *New Avalon* constituents. Leah, Natalie, Sonia, Georgia and Ellia were going to get together when the Rangers were meeting on Friday to work on their doll projects and sort out teaching duties for the Outreach projects. They'd all worked with Leah for many years and each was a great teacher in her own right. One project was to start training Shelley and Jenny to help out too. It was thought that Katia best wait until further along with mothering. Leslie's niche had been carved out at the studio, and Christina, because of her duties in the Assembly and Marin, would be pulled away for big, consistent chunks of time vastly more important to the future of all new systems than teaching assistance.

"I need to chase down Nick to see how Trynel was doing today," Leah declared, as she dished up the dinner she'd put together that night. "I assume, since he hasn't chased me down, that she's still alive."

"No need. I went with him," Chris replied, shaking and applying his homemade garlic and lime salad dressing.

"Cowboy! Why'd you let me go on blabbering about my day when you had a report from the *Woodland Folk*?" she demanded, feeling especially fragile.

He set the salad bowl on the table and drew her in for a warm cuddle. "We've got all night, lass; that is until tango lessons. He gave her a deep, gratifying kiss whilst running his hands around under her sweater. "I love to hear your review of the show. Then I go watch it for myself on YouTube. I'm becoming a savvy solutions–oriented fan," he grinned.

"We haven't had sex since Tuesday night, cowboy. Is there something wrong with us?" she asked, in jest.

"It's not for lack of desire, lass. I for one have been three times over the ridge with Thunder in two days. We're both feeling the strain and my brain's been working overtime between cottage industries and the illegal fostering of some deserving kids," he offered.

"To say nothing of the singing, directing and acting four days a week," she added. "Rehearsal was great this afternoon, by the way."

"Aye, but that's all joy for me, and you? It was the only scene I was worried about, what with the level of emotional engagement. You were terrific, lass. That said; I reckon I don't multitask as well as you do. You're amazing, you know," he added as they sat down to eat.

"My emotions are real and raw at the moment, cowboy. It does make the acting easier. As to my skills at multi-tasking, I've been having fun *delegating* tasks lately. Although, it does turn out I'm the only surgeon and purveyor of pharmaceuticals here. I found I couldn't give the show 100% and be that dedicated doctor at the same time. It was a subpersonality conflict of interest, if there ever was one," she sighed.

"You handled it well, lass. So, here's the report: Nick sat a long time with Trynel this morning. She's a bit feverish still, but alert and mildly agitated. Her pulse is wiry. She's taking her meds and, according to Sissi, is secretly very grateful for the painkillers. She'd been in agony before you came to fix her up and she does remember that. She doesn't remember the accident though," he reported.

"That all sounds normal. She'll feel a lot better when the antibiotics start wiping out the infection. The fever will drop and she'll have more etheric force to deliver to the bone. I'd be more than agitated with a leg I couldn't move. She's a trooper, in that regard."

"That's for sure. I can't imagine a woman having lost that many children going on with life in any version of normal," he said.

"I doubt it's normal, cowboy. Her only option is to opt out and she would never do that to her children. You're right to get the little ones out of there while she's mending her leg. She'll be up on it way too soon trying to serve them. Sissi will grow in her gifts through her service, earning her right to be who she's meant to be one day."

"What is it about the girl that so attracts you, lass?" he asked.

"We've not discussed the surgery, you and I. Sissi was as steady as Gibraltar holding space and assisting with sterilization and continual cleanup. She has the temperament of a great nurse, like Jane Fuzzy Wuzzy," she noted. "But, the kicker is that I had called in Archangelic assistance, and *she* saw them."

"Seriously? What happened?" he asked, his interest piqued.

"Significantly? Archangel Michael thrust that sword of his into Trynel's leg. A tremendous light entered it, but to what end, I've no idea. I'm anxious to see the bones tomorrow. I was able to use my etheric vision to view the two tibia fragments and set them. The bone you saw was the tibia — not an easy, clean break, but it may mend. The smaller lower leg bone, the fibula was crushed and all but the two joint ends, knee and ankle, were destroyed. Even if the tibia mends correctly, she may not be able to walk."

"Sissi told me you were the answer to her prayers. I reckon she knows how to manifest. She didn't say anything to me about the *other* angels," he said, with a wink, "but greatly admired your skills."

"R-r-right, cowboy," she drawled. "Tomorrow will be your fourth journey over the ridge unless you're going to send me over with Nick instead."

"You'll not be alone lass. All of the Rangers and Jim Taylor are coming with us to get the farm and house in order. We'll be using all our horses and Jim's donkey, which he suggested they could keep for the kids' journeys back and forth. He can rig her up with donkey baskets, like big saddlebags, to carry quit a bit. We're taking chain saws, petrol, axes, wedges, hammers, nails ... the works. If we give it a few Saturdays and Sundays, we should have them all fixed up."

"Chris, that's wonderful. Will Zacker accept it?"

"He's got no choice. He can't do it alone and, according to the locals, winter will come at some point and crops won't grow again until next spring. He's a proud bloke but I reckon he'll be grateful. I did warn him."

"Will the kids come back with us then?" she asked.

"The two little ones could. It will work best for them to be meeting our boys at the springs late morning and they could come down to *New Avalon* with them. Tommy and I'll have a good yarn with Zacker about the plan and I'm hoping you, as Angel Jane, will set Trynel's mind at ease that they'll be well taken care of and come for their visit Saturday morning. The Rangers will split into two work teams, so as not to abandon *New Avalon* for more than tomorrow. The kids can come back with the Sunday crew and we can split you and Nick to give Trynel coverage and Sissi a break. What do you think?"

"I'm thinking Holly and I might come home early. A whole day over there feels over the top. Sissi has the household in good order. If we just bring in some supplies, she'll be good. Does that suit?" she asked.

His hesitancy at letting her come home alone was palpable. "I'll see you to the springs, if you don't mind, lass. I could give you the rattlesnake lecture you gave me to make my point?" he added, with a grin.

"No need, cowboy," she conceded. "I'll stay and explore the forest with the Sissi. We can collect kindling for starting fires. We'll get a routine worked out and after Trynel is in a cast and there's no infection, I can come every few weeks for a short visit. Maybe we can visit mid-week to see how they're going and give Sissi a little relief."

Aye, lass, that's a better idea. Now, Tommy's turned up the supplemental heat in the farmhouse and Demetri will go down there with a crew of our women to get it cleaned up and livable. We'll take care to fill the woodshed, the fridge and the pantry. We've a loose consensus through Ranger consults at home, but Demetri wants a vote at the community meeting to affirm his move."

"I agree. It should go down in the records of *New Avalon*." She reached out to touch his hand, "Tell me, cowboy, how all of this has made you feel. You've stepped up, taking on a huge responsibility."

He thought about it for a minute, taking her hand in his. "It's not been in my comfort zone, lass. However, if I couldn't rally the Rangers and organize the kids' protection, the tragedy I foresaw for the *Woodland Folk* would've been on my karmic plate. It's as simple as that. They would not have made it through this winter. The more I observed, the more I was convinced of that outcome. The kids might've come to us, and did, in their own way, initiate all of this by coming out of the forest at the springs. Spirit works in mysterious way, if we surrender to it. Zacker isn't evil. He's been misled. I think he'll pull through this into proper manhood."

"Cowboy, you're gosh-darn amazing," she purred. "Dragon Lady would have gunned him down in a heartbeat if she'd had her classy rifle and knew how to shoot it."

"You can tell her for me, we'll not be restoring the divine feminine that way," he grinned, pushi,ng his empty plate away then pulling her around into his lap.

part three: community action

chapter 7: the canary caper

The Church of Tango took care of the lack of sex and laughter, and made for an energetic start the next morning. Leah and Nick were at the clinic early, packing up the materials for varying degrees of adjustable, full-coverage casting without plaster, padded bracing, herbal and medicinal supplies, including what she had, which wasn't much, of the 'morning after' pill. It was, unfortunately, the least she could do for Sissi under the circumstance. Nick packed up more comfrey and horsetail, wondering if the *Woodland Folk* knew of the plants so common in European herbal medicine. He'd take a look around for the frost-killed remains, not that it would help in the moment.

When they arrived at the barn, they found all of the horses — save Lucy — saddled and ready to go. The men had backpacks filled with tools and building supplies, and Jim Taylor's donkey loaded up with chain saws, axes, fuel and a sack each of potatoes and whole grain flour. Nick had taken the medical supplies in his backpack and Leah quickly stuffed Holly's saddlebags with wholesome, strengthening food, clean tea towels, and odd bits like yeast, soap bars and matches. Everyone had packed a lunch, to keep that simple. A few of the men were armed and everyone seemed in high spirits.

When they came over the last ridge, the group stopped in a clearing to get the lay of the land and check out the small farm on the hill to the north. It was a wee oasis in a sea of conifers. Leah couldn't help thinking that they all would have perished, Trynel first, had Mike and Rob not climbed to the springs that day with Candace and Perry. No one would have known they existed with Mr. B gone. *Heartfelt Sigh.*

The men would focus on fencing and firewood today, and the following Saturday, then round it out with house repairs and improvements on Sunday next. Much could be done to improve the cooking hearth with cement and a decent grate. They came into the farm clearing, Thunder in the lead, around nine o'clock that morning. Chris felt the horses would be fine grazing what they could find on the perimeter if the men kept their ears alert for distress, and visual checks with head counts were made from time to time. They would use the donkey for hauling logs, if needed, and otherwise let her run with the herd. The children piled out of the house to greet them, and to find both Chris and Tommy able to communicate in Low German. They helped with getting the food into the house while the men split into woodcutting and repairs teams. They would switch chores after lunch. Zacker was at the far side of the pond when they rode in, tending to the sheep he'd moved to empty the main paddock for fence repairs. Wanting to establish a work plan for the day, Chris and Tommy went to meet him as he walked towards the house.

Nick accompanied Leah inside to help check on their patient. He would catch up with the repair crew after he'd finished helping Leah. Trynel was alert and propped up in her bed against a pile of sheepskins. A good fire was burning in the hearth and a teapot with cozy sat on the nightstand. Trynel was meeting Leah for the first time, consciously. To Leah's eyes, she looked like an exhausted woman of 50-60 years, when in fact she'd have been no more than 40, likely younger. Sissi had brushed her mother's hair back in a bun and dressed her in a clean nightshirt. She'd still been in her rugged outdoor work dress when Leah had operated on her leg.

Chris had met Trynel the day before, when he and Nick had come calling. He walked in, with Zacker trailing behind him, to translate the meeting and treatment strategy that Leah wanted Trynel and Sissi to understand. Trynel was very grateful for their help and the strong spirit they brought to their family. She was in no position to refuse allopathic medicine on any dogmatic grounds, whether Zacker felt that way or not. She was determined to recover and resume her farm and motherly duties. That gave Leah pause. As gently as possible she had Chris explain that her recovery if all went especially well, would take the entire winter at the least. Her fracture was very serious and the more fragile crushed fibula bone in the leg might be of no use whatever — and it was critical to the workings of her knee and foot. That was the reality of it. Trynel was shaken, though knew full-well she wasn't in good condition — even before the accident. She was still running a moderate fever and would be feeling very frustrated at immobilization.

Chris explained that their community of men were here to get the farm work and woodpile caught up and that these same men would return in smaller groups in a week to finish up. They'd be ready for winter. She was grateful but concerned for the children who needed her to take care of them. Sissi, so helpful and confident, was yet a child herself.

A better opening would never present itself. Leah offered her bedside chair to Chris who, after dismissing Zacker, used his everyday, kind and compassionate magic to convince her that they'd be well taken care of in *New Avalon* until she was stable and on her feet again in the spring. Jürgen and Zenzi could come to visit their parents once a week until snow blocked the trail. Chores were minimal in winter and they would be well stocked with food and wood. The children would eat well and have playmates with whom to share their skills at handcrafts and foraging. Chris masterfully held her fears and sorrow at separating from the children and wove them back into a sunnier picture of the future than Trynel had ever thought to imagine.

Next, Trynel was concerned for Sissi's future (that made three of them), her coming into womanhood and finding a partner. Again, Chris soothed and calmed her, suggesting that Sissi was a very bright, beautiful girl and, if she were to spend most of her time in New Avalon after Trynel was stable, she would likely find purpose and partner without a problem — and in a community that shared family values, had an abundance of good food, and interesting work to pursue. Trynel received his advice and agreed to give it a think while Chris was out working. *What a charmer you are, cowboy,* Leah thought with her warm inner giggle. Sissi had been listening with great interest. It was probably a good thing that Leah was staying for the day with plenty of time to pull Sissi aside for a private chat.

That, settled, for the moment, Chris went out to split wood while Nick assisted Leah with cushioning the leg to remove the brace and padding for wound inspection. Once again, Leah called on the higher world help to assist her medical training and vision. Sissi stepped back to witness the scene at the bed in silent wonder. The sutures were holding well, the surgical end of the wound was already mending and the jagged end partially, with substantial areas of inflammation. She gloved her hands and cleaned the entire wound again, dabbed it dry then applied a thin layer of antibiotic ointment to the healing wound and a lavish layer on the inflamed portions. Trynel had leaned back to stare at the ceiling. Little did she know, that Archangel Raphael was cradling her head in his cupped healing hands. It was likely why she did so well with the manipulation of the leg.

Leah, sitting along Trynel's right side, asked Nick to hold the space for her to enter trance state to look at the bone mending. And while he was doing that, Sissi was to start making a new poultice of comfrey leaves to wrap the fracture site. The bone was knitting together nicely — to her 'sight'. As long as Trynel kept the leg immobilized, she felt it would mend completely, but not without typical seasonal aching and myalgia. Leah changed positions, taking her chair to the opposite side of the bed to view the fibula. She'd a good 'mental x-ray' from Friday's viewing of the crushed bone. It seemed the same taken as a whole, but she looked carefully, laying across the bed to view the proximal end of the fragment up close. She saw something extraordinary. Still with tendon and ligament attachments at the knee, the bone showed new bone growth at the distal fracture site. Checking the distal bone fragment still clinging to the ankle, she saw the same phenomenon proximally. No instant miracles from Archangels Michael and Raphael, but rather the forces for the body to miraculously heal itself.

She sat back in the rough-hewn chair, eyes closed, in a prayer of gratitude. A few tears dropping to her cheeks before she opened her eyes to Nick's questioning gaze. *Later,* she mouthed. Then, moving back to Trynel's right side, where she could view and work with the wound. She asked Nick to help again from the opposite side as they bandaged the wound, applied the poultice, wrapped the leg, and secured it in the adjustable cast right up over the knee and down to cradle the foot. She was careful to align the fibula bone fragments, although distant, with each other. Trynel wouldn't be able to move the healing bones, ankle or knee and was to stay in bed, adding no weight to the injury. She and Sissi could work out the logistics for using the chamber pot, which she saw stashed under the nightstand, as well as frequent maneuvers to avoid bedsores.

The medical procedures exhausted Trynel, who easily slipped off into a nap as they finished. Leah urged Nick to get out with the men, while she and Sissi cleaned up. He was happy to be going outdoors — mostly since the hearth put excessive smoke in the house — and would come if she called him. That left she and Sissi to clean up the medical waste into a plastic bio-waste bag and go over her stash of medications and herbs, replenishing them. She doubted she would be back before 10 days, and it wasn't likely she'd be needed. Nick would come back in six days to check on the wound healing and apply a fresh poultice.

Leah and Sissi took a pot of peppermint tea out on the front porch to unwind This provided the perfect opportunity for Leah to give her the 'morning after' pills and explain them. She wished she could do more. Chris was working it out but, for now, she needed to help her mother.

Sissi was grateful to have just her mother and father to cook for and her mother to tend. The littler ones were wonderful, but a handful, and would have a grand time with the other children. Leah assured her that she'd be joining them as soon as her mother's leg could carry her own weight with crutches and without pain, leaving her parents to make it through the winter together. Sissi brightened noticeably with that assurance.

She wanted to know what Leah had seen in the leg when in trance and how she did that. *That was a bloody challenge to explain*, she would tell Chris later. Sissi thought she might practice seeing in that way. Well, why not? If she succeeded, Leah would put her to work at the future medical center instructing the doctors, who wouldn't have grown up in the wilderness, opened by the less opaque veils of the natural world.

Out on the land, the men worked steadily, accomplishing a great deal before they brought out their lunches, gathering around the front porch to rest and eat. Leah and Sissi had filled a big pitcher with spring water to replenish the men's water bottles. Fresh water was readily available because they'd built the cabin in close proximity to the hillside spring.

After cutting and splitting the wood left at the accident site, they'd found no shortage of downed trees in the immediate forest. Sassy, the donkey, hauled the big pieces of cut trees out into the open for splitting and the pile of wood was as high as the cabin eves by lunch. In the meantime the repair crew had finished the paddock and moved to rebuild the woodshed, which was close to collapse. Tommy would rustle up some shingles and roofing paper during the week to finish it off, but it was ready for wood stacking – a job Sissi enjoyed and would take care of during the week.

Sissi and Leah had packed up lunches for Jürgen and Zenzi, sending them on their way to meet the boys at the springs, with instructions to go home with Rob and Mike, who would take them to the farmhouse for a visit to *New Avalon*. They were wide-eyed with excitement and started out on their journey at a gallop. The sun was warm enough for Leah and Sissi to sit down with their lunch outside the gate, a short distance from the men. Leah had brought two roast beef sandwiches and a container of raw veggies and sunflower seed dip to share with her. Although careful not to show the depth of her hunger, Sissi ate it all eagerly. Sissi's mind was filled to the brim with questions about life in *New Avalon* and Leah's work. Having no easy way to explain television to her new friend, Leah stuck to doctoring, garden helping, beekeeping, horseback riding, and community functions – all of which had strong appeal. It was good to see Sissi laugh at Leah's adventures riding Holly, and Leah learned that Trynel kept bees in hollowed-out logs for honey and candle wax.

Chris continued to keep a watchful eye on Zacker, who spent the better part of his lunch staring at the women. Leah would remark about her discomfort later, when they were back at home – the unspoken, intuitive reason she'd not wanted to stay. When Sissi got up to refresh the spring water, Zacker's eyes did not follow his daughter but stayed focused on Leah. Chris could read the energy easily enough and would bide his time for the opportunity to enlighten his wayward soul.

That moment came when Leah walked to the spring with the pitcher after his group of men had taken up the wood splitting. He and Zacker were leading Sassy out of the forest dragging a big slice of ponderosa to the cutting area. Forgetting where he was, what he was doing, and whom he was with, Zacker stopped in his tracks literally salivating over Leah, who'd dressed modestly in jeans and a baggy sweater. Chris felt Zacker to be decidedly more animal than man. Like the bloody mongrels, he'd no social skills, whatsoever. Unlike those varmints, he exhibited instinctual urges that were, in Chris' opinion, unprecedented displays of regression. He'd never seen anything like it ... and, he'd seen plenty.

When Zacker came out of his licentious trance, Chris was leaning over Sassy's back with his hands clasped, waiting. To his credit, Zacker did flush slightly at the sight of Chris's steady gaze. Chris was slow and deliberate in approaching the moment he'd been waiting for – *second in one day ... bloody astounding!* He was ready to stretch the Low German with a few gestures as needed.

"Zacker," he began, riveting his gaze to lock the clod in his power, "it occurs to me that you've been lusting after my wife – a beautiful woman, I agree, but one for whom I've the utmost respect and love. I stand forever faithful, and in service to her, with support and protection in whatever way is necessary. Now, I reckon, in times past, perhaps more familiar to you, I'd simply have to beat you to a pulp or hang you from the nearest tree to defend her honor. *(Pause)* Would you like to discuss this uncontrolled, wanton desire you have for women, including your daughter, who is yet a child?" This he delivered while slowly and deliberately clenching and unclenching his fists.

Zacker looked immediately sober, although defensive. "That's how I am — always been that way," he offered, with ignorant pride.

"That's a lousy excuse for criminal behavior. You took your wife in violence and you've marked your girl likewise to covet her and destroy her life. These are the actions of a man who may desire women, but who hates them at his core," Chris hammered on. "What've you to say to that?"

"You can get off my land and take your people with you," he replied, belligerently, standing his ground, hands on hips.

"That so?" Chris countered, with a hint of a grin. "You happen to be squatting on land belonging to the citizens of the United States of America. Though, you've the right to be on it, you don't own it or anything you've put on it. You are a guest of your fellow Americans — that's assuming you are a citizen. Now, we *could* leave, right now, as you've requested and kind-heartedly return in the spring to bury you. Your choice."

Stubborn silence and a stony face was all Zacker could muster in return. Chris continued: "That settled, why do you hate women? Do you need to get even with women because of your mother?"

A twitch of Zacker's cheek reminded Chris of Thunder's withers in reaction to each test of his training — *a damn good metaphor for the current situation*, he had to admit. Thunder, the stallion amongst the mares, had been a bit of a blockhead himself.

"Did she beat you, Zacker?" he challenged. "Did she break the furniture over your thick head?" he went on, and on, and on … until a tear dropped out of Zacker's right eye, his shoulders sagged and his arms fell to his side. A half a tear was enough for Chris. He'd heard more than one family story of strong German mothers who had used violence to keep both boys and husband in line — for hatred of their own fathers. The opposite story — that of the controlling and abusive German patriarch — was the one Zacker was playing out. And it was all too common. Chris enlightened Zacker about the way those two patterns were forced to alternate generations, especially when people held fast to the old ways of thinking.

After that sank into Zacker's rock hard skull, Chris stepped around the front of Sassy, grabbing her lead, and let him have it up close and personal. "You've got a dangerous weapon dangling between your legs, son. You can let it rule your life or you can learn how to use it responsibly. You've fucked yourself a substantial graveyard up the rise and your woman's vitality is spent. You've the capacity in that weapon of yours to bring her life force — the vitality you lust after in my woman — or you can suck it right out of her. If you can't learn to use it with respect, and, one day, reverence, I'll be happy to hack it off — and Leah can tell you'll I'll have the misfortune to faint at the sight of the blood I let doing it." Chris paused, letting that sink in. "Alternatively, we could have her surgically remove it for the betterment of mankind."

Zacker instinctively grabbed his genitals. Chris crossed his arms in front of his chest and stood his ground waiting either to deflect a punch to the jaw or inwardly applaud another tear. He got the tear and a weak response. "How?"

"You're in luck, because I've a plan. We'll be taking the children off your hands for the winter, providing Trynel is able to get around the cabin by then," he raised a hand to Zacker's forthcoming protest. "Until that time, you'll keep your hands off your daughter, learning to respect her sovereign right to a life of her choosing. Women in our world are meant to be equal in every way to men, Zacker. You're living with 19th century thought and behavior. You'll be well stocked with supplies to make it through the winter together and this confiscation of your children will give you and Trynel the time to start over, with respect and love, if it's there. If you can't learn to support her in every way, defend her to the death, care for her as a loving partner, and release her to her own joys and sorrows in life, she'll be given the opportunity to leave you here alone and join her children in *New Avalon* in the spring. I'm not of a mind to let her be the seventh grave at the edge of the meadow.

"Furthermore, I'm happy to fill in where your own father failed for both you and Jürgen. And Leah is happy to model a well-loved woman to Trynel, Sissi and Zenzi. If you choose to look upon Leah as a sex object, it will cost you dearly. In addition you have nine good men here, all committed and loving partners, to be your brothers when you can measure up to them. Do we have a deal?" he asked, firmly.

"Do these men know about Sissi?" he asked, sheepishly but also acknowledging the weight of his crime within a community of good people.

"They do not. She shared her story with Leah and Nick in confidence, and Leah confided her sorrow to me — and there'll be no punishment to her for having done it. No one else needs to know until you're ready to talk about it. I can't say for sure if any of my brothers observed your lust for my wife. No one's spoken of it to me."

"Why do you want to take my children to your community?" he asked, not quite putting two and two together.

"To protect them from you, for one thing. It wouldn't surprise me if you've fucked the ewes. Beyond that, they'll have a chance at life. There's no life for them out here, Zacker. Be honest about that," he insisted.

"You're willing to teach me to be a good husband and father?" he asked.

"Until the snow flies, we'll practice the art of husbanding — a beginner's course. Then we'll see what rises up with the rebirth of nature in the spring. What you don't want to have is a pregnancy. I'll bring you a way to prevent that. Trynel hasn't the life force to bear another child — to raise or to bury. There you've got lesson one, respect for the dominion that is her body. It doesn't belong to you anymore than this property does. She must be willing in sex, not powerless to your dominance. Until Leah decides that Trynel's able to stand on her leg without any possibility of harm, you'll refrain from sex altogether and spend the time contemplating what we've talked about. Lesson two: Sex is a sacred act. We'll get to that another day. Let's get back to work now." Chris released his tension with an enormous shrug of his shoulders. He'd actually transported part of himself back to Tyrol to manage the language barrier and hoped he hadn't bungled it up in even a minor way.

Holly and Leah, both anxious to be back home, were the first to head out. That left Chris to bring up the rear and chat with the Rangers one at a time during the return trip. The men had accomplished an enormous amount. A number of log–length rounds of cedar had been rolled out into the woodcutting area and set on end for Zacker to split, as he could, and there were now two big piles of split wood to keep Sissi busy. That, and what Zacker needed to finish, would probably do for winter.

Tommy and Will looked at the interior of the house to see what improvements might be made. Tommy felt it not a huge project to bring water in from the spring with a small solar pump to assist the gravity flow. The incoming pipes would need winter insulation. A tap could be added on the food prep slab of wood against the back wall of the house with a dishpan under it. A single solar panel could provide several ceiling light bulbs, which would cut candle and oil lamp smoke, and conserve animal fat for cooking. Those improvements were added to the list with a hearth-cooking grill for pots or direct grilling and an inspection and cleaning of the chimney and flue in the form of simple demonstrations with instructions for Zacker to repeat twice a year.

Of all of the men, only Will mentioned his unease at the way in which Zacker had looked at Leah during the lunch break. He'd been her protecting male at *New Avalon* prior to Chris' return, and would likely always share that privilege with Chris. Will and Leah had a profound love for each other that Chris understood and nurtured. Like her relationship with Joel, there was something very deep and old at the root of it. He felt it for both of these men as well.

When the entourage came down the hill onto the horse trail, Jim Taylor and Sassy headed down valley, toward his place, along with Chris and Leah, who would check on Demetri and the children at the farmhouse. Everyone else turned north to *New Avalon* and the stable. After expressing their gratitude to Jim for his brotherly assistance, Leah and Chris turned into the drive of *New Avalon's* second original farmhouse. It was a typical square two-story farmhouse with a bedroom on the main floor along with a half-bath with shower, the kitchen, dining room and living room, and then three more bedrooms upstairs with a full bath and, on top of that, an attic. When Demetri opened the door to welcome them, they found the children, in the living room, decorating a fresh-cut fir tree for Christmas. They'd taken their first real bath, with head washing, under Shelley's supervision, leaving a profound ring in the tub and splashed water everywhere from all of the fun they'd had. After making haircut appointments for the kids with Demetri, Shelley had left for home, with a pile of filthy clothes to cleanup before Saturday.

The mothers in the community had pooled hand-me-down or borrowed kids' clothes they thought might fit Jürgen and Zenzi. To see them without their thick layers of homespun and skins confirmed what Leah had anticipated — general malnourishment with slight abdominal distention. She would give them thorough physical checkups at the clinic, later in the week. In the meantime, raw goat milk was a great place to begin rebuilding, and the community dinner a timely follow up. They were, otherwise, beautiful children of great clarity, luminous eyes and lively spirits.

Demetri was busy cooking a dish for the community dinner but had baked Greek anise biscuits that afternoon for tea with the women helpers. The children were enjoying the leftovers, with milk, while hanging natural ornaments made by the homeschool children on the tree. The house was filled with warmth from the woodstove and Demetri seemed relaxed and very much at home. He poured them each a glass of red while Chris stepped in to translate for the children and Demetri — to make sure they knew he'd be their caregiver, and to ask if they needed anything else. The children were very content, loved Demetri and is biscuits, but felt starved from the smell of roasting lamb coming from the oven. They'd be surprised at the food available to them at the dinner, where the roast was headed. Demetri had borrowed an electric cart to transport them back and forth until they got the lay of the land to walk, and maybe learn to ride bicycles.

Before Chris and Leah left, the children dragged them upstairs to see the bed they would share, with its big soft *doona* and pillows. They sat down on the bed with the children to see what they'd brought from home to share with the boys at the springs for wilderness show-and-tell. Zenzi had brought a rabbit she'd made from lamb pelt — the stitches sewn with her mother's one thick needle. *Needles — another 'bit and bob' Trynel would appreciate*, she thought, adding it to her mental list. Jürgen had made a bow from animal gut and a springy, but strong, sapling. His arrows were made from straight oak sticks, bird feathers and genuine Indian arrowheads he'd found out foraging. Chris was very impressed with their handiwork, and most interested in the arrowheads.

As the sun set, with the suddenness common to valley living, Chris and Leah had to be on their way to prepare Thai Beef Salad (*what else?*) for the dinner. Chris promised to take the kids to the stable for a ride on Cinnamon the next day after school. Rob had already agreed to come down the road to tutor English after his day ended at the studio. The children seemed to be happy with everything and immediately taken with Demetri, who was pleased with that report.

Leah felt her heart open wide to her Ruby Brother as he set about having his vicarious experience of parenting. Personally, she thought it a phenomenal match and would, perhaps, result in the kind of apprenticing Demetri had never dreamed possible. Jürgen and Zenzi, after all, had demonstrated some extraordinary skills of deception in the forest at their first meeting with Rob, Mike and Joel's kids.

She fell into silence on the ride home and at the stable, where Alex took Holly for her grooming. She walked home alone to get the salad going, while

Chris made sure all of the horses were properly groomed and fed. The Rangers had been thorough from the start to the finish of the workday. They'd be a hungry lot at community dinner. When he did get home, he went straight for the shower, noting Leah had done the same and was still lost in her soul's space. He came out with a dusky-purple towel wrapped at his hips whilst drying his hair with a hand towel. Ordinarily, this would have set off the Bee Mistress for a good bit of fun, but not tonight.

With this verification of her broody mood, and inward journey, he stepped up beside her charging energy into the back of her neck. Leah hung her head receiving his gift fully then dropped her knife and turned to sink into his bare chest, unleashing a torrent of tears.

"Aye, lass, let the rain pour down — drain the sky," he crooned. "You were in high service to humanity — impeccable as always, in all ways."

He rubbed her back and reached for the ever-handy tissues as she worked through the catharsis. She'd handled herself masterfully for a woman who spent the bulk of her time with the best of humanity. When the tears subsided, he raised her chin and kissed her forehead. *Zing!* The hint of a smile appeared, as he tickled her soul.

"Cowboy, how can being visually raped by a complete animal be high service to humanity?" she begged.

"Well, lass, it turns out there's merit in salvaging a fellow human who's teetering at the trailing edge of the bell curve."

"I won't argue that as duty, but I didn't do anything for him, cowboy. I'm not sure I did much for Trynel and I feel awful about having left Sissi there with him," she said, backing away to blow her nose.

"You wouldn't have known it lass, but you opened the door for me to begin a discourse — when you came out mid-afternoon for spring water. I'll admit you looked good to me for a roll in the hay at that point in the day," he said, with a grin, "but Zacker's tongue was hanging out far enough for me to grab it. And though it was full of lusty drool, I hung on and gave it a good twist."

She'd no choice but to giggle. "He'd end up in the animal kingdom if he fell?"

"Or between the worlds, just as Lucifer ended up between the world of angels and men. Angels aren't capable of physicality; Lucifer couldn't fall all the way — not true with humans and the animal kingdom. That's where the apes came from, remember?"

"I do remember that. I just never imagined encountering it. I gave Sissi 'morning after' pills, Cowboy."

She shouldn't need them. If she does, I volunteered you to saw off is pecker," he said, deadpan matter-of-factly.

"*Cowboy!* How could you?" she asked, genuinely aghast.

"Aye, I did tell him I'd do it myself, but it occurred to me that I'd probably go wobbly … so I offered your services," he said, with that grin of his.

"I could almost feel sorry for him."

"Nat. He is so thick I had to be graphic to get anything across. I think he'll come around. If not, I promised him we'd come back for Trynel in the spring and leave him to rot."

"Is that supposed to make me feel better?"

"I hadn't thought of that, lass. I was thinking it might make Trynel feel better, though."

"Well, I agree. It's good to have options when you've so little power."

The children fit right in at the community dinner, eating a great deal and trying all sorts of food they'd never seen before. After the meal, Zenzi wanted Chris to say something to Demetri for her, so came by their table where the two Ruby Brothers were having a chat over tea. Leah and Georgia paused in their conversation to listen in. Zenzi wanted Chris, Leah and Demetri to know that she and Sissi had both been with Demetri in a dream many sleeps ago, and that Leah had come to Sissi as an angel in a vision she'd had while praying for help to come. Sure she would come, Sissi waited for Leah, rather than sending the children on their own to *New Avalon*. They'd not foreseen Chris, making him the most wonderful surprise of all.

Demetri sent them into peels of laughter when he shared with them the details of the dream they'd been in *together*. Their sharing included big hugs and kisses for all of the adults and a swift return to play with the community children. who wanted to show them their classroom. Georgia was looking forward to having them in the school, certain that children of their obvious supersensible consciousness would pick up the language quickly.

Leah's Monday morning Skype session with Joel was a fun loving recap of his Thursday show wherein he admitted his conversion to community. After updating him about the *Woodland Folk*, for the benefit of Candace and Perry, she clicked the 'hang-up' icon completely free of the residual energy hanging around from her pivotal but unpleasant role in the Zacker affair. She went on to outline a strategy for pulling together the four sacrifices of Christ Jesus, four crucial stages of evolution for man and man's developing brain, and then the rainbow body correlation and implications. With good strategy and foundational information, she hoped to be ready to engage Chris in a meaningful discussion of the first sacrifice sometime during the week — ah well, most likely not until Saturday.

On Tuesday evening, the community meeting was an especially lively affair. Sonia began with the results of the food survey, which were no surprise. The consensus was to shorten the radius of what they considered local, grow as much of that outlying produce as they could, and make concessions for sugar, tea, coffee and chocolate as long as they were available through distributors in Sacramento. Everyone was positively oriented towards the proposed extra-tall greenhouses for citrus and avocado production, trusting that Sonia would figure it out. Climate change continued to make it more feasible in their sheltered, sunny valley.

Natalie condensed her reports on apprenticeship and teaching assignments for the Outreach projects and Will and Tommy gave a glowing report of the Inner City initiative in San Francisco. Chris' proposal of cottage industries was well received, and sparked an immediate discussion of a good many more possibilities. Natalie was scribbling hasty notes to guide Harmony Valley participant selection.

Demetri was given a rousing consensus *Yea!* on his move to the now bustling, old farmhouse and caretaking of the *Woodland Folk* children. Everyone had been down there to help out as they could. Finally, Nick's library proposal was approved without dissent and the tribe would think over his and Leah's idea that they become a baseline group for the new Rainbow Body medicine. They'd be ready for a discussion in January.

And then, Will got up to propose the active participation in sorting out *Social Threefolding* for *Harmony Valley* and its subsequent application to many other projects. A good discussion followed with Will, Natalie, Paula and Leah drawing examples of violations of the basic principles from present day news headlines. They weren't hard to identify. Everyone saw the need to hash it out for the homeless but also for themselves with an incoming second community. When all was said and done, the community had divided itself into the three spheres both to dramatize overstepping boundaries and defending them on the scale, and in the context, of a growing community. Will would head the judicial sphere with Leah, Mitch, Tommy, Ellia, Paula and Christina in his camp. Nick would head the cultural sphere for Georgia, Natalie, Katia, Stu, Chris, Demetri and Greg. The economic sphere would be under Bernie's leadership with Sam, Leslie, Jenny, Spence, Shelley, and Sonia participating. The small groups would meet to begin defining each sphere and how that would look in *Harmony Valley* before acting out some conflicts. They would work on it, as they could, through the holidays and begin discussions after the January community dinners, with a goal of coming up with rudimentary guidelines by the end of January.

Leah had nothing new to report other than the fact that the Christmas and New Years Saturday *Light on the Crisis* shows would be artful recaps of the most wondrous moments and themes of the past six months. The Christmas show theme would be *'gifting'* and the New Year's theme would be *'the best of 2011'*. Following a round of cheers and promises to meet in the theater for buttered popcorn to watch the two shows, she expressed her gratitude at so marvelous and magical a year, and her intent to give her all to grand-parenting over the holidays. She added a reminder for everyone that the selection process for their sister community at valley end would be the top priority for the January meeting.

Leslie, who was chairing the meeting, passed out a community events calendar for the holiday season.

- December 21: Dress rehearsal of the play.
- December 24: The presentation of the choir on Christmas Eve beginning with a children's event in the apiary at 7 pm.

the canary caper

• December 25: The presentation of *Oklahoma!* at 2 pm in the community room, followed in the evening by the community Christmas dinner.
• December 31: Preparation of the Three Kings BD prep, for those interested, 11:30 pm until 12:30 am (the hour encompassing the transition to the New Year)
• January 1, 2012: Home visitations and blessings on New Years' day, followed by the first Community dinner of the New Year.
• January 6: The stirring and application of the Three Kings BD prep to the land, for those interested in participating, beginning at 1 PM, on horseback, followed by a bonfire and ceremony.

Sonia enthusiastically described the Three Kings prep and application to the meeting attendees, and the urgency of applying it, given the continued desecration of Mother Earth and harm to the nature spirits. She sat down to a low rumble of conversation amongst community members and then Leslie, gavel in hand, asked if there were any further items for consideration before meeting's end.

Greg stood up rather gingerly apologizing for having been so engrossed in the meeting that he forgot what he was meant to present. Everyone laughed, as this was typical of Greg. He joined in the laughter, and then informed the group that those requesting WWOOFers get that information to him within the next week. He'd gather the data and put out an email of their needs and a submission editing date when he had all of them — hopefully at the next community meeting. Then he added that Gayle and Jim Taylor had made a decision about their readiness for community and would like to be considered for *New Avalon II*. Jim was scheduled to attend the Rangers meeting on Friday evening and admitted to Greg that the community effort to help the *Woodland Folk* had sealed the deal for him and Gayle. They were ready to negotiate their space in the community using their farm equity as full or partial payment for their home. Greg reminded them that the farmhouse could then be used for the new, combined school as had been previously suggested, by someone or other. Everyone laughed again, and gave a round of light applause to show their approval of Jim and Gayle's decision. Leah promised to give Jim and Gayle priority on the list. In the meantime she asked for a vote to include Jim and Gayle in the holiday festivities and received an easy consensus before the gavel fell.

The *Light on the Crisis* Saturday show topic, 'canaries in coalmines', lit a fire amongst all the staff, which spread across the courtyard to Will and Sam. By Wednesday the studio was full of canaries. Could there possibly be that many warning signs of disaster out there? Indeed. Leah saw an opportunity to *go local* that she couldn't pass up. Staff members were asked to thoroughly research areas of interest where canaries were appearing. For example, Will had been watching the commodities and bond markets, especially precious metals as they related to fiat currencies. Canaries were chirping loudly in the markets. Sam was keeping a close eye on inflation/deflation, the Federal

Reserve and their QE2 program, and the numbers rolling out of Washington regarding job growth, unemployment/underemployment and disability rosters, consumer spending, and the deficit. Natalie, naturally, was hyper-aware of the homeless crisis and hunger — right at home. Paula had already begun a yearlong campaign to track and tally the lies coming from the mouths of presidential hopefuls. She might need a bank of memory sticks to store and catalogue them on her computer. Matt had a keen interest in so-called entitlement program reforms, retirement fund raids and Ponzi schemes to milk the dwindling American middle class of any remaining wealth. There was much to be cautious about and much to consider, as the stage was set for 2012.

Leah proposed that on Thursday, after the taping session with Willow, she would interview the staff members about their research projects. These short videotapes would be used to introduce each topic to their panel on the Saturday show. Energy levels soared, experts were consulted by phone or Skype interview, computers in the studio and the tech room were working overtime cranking out data, and heads were put together to come up with short reports having huge impact. Each report was to end with a leading question for the panel. Ordinarily camera shy, Natalie reluctantly agreed to be filmed — a huge concession on behalf of the homeless — and the millennials were excitedly supporting each other through their first appearances on the air.

Seeking relief from the mayhem she'd created, Leah took off a bit early for her check-in with Nick at the clinic. He was with a patient in his chiropractic treatment room prompting Leah to take a seat at the front desk to go through messages and the mail. At the bottom of her pile of sorted mail, she found a parcel from Elliot Davis. It was a book, of course. Under the brown paper wrapper, she found he'd wrapped it up for Christmas and attached a gorgeous card – a watercolor painting of children around a Christmas tree in the ethereal style of art associated with Anthroposophy — and the soul. She would pass the card along to Mandy who would love it as much as she did. His message was brief.

"It feels time for you to read this, Leah. Don't wait for Christmas to open it — with much love, Elliot and Jan."

Leah felt the charge of the book as soon as she'd picked up the parcel. Archangel Michael's book would have to wait. While holding the still-wrapped gift, she took a deep breath and closed her eyes in meditation, in expectation of clairvoyantly connecting with Elliot Davis. Instead, she found herself in an intimate group of people listening to a dynamic speaker — undoubtedly Rudolf Steiner — lecture on ancient Lemuria. The vision faded. She could not hold that clairvoyant space because it was a spontaneous gift — a priceless gift. Whilst reading the book she was about to unwrap, Leah would hear his words once more in the context of the bigger picture. After wiping tears from her cheeks and the wrapping paper, she carefully unfastened the tape at one end of the parcel and pulled out *Cosmic Memory*.

Chris found her curled up in her chair halfway through chapter one when he arrived home for lunch. He looked at the title after giving her a warm kiss. "I thought you were going to wait on that one, lass?"

"Elliot knew better, cowboy. And, I had a nice affirmation from Dr. Steiner that it was time. I guess that was the meaning of the vision, at any rate. Unless I had actually been there in the lecture I found myself in." she added, curiously.

"That might be something to explore," he said, flopping onto the sofa.

"Too much cosmic love, last night?" she asked, raising an eyebrow.

He grinned, while gazing at the ceiling. "Not possible. I had to fill in for Greg with the WWOOFers to get hay out to cattle. He threw his back out and nabbed me on his way to Nick's."

"That explains why Nick missed our daily chat and I got a leg on this chapter. The energy at the studio is so extreme, I bailed," she giggled.

"Have you got some hotshot guest coming in this week?" he asked, curious about the excitement.

"Our guests are hardworking whistle blowers who never get press. No, I'm enlisting the staff to up the bar. They'll be asking the leading questions through taped reports on topics of interest to them and the panelists."

"You've got your whole staff on the air? Are you taking the day off?" he queried.

"No. I'll be in there for the bees. Why is it I'm the only one interested in bees?" she mused.

"That's not true, Goldilocks. You've got the three bears interested in bees," he laughed.

"Interested in destroying them. They're not on the bee's side."

"Sounds to me like you've given your young staffers a real opportunity to shine — nice Christmas gift, lass."

"And more delegating, for Dragon Lady. I like the way Joel gives the young investigative reporters a chance," she replied. "And, maybe I'm getting ready for spring, when we're likely to go daily," she reflected.

"There will be a crowd for the replay on Sunday. I'd better get there early," he smiled, drifting into a well-deserved nap.

"R-r-right," she drawled, directing her attention back to her book. He'd not be ready for lunch any time soon.

That night the community thespians and musicians rehearsed the last scene of Act II, Laurey and Curly's wedding. It is complicated by the appearance of Ali Hakim and Gert who were married shotgun–style, and Jud who attempts to kill Curly with a hidden knife. As Curly dodges the knife, Jud stumbles and fatally stabs himself. The wedding guests hold a trial for Curly at which evidence is presented, and he is acquitted. When the party resumes, Curly stands up from the wedding dinner for his solo of *Oklahoma!,* which leads into the whole cast version as everyone gets up to join in. At the end of this last scene, he and Laurey step out of the house to sprays of rice and confetti and are able to leave for their honeymoon in the surrey with the fringe on top while Ellia and her accompanists begin to play the grand finale. The non-musician cast returns for bows and the last round of *Oklahoma!*

It was a long rehearsal but one in which a great deal was accomplished. Chris drove the cast hard since they would be skipping Saturday rehearsal to help out the *Woodland Folk*. He was adding a rehearsal on Christmas Eve to make up for it. The Bee Mistress was in her mastery, having anticipated this wedding for some time. It was a good bit of fun, though the seamstresses once again pressed Leah to make a decision on her dress. Chris's role eased, allowing him to devote the lion's share of his time to the court scene, extracting as much sober, subtle humor from the actors as he could, and then to the choral arrangements at the end. Stu, Greg and Mitch had rigged up a battery-powered surrey much to everyone's amazement.

The two exhausted 'stars' of the show lay in bed together that night holding hands while settling in to sleep. Chris, sensing Leah midway between the alert state and sleep, squeezed her hand. "Where are you, lass?" he whispered, "right now."

He gave her a start. "I don't know, cowboy. I was somewhere. I wasn't asleep. I wasn't in a clairvoyant space, nor was I here."

"Remember anything?" he asked.

"Nothing, except that I really *was* someplace. Where was that place? Do you know?" she queried, raising herself up on her elbow to look in his eyes.

"I reckon you go there a lot, like you just did, lass."

"I think you're right, but why can't I retrieve anything?"

"Aye, your higher self is protecting you — until you're ready to enter consciously."

"Is that the etheric–elemental world?" she asked, sinking back into her pillow.

"It is. It can feel like a parallel reality but you can't remember details, just that you've been somewhere very much like here. You can feel deeply involved in living life there."

"Exactly. I do remember feeling that, and the sudden thrust back into this reality. So, I'm still protected and not ready to enter the etheric? Which, I assume is the earth's etheric accessed with my own etheric body?"

"Yes, no and yes," he chuckled.

"I'm ready?" she asked, just to be sure.

"It seems so. I wouldn't have been able to track you otherwise. Let me check out where Demetri is with this initiation. It might be time for both of you to pursue it. We could work together with him."

"That would be wonderful. I assume this is necessary for etheric mastery?"

"Of course, though he'll not be pursuing the experience clairvoyantly — at least not at the outset. We each have our gifts to help us build the bridge. Demetri is extraordinarily clairsentient. He really *felt* the dragon's fire when his teacher was training him."

"And, I suppose he really *felt* his brother's suicide," she said, lost in thought. Leah would have described her consciousness state, scientifically, as hypnagogic, but such terminology had no place in the work they'd be doing there. She felt immediately more comfortable about the pending challenge given the prospect of Demetri's participation. They snuggled up together, drifting easily into sleep.

It was Paula's task to review and edit the first drafts of everyone's 'canary in the coalmine' report. She sent most of them back for rewrites and passed the lot onto Leah by eleven o'clock the next morning. Leah, Stu, Leslie and Natalie had just finished reviewing the interview they'd taped with Joel for the show when he'd been in *New Avalon*. That 15-minute segment would be the hinge between the news and the panel discussion. A good many of his points were on the discussion table, but with his unique 'Joel spin' there'd be no repetition. The staff spent the afternoon in front of the camera with decent results, though a few nervous novices suffered the embarrassment of re-tapes. "All in the game," she assured them, calling it a wrap at five o'clock. They were ready for rehearsal the next day save the updated news analysis that Paula would hand her in the morning.

Chris was out the door to choir practice right after dinner that night. Leah wished them all a splendid time singing, cleaned up the kitchen, made a pot of *Melissa* tea, lit the fire and curled up in her chair with *Cosmic Memory*. She'd been anxious to get back to it all day — *more conflicts of interest*, she thought, with a smile. For some reason, Steiner had written the book himself, meaning that she was reading a good translation of his writing rather than a stenographer's recording of it, or worse yet, someone else's comprehension of yet another persons' notes of his lectures. Oddly, he'd started with Atlantis and gone backward in time through a transition period and then to Lemuria. As she continued to work through the book she would find that he'd arranged the book such that it defied common logic but activated memory in an amazing way. The information and terminology weren't easy to grasp, making her grateful for her youthful interest in Theosophy.

Leah made a pact with herself to read through the entire book once without picking up a pen to underline or take notes — nor would she discuss it. She would let it wash over her however it was meant to. When she heard Chris singing *Hark the Herald Angels* on his way to the front gate, she tucked the book into her knitting basket, and took up Mandy's doll.

The Saturday show launched a huge shift in consciousness amongst its viewers. In the end, they were asked to be watchful for signs of collapse and report them to a members-only, 'no comment' blog that Stu had set up on the website. It was called *Canary Sightings*. Working bloggers would become members — *Canary Watchers* — signed-in with emails, fictitious names, and committed to the project wholeheartedly. Others could follow on Twitter, Facebook and/or click on a weekly staff commentary newsletter entitled

Canary News at *Light on the Crisis.com* to get reports. The newsletter would report legitimate signs of collapse and the most poignant blog entries with staff comments. Their newly hired young staff would take on these projects, with veteran oversight, to hone their research skills. Paula's 'truth or lie' detection skills would be put to the test analyzing the blog comments before getting a genuine workout with the Republican primary season, which was already ramping up.

In other words, a discourse was to begin between those viewers who would become committed observers of the many and varied aspects of collapse and the show staff, while their whole viewing audience was able to engage on some level. It was, at once, the creation of an on-the-ground reporting team of some magnitude and an early warning system to monitor collapse through the observations of the most conscious and committed amongst their viewers. In announcing this at show's end, Leah made it clear that conspiracy theory had no place in this discourse, nor did profanity, lies, surly comments and personal opinions. Any such blog entry would be deleted, and the blogger would be banned. They were simply to report the facts like good journalists. *Wow! If they can all learn to operate within those guidelines they'd stand a good chance of attaining consciousness soul!* Leah marveled, to herself.

All of this bubbled forth from Stu on Friday morning as he was putting the show segments together. It sparked a profound discussion in the film department, which spilled out into the whole studio and on into cyberspace. It seemed like a great idea, especially since the studio would pick and chose what to comment about in the newsletter. They would let the blog members thumbs-up or thumbs-down their fellow bloggers' entries to preliminarily sort out their impact. This would give them a voice in return for their attentive investigations. Leah thought it a great exercise for both their young staff and the viewers, but was really taken with the grassroots level of participation being called into service. That was where all change began. The world needed truly conscious grass-rooters, and the show needed to report all of the news, especially the news that corporate-run media ignored.

The entire studio and banking staff journeyed over to The Lodge with their show guests, putting together a spontaneous luncheon and extended discussion about system collapse and those 'smarter-than-us' canaries. Leah kept notes to share with Joel during their Monday Skype session, listening carefully to the guests' local-level concerns.

Stu, motivated by the potential benefits of technology, had not, with the blog, intended to give them a measure of the impact they were having on their viewers, but so he had. Their blog would bind together an intelligent, progressive force to be reckoned with. For better or worse, he'd put foot soldiers and spies on the ground — and legions on Twitter and Facebook to lend their support. A movement began on December 10, 2011, and it had a life of its own. They did raise their glasses to acknowledge that magic was afoot.

Leah rode back to *New Avalon* in a daze. Alice was excited about their new adventure, the Bee Mistress was quietly tapping into destiny, Jane was recounting the varied odd and spontaneous ways that events had begun unfolding in *New Avalon* of late, and, curiously, Dragon Lady was nowhere to be found. *Just as well. May Archangel Michael bless and protect us all.*

Half the men, including Chris, were over the ridge helping out the *Woodland Folk* while the show was on the air. They'd taken Jürgen and Zenzi with them and expected to return before sundown. The children would come back with the other half of the Rangers, including Will and Stu, on Sunday when they took their turn helping out. Tommy would be over the ridge both days seeing to the water and solar installations and supervising the shed roofing, grill installation and chimney cleaning. The men wanted everything to be in place for winter by the next weekend so as not to interfere with visiting relatives for the holidays. It didn't look like they'd get any precipitation in December. However the one thing the weather was — was unpredictable. It was best to be ready for anything.

Leah dove right into her reading when she got home. After finishing the Lemuria chapter, she decided to map out a few ideas before moving forward. She gathered her notes and references for the four sacrifice research on the kitchen table and began imagining and noting what the characteristics and behavior of man might have been during the period of the first three sacrifices. Somewhere, in the midst of her absorption in the story, she remembered promising Leslie that she would, *absolutely*, remember to look into the wedding dress situation for the play, and let her know that evening, so Leslie and Katia could work on a new dress if need be, on Sunday. The chances of her remembering again were slim, so she took a break to do it.

Luggage, Christmas decorations, and a box full of children's games had to be pulled out before she could wedge herself into the end of the double-door closet to grasp the dress, which was stored in a cloth dress bag against the outer wall of the house. Leah pulled a clamp-on hook off the closet shelf and fitted it over the closet door with one hand. After hanging up the bag and dusting it a bit, she unzipped the front of the bag to slip it off the dress. She'd not beheld the dress since she'd returned from Peru with it. In the beginning it didn't seem necessary. In Chris' absence it would have been too painful. With his return, it seemed superfluous.

She removed the protective bag and felt, regardless of the outcome, that she would wash the bag before re-stowing the dress. She took the bag to the laundry basket and came back into the bedroom, flicking on the overhead spots for the closet to take a good look at the dress. It was luminous still — the lights picking up the facets of the tiny diamonds, which were splashed clear around the satin-like skirt, like the stars of the Milky Way. The many little rosebuds lining the plunging neck, the wrists, and hem had dried in place but were still faintly pink. Though she'd been curious about the composition of the fabric in Peru, she now knew that it wasn't from this world — and she'd no real need to know. It was charming how the passage of time shifted priorities and preferences. If her body had changed she imagined the dress would somehow accommodate it. After some long minutes of reflection while seated on the end of the bed, Leah deemed it necessary to take a shower and wash her hair before slipping into such a luminous gift. She might have been stalling. She might have been stalling all along — putting it off until such a late date. *Whatever!*

She emerged from the bathroom in bra and panties with her wavy blond hair partially dried. After unfastening the long row of tiny diamond buttons down the back of the dress, she stepped into the skirt and pulled the drop-waist bodice up around her. Her arms fit well into the long sleeves but she was only able to fasten two buttons at her waist and one at the neckline without assistance. It would have to do. *Pretty fancy for Laurey,* she mused, moving to look at herself in the wide bathroom mirror. As she flicked those lights on, and stood back from the mirror to have a look, the entire row of buttons fastened themselves and all of the rosebuds refreshed themselves to their original blooms. Except for her damp hair, she looked every bit an Arthurian Lady about to be wed.

Leah stared in the mirror, amazed. The dress fit perfectly. It was gorgeous — and way over the top for *Oklahoma!* Relaxing her eyes, deepening her vision, she tapped into a sequestered memory of her higher world marriage to Chris. She so thoroughly stepped forward to claim the entirety of the memory that when she and Chris stepped up together before Sananda and Lady Nada for the ceremony, in the great temple of the Kumaras, the sight of the Masters thrust her back into an interview with them, as Jeshua and Magdalen, in a beautiful Sapphire audience room where she'd been taken after arriving in the Great Central Sun. She found herself wearing the ruby red dress she'd been given to wear to the Ruby Order's meeting with the masters before the disc of the Sun. Leah had previously remembered sitting in the same chair from which Chris had just disappeared — the Siege Perilous, at the round table — and nothing beyond that moment until their return together.

She saw herself sitting at the feet of Jeshua (Lord Sananda), and Mary Magdalen (Lady Nada), receiving her mission. Leah listened to their every word, hoping she would return to earth reality with the memory intact this time. After that conversation with her beloved teachers was completely recalled, she found herself back again before them in the marriage ceremony in the wedding dress. Her last recollection was the glorious choir and their exit down the aisle of that unimaginably beautiful temple before re-entry into this reality. After their reunion with the Ruby Brothers, their circle rejoined the women, including Natalie, Sonia, Ellia and Georgia, who'd been holding sacred space for them. Had she missed something between their vows and that exit? Perhaps, but she grasped all she could, especially the sight of Lord Sananda and Lady Nada in their luminous robes and tall Kumara bodies — and Chris, so dashing in black with his ruby cape.

When the vision faded, she found herself in the living room, standing in front of the picture of their wedding day, when back in the Valley of the Blue Moon, which sat atop the secretaire. Tears of joy sprang from her eyes as she carefully recalled all she'd remember from the Siege Perilous to the exit from the temple and return to the Ruby Brothers sitting at the round table before the Sun disc. She held the picture to her heart and wept in gratitude for the recall of the most beautiful day of her life, which, surrender after surrender, had led to reunion with her beloved.

As if on cue, Chris burst through the back door, kicking off his boots to rush into the house looking for her. He stopped in his tracks as she whirled around reacting to the commotion. Then he fell to one knee as tears filled his eyes. He bowed his head in deep respect for his beloved and the two Masters who stood behind her.

"Oh Chris," she cried. "I've remembered our wedding and a wonderful meeting with Lady Nada and Lord Sananda before the marriage. Darling, I've remembered!" she cried. "You are Mana Sanar, my Lord of the Ruby."

Chris waited for the vision of the Masters to fade then came to gently wrap her up in his arms. "Aye, my lass, my Sanara. I'm so proud of you. Something profound must have happened to bring this about — not just the dress. In the midst of helping Tommy with the water project, I felt an urgent need to come home, figuring you were in some danger. Thunder is hitched up out back and the others will return in good stead."

"No need to worry, darling. I want to tell you all about it," she said, before returning his tender kisses.

"Our luck that we have the rest of the day and evening together to discover the whole of it." He hugged her and twirled her around, wiper her tears and then held her at arms length to look at her again. 'Laurey?" he asked.

"Heaven's no, cowboy!' she exclaimed, laughing. "I must change and make a quick run down to Leslie's to ask her to sew a dress for the play. Chris, this dress isn't even from this world. I must zip it back up in the bag to preserve it. We may live long enough to watch Mandy walk down the aisle in it."

"Of course, we will. Do you think the roses will come alive again for her?" he laughed, lifting her left hand to see the detail around the sleeve.

They both looked down at her wedding ring with its 'rivers of gold' wrapping around it. "This feels complete," she whispered, looking up into his eyes.

"Just one more for the Bee Mistress, remember? Do you suppose that was the trigger? We finally got to the wedding scene in the rehearsals?"

She squeezed his hand. "Wait until you hear about my last couple of days, cowboy. We'll need to sort a few things out to get to the bottom of this but I have some good hunches — and, such remarkable timing. Can you unbutton the back of this dress for me ... again?" she smiled, enchantingly. "I thought I would have to sneak over to Nat's and ask her to help me."

Chris laughed, remembering that night in Peru when they finally consummated their love. "With pleasure, my love. How did you get them buttoned?"

"I didn't. The dress button itself," she beamed.

Chris journeyed back to that day and unbuttoned the dress with reverence. He kissed her lightly on the neck and gave her a little push towards the hall.

"I'll take care of Thunder while you meet up with Leslie, lass. I'll meet you back here soon."

He was pulling his boot on when she screamed out in fright. He found her backed up against the wall in the hall, one hand to heart and the other pointing towards the bathroom floor. He rushed down the hall to protect her, sure there was some menacing spider, or worse, one of her fearsome snakes, in the bathroom. She was speechless and barely breathing. Crumpled on the floor of the bathroom, as if she'd just stepped out of it, was the ruby red dress that had been left behind in the world of the Kumaras.

"Shivers," he breathed. "You have got a story to tell me, Lass," he said, as she collapsed in his arms.

When she'd caught her breath and stilled her heart, he picked the dress up to look at it full length. "Made on planet earth," he laughed, with that crocked grin of his. "And, just in time for tango night, lass."

Leah's soul was replaying some sobering words spoken by Lord Sananda during their higher world wedding:

"I send you back to earth to snatch the pearl from the mouth of the dragon, for humanity and the planet."

Her body relaxed as she let out a big breath and looked in his dancing eyes. "I'm so grateful for your humor, cowboy. You bring the balance to my life, when I most need it."

Chris would be some time getting Thunder squared away, giving Leah plenty of space to tenderly hang both dresses in the closet, the wedding dress to await a clean storage bag and the red dress? Well, she'd see about trying to dance in a long slim skirt. She reckoned Chris was just balmy over the dress and it would be a short night. *Giggle.*

Before walking down to Leslie's house, she brought the Christmas ornament box out into the living room. There were decorations to be placed here and there around the house and her share of ornaments for the community center tree, which they would decorate during the Sunday dinner. The box of children's games had been saved from her childhood and rescued from the fire at the family home. David and Mandy would look for them on the bottom shelf of the bookcase. She tucked them into their holiday home there, removing her collection of Med School books for transport to the new clinic library. She noted that Chris was nearing the end of Nathan's last series of adventure stories — just in time for their arrival. Leah allowed a small excitement to begin building in her heart at the thought of being with them all again, in less than two weeks.

Leslie was relieved to have a decision on the dress and showed her the pattern they'd found through a period costume service. It was a full-length dress with petticoat and layered short overskirts front and back. The dress bodice went up to the neck with a standup choke collar, and had a laced overlay of the chest. The sleeves were puffed at the top and slim at the bottom. Leslie and Katia would use lace and beading to trim it up and attach an abbreviated bustle to the waist at the back. It looked quite authentic for the period but Leah worried it was too much trouble to go to for one show.

"All of the costumes will be used again, Leah, or they can be reworked. Don't forget Chris has *Carousel* in mind next," she laughed.

"Well, it has been fun, hasn't it?"

"It's been a blast! Your man showed up, with his bag of tricks, when we might have been getting a bit ho-hum with our good life. He's lit a fire that won't be going out any time soon."

"I can't argue with you, Leslie. It'll be nice when he gets that barn rigged up for theater. Maybe we'll do *Oklahoma!* again, with a proper stage one day."

"A great idea. So does this dress suit you, darling?"

"It's gorgeous, Leslie. Let's go for it."

"We'll need you to try it on for hemming at some point, but for now, you're free to go."

Leah gave Leslie a hug and put her coat on to walk home. Out front of Leslie's she ran into Nick who was hunting her down to give her a report on Trynel. He told her Chris was helping the men with the horses and would be home soon.

"Thanks, Nick. How *is* Trynel?" she asked as they began walking towards Nick and Georgia's house, the first on their side of the commons.

"She sends lots of love and gratitude, as does Sissi. Trynel was sitting up, eating well, had a little bloom in her cheeks from all the good food, and reported that she could feel the wounds healing and the bone knitting."

"Why am I not surprised?" she asked with a smile.

"She is an extraordinary woman, Leah. Her fever is gone but she'll finish the course of antibiotics as you suggested. The wound looked good with my normal vision and I'll be interested to hear what your sight picks up when you go over the ridge. I took more comfrey for poultices and for tea and gave Sissi the pain pills for you."

"It's amazing to me that she could feel bone knitting whilst on pain killers," she commented.

"They've backed off on them quite a bit. She would rather 'feel than not feel' — her words — and, apparently, she has a pretty high threshold for pain."

"She must. That sound really good, Nick. Thanks for tracking me down. Chris and I will go over on Wednesday. Did Sissi give you an idea of what they might want us to bring?"

He laughed. "Trynel is knitting sweaters as well as bones. You might bring her some yarn or dyed wool for felting. With her feet on vacation, her hands are working overtime," he laughed. "That and whatever food you think they could use. She didn't give me specifics."

"I'll send Chris with a list of questions tomorrow. I have a good stash of yarn and wool to send with him too."

They parted with a quick kiss on the cheek at his garden gate and Leah continued on home. Chris found her studying the big spread of her notes on the dining table when he returned. She'd put chicken in the oven to roast for Saturday dinner and had made a fresh pot of tea anticipating his return. When he'd showered and changed to clean jeans and a lightweight, black, V-neck sweater, he pulled a chair up next to her, poured a cuppa and asked how her inquiry was going.

"It's going well," she reported. "I would actually love to have a first chat about it tonight, if you're up for it."

"No worries. I'll take a power nap while you finish dinner. Shall we talk about your experience today as well?"

"Do you have time right now?" she asked, eager to get his take on it.

"Sure do, lass," he replied, getting up to move across from her. He insisted on full eye contact for important discussions. "You can start with the trigger, move to the recall and end with explaining how life set it up for you."

"R-r-right. Sounds like an interview, cowboy?" she laughed.

"I don't want you to leave anything out," he grinned, loving the idea of turning the tables on her.

"Okay then. The trigger wasn't the dress so much as seeing myself in the mirror *in* the dress after it was magically buttoned up and the roses bloomed. Where I arrived first in the recall was the marriage ceremony in a stunning temple, with a full house and Lord Sananda and Lady Nada officiating."

"Of course. That was where you showed up in the dress — like an angel of light, I might add."

"And *you*, dashing to the max, cowboy." She waved her hand in front of her heart as if to fan away the heat invoked with the memory. He laughed heartedly as she continued. "Well, anyway, it was when we stood together before them that I was taken further back in the experience to a private audience with them as Jeshua and Mary. This took place in another beautiful but smaller room not long after I arrived there, I reckon."

"I had a similar experience with them after time in a healing room getting accustomed to the higher realm," he offered.

"I have a vague recollection of that too, and it was Lady Nada who was helping me there. So, this audience was about my mission and how I had to go back to serve. On top of that being disappointing in the moment, I was required to surrender any attachment to your being part of it, but was assured I'd be well protected. There were words about the scope of the mission and mastery of the physical body. He said quite a bit about the Kumaras and how all those who he'd instilled with aspects of his Kumara self would need to fully ascend before he could. That worried me a great deal — all of it. Chris, I feel, definitely, that I'm running out of time to do that in this life. He seemed to indicate that it was necessary."

"Much to be said about that later, lass. Go on."

"Well, I agreed to what he said and the interview ended. I might add that I was in the red dress for that part of the recollection, and then I was back at our wedding in the wedding dress. The wedding was beautiful but, again, some very lofty expectation for mission accomplished. Can expectations like that change?" she asked.

"Later. How did it end?" he asked, pressing on.

"There was a fuzzy bit there. I do think there are parts I still cannot recollect. Be that as it may, we turned and, not looking back, as Lord Sananda instructed, left the temple midst an amazing choral presentation by the beings filling the temple. We walked out of the temple into a blue light that took us back to the inner sanctum of the Sun Temple in the Valley of the Blue Moon, where the Master Saint Germain and our Ruby Brothers greeted us. The rest I had good recall of prior to this experience. I came out of it holding our picture to my heart in the living room where you found me. I don't know how I got there."

"How much time passed, do you reckon?" he asked.

Leah had to think about that. She'd returned from the luncheon after three o'clock. "When did you arrive home, Chris?"

"That would have been around four-fifteen. Everyone else was back by sundown."

"Okay. I didn't remember to try on the dress until I'd launched into this work then I mucked around trying to get it out of the closet. Then I decided I needed to shower before I could put it on. I would have to guess that the actual recall was less than 15 minutes. My hair was still wet when you stormed in."

"You make it sound like the Marines," he grinned.

"You did seem on mission," she laughed.

"I was. I had my own chat with Lord Sananda while galloping through the forest. I set out on a strong intuitive hunch and he came along to validate it. Thunder knew the way back. It was the pitch of the trail down the hill from the spring that brought me out of it and nearly out of my saddle."

"Do tell!" she exclaimed, eyes wide.

"Lord Sananda urged me on. I do think he wanted me to find you in the dress and I'll admit it shifted something within my soul when I did. You were in your full Sanara presence, lass, the goal of all your hard work. And they were standing right behind you." She gasped. "We should both have hope renewed," he concluded.

"I *do*, as long as I keep my head out of the logistics," she smiled.

"That makes two of us," he conceded, with a grin.

"Was that the gist of it?" Leah asked.

"No, lass. And there will be more at a later date, but for the moment, he wanted me to know that a great deal has changed since we received those audiences and wise words on our wedding day. Mission is in flux, opposition has intensified, expectations have shifted, and the future is less certain than it had been. The dark forces have gained a massive level of control over the financial sector worldwide and are entering the realm of governments more fully through that control. The steady increases in global wealth inequality are a measure of their success for they'll first impoverish the majority of the people on earth … and then they'll destroy the class of 'so-called' superwealthy they have created."

"That and the presence of former bankers as heads of state … to what end, cowboy? Enslavement?" she pressed.

"Apparently it seemed the easiest way to curtail the evolution of consciousness through fear of survival," he replied.

"I thought the dark brotherhoods were on the same track as the rest of us but wanted to control the process of evolution. This is far more sinister."

"I didn't say the brotherhood, lass, I said the dark forces. They're quickly overcoming the dark brotherhood, defeating them at their own game handily and using them as puppets."

"What does this mean for the Ruby Order and our endeavors here, Chris?"

"For starters, I'm no longer on vacation," he began, drumming his fingers on the table. "It's obvious they're pulling some of the Order together here. We should expect more of that. Joel's apprenticeship and Demetri's presence are just a beginning. The other bit for you and I to get clear on is that Lord Sananda's references to expected mastery weren't meant in the concept of this reality's time. He speaks of the supersensory world — another thing entirely. This fight will go on for thousands of years, lass, with or without us being here. But, and it's a big 'but', the work we do now for the evolution of humanity will affect the outcome. Sure, the Order will course-correct as needed, but how the coming time of global collapse is framed is critical. It can lead to thousands of years of tortuous decline or thousands years of evolving empowerment."

Leah jumped up and began pacing back and forth. "I could feel this coming, cowboy. Certain things made no sense to me — like physical mastery in this lifetime. I can assure you that I'll not be stopped in the pursuit of my personal work but it does free me from a preoccupying concern. That will give me even more energy to move this mission forward. And I can see what you are talking about out there. What is happening in Greece is just the beginning. The power brokers will choke them out of every last bit of wealth. Their growing pile of bailout debt will enslave them. It's as if the Greeks, who birthed it all, are modeling the theft of democracy for the rest of us. And at the same time, consciousness is awakening, beliefs are shifting, and we cannot let this weaken our resolve to bring about great transformation during the collapse."

"And the Arab world?" he asked.

She stopped in her tracks to stare at him. "I won't even speak of it, Chris. I trust you're not going back there. I can see now the Destiny of America and how the core values set in place by our Founders are being twisted and contorted into a status quo more in keeping with the destiny hovering over Greece, Italy, Spain, and a growing number of other countries. It makes me wonder if the whole idea of the EU was a set-up. But, I'm not going conspiracy here — just the facts." She sat back down again and poured another cuppa for both of them. "That brings me to this glorious insurrection that took place at the studio yesterday and today," she grinned, rubbing her hands together.

"My curiosity is piqued by your obvious solidarity with this insurrection," he grinned. "Do tell."

"Stu pulled off a coup, though he never intended it that way," she smiled. "He had this stroke of genius to get our more astute viewers to start a blog of their observations of collapse — looking for the *canaries in the coalmine*

– the theme of today's show. The entire staff jumped onboard and helped him establish the guidelines to keep it in integrity. An e-newsletter will go out periodically to our mailing list with the best of the blog entries and our comments. Anyone can read the blogs but only members can post and vote. Everyone else can be 'vocal' on Facebook and Twitter. So no one is left out and we get the really observant folks to help us monitor the collapse. It's participatory. And, I have a strong intuition that it will evolve into first class investigative reporting. The staff will truth–check everything and maintain our control over the blog."

"But it does put reporters on the ground for you, right?" Chris interjected.

"Exactly — an army of them in every nook and cranny, cowboy."

"Brilliant. Couldn't be better timing I reckon. I wonder though, how you and Natalie can take on any more, lass. You two carry on with a mind-boggling number of projects already."

"Well that's where the coup came in. Our young staff snatched it right up. They're going to add it to their workload with a little oversight from us. Paula is keen to hone her truth meter and everyone was so turned on about being on the air reporting and questioning today that they don't want to stop. So they'll put the newsletter together and Natalie, Stu, Will and I will check it all out and sign off on it."

"I still don't get why you're call it a coup?" he asked.

"Dragon Lady would never have let this happen, cowboy. She had her back turned, or she's stuck in the elevator, or she bailed completely," she laughed.

"Maybe she's seen the light, lass. It makes me think it a good time to start that work with Demetri too ... if you're ready?" he added looking over his teacup at her.

"I'm ready to talk about it with the two of you. My instinct is to play it by ear with the children here for the holidays. I'd prefer to be in my body and in good humor for their visit," she smiled.

"We can't control it, lass. You've set it in motion with your intent. We'll see how and when it unfolds."

She stared at him, blank-faced, for a moment. "What does this work look like, cowboy?" she asked, hesitantly.

"Let's save that for our chat with Demetri," he suggested, reaching over the table to take her hand. "For the moment, just know I'll be there for you — and, if you're lucky, Dragon Lady will still be in her passive zone. For now, let's try to embody the experiences we had this afternoon. The recovery of your memory indicates a frequency shift for you, lass. There's a story there worthy of some investigative reporting."

"You're right, cowboy. I never thought past recovering the memory and all the bliss that came with it. I couldn't even tell you if it was the actual memory."

"How do you explain the presence of a sexy red dress hanging in our closet?"

Leah fell silent as she thought about that. "It must be time for your nap," she suggested.

"R-r-right," he drawled, pulling himself up from the table.

Leah returned to her notes as he made his way to the king's sofa. She was keen to have a short discussion about the first sacrifice after dinner. Investing more time in researching without Chris' input would be foolish. She was hoping he could fill in a few blanks and steer her in the right direction. She glanced up at the Golden Queen's altar in the niche whilst opening her soul to any streams of wisdom coming through the Bee Mistress.

chapter 8: democracy in peril

Chris built a fire in the hearth while she poured the wine. They settled into their discussion positions aware that they were still in very expanded awareness from their separate encounters with the higher worlds. Harry, who'd shown up for dinner, curled into his cuddle ball, next to Chris.

"It seems the perfect time to begin this discourse," he remarked, lifting his glass to toast with her.

"It does. I'm entering this exploration with a good many unknowns. May it prove fruitful for this community — in time," she proposed, reaching over to touch her glass to his. "Thank you, Chris, for helping me steady its course."

"Yeah, look, I'm eager to engage this with you, lass. It's a great project and I relish the opportunity to revisit the mysteries."

"I'll not push the river on this, cowboy. I've no intention of digging deeper than I'm able — taking it as it unfolds. I'm hoping it does open a door to more depth, though."

"Your intentions appear impeccable. What have you got there?" he asked, with the hint of a grin.

"I have to say, for starters, that everything I thought I knew about *The Fall* has either been trashed or radically revised whilst reading the first half of this book," she began, touching the book Elliot had sent her, which was resting in the knitting basket. "I reckon that was a good thing, but a real mind scrambler, especially considering the quest I'm on. That said; we have to start the story well ahead of *The Fall* with a slowly evolving epic journey that started in early Lemurian times. When this epoch began, we were animal-man, not entirely human as we are now. However there was also a separate animal kingdom. Man has always been man — more on that later.

"Tremendous and continual changes were happening on the earth all through this and the previous epochs, the Polarean and Hyperborean. There had been a traumatic shift in late Hyperborea when the sun, which was joined with the earth and moon at that time, extruded, causing adaptation to sunlight and an external source of heat. There were animals in body that adapted or went extinct because of that and our creator gods, the Elohim, worked with our ether-astral bodies to add the rudimentary sensory organs for light and sight. Mind you, I may be talking fiction here but am weaving in a lot written in the book, which was clairvoyantly researched and based on the ancient mysteries."

"It seems a good story, lass. I wouldn't worry about the fringe details so much as what was happening with the human line. Go on," Chris encouraged.

Leah sighed. "Thanks cowboy. Maybe this will get clearer over time and maybe seven or eight re-reads of the book," she smiled. "It seems, when Lemuria began, that there were mineral, plant and animal realms, which had all been adapting to the cooling and hardening of the planet. It was a slow process, which allowed this to occur. We also had animal-man bringing the human line forward from having been 'astral/animal' in moon time. I can actually get a good representation of that split with the animals with our old friend, the bell curve. In fact this really is the visual for the evolutionary process. Period. On 'Old Moon' — an evolutionary time prior to this earth journey during which we received our astral body — man was in a bell curve with the animals, we all lived 'Old Moon' as animal in ethereal–astral bodies. Those who had advanced spiritually were on the right of the bell curve, and those who lagged behind were on the left. This turns out to be a key to evolution. After we came to earth, those on the left sacrificed themselves to stay behind as animal and those on the right took a leap to become animal–man on a new bell curve. This would have previously happened when mineral sacrificed, staying behind while mineral-plant went forward and mineral began sustaining plant evolution on 'Old Sun'. A new bell curve was created for the plants. Subsequently, plant sacrificed, staying behind, while plant-animal went forward into animal evolution on 'Old Moon'. A bell curve was created for the animals and the mineral-consuming plants became their sustenance. In earth evolution, the astral–animals of our line sacrificed to allow man to go forward, initially as animal-man, who is still fully evolving into man today. The plant-eating animals offered themselves as sustenance for man, and evolution went forward. It's important to note that this lineage, still in existence, from mineral to plant to animal to man, is our lineage. Humanity was always there.

"So the minerals, plants and animals, each in their turn, densified on the hardening earth and quit evolving as each reached their limit of densification. There was much animal extinction, but many of the lower animals still exist at their halting places. That happened to the plants well before the animals experienced it and they became immobilized and rooted in the sustaining mineral world of earth. I have skimmed ahead enough in the book to know that the Polarean epoch would have had a Saturn imprint and upgrade of the mineral world, though huge hardening would occur further on as that world was established in physicality. Then the Hyperborean epoch, a Sun repeat, would have been a stabilization of the plants in physicality, and Lemuria was the time when the animals were transitioning. *The Fall*, by my reckoning, did not occur until the middle of the Lemurian epoch. Here is where I got an assemblage point tweak. One can't help imagining a sudden collapse when we encounter the words, *The Fall*, but, in fact, it was prolonged and a good many important events occurred within it.

"Celestially, the moon was extruding from the earth. I cannot wrap my head around this and imagine anything on earth surviving it. Maybe you can shed some light after this part of the story, but I find myself imagining this in a spiritual way, that the ether/astral body and spirit of the pre-existing moon was birthed of the earth, so to speak, and went out to form the body orbiting around the earth. When the sun extruded we weren't in bodies of substantiality yet and perhaps there was a similar process of extrusion, but then the moon was cast away by Jehovah (an Elohim), as the story goes, throughout the first half of the Lemurian epoch, when there were plants and animals in physicality — mind boggling," she exclaimed, looking his way.

"I think you can assume that most of the animals going forward weren't yet in physicality, lass," he said, soothingly, knowing she'd be anguished at the loss of diversity and life forms.

"Bless you, cowboy," she sighed. "I assume that we were all meant to experience some form of physicality here on earth but that it wasn't meant to be a full-on sensory experience. So, as the moon gradually extruded, the animals adapted, or didn't, and the bell curve began to spread out according to advancements through adaptation. Now here is a real piece of news — to me, at least. Apparently, our creators had given us a nervous system on 'Old Moon'. It was likely the energetic/etheric basis for our CNS, and would have guided the budding of the Reptilian brain during this adaptation process. It must have been intended to facilitate internal responses to the environment, but that's a guess. The other astonishing revelation is that the Superhuman Moon Gods and the half-human, half-Superhuman Sun Gods were advanced or ascended forms of humanity not originally from the angelic world to which the Moon Gods now belong. It also seems obvious that we don't ascend *en masse*. That's for further research.

"We arrived in Lemuria in a bell curve spread, wholly contained in the ethereal-astral realms with bodies of gas-like substantiality based on the Phantom, a perfected human template that had been gifted us during the 'Saturn' stage of earth consciousness and upgraded throughout all stages of our evolution. The Moon Gods (Superhumans wholly connected to Spirit, or we could say fully ascended humans who'd moved into the angelic realm) were at the far leading edge, followed by the Sun Gods, (half-human angels connected to Spirit and to Man or, I would venture to guess, striving to be both), then animal-man with some potential Spirit connection and on down the curve to the lower animals.

"Let me just add that after the sun extrusion at the end of the Hyperborean Epoch, animal man began being guided by the Moon Gods, our fully Ascended Masters, through a time called the Fire Mist, which went on until the end of the moon extrusion of the Lemurian epoch. They worked directly with man to instill within him the organs of thought and understanding — paving the way for our astral bodies to split, making room for the future intellect. During this time the Sun Gods could not influence this process of evolution — meaning that it was guided, impeccably, from the spiritual world, of which the Moon Gods were wholly a part. It should also be said that when the sun extruded, a huge spiritual family, including the Elohim, went with the sun. Christ, the Sun God, is the regent of the Elohim. The Elohim are a part of the Powers Hierarchy, the Spirits of Form — our creator gods. We grieved that loss and our frequency fell because of it, but they could no longer remain on earth. They continued, and likely still continue, to work with us from the Sun, Venus and, perhaps, other planet and stars.

"Then, at some point in the first half of Lemuria, a monumental event takes place. It's another evolutionary leap with the back end of the animal-man bell curve sacrificing to allow man (the leading part of the curve) to go forward with the Sun Gods in the lead. This happened in the spiritual world. The bell curve fractured, and from then on the animals spread out on their bell curve and man went forward, beginning a new bell curve with their ascending members leading (at that point just the Sun Gods). They'd cast down what would become the lower animals. With their fire mist mission completed, the Moon Gods were free to join the angels as ascended beings from our lineage (my assumption), but worked with us from spirit world to develop reproduction and nutrition/digestion connected with the lower half of the split astral body.

"Another stream going on over time was the transformation of reproduction from dividing ourselves into two, to an asexual budding off or birthing and nurturing of an immature offspring, which occurred in the fire mist times, and on to the division of the sexes, which was necessary in physicality and concomitant with the splitting of the astral body. This would have been previously initiated for the plants and then the lower animals as they began to harden into physicality. The Moon Gods oversaw reproduction in man and designed the sexual act as a spiritual practice — selfless service dedicated to the future of humanity and earth. I reckon all of this was in place prior to The Fall in bodies that were gradually feeling the densification that had hit the lower animals hard in more susceptible locations. Man was in a more protected environment than many of the animals."

Leah paused, to take a drink of her wine. "Sorry this is so long, cowboy. I find researching this complex hinge between this reality and spirit world to be more challenging than anything I've ever tackled."

"I understand, lass. There aren't a lot of toeholds. Just remember that toeholds in the maya are illusory. You are searching for the real deal — the truth." He'd had a sip of wine as well, but sunk back into the sofa closing his eyes again.

"A timely reminder, thank you. Onward ho!" she sighed. "Within a third but related stream, and simultaneous with the fracturing of the bell curve, man went forward with the more complex, split astral body I've been referencing, which translates as the addition of the intellectual mental body. This would have been another gradual evolutionary development in the rainbow body begun in the fire mist and carried forward. It's thought that even in those early Lemurian fire mist times, we began to experience death, reincarnation and karma when we began creating new humans from within rather than splitting ourselves in two. Souls were beginning a process of individuation likened to the branching of a tree. It's suggested that we were all one pool coming into earth evolution and that from that pool of group soul all the kingdoms of nature evolved with man instrumental in their creation — dull as we were. We might think of man embodying the lower forms of his tree even as these Sun and Moon Gods worked from within us. Why wouldn't the same process exemplified in our own creation be occurring for the lower of our hierarchy with our assistance? It seems to me that we would be to the highest animals as the Sun Gods are to us, and to the plants as the Moon Gods are to us — just a thought," she murmured. Chris grinned, didn't comment, but did give Harry a loving rub.

"With this astral split, we were distinguished from the animals because we possessed a mind. Our newly split astral body was immediately seized upon by the Sun Gods, who were attracted to our instrument of understanding. They took control of man's intellect, while the Moon Gods ruled the lower, emotional–astral body and, within it, the processes of digestion or metabolism and reproduction. The Moon Gods worked externally sending love out into the world through our lower astral body and the Sun Gods moved us within, bringing wisdom to our minds in the intellectual-astral body.

"In this semi-physical world, our brain began developing — surely beginning with the brain stem and Reptilian brain — to cap the etheric templated nervous system we'd already acquired on 'Old Moon'. I'm not certain I can say this is true, but it seems that these additions might have occurred in our etheric blueprint to be born out in the physical world over generations. Alternatively, we might imagine some gene manipulation, perhaps through viral DNA. At any rate, we spread our bell curve out again with the Sun Gods on the leading edge and a continual drop off at the trailing end as evolution proceeded through the moon extrusion. It must be noted that the Sun Gods, our precocious advanced guard, didn't receive the understanding gifted to us by the Moon Gods, in the fire mist time. I reckon that's why they seized control of our intellectual-mental bodies as soon as the fire mist period was complete and the split astral body made that possible.

"Man's developing personality was then controlled by the Sun Gods, who, *surprise*, are the Luciferic beings — the Bringers of Light. They'll complete their development through humanity's evolutionary process. In that way, we'll redeem them. That point in time, when the astral body split, the moon extruded, and we had to adapt to densification and cooling, was *The Fall* — when Lucifer rescued us and gave us freedom of choice and good and evil were born. The Luciferic beings caused us to turn our attention to things of the earth by stimulating those thoughts within us. It sounds like an ongoing, completely vicarious, experience for the Sun Gods who still haven't acquired the understanding of the Moon Gods. They're truly fallen angels and we've that same potential because of their actions. Our "I" holds no guarantee of impeccability. We must acquire it ourselves. We do have them as a reminder of spiritual loss, but that would only work if people really understood our relationship with them.

"When the moon finished extruding there was another great cooling and hardening on the planet. The Moon Gods worked with our lower being from the higher worlds, while the Sun Gods drew closer to the evolving physical reality into which we were being drawn. It must be said that they'd an ego investment in our minds as well. Perhaps that temptation led them to stage a great rescue of humanity by taking us to the moon and other planets when the hardening would have destroyed the forms we were embodying. The Spirits of Form/Powers/Elohim would have been working with prototypic bodies then and must have been doing that on other planets and the moon as well because, it's said, we experienced a physicality elsewhere before we were brought back to inhabit viable bodies on earth.

"And that was *The Fall*. It wasn't sudden but there was a time when all but the future prototypes of the human form had been destroyed. Had the Sun Gods not rescued us we might have hardened beyond the hope of future evolution and been stuck here incarnating into hardened bodies incapable of further brain development. It was their ego that caused our full descent, or *The Fall*, into the sensory world. Their eagerness to run ahead and push the flow of evolution caused them to falter and rebel against the "I" that could not err. It finds them trapped between our world and that of the angels, where the Moon Gods, dwell with the other angels. It also presents us with the option to bungle our own evolutionary journey, as we have received and must master our "I" beyond error ... or not.

"A slightly later complicating factor of that evacuation and return was that a good many on our bell curve were thrust down into the animal world because they'd no connection to spirit and/or bore bad breeding material for the rest of mankind who had, at least, some flicker of spirit–connection. So there was yet another bell curve fracturing and the higher mammals, described as man-like, fell, becoming the leading edge of the animal bell curve. I take man-like to mean they had a brain and similarly develop organ systems as man did then, and which they all do today. The lower animals and these mammals continued to evolve but the process was limited by the hardening, and comparable brain complexity with man never happened for them. Our evolving brain is our link to spirit. The previously thrust–down animals never experienced *The Fall*. I have no clue about the primates, in that regard. The animal's reality, which remains in *group soul*, is astral, which is a higher vibrational world than this world of physicality. In one chapter, I read that the ants and bees around us are organs, in this reality, of beings that exist at elevated consciousness — beyond the human experience. The *bien* is one such elevated consciousness.

"The aftermath of *The Fall* would have been extremely traumatizing despite the good work of the Powers to provide us with our soft malleable bodies and brains with frontal lobe potential. Still very animal-like, we engaged and spread out on our bell curve, reproducing like crazy — a best guess, based on the fact that the syphilis and gonorrhea miasms began then — until those frontal lobes began to bud in those of us traveling on the right side of the bell curve. Then the primates dropped off our bell curve as regressed humans to take the leading edge of the animal bell curve. After having caused *The Fall*, The Sun Gods, with Lucifer as their Regent, were no longer on our bell curve, and they have no access to the realm of the angels. As I indicated before, they're stuck between the hierarchies until redeemed by mankind. As you'd expect, Steiner did indicate that the evolutionary process is ongoing, pointing out that there are many savage humans still hanging on to our trailing tail. I'll refrain from mentioning names." Again, a grin emerged for a moment.

Chris grinned, but didn't open his eyes. "Let me just insert into this part of the story that in more evolved times, those falling off our bell curve have, like the Sun Gods, been caught between the worlds — as sub-humans. Keep that in mind as your research continues."

"*Shivers*. Will do, cowboy," she replied, scribbling some notes in the margins of her notebook. "That brings me to ask again when the first sacrifice of Christ Jesus, to stabilize our senses, took place. There are two conflicting options for this answer. It was written that animal–man was already erect in bodies not yet hardened, which would have been well ahead of what I just described as *The Fall*. The first sacrifice is honored when a child stands to walk. Though our *pre-Fall* forms weren't physical, they were erect, making that a possibility. However, I lean more to our return into denser physicality, when the senses were awakened in this physical world. We were then forced to inhabit carbon-based bodies (the volatile perfected phantom had been corrupted), which were subject to organic disease and death. In addition, the Elohim had sequestered the higher aspects of our etheric body in the spiritual realms, meaning we were minus our higher self — an archangelic consciousness (I believe), which would need to be regained through spiritual mastery.

"As a result, our souls, already cast onto the wheel of karma when the sexes divided, began to stumble and grow in wisdom by means of our own intellect and free will. I would suggest that this first sacrifice stabilized our growing sensory-neural system complex and made the sensory world bearable through neuropeptide and hormone feedback loops and a likely stabilization of the nadi–nerve trunk junction. I might add that it would have made life more enjoyable and promoted procreation. To man, it would have felt like a miracle that made sense out of chaos. He stood up amidst the maya and looked to the heavens, perhaps more aware of the intervention of the gods than anyone is now. It's likely, otherwise, that man's evolution would have ended right there on all fours, at least with the earth. *The Fall* definitely lies on Lucifer's and all of the Sun Gods' karmic shoulders. All of them could as easily have made the choice to be angels. That's free will for you," she suggested.

"And that's really simplistic, cowboy, but possibly close to the truth of it," she concluded. "It makes sense that the sacrifice occurred with the full descent into the physical world, though exactly when that happen, I've no idea — mid-Lemuria will have to do."

Chris, who'd been taking it all in with eyes closed and head resting on the back of the sofa, came back to life, sitting up to take a sip of wine.

"That was a big moment in human evolution, lass," he remarked. "Do you see the potential for patterns to form in the story ... as it goes on, or haven't you speculated about that?"

"I do. Just from the overview of the sacrifices that I'd read in the Fifth Gospel, I could see that each one corrected aberrations in a layer of the rainbow body. In fact, they went right up and out the rainbow body just as each epoch started with an upgrade of each body in that order — the order in which they'd been created."

"I reckon the hierarchies weren't expecting the Luciferic Sun Gods to have enough power to side-track evolution," he mused.

"It does seem that this first sacrifice facilitated an unexpected and immediate adaptation on the physical body level. Surely the split in the astral was intended as part of earth experience, and the need for the division of the sexes was foreseen and acted upon on the etheric/astral level. The impact of the sensory world on our nervous systems was unforeseen, and thus the intervention of the Divine," Leah added.

Chris nodded in agreement. "It puts a twist on the story to know that the so-called 'fallen angels' were humans who impetuously ran ahead of the bell curve, trying to catch their ascended Moon God brethren," he added. "Their fascination with our intellect, because they weren't with us to get a split astral body with a mind, and the temptation to explore that through us, won out over full angelhood. We can take that lesson to heart," he said, with the hint of a grin. "The angels have a different rainbow body anatomy than humans."

"R-r-right, cowboy," she drawled. "The other obvious pattern is the advancement of our brain, our connection to spirit. I reckon this sacrifice stabilized the neocortex as well, allowing the frontal lobes and neocortex to continue growing in humans while the primates kept what they had to varying degrees as they were lobbed off our bell curve. These lobes are what truly distinguish us from the rest of the animals. Realistically, we were only functional on a Limbic brain level and likely building the connection to the right hemisphere of the neocortex. There was no memory until later in Atlantis, which indicates that the hippocampus and amygdala, if present, weren't fully functional in Lemuria. The casting down of the primates seems to be concomitant with the end of brain advancement in the animal world. We've gone ahead with our brains expanding the neocortex and its frontals, and eventually adding the prefrontal lobes and, along with them, the spiritual-mental body somewhere along the way — a third layer of the astral with its potential to bridge to spirit."

"Aye. In your imagination, what do you think was going on at this time at the lower bridge, between the etheric and the soul?" he asked.

"Great question, cowboy. We know that the bridge exists in the higher animals though I don't know if they can overlap soul with body and live soulful lives in this reality. I doubt this, but the bridge is there because the higher animals express feelings. Furthermore, this bridge likely existed prior to *The Fall*, when we were in astral/etheric bodies of gradually increasing density. What came with *The Fall* was sensory stimulation in a carbon–based body. For this adaptation step, I vote for an upgrade to the *physical/etheric bridge* — the nadis — which made the connection to the nerve trunks essential for the feeding of animating life force into the physical body and, with that, the conduit for emotional impulses to move through the etheric and into the physical to stimulate the cascades within the hormonal and neuropeptide loops. We would have had glands, and the nodal points along the spine, where the neuropeptides are plentiful."

That makes sense, lass. I would imagine the sudden awakening of sensory organs would have been a real shocker for our primitive ancestors."

"It makes me think of certain movie trailers at the theater — visual and auditory over-stimulation is actually deafening our sensory responses to normal stimulation — Lucifer diving too deeply into the physical, for sure."

"They certainly get your attention, though," he laughed. "To get back to it, here, you have a pattern emerging with the rainbow body, the developing brain, and adaptation, no?"

"Yes, indeed. I'll make certain that I watch all three streams as I move on. Furthermore, I have a feeling that these sacrifices have meaning to us on the spiritual path in a more or less initiatory way. I've no real clue about that yet but I'm not very far into this research."

"Aye, that's a good stream to consider. You're aware that we ascend through the frequencies just as we acquired them in the story you're compiling. Then, in mastery, we work our way backward in partnership with spirit, mastering the physical body in the end. Keep your mind open to that paradox. The most challenging initiation will likely relate to our most ancient past as a reflection of our physicality and reclamation of the perfected phantom."

"Well we know that was one gift of the fourth sacrifice so all roads should be leading there. Furthermore, we can't expect to master the etheric without earning the reintegration of the higher self that's been sequestered. It looks like the rest of the book explores a past more ancient than Lemuria or even the ancient days before that. The next chapter is entitled *Saturn.*"

"Brilliant! Can't wait to see how you work that into your story. How are you doing with the four topics you set out to explore?"

"Hmmm," she hummed, turning to a tagged page in her notebook, "The first was human behavior before and after the sacrifice. To be honest, man before this sacrifice is a bit hard to imagine — maybe an ape-like creature on two imaginative 'feet', but without a real skeletal system and a complete prisoner of his out-of-whack senses. That's a challenge. Although, I don't doubt it. Accompanying this would be a widening stream of the mature right hemisphere's gifts of dreaming, creativity, intuition, and a fascination with novelty, which becomes the driving force of evolution and the potential of the new frontal lobes. That ability would be spread in a gradient across the bell curve. The strengths of the right hemisphere would, over time, support the maturation of the left hemisphere, which represents the intellectual–mental body in this reality. I'm sure we'll see this play out in the later sacrifices.

"Fetal development mirrors evolution, as does child development. If we draw from that, we can conjecture that *pre-Fall* man lived in a fantasy world, just like the child between birth and seven years of age. The maturing of the right hemisphere and the emotional-mental body coupled with the distinction of the intellectual-mental body that occurred with this first sacrifice would be similar to the leap a child makes at the seventh-year transition. This transition is celebrated by the emergence of their very own teeth and their very own sense of self — individuation.

"After the sacrifice, humanity — again with the gradient on a bell curve — has the brain capacity to remember dreams and experiences, the mature instinct to nurture the young, a drive to see what's over the next hill, and an emotional connection to each other — the incentive for community. He's upright, strong, curious, intuitively inclined with little retained knowledge, but he's productive both in progeny and the art of manifestation. I'm assuming the left hemisphere has its day in the Atlantean epoch. This Lemurian man is a great builder with increasingly useful opposable thumbs and primitive thought processes developing to go with them. I characterize this sacrifice as a crucial correction to the physical body to accommodate an evolutionary leap that rippled through the rainbow body, as it existed at that time. I have a lot more work ahead of me to get a deeper understanding of the gifts' significance."

"You've a powerhouse up in that intellectual-mental body of yours," he remarked, baffled at all he'd just heard. "What were your other points of investigation?"

Leah back-peddled through her trusty notebook to the tagged list she'd made not long ago. "*Esoteric initiations and the after death journey/initiatory journey* was number three, following the *before and after behavior of man*, and the *correlation of the dysfunction with evolution*. I've little to go on for the esoterics at this point but some leads. And, I hope to have a follow-up discussion with you quite soon about man's behavior later in Lemuria. Number four asked for *greater understanding of the Kumaras and Sananda's role*, which is obviously major, in this story of the sacrifices. There are likely some fascinating co-creative efforts between the Elohim of the Powers and the Kumaras. Honestly," she laughed, "after today, my Kumara plate is full — for the moment."

"I'll look forward to the esoteric research and would urge you to focus on the late stages of Lemurian when the advancing front of the human bell curve were gathered in one place for a kind of leadership training with their own ascending masters and higher beings. You've a nice platform for it there, lass. In the moment here, I'd like you to tell me how you imagine the Jesus being who heard humanity's call for help and petitioned the Sun God to use him as a vehicle for the redemption of our physical body?"

She sat there staring at him for a long moment. "Beautifully put, cowboy. You take my breath away. It's not challenging to imagine his compassion, but who was he really? Steiner mentions in passing in one book or another, that he was an 'Archangelic-like' being. We know he is a Kumara — now. We don't know if he was a Kumara then, but he is now. The Kumaras, as near as I can tell, are a branch of the Elohim associated with Venus (now). The Elohim are part of the hierarchy of Powers, the Spirits of Form, and our Creator Gods. We remember them from the story of Adam and Eve and the creation of our prototypic bodies.

"Being a Kumara puts him well-above Archangelic consciousness — now. That begs the question: Is it possible that he began this journey as an Archangel, who was ascending from the right end of their bell curve, and through his selfless sacrifices, became an Archai. Then, before the fourth sacrifice was embraced, he was elevated by the Elohim for his repeated selfless service to humanity. I could imagine that he became so integral to their success that the Kumaras, the planet tamers from Venus, embraced him as their own."

"Beauty, lass. Let's work with that big imagination of yours. It's got some meat on its bones," he grinned.

She dashed off a few notes. "Do you think I'm crazy for imagining that there's a connection between our past and our journey to spirit?"

"There is. Pay attention to the third hierarchy. You'll find we're all on the same road home, whether we are third or fourth, or have wings or brains or identical rainbow bodies. I reckon you'll get a bit of that in the rest of the book."

"Oh it's already there — and fascinating. I'm just on my first read. In what I've compiled here so far, we don't even have Ahriman's entry into our evolutionary story."

"I'm not sure when your finding the time to put all this together, lass, but I do appreciate it. You've got a show to put on every week and in my memory, which is brief, you used to devote your work week to that."

"Well, that's shifted, dramatically, with Paula. She is a real dream–come-true for me. What's more, this next show is the last before a nice break, and it's another show where we can draw in community — all about local food and local farming. I'm aiming to have the fourth sacrifice outlined by Christmas. It seems an important deadline for me, personally."

Chris got up to stir the fire again then stood behind her to apply a shoulder rub. She gave herself over to the much-needed relaxation.

"Have you got some ideas for our *Threefolding* role-playing tomorrow night?" he asked.

Leah tucked her notebook into her knitting basket alongside Mandy's doll, which was finished but naked. She took up a wee bit of knitting and answered is query. "I have too many ideas, cowboy! I want everyone to help out. What Lord Sananda told you about the near future should spur us on. It's easy to see the thick overlay of fear and insecurity shutting people down. The answer is community. The need is to break down the barriers and knit strong community from difference."

"*Harmony Valley* seems like a grand experiment in that regard, lass. We'll have the commonality of homelessness but as soon as they're comfortable, don't you reckon their past differences will prevail?" he asked.

"Of course. That's why we need to set up systems that protect them from failure. We need to knit community from their strengths not their weaknesses, and the project needs to succeed in everyway to provide a positive outlook for the future. They'll all have to take part in their government and culture as well as their economic success. When they do find prosperity, the will to put that back into the community has to be there. Alternatively, there needs to be an exit strategy in place. It's a grand experiment with a small chance of success if you look at the stats. We've got our work cut out for us."

"What do you think about instilling them with a greater purpose?" he asked. "*New Avalon's* success is tied to a common mission — granting a part of that is the community's survival."

"You're right, cowboy. It has to be more than a better, more secure life. I don't see how that can be assigned, though. While we continue to work with them, all of us will have to be on the lookout for the kind of strengths that lead to mission."

Chris returned to his seat at the end of the sofa again to finish his wine. "What are you knitting now, lass?" he asked, breaking the energy in response to a sudden and keen desire to move on to tango lessons. "I thought you'd finished the cardigan," he added.

"It's a sweater for the doll, mate," she laughed. "It won't take near as long."

"Aye, she'll look better with clothes. She's a beauty as she is, though — very soft energy."

"Okay, I get that you're ready to dance," she smiled, looking up from the knitting.

"Imagined a good many times with that dress on you, my beauty," he grinned.

"You win. But first, I'd like to apologize for my knee-jerk reaction to your having brought up the Middle East this afternoon, cowboy. That was inappropriate. If it's part of your new mission, so be it. You'd think they'd send some younger blood, though. I'm loving you being right here, where I can reach out and touch you every day."

Nay, lass, that's not my mission this time around. I do worry a bit about the explosive nature of the politics, though. It seems to have gone viral throughout the region."

"It was inevitable, I reckon, and then after you boys finished up over there? Well, you know the story. Anyone awake is worried about it. Did Lord Sananda give you a mission clue?" she prodded.

"Not a clue — an overview. Has Steiner been writing about the transitions between Lemurian and Atlantis and then between Atlantis and this epoch?" he asked.

"In detail. He was careful to point out that only a small band of inspired humans and masters — and in the old days, embodied hierarchy, which maybe were our ascended ones — fled to safe land and held the mysteries intact. They must have been extremely dedicated, hearty … and brave."

"Well, lass, we're to initiate that mission," he said, matter-of-factly.

"So soon?! Cowboy, there are over five thousand of years left in this epoch," she replied, noticeably alarmed.

"When you reread the book a second time, you'll likely see that the Semites of the Atlantean epoch preserved the mysteries for this epoch and they did it from precisely the epoch period we find ourselves in now. Most often, the integrity and evolutionary progress, which is steadily built to a high point during the epoch, corrupts as the epoch comes to closure. Epochs always end in the ultimate, appropriate version of cataclysmic collapse — a cleansing — and a return to the spiritual world for most everyone."

"I do remember something about that and will reread it before going on. What does this mean … and with a third of the incarnate Ruby Order actively engaged with *New Avalon?*" she asked.

"I've no clue about that serendipity. We'll rely on the Order for those logistics and assume responsibility for what happens on the ground. Those assigned to actually hold the mysteries are likened to warrior monks who know well the value of their keep. What we'll need to do is create a safe place on the planet for their lineage to sequester those wisdom teachings and mysteries for the future. We must assume that there's an imminent danger of their exposure — or that it's just time for them to relocate.

"Now, if you'd care to surrender to our redeemed human senses, why don't you hustle in there and put on that dress?"

"Okay, cowboy, one step at a time. It's good to know the big picture and I'm glad you'll be spinning energy here, for the time being. I'll now surrender to your irresistible offer of romance," she laughed, tucking the tiny sweater into her knitting bag.

Most everyone came to the rerun of the show that Sunday afternoon, and though Natalie good-naturedly took a bit of razzing, it turned out to be an excellent introduction of the studio's young staff to the larger community. They were all asked to stand up and take a bow at the end. Leah was not only pleased with their research and reporting skills, she was instilled with their enthusiasm such that the small worry she'd been harboring, about not being ready for a daily show come spring, completely dissipated.

Zenzi and Jürgen had been returned to Demetri by the second group of Rangers, who pretty much finished up with the improvements to the *Woodland Folk's* cabin, fencing, and food stores. The children burst into the community center excited to see their new friends, who were waiting for them before starting the line for dinner. Chris and Tommy had their heads together, catching up on the *Woodland Folk* project while Bernie, Nick and Will went over an objectives outline for the small group discussion of *Social Threefolding* in *Harmony Valley*. Leah and Natalie were communicating a loose format for the Melissae meeting on Tuesday evening to all of the women, including Paula. They would begin with a circle discussion, during which handcraft projects could be engaged as they talked and listened. Then there would be an unspecified need for yoga mats and meditation cushions after which they'd end with a sauna, sending Katia home to bed. She was sporting a nice little baby bump and that magical glow of a wholesome lifestyle pregnancy.

After dinner, the children played together in their classroom while the adults held their first group meetings on *Social Threefolding*. The aim was to come up with a comprehensive list of boundary conflicts that their sphere might imagine initiating to diminish the sovereignty of either of the other two spheres. They'd all been contemplating this during the week and agreed it had been a wonderful exercise to illuminate the boundaries of the spheres in *New Avalon*, where it had been natural to assume and respect them. *Harmony Valley* would be quite different and they all felt these thought processes and dramatic enactments would greatly assist with the expansion of their own community down valley.

Stu would interview the group members from each sphere in the next few days, giving them time to summarize the work from their small group meetings for the camera. That gave him the chance to participate in the moment. When they presented the dramatizations, he would film and follow up with interviews of those acting out the conflicts. He'd have plenty of material for Matt to work up an instructive video, which could be interspersed with theoretical conversations engaging Leah, Will, Natalie, and Tommy who were implementing the concepts. Leah suggested that Elliot might be called upon for a deeper, more experienced, perspective.

Bernie chaired an economic sphere group that included Leslie, Sam, Jenny, Shelley, Sonia and Spence. They were the equivalent of a small business sector in *New Avalon* with Sam as the link to the bank. Will had already established banking parameters whilst putting his proposals together for the Inner City banks and helped Sam adapt them to *Harmony Valley*. Sam took a few minutes to give an overview of the banking.

The bank would be a member-owned cooperative and all adults in the community would be equal shareholders. It was meant to serve the community through its services and through local investing of community savings and income. The bank would manage community funds in three divisions; an insurance, retirement and tax fund, an emergency, or rainy day, fund for the unforeseen, − both personal and community − and a community fund for maintenance, improvements, investment and expansion, etc. Decisions for funding would be by consensus approval within each sphere's governing circle and then by representative community approval. Currency would be similar to *New Avalon* with quarterly divestment of personal accounts and dispersal of demurrage currency to these three funds in proportion to their expected fixed and imagined needs. As such, the bank was a servicing bridge between the three spheres and not a member of any of them.

Will had laid out a broad outline indicating that each sphere would have a governing body of adequate size and representation akin to an elected board of directors or chamber of commerce or, for government, a legislature.

In addition, there would be representatives from each of those circles within a community Circle of Friends who would oversee the balance of the spheres. Within each sphere there would be smaller circles, or committees, to facilitate sub-sections of the spheres, for example, the schools, the greenhouse operations, the farm, the courts, security, medicine, housing and so forth. Formation of all representative circles would be from the bottom up through the democratic elective process, including, and especially, within the worker-owned cooperatives.

Bernie opened his circle to a discussion of possible infringements the economic sphere might impose on the cultural sphere. Spence proposed that the economic sphere, which is meant to be concerned with meeting community needs with the responsive flow of goods and services, might overstep its bounds by producing more or less than was needed. This would open up market manipulation and a surplus/scarcity model. Rather than a flow of goods and services, that could produce price fluctuations that did not reflect the actual value of the product or service.

This discussion went on to include the need for mobility in the work force to keep supplies and services fluxing with the needs. That would spark diversity and imagination in the workers who were, after all, the owners of their economic venture, especially with variable seasonal requirements.

Shelley wondered about commerce trying to influence the educational aspect of the cultural sphere to turn out more technically oriented workers while downplaying the humanities. Her query brought up a discussion about the current model countrywide, which was downplaying skills not related to corporate demands or recommendations.

They all wanted to make sure that the banking system served the people and that any community funds invested were with ethical, sustainable efforts that served humanity. Sam was sure Will had taken care of that in the bank's mission statement and board guidelines. The bank was meant to serve all of the spheres equitably.

How the economic sphere might overstep boundaries with the judicial sphere was all too apparent at local, state and national levels of government. The economic sphere must not lobby for gain, although their requests must be heard and answered. This might happen through manipulation of labor laws or assumption of greater overall influence through financial success, which might lead to arguments and demands for a greater cut of community funds. Any suggestions to privatize either the commons or aspects of the judicial sphere would be monitored and rejected by the governing body of the judicial sphere and the Circle of Friends.

Likewise, they would safeguard against the economic sphere coercing government to drop regulations that protect the other spheres. Leslie took comprehensive notes for the group discussion, which would be sent to all community members by email. For the next meeting, Bernie and Jenny would write up a rough draft of guidelines to keep the economic sphere in balance. Their consensus warning for the economic sphere was: Labor isn't a commodity. All economic endeavors will be worker owned and run cooperatives. Profits beyond a living wage are pooled into community endeavors and entitlements.

Nick chaired the cultural sphere team, while Greg took the notes. Their circle also included Georgia, Chris, Natalie, Katia, Stu and Demetri. They began by listing the different aspect of the commons as was originally intended in a democratic system. Firstly, it was stated that *Harmony Valley* was held in a Land Trust. That eliminated any ownership of land, even by the community, anywhere within the Land Trust bounds, which was all of the land donated by the Wilson's and a separate woodlot. As for aspects of the Commons, they came up with education, medicine, fire protection, security, parks and recreation, libraries, museums, arts, religion, neighborhoods, the community center & activities, the forests and environment, water, energy, and insurance with the right to provisions in the community plan for health care and engaged retirement.

It was also understood that this sphere would eventually manage the flow of members into and out of the community. This would include a way in which personal equity was built up, perhaps through a portion of an interest free 'mortgage' payment, not unlike Mitch and Katia's arrangement, that ensured a nest egg for those who chose to leave or retire in another part of *Harmony Valley*. Taxes on such earnings would have to be sequestered and paid at the time of withdrawal as well. All aspects of the commons would be free, as rights, to members of the community, who serve in their administration and defense so long as they remain in the community. When its systems became sustainable, its *Social Threefolding* spheres in proper balance, and its limits of growth reached, *Harmony Valley* would no longer need the non-profit shelter of Outreach and would, hopefully, become a model sustainable bottom-up town. The process, from inception to fulfillment of this expectation, should be meticulously documented.

The circle spent most of their allotted time defining the commons in detail. *Harmony Valley* wasn't a welfare or charity-based community. All adults would be encouraged to work in areas that fulfilled them at a common wage that would easily cover their needs. They felt that family and community size would limit itself through lack of pressure in a sustainable society and the physical boundaries of the land. However, it was an experimental community that would operate under an oversight board from *New Avalon* until well established. When looking at the ways in which the cultural sphere might overstep boundaries into the judicial or economic, it became apparent that the job of this sphere's citizens and managing board would be to protect the sphere from invasion by the other two spheres so long as all aspects of the commons remained free of charge. Keeping money and politics out of the commons, along with stringent oversight of the three community funds by the bank and board, were their key statements.

Will led the judicial sphere group with Ellia taking notes. Others in the group were Leah, Tommy, Mitch, Paula and Christina. They defined the sphere as one of elected governance, lawmaking and enforcement — including labor laws, regulations and deregulations, protection of human rights, due process and representation under the law, and, above all, service to the community. Guidelines were suggested to keep the economic sphere from influencing legislation in any way. Every elected legislator was also a member of the community cultural sphere with family members and friends (and perhaps themselves) in the economic sphere. Legislation would be made for the common good, protecting sphere sovereignty but without interference. One safeguard already in place was the bank's oversight of the three community funds. They would not be under the jurisdiction of the legislators but under the board of directors of the commons and the Circle of Friends, with bank protection of the funds.

The judicial sphere would respect economic enterprises while safeguarding the community and commons from economic sphere abuses, like contamination of the water or violation of workers rights laws. The legislators would set a fair price for power bought from the commons, space rental in buildings and the use of property belonging to the commons much as the studio contributed to the community funds in *New Avalon,* and petitioned the community for expansion and purchase of new equipment, hiring of new employees, and so forth.

The judicial sphere had no influence within the cultural sphere beyond its duties already stated. It wasn't meant to influence education, medicine, agriculture or the environment, for example, as was common on the state and national level. Concluding statements were made about keeping money out of politics, defending the rights of the community and its individuals, and enforcing the laws governing the community with due process. It was advised that each sphere watchdog the other two spheres for boundary oversteps. It was going to be a learning experience for everyone.

Will brought the discussions to a close by asking that each sphere come up with its own rules of governance and a kind of bill of rights, to define the boundaries of the sphere, by the next Sunday's meeting. They would take a break for the holidays and resume with a combined group discussion on January 8th. He granted that *Harmony Valley* would resemble a charity during its inception and initial cycles of growth. There was no way to avoid that, but he felt the way the model had proved itself in *New Avalon* bode well for the overall undertaking. For the moment, the selection process, in good hands with Natalie, held all of the possibilities for a bright future, although, realistically, there'd be problems aplenty.

At the studio, on Monday, after a good-humored Skype session centered on the canary coup, Leah and Joel taped two *Light on the Crisis* interviews with Stu and Rob. The first, to be aired that Saturday, followed the theme 'think globally, eat locally', with a close look at how GMOs come into play on the dinner table. The second, for the January 7th show, would fit a theme that was forming around 'what you can do'. That show would draw attention to carbon footprints, backyard gardens and apiaries, ways to make your home energy more efficient and some exemplary examples of individual and community change.

Natalie spent the morning at the bank, going over her plan for interviews and spiritual work in San Francisco with Will. The new year would be a big one for Outreach and she wanted Will to help her come up with a format that would work in any Inner City project, with or without her. She returned to the studio to find Leah at her desk listening to Paula's plan for 2012. They invited Natalie to pull up a chair and join them. In addition to her newsroom duties and participation in the canary blog, Paula was pitching her fact-checking idea to Leah. If there was one thing *Light on the Crisis* stood for, above all others, it was speaking truth. As long as she was monitoring all news sources in the US, al Jazeera and the BBC, Paula was proposing that they subscribe to a number of data compilation and archival news sites as resources to fact-check the politicians as the 2012 election season unfolded. She knew Leah wasn't interested in engaging the political races in the same way Joel intended to, but she thought it useful for the blog, where their viewer canary sightings would have to be verified, and for occasional special interest slots on the show where truth was in question.

Natalie couldn't believe Paula actually *wanted* to take on such a big project — an indication that she'd not got to know Paula very well yet. Leah, who was in favor of the idea, questioned Paula in a way that honored her apprenticeship, while it gently revealed more of Paula's depth of spirit. She'd obviously been brought up with moral discernment and a willingness to put herself on the line for truth. They learned that her dad had been a Montana state senator for thirty years, before a shocking defeat at the hands of big money and a smooth-talking, forked-tongued liar with an agenda that would open protected state lands to big oil and gas. Paula had lived through those lies — had felt the power of money crush the truth. Her father took his defeat graciously, while a warrior for the truth and light was birthed within his daughter.

"This is a big undertaking, Paula," Leah pointed out, "and I do see how it dovetails with your news duties, but I can't quite envision the final product."

"Right. Well, I see two avenues at the moment for this endeavor. Firstly, we have to check what our canary spotters are reporting. We do have the thumbs up and down vote of the other bloggers and the facebook and twitter input from the public at large, but if we're going to keep the post and comment on it, we'd better make sure it's true for the sake of our own integrity."

"Agreed. And, there will be a number of us to sign off on it. You might want to consider tracking the valid sightings to get a pattern of collapse for the systems observed."

"Yep … thought of that one. Matt and I are looking at a way to write a program to help piece that map together. As for reporting the facts versus the lies, it ought to happen the week that the lies were spoken or written — so, on a weekly basis. It might actually be helpful to have archived videotapes of these lies and political gaffs for future reference on the show. I think the column in the e-newsletter and the show segment should be call *Oh, Really?"*

"I love it!" Natalie laughed. "I think it will fly, Leah."

"I do, too, Nat," Leah said, cautiously. "But let's see how it looks before we give you the go ahead, Paula. Why don't you get to work on it and have Rob make a film clip for us? The Republican presidential race is already beginning amidst a good many questionable claims to fame."

"Fair enough," Paula beamed. "That should be fun to put together. We'll get on it," she said, getting up to go. "Thanks, Leah — and Natalie. You won't regret it."

"I know that for a fact," Leah agreed.

After Paula had dashed out, Leah turned her attention to Natalie. "What's on your mind, sister?" she asked.

"Dog-sit?" she queried, with a broad smile.

"Of course. Harry's like our foster child as it is," Leah laughed. "What have you got planned, if I might ask?"

"A New Year's Eve ball in San Francisco with Chuck. It's a big yearly fundraiser for the Democrats and he'd like to have me on his arm for it this year. We've not ironed out the plans yet, but, somehow, I'll need to find a dress," she said, cheerfully.

"Your first official function with Chuck, Nat. This is big — and you'll stay at his home in Palo Alto?" she asked, so happy for her best friend.

"We will. We do want to be back up here for New Years Day and the house blessings, so it will be a short trip down to the Bay Area."

"We haven't any studio pressure during the holidays, Nat. Take as much time as you want. Joel takes the week off for family so we don't even have that interview to worry about. And Harry, as you know, is most welcome to stay with us."

"Okay. I'll let Chuck know. We'll see how his other obligations unfold. He already has his flight back to DC from Medford, so we'll round-trip it down to San Francisco. After Christmas day our community activities have a little lull too."

"That's right, and Mandy and David will be here to keep Harry on the go."

"How is your big research project going?" Natalie asked, eying the stack of notebook, book and papers on Leah's desk.

"Which one?" she laughed. "I'm looking into some new medical models at the same time I'm knee deep in human evolution and the role of Christ Jesus in it. I'm not certain where any of it's going, or even why I'm so interested in the latter project, but it feels important for me and for the Melissae."

"Will we hear something of it in circle tomorrow night?" Natalie asked.

"Too many missing pieces at this point, Nat. In fact, I'm going to have a good chat with Elliot after lunch about it, and leave early to get a leg on the next bit of research — choir practice for the rest of you, remember?"

"With pleasure. Chris is amazingly gifted with voice and music — well, what's he not gifted with?" she pondered.

"He couldn't make a decent Anzac bikkie — even if his life depended on it," she whispered, as if giving away a deep, dark secret.

"He's lucky he can get away with eating them," she whispered back, getting up to leave.

"That's where his extraordinary discipline comes into play," she laughed.

After lunch, Leah applied herself to the show outline and had a brief chat with Natalie about the guests — all local farmers, including their favorite purveyors of Zinfandel, Max and Julia Cummings. The last live show of the year was going to be informative, casual and, likely, a lot of fun. Feeling quite good about that, and with two Joel interviews on tape, Leah took a little time out to go over her notes on the four sacrifices of Christ Jesus before placing her pre-arranged call to Elliot Davis. She was sure he'd add color to her vision of the past. When home for lunch, she'd lit a candle on the altar of the Golden Queen requesting that she hold a good space for their conversation, and had asked Chris to do the same. He'd been working on his project all morning at the kitchen table and planned to spend the afternoon at the stable.

Following a brief catch-up with each other, she gave Elliot a concise summary of what she'd discussed with Chris about the sacrifice during the Lemurian epoch. When done, she assured Elliot that she'd a good many puzzle pieces to fit into the big picture and admitted that the scope of the project was giving her reservations. As a neophyte she felt completely out of her element save for her passionate interest in the puzzle itself.

"You're not a narrow thinker, Leah," Elliot began, with a chuckle. "You are on the right track and, frankly, the correlation with brain development, though a cornerstone of evolution, seems never to make it into written or spoken thought about these sacrifices. I encourage you to continue that trajectory of thinking, as it will likely be fruitful."

"I will, Elliot. The phases of childhood that are so well developed in your society and the Waldorf school curriculum correlate beautifully with embryogenesis and brain development. And, embryogenesis and child development retrace our evolutionary journey each time we incarnate."

"Quite so. What feelings do you have about the missing pieces then?" he asked.

"Mine is the 'forest for the trees' dilemma, Elliot. It feels right under my nose. I've yet to get a good handle on the previous forms of earth — Moon, Sun and Saturn — but feel it has to do with those ancient incarnations of earth and how this story is a reflection of those long ago times as we surely bear them within our rainbow bodies. Does that make any sense?" she asked, trying not to cross over her own tracks, causing further confusion.

Elliot was right with her. "I can think of more books to send you, Leah, but try to digest the end of *Cosmic Memory* first," he advised. "Read it a number of times. What I'll do is give you the essence of one lecture in a book I have in my mind for you next. Dr. Steiner loved to speak of this Christ mystery around Christmas time — like now — and in this series of lectures, he built up his rhetoric, adding subtleties, to open the flower fully in the last lecture."

"I'm wild with anticipation, Elliot," she replied, adjusting her ear buds. Then taking up pen to paper, she awaited his thoughts.

He took some time, putting those thoughts together before speaking again. "In the third sentence of this lecture Dr. Steiner suggests ... *we need a school of selflessness for our culture.* That's your clue. Follow it through the four sacrifices as you research, using the following ideas to form the basis for your reasoning.

"The first sacrifice became necessary because, as you correctly stated, our senses were thrown into a state of agonizing hypersensitivity. Now consider man at the time, still animal-like and in image consciousness, remembering that up until the more recent time when the "I" descended, we really had no feelings or thoughts of self or ego even though, through all those many millennia, those soul capacities did develop. Early on, we had selfish desire and as our consciousness ascended into the intellect, we had selfish thoughts aplenty. Later in Atlantis we had an emerging sense of self but it wasn't really our true "I". It's the true "I" that draws our higher self to us. That potential did not exist until our present epoch. Does that make sense?" he asked.

"Absolutely, Elliot. I recognize that false sense of self as a kind of cultural "I". Go on, please," she replied, quietly.

"Into this rational sort of development, or adaptation to the world of physicality, we must not forget how we got here. It would never have been necessary had Lucifer not become invested in our proximity to the material world, driven by his desire for a vicarious experience of being truly human. This opportunity was denied him on Old Moon for his brazen and rebellious behavior in freedom questing and, frankly, really bad timing on his part. He ensouls a kind of arrogance that you will find in the cultural "I" of which you speak. As a consequence we fell into deep materiality and he and his legions have helped us and meddled with us since. What Lucifer wasn't mature enough to acquire impeccably in Old Moon time, we were meant to receive in this Earth time — the true "I". And we have received it, but within a world corrupted by his and Ahriman's presence — a world in which evil and error exist. At the moments of these four sacrifices, humanity, though growing in awareness over time, wasn't conscious enough to resist their self-serving vicarious experiences."

"And what were those experiences, Elliot?" she asked, sure that she'd missed the point completely.

"They've not the ability to tamper with the holy space of the True "I" within consciousness soul, Leah. In fact, that holy space, our sanctuary of higher self, was sequestered in spirit by the Elohim, because they knew it would become vulnerable to the interference of Lucifer and Ahriman as humanity evolved. It was restored to us, as a potential, with that sanctity, upon the fourth sacrifice when the "I" itself was in jeopardy. I trust these thoughts are already working in your soul, Leah. What I would ask you to consider is the nature of their quest with humanity. In their own ways, they desired to experience being human. Lucifer's desire drove him deep into our physicality — deep into our senses. Then, in early Atlantis, they both (and I speak metaphorically of their legions of followers and their overall consciousness) worked their way into our etheric bodies. In later Atlantis, Ahriman, the prince of black magic, tried to possess our soul faculties, and finally in Roman times, when the "I" was fully coming to us, they would have seized upon it."

"And each time, the Jesus Being embodied the Christ and sacrificed himself to prevent it?" she added, not certain she was correct.

"Yes. However, our adversaries weren't without some success. A good many humans were thrust downward in evolution due to their actions and that's ongoing. There are many, actually most, who unconsciously embody the false "I" as their true "I" and are subject to their influences. We were restored to the possibility of using free will to find our way home but obstacles were built into the journey by these opportunistic beings. And, I'm not saying that it wasn't meant to be. It was and is. And, they've brought us great gifts as well. Now it's for you to define what remains of them within us, and to find the commonality they brought to these assaults on humanity. Good comes of it, but at what price?"

Leah sat back in her chair, allowing what he'd said to wash over her. "Elliot, Ahriman is a high being from what I understand."

"Correct. He operates from the eighth sphere."

"He would have an "I" incapable of error, if I understand what I have read thus far."

"Indeed. *The Fall of humans by Lucifer's actions, is Ahriman's karma.* I believe that's a direct quote from Dr Steiner. Ahriman was a necessary counterforce to Lucifer in this state of materiality."

"Yes. I do recollect reading that and observe that polarity within the rainbow body — that delicate balance that maintains health," she said, recalling the battle for Demetri. "And, Lucifer received an "I" but, by his choice to turn away from the divine plan, it was corrupted and fully capable of error — enter good and evil. Correct?"

"Correct. He fell, along with his legions. Do keep in mind that he hasn't a brain."

"The human ego was forming much like a child's during these ancient times. I can imagine it being naïve and vulnerable to Luciferic selfish desire and ill intent. Could it be that they used their corrupt egos to knock our intellects off course? That could be a powerful means of intervention. What would happen to a dog, for example if we forced our "I" into their soul? Especially if we had an "I" with no moral fortitude?"

Elliot chuckled. "I'll leave you with that, Leah. I dare say Dr. Steiner would have welcomed a good chat with you."

"Who's to say he hasn't had one, in the depths of dreamless sleep?" she laughed. "Thank you, Elliot. This has opened up new avenues of thought for me. I'll run this all past you again when I've come through the fourth sacrifice with my research."

"Any time, Leah."

"Do have a lovely Christmas celebration, Elliot, and give our love to Jan."

"Thank you, my dear. And you must convey our blessings and good cheer to your community."

"I will. Blessed be, Elliot."

Leah pulled out her ear buds and swiveled around to stare out the window at the forested ridge rising along the road. Her thoughts were racing. *If Lucifer's desire to experience the material world inspired him to thrust his ego into our physicality at The Fall, what would that look like? What would it feel like? Could we start with over-stimulation of the senses, perhaps? Did the senses take on his extreme egocentric selfishness? No wonder we need a school of selflessness. We would have been weeping and gnashing our teeth trying to get the attention of the hierarchies to help us. And, who heard us? Jesus – an archangelic-like being imbued with selflessness and a desire to serve humanity. Did He petition the Lord of the Sun to use his being as an instrument of our salvation? It would not, in the least, surprise me.*

When he arrived home, Chris found Leah bent over her work at the kitchen table. He peered over her shoulder to see a series of bell curves plotted along the path of human evolution – a good guess. He nuzzled into her neck with a good many kisses until she dropped her pencil in a fit of giggles.

"I'll spare you my icy hands, lass, but I'll be back after a hot shower."

"Great, then we can leave Thunder out of the equation," she laughed.

"Not Thunder, but I get the point. I was seeing to Moonshine's comforts. Expectant mothers have high priority in *New Avalon*. We're starting to bring her in early on the cold nights with good hay and a handful of oats. That brings Katia to mind. How's she going?"

"Quite well. She'll have a healthy baby and we can hope for an easy delivery, but you never know. When do you start calving for her?"

"She's got the girls spaced out starting in February – could be some all-nighters but a lot more fun that hunting down mongrels."

"Don't remind me. I hope you'll have some wind-down time tonight to hear my final bit on the Lemurian rescue of mankind."

"I'd love to hear it. That reminds me. I'll be spending tomorrow afternoon at the piano in the community center working on the play, if you'd care to join me for a duet or two."

"Hmmm. That's probably a good idea. We'll barely have time to fit in dinner on Wednesday before rehearsal. Okay, cowboy, into the shower. I'll be chopping stir-fry veggies when you're done. I don't want you to be late for choir."

Chris gave her a quick rub on the shoulders and a zing of a kiss on her forehead before heading for the shower. By agreement, they'd not discussed going over to the *Woodland Folk* to check on Trynel on Wednesday. He was glad to know it was on her mind and schedule, though.

After he left for choir, Leah continued to apply herself to the interwoven picture of the first sacrifice, until, exhausted, she ran a bath for a good meditative soak. While sinking in and out of *Melissa*-scented bubbles, she found herself sinking in and out of that in-between elemental world, again, without a single retrieved memory. Then, after falling sound asleep several times for a second or so, she finished her bath, slipped into her robe and whispered a short request for clarity as she passed the Golden Queen's burning candle on the way to the living room. She absently lit the fire that Chris had set for her and flopped down in her chair to await his return.

How did she feel? Odd. *Have I become so obsessed with this search for truth that I've lost the light-hearted magic of life?* She asked herself. It was winter, a time for deep introspection and this sort of project was well within her mental capabilities if not her spiritual depths. *What is it then — this agitation I feel deep within, like a ticking clock? Is that White Rabbit back again?* Honestly, Leah felt like her well-directed research was helping her avoid something — something that felt like a gathering storm. It gripped her heart with dread. *Where is vision when you need it?* She demanded. She would have clear sight for those she loved. That wasn't a concern. It didn't feel like social uprising, which was going through its own season of introspection. *No. It's within. It's that awful door of initiation playing with my ego. Where is Dragon Lady? I fear she'll be shattered in a million pieces. Where and why have I tucked her away?*

Closing her eyes, Leah went deep within using the Bee Mistress' skill and Jane's grace to navigate to the bridge. Dragon Lady wasn't there, and Little Alice, now growing up rapidly into Adult Alice, was agitated. She'd found the source of her agitation but she hadn't found Dragon Lady. She didn't know how to navigate the space between the lower and upper astral — if, in fact, there was a space of transition there, but the Bee Mistress searched the lower astral through every metaphor she could imagine looking for Dragon Lady — to no avail. She did, however, come upon an open portal in her intellectual-mental body. Had she fled ... got away somehow? She stood at the portal and called out for Dragon Lady, reminded of the many people she'd known who had childhood personality aspects, that had fled during childhood abuse, still living outside their fields. She'd not be too far away, out in the collective ... *I hope.* Acting within metaphor, she threw a line out the portal intending that Dragon Lady grab it. Then she began to reel her in, imagining that Dragon Lady had recognized and grasped the lifeline. What she reeled through the portal was a big bamboo cage with a whimpering Dragon Lady curled up on its floor. Once Dragon lady was completely back within her field, Leah invoked Archangel Michael to place a guardian at the portal — forever more.

A quick inspection revealed that there was no way out of Dragon Lady's cage, though she seemed less upset just to be back within Leah's field. She promised her some sort of rescue from her predicament, in time, and excused herself to journey back into her body, which was curled up much like Dragon Lady's in her chair. Tears streamed down her cheeks as she built the dwindling fire up again. *My God, how have I failed to see this tragedy unfolding within me?*

Chris found her sitting on the rug, hugging her knees and staring into the fire. Singing a gentle refrain from *The First Noel*, he came to sit beside his entranced wife — at which point she collapsed into his sweetness and strength feeling more helpless than she ever had in her life. When he finally got the whole story out of her, whilst snuggled on the sofa together, they set about trying to piece together the events that led to Dragon Lady's escape ... or abduction. That remained to be determined.

"Now, lass, try to think of the last time you remember Dragon Lady acting out?"

Leah gave that considerable thought. "I've been making excuses for her or imagining that she is biding her time of late. I would have to say the last time I really felt her, and not some imagined reformed version of her, was when Sissi took me to the graves. I swear Dragon Lady would have killed Zacker if she'd had the means. I'm ashamed to admit that, twice now, but Dragon Lady has a real issue with abuse of women and that despite the more male nature of her character. It might have something to do with her lashings at Monticello."

"Do you recall how you felt at the graves?" he asked, giving her a squeeze.

"It occurred to me that I might actually explode. That's what if felt like, cowboy — rage-induced spontaneous combustion."

"Thank you for your honesty, lass. I reckon she poked her own hole in your astral body in the process. That was some kind of cosmic button push, alright."

"Who put her in the cage, if I might be so bold as to ask, magus? And why hasn't it got a door to get her out?"

"Yeah, right. I'll point out that she's back in your field now, and could be questioned about that. I'd guess that it's self-imposed.

"Why … on earth?" she queried, honestly confused.

"Shock, fear, dread, hatred, rage, cowardice, selfishness, egotism? How about unforgiving, and lacking compassion? Mix and match."

Leah stiffened at his boldness, but, painfully, owned it all on behalf of Dragon Lady. His heart was wide-open and pulsing white light. Chris was surely the one to stand by her at the gate of death and future life, but she knew well that her own soul would create the circumstances of initiation, as had just been demonstrated beyond doubt.

She agreed to present a summary of her new findings about the first sacrifice over breakfast as they slipped between the sheets to renew their fierce, unwavering love for each other.

Over whole grain buttermilk pancakes and sausage — a delicious luxury considering the hens' winter egg-laying moratorium — she laid out what she felt as initiatory in the first sacrifice.

"For starters, cowboy, once we'd fallen into the material world at Lucifer's hands, we actually needed Ahriman to hold the yang to Lucifer's yin, the two poles of this reality. So that's a given and remains with us until we redeem Lucifer and, I imagine, take the yin pole ourselves. Ahriman will be with us until the end of the material world, as I understand it. We'll redeem him through our physical mastery.

"Along with that necessity came Lucifer's reckless plunging of his immoral ego into physicality through us. Apparently, he did manage to imbue our sensory organs with his egoism as a result and that subsequent selfishness was what the first sacrifice of Christ Jesus reversed. Lucifer made our newly installed sensory organs selfish, and that sense of self nearly destroyed us.

Imagine being self-conscious of seeing with our eyes, for example? We'd go mad.

"Now, what really interests me about those sensory organs is how we got them. If we go back to the Saturn evolution of the earth, when we humans were first created by the Thrones' sacrifice of the pouring of their physicality into us, they gave us the template of the phantom. Then all of the hierarchies added their bits to it over the span of the Saturn stage of consciousness. We humans were unconscious/comatose but were able to participate at that level of consciousness, none-the-less. When it came time for the Archai to make their contribution, the Saturn stage was in the middle of the fourth cycle. Actually this was the Saturn equivalent of the timing of the fourth sacrifice of Christ Jesus in this earth stage of consciousness. During the span of the mid-fourth to mid-fifth of each evolutionary stage, the hierarchy next in line to receive the "I", as part of their own evolution, received it, and subsequently had the experience, through us, of being human. For the Archai this would likely be referenced through our physical body. Lucifer, an advanced human, was in this stage with the angels and the Moon Gods during Old Moon consciousness, when he turned away from the impeccable evolutionary journey of the angels to explore materiality. He was at the stage of experiencing being human through our creation process as we received our astral body, but he wanted more and influenced other advanced humans to join him.

"Back to the story ... what the Archai gifted us during Saturn stage was the germ of our sensory organs and selfhood, and with it, selfishness — all rudimentary. They have stayed with us through our evolution and are also called the Spirits of Personality or Darkness. So here is my correlate: what they implanted within us was the germ of the organs that Lucifer later corrupted. They allowed us selfishness at the same time they allowed us ego and sensory organs. At the time, these gifts weren't intended for a material world but — a guess —as organs of the soul. I'm expecting this to be another stream to watch with the four sacrifices, Lucifer and Ahriman, and the gifts of the Archai through the stages of consciousness. It was during Saturn consciousness that we received the physical body phantom. It's also impossible to come away from this story without a profound sense of what the Thrones sacrificed to birth us into being. They were our true creators.

"Well, cowboy, what do you think?" she asked, laying down her fork to pour a final cup of tea.

"Not bad, Sherlock," he said, with a slightly crocked grin. "Can I ask where you're going with this story? A documentary?"

"R-r-right," she drawled. "It's between you and me, laddie — and maybe Demetri and Joel. However, I see how it's reorganizing my assemblage point. And, there's something to be said about the way in which that might reframe my thinking and affect not only my spiritual path, but mission. So, do you think I should devote any time to rescuing Dragon Lady from her cage?"

"Waste of time, lass. Remember, there's no door until she creates one."

"On that note, I'll be off to hash over the judicial sphere's guidelines with Will, before I show up at the studio. Remember, I've a short lunch today with school duty from two until three. We're practicing our presentation of the Christmas story for our ceremony in the apiary."

"No worries. I'll walk you up there and get an early start on the piano. Will and I will have the sauna ready for your women's group at 9:30 tonight, if that suits?"

"Fire and ice," she laughed. "A perfect way to end our last meeting of the year."

Will was working with a governance model that assumed at least fifty-percent occupancy of *Harmony Valley*. He and Sam were also drawing up the guidelines for the banking system, which would be a non-profit member cooperative with any money made being funneled into the three community fund accounts, as would be the case with all profitable ventures in the community. The community as a whole would operate as the umbrella non-profit. He suggested that Leah and Natalie get to work on a back-up plan for the spiritual work should greed start to sprout up or be planted amongst community members from outside interests. She assured him that she and Natalie had already talk about how that would be approached – in the simplest way – with an equity buyout option to leave the community. And yet, that was something the mature community would have to thrash out.

At the onset, everyone was agreeing to be part of an experimental model in which money did not have the power of speech and commerce was all worker-owned cooperatives. Profit-oriented corporations had no place in *Harmony Valley*. As long as the happiness quotient was in good stead and commerce oversight was persistent, problems ought only to be periodic. Installing a neighborhood version of this plan in the middle of a big city was the kind of challenge that fired up the best of Will. He shared with Leah that he was keeping a meticulous diary of both the *Harmony Valley* and Inner City projects, knowing that the documentary versions of these Outreach projects would likely miss the fine points important to the very nature of the gift pyramid.

On the strength of over 200 years of sparring between the judicial and economic spheres in America, and the takeover of the cultural sphere by both of those spheres (or one via the other), rigid guidelines would be put in place to safeguard boundaries and, thus, democracy. The voice of economics would be heard at the level of how it serves the community and, since the community wasn't built on hierarchy, that would mean everyone equally. Everyone was a member of the cultural sphere, shareholders in the commons, but, in America, and everywhere else that claimed to be a democratic state, the bankers and government officials had not only blurred the boundaries of the spheres, they'd forgotten their own obligations and accountability to the commons. To compensate for this deliberate sabotage of democracy, they lied. They lied so well they believed themselves and the lies became their truth until, presently, they had their own version of the commons and were able to exclude the rest of the culture from it. It seemed that the maya had deepened in many ways.

Into Will's broad outline, he would incorporate the consensus recommendations of the community as they went through the process of enacting conflict and resolution, and the definitions of rights and duties, after the community dinners. Bernie and Spence would have an outline for the economic sphere, and Nick and Stu were covering the cultural sphere. Leah was awed at the level of detached wisdom pouring out of Will. She thought about Greece, and soon Italy, under the leadership of banking technocrats and her eyes welled up with tears.

"You okay, Light Beam?" he asked, reaching into a bottom desk drawer for a small box of tissues he kept there for her.

"Sorry, Will," she said, reaching for a tissue. "I'm having a moment. At times, all that we hope to accomplish seems daunting to me. I feel exhausted at such moments and would, honestly, prefer to be a witness without such an emotional stake in the outcome of our initiatives."

"I know how you feel but will remind you of your role as standard-bearer for this whole gig," he laughed. "Just hold the space for us, Light Beam. I can feel the inspiration coming through and give you a lot of credit for that."

"I wouldn't, Will. I'm happy to hold space but what you're bringing through is wisdom and the gifts your soul carried into this life. I'm heartened that access to it has begun to flow for you."

"Due in no small part to you, and your man's, faith in me — to say nothing of your steady assistance with my personal work *and* your lending library of Jefferson's writing. And, I must add Demetri to that list. I've had some remarkable insights about my own life since he stayed with us. Well, let's add Elliot, as long as were at it," he laughed. "Every time I see him I feel inspired and, somehow, accelerated. I have no idea how he does that but he's damn good at it."

Leah smiled, broadly, while tossing the tissue in the wastebasket. "You can say that again. He gives me only what I need to help me find my own truth — the mark of a good mentor."

"That's it. That's exactly what he does. You do that too in your own way … and Chris? He's a master."

"I partly understand Chris. He can be fully engage, envision an outcome, and attain it easily because he never attaches himself to it. He's not emotionally bound up in it — like the theater project. He joyfully pursues it, giving it more than his all, in the moment. Then, he doesn't carry it with him to influence his participation in marriage, community, work with the horses, or the play, for example. He's like that with everything. And, he's an impartial sounding board. I'm not there yet."

"Me either," Will affirmed. "Everything he does makes a difference to all of us, though, as if he's able to continually balance the energies here."

"Grace. I think of that as grace, Will. Or, as the Navajo like to put it — he walks in beauty — even through the horse shit."

"Well put, Light Beam, but kind of odd for someone who was a success in theater and film."

"He would be again, if he pursued it, Will, but he'd not engage the system. Good lessons for all of us trying to bring through the grace."

"You've inspired me to finish this up and apply it to the Inner City projects," he winked.

"I'll run along to work then," she said, gathering up her notebook and pile of papers. "I love you very much, little brother."

"Back at ya, Light Beam," he said, leaning over his desk to kiss her cheek.

Chris had worked his way through a good many songs while Leah coached the children on their Christmas story presentation. Apparently, he was satisfied with the score for the play because he'd moved on to Mozart by the time Leah slipped into the community room from the children's classroom. Though not the same piece he'd been playing the last time she walked in on him, she barely had time to sit down before floating back through time to Monticello.

Dolley Madison was, once again, playing the exact Mozart piece that Chris was playing on the piano, but on the harpsichord in the sunny parlor. Leah easily got her bearings and moved through the door of Jefferson's bedroom looking to see if he was in his cabinet with James Madison. He wasn't, but she heard their voices and followed them to the greenhouse off the passageway to his library. Jefferson was pruning a potted orange tree, while Madison read aloud a letter he'd received from President Monroe — Jefferson's most beloved protégé. Jefferson laughed repeatedly at what must have been political jokes — very much enjoying himself. Leah's interest, had she been able to speak with him, would have been his take on the establishment of a purely democratic system in *Harmony Valley*, which, during his life, wasn't part of the United States of America.

Leah realized that she could travel back indefinitely and never communicate directly with Jefferson. The closest she'd come was when she'd slipped into the body of her former slave self, both at her first visit and when she'd been whipped. She decided to go looking for her former self and found her right around the corner, dusting books in the library. In a daring, and, doubtless, risky act of possession, she merged her consciousness with that of her slave self. Her tranquil act of dusting books gave way to a surprising level of agitation. The woman became frightened and went straightaway to Mr. Jefferson to ask for help. Leah felt herself looking through the woman's eyes and sunk deeper into her sensory world to give her voice.

She boldly ran to stand between the two men and heard, in her present voice, the plea: "Please, Mr. Jefferson, we're in peril. Please help us with the precarious future of democracy!"

Jefferson was momentarily stunned knowing full well it wasn't his slave speaking to him. And, perhaps, he could see a cloudlike image of Leah for he spoke directly to her senses with unsympathetic candor and more than a little irritation. "Madam, speak to your banker!" He waved off the slave woman who, upon Leah's withdrawal of consciousness, was profusely apologetic herself. Jefferson acknowledged her confusion and suggested she make a trip to the kitchen for a cup of chamomile tea to calm her nerves. Jefferson watched her as she slipped back through the passageway heading towards his library. He shook his head and turned to Madison with his apologies for the interruption. "She seems possessed at times," he murmured.

"As do you, my good friend," Madison replied, from under raised brows, "unless you've initiated a banking venture amongst your slaves."

The two men had a good laugh as Leah found a chair in the library, where she initiated a decidedly rocky ride back to *New Avalon*. She came back into her body on the floor with Chris holding her hand pulling her back. He helped her up and back into the chair where her journey had started, while she moaned and groaned, feeling truly uncomfortable in her body. Chris stood behind her with one hand on the back of her neck and the other on her third eye until she stabilized.

"Shivers, lass, would you please *not* try that again. I'll swear off Mozart if that'll help."

"I'd guess you and Jefferson are in agreement about that, cowboy," she moaned. "He's given me no alternative but to stay in the here and now."

"Did the two of you actually communicate?" he asked, pulling a chair up in front of her.

"We did. It wouldn't surprise me if I embedded myself so much in my former self that he not only heard my voice, but actually saw me present day. He was shocked and maybe a little fearful. I'm guessing about that, given the tone of his voice and immediacy of his command."

"He commanded you to get out?" he asked.

"No, he yelled at me to *speak to my banker*, which so shocked me I withdrew from the woman who beat a hasty retreat to his library. He and Madison ended it all in laughter after he'd sent the slave woman away. I don't think I caused additional grief or punishment for her, but I could have — can karma travel backwards, I wonder?"

"I'd be more concerned about your banker, lass. I'm assuming he meant Will."

"Will is my banker and he is currently feeling quite inspired about the *Threefolding* plan for *Harmony Valley*. Do you suppose Jefferson is one of the sources of his inspiration?"

"Doesn't that make sense to you? He's read nearly every book you have of his writing," Chris suggested, moving back to the piano.

"It does. My ego needs to back off from being any source of inspiration in our relationship. It's fitting and more natural that Will be inspired from within — and, he's doing an awesome job with the planning," she mused.

Great. That's one less ego investment to get in your way. Now, how about our duets?" he grinned. "The banking can wait."

And it did wait, as her soul inwardly processed her final flight back to Monticello. That task preoccupied her as she and Chris journeyed over the ridge the next day to check on Trynel, Sissi, and her foremost button-pusher, Zacker. She resolved to hold that space for Will's work without complicating his life with her story. He would attribute the inspiration he'd acknowledged to the wisdom found in Jefferson's writing, his relationships with the community members and Elliot and, rightly, all of the political experience he'd gained in his own life.

Chris, in turn, held space for her process and spent his own meditative time intending the best possible outcome for the *Woodland Folk* over the coming winter. Presently, the trail was as clear as a summer day but winter snow would eventually make it impassable. He felt Trynel in need of help for another month but would rely on Leah's examination to reassess that estimate. At that time, the second phase of the kidnapping process would take place with Sissi's removal to *New Avalon*. She'd be leaving behind a full larder, a full woodshed, and, hopefully, a mother on crutches and a father invested in his wife's survival. He'd get Zacker out of the house on tasks they'd planned as quickly as he could, offering Leah an agitation-free space to conduct her examination and ministration to Trynel's mending leg, and soul.

Wrapped up in a knitted shawl, Sissi ran out to greet them as they dismounted Thunder and Holly. They were towing along Sassy with more food stores including a good many jars of meat that Jenny and Shelley had pressure-canned. There were also wheels of aged cheese and some fresh dairy products for the next few days. The outdoors was serving as the perfect refrigerator at the moment but that wasn't reliable over the whole of winter. Sissi led Sassy right up to the front door with her bounty, wrapped her lead around the porch post, then returned to give Leah the most enormous hug and kiss, and helped her with her medical bags. Leah was equally elated to see Sissi and heartened to hear about her mother's progress as they made their way inside. Chris took care of the horses, and then, spotting Zacker near the pond, took off to provide the necessary distraction for the practice of visionary medicine.

Leah found Trynel sitting up and eager to communicate. Her blonde hair was pulled back neatly into a bun, her cheeks had the first bit of color Leah had seen, and her eyes looked well rested, with a mellow glow. All of that and her demeanor, gave Leah hope that healing was proceeding well and that she was, at least marginally, comfortable. The hollowness below her cheekbones was filling in too, indicating some weight gain and fluid balance. Trynel was a handsome woman with a lovely smile and delicate features overall. She was soft spoken and eager to share.

Although, Leah was told, Trynel had been increasing her English vocabulary daily, it was important to be accurate, so Sissi acted as interpreter. If they still had difficulties, they agreed to call Chris in to help out. Leah felt that could be done at the end of the examination if she had questions. And so, she sat on the chair next to the bed holding Trynel's hand and listened to her speak through Sissi. Since Nick had been there to check on her, she was eating well and especially enjoying the beef. She'd not had red meat in a long time and felt that eating it strengthened her blood almost immediately. She needed the pain medication rarely, when she couldn't sleep, but felt, truly, that she was sleeping her life away. She laughed softly with that release of guilt and admitted she'd not had good rest in years, maybe since Sissi was born.

She'd been knitting — had made the shawl for Sissi — and was rereading the few books they had in German. Leah presented her with more yarn and a community pool of sewing odds and ends. There were plenty of fabric scraps from the making of play costumes to offer her as well. She immediately began envisioning a patchwork quilt and was elated with all of the gifts.

Leah check medication supplies and agreed with Sissi that they didn't need more. Then she set about examining the leg, first removing the brace with Sissi's assistance. Her surgical wounds were well healed. Leah removed the stitches and gently washed off remnants of antiseptic. Even the jagged stitching looked good though she'd have a nice scar as an external reminder of the accident. Then she turned to the mending of the jagged break in the bone, softening her sight to see how the bone was setting. Leah sat back with a sigh of relief and announced that the progressive bone knitting was exactly where she wanted it to be. Trynel admitted that she could feel the knitting as it happened.

"I'm not surprised," Leah laughed, while moving to the opposite side of the bed for inspection of the fibula. "Now, if you've manage to knit this one, I'll know you're a miracle worker, Trynel."

"I can feel that one too," Sissi translated. "It's growing and feels very itchy inside the leg."

Leah had to raise an eyebrow to that one as she lay across the bed to exam the bone with her sight. Indeed, both bone fragments were growing towards each other. Leah thought she saw more. She shaded rays of sunlight with her hands, prompting Sissi to hold her shawl up to block the sun from the window. With this help, Leah could detect an etheric stream of light connecting the two growing bone ends. The path of healing was being organized on the etheric body level through the body's own capacity to heal, aided by the higher beings who continued to hover around Trynel day and night. Leah held the joint ends of the bone, at knee and ankle, in her hands and sent in as much healing power as she was able. She'd absolutely no idea how to handle an unprecedented bone healing, except to yield to the powers of the body and the hierarchies. She accepted that this woman was obviously important to the divine plan and would continue to keep her leg immobilized until the bone had knit. Thank God, for the brace and Trynel's ability to feel progress, which maintained hope and vigilance.

Leah went about her business, cleaning up and repositioning the leg in the brace with plenty of cushion. The tibia, though knit, would not be healed completely for a good many weeks and the fibula? Well that depended upon the rate of bone growth. If it continued to grow at the rate she was estimating, it was possible that the brace could be replace by a cast that immobilized the leg from above the knee to the middle of the foot, but allowed Trynel to move around in bed and very, very, gradually make use of crutches. She would be housebound for the winter and might be able to bear weight on the leg, with the crutches, beginning in February or March. Through the initial stages of mobilization absolutely no weight could be applied to the leg, meaning one legged crutching around the house.

Trynel, radiant with hope, would pray that the snow held off until she was ready for the crutches. In the moment, she would take a little nap. That gave Leah time to introduce Sissi to a sack of beef bones she'd brought along with a bottle of apple cider vinegar. She was to boil up bones with a splash of vinegar to make bone broth for her mother. It was rich in minerals and essential fats for healing and bone building. Sissi was to see that she'd a good bowl of hot broth morning and night perhaps boiled up with roots and onion in the broth and flavored with salt and herbs. Temperatures were cold enough to store the surplus broth outside. They unpacked the yogurt, milk, butter, cheese, canned beef, potatoes, turnips, parsnips and carrots and a sack of greens – kale, chard and lettuce – and three loaves of whole grain bread. Nick would be back just after Christmas to check on Trynel and bring more fresh food.

When they were finished putting away the food, Leah spread a lunch out on the table and the two of them sat down to eat and talk about life in *New Avalon*. Sissi was devoted to her mother's recovery at the same time excited at the prospects of a new life in community. Jürgen and Zenzi were bringing home wonderful stories, especially those about living with Demetri. They were careful not to share them in front of Zacker, who was strangely quiet and withdrawn most of the time.

Chris had loaded Sassy's packs with a few tools, scrap wood and insulation to help Zacker repair the chicken coop and duck shed. They insulated the walls of the coop and patched up the duck shed to keep snow out. After a bag lunch at the wood chopping station, they introduced the chickens to a used feeder and a water station, which Ellia had donated to assure a food and water supply when deep snow isolated the coop for a time.

Chris began their work talking about the moral responsibilities that ought to come with maturation into manhood. This, Chris deduced, was where Zacker had missed the boat. Then, while working together, they journeyed back through his boyhood together, followed by puberty, and then his coming of age. Though many stories began with normal boyhood adventures or interactions with others, each ended with his mother's blind rage and abuse. Fear and loathing gradually dominated his emotional life – directed at his mother but gradually transferred to all women. He saw his father as a weak man trapped in a hellish reality of his own making. He'd felt pity for, and was humiliated by, his father but, above all, there remained disgust and hatred. Zacker had vowed it would not happen to him. It didn't, and before long he was shipped off overseas before a growing history of sexual assaults caught up with him. Zacker's was a complex, but understandable, story of horrific parenting.

Chris consumed Zacker's emotional baggage as it poured forth. He digested it and spat it out for the earth to process into new life forms. With each chance to touch Zacker, he infused him with light and healing energy. He noticed that Zacker began inviting those chances as a softening or melting process began to take hold within him. There wasn't a better stand-in for love and compassion when it came to healing a life lived in error. Zacker was retracing the steps he'd taken to the trailing edge of the bell curve led by a man he was, at least, learning to hear. The 'who, why, and what' of Chris' presence would remain well beyond Zacker's comprehension. That gave Chris many more degrees of latitude than would have been available to him with a conscious man.

When Sassy was packed up with Chris' tools and *New Avalon* recycling (empty canning jars and veggie sacks), Chris came in to see Trynel and help Leah with her medical bags. Trynel was awake and full of cheerful news of her recovery. Her natural beauty and depth of soul wasn't lost to Chris as they caught up with each other. When he'd asked Zacker how they managed to have chickens and ducks with little protection from predators, he'd laughed and said Trynel had created invisible fences — sturdy fences. Now he put the question to Trynel, who blushed noticeably, and admitted that when she was a girl she'd been taught the old ways by a village healer — ah, well … *sorcerer* — with whom she'd become acquainted.

"That should be no surprise to a man whose wife commands the angels!" she exclaimed, with dancing eyes.

Chris had a good laugh and gave her hand a squeeze as they said goodbye. He promised to come back with Nick after Christmas, and with Leah, the first Wednesday (just three weeks away) after the New Year. He'd checked the long-range weather forecast and it look like good weather for continued visits into January. Leah gave Trynel a hug and kiss on the cheek before they left the house with Sissi. She held Sissi close to her heart before letting her go with a kiss to the forehead. Chris had stowed her medical bags and brought Holly around for mounting.

As they turned to go, Leah saw Zacker, who'd been hiding at the side of the house, step up on the porch. He removed his hat and gave a recognizable nod of respect to Leah. She acknowledged him, feeling the slightest trace of repentance in his gesture. Chris assured her that Zacker's actions were voluntary and a pleasant surprise to him as well. That was all she wanted to say, or hear, about Zacker until she visited Trynel in early 2012.

The community was now in the final stages of play rehearsal, going through the entire play that night and again on Saturday afternoon. Then the following Wednesday was dress rehearsal and the play on that Sunday, Christmas Day. Everyone was excited and in excellent voice. The cast had their lines down, which allowed Chris to improve on their performances with subtle but amazing changes in inflection, body language and gestures, use of props, and harmony on the choral numbers. He built the emotional charge up to the court scene after Judd's death then discharged it with humor. That scene flowed easily into the departure and the grand finale with the whole community. They applauded for each other and started all over again for a second round, with fewer corrections and Chris in full form as Curly. Everyone had a bit to work on over the few days until the second full–run rehearsal, including final alterations of costumes by Leslie and Katia, and final work on sets for Bernie and Greg. There was high-spirited conversation as they all walked home around the commons. The stars of the show were sound asleep within half an hour of opening the front door.

Leah and Joel were laughing their way through a Skype makeup session at nine the next morning. He'd written a piece for his show about the technocratic takeover of Greece, and that projected for Italy. How he managed to make something so infuriating seem cynical, and then funny, was beyond Leah but she very much enjoyed the story. He'd be running it at the end of the show that day, after his live interview with her about the Canary Project, recapping some points from the interview he'd taped on the related show when at *New Avalon*. They went over the details of the project again and she reported a good response to the blog and newsletter idea, with six blog members so far and heaps of tweets and facebook comments. Paula and the rest of the millennial crew were checking out the bloggers as best they could and the few blog entries thus far.

After Joel's live segment, at three-fifteen that afternoon, Stu and Rob were taping the last *Occupy* summary of 2011 with Willow and Leah. Willow was taking a long break, and would pick up her reporting work again from *Occupy* initiatives meant to be springing up around the country in late winter. She was morphing into a reporter on wheels for both shows.

It had been a full day of work for Leah when dinner rolled around. Chris had taken on the cooking while she gave the house a quick cleaning and put clothes in the washer. He'd be off to choir practice after dinner and she'd be spread out on the kitchen table immersed in the second sacrifice of Christ Jesus. She was intent on a good discussion Friday night when neither of them was otherwise occupied.

"What do you make of Trynel's skills at sorcery, lass," he asked as they sat down to a bowl of chili and a salad.

"I'd be interested in knowing more about her past, cowboy. It seems to be working for them. There'd be dead chickens over here, for sure. The children are quite gifted as well. It's curious, isn't it? — A woman like Trynel in the middle of nowhere using high skills just to stay alive?"

"I suspect a little karmic repay there," he replied. Then, skirting any discussion of Zacker the object of the proposed karma, he changed the subject. "How was your women's group on Tuesday night. You've not mentioned it, lass."

"Oh, it was wonderful. We're all finished with our projects for the children now. Georgia helped me with Mandy's doll's hair and loved the dress and sweater I'd knitted for her. We talked about relationships, which are getting better all the time," she added, winking at him. "And, the sauna was, as expected, fire and ice — divinely restorative and cleansing. Thanks go to you and Will for that. Did you take a sauna while we were meeting?"

"You didn't pick up our scent?" he asked, laughing.

"All you could smell was the intensity of the fire and how that makes the iron of the stove smell really hot — that, and the cedar oils from the sauna walls. It was great — and such a welcome addition to the community."

"You'll be happy to know that Tommy joined in then, enjoying the fruits of his labor."

He'll miss it and the Ranger meetings when he moves to Marin for the Inner City project. That reminds me to return the two-way radios to Shelley," she added.

"Already done, lass. We didn't need them going over the ridge but I'd not let anyone go without them — except Zenzi and Jürgen, who are like homing pigeons no matter which way they're going."

"Don't forget Thunder's trusty lead. He's turning into a truly magnificent stallion, by the way. I think Holly's keen for him," she mused.

"He'll be after all the mares comes spring — a real handful for an old bloke like me," he grinned.

"Awe, you over-the-hill cowboy," she crooned getting up to refresh the plate of cornbread.

He pulled her down for a deliciously naughty cuddle, then, catching the time on the kitchen clock, hustled to finish his meal and get out the door for choir practice.

"Our dalliance has dashed my hopes of setting a fire for you, madam," he said, in his best British butler accent, whilst zipping up his down jacket.

"Not to worry, James," she countered. "I'll be spreading my research over the kitchen table tonight, anyway. Don't forget your lemon water, mate," she added, handing him a glass bottle of water with lemon slices. He had all those involved in singing projects on lemon water before practice to clear their vocal chords.

"Joyeux Noël, Madam," he sang out, hurrying out the front door with his stack of sheet music.

In bed that night, they arranged a Friday evening discussion of the second sacrifice, which took place in early Atlantean times. He promised to get himself in the right frame of mind for that and to both cook and cleanup so that she could continue putting it all together. They would start early to work her pre-show download into the latter part of the evening. It was a busy life, to be sure. To help him out, Leah would set up the slow cooker with a beef brisket before leaving for work. He'd be off to the stable after finishing the wash and stoking the boiler out back — his morning duty for theirs and Natalie's radiant heat. He'd heard tell that would be twice daily after it really got cold.

The next morning, the studio was bustling with activity in preparation for the last live show of the year. That would be followed by a Christmas party luncheon for the staff and their guests (local food producers and organizers) at The Lodge. Leah and Paula went over the week's news, picking out the stories most appropriate to the *Light on the Crisis* mission, including last minute legislation in the US congress and the California Assembly, before the holiday recess. She'd let Will cover the big bank nonsense and make sure Paula had up-to-date, accurate information on the takeover of Greece and Italy by the technocrats. That assault to democracy was of particular interest to Leah. In fact, it got her steamed up enough to stomp across the courtyard to speak to her favorite banker about it.

"Hey, Will. I need an ear to hear my rant about the systematic takeover of the EU by the banksters," she announced, earnestly.

"Light Beam, allow me to bear witness to your rant," he laughed. "I intend covering the economic ramifications of technocracy during my five-minute piece tomorrow."

"That's good news. Make sure you and Paula have some continuity so you're not repeating each other."

"Will do. Now, what's on your mind, sister?" he asked, sitting back with his feet on his desk.

Leah stood before him, and then began pacing back and forth. "What the hell is going on, Will? Is this the first in a long series of failures of the democratic process? It's a small scale version of the mess *we'll* be in when the banking powers start pulling the plugs on *us*, put their puppet in the White House, cash in on their campaign investments in our greedy congress, and impose austerity of this scale on the working people of America. Didn't we learn anything from Iceland and Ireland? It worries me that we'll not be able, or strong enough, to pull off true democracy in our Outreach projects. We're losing it daily in Washington. Realistically, we're a country run by Wall Street. Correct me if I'm wrong."

Leah plopped down in the chair opposite Will, with tears streaming down her cheeks. He silently passed her the tissues, realizing she was in an uncharacteristically fragile place the last week or so, and might have more than Greece to get off her chest. He sent out a silent plea, asking for all the help he could get to restore the very core of their community to her usual 'pillar of strength' emotional state. In the back of his mind was a real curiosity about the cause of her strife. Surely she and Chris were getting along famously. That would be his shortcoming with Sonia, but likely not Leah's with Chris. *Okay. Let's get to the bottom of this,* he resolved, taking a deep breath.

"Let's go sit with your gold, Light Beam," he suggested.

"What? Why?" she asked, taken by surprise.

"Trust me," he whispered, coming around the desk to give her his hand.

After locking the entrance door, they walk down the stairs to the vault, which he proceeded to open, deftly working the tumbler in the door. He pulled a couple chairs over to each side of the pile of gold ingots and sat her down on one of them — with the tissues.

"Light Beam, imagine that you're the queen," he began, glancing at the golden scepter she kept on top of the stash, "and that this is your gold and the gold that represents the sovereign wealth of your kingdom."

"Except that this gold could actually be recalled by our own government in a monetary crisis," she reminded him.

"Never mind that for now. At least it's here. I check on it every day, as a matter of course, for this community. Now if the Queen of England were to go to the vaults of England's sovereign wealth, she would find that a great deal of the gold would be missing. Of course, she likely knew about the Brown government's selling of that gold at auction at the lowest possible price before the last boom. In fact that sale likely spawned the present boom, and gold soared from the mid to high 200s to the 1600s of today. That was a decade plus ago. The British public wasn't fully informed until recently. He sold the gold to the banksters who picked it up at that low price to cover, through a subsequent boom, unreported losses in their own gold reserves. They sold it when it was high and made enormous profits — 100% manipulation. London banking remains the least regulated of any major banking center. This amounted to an unpublicized bank bailout, and it wasn't long before the financial crisis hit Wall Street — our own bastion of corruption, as you know.

"Who knows but that a great deal of the gold in Fort Knox is missing, and much of what is there doesn't belong to us. The governments of this world, like the citizens of their countries, were brainwashed into thinking they could borrow, on easy credit, beyond their means. For the public, it fed an insatiable desire for stuff, playing on our universal beliefs about scarcity and the dream of winning the lottery in life. We were given permission to have our heart's desires. The whole situation began resembling a casino. So now, the swindling banks continue with their unregulated, unethical practices and the public in the UK pays the price with austerity. That contrived bailout will never be repaid and if the Queen and her subjects want their gold back, she'll have to buy it at a very high price or wait for a bust, which is likely on the horizon.

In Greece, the same thing happened. JP Morgan Chase, Goldman Sachs and other banks developed financial products that allowed the governments of Greece, Italy, and possibly other countries, to hide their borrowing. These countries spent beyond their means for years while appearing to meet the Debt to GDP ratios of the EU monetary guidelines. The lion's share of wealth went into the pockets of the 1%. When all of this came to light, the bailouts began, and the stiff austerity packages demanded by the IMF, EU and ECB that accompanied them were laid on the Greek people, who had their own debt to GDP ratio problems, but with little understanding of how they'd been duped. For starters, I wanted to assure you that we do have our gold here, though I know you weren't the least bit worried about that."

"Well, you're right about that, Will. And, I get the lack of regulations there and here, so what does this have to do with the end of democracy?" she asked, a bit confused.

"If you want to make a man your slave, you steal his wealth and indenture him to your desires. This isn't a new story and it's a pretty simple one. People become indentured slaves of the banksters through debt, and so do countries. Countries are very wary of suggestions to use their sovereign gold as collateral for the sale of bonds to raise money for debt repayment. The fact that economists and bankers would suggest that they do that is an enormous red flag. Greek hasn't that much gold in reserve but Italy has a massive amount — Spain nearly as much — much of it stolen from Don Eduardo's ancestors, you'll recall. This unfolding crisis in the EU bears close scrutiny. We're very likely looking at a strategy beyond the realm of shadow banking."

"Are you talking about the power brokers, the power elite?" she asked.

" Listen, when we bailed out Wall Street, the banksters paid back, or are in the process of paying back, those bailouts by stealing money from investors, stealing homes from mortgagees, stealing from savings and retirement accounts, and stealing bank charges and inflated interest from credit card users, to say nothing of making high-risk investments. Those are but a few of the crafty ways the banking casinos actually stole money from taxpayers to pay back the bailout *from* the taxpayers. Who are the losers in this little caper?"

"The taxpayers — *We the People* — obviously," she concluded, getting a bit hot under the collar.

"Directly and indirectly, in a lot of different ways, and it's an ongoing story. Greece will continue to need bailouts. It's not possible for them to re-invigorate their economy and make a complete recovery from the edge of what should have been default. After years of imposed austerity, insurrection, suicides, the wealthy absconding with their loot, and now the replacement of their leader with a technocrat, the banksters have the people where they want them and they're one big step closer to their goal. That's my guess at any rate."

"What's the goal, Will?" she asked, quietly. "Enslavement?"

"Distraction. The enslavement is a given. The power brokers want to end up at the door to the vault with the 'freely-given' combination."

"The sovereign gold?"

"The sovereign gold. Fallen nations, with no hope of recovery, will have nothing left with which to pay their debt except the gold. They may choose, at that point, to default. You have to understand the power of credit ratings to know the pressure put on a country to avoid default. The credit rating agencies, by the way, were major players in the financial crisis and continue to wield an unwarranted amount of power over countries. In Greece, the people have already lost their freedom to personal debt, and now to shame, job loss, and the side effects of insurrection. The IMF, EU and ECB will come calling to collect on their loans. These three financial institutions, together called the Troika, hold more gold reserves than most nations, with the exception of the US — if it's really there in Fort Knox. And, there's a long history of bankers using debt as political leverage. They'll likely suggest more loans and more bailout money now that they've one of their own making the financial decisions for the country. It reminds me of the World Bank loan program to developing countries that loaded them with debt they couldn't repay. It bought a lot of leverage for our government and its corporate bullies, who dove in to steal the natural resources."

Will, who'd been quite animated and passionate in his discourse suddenly became still. Leah looked at him, expectantly. Startled at his appearance, she audibly sucked in air and raised her hand to her gaping mouth, as he looked her square in the eyes.

"*Experience declares that man is the only animal which devours his own kind,*" he stated.

Leah was staring into the eyes of Thomas Jefferson. Will had somehow morphed momentarily into Jefferson to deliver that undeniable truth. And, before he disappeared, her former slave master, winked at her playfully. *Speak to your banker, indeed!* She thought.

"Hey Light Beam, are you okay?" Will asked.

She gained control over herself quickly, actually wanting to retreat to solitude and a chance to process what she'd seen. It was no clairvoyant mistake or Luciferic trick. Will had taken on the voice of Jefferson, exactly as she'd heard it clairvoyantly at Monticello.

"Sorry, Light Beam. I get a little carried away when enslavement is involved in a story. You look like you've seen a ghost," he said, apologetically, with palpable concern.

"I'll be fine, Will. Can I ask you to include this in your report tomorrow, or at least hint at it for future reports. People need to hear this angle on the European debt crisis. They need to think out of the box."

I can suggest it. I've no fear of the banksters. They're pawns of the power brokers and not very bright. On the other hand, the power brokers, at some point, would want this little pile of gold, Light Beam. So let's be careful."

"Of course. Do what you need to Will. I support you fully."

"Did I say something to upset you? I felt a little overpowered for a moment there."

"You made good sense, little brother," she smiled. "I feel like we're in good hands here, and with Outreach now. Maybe I can settle down a little bit. I do feel a dark cloud hovering, but that could be personal. Chris has a plan to straighten out a little of my esoteric education," she laughed.

"Sounds like fun. I'm happy to be loitering around with my subpersonalities," he admitted. Then he put his hands on the gold and looked her in the eyes. "There's a magnificent vibration in this stuff, Light Beam. It holds a nice space for our service. I'm totally committed to upholding a model of true democracy here and in all of our projects. Presently, in the world, *We the People* are missing from the equation in all but a few instances. Here, *We the People* are the beginning and the end of all our efforts."

"Again, Will, I love you so much," she said, picking up the scepter of Qoyari, which was resting on the stack of ingots. "This belonged to a well-loved Queen, a true mother to her people, who safeguarded the sovereign wealth of the Incas, my friend. Perhaps she is helping us on our quest."

Leah left Will at the bank and walked back to the studio to shut herself up in her office. Before she tried to process what took place in the vault, she got online and searched for the words Jefferson had spoken to her, through Will. Indeed they were — Thomas Jefferson to Edward Carrington 1787. She closed her laptop and her eyes. Jefferson had done the same thing to her that she'd done to him. How could that happen? She'd not actually contemplated how she'd been able to slip into the slave woman in the first place. There was a soul affinity to be sure. On the dark side it was a possession of sorts, driven by her desire for counsel.

Where did she take counsel? Chris had no personal interest in politics or economics. Joel was interested but took his counsel from all sides of the economic and political spectrum. Truth be told, she always walked across the courtyard to Will. Before there was a courtyard, she sought his counsel over the phone or in arranged meetings. He'd guided those aspects of mission since before the get-go. And, she had this enormous love for Will that, at times, overwhelmed her. He wasn't a replacement for Eric, her erstwhile brother, but a soul she'd known a long time — that deep kind of love and respect.

That begged the question: How did Jefferson manage to possess Will? For her part, it wasn't like her soul was a stranger to the slave woman. She'd been the slave woman — although not as her current collection of subpersonalities. However, at the very least, Dragon Lady had been there. It was easy enough for that slave woman to give her a great deal of clairvoyant information about that life using threads of unhealed karma still in her soul. So, was it possible to jump to the future? Could her slave woman suddenly move in to replace her present soul for some short moments of time? Could she pop into a future life being lived in the timeless universe? If she were between lives, maybe? Jefferson had been dead for nearly 200 years.

Was it a comfort to her that Will was able to be an unconscious conduit for Jefferson's possession, if that accurately described it? He was doing well enough just being inspired by Jefferson's writing. Will's timing was impeccable. He was engaging mission steadily and with amazing productivity. She hadn't the answer. A chat with her husband was imminent.

After rehearsal and a check–in with Nick at the clinic, as was her habit, Leah left for lunch intending to spend the afternoon on her research. She and Paula would finalize the news, discuss it at eight the next morning, and then put it into the teleprompting program for Stu. The tapes of Joel and Willow were already in the program sequence, having been reviewed by the staff at rehearsal. The guests — locals, who would not be staying overnight — were confirmed, as was one on-call alternate. She'd not be missed as the staff assumed their pre-show duties. Her task was to relax, let it all sink in, and then ask for guidance under the stars.

She was already spread out on the kitchen table when Chris came in the back door. "Need anything before I knock off my boots, lass?" he asked, opening the laundry door to greet her.

"Perhaps a therapist," she replied, with a broad grin.

"Interesting morning, was it?" he laughed.

"Quite. You could put the clean towels into the dryer while your handy there."

He knocked off his boots, stowed his jacket, loaded up the dryer and came to give her a cheery hug and kiss. "I've had a great time at the stable, lass."

"What could be going on at the stable in January to make you so jolly, cowboy?" she asked, wiggling away from the chilly hands working their way up under her sweater.

"Aye, the usual cleaning up, then I finished Nathan's last book, which, compared to his first, proved the fellow is on the right track with the adolescents — can't wait to meet him."

"He's excited to meet you too, darling. Sounds like a good morning."

"Aye, well that was just the first part of the morning. I like to use Friday mornings to check in with the brotherhood," he admitted, to her raised eyebrows and widening eyes. "Especially now that I'm back on active duty," he laughed.

"I had a suspicion that the stable had become some sort of Temple of the Magi," she giggled.

"I reckoned you'd figured that out months ago, lass. At any rate, I found myself sitting across a desk facing St Germain."

"Do tell, cowboy," she replied, more than curious about the timely nature of the visit from the head of the magi and the oddity of an office setting.

Chris fetched a kombucha from the fridge and sat down across from her. "Yeah, well, he's pleased as punch with Demetri's recovery, and his tenure as a surrogate dad. Your facilitation of his rescue has gone down in the magi record books, by the way," he added, with the hint of a grin.

She burst out laughing, then, lost for words, or the desire to comment, waved him on with his story.

"Right. He's also pleased that we've connected solidly with Joel but he did ask that you be watchful of a tendency there towards ultraliberal ideals that might actually lead to some sort of bloody insurrection. Joel is on track to hugely influence the public but he's still in a place to be easily influenced by the power brokers who play the extremes on both sides of the aisle. That was how he put it. I trust that you know what that means."

Leah nodded, thoughtfully, recognizing yet another aspect of mission needing oversight. Fortunately, she and Joel had an open-hearted working relationship that lent itself to course correction.

"Go on, cowboy," she urged.

"That was a routine sort of exchange, and then he began ranting about the power brokers and the way they'd corrupted the banking systems. He feels the work with *Threefolding* isn't going to be easy but will provide the infrastructure to revolutionize society. Of course, he'd had many a discourse with Steiner in his day, so this isn't a surprise. What does surprise me is his suggestion that Will be groomed for a political career. The Will I know and love would be alarmed at such an idea. You know that side of Will better than I do, lass. What's your take?"

Leah's mouth was gaping open for the second time that day.

"Are you okay, lass?" he asked, at a loss to understand her reaction.

"We may both need a therapist if we can't work this one out, my lad," she said. "It's time you heard about my interesting encounter with Will today."

"Do tell?" he grinned.

"I played St. Germain's role and went over to vent my concerns about the European Debt Crisis, the corrupt banking institutions, and the imminent end of democracy," she began. "I was preaching to the choir, of course, but he does listen attentively. Then he proceeded to take me to the vault to sit with the gold. I assume it's holding a space for our endeavors. He then explained the power brokers intentions in Europe, or at least a fraction of those intentions, and, in the process, at one point, he completely morphed into Thomas Jefferson to make a point. You will remember he'd reprimanded me — chased me off, really — suggesting I see my banker."

"I'm surprised you waited three days to do that, lass, but go on," he grinned.

"Wait a minute, cowboy! Does this make any sense to you? Not that Jefferson would attempt to speak to me through Will. He more or less suggested that. But, how did he do it? Is his soul out there with the brotherhood and able to take possession of someone like Will, even for a few seconds?"

"Apparently so," he replied.

"That's a lot of drama to go through for what he delivered - basically a statement about man's inhumanity to man — the obvious. So what gives here? Is Will going to channel Jefferson and lead the way back to the democracy of the Founders, which, incidentally, will not work in today's world?"

"The brotherhood doesn't waste time retracing steps, lass. I think we need to give Jefferson credit for having kept abreast of this mess from the soul state — at the very least. And, I expect he's no laggard when it comes to progressive ideas. You seem confused about how his soul could take possession of Will, even for a moment. I'd suggest it would be a lot easier than you going back to possess someone you'd been 200 years in the past."

"Dragon Lady knew the way, even from her cage," she sighed. "But, that doesn't explain the present situation. I don't doubt that we need Jefferson's vision and wisdom, and I'm fine with hearing that from Will instead of Jefferson himself. It just feels like we're missing a piece here, cowboy."

"You're missing a piece, lass. Has it not occurred to you that at least part of Will *was* Jefferson?"

"Seriously? No. It never crossed my mind. Is it true?" she asked, dumbfounded.

"True blue, lass. Your slave master has come back as your banker, and a man of color, at that."

"Oh my God. And a man I love to the core. We must have done some patching up along the way, if that's the case."

"An outwardly inconsequential life as loving partners — genders reversed — with Rosicrucian inner circle connections to your beloved Steiner. I leave the rest of that for you to clairvoyantly explore. What is important here is that Will know nothing of this revelation, but he be gently guided into the political sphere. He'll be very adept once he accepts that part of his mission. Everything he is involved in now is preparatory. Hey, he's earning the respect of a good many influential people in California, is he not?"

"Absolutely. And, our viewers adore him. I don't have to tell you he's a magnetic, charismatic fellow. What I do have to tell you is that he sincerely hates politics."

"Like the Boss said, it'll grow on him. And, like Dragon Lady, his Jeffersonian subpersonality is but part of the complex ego that is Will," he reminded her. "How does this make you feel?"

"Dizzy. It does answer a lot of questions for me, although I'll need time for that to sink in. And, it raises umpteen new questions about the future that I'm excited to explore. I so like this idea of a bloodless revolution. Jefferson was a firm believer in revolution as a cleansing ritual for democracy. He didn't mind that it was bloody, but I do."

"So how does this make you feel about *Harmony Valley*?" he queried.

"It's the most important thing we're working on, cowboy. We need to get it right — *perfectly* right. We need to have a lot of happy, increasingly conscious people living in that valley, and soon," she concluded, her eyes looking dreamily into the future.

"Great. Can we have lunch now? I'm bloody starved to death," he pleaded, with exaggerated drama.

"A bloody good idea, mate," she laughed. "Let's celebrate. There's a master in our midst."

"In the making," he reminded her, as they both stuck their heads and hands in the fridge to pull out all the sandwich makings and the pot of leftover chili.

"Hey, cowboy!" she declared, suddenly illumined. "He'd be Order of the Ruby, wouldn't he?"

Chris set the food down on the counter and took her in his arms. "One day, my love," he offered, kissing her forehead.

"Of course. There are already twelve of us in circle. Who will go for Will to rise?" she wondered aloud.

He held her close to his heart and sent a blast of energy into the back of her neck.

"You! Oh Chris, I've got chills all over. He'll take your place as Lord of the Ruby, won't he?" she whispered.

"Aye, my sweet lass. We'll return to the stars in due time. Can you hold a space for this extraordinary transition to unfold, naturally?"

"With all my heart and soul," she wept.

chapter 9: truth be told

Chris took off to help Bernie and Mitch with set designs at the community center that afternoon, while Leah dove back into the second sacrifice material — with little spells of wonderment at the magic unfolding before her eyes. At one point she had a sudden yearning to speak with the bees about it all and wandered down to the apiary for a visit. She didn't stay long — just long enough to run energy with each of the biens, to tell them of Will's integral role in the future, and to fill herself to the brim with the kind of hopeful focus that the bees inspired. She'd invited Harry along and they continued on for a walk along the river to the stable.

She decided to walk through the orchard and the community gardens, instead of cutting through the paddocks, and found Sonia and Ellia with Demetri in the greenhouse. Warm hugs were shared with her friends who were maintaining the gardens during the winter — without extra help. The sight and smell of rich earth and flourishing winter greens, with the background sound of the fish tank aeration pumps, provided those stopping by with a blast of summer, even as the winter solstice loomed four days away. Leah felt thoroughly rejuvenated as she left the greenhouse and pleased with an invitation to lunch, along with Chris, at Demetri's farmhouse on Sunday at noon — Greek food was on the menu. *Delightful.*

The horses were all out on pasture enjoying a sunny afternoon when she and Harry slipped in the front door of the stable. Leah stepped into the tack room, sat on Chris' chair there, and sent streams of gratitude to St. Germain and all those off-planet holding space for their mission. That felt like completion, to a woman who liked the idea of completion, but then a beautiful light came down through the roof of the stable to engulf her. Within that light she felt a strong impulse of courage and the need for authenticity and impeccability — like she'd never felt it before. There was grace to be sure, but then came awareness of the worsening storm in her psyche that was beginning to feel like a hurricane.

When they got back to the house, she went straight to the altar of the Golden Queen asking for her blessings. She then felt the storm clouds organize themselves into a hurricane swirl around her, while she stood her ground in the eye. When the forces of her soul's turmoil had calmed there, she heard a whisper in her ear: "Best I could do Bee Mistress. Maintain your focus and stay alert."

Although instinctively wanting to run, or at the very least cry out for help, she, instead, calmed in the storm's eye. With strengthened determination and the cleansing power of a good hot shower, she re-engaged the work before her as the most important of her many tasks to complete.

In the midst of that task, she began to see the great evolutionary drama being played out on earth through humanity. The hierarchies had not been able to appear on earth for a very long time, although they could influence the direction of humanity in a good many other ways. Before Chris arrived home to finish up the dinner she'd been minding in the crock-pot, she was well into the third sacrifice with her notes and diagrams and confident she could be through Atlantis ready to contemplate the fourth sacrifice — Golgotha — over Christmas break.

When they were settled into their discussion positions after kitchen cleanup, Chris asked her if she'd talked to Nathan lately about their visit.

"I did, briefly. He called this morning before Paula and I started in on the news that led me to Will at the bank ... and, well, you know the story. Good grief, this has been a long and interesting day," she sighed. "Back to his call. They're driving for sure. The weather looks fabulous across the west so we can expect to see them Thursday late afternoon. He really wanted to let me know that Mandy had put a winter hat on her list for Santa and that David was more in need than she was. Hence the knitting basket and needles are out again," she laughed, glancing at the filled basket next to her chair.

"In your spare time, lass!" Chris declared. "What can I do to get their house ready — stoke the boiler starting the day before, perhaps?"

"Lovely of you, cowboy, but, for practical reasons, Greg keeps both houses heated throughout the winter. You could give him a hand, though. It would take more energy to heat the cold water up again and all the furniture and bedding, plus we can't be having frozen pipes. I was intending to take their rent out of my year end surplus, though I've no idea what's there for it."

"You could make a down payment on a house if it came to that," he laughed. "I've been using my account for all the food, our share of the electric costs and cooking gas. What else can we spend money on but the kids? It's money well spent. If you gave me a list of groceries for the guesthouse, I'd be happy to contribute that as my share of their visit. They'll be strapped with petrol and motel costs to make the trip."

"That'd be so appreciated, darling. I'll ask Julie to email a list of food to have on hand and print it out for you. We'll have them here for a good many meals, they'll want some with friends, and then all the community events and dinner parties will take care of the rest. Nathan and Julie are good friends with Christina, Spence, Stu, Leslie, Nick and Georgia because the kids play together constantly, when David and Mandy are visiting. The influx of visiting grandkids and nieces and nephews makes for a mob of young ones on the go from sun up until bedtime."

"Do we get an accounting of the community fund at year end when the last quarter of our demurrage currency contributions pour in?" he asked.

"We do — at the January board and community meetings. Everyone has been mindful that we need a great deal to get the second community off the ground. My house down payment will be but a drop in the bucket. It's a big project."

"Aye. I'm conscious of expenditures with my project. Except for a couple of big beams, I've decided to use all recycled wood in the transformation of Mr. B's barn. Tommy turned me on to all the dumps in the county where they take it in and sell it back. He suggested I put the word out about the beams at the Grange Co-op ... might be some farmer's barn falling down with good beams. Greg and Bernie went to the dump for set materials, as it turns out. They've done a great job creating our Oklahoma farm scenery. Then there's Mr. Bs house that needs to come down for the community center."

"Excitement is building for the play, cowboy. I can tell you that. We have a mob of people coming from the greater community as the local grapevine reports. You know, tomorrow will be a big, big day for both of us. Shall we get on with this?" she asked, rustling a few papers in her lap. "It's far more concise than the first sacrifice presentation. There was so much evolutionary background to consider with that one."

"I'm keen to hear your second story, lass. Lay it on me," he grinned, sinking back into the sofa with closed eyes.

Leah took a few seconds to surreptitiously adore him, then organized her papers and began. "I need to begin by conjecturing what humanity looked like through the transition from the Lemurian epoch into the Atlantean epoch. I would assume this took place over a long period of time during which a lot of people perished, along with animal and plant species, in Mother Earth's explosive rearrangement of continents and oceans. It was written that those who would take the mysteries forward were an advanced colony under the guidance of enlightened beings — if not embodied hierarchies. Theirs was a place of stable land where temples and mysteries school were plentiful, compared to the rest of Lemuria. And, this isn't to say that people didn't survive the fiery transformation of the earth in other places. Lemuria was spread around the globe and surely large groups and whole colonies survived in isolation to begin again.

"In that safe haven, I'm going to place the leading edge of the bell curve, along with many striving in that direction as students of higher knowledge. It reminds me of the Inca colony at Machu Picchu in more recent times. The spirituality of that time was based in nature. There was great respect for the mineral, plant and animal realms and likely adoration of the higher beings guiding them. The elements would have had enormous respect since humanity and all life seemed at the mercy of fire, wind, water and an unstable earth. The sun would have been worshipped as the giver of light and life. We can see these truths coming down into the early civilizations of our epoch and I suspect the origins were pre-Atlantean. I want to connect this place to Madagascar and North and Western Africa, which was likely not a desert in that epoch. We know that Lemurians populated Africa, Australia and the Indian subcontinent and that central Lemuria had been where the Indian Ocean is today. We see this black race's lasting imprint amongst those of the red race, which originated on Atlantis.

"Keep in mind that our skeletal systems weren't hardened at this point. There's no pre-Paleolithic evidence of these populations and likely their temples have been destroyed, but remnant people remain with us today to remind us of our past. They'd no fear of death and felt it a privilege to sacrifice their life for another. In time, the Atlantean empire would be more solidly in what is now the Atlantic Ocean, spreading from the Southern Mediterranean to the mid-point of the USA in width with colonies worldwide. The center of leadership migrated west as that mass of land stabilized. Our indigenous people today are remnant Lemurians, Atlanteans, Lemurian–Atlantean combined remnants, or those remnant people who interbred with the Caucasian race. I would assume that the red evolved from the black race and that the white and yellow races evolved from further interbreeding, mutations and natural selection due to climatic conditions. My soul wants to suggest a starseeding here and there to help out evolution."

She caught a hint of a grin with her last sentence, had an inward giggle, and went on. "So that's the lay of the land ... shaky as it must have been. Looking at the so-called (by me) history of evolution preceding this transition to the Atlantean epoch, I feel certain that we would have lost, at least, the last half of our bell-curve to the catastrophic end of Lemuria and that that was no mistake. The pattern within the records indicates that to be providential for humanity's future. It seems we need to slough off bad genetics and regressed brain development when new epochs begin. And, I think that has everything to do with steady, progressive brain growth, intelligence and the development of additional brain faculty, as we witness with the frontal lobe addition in Lemuria. All of that increases the odds of our vital reconnection to spirit. The maturation and mastery of these brain improvements was a mighty slow process as is reflected in the development of a child. We can see that the overlap in the stages of brain development in a child is a reflection of the overlapping of human evolution over epochal transition. It's all rather magical, if you ask me, but don't ask me or I'll get off track here," she sighed. "There's so much."

A raised eyebrow was all she got in response to that comment. "Onward, ho! We have a new bell curve spreading out over Atlantis and no new additions to the rainbow body to be concerned about. However, we do have Luciferic

truth be told

beings in our intellectual-mental bodies, presumably having a field day with those not under some spiritual supervision. Surely they were helping humanity, as we had no capacity to think at that time. As was the case at the beginning of our present epoch, some real wisdom flowed through from the Bearer of Light to give the Atlanteans some true mastery over life. This, I have read, was in the form of harnessing the energy that lies dormant within a seed. I doubt this happened right away, given that the epoch began 12 million years ago, but as civilizations rose and fell, this came into being. Just as the Lemurians had mastered building by (I'm guessing) guided brute force, the Atlanteans used energetic power to build, to have industry, to advance research into all aspects of life, including — surprise — powering their airships. It was in these airships, I presume, that Aramu Muru dispersed temple-trained late Lemurians to Tibet and the Andes long before the sinking of the Lemurian lands. That, you will recall, was part of Don Eduardo's story of his people when we were in Peru."

"Quite so, lass. I've wondered how he powered his ships. Interesting," he said, waving her on.

"So, we know Lucifer was at work in our intellectual-mental body, along with the good angel Moon Gods holding sway in the emotional-mental body whilst protecting our reproductive fire. Gosh, we should put them on our reproductive rights, now!" she exclaimed, dashing off a note to herself, while a grin stole across his face once again. *Not a bad idea,* he thought to himself, and then aloud: "We should have had post-it notes for such inspirations back in Atlantean times."

"R-r-right," she drawled. "I'm diving into the meat of the story now, cowboy. Hang in there. You'll remember that Lucifer's actions at *The Fall* became Ahriman's karma. This translates in a lot of ways but, most significantly, that Ahriman was given the task of holding a necessary polarity against the Sun's emissions of light and life force in order to stabilize physical reality. He is the dark side to the Sun's light, which would not have been necessary if we'd remained etheric/astral beings of some substantiality — real children of sun and moon. I imagine that polarity being needed in man's physical structure and in all living things in this reality.

"Working with the law of cause and effect, we know that the effect necessitating this sacrifice by Christ Jesus was a threat to our life organs. Our souls would have been thrown into deep desire or disgust. That which modulates those soul 'qualities' is the etheric body. And, Steiner does state — somewhere — that this sacrifice was at the level of man's etheric body. It fits the rainbow body pattern of stepping out the rainbow body one layer at a time, adapting them to life on earth. What is more, it makes sense in the context of esoteric medicine. At first read, I admit I assumed the life organs to be those in the physical body but, alas ... not so simple. Our life organs are, literally, our chakras. Through the meridian system, life force is delivered through the chakras to their paired organ and gland. So we have to look at life organs as, for example the base chakra, kidney/bladder and adrenal glands. There's an organ and gland for each chakra. Another example is our higher brain, the pineal gland and the crown charka. I'm uncertain how aware we were of the chakras, especially the higher ones at that time. We didn't grow into our intellect until the latter parts of Atlantis — except for those in the temples and schools of higher learning. On the other hand, the concept of a chakra would have made more sense to us then than it does now.

"The cause that created the need for this sacrifice? We know it has to do with Ahriman and Lucifer. We know the manifestation of the sacrifice in man was the ability to speak — a temple inspiration surely, as the women there were working with sound. Where I went with this missing puzzle piece was back to Demetri's healing. I can easily imagine the Ahrimanic and Luciferic forces doing battle in the heavens, each wanting dominion over man, but I can also imagine man experiencing that within the rainbow body. That would look something like the tug of war for Demetri's etheric body that we witness and, hey, if he nearly lost his, we would nearly have lost ours back in those days. Desire and disgust, translated over ongoing evolution, might well look like mental illness and organic disease today. We know those two forces have the ability to affect us in exactly those ways.

"We can now appreciate how the etheric body modulates the soul's antipathies and sympathies. When in balance, its meridians and chakras deliver a steady rhythmic supply of life force to every cell in our body and maintain proper function of the organs and glands. In disease, imbalances in the delivery of Qi or life force are apparent. Let's assume that Christ Jesus sacrificed himself in the astral to save our etheric bodies — pure and simple. Without that sacrifice we would have been forced to retract from physicality and would have been as lost as the fallen angels between the worlds.

"I reckon we were well into maturation of the right hemisphere then, having mastered the limbic brain and subjugated the reptilian brain to its control. The left hemisphere was continuing to develop. That's about the four-year-old stage of brain development midst the most important years of emotional stabilization — the widening and shoring up of the bridge, cowboy. In a nutshell, this sacrifice stabilized our etheric bodies and allowed the smooth flow of life force through the meridians and chakras to give life and health to our physicality.

"Another way to think of the calamity that precipitated the need for sacrifice is that Ahriman and Lucifer made our life organs selfish — self conscious — by forcing their ego into them. The sacrifice moved our life organs back into the realms of the unconscious as selfless servants to our future evolution. My God! It's so beautiful, I could cry."

And she did shed a few tears before going on. His heart pulsated in empathy and her astral body relaxed. "I imagine this sacrifice allowed the leading edge of our new bell curve, which had spread out through a gradient of brain maturation and consciousness, to move into the beginnings of left hemisphere maturation. That would have led, with guidance from the Masters, to the discovery of the life force in seeds. It was another big leap. And, we spoke — not intelligently, but words began to be associated with feelings and objects much like those of a small child. I would not be surprised if this resulted in a densification of our skeletal system, but that might have been unrelated —

pre-programmed into the Saturn return of the first Atlantean cycle.

"I see a real theme, in this sacrifice, of the ancient time of 'Old Sun'. If 'Saturn' evokes sacrifice to move evolution forward, 'Old Sun' evokes bestowing life force on earth, fueling the energetics of living for the future. And that's captured in each and every seed by the purest of etheric life on earth, the plants.

"Of course, just as with the assault on our physical bodies, there's a lingering malevolence as a result of their selfish and arrogant battle for our ether bodies and the rescue of our cosmic magnificence by Christ Jesus. It's the Ahrimanic double within the etheric body of each of us. We have adapted to the life-giving grace of our bestowing sun, but we walk with the shadow of our own accountability."

Leah set down her notes on the table and took up her new knitting project — a quick winter hat for her darling, comically intense, seven-year-old — Mandy. It would be made of thick multicolored yarn from green through the oranges, then the pinks and magentas, to the purples and the lot all over again. The yarn was flecked with sparkling silver thread, like the flashes of light from her eyes.

"I've no argument with any of that, lass," Chris said, sitting upright and picking up her notes. "It seems that each part of our rainbow body, created in divine perfection by the hierarchies, has undergone corruption and redemption. It's likely a consequence of physicality, but I look at our journey here as a tremendous learning for the hierarchies. They've stretched themselves and grown in the process."

"And suffered some bell curve losses of their own. Say more, cowboy," she urged.

"There's a substantial group of rebels from all levels of the hierarchy and a long chain of events in their world that precipitated physicality and free will. I dare say this is the furthest any of them will have traveled into density. Furthermore, they've actually called upon the Son of God to intervene on our behalf. My suspicion is that there's more to come before we get out of here, free of both Lucifer and Ahriman, who, with all the fallen rebels, will be redeemed. I don't want to know or even guess what that's about. Our strongest position is the here and now. So be thinking how we apply this to the present."

"I thought that might be your department — given that Demetri and I stand at the brink of our etheric portals. On the other hand, we're karma yogis and yoginis at *New Avalon* — taking action in the present for the future of evolution. And, by the way, we're expected for lunch on Sunday at his house."

"Quite right. Being present in the etheric body is the next level of mastery for you."

"I'll remind you I've some unfinished business in the astral," she sighed — a reminder to have a chat with Dragon Lady soon.

"Look, we'll have a good introduction to the initiatory work over lunch — soft lecture style, questions and answers … if I have them."

"So you two cooked this up together?" she asked.

"It was Demetri's suggestion. He's wanted to repay our hospitality since he moved in and thought this a good opportunity. The children will be over the ridge until later in the afternoon and he and I have an assignment for the cultural sphere to work on in the morning. I'll ride a bike down valley and you can bring a cart to pick me up."

"Good thing I ran into him this afternoon in the greenhouse. I might have missed it altogether," she teased.

"Nay, lass. He told me he'd talked to you. He came by the community center on his way home to help us raise the set wall. What were you doing in the greenhouse?" he asked.

"Just needed a break from all of this. Harry and I visited the bees too. We were careful," she said, looking up from her knitting to find him studying her. "It's not like I have to confess everything I do to you … or maybe it is, but we went to the stable too — to thank St. Germain."

"Ah, the truth is out," he laughed, slapping his right leg.

"What? You know everything that happens in the stable, whether you're there or not?" she asked.

"It's as much your stable as anyone's in the community, lass, or should I say, Alice. I'm glad you sought out St. Germain. As for my supersensible powers, Greg and I had to get some tools from the barn and I happened to notice you leaving."

Leah let her knitting fall into her lap. "So here's the downside of life in the present moment, cowboy. I think I mentioned this gathering storm I feel around me. I can't put my finger on it other than it's on a personal level. When I was in the tack room, a blessing came through — quite beautiful — and then thunder and lightening as the storm began surging. I came right back here and asked the Golden Queen to help me. She did what she could but this is something I have to face. I was a little worried about visiting Trynel, then worried that someone I know and love might suffer a serious illness, then worried about lunch with you and Demetri and this initiation work. So it seems I'll be worried about every little thing, real or imagined, until I really have something to worry about."

"I assure you lunch is nothing to worry about. I can get you that far down the road, lass. I did promise to be there for you, and I will be. How do you stand with it now?"

"The Golden Queen organized the storm to allow me the eye … for now."

"Good of her," he winked.

"I'm grateful for her. I would otherwise be worrying about the bees making it through the winter," she said, rolling her eyes heavenward.

"I reckon it's time for your download, lass. Last show of the year then two weeks off the air."

"Except for the fifteen-minute news segment. You're right, I'd better get my sleeping bag," she said, stashing her knitting and reaching to gather up her notes. Chris handed them to her with a heart-warming smile.

" You've had a day for the record books, lass — Akashic, and otherwise!"

truth be told

Saturday's show was a testimonial to resourcefulness. Few of the panel members knew each other but all found themselves with a common goal — their local economy. Leah's interview with Joel focused on needed changes in the Agricultural Department and the Food and Drug Administration. The former was top-loaded with 'revolving door' Monsanto executives while the latter looked like a branch of the pharmaceutical industry. A campaign was underway to move farm subsidies from Big Ag, which had plenty of resources, to small organic farmers, who were the hardworking minority devoted to sustainable agriculture and restoration of the land destroyed by Big Ag. The panel discussion began with an interview with each farmer or grower providing viewers with five different effective and profitable approaches to sustainability. Farmers markets were discuss, as well as local food clubs, direct sales to groceries, restaurants and consumers, whether in person or by internet mail order. It was concluded that the driving force behind any of their successes, aside from good agriculture, was the education and participation of the public.

From there, they moved into an open discussion of the challenge before them — the food industry, the industrial farming corporations responsible for the destruction of the soil and our health, and the brainwashing of the public by both, especially since the Citizen's United decision. After the show, at the Christmas luncheon with their guests, Leah and the entire staff, including Will, whose financial report had raised a few eyebrows, engaged in small group conversations with appetizers, then a larger discussion at the lunch table. In the end, it was agreed that they needed to take action on the GMO (Genetically Modified Organism) front. There were rumblings from different sectors of the State of California about the need to enforce food rights and create them if they were lacking. Leah concluded that the farmers present, and many who weren't, were energetic activists for sustainable change.

Stu proposed that they form a coalition and create a website devoted to this issue with links to Light on the Crisis and all of the farmer's websites. The farmers would encourage links with other sustainable farmers and organizers for food rights, forming a solid network of concerned citizens. The millennials offered to investigate campaign contributions to individuals, organizations and potential ballot initiative movements as the future unfolded as well as the lies generated by Big Ag to brainwash the public into complacency. Leah noted that her young staffers were looking and sounding more and more like a force to be reckoned with, especially with media investigation. Their tech skills were paying off for Light on the Crisis — why not for the larger community? She also noted that they'd been clustered around Will during small group discussion, interrogating him about his knowledge of Wall Street trading and the banking services industry.

Community members went straight to play rehearsal, leaving the millennials and a group of young local growers eager to help with cleanup. Chris raised the bar once again, asking more of his troupe than they'd thought possible. In fact, the entire production was looking and feeling quite professional. Voices were strong and clear and everyone was backing off from the other pressures of life to bring forth a first rate production — and, in good health. There were no understudies, prompting a short lecture from the director about getting to bed early, eating well but not overeating, and asking for help when it was needed. Everyone was pleased with the sets, commending Bernie and Mitch for the attention to detail that made minimalism succeed. There were costume alterations to be made, but they were minor and could be picked up at Leslie's (women) and Katia's (men) before Wednesday night's dress rehearsal.

Leah bowed out early to get dinner in motion and step up her housecleaning efforts in preparation for visitors. She'd left Chris, in his element, attending to small insecurities, a few adjustments of score to voice where he'd noticed needless strain, and another run through the dream dance sequence with Katia and Mitch, now that the set was in place. He encouraged them to practice a few more times before dress rehearsal and arranged with Ellia to accompany them. They'd done a beautiful job but Chris' director's eye had noticed a slight hesitancy when near to the newly placed farmhouse walls. A few more rehearsals, and added floor marks, would do the trick. She heard about all of that over dinner during which she, thoroughly exhausted, was granted an early tango lesson and good night's rest.

For Sunday lunch, Leah decided to drive her hybrid car down valley rather than an open golf cart. She'd not take chances with a cold when weather was changeable, the children were coming, and she was lead in the play *and* the community doctor. Her morning had been spent hosting Natalie and Harry for breakfast, engaging another laundry day freshening bed linens for the guest house, and working on the third sacrifice, which she left spread out on the table to join Chris at Demetri's.

The two brothers had been spread out on his table, plotting out their contributions to the cultural sphere's Bill of Rights. They'd been asked to cover the arts and religion/spirituality. It was hard for either of them to imagine the kind of diversity the homeless population might bring to either of those cultural components. They did know what would happen if religious extremists or zealots infiltrated the judicial sphere. That was an old story. What they hadn't anticipated was the need to curtail economic interests for religion. People were free to worship, as they liked, but not to make money through religion. But, what religion didn't? They were amongst the wealthiest property owners — tax-free and regardless of the population's interest in their beliefs. They were both scratching their heads on that one, when she arrived for lunch.

Demetri served a wonderfully nourishing lamb-rice-spinach soup, enriched with lemon and egg, and plates full of Greek finger foods and French bread, which was close enough to the crusty bread of Greece for him. They talked about his life with the fish and the children and how Sissi's arrival would shift the energy in the house. He'd quite enjoyed being their caregiver but was also open to Sissi assuming a big sister role with them — especially at bath time. Leah assured him Sissi was holding in her excitement to be there for her mother, but was full of wild imaginings, thanks to Zenzi and Jürgen's stories of life with Demetri.

When the dishes were washed and food put away, they sat at the table again to listen to Chris, each with a pen and paper to take notes. Demetri had a pot of tea steeping in the center of the table and three cups sitting nearby.

Chris led an invocation, calling in the leadership of the magi and the Ruby Order to witness the first meeting of their tiny mystery school. Their purpose, for this day, was to assess the consciousness level of present attainment, define what preliminary work needed to be done, and then provide an overview of the first initiation. Each of them was already aware of their discipleship, whether they called it such or not. Of course, they'd done as much or more in previous lives but each life required that each step be accomplished again before further advancement.

"Demetri," he began, "you had a setback not long ago due to emotional trauma. Your subpersonality, recently arrived in your consciousness soul, tumbled back a bit as a result. Because you and Leah exchanged soul–contracted mutual healings, you didn't lose as much ground as you could have, and she was freed of an onerous obstacle to her lagging subpersonality's ascension. These subpersonalities or tendencies, if you prefer, are your highest priority. Your astral mastery must be complete — including integrated personality and the presence of your higher self — before this initiation can be completed.

"You've both done amazingly well moving through most of the preliminary steps. We can go back to cover the preparatory steps, like body-soul-spirit health and well–being but those were rudimentary for each of you — ages ago. Your slip-up, Demetri, was a karmic debt with your brother that could not have been anticipated through self-awareness, just as Leah's implant carried a big karmic imprint several lives forward. These are exceptional circumstance, well beyond the typical rudimentary training for the path.

At the present stage of the path, you've both moved through Fire giving you a transparent, supersensory view of your fellow man, animals, plants etc. I think you'd agree that you can anticipate their needs and satisfy them without intervention from mentors?"

They both nodded and Chris continued. "This gives you courage, self-confidence, endurance and a magnetism normally not attainable to our average man or woman. For example, Leah this includes your clairvoyant gifts and Demetri, your affinity for magic. An advanced attainment in this area is the ability to read the script of the Akashic records and communicate in that way to other initiates and mentors. This unfolds when you are ready, as does so much of the path.

"We don't finish one of these steps before we start another, but rather engage them simultaneously. Leah, I believe you would simply refer to the lot of them as the work of astral mastery. The second is Water, which gives us discernment but, to attain it, we must clear our memory of this lifetime up to the present moment, and move beyond desires and addictions with an astounding amount of self-control. Truth is the guiding principle, thus all of the illusion and baggage of life must be abandoned to live outside the maya.

As a general rule, the school of life puts this one in your face whether you ask for it or not. Leah, I would remind you of the Bee Mistresses options of the two paths. The higher self defines this path, which is beyond the maya. This passage provides us with impeccable judgment based on sound ethics and morals.

"Then there's Air, which calls us to action. This action is without indecision and without doubt. Life is the school for this one too, and we know well when we have moved decisively with positive outcome. It's the greatest affirmation on the path. When these three passages are complete, we move fully into the Consciousness Soul, connecting with the Inner Sanctum of our Higher Self. Naturally, this one isn't complete for either of you because of the lagging subpersonalities. However, your other subpersonalities have ascended decisively, with favorable outcomes. Here we receive wisdom, and with it the maturity to walk the path in silence and humility. This is the point where living in the present becomes the way of life. We must continually remove the veil of memory that would attach us to the past. At the same time we must live with the teaching always in our minds and hearts that we become one with the higher mysteries. Here then, we build the bridge to spirit."

""I'm a little confuse how we arrived at the bridge to spirit instead of the door to etheric mastery, Chris," Leah asked. "Are they one and the same?"

"Not. Consciousness soul and *manas* must merge — literally consciousness soul is transformed into manas. The bridge must be built. Remember, we become spirit-filled consciousness soul?"

"Right. Do we master the *manas*?"

"There's no need, or way, to master spirit world whilst on earth, lass. It's an archetypal world of gifts given for complete astral mastery. *Manas* is the intellectual spirit world — the first layer of the third part (spirit) of the rainbow body. Spirit world is the home of the good and true and the truth of every life we've led. The path gifts it to us but, at the same time, directs us back to the etheric body for mastery. Remember the paradox of initiation?"

"I do. Demetri, are you getting all this?"

"Yes, my sister. My dragon of a teacher rammed it into me — likely before I was ready, but there it is," he laughed, tapping his third eye.

Leah poured tea for the three of them and sat back savoring it.

"Now, lass, the secret of success with any stage of mastery is to surrender to it and patiently await the work spirit and your true "I" send your way. It isn't like med school."

"That would be too easy," she laughed.

"Right, then, that's the preparatory work for entering etheric mastery. Now, lass, remember those times when you'd slip into another world but couldn't remember it?"

"Quite well. It keeps happening to me, cowboy. Now you'll explain it, I hope?"

"I'll try. Remember you've an etheric body and then there's the etheric body of the earth — the elemental world. There's a thin veil separating us from the elemental world. Likewise there's a thin veil separating us from our own etheric body. But, it's as if you are knocking on the wrong door, lass — lifting the wrong veil. Did Alice in Wonderland do that, too?" he asked, with the hint of a grin, as that suddenly occurred to him.

"Alice knocked on a lot of wrong doors and pulled away a lot of risky veils, cowboy," she laughed. That was lost to Demetri of course, so they didn't linger.

"You can't remember anything, though you have a notion it's another reality or parallel reality to this one. That's because it's real, but you've tried a door that doesn't suit your state of consciousness. The etheric world must be accessed from the astral not from this reality, especially if we want to remember and work with it. Your mind and memory are in the astral not here. From here, it would not make sense. That's why you'd find a good many books out there about conscious dreaming or controlling your dreams. Ordinarily we're not conscious in our dreams and just remember the flash sort of stuff that we pick up coming back in through the etheric body. The etheric body is the image body — you know that — while the astral, the soul/mind, is the body that can access and remember image. So where our exercise will begin, as you finish up with your subpersonalities, is dreaming."

"I'm a professional dreamer, my brother," Demetri assured him. "I have been keeping records for many years. It feels like a separate life that's very similar to this one."

"You're in, Demetri. It's similar but it can be more illumined. The idea, over time — and that could be lifetimes — is to bring that consciousness into this reality to have access to the knowledge here."

"Now that sounds like the *manas* còming through, cowboy — spirit-filled consciousness soul — bringing spirit into this reality."

"It is, lass. The reality we access in the etheric body as a process of mastery will not only tap into spirit world, it will allow us to control the etheric forces within our body and within the bodies of others. Your interest in medicine might be piqued by that information."

"Darn right, it is. So what's the hitch? I have some dreams that seem very real to me for understanding a situation or problem solving, but they don't feel illumined."

"I expect that we need to have access to that bridge, my sister," Demetri offered. "We need to be fully integrated with our true "I". Is that right, Chris?"

"Quite right, Demetri. But there's no harm in practicing holding on to dreams because the level at which these images play is the dreamless sleep stage, not the flash images you're remembering as you come back in or go out in sleep." It's reminiscent of the 'Old Sun' stage of consciousness, during which we received our etheric bodies. I'm sure you'll run across this at some point in Steiner's writing, lass."

"I have read about 'Old Sun', but not yet with this connection to dreamless sleep. Thank you, Chris. So, first we get to remembering dreams from this stage of sleep and someday they'll be illumined?" she asked.

"Close, but not quite. The skill gained remembering from the dreamless sleep stage of consciousness will assist in bringing through the images from the etheric body. But firstly, we must attain oneness with our true "I"; secondly, we must have crossed the threshold of the etheric body — the correct door; and thirdly, we must have confronted the Guardian at the Threshold. That's where the courage comes in handy."

Leah had a queasy feeling in the pit of her stomach. "Do tell."

"Well, that would be our shadow, lass, our dark and ugly nature that will lay us flat on our face."

"That sounds like Ahriman to me," she said, her throat catching a little.

Demetri looked altogether grim. "I've smelled him, twice in this life. You have clairvoyance, Leah. I have clairsentience with olfactory hypersensitivity. I smelled the rat in Iran when Chris lost his mastered double. I smelled him in the corridor where I was waiting for you, brother. And, I smelled him again in the apiary when he tried to snatch my life — he has a Mephisthophelean smell — the smell of hell."

Leah poured another cup of tea for herself, thinking it might calm her. Chris was well aware of her anxiety — could almost here the thunder in her personal storm. "But cowboy, this ugliness is us. We need to own it and heal it through karmic action, no?"

"True. However, it's Ahriman who embodies that ugliness and relishes the opportunity to confront us with it at the moment of death or initiation. Remember, he has the power of numbers and can duplicate himself in each and every human being — ala Mr. Smith in *The Matrix*. Only our true "I" can survive such a confrontation and continue living in this reality."

Leah took a deep breath. "Okay, I get the big picture. I, for one, have work to do in dreamtime, and with my recalcitrant rebel, before taking that step. Perhaps with the connection to my true "I" and spirit, and some expertise at dream navigation, I'll actually embody the courage needed to confront the guardian."

"You'll likely have ample opportunity to own that part of yourself. Higher self will push you to it. It has no place on the path after this initiation and so, both the approach to the threshold of the etheric and crossing of the bridge to spirit have a simultaneous timing. They also require knowledge of, and healing of, the immediate past life," he added, as an aside.

Leah looked at Demetri to see if he'd comprehended what Chris had spread out before them. "We'll have learned to love ourselves, Leah, right after we learn to hate ourselves," he declared, soberly.

"Witness my request for a reprieve until after Christmas Day, gentlemen. My higher self has to be sympathetic to community responsibilities."

"There's no harm in trying, lass," Chris suggested. "What will happen in the etheric world, after the threshold, is a more vivid reality than this one — luminous, in fact. It's in the elemental reality that the Christ will appear to us as an astral being. He inhabits the elemental world of the earth as an astral being and has promised to inhabit our own etheric bodies in time. As we proceed with mastery of the etheric, the veil between this reality and the elemental world thins, and then falls."

"Christ consciousness?" she asked.

"Aye. And that consciousness of fifth dimension is native to the *manas*. Christ is called the second Guardian at the Threshold. Now, when you finally enter the etheric you will need to find an anchor or root from which to explore and expand that reality. You always want a landmark, especially in the beginning. Trying to become conscious of these two realities simultaneously is quite difficult. You might try to identify a familiar landmark in the astral dreamscape for practice." Chris stretched his back, twisting from left to right, then stood up. "That's really all I care to say today," he concluded, knowing full well he'd be grilled for days by his sweet lass.

Chris stowed the bicycle inside the back garden and walked over to the stable, promising to come home with fresh herbs from the greenhouse for Thai Beef Salad. It was community dinner night with the second round of their *Threefolding* discussion afterwards. Leah finished drying and folding the bedding for the guesthouse, then dove back into the third sacrifice, albeit with a post-it pad next to her for pressing questions pertaining to her first moments in their fledgling mystery school. By five o'clock, she'd wrapped up the third sacrifice to her satisfaction and stopped there until she could run it by Chris on Tuesday night. He found her broiling the beefsteak with a glass of Zinfandel, when he poked his head in from the laundry room. She came to take the herbs from him, along with a sweet welcome-me-home kiss.

"Can I pour you a glass of red, cowboy?" she asked, returning to the oven to watch the steak.

"I'll have a beer, lass, but I'll take a few minutes to stoke the boiler. I need a shower, too, before we go."

He backed out the door again, leaving her feeling the slight shift in their relationship — all in her mind, of course. She'd just stepped onto a path of some magnitude with the love of her life in the driver's seat. How would this affect their marriage, their playfulness, and their love–making. He'd be unchanged, steady as a rock, shocked that she felt anything. While he was in the shower, she took a quick trip within to have a chat with her caged controller — the likely source of those unhelpful feelings.

Dragon Lady was suffering in her isolation and delighted that she'd been heard or felt in the outer world. But, the Bee Mistress gave her no wiggle room. She asked her point blank if she'd been around in another life for true initiation. The answer was no. She was a warrior, not an initiate. Yes, she'd been present in discipleship and had learned a lot in the process. She preferred male lives, was set back by the slave life overshadowing the present life for her, and the current life had become a real challenge. Her opinion was that it was pretty high-minded ... if anyone wanted to know.

That was all very interesting. Leah wondered why she'd never asked before. The Bee Mistress went on to explain how Dragon Lady was holding up a great deal of progress for Leah and the community. Her leadership was needed but not in its present or past form. Her competitiveness with Chris would prevent her release from the cage and an initiation needed for Leah's mission. *That,* she blasted at her, *was enough karma to set her back to the slave days!* Dragon Lady was to contemplate beliefs that were blocking her participation in the mystery school initiation process and judgments born of selfishness instead of truth. For Leah's part, it was nice to know that Dragon Lady had never experienced being part of an integrated personality. In fact, that explained a lot.

The salad, made on automatic pilot while she went within, was ready for the thin slices of steak (Chris' specialty) and Thai dressing (her specialty) when he emerged from the shower. He showed up in the kitchen in his dark brown v-neck sweater and, of course, black jeans, ready for a good cuddle, a cold beer and the sharpened chef's knife. Leah moved to the big stone mortar and pestle to pound chunks of palm sugar for the dressing. Her remaining ingredients were all lined up at the back of the counter making it another autopilot task. They chatted about the ponies and then the *Threefolding* task that lay ahead that evening.

When they arrived at the community center, Leah sought out Stu right away. He was organizing cameras and mikes for the final statements from the groups that evening.

"Stu, I have an idea for the holidays," she announced.

Typically, Leah's ideas mobilized the whole community into action. Stu was looking for some down time with the girls and Leslie. "What have you come up with now," was his wary reply.

"Nothing big," she laughed, knowing exactly how he felt. "I was wondering, with all the kids here, especially so many pre-teen and older boys, if we could run videos every evening in the theater for them."

"Great idea, but an odd one coming from you, boss," he laughed.

"Right. Well I want to watch them too. I was thinking of the whole *Star Wars* series. It's been years since I last watched them. I'm forgetting some of the take-home messages — like the wisdom of Yoda."

"Yeah, I could brush up on those, myself," he replied. "We could run them late afternoon, around sundown, so the kids could have a full day of play together first," he mused. "I can have them ready and any one of us can run them. Hey, we could put Rob in charge. I'll bet he'd love to see them again."

"Yeah! Parental discretion for the littler ones but I reckon the older kids have already seen them."

"Why don't you make an announcement when our groups are meeting. Then the parents can have some time to decide about attendance. We can let our staffers know tomorrow. Some are going home to family but I know Matt is planning to be here."

"I like that, Stu. Paula and Sam will go to Montana after Christmas and would likely be keen to see the films. Thank you. In all fairness, we ought to have a few special movies for the girls. I'll ask Leslie and Georgia to give that a ponder."

Thus, imprisoned Dragon Lady would get her lessons from Master Yoda, starting on Friday afternoon, while the Bee Mistress held the space seated beside her beloved mentor. As it turned out, the most enthusiastic response

truth be told

was from Demetri, who gave Leah a cheer of approval when the idea was put forth. She was hard pressed to keep a lid on the giggles.

At one point, during the *Threefolding* discussion, which now included Matt and Rob in the economic sphere, Leah raised her head up out of the judicial huddle to check on everyone. All three groups were actively discussing issues — all at once, and loudly. The children were having an equally boisterous game — laughing and squealing from the classroom. It was a good measure of the holiday mood sweeping through the community. Her judicial circle was compiling a thorough list of rights and duties and another of rules and regulations, which Will had suggested as a strategy for all the spheres. These would be presented at the end of the evening and shared by email with the community for critical analysis. Soon the roar began to organize itself into the written word, signaling that they were nearing completion.

After calling a quick break, Will pulled a slate blackboard out of the noisy classroom and drew a picture he would fill in as the circles reported. He was going for a 'big picture' view of the community that might help the visually inclined amongst them and evolve into a handout for future *Harmony Valley* residents (see Appendix B). Using different colors of chalk he began by drawing an enormous circle touching the edges and the top and bottom of the slate. At the center he drew a small circle, maybe six inches in diameter and labeled it Circle of Friends. He then created a bull's eye around that circle ending with three bands around the circle and a lot of open space out to the edges of the 'big picture' circle.

The huge circle he then divided into three pie slices bringing the lines right up to the circumference of the Circle of Friends. He labeled the pie slices Economic, Cultural and Judicial, and labeled the left and right of the board outside the community as The Outside World. The outermost ring of the bull's eye, which interface with the large pie slice of the sphere, he labeled in each of the three segments as 'The People's Bank', then he erased part of the line to create a channel at all three junctions indicating that the bank served all three sectors with interactive service. Finally, he drew a triangle under 'The People's Bank' in each segment, tagging the three of them with a different label in each sector. The economic tag read 'collection', the cultural read 'dispersals' and the judicial read 'allocation'. These triangles symbolized the three arms of the community funds, which the bank would collect, hold and disperse as part of its service.

"How does this work for a scheme, folks?" he asked. Most of the women expressed gratitude for the visual while, not surprisingly, the men held their opinions until they knew where Will was going with it. He asked everyone to absorbed the reports, making notes of further recommendations and ideas, rather than trying to recreate the drawing or write all the points down. He would supply everyone with a copy of the finished drawing for contemplation over the holidays. Matt volunteered to generate a professional color graphic with the studio software, which met with immediate approval. Will sat near the board to add what each team presented to each sector's big empty pie slice.

275

Bernie, representing the economic sphere, began the summaries. As requested, the group had separated the report into two lists — rights and duties, and rules and regulations.

"Here's what we've come up with for the rights and duties," he began. "The Economic sphere workers have the right to be heard, the right to job mobility, and the right to further education. The sphere itself has the right to petition for funding to cover needed expansion and research of good ideas. This can be community-backed funding or qualifying bank loans. They also have the right to petition their grievances within the sphere or with other spheres through the governing body of the sphere, the Circle of Friends and, if necessary, through the judicial court system. The businesses have the right to argue the need for certain regulations and the duty to comply with the community decisions regarding them.

"Now, on to duties. The businesses have the duty to produce what is needed rather than profit-driven production. They have the duty to be energy efficient and green at every step of production and delivery of goods and services. They have the duty to comply with regulations and inspections by internal and external (federal, state and county) oversight bodies. They have the duty to keep goods and services in circulation with seasonal or cyclical adjustments made clear to the community. They have the duty to produce the highest quality products and services for the community and outside markets.

"Spence is going to go through the list of regulations and rules for the economic sphere. Thanks, folks," he said, taking his seat amidst sounds of approval. Will had written condensed versions of Bernie's summary under the headings of Rights, which was subdivided into Workers and Businesses, and, under that, Duties.

Spence took the floor, noticeably more self-conscious, but ready to do his part. "We've got a pretty good list of rules and regs here but would appreciate suggestions if we've missed anything obvious. We're assuming this is a work in progress.

"We came up with the following rules: Equal Pay — Equal Say, which speaks to the co-operative structure of the businesses; All profits will end up in the community funds, for dispersal through consensus agreement by the Judicial Sphere and the Circle of Friends; Ecological guidelines are followed at all times; Labor is not, and will never be, a commodity; No individual or business is permitted to give gifts, bribes or donations to sway the opinions of members of any sphere; the first priority of the economic sphere is to serve the community; this sphere follows strict safety standards.

"In terms of regulations, the list is shorter. We would like to see oversight in the areas of research and development, efficiency, cost analysis, marketing, sales, and accounts payables and receivables. These could be members from other businesses within the sphere or those appointed by the Board of Co-ops, as we have called the governing body of this sphere. There should be price regulation guidelines, though if we're following the *New Avalon* model the prices within the community will not vary. However, those to the outside world could be monitored and adjusted.

" Thanks, y'all. Bernie will finish up," he concluded, taking his seat.

Bernie stood again for the wrap-up. "In addition, we suggest that the judicial sphere organize a consumer affairs subcommittee that seats advocates from the cultural sphere and legislators. This group could offer another level of oversight to the economic sphere. We're also not especially clear about whether this sphere includes the farms, gardens and orchards in addition to all cooperative businesses and sole proprietorships. If we can all consider this for next time, we'd appreciate that.

"Within this sphere, we suggest subcommittees for agriculture, market gardens, small businesses, and manufacturing. Let us know if you have other ideas there. Once again, the sphere's governing council will be called the Board of Co-ops. We're thinking maybe six representatives from across the sphere and recommend that this board and the sub-committees be rotated appointments so that everyone serves in turn, but without overlap. Because this is a co-op venture, we feel that a proposal will start at the subcommittee level with a super-majority vote of approval by that sector before it moves on to the Board of Co-ops for approval where a super-majority or consensus vote would be needed to take it to the Circle of Friends.

"Could we also recommend that those serving on the Circle of Friends be evenly divided from the spheres and, once the community is rolling along, that they'll have served coming up the line from subcommittee to committee to have gained the experience for the Circle of Friends. I'm not sure what you have in mind for all that, Will, but we thought it good to throw this out there now. Thanks everyone. That'll do for us this week."

An affirming round of applause followed as Will finished writing the subcommittee names within the Economic pie slice. The Board of Co-ops was put in the innermost circle around the Circle of Friends. *Harmony Valley Threefolding* was taking shape.

Nick rose next to present for the Cultural sphere. "For Cultural, we, and I'll use the word we throughout for *We The People,* have a good list of rights and duties, starting with the right to enjoy life with moderation. There's also the right to express the needs of the people to the Economic and Judicial sphere. That's also a duty. We would also include the right and duty to express the need for regulation and deregulation, as that's needed, and to present grievances to the Judiciary sphere for review. We have the right to demand the quality the Economic sphere is meant to deliver. We also claim the right to be heard and remind everyone that it's one person and one vote, when voting is used for decision–making. Businesses have no voting rights in elections, though their workers have voting rights within their co-ops and in the community. We have the right to all aspects of the commons and in turn the duty to see that it's maintained, protected and cherished. That includes but isn't limited to, housing, community gardens, sewage treatment, water, power, food resources, the community center, parks and recreation, and the natural environment.

"We have the right to law enforcement, a voice in making and amending those laws, and a right to 'police' and fire protection — whatever form that takes. Finally we have the right to all the benefits of the commons at no cost, as just compensation for our contributions to the community funds through our labor. That includes education, food distribution, transportation, medical care, retirement benefits, local postal service and delivery, communications, arts and theater, community garden space and the farms, the woodlot, orchards and gardens — as part of the commons, not the business end of it. To that we would add a reasonable range of tools, supplies, and heavier equipment. We're not exactly sure about how utilities will look when all is said and done. That would be another topic to take up next time after consideration between now and then.

The general benefits just listed are suggestions for subcommittees within the cultural sphere with the addition of 'spirituality'. We feel religion can be better fulfilled with local churches outside the community, perhaps with free Sunday transport, and that the community can maintain the chapel in town center for non-denominational meditative spiritual connection. We feel each of the four neighborhoods should have a sub-committee as well, or, if more practical, the total of the neighborhoods, to deal with home repairs, maintenance, garden planning and mobility within the community. We do have some concern about utilities being regarded as commerce and feel strongly that they should remain in the cultural sphere. Teachers, for example, get paid from the community fund in *New Avalon,* and we all pay our share of utilities to the community fund. We also suggest that the laws from the judiciary to protect citizens follow typical criminal and civil court guidelines.

"For rules and regulations, we came up short since rules and duties in the commons seem redundant. We could come up with standard guidelines for the filing of a complaint or making a proposal of some sort, or guidelines to get information leading to an appropriate reference point rather than causing a run around. We established a rule to safeguard the rights to water, power, etc., treating them as precious commodities provided by the earth and cosmos. We can also decide that a person be allowed to go on in education as far as they're able, for free, as is the case in Denmark. This would mean that someone capable and eager to pursue medicine would be sent to a university at the community's expenses in return for a promise, in contract form, to return to serve the community for so many years. If the contract is broken the debt must be repaid.

"In January, we should discuss how to separate agriculture into two divisions — the economic surplus that might not come directly to the people and the feeling that the land and animals belong to the commons. We might also discuss a way in which a percent of a person's home rent, paid out of their wages, might accrue in an equity account available to them in US currency if they should leave the community. This percent could increase over time, encouraging longevity, and would, in all cases apply to their old age care in our future retirement community. I expect that Will has plans to hash out a deduction schedule for their wages to establish a firm, expected amount with excess quarterly account balances, and supplemented by the economic sphere donations, going into the community funds as well. It might take these folks a while to trust that system. One last point, as hard as it might be, is to strive for a span of generations in the final population, making sure we have some young people to balance out those who are aging or debilitated. Okay. There you have it for the Cultural sphere. Thanks, everybody."

Nick got a round of applause while Will finished writing in the Cultural sphere's sub-committees. "What were you going to call your board or council, Nick?" he asked.

"Oh, sorry about that, Will — my omission. We tossed around a few things and came up with The People's Council."

"Thanks, Nick," Will said, with a smile, while writing that into the inner sphere ring. He really liked that name. "That brings us to the Judicial sphere which I've been asked to present," he began standing in front of the board with his notes. "I'll be jotting down summaries on the board as I go along but will write this up in total and send it out to everyone, which might be a good idea for all three spheres, in addition to the graphic that Matt's agreed to create.

"Let me begin by stating the three functions or duties of this sphere as Steiner defined them. They'll be no surprise to any of us. First, there's the protection of human rights. This would include labor as well as those unable to contribute with their labor, for example new mothers, the children, the ill and the old. This is a broad category and one for which laws must be written.

The second duty of the Judicial is the regulation and de-regulation of business, which includes the oversight needed to keep the Economic sphere from reaching into the other two spheres.

The third duty is to enforce the laws, which are made on behalf of the people by the Judicial sphere. This is accomplished through the regulations but also through prosecution in a court system that's also part of this sphere. Here we note the difference between the police, who are in service within the Cultural sphere, and the court system, which enforces the letter of the law in the cases brought before it by the Cultural or Economic spheres. We suggest the court operate with the choice of a three-judge panel or a judge and jury. The juries will be drawn randomly from the adult community, the judges will be appointed by consensus of the legislative body, which will be elected by the people to serve one-time fixed terms. We feel the judge or judges ought to have some knowledge of the law, a sense of justice, and wisdom.

"Here we need to make the distinction that the Judicial system in this community is meant to handle minor offenses, misdemeanors, and that serious offenses would come under the jurisdiction of the county sheriff and be prosecuted in the County Court in Yreka. Anyone convicted of a misdemeanor will suffer the punishment allotted by the court, which might include expulsion from the community. If convicted of a serious offense, in Yreka, the community judicial system will exact its own punishment at the community level. This is all very complex and bears a lot more thought and work, but this is what we've arrived at for law enforcement at this time. In *New Avalon* I think we can all agree that if anything of this nature did occurred, we'd thrash it out at a Community Meeting. In *Harmony Valley* we'll have a larger population with a wider variation in moral character. It will have to sort itself out.

"In terms of laws to have in place, we'll need to spend more time working out details. I think we can agree on no firearms, recreational drugs, hard alcohol or prostitution. I would also think it wise to store prescription drugs in *New Avalon*. These rules alone will need to be watch – dogged to prevent a black market. We can't assume innocence with residents. Hopefully, Natalie's sound judgment in selecting residents will lessen the need, but I think we need to be forthright about human nature. I'm not sure what can be done to prevent marital hanky-panky," he laughed, "beyond people actually embracing the spiritual work, which isn't enforceable.

"Now, if I list some duties and rights, they might look like the oversight of the Economic sphere, the making of laws on behalf of the people, and providing free counsel for court cases. For labor, we can include regulation of fair hours, wages, advancement opportunities, education and mobility within the Cultural and Economic spheres. This might also come into play if labor strikes, or we need to hold hearings on grievances. The Judicial will rule on all oversteps and challenges to the laws and make or amend the laws as needed.

"Most importantly, it's the function of the judicial sphere to allocate the community funds as dictated by the Circle of Friends. As we've discussed in the past, there's a *fixed fund* for retirement, taxes and insurances, like fire and natural disaster, liability and universal health care. There's the *emergency fund* for community and individual unforeseen crises, which ought to maintain a base–line level with yearly spillover of excess into the third fund, which we called the *community fund*. This is allocated for wages of the Cultural sphere laborers, including teachers, bankers, farmers, fire and police, landscapers, improvement and maintenance of housing, utilities/infrastructure, and the commons, in general. We should consider this fund fed from three sources: business profits, wages, and grants and gifts. We can work out the fine points there at our next meeting. It should be noted that all judiciary, legislative, subcommittee, council and Circle of Friends assignments are required, unpaid community service positions.

"Additionally," he continued, nodding at Bernie, "I would recommend that there be a business expansion and maintenance fund held within and managed by the Board of Co-ops, with Judicial sub-committee oversight, allowing a portion of profits to be allocate for maintenance and improvement of the businesses without needing to channel requests through the Judicial branch and the Circle of Friends for approval. Any process within the Economic sphere is initiated by the workers, moves up through subcommittees and then to the Board of Co-ops. It's a pretty good democratic process on its own, but we should talk more about that when we're all together again as a group.

"Major expansion or new business would be excluded from that proposal and year-end surplus not approved by the Circle of Friends for expansion or new business, would spill over into the community fund. The community should have tangible evidence of the benefits of the Economic sphere. The purpose of business expansion is the betterment of community, period. There's much to be worked out there. Further expansion of the community might come through a combination of business profits, grants and gifts, and unused Cultural sphere funds. For next time, as an exercise, we might consider how the community might build a new theater or clinic. Part of that should come from business as profits from their labor, part from their wage contributions and part from grants they might receive. Beyond that, we're looking at a retirement community and aged care facility as satellites of the main nuclear community. They would both provide more employment for the working members as the elders leave the work force.

"As for rules and regulations, this sphere creates them when they're needed to maintain the balance of the spheres and the rights, health and safety of the commons. This sphere has no control over the Cultural sphere activities save law and regulation enforcement and, if needed, judgment. This sphere recognizes the need for the people to organize initiatives and present them to their elected legislative body. If this process begins to resemble lobbying for individual or small group agendas that don't benefit the community in general, this sphere can bring such lobbying efforts to the attention of the Circle of Friends for further discussion. In all ways, the community, business and legislature maintain themselves within the legal laws of Siskiyou County in the State of California, and United States of America as we do in *New Avalon*.

"Sorry to be so long-winded folks. I can see we're all tired. I wanted to get a good leg on this before the San Francisco project draws me away, periodically. So I'll end with a list of possible subcommittees for the Judicial sphere that will sound a bit like our government's: appropriations, law enforcement, oversight/regulation, consumer affairs (I liked that suggestion), labor rights, common rights, and community affairs which might include diplomatic relationships with the outside world."

Will finished writing the subcommittees in the judicial pie slice just outside the banking ring, then turned around to bring his presentation to conclusion. "I'll wrap this up by inserting our choice of Legislative Council for the governing council name. So now we see the Circle of Friends being informed and informing the three sphere 'councils', the 'councils' interacting between their sphere and the Circle of Friends on behalf of their subcommittees, which communicate with the workers, citizens, and legislators, as the case may be. The bank acts in service to all three spheres with its own rotating board of directors coming directly from the commons. We have plenty of loopholes to fill here, more ideas to put forth and problems to hash out at our next meeting, which will be January 8th, 2012. Over the holidays, we'll get the summaries and the dazzling color chart to all of you for your consideration and preparation for that meeting.

"If you ask me, we've grasped the *Threefolding* concept and its application. So let's get ready to fine-tune it next time. In the meantime, let's all enjoy the holidays and celebrate the end of a really wonderful year."

That brought a rousing round of applause from the weary group and a bursting forth of children from the classroom. They were all on school holidays and pleased as punch to be staying up so late to play. And, they were all *starving*. Their mothers pulled the leftovers out of the fridge to let them have at them and would stay behind to wash up again. They'd have done the same at home.

The studio staff wasn't on holiday though the lack of pressure of a full show was apparent. Stu and Rob were still putting the Saturday composite of 2011 show excerpts together with the theme of *'the gift'* and Joel still expected a live interview with Leah on Thursday. Paula's news analysis job was full on though the holidays typically silenced the politicians and eliminated global crises. She was into a little investigative journalism to make up for the slack.

Monday morning found Leah and Joel in a scheduled Skype session. He and his family were off to the Virgin Islands on Saturday morning. His show would play repeats between Christmas and New Years, when his viewers, more-or-less, expected him to take a break. Then, he would be back on the air January second. Leah shared her concern about the European Debt Crisis and listened with a critical ear to his take. It was ever so slightly more radical than Will's with more focus on the violence on the streets — insurrection. She didn't bring up the sovereign debt or refer to the World Bank's history of exacting bondage or resources for debt. Instead, she asked him how they might avoid insurrection at home.

"Why avoid it?" he asked. "I do favor revolution when it's needed."

"I don't disagree, Joel. However, there are bloodless revolutions and there are bloody revolutions and, let's face it, the American public, no matter how many assault rifles they've piled up, hasn't a chance if they challenge the federal government. The states that might stand up and fight the feds are some states where big oil and gas would fight for the opposite values of the people's insurrection. Ghandi fought globalization by demonstrating local sustainability. He spun his cloth and wove the cotton, and it wasn't GMO cotton."

"Oh, come on," he moaned. "Ghandi was a saint. This is America, Leah."

"It *is* America, Joel. We don't have to be saints to demonstrate resiliency although we do have to live up to who we are and what we're doing here, I'll remind you," she argued, on behalf of the Ruby Order. "Our stuff-filled culture has forgotten our strength, and a good many are young enough to have never experienced hardship or remember their grandparents' stories of it. We don't have to be victims of this global economic disaster."

"I get that point. I'm all for the community work Kim is spearheading. On the other hand I want to look for ways to bring the banksters to justice for their crimes. They're treated like kings instead of the criminals they are."

"I agree, Joel, but you can see that insurrection isn't affecting the bankster in Greece — at all. The root of the problem is income inequality. If the people want to fight, they should do it through product boycotts, making goods locally and buying them locally and reframing lifestyles to do without the food that doesn't grow in their climate, the goods that come from overseas — like that. I realize the Greeks aren't in a position to do that now, but we are. Those holding investments can divest and reinvest ethically and/or urge their retirement funds to do the same. This is bloodless revolution like the one in South Africa that finally stopped apartheid. If the government had wanted to avoid the whole thing, they could have bailed out the people instead of the banksters."

"Maybe you should do a show on this theme, Leah. My staff would agree with you, I have to admit. Maybe I need to look into the alternatives. The millennials will fight for what's right but they don't need to die for it. Maybe it would help change the way conflict is resolved in the developed world."

"I like that idea, Joel. Could you engage your staff in focusing your Thursday show, including our interview, on the same topic as our show, but from your perspective?" she asked.

"Sure could. I'm thinking along the lines of the 1%/Republican campaign to bring the jobs back from overseas now that they've killed labor unions and thrust the middle class into poverty so they'll work for less than the Chinese," he offered.

"That will fit and it's more your style than spinning cotton," she agreed.

"In fact, we might have our two staffs share information and research just to give it more weight, more credibility. They'll sort out what to emphasize and how to avoid dual coverage."

"They'd love it. After the first of the year, we're going to include a five-minute analysis of political lies and what the truth really is. Paula is spearheading this one for the 2012 election and already has a cache of taped guffaws from early primary rhetoric."

"You're going to deliver the goods?" he asked, referring to her general disinterest in the election.

"I'm actually thinking of making it Paula's spot. She's the 'canary sighting' champion as well."

"You might be able to syndicate it. I'd pick her up if it looks authentic."

"Interesting idea. Let's see how it goes over with our viewers. One thing we can rely on is her radar for the truth or lack thereof. The value of truth can't be overestimated."

They went on to chat about the *Threefolding* project in *Harmony Valley* and the application it would have to all the projects as a sort of Community Constitution that could be amended as on-the-ground experiences from a lot of projects were analyzed. They could both see the value of experimental democracy within confined local communities ... as if it was early America getting a second chance. She hung up realizing that the tone had changed in their usual system–bashing sessions to one of solution and mutual assistance. What didn't dawn on her, in the moment, was the importance of this new awareness, and the tasks it necessitated with Joel, to Dragon Lady's freedom and transformation.

After she and Joel wrapped it up, Leah had a chat with Natalie about the guesthouse situation and her desire to pay for Nathan's rental out of her NAD account. No problem there. They got on the computer and took care of the transaction right then and there. Then they talked about the *Threefolding* work and the suggestion of a greater age span amongst residents than the homeless population might give them. With so many young people stuck living at home, with a mountain of student loan debt, she thought they might put out a call through the show's website to see who might be interested in co-creating the future with them. They could use the money they earned at their jobs to repay the loans, and she was sure the farm and food production side of the project could use their energy and novel ideas. They could run it by the Outreach board when they met on January 5th. She would give an estimate of homeless applicants and some interview results then as well.

Chuck was arriving on Wednesday evening. He planned to go ahead of her down to the Bay Area to meet with constituents on December 29th and 30th then pick her up at the airport around noon on New Year's Eve for their shopping trip. He remembered where his wife had found her gowns and made an appointment for Natalie and reservations for lunch. She and Georgia were going over makeup tips for such an extravaganza and Shelley was sending her off with a fitting hairstyle. All she had to worry about was worrying. They had a good laugh over that one, but Natalie had stunning good looks, an abundance of poise and charm. Leah was sure she'd have a great time though she wasn't going to be gone much more than a day.

Her next stop was the clinic where she checked in with Nick. They had a good talk about the work his group had done on the Cultural sphere and he liked the idea of recruiting millennials who would be homeless without their parents help — and likely a good many were homeless, come to think of it. A lot of the *Occupy* participants were on the streets or piled in with friends. She gave him a few tips about Trynel for his trip over the ridge on the coming Monday but, otherwise, neither of them had anything medical to report. With the influx of visitors from the outside world, he expected some colds after the holidays but the flu season, if there was going to be one, wouldn't be hitting until the temperatures fell. No one felt comfortable talked about the lack of precipitation anymore, not wishing to add negativity to a serious situation.

When he arrived home for lunch, Chris found her, once again, spread out on the kitchen table with her work on the four sacrifices. He and Tommy had hiked up to the wind power generators on the west ridge to make sure everything was working right. He cherished the time spent with Tommy whom he'd miss having around fulltime after his project started in the Bay Area. Tommy held a strong but silent spiritual anchor for the community that Chris truly appreciated. His presence in the Ranger group greatly enhanced the worked they'd been doing because Tommy had close ties, his whole life, to spiritually grounded male peers. The Rangers were keen to have their meetings the day after the Outreach board meetings to make sure he'd be there at least once a month.

After lunch and a short power nap, Chris and Greg were over to *Harmony Valley* to check fences and water the orchard, berries and some greenhouse production for Sonia. Tommy would be over there working on the solar power farm with some of his crew. He had three building crews on various projects including the barn, hotel, and WWOOFer/Apprentice compound. *Harmony Valley* was taking shape both in the minds of the community, due to the *Threefolding* work, and on the ground.

Leah returned to her work on the kitchen table after lunch, hoping that choir practice time and the following afternoon would bring her research to completion. She had a date with her husband to present the third sacrifice on Tuesday evening and he had a date with her for cosmic loving right after their discussion.

As they lay in bed together Tuesday morning, Leah related an interesting dream. She'd found herself in the garden of Master Mukda's Ashram sitting by the pool where she'd had a profound meeting with her friend, Bryan, during a dream in Peru. Bryan died in service to the mission on that journey, but not before he'd done a lot of spiritual work on himself — in this reality and the dreamtime. As Leah recounted to Chris, she'd wandered through the garden unable to find the door to the Ashram so turned to admiring the beauty of the flowers instead. A beautiful deep lilac bearded iris bowed before her allowing a golden path of light to spill forth from its center. She felt she could have followed the golden path, but didn't. Then just before awakening, she was in a dream choosing greeting cards from a left to right scroll on the Internet. She came to a card with a yellow bearded iris and it bowed, offering her the same path.

"Interesting, lass," he said, holding her in his arms. "What do you think or feel about not finding the door to the Ashram, and where do you think that golden path might take you?"

"Well, I was contemplating that whilst waiting for you to wake up. I've been through that door before, but always to meet you there for sparring and then to go to Master Mukda, whom, I assume, is no longer there. I reckon that must be an upper astral place inside, but not in the garden. The flower is totally different. It doesn't need to be in the garden there, unless that's a landmark for me, but it's an etheric being without an astral body so I'm thinking it will lead me to the elemental world. The Guardian at the Threshold, which the path might lead me to, still confuses me. Is it my etheric field or the collective-elemental world? You might clarify that for me, darling," she suggested.

"You're right not to expect Master Mukda there. He's gone fifth dimension on us. And, though you referred to it that way, it wasn't his Ashram, but an Upper Astral Ashram for the Ruby Order. That's why Brian was only in the garden, which you might think of as the astral landmark with lower and upper astral portals within it — like when you went into your image in the pool?"

"Ah, yes, I do remember that. I also remember being with you and Master Mukda when we passed a being of great light with four bodyguards as we were walking down an interior portico."

"You saw him. We didn't. I expect he was important to you and not to us, and that he crossed over from a higher dimension. Mukda might have taken that walk in the opposite direction when he left. Once you are integrated in consciousness soul, the Ashram doors will appear and you can enter consciously. Until then, I can make that happen for you if we need to go there."

"So how about the elemental world?"

"Until you walk that path, I can't rightly tell you where it goes. It might lead to the elemental world or it might lead to your etheric body and the Guardian. You only need to meet the Guardian at the Threshold once and then both realms are open to you."

"What a great help you are," she teased. "Should I take the walk or not?"

"It does seem like an invitation. I imagine you'll know when it's time to take it."

"I've never seen it before. It must have something to do with the path right now, then. Okay, cowboy, I'll see if it appears again. I'm intending to find my landmark. I have the pool — though I didn't try to use it — and now, perhaps, the flower."

"I think you can assume that the Ashram is your landmark, lass. I'm glad you found it without a struggle." Then he gave her a squeeze and whispered in her ear, "Can't wait to fly away with you tonight."

"After I bore you with the third sacrifice?"

"You are not at all boring. I've never given a thought to brain development when pondering these mysteries. I find it fascinating," he replied, showering her with kisses.

"That's pretty much what Elliot said too. We wouldn't need or have a brain if we hadn't crash-landed in materiality. It seems the likely touchstone for the rainbow body and the hierarchies and a good measure of our progress as well."

"On that note, I'll put on the kettle while you get organized for yoga."

"Thanks, cowboy. I'd be lost without you."

"Not likely, but I *will* be there for you, lass."

part four: joyeux noël

chapter 10: oma & pops

Leah and Natalie spent an hour on Tuesday morning filling in calendar page printouts for the first half of 2012. The goal was to see what else they could take on without compromising the show or the community. Natalie had adequate help teaching the Outreach Community Program and would take on Kim's group herself. She was still revamping the program to apply it to the Inner City projects and did have Sonia and Georgia eager to help out with those weekends when they got going. Beyond that, there were the apprenticeships. If all went well, those coming in for that training would help free up the community from their everyday jobs to help with Outreach.

Will wandered in as they were trying to come up with a schedule for groups waiting in the wings. There was a long list of inquiries but no assurance they would pan out long haul.

"Hey Will. Are you here to volunteer for additional selfless service?" Leah asked, pulling his leg a bit.

""I'm maxed out, Light Beam. I'm here to let you know we'll definitely be audited. Nothing to worry about but the Feds will be in here snooping around."

"Don't you file the non-profit tax report in May? How could you know that?" she asked, puzzled.

"Well, there's the steady stream of donations that has piled up to a hefty sum, and then there's this little end of the year gift courtesy of Ali Cat," he said, waving a check around in front of them.

"Let me see that," she laughed, grabbing it handily. "Holy shit. You're right about the audit. Any strings attached?"

Natalie grabbed it from her since no one was forthcoming with a total — $3 million dollars. "That'll butt-kick any number of projects. End of the year tax write-off?" she asked.

"You bet. It came with a note to cash it right away so it clears by year-end. Strings? You could say that. It looks like LA's Inner City project will get off to a good start. And get this: he wants to donate his mcmansion in the foothills for the community farm. Ali wants to be the first resident of the Inner City project. *New Avalon* had more of an effect on him than I'd imagined."

"He'll be fun in the Outreach program," Natalie laughed. "I can hardly wait for that one!"

"You're right about the audit, Will," Leah concurred. "Are we current on all our licenses and inspections here?"

"No worries," he replied, "to quote your cowhand."

"Cow*boy*, Will," she corrected with glee. "I have a feeling they'll be watching us like a hawk with *Harmony Valley*, but you'll be golden with the Inner City projects because local government is behind you."

"They're behind us here," he protested.

"Don't count on it. Always remember this is a red county until we over-populate it with progressives. They could start nit picking non-profit exemptions and tax breaks, building codes, inspections — you name it. Imagine what we would owe them in property taxes alone if we lost our non-profit status over there."

"Okay, Light Beam. I have been sufficiently warned. We'll bend over backwards to meet requirements *and* make some attractive improvements to the county. I bet we'll attract a lot of organic farmers and ranchers to the area."

"You're probably right, Will. I'd so like to keep a low profile but who would that serve?"

"Us," he replied, with a chuckle. "Later, eh?"

After Will left Natalie's office, she looked at Leah. "Could we not make up anything extra to worry about, girlfriend?"

"Sorry, Nat. I'm in a worry rut. I'll find my way out of it. You don't suppose it has anything to do with what we've written all over these calendars do you? And likely going daily in the spring?"

"Listen to your banker," Natalie advised, unknowingly sounding a bit like Thomas Jefferson. "*No worries.*"

"It was an awesome donation. I'll call Mr. Cat on Christmas to thank him," she conceded, with a big smile.

Chris and Leah caught up about Ali Cat, Joel, and the state of affairs at *Harmony Valley* over dinner. Chris had placed the food order for the guesthouse and would see that the kitchen was stocked on Thursday morning. They'd not made any firm plans for activities except that Nathan would be invited to the Ranger Christmas party on Friday night, along with Chuck *and* Sam. *Those two are worming their way into everyone's hearts,* she thought to herself. *It seems Sam and Paula will be here long haul!* Leah shared that she'd need to work Thursday afternoon for Joel's interview, and then a fifteen-minute news segment for Saturday's show, which could be taped well ahead of the show that day.

When she and Chris sat down for the third sacrifice discussion, it was with the satisfied feeling that a good coconut curry provides — followed by a pot of lemongrass tea. It was still early in the evening as they settled into their nests to sip tea and hear her story of late Atlantean times.

"You ready, cowboy?' she asked, setting her empty cup on her mother's tea table, which was placed between them on the carpet.

"Aye, and expecting another interesting tale, lass," he replied, taking the last sip of tea, for the moment. The pot sat in a cozy, promising a second cup after she finished.

"Right, then. Here we go. This third interference with our evolution, which was said to be Ahrimanic — Lucifer was involved but not directly, from what I surmise — came late in Atlantean times. I'm guessing this was in the last era of Atlantis, during which the Mongol civilization rose and fell. It was known to be a time when black magic came into being, which fits the Ahrimanic picture. In particular the Mongols were trying to recapture the ability to extract energy from seeds and resorted to black magic trying to make this happen. This tells us the whole epoch was in decline, which, as you pointed out, is to be expected as any epoch nears its end, but also that they'd lost the art at some point in the past. Man would have had hardened skeletons by this time. There were extensive temples and mystery schools spread around the globe, some populated by the most conscious amongst the Semite people. Atlantis was a far-reaching civilization. Although, we think of it as an island in the Atlantic, it covered the globe with large and small colonies that interbred with Lemurian remnants to further racially diversify humanity.

"During the Atlantean epoch the western US would've been under water except for remnant Lemurian lands — a string of islands on the Pacific coast, which likely included the Cascade volcanoes and this valley. Some huge earth changes occurred at the end of Atlantis — the great biblical flood was the result. It must have been a massive cleansing with another re-ordering of the bell curve, but that's ahead of this story. This story chronicles aspects of the decline. Ahriman attacked the soul of humanity. It's written that our soul forces of feeling, thinking and willing would have become disordered to the point of madness. Another way to put it is that they would not have developed in an orderly way. A lot of what I'm going to say is my own speculation. I haven't read anything yet to confirm my suggestions, which arise from logic and my understanding of the rainbow body. I welcome any corrections and clarifications, cowboy."

He gave her the 'okay' sign from his meditative state and she continued with the story. "How we would have looked, and behaved, read like a battle between a rising willfulness, seized by ravings (as it was put) as the intellect scorned the will. I could also imagine the feelings and intellect in conflict with the will and with each other. It was a time when intellect was beginning to awaken. Ahriman thrust it into a state of selfish egoism and self-absorption. I'm jumping ahead a bit but will pick that thread up later on. Ahriman's interference in our evolution, though necessary to physicality, created evil and opposition. If the 'Old Sun' time was about 'gifting' and the genesis of our etheric body, this would reflect the 'Old Moon' stage, related to the genesis of our astral body. We also need to keep in mind that it was on 'Old Moon' that the Luciferic angels refused the "I" that could not err, and brought in free will and the option of rejecting the gifts of the hierarchies. This 'renunciation' of gifts on 'Old Moon' gets projected into humanity as the selfishness and egoism driven into us by Ahriman's desire to chain us to materiality — the polarity he is meant to project. That desire was accompanied by a deep dive into our astral bodies and our collective astral plane. According to Elliot, the inception of 'renunciation' on 'Old Moon' imposed itself on humanity as an astral trap of unending images. That created image consciousness, the 'Old Moon' gift to our evolution. We were ripe for black magic, that's for sure — and, one day, Hollywood!

"So, this potential human madness, created by Ahriman's overreach into our astral bodies, attracted the attention of the hierarchies, and in particular our compassionate savior, Jesus, to request once again a Christ 'embodiment' and sacrifice in the higher realms on our behalf. What is amazing is that we actually have evidence of this sacrifice in the Greek myth of Apollo, the Sun-Spirit. He was their version of Christ, who calmed the disturbed Sibyls and healed the aura of the earth. In Christian myth this is remember as St George and as Archangel Michael slaying the dragon.

"It feels safe to say that Ahriman has been cast out of our astral bodies, which are still the realm of the Moon God angels in the feeling aspect and the Luciferic beings in the intellect. One can imagine where we'd be if Ahriman had taken over our will and had access to our incoming "I", but then this takeover is still a possibility if we falter and become 'possessed'. I'd like to assume that this sacrifice normally limits him to our etheric body and that it probably installed him as the Guardian of the Threshold there, as the price we paid for this redemption. Instead of penetrating our will forces directly, he engages them in the materialistic creations of the material world, often to the point of addiction so severe as to command the will forces indirectly. I could be wrong about that, but assume that the egoism and longing, that accompanied his interference, stuck to some degree and played a great role in deepening our life experience as well as our death experience. If we're going to step up consciousness, it must be concomitant with stepped up accountability.

"That brings me to propose that this sacrifice facilitated a further split of our astral bodies, adding consciousness soul to the complete picture. Now this is tricky. I can't find anything written about it thus far but it makes sense that this was either in the works by the hierarchies and actually created the crack, so to speak, for Ahriman to wiggle into our astral body, or it was a result of the sacrifice. The upper astral body, or consciousness soul, split from, or budded off, the lower astral bodies, creating a higher frequency astral body for the incoming "I" in the present epoch. A third bit about the rainbow body would be the way the three layers of the soul communicate with each other. If we equate the lowest astral body with feelings, and the middle body with thinking, then this third and highest body would be equated with the will forces. This was affected by Ahriman and Lucifer's egotistical meddling.

"I propose, then, that the third sacrifice stabilized the interfaces between these three layers of the soul. As expected, this sacrifice saved our astral bodies (our souls), such that wisdom flows into our feeling, thinking and willing, which must be a reference to the beneficial work of the hierarchies. The only difference at this stage between consciousness soul and the emotional and intellectual layers was frequency. From what I've read, thus far, in the book about Michael, the war went on in the collective astral until the late nineteenth century when the dragon, at last, was defeated and cast from the heavens to the earth.

"For humanity, this sacrifice preserved the evolution of speech into language — crafting speech into language and image-based object consciousness, which was the Atlantean epoch's overall achievement in consciousness evolution. Whereas the second sacrifice safeguarded our ability to bring speech forth, this one opened the door to communication and a new experience of relationship. Although, I do recall a biblical reference, — *I will confound your speech*, — which actually seems to have taken hold of us, especially in relationships," she laughed.

Chris lay back in the sofa with a grin on his face. It was true that we misunderstood each other more often than not.

Leah went on. "That brings me to the brain. This salvation of language speaks to mastery of the right hemisphere, which I would expect at this stage of evolution. We would already have been exploring the left hemisphere, which was likely fully developed but not yet the focus of evolution. I feel this sacrifice made it the focus. And, as a result, the corpus callosum was either stabilized, matured or came into being. It communicates left to right and back again. The other interesting piece is that thirty thousand years ago we began to bud the prefrontal lobes, the transcendent brain, off the front of the mature neocortex frontal lobes. To relate this to childhood, the left hemisphere starts maturing at seven and is finished at twenty-one. Twenty-one is the age when the "I" is meant to descend into consciousness soul. Well, that would be in a perfect world. So, roughly, in late Atlantean times, we were right around the 15 year-old stage of development where, these days, children chose between the cultural "I" or the true "I" in terms of their life trajectory. That's going to come up more with the fourth sacrifice. At our present stage of evolution babies are born without the prefrontal lobes, which begin developing after birth. This newest brain's development is wholly affected by the infant and toddler's life experience.

"Returning to the theme of selfishness; I believe that having the Ahrimanic ego thrust into feeling, thinking and willing would have turned the soul outward. We would have lost our inner world as it now exists, and our hope of transcending this world. We would be in that trap of endless images, brought about by Lucifer's renunciation of the "I". That would also have meant that the descent of the "I" which occurs in our epoch would not have happened.

"To wrap it up … as we've previously discussed, Manu, the higher being guiding the advanced temple and mystery school of the Semite people, led their most advanced disciples and initiates to safe land in the Himalayas. It must have been a journey over many years – perhaps decades – with the deposition of wisdom along the path they followed. We'll start our last discussion with that journey but I'll remind you now of what you'd shared awhile back with me. These Semites were the high civilization of the 5th Atlantean age. They were at the same position in the cycles of the epoch that Western Civilization holds right now. Atlantis was largely swallowed up by the great flood, which trimmed up humanity's bell curve massively, at the same time it changed the map of the globe completely. Thanks, cowboy. You've held a beautiful space … and you're still awake!" she laughed, setting her notes on the table to fill their teacups.

He opened his eyes and propped himself upright again to take the cup she was passing to him. "Thanks, lass, and I'd say you've done it again. I don't see any glaring contradictions to what I was taught and, again, I do like this connection to brain and child development. I think you're right about the third layer of the astral coming into being around this sacrifice, but I've no hard evidence to clarify that for you. I'd suggest that, along with Ahriman's presence as the Guardian at the Threshold, it's likely that the veil fell between the lower and upper astral giving consciousness soul access only to disciples."

"Brilliant, cowboy. That's definitely a distinction to acknowledge. If it had been accessible to those humans living in the cultural "I", the fallen ones could have gained access," she said, jotting on a post-it note.

"I could add something to your story of the hierarchies and the past stages of earth evolution," he offered.

"Please do," she urged, taking up her pen and notebook.

"It has to do with the expression of the earth's evolution within the solar system the hierarchies have created. In Saturn time, when the Thrones 'sacrificed' themselves to the Cherubim, time was born and the Archai, the hierarchy right above the Archangels, were receiving their "I". They came into 'being'. These are the Spirits of Personality who have given us our "I" three grand cycles later. You covered this nicely during our last discussion. The Archai are often called the Time Spirits. That all took place during earth's Saturn-stage of evolution. We can think of the Thrones as a frothing sea of courage and the Cherubim as radiant wisdom. We can equate sacrifice with fire/warmth and, in this reality, can associate it with the maya.

"During the second state of earth consciousness, 'Old Sun', we find that the act of sacrifice opens us to surrender and that, in turn, opens the way to higher consciousness. And here is where your 'gifting' appears – grace – the pouring forth of ones gifts, selflessly. You called it bestowing. The Dominions, the hierarchy just beneath the Thrones, were most active and instrumental on 'Old Sun'. They're the great 'givers' of the cosmos. During this 'Old Sun' cycle the Archangels received their "I" and have since become the 'givers' of light. There were, during those ancient times of our creation, those Cherubim who renounced the gift of the Thrones and, in so doing, created eternity – no time.

We can say that in one word — space.

"We have time and no time, we have 'offered sacrifice' and 'renunciation of that sacrifice' by some. When we move on to 'Old Moon', from air to water, the renunciation of Old Sun causes a resignation and 'longing' — egoism or self-absorption, which came out in your story. What's more it created a need to be embodied by those whose sacrifice was accepted. This was a state of condemnation from which the Mights, those who were most active on 'Old Moon', released us by bringing us image consciousness — the gift of 'Old Moon'. As it turns out though, this created pain and suffering and further entrapment in the endless images that you spoke of. Our take home message here is that the hierarchies, the gods, call their opponents into being to balance their acts of creation.

"Ahriman was no mistake. As you described before, he came forth to balance the Sun's creative light, and in so doing, the solar system, earth, and life upon her, could take form in the physical world. Lucifer's renunciation of the "I" and quest for free will was born of the renunciation of the Thrones' sacrifice by some of the Cherubim. We get a picture of creation that's not static. Just like that yin–yang symbol of the Tao.

"In summary, so far, we have Saturn/fire/sacrifice/our physical body, Sun/air/gifting/our etheric body, and Moon/water/renunciation-resignation-longing/the astral body or soul."

"Oh thank you, cowboy. This is a wonderful addition to the story. Have you more to offer at this point?"

"Not," he replied. "You'll be finding this in Steiner's writing I'm sure. Have you anything more to offer?" he asked.

"Well, I do have one observation and a couple of questions. You didn't disagree with this sacrifice's remnant antagonism, if you will, being Ahriman as the Guardian of the Threshold. Lucifer stands in the way of our astral mastery and Ahriman stands in the way of our etheric mastery, as I see it. Here I'm beginning to see the application of this story to initiation. Care to comment?"

"Not," he grinned. "I'm happy to witness your imagination and inspiration unfolding."

"R-r-right. Question two then," she continued, looking up from her notes to meet his gaze. "Do you reckon Cro-Magnon man, and other primitive human's we've discovered, fell off the bell curve as regressed humans or were they genetic lines that couldn't adapt as well as the line that went forward?"

"Likely the latter, lass. They seemed not to be regressed humans showing up as animals. Scientists would look at that a little backward and call them our early ancestors but they're not like the apes, that definitely ended up in the animal bell curve. I think we can assume there were more dead ends than not, as we evolved. Most of it was probably failure to keep up with brain development, don't you think?"

"I do agree with that. We had to adapt continually but the measure of our success was most likely the advancement of the brain. That would have given us an enormous advantage, especially as language developed and thinking.

I'm nearly finished with the fourth sacrifice and will be before the kids get here. When we have an evening next, I'd like to finish."
"I'll look forward to it, and whatever you decide to take up next."
"I might give the esoteric a rest while we figure out *Threefolding*, but we'll see. I'll get back to the Archangel Michael book for sure."
"Where would my beloved Jane like to go, tonight?" he asked, shifting the energy to sacred love.
"I'll leave that to you, my dearest, but I would like to check on my crew at the bridge on the way back, just to let them know Dragon Lady is still alive. Do you suppose we could start at my landmark, the Ashram?"
"That can be arranged. How about we start in this reality with mutual massages? I think we both deserve a good rub."
"Oh, yes! I'll warm the oil and you can break up the Anzac bikkies for our welcome home."

During her Wednesday morning Skype with Joel, Leah got his commitment to record two more interviews for upcoming shows. They'd already filmed the interview for the 7th, so she assigned him the theme for the 14th — 'are you prepared for climate change?' and, for the 21st, 'four megatrends'. Joel would cover the political aspects as features on his show throughout the week ahead of Leah's show. They would discuss them from his angle on his Thursday show, and then she would cover solutions on Saturday, including her interview with him. The four megatrends were economic instability, violence (including terrorism), depletion of earth's reserves, and poverty (including wealth inequality). They agreed on overviews for that show, since these four trends were worthy of separate coverage. Rather than waiting to have viewers tell them that, they assigned those four trends to the following four weeks as her show themes and his weekly features — titles to be determined.

With that settled, they talked about the obvious deepening of their collaboration and his willingness to approach the program director at *freedomofspeech.org* about back to back daily shows in the spring, which would be looming large on the horizon once the holidays were over. That was fine with her. Natalie's new assistant would start after the first, as would another tech hire for Stu. A one-hour daily show would give her time for greater depth with individual interviews, spread out the *Occupy*, Economic, and Truth in Politics reports, allow deeper news analysis and assure a 45-minute panel at least once a week. Myriad great ideas sprang into her mind, after they'd closed their session with holiday wishes in both directions and his promise to email the interview outline for their live interview the next afternoon.

The millennial staff was left in charge as Stu, Leslie, Natalie and Leah went home to change into work clothes, pack lunches and join the rest of the community in the greenhouse for the big year-end cleanup. This was the way the community celebrated Winter Solstice. They would be washing and sanitizing pots and trays for spring seeding, hauling in compost to mix in with Sonia's potting soil, and generally sprucing up the office, sorting and washing room, and the greenhouse itself. They hauled buckets of spent plants and weeds to the active composts outside, which Greg, Chris and Will were in the process of turning with forks and the garden tractor scoop. Tommy help Demetri check and service all of the fish tank pumps, the solar power installation that ran them, and the heater. Shelley and Ellia organized and inventoried the seed bank to give them a ready reference for spring seed orders. The catalogues were already rolling in from the seed companies. Katia pulled out excess saved seed to send over to the Transition Town folks in Mount Shasta for community sharing, and Sonia went through her desk and all the bookcases in the office sorting and cleaning. She would spend time over the holidays compiling data about the year's production and losses for the January community meeting. When the studio crew showed up, Stu and Leslie were put on task with Nick, Mitch, Bernie and Jenny cleaning the wooden trays and benches with power hoses and vinegar washes.

Leah and Natalie took on the mixing of potting soil — good therapy for a woman whose traveling man was going to show up that night. Natalie still got jittery the day Chuck was to arrive — attributing it to the long distant nature of their blossoming partnership. For her part, Leah was glad for Chuck's visit, sure that he would give Holly a lot of good exercise and Chris a riding partner of exceptional merit. Other than her trips over the ridge to see Trynel, she'd not been riding for some time. But life was about to shift again. With the passing of the holidays, there came not just the greater likelihood of snow, but also the return of evenings with Chris. Although, she was sure Chris would find some creative, but less intense, ways to keep the community singing, dancing and acting.

The group finished up, in high spirits, and to Sonia's satisfaction and grateful praise, by four in the afternoon. They would all meet again at the community center that evening, with their costumes, for the dress rehearsal of *Oklahoma!* Leah had been back for a fitting of the wedding dress, which Leslie would bring to the rehearsal. Up until the last scene, she would either be wearing denim overalls with a red-checked shirt or a high-collared yellow gingham frock with a lace-trimmed white bodice and full floor-length skirt. When the women gathered together that night it was with a fair amount of excited giggling and sincere kudos for the seamstresses. They formed a pastel rainbow of florals, checks and solids, with as much style variation as the patterns and imagination had allowed.

The men stood across from them with arms crossed, in loose muslin shirts and farmer cotton duck pants or cowboy jeans. Chris had found a pair of ankle-length leather chaps in Mr. B's barn, which made him look authentically Curly — except for his hair. Shelley thought some gel could be applied to loosen up his natural curl and promised to bring him a jar for experimentation the next day. He took them through every scene of Act I separately, with a serious critique of acting, singing and accompaniment. Then they repeated the entirety of Act I, with a few more comments, before moving on to do the same with Act II.

When scene three began, with Leah's costume change to the wedding dress and Chris in a black suit coat and pants, the two of them acted as if they were falling in love all over again. So much so that the women wept through the wedding. Of course, they *were* falling in love again. This was his marriage to the Bee Mistress and though it was only a rehearsal, she was sure they could fall in love again on Christmas, when the real marriage would occur. The finale was glorious. Everyone had a hard time falling asleep that night though they were all genuinely exhausted — everyone except Natalie, who curled up in the embrace of her lover to slept like a baby.

Chris and Chuck were off like a shot the next morning. Chris promised to be home for lunch, and then make his special pickup of food from Sonia and Jenny to stock the guesthouse. He was in line with everyone else welcoming family and friends, having been given a three o'clock warehouse pickup time. He also had a warm invitation from Sonia to stop by for the veggie box anytime after two. He'd make another trip to the brew house to stow some beer, cider and kombucha in the fridge along with the raw milk and apple juice for the kids.

Leah had worked on, and completed, the fourth sacrifice summary by lunch, while multitasking the filling of the cookie jar with freshly baked cowboy and Anzac cookies. After putting all of her papers in the first drawer of the secretaire, she grazed her lunch while planning and organizing dinner for six. Though she'd not seen the children since Memorial Day weekend, she imagined them around the table and took special care to see that their favorites would be served. Dinner would be a beef rump roast with extra cheesy-creamy scalloped potatoes, snap peas lightly steamed and served with butter, spinach soufflé and tossed salad.

For dessert, she had a surprise. In the fall, she'd asked Katia to stash a quart of caramel crunch ice cream in the warehouse freezer for her. Katia had it delivered to Natalie with her Wednesday box. It was hiding out in Natalie's freezer for a quick neighborly pass before dinner. Leah would run the transaction the next day so her transaction–checking husband and ice cream aficionado would be as surprised and delighted as the kids. These were the small perks that made community an even greater treasure.

Nathan's ETA of four o'clock left Chris to head up the welcoming committee. She might be there if they were late but she had a date with Joel at three-fifteen live and would be hard-pressed to wrap all of that up in time.

And so it was, at four-fifteen, as she wandered down West Commons Lane towards home that a gorgeous, copper-headed little girl came running down the walk towards her, joyfully screaming, "Oma, Oma! We're here!" She grabbed Leah around the waist, nearly bowling her over. Leah wrapped her arms around Mandy, holding fast, while they shared a good cry.

"Oh, Mandy! I have missed you so much and look how you've grown!" she cried, squeezing her close, and then letting her go.

Mandy smiled big, revealing, and pointing out, the site of a missing front tooth. "Look, Oma! I'm seven for sure now."

"You definitely are, Mandy. Tell me … have you met Chris?"

Oma and pops

"He's not Chris. He's Pops. He told me so," she said, matter-of-factly with a big grin.

Leah laughed inwardly. "That he is, my treasure. Where's David?"

"He and Pops went to see horses with Daddy. Mommy's putting things away at our house. Can we eat with you tonight?"

"That's what I've planned," she said, turning to walk, hand-in-hand, the rest of the way home. "Would you like to help Oma cook?"

"Of course!" she replied, looking up at Leah with her huge green eyes. What manner of genetic crapshoot went on in the egg and sperm that became Mandy could hardly be imagined. Her hair was genuinely copper with Leah's wavy curl. Her eyes were true green with a slight almond slant, her cheekbones were high like her mother's but her skin pale with some freckles sprayed across the bridge of her a nose that resembled both Leah and Nathan at that age. Her personality was all her own and of great fascination to Leah as she watched it differentiate over time. There were aspects of Mandy capable of taking over Leah's job on the show. She could be demonstrative, bombastic, enchanting – even magical – as well as demanding, business-like and manipulative, or as quiet, soft and cuddly as her Teddy. She was 100% seven-year old.

Her brother, David, on the other hand, looked like he was born in Tokyo – with all the dominant genes at play. He was bright, active, fidgety, amazingly creative, detail oriented, and a great lover of books and horses. And, he was, predictable – what one might expect from the parenting of Nathan and Julie. Mandy was just the opposite. *Straight from the stars*, in Oma's opinion. Which star? She couldn't quite put her finger on it. It never occurred to Oma that Mandy was very much like she'd been at seven – an unpredictable whirlwind. *Big surprise.*

Together they put the roast in the oven, then washed and scalloped the potatoes, with their skins on, using the mandoline. Finally, they got to the good part – shredding cheese, melting butter and putting the sauce together with Sally's cream. Mandy loved Sally almost as much as Leah did. She would find that Pops was an ardent admirer as well, when that ice cream appeared for dessert. Once the potatoes were in the oven baking, they pulled the strings off the snap peas, to have them all ready to steam, and made a nice salad of greens, table ripened tomatoes from the last of the hothouse crop, red onions, carrot peelings, kohlrabi, cauliflower, and radishes. Cucumbers were, regrettably, off the menu until spring. The last of their efforts went into the spinach soufflé, which was meant to come out of the oven to a full table.

Mandy set the table – although Leah handled her mother's wine glasses – and made a centerpiece from Oma's small box of odds-and-ends Christmas decorations and drawer-full of candles. While she worked on that, Leah slipped out the front door to pick up the ice cream. Chuck answered the door with a big hug and kiss – and a guilty admission that he'd taken a small sample of caramel crunch before Natalie slapped his hand. It wouldn't be missed. With many thanks to Natalie, she rushed home with her booty and stashed it in the freezer behind some packages of meat. Mandy, completely focused on her project, had no idea she'd left. Soon, Mandy declared herself done with the table décor and ready to cuddle into Oma's favorite chair, with her, to read a book.

And, that's where Pops and the rest of the tribe found them. They'd stopped at the guesthouse to pick up Julie, who looked a little tired but as young and beautiful as the day she and Nathan had married. They poured in the front door— *starving* – to be tantalized by the aroma coming from the oven. David came over, eager to receive his hug and kiss from Oma. He sat on the arm of her chair while Nathan came to give his mother a bear hug and kiss, after she rose to meet him. Julie was right in line to complete the greetings, graciously thanking her for the guesthouse and letting both Leah and Chris know how much they appreciated the stocked fridge and cupboards, fresh linen and sparkling clean house.

Over dinner, Oma and Pops got caught up on everyone's activities including Mandy's school play — she was a shepherdess, David's horseback lessons — he'd had his first canter, and Nathan's latest writing project — a mystery, of course. Nathan was the stay-at-home dad, while Julie worked. She dropped the kids at Shining Mountain Waldorf School and he picked them up and saw that they got to their after-school activities.

They wanted to know what was happening at *New Avalon*, including all the Outreach projects. The kids were wide-eyed at the story of the *Woodland Folks* and keen to meet Jürgen and Zenzi as soon as they could. Chris promised to see that that would happen the next day. as well as a nice ride down valley for anyone interested in horses. David was keen. The ice cream, with cookies, nearly brought tears to Chris' eyes ... or so he said, as he savored every spoonful. Leah let him know that was it for Christmas presents! His reply? *"Beauty."* His comment attracted an odd look from Mandy, who then studied her ice cream, assessing its beauty. With a subtle shake of her head, she dove in with great enthusiasm.

Tired from the two-day drive — that day from the middle of Nevada — Nathan and Julie bowed out with the children after the dishes were done. They'd made plans to ride the next morning and have dinner at the guesthouse that night. While the men went off to the Ranger's Christmas party after dinner, Leah, Natalie, Julie and the kids were going to make the luminaries and candle holders for the Christmas Eve ceremony in the apiary. After they completed that task, Mandy had a few games in mind before bed. Friday was looking like a fun-filled day.

As it turned out, Leah gladly relinquished Holly to Chuck the next morning when Mandy decided to have a play day with the girls instead of horseback riding. Leslie's Celeste and Suzie showed up on her doorstep to invite her at around eight o'clock. Then they knocked on the other guesthouse door to invite Mitzy, Ellia's seven-year-old granddaughter to join them. Emily, Spence and Christina's eight-year-old and Nick and Georgia's Kate, who played often with Celeste, would join the girls when they were finished helping their mothers bake Christmas cookies. All of the community children, including Jürgen and Zenzi, had a last practice for their presentation on Christmas Eve after lunch. Georgia invited Mandy and David to be part of that.

Later on, Nathan, Chris and David were up to something secretive with Tommy and the boys. With the boys preoccupied and Mandy off Leah's radar until dinner, she found the time to finish their winter caps and wrap their gifts. She'd also committed to catch up with Paula at the studio for a news update, then on to Star Wars at four o'clock with most of the men and boys in the community and all the millennials, followed by the viewing of Joel's last show of the year, at the studio, with Chris.

From the get-go, the community consensus was to preserve the forest for the seven generations to come and limit Christmas trees to the Community Center. Now, they also had The Lodge, full of family and friends, where a second big tree stood in the vaulted ceiling of the great room and a small tree — this year at least — at Demetri's house for the *Woodland Folk* 'orphans'. Jürgen and Zenzi would stay for the Christmas Eve ceremony before trekking over the ridge to visit their parents over Christmas Day and night. They would come back with Chris and Nick who were scheduled for a visit on Monday.

Christmas tree decorations had been pooled, just like the tools in the community tool shed, and everyone had helped the children decorate the tree in the community center the first weekend of December. The millennials had worked their magic on the tree at The Lodge. Presents for the children would be opened at the community dinner Christmas night. The rule was one each, all natural, typically from their parents. At home, they would receive the gifts from grandparents and other family and friends, all of whom embraced the need for natural, creatively inspiring toys.

While she finished her knitting projects, Leah's mind wandered back to her own mother, who'd taught her to knit. Nathan's Oma had made the sweaters and caps that he'd worn as a child, when she hadn't the time to knit them herself. In retrospect, a good bit of her free time she'd devoted to selfish pursuits. Her mother knew that but had expressed no judgment of Leah. Were all children takers from their parents until they woke up to their own children following that patterned behavior? She'd asked her about that in her old age and her mother shared that she'd been that way herself, especially when Eric was little. She'd chalked it up to youthful dreams and unfulfilled desires, which melted away over time. Yes, Leah could relate to that.

She acknowledged that she came from a line of really beautiful women who were both strong and soft, yang and yin, fierce and gentle — anchors for home, family and community. Her mother's service to others had been a curiosity to Leah in her youth, but exemplary as she'd matured, and now, the sole focus of her life. To have Chris partnering with her in that service brought tears to her eyes because she knew that had not happened for her mother. Not that her Dad didn't allow female 'distractions and diversions'. She got up and lit the candle in front of her mother's picture on the bookcase and then Betty Morrison's in the niche of the Golden Queen, thanking them both for being amongst the brood mares that would bring forth future generations of conscious women *and men*, to topple the patriarchy. The job was, by no means over, but it was well under way. *Hallelujah!*

The Rangers had a great night together sharing the holiday brew Chris and Nick had dreamed up. Chris was still in a playful mood when they cuddled together in bed that night and decided to engage her in a little recapitulation of Star Wars. "So, lass, what did you learn from Yoda today?" he asked, propping himself up on one elbow to gaze at her with his endearingly crooked grin.

R-r-right," she drawled. Then she thought about it for a few seconds. "I would say that I noticed a marked change in my interpretation of the whole affair with little Anakin. When this movie first came out, I found Qui-Gon Jinn the perfect Jedi. In fact, I remember discussing it in circle with my students. He was a warrior of great merit, but he was also gentle, especially with Anakin's mother, firm in his belief about Anakin fulfilling the prophecy, enough so that he followed his own truth instead of the Jedi Councils'. Now I interpret this differently and probably correctly, though it might be, deliberately, open to interpretation."

"How so?" What's different now?"

"Now I see why the Jedi had an age cut-off for training, no matter how many bloody mitichlorines one has," she laughed. "Maybe it's that very gift of Anakin's that gave him a precocious ego, which, as we know, trips him up big-time in Episode III. I would call him a bit of a smart-ass now, though that wasn't completely lost to me when I first saw the movie. I also see Qui-Gon Jinn's treatment of Anakin's mother as being self-serving rather than compassionate. The boy could have used a strong mother, even if she was a slave, for a few more years. Of course, the bizarre place in which they were living didn't help his personality one bit. And, as a Jedi, Qui-Gon Jinn deliberately defied the wisdom of Yoda and the council who advised against it. Further, he bound Obi-Wan to a death debt that turned out to be a ticking time bomb. He wasn't an impeccable example to his 'young Padawan learner', but then that can also be the divine plan. I'm reminded that Jefferson's wife made him agree not to remarry. He honored that wish but might have been better off with a wealthy widow to help with his debts," she laughed.

"You remember that?" he asked, astounded.

"From a book I read, cowboy," she replied, rolling her eyes.

"Ah-ha. Well, that's a commendable analysis, lass. What did you hear of Yoda's wisdom?"

"Are you talking to Dragon Lady, cowboy? I can feel her stirring and I do want to sleep tonight."

"Of course, I am. Isn't she the one watching the movie? Wasn't that the aim for showing them?" he laughed.

"She did watch, but Jane is doing the interpreting for her. I reckon she's getting it. So, Yoda, huh?"

"Yeah, Yoda," he said both as an affirmation and a command to the higher aspect of Dragon Lady.

She sighed. "Take *'hard, the dark side is to see.'* Like me, at the original viewing of this movie, most of us agree that evil can be sneaky and we're fooled by it often in this life. Now, I see that Yoda meant it as a reference to the Ahrimanic within each of us, which is even more elusively veiled. Yoda saw that in Anakin — or, at least, he saw enough to describe his future as clouded and his fear palpable. One wouldn't expect a kid his age to have quite that obvious a shadow. It must have been all those mitichlorines," she smiled.

"Gold star, lass. Go on," he smiled.

"Gee, thanks for that. What else? The piece about fear, anger, hatred and suffering, and *'fear is the path of the dark side'* were obvious warnings to anyone watching. Steiner would warn that embodying any or all of these is the best way to keep wisdom from ever knocking on your door."

"Agreed. So what's your take home message for Dragon Lady? Answer that and I'll put you to sleep."

"Great. I'm going to need help now that you have my mind spinning," she laughed.

"It's best not to wait, lass. We've got a lot going on right now," he reasoned, "and five more movies."

"Okay, I would say the take home message is *know and watch your blind spots — all of them.* Qui-Gon Jinn was defeated, killed, by the Phantom Menace. And, that after Anakin declared that the Jedi never die."

"Blind, he was, and stubborn to the end. Pass that on to Dragon Lady before I knock you out."

"She heard you, cowboy. That doesn't mean she 'gets' it, but she'll think it over," she whispered, drawing him down for a kiss.

It took him less than 20 seconds to redirect her internal dialogue.

Leah left Chris in bed the next morning, sleeping off the Ranger's party. She needed to be at the studio for a live news report and introduction of the Saturday show, 'the gift', which Stu had all ready to transmit. They'd all watched it on Thursday before the live broadcast with Joel. Stu's gift with film was evident and spawned further anticipation of the documentaries he and Matt were putting together. His latest hire would be coming in to manage manufacturing and distribution — both digital download and disc — of those and future films.

When she returned from the studio, she found a note indicating that Pops was, once again, with his and Tommy's male contingency, finishing up a community project. *Fair enough, cowboy,* she thought, smiling at the x chain below his name. They were 'on' for an early dinner before the ceremony in the apiary. She had a leg of lamb defrosted but would put off preparing anything. Mandy had made her promise to wait for Julie and her to help with the meal and, further, had extracted a 'cross-her-heart-hope-to-die' promise to let her help put the luminaries out at the apiary. She and her mum were spending the morning at Spence and Christina's — Mandy playing dolls with Emily, and Julie getting to know Christina better. Spence was at the bakery piling up loaves for the big weekend.

Leah, blessed with a little free time, was happy to use it cleaning the refrigerator of piled up leftovers, which she laid out on the countertop for the 'boys', with a loaf of fresh-baked bread snatched, for four NADs, from the coffee house after her studio work. They would no doubt come home *starving* from their project. She'd just made enough room for the leftovers that would accrue that evening, when the 'boys' came noisily through the back gate. Out came the mustard, mayonnaise, lettuce, tomatoes, and dill pickles. Yep. They were *starving*, and in high spirits from their 'guy time' together.

Leah reveled in the swelling of her heart as she observed the easy fellowship between Chris and Nathan, and the way in which it included David. Nathan who'd looked stressed to the point of thinking he was getting the flu when they arrived, was rosy-cheeked, amazingly engaged and filled with laughter. Surely, her magus was up to some much-needed healing there. An evening with the *New Avalon* Rangers would have been an unprecedented experience for Nathan — and that after the grand tour of *New Avalon I* and *II* on horseback. Nathan and Julie wanted to see *Harmony Valley* on Tuesday and Nathan had already committed to accompanying Nick and Chris over the ridge on Monday. David was enthusiastically signed on for soccer on the commons with the older boys, the millennials, and the over-wintering WWOOFers.

As soon as Mandy heard them talk about the trip to the *Woodland Folks*, she began an unrelenting, afternoon–long campaign to go with her Pops, Dad and Uncle Nick. Leah could not comprehend why she was hell-bent on doing it until her dad's curtailment of the harassment, just before dinner, brought on the tears that had been threatening since the launch.

"I must meet Sissi. I must!" she insisted as her passionate, young body cried out. And, she did this whilst strategically throwing her arms around Oma, typically her staunchest supporter.

All Leah could think of was Zacker, and Mandy's innocence and wild beauty. Chris was fully aware of her emotional angst. He stepped in to sit Mandy down on his knee at the set table to sort it out. She allowed herself to be cuddled by Pops for the very first time, and calm descended on the household. She'd listened attentively to the G-rated version of the *Woodland Folk's* story, had met Jürgen and Zenzi, and saw, in her minds eye, this vision of Sissi — and described her, in detail, to a tee, mind you. She didn't know why, but she and Sissi needed to be friends.

Leah sat down adjacent to them. "You saw this picture of Sissi in your head, Mandy?"

"I did, Oma," she answered, with sobs far milder than at the onset of the drama.

"Well, I suggest we all think this over," Oma said, winking at Nathan. "There might be something to this remarkable, spot-on vision of Sissi. She is a warm and beautiful girl, to be sure."

"That she is," Pops affirmed. "We'll be sure to talk to you about it tomorrow, Little Dragon," he told her, winking at Leah.

No one saw the slight roll of Leah's eyes as she bent to give Mandy a kiss on the cheek and suggested they get on with the wonderful Christmas Eve meal Mandy had helped her cook for them — before it got cold. They still had to place and light the luminaries for the ceremony before anyone came, she reminded her.

That did it. Order was restored, for the moment, and a wonderful meal was served. Mandy and David sang a grace from their school repertoire before Pops carved the meat. Oma's soul had been given a jolt with Mandy's vision, nearly ruining her appetite, but she did enjoy the meal and managed to drop a bucket load of hints favoring compromise, for Nathan's benefit. Chris was inwardly amused and outwardly at play with both of the kids.

When the dishes were done, Leah, Julie and Mandy gathered the white luminary paper bags, tea lights, and hand-held candles, with their paper drip trays, together in one big-handled cloth bag. The men had gone ahead with strong flashlights to check for bears and unlock the apiary. When the women came down the hill they saw more lights flashing around in the apiary than Chris and Nathan had taken with them. It was otherwise pitch black and impossible to tell what was going on. Mandy lit their way down the hill and into the apiary with more drama than attention to safety — tripping once on a rock, but righting herself before she hit the ground. That caused her to focus the light on her own footsteps instead of Leah and Julie's. They were hard-pressed not to burst into laughter whilst making there way down the hill holding onto each other, relying on Leah's 'knowing' of the way.

It wasn't until they were in the apiary that they could make out Tommy and his boys there with Chris, Nathan and David. They all turned their lights off while Leah gave the Wiesner men a big Christmas hug, and thanked them for coming to help out. She turned around facing the hives in the pitch dark to begin setting up, when suddenly all of their flashlights went on at once. She was standing in a half-circle of eight tall hives, instead of four. Leah gasped at the sight of a doubled apiary, all the new hives on sturdy benches facing the east with Carmella, Lucinda, Sophia and Geraldine's hives in the middle.

"Oh my God!" she cried.

"Merry Christmas!" the men and boys cheered.

Chris put his arm around her, sensing she was overwhelmed. "And a good wedding gift for a Bee Mistress?" he asked in a whisper.

Tears were rolling down her face. "Look at me, you boys. I haven't even heard the first Christmas Carol!" She pulled tissues out of her pocket and gave each of them a kiss on the cheek.

When she came to Tommy, he said, "I'll not be around much the rest of the winter, Leah, though I would love to have had that time together."

"It would likely have taken all winter, Tommy." And turning to face them all, "Look, you guys, you've done two boxes for each hive and copper roofs. This is so incredible."

"I'll trim them down to one box each tomorrow, lass. We have one more box for each hive in the shop still. I think they'll stack up nicely in the garden shed until you need them. You and Tommy can build extra boxes for your four queens in the spring."

She turned around to find Mandy sticking her nose in Carmella's hive. "The bees are sleeping, sweetheart," she said, coming to squat beside her.

"I want to see the bees, Oma," she insisted.

"Well, they don't come out at all in the dark, Mandy. We could come back on a sunny afternoon. How's that sound?"

Mandy was pouting something ferocious. Just then a bee came to the door of the hive and flew out to land on the end of her nose. Mandy showed no fear and allowed the bee to crawl up the bridge of her nose to her forehead. Leah blinked to make sure she wasn't imagining what she was witnessing. The bee made no attempt to sting her, but gave her a wee bite on her third eye. Leah sat back on the grass, flabbergasted, as the bee walked back to the tip of her nose and flew into the hive.

"Are you alright, Mandy?" she asked gently, as her brave little granddaughter turned her brilliant green eyes to meet her own brilliant blues.

"Yes, Oma," she said solemnly. "It was just a bee kiss. I love the bees, Oma. I want to live in the hive."

"You're family would miss you, darling. How about we discuss that later and get the candles lit before everyone comes down in the dark, stumbling over stones? After all, living in community is living very much like the bees. We all have to take care of each other."

They placed and lit luminaries along the path beginning in the oak grove, then through the frozen *Lacy Phacelia*, down the hill and into the apiary, and then lit one luminary in front of each hive. There was plenty of magical light. Mandy stood at the apiary door and passed out tapers with drip papers to all who entered. Nearly 50 bundled-up adults, including their added guests, the millennials and the Taylors, stood facing the hives in front of the east fence, with the choir members in the center rows by height, leaving room for the children to stand before them. When everyone was assembled, with Leah and Georgia flanking the children, the choir opened the ceremony with Silent Night. Everyone sang with them, though Leah wiped her eyes a great deal. The choir was beautiful, their harmonies perfect, and perfectly attuned to the twinkling stars overhead.

Next, pairs of children took turns telling the nativity story, from the gospel of Luke, to the bees. Mike, as the spokesman for the group, addressed each of the queens, asking for their kind attention. Paul and Mark began, by speaking of the Babe's lineage from Adam, Abraham, and David, and then through the line of David's son, Nathan. His parents were from Nazareth. They were poor people but filled with love and a knowing of the gift they were bringing to the world. That, as Emily and Suzie declared, was because an angel, Gabriel, had appeared to his mother, Mary, to announce that Jesus was coming to be her child. Joseph, her husband, had to leave home, with Mary, and travel to Bethlehem to be counted in a census. He put Mary on a Donkey, like Sassy, because she was heavy with child.

Little Celeste and Kate declared that Baby Jesus knew his name and spoke in a special language to his mother, even when he was just born — and she understood that language from the stars. Then Jürgen and Zenzi, in fairly good English, told the bees that this Baby Jesus had the soul of both Buddha and Adam, who had not experienced humanity's *Fall*. He would be pure and filled with love and promise. David and Mandy ended the story by declaring that the family returned to Nazareth where Jesus grew into a fine young man who was a carpenter, just like his daddy, until he was called into the world to begin his great work. Then Mike led them, singing *Oh Little Town of Bethlehem.* Everyone stood in the apiary, silently looking at the stars, honoring the children's sincere honoring of the birth of humanity's savior. It was a priceless moment for community.

When the children were finished, and with cold penetrating the thickest of coats, the choir stepped in to warm them through and through with *O Holy Night!* This brought on a torrent of tears for Leah, who was comforted by Mandy's grasp of her hand. Their audience was spellbound at the magnificence pouring into the surrounding night — so much so that they all fell to their knees when the song commanded it — *fall on your knees.* As she fell to her knees, Leah looked up to see the Archangels surrounding the apiary with Michael, her champion, front and center — *O hear the angels voices.* The light poured down from Michael's sword in blessing, most intensely upon the hives and the children — *O night Divine, O night when Christ was born.*

The spell remained unbroken for some time after they'd finished singing. Then Leah and Georgia silently led the children along the path of luminaries back up the hill, past Rob and Stu, who'd filmed and recorded it all with a special night camera and a couple of good microphones they'd hung on the apiary fence. The procession continued behind the houses of West Commons Lane to the community center for the choir performance. There were hot drinks and Christmas cookies for everyone as they prepared for the concert. Stu was already set up to record and film the choir and the play the following day, and most of the community was in the choir, so seating arrangements were expedited easily and the singing began, on time, at eight o'clock.

Leah lay in bed completely spent. She'd not cried that much since her mother had died, though this was joyful instead of grief-laden crying. Chris declared it a good cleansing — of her tear ducts, at least. He snuggled in beside her with that afterglow common to performers who'd put on a hell of a good show. And they surely had. She was very impressed with the respectful way in which he directed the choir and the eager way they responded to him. His voice was their strength ... their harmony his nectar.

"How do you manage Easter songs?" he queried, peering down at here red, puffy eyes.

"Oddly enough, I'm fine with resurrection and really never understood my reaction to devotional Christmas songs until now. Especially, knowing something of the four sacrifices," she reflected. "I'll be there for choir practice," she smiled, stroking his cheek, "if only to hear you sing with all the stops pulled out."

"Tomorrow should be interesting," he offered, looking ahead to the play.

"Especially if my eyes don't clear up from a good sleep. Merry Christmas, my beloved," she said sincerely. "Our first Christmas together *and* tomorrow? We wed again," she giggled. "I loved the present from all you fellows. I had a wee worry in the back of my mind about having hives for swarming season."

"Brilliant. You can strike another worry from you list, lass. Let me put you down now," he offered, placing his hand behind her neck. She became flooded with calming warmth.

"This is getting to be habit-forming, cowboy," she smiled, drifting off.

"I need you tomorrow, Laurey. Sweet dreams," he whispered pulling her into the curve of his body.

Morning tea was followed by the ceaseless flow of lemon water, for both of them. Mandy, who'd fallen asleep near the end of the choir performance, tumbled in the front door around nine on Christmas morning to discuss her bee kiss with Oma who was still in her blue robe. Leah had a close look at Mandy's forehead. She pronounced the wound a 'loving kiss', when, in fact, it was an outright bite. She'd never had a bee bite her, though she thought, perhaps, they could. Perhaps the bee would have stung her but knew the limits of her age. Leah rubbed a little healing paw-paw ointment on it.

She pulled one of the dining chairs over to the niche of the Golden Queen and asked Mandy to climb up to have a look at her altar. She asked who Betty Morrison was and why she was in the niche. "She kept bees, Mandy, when I was a little girl."

"Is that you with her, Oma?" she asked.

"It is. She showed me how she kept the bees. I was quite curious about the bees in my mother's garden. Mrs. Morrison was our neighbor and her good friend. She lived right down the road."

Mandy picked up the golden bee and then the small stamped gold bar, looking them over very carefully. "Someday you'll give these to me, Oma," she declared.

Chris raised an eyebrow to that one. "You reckon, Little Dragon?" he asked, from the table.

"I dreamed about them last night, Pops, and a really big live bee that was all gold. She kissed me on the forehead too. I told her I loved her before she flew away, and I woke up." Oma was looking very perplexed. "Can we go see the bees when the sun's warm, Oma?" Mandy asked.

"Of course, darling. But please don't go there with out either Pops or me. We have big bears that come looking for honey. The fence is electric to give them a shock and it would seriously hurt someone your size. So promise to stay away?"

"Yes, Oma. I want you to go with me, anyway. The gold bee loves you too. She told me so."

"Okay then. How about you run home until time for presents? That will give Oma and Pops time to take a shower and get dressed. We're going to entertain you this afternoon with a theater play."

"Wow! With more singing?" she asked, eyes wide.

"You bet," Pops told her, with a grin. "I'll want a fair review from you at dinner."

"No worries," she laughed, catching on to Aussie talk.

After she left, Leah stood staring at the altar for quite a spell. She was having a chat with the Golden Queen. Finally she turned to Chris who'd been intently cutting up more lemons.

"Aye?" he queried, cocking his head to look at her.

"Cowboy, how am I going to mentor the next Bee Mistress long distance?" she asked.

"Mandy's only seven, lass. You can wait until she's grown can't you? Are you certain?"

"Quite certain. Chris, think of the Jedi rules. Imagine if Mrs. Morrison had really taken me on, like in the old days, in the Bee Mistress' circle of women. I wouldn't have gone so far astray and come so late to my power."

"Don't you reckon that was meant to be, lass? You've been having exactly the experience you called in, no?"

"I could have made better choices, cowboy, and still worked off the karma. Mandy's gifts are opening before our eyes, right when mine were shutting down for a good bit of my life."

"You've got a point there, I'll admit. She's not in such a bad place at the Steiner school though."

"That's true, and with a dad who adores her and mom who finds value in her personality, if not the gifts."

"Well, lass, to be honest with you, I've kidnapped my quota of kids for this year and taken on enough abandoned horses, so why don't we see what unfolds and give our psyches a rest ... at least, for the moment," he grinned, transferring lemons from chopping block to bowl.

"You're right. We need to get on with a very big day," she smiled. "It's funny how life plays with us, though. This is altogether magical."

"I couldn't agree with you more. Here, have some lemon water," he said, jamming a lemon-filled water bottle in her hand.

The children came back, with their parents, to open their new hats from Oma. And from Pops, some wood whittling he'd been working on at the stable — a complete surprise to Leah. For David, he'd carved a snake from a beautiful piece of curvy *Manzanita* wood. And, for Mandy, a hand-sized bee with her wings folded on her back. He'd attached antennae, made of fine springs from Tommy's junk drawer, with small wood balls on the ends. The carvings were perfectly beautiful. He gave Leah a wink when Mandy opened the bee. *How did he know?!* They were going to reserve Oma's other gifts for the children's gift opening after dinner, but Nathan had a big box from Mom and Dad.

It turned out he'd been carving as well, and the children had before them the task of assembling a gnarly oak tree that had five separate little worlds within it. He'd seen one at a Waldorf handcraft sale and worked with the carver to do it himself. They would have many hours and days of pleasure fantasizing and rearranging the moveable parts. Chris and Leah left the four of them there, scattered around on the blue rug building together. They packed up their costumes and snuck out the back door to meet the other thespians at the community center.

In spite of the fact that the entire community was in the play, it was standing room only in the community center — partially due to a shortage of chairs. All the visiting family and the millennials were respectfully lined up in the rear, ready to stand if need be, and to help those who needed assistance. Burt and Alice Wilson were in the front row, with their entire family, and extended family, flanking them. Everyone involved with *Harmony Valley* had come including Ed and Shirley Prescott and the girls. The Vintners and their visiting entourage sat on the carpet with two babes in arms. Gerald Red Hawk had brought half the tribe, and many of their local veggie and coffee customers wandered in for a more intimate experience of the community than the storefronts and farmer's markets. Gale and Jim Taylor brought their family and Mr. B's sister, Maud, came with her daughter. The young children were sitting on the lined-up buffet tables to get a better view.

As the lights dimmed, the din of conversations gradually ceased. When it was completely dark, the audience heard them pushing props out and uncovering the set, which had been shrouded. Ellia began to play the Overture, then the other musicians joined in one at a time. As the Overture trickled off, the back of the makeshift stage gradually up-lit up as a painted rural scene, while Chris launched into *Oh What a Beautiful Mornin'*, *acapella*, from the shadows. Ellia began to accompany him as he stepped out into the stage area. The lights came up gradually to reveal a cabin with Leah/Laurey sitting on the front step in overalls and a red-checkered shirt, her hair pulled back in a ponytail tied softly with a red ribbon. Jenny/Aunt Eller, wearing an everyday ankle-length dress, was churning butter near the front of the stage. Chris, wearing the chaps and his worn leather hat, wandered over to casually lean against the front wheel of an old farm cart they'd rescued from Mr. B's shed, then engaged Aunt Eller as the song continued.

Two hours later, the audience would not cease applauding their shockingly good performance, and the cast could not stop laughing at what outrageous fun it had been. They put down their lemon water and brought out the beer and wine to celebrate with each other as the audience thinned and community gathered.

Leah, Chris, Natalie, Leslie and Will had spent a great deal of time with visiting friends, meeting new people in the area, and thanking everyone for being wonderful neighbors, and in some cases, supporters, of the community. Stu got it all on film. As the last guests had left, everyone pitched in to clean up the center and ready it for Christmas dinner at seven. When they left for home to start cooking at around five o'clock, the tables were dressed and set, and the buffet line had been readied with its table clothes, chafing dishes and hot plates.

Leah had drawn a dessert card when they were divvying up the cooking chores. She chose something her mother used to make for her birthdays, part of which she could make ahead. That was what she'd been doing in her blue robe that morning. A sponge cake lay covered on a cooling rack awaiting the next steps, which were the making of thick caramel, the whipping of thick sweetened cream, and the conducting of a search through her baking cupboard for the slivered almonds she was certain were there — somewhere.

Chris was meant to bring an appetizer. After a chat with Spence, when he was pumping iron earlier that week at the bakery, he settled on Parmesan *crostini* using freshly baked French bread slices. The secret was to use a lot of butter crisping the bread in a fry pan before letting the cheese ooze into each slice under a broiler. They were wonderful served at room temperature with an optional side of sun-dried tomatoes in olive oil and basil.

As he fried his buttered bread, Chris watched the unfolding dessert assignment with interest. It didn't look altogether different from caramel crunch ice cream except for the cake. The making of caramel sauce was a revelation to him as was the use of a candy thermometer to monitor the soft stage of caramelization. Leah's mother had used some boiled sweetened canned milk for the recipe, as was the fashion of her day — not unlike a spread that was sold in Aussie groceries nowadays, but *New Avalon* would not be stocking either item. Instead she used organic sugar, butter and heavy cream. It was butterscotch gone to caramel, she explained to her fascinated, finger-licking, cowboy. It helped to have had organic chemistry lab in Pre-Med, she confided. The rest was easy. Start with a 4 x 14 slice of homemade sponge cake centered on an attractive rectangular platter. Coat that with a thick layer of caramel, followed by a whipped cream layer and repeat until you ran out of cake three layers later. The last layer of whipped cream on the top and sides was brought to soft peaks and sprinkled with slivered almond. *Voila!*

He was playfully worried about being at the end of the food line, sure that he'd miss out on his slice. They negotiated a compromise. The cake would be sliced very thinly and not served until all the kids had stuffed themselves beyond belief. If, in the end, he'd been denied his slice of cake, she'd make another on New Years Eve, when it would be just their family and Harry at dinner. Furthermore, if that turned out to be the option, she'd teach him how to make it himself. *Well done, Yoda!*

When the kids met them out front to walk to the community center, Nathan looked at the cake with thoughts similar to Chris' running through his brain. "How could you, Mom?" he said, aghast.

"Good question, son," she replied, as if giving it serious thought. "Next year I'll engage you two fellows and Sally to help be make a ten footer! In the meantime, you can speak to Chris about the backup plan. Mandy, would you like to carry this bag for me?" she asked, handing her the sack with their wrapped gifts in it.

"Men ... right?" Mandy asked, looking up at Oma, with knowing eyes. "It's just a dessert," she added with a roll of those eyes at her dad and Pops. Leah and Julie burst out laughing as the tribe turned earnestly towards the Community Center.

As Leah had anticipated, there was a great deal of food on the buffet with appetizers already set out for nibbling. After asking Mandy and David to put their presents under the big tree, where they could find them later, she slipped the cake into a sliding door fridge for desserts and helped Chris set his *crostinis* out with the other finger foods. Julie had made Tilapia Sashimi with dipping sauce as a main course, which she stashed in the big fridge. Then they went looking for a glass of red each — 2009 had been an excellent year for the Cummings' Zinfandel. The bar was open with Demetri serving drinks. He had energy to burn, having had no interest in singing, dancing or acting with the thespians. He'd thoroughly enjoyed watching it though, and promised to be there in the audience at future performances. Given the lack of *fillo* dough in *New Avalon*, he'd made an apple strudel — sort of — for his dessert contribution. It seemed the German influence was working its way into his Greek cooking.

On Christmas, the children sat with their families and extended families at the big round tables. Mandy counted the chairs and then their family, and realized they needed two more people at their table to fill it up. She asked Oma and Pops if she could pick some friends to join them. Leah thought of Natalie and Chuck with Harry (who took a seat under the table), Will and Sonia, or dropping a chair to embrace Demetri, but decided to let Mandy chose from her new friends, knowing that none of their neighbors, and especially not Demetri, would be offended by an exclusion. Pops was sympathetic to her request and admittedly curious to see whom she'd go and collect. Mandy was craning her neck looking around at everyone, and even stood on a chair to get a better view, before flying off towards the doors waving her hands. She came back dragging Paula, who had Sam in tow with a huge kale salad.

"Hey, everyone, Merry Christmas, again," Paula said.

Leah looked at Chris, who couldn't suppress a grin. "Peas in a pod, I reckon," he whispered to Leah.

The children opened their gifts between dinner and dessert. All of the girls received the dolls the women's circle had made for them, including a hastily made doll for Zenzi that she would receive from Demetri the next day when she and Jürgen returned. When Mandy opened her doll, she was startled … and then overjoyed, to see that Oma made a doll that look just like her, with unruly copper hair, green eyes, and high cheekbones. She had on a hat just like the one Mandy had received that morning, and a lime green sweater the same as Oma's present from last Christmas. She brought it back to the table to show Pops, who hadn't seen the finished doll. He shook his head, smiling in wonderment.

Paula was quite taken with the doll and told Mandy she wished she had one just like it. Mandy thought about that for a minute and then offered the doll to Paula — for keeps. Paula was taken aback. She'd not meant it that way. Furthermore she was astounded at Mandy's generosity and detachment. She looked to Leah for help.

"Seven-year-olds take things quite literally, Paula," she said, unperturbed that Mandy had given away the doll she'd made for her before running off to play with the girls.

"I see," Paula replied, filing that one away for the future. "What really amazes me though is that she thought it over, and then made that decision. She wasn't the least bit attached to it."

"That's also the age, but add to that the Waldorf schooling, which has an emphasis, in the early years, on sharing. None of our kids here feel like they need to own something. They have access to whatever they need and share their toys like family."

"Will you figure out a way to get this doll back in Mandy's hands ASAP?" she asked, trying to pass it back.

"Why don't you give it some thought first? See what you can come up with that would work for Mandy," she suggested.

Paula looked distressed, but Leah turned her attention to David, who'd come back to the table in his new navy blue cable cardigan sweater. He stepped between Leah and Chris' chairs so that she could check out how it fit. "Pretty good fit, darling," she concluded.

"And it matches my new hat," he smiled. "Thank you, Oma. I finally outgrew the old red one you made."

"Lucky for you a little birdie told me that," she laughed. "What's that you're fussing with David?"

David had his hand down in the right pocket of the sweater and pulled out two arrowheads. "I found these in the pocket, Oma," he said, showing them to her. She'd not noticed the special surprise when she'd wrapped the sweater, but knew exactly where they'd come from.

Oma nodded her head toward Pops, who'd been watching their interaction. David turned around and fell into Chris' open arms with his prize arrowheads. The two of them had a talk about where Pops had found them and a promise to take the horses out on a ride to look for more. Pops also recommended that he show them to Jürgen who had quite a collection of his own. Nathan and Julie were nearly in tears. David had found his first real live hero. *Geez! If they only knew,* Leah thought.

When it came to the desserts, the caramel sponge cake was long gone before most of the adults in the community got to it. As it turned out, Nathan and Chris had made a pact to take the end of the line so they wouldn't get any, knowing the prize they'd collect on New Years Eve. They promised Chuck they'd sequester a couple slices for his and Natalie's return from the New Year's Eve Ball the next day. *Hmmm, the Fellowship of the Caramel Cake was growing.*

Chris called Nick over for a serious discussion about the upcoming horse trip over the ridge. Billie was staying home with Georgia since she wasn't teaching, and Nick and Chris agreed that Mandy wouldn't over burden Moonshine if she did come along. Julie, who had no idea Leah was reticent, was fine with the idea. It would be easier for Nick to cradle her bareback than for Chris to try it on a western saddle, and Nick was agreeable to that. Thunder wasn't far enough along with his training to take the chance. Nathan and Chris turned to Leah, who'd been listening with interest, for the final approval. She turned inward, where her caged Dragon Lady struggled to express her fear, anger, and hatred — all directed at Zacker. *You are standing in the way of wisdom, my warrior,* Jane told her. And then the Bee Mistress step into to shake her cage whilst chanting, *Fear is the path of the dark side, you fool.* Little Alice might have taken comfort in a jailed Dragon Lady not that long ago, but now she looked anguished. True, she'd grown up quite a bit, but the little girl who'd been so invested in freedom and magic would never leave her. And, that little girl had never felt fearful of life.

Leah snapped out of her inward journey, refocusing her eyes on those awaiting her opinion. "Mandy has much to gain by going and I have much to gain by letting her go," she smiled. "Have a great time. Julie and I can pack lunches. How about David," she asked, noting the broad smile plastered across Pops' face.

"Tommy and Rob are taking the older boys for a hike in the Marble Range," Nathan offered. "They were even talking about an overnight."

Chris heard Nathan's soul making a compromise. "Listen, Nathan, if you'd rather go along, and it sure sounds tempting, Nick and I can make the day trip on our own — up to you. I'll see to Mandy."

"That does put me in a bind. I wanted to spend some time getting to know Nick, but I'd love to do the same with Tommy. What do you think, Jules?" he asked, turning to Julie for her take.

"I'm fine either way, Nat. Actually, I might go along with Nick and Chris, if you don't," she admitted. "I'm curious about Sissi and Trynel, myself, might be able to help in the kitchen, and do love to ride."

Isn't this interesting, Leah thought, catching the quiver of a grin from her husband.

"Let's get Tommy over here," Chris suggested, looking around for him.

Leah went back to the buffet to get dessert and tea. On the way, she was stopped by Georgia's mother, Adelle, who wanted to rave about Leah's performance in the role of Laurey. *My God, I've forgotten it even happened. What? Four hours ago?* They had a lovely chat, and Adelle reaffirmed her and George's interest in joining the new phase of community. Leah assured her they were at the top of the list and that the community was very much in need of their skills. They'd be contacted after the next community meeting, which was on January 10th.

When she arrived back at the table with her tea and 'sort of' apple strudel, Nick had left and Tommy had joined them for a Marble Mountains discussion. Tommy felt, with another adult along, that they could easily do an overnight. If Nathan wanted to join them, the boys would be doubly excited about the adventure. Done. Julie would go with Nick, Chris and Mandy. They would be back in time for Star Wars. *No worries, Oma.*

Nathan went off with Tommy to hustle some camping gear for the trip and let the boys know what was going on. Some big cheers went up when the overnight news was announced. Chris put his arm around Leah, asking if he could get her anything.

"A bed and pillow?" she laughed, resting her head on his shoulder. "I'm fading quickly, cowboy."

oma and pops

"We can go," he offered.

"I'll do some cleanup first. We still have Paula, Mandy and the doll to bring to resolution before I can break from holding space," she smiled.

"Sure you're okay with tomorrow, lass?" he asked.

"Yes. I'd say the lessons from Episode I have been integrated."

"Aye. I'll be looking forward to the after affects of Episode II then, though I can't rightly say I remember it."

"Me either. That's why they're such a good butt kick," she laughed.

Paula returned to the table to inform them that Sam was now on the Marble Mountain expedition. She was going to map out her strategy for 'Oh Really?!' with the extra time he'd afforded her. He loved winter backpacking. When Mandy ran up to check in with all of them, Paula called her over for a chat.

"You know, Mandy," she began, hugging the doll to her chest, "I realized I didn't want your doll — though she is very beautiful. What I really want is my own baby, my own little girl, just like you."

"Really?" Mandy replied, with wide-eyed approval.

"Here's what I'd like to do. I'd like you to care for your doll while Sam and I see what we can do about our own baby. We've been talking about it for some time. Then when our little girl is your age, maybe you would share your doll with her. What do you think?"

"And maybe I can baby-sit for you," she suggested eagerly, acting ever so grown up.

"Great idea, Mandy," Paula laughed, tucking the doll back into Mandy's arms. "She is an incredible doll in many ways, and she's so happy you'll be looking after her for now."

Mandy cradled the doll, then turned around and asked Oma to hold it for her while she went back to play with the girls.

Chris leaned over and whispered in his favorite newscaster's ear whilst Paula walked away to find Sam. "Young Padawan learner she is, Master Yoda. She's just negotiated the first of many compromises — and with a Little Dragon, no less. She'll do well with presidential candidates."

"Why me?" Master Yoda asked, in a clouded moment of doubt. "Oh bloody hell, why *not*?"

Oma and Pops took Mandy and David home with them while their parents collected backpacks, sleeping bags, a tent, and bed pads from various community members, and a food list from Tommy. Chris offered to fix them up with flashlights, water bottles, and other bits and bobs. Mark would send an extra quilted vest home to David, for under his winter jacket, along with a pair of warmer hiking socks. Thinking of warmer clothes for Nathan, Chris went to the bedroom closet looking for a heavy knit cardigan he'd found at the second hand shop in Yreka. He came out sporting a handsome 'Marlboro Man', genuine shearling, riding coat.

"Hey, look, Oma! Santa Claus must have left this in our closet. Can you imagine?"

315

"I can!" she cried out, coming to check it out. "I can picture him sneaking in here while we were gone. That's what happens when you don't lock your doors," she laughed, opening her arms for a really warm hug.

"I'll give Nathan my winter jacket for the hike. This one's going to need breaking in tomorrow," he grinned.

"Good idea, Pops," she affirmed.

He took it off and looked at the label. "Cheyenne, Wyoming, lass — land of the wild Mustang herds. Santa must have a workshop there. Those elves have done some mighty nice stitching. Hey, this gives us a pattern for *Harmony Valley*," he said.

"I wouldn't advise taking it apart, cowboy. We can get another one from a real store if it comes to that," she winked.

David and Mandy were building their tree house with their ears wide open. She still believed in Santa. Why not? Look at what he can come up with! Her biggest gift was happening in the morning when she got to ride bareback with Nick, a *real* Indian, on Moonshine, the prettiest horse in the world. Holly had been hugely overwhelming for her, but Moonshine was quite plausible for a favorite horse.

After they'd collapsed in bed that night, Chris officially thanked her for the jacket. She didn't need confirmation of his delight but relished it nonetheless. She thanked him for the Bee Mistress' wedding and for bringing the community to a new level of vitality through the sharing of his talents. When asked what he would do next, he announced a plan to resume play practice on Wednesdays, starting in September, for next year's presentation of Carousel. Then he added that there'd been a consensus vote to continue the choir practices on Thursdays, alternating with a new initiative — dance classes. It was time the whole community learned the tango.

"Oh, really?!"

chapter 11: "do, or do not"

The easterly trip over the ridge didn't get organized until the men and boys on the Marble Mountains expedition were sent off, in two vans, towards the west. Cupping his gloved hands like a stirrup, Chris gave Mandy a boost up to Nick on Moonshines bare back, while Julie and Leah stuffed saddlebags with food for lunch and gifting. After a few last minute instructions to Nick about Trynel's examination, Leah held Magic steady while Julie mounted, kissed her sheepskin-clad cowboy goodbye, squeezed the hand of a rapt granddaughter, and then waved them off from the farm road in front of the stable.

What to do with seven hours of complete freedom, she asked herself. What popped into her head was a reference, from a Casteneda book, wherein Don Juan declared that walking was the best way to access the past, which was, according to Don Juan, stored in our calves. She might debate that metaphor but felt, as a whole, he was right. She went home to get properly dressed, let Natalie know where she was headed, and set out on a long walk to the nearest town ... well, crossroads. She couldn't remember its name, if it had one, but knew it well since the Cummings' vineyard was just beyond it. With her small notebook, a pencil, and sandwich in one pocket and a filled water bottle in the other, she tried to walk consciously aware of the past. In particular, Leah was interested in the origins of Dragon Lady's fear, anger, hatred, greed, and envy ... the lot.

About a mile into the walk, Dragon Lady reluctantly began unloading her story. In addition to the slave life with her favorite president, Leah had lived as many lives possessed of his kind of power as she'd had living the slave's oppression – with Dragon Lady on board, for the most part. The details were irrelevant, in the moment, but in the Akashic if she cared to research them.

The pattern wasn't irrelevant. Dragon Lady was up for a life of power this round and hadn't been able to pull it off — yet. In fact, since Chris had arrived on the scene, her hopes seemed dashed. This was also her first time out with characters like the Bee Mistress and Jane. They, to put it mildly, confounded her, though she'd thought she was getting somewhere with the Bee Mistress prior to her recent illumination.

It occurred to Leah that Dragon Lady had not really had the opportunity to tell her story. She'd been too busy being the entire judicial sphere of her life — prosecutor, defender, judge and jury, but also a legislator and, it could be argued, a petty tyrant. And thus, an internal dialogue was initiated, between Dragon Lady and the rest of her, on the road to, what turned out to be, Sheldon. Jane, Alice and the Bee Mistress pitched in to begin sorting out Dragon Lady's stubborn, near-dictatorial investments in the outcomes of Leah's life. Right off the bat, Chris was identified as the biggest button-pusher to ever come along. Dad and Eric had been oblivious. Chris was superconscious and a deliberate pot-stirrer — in Dragon Lady's opinion.

She'd grant her that. The rest of her very much liked the outcome of those button-pushes. As she walked, she discovered that Dragon Lady's fears were diverse. Currently she feared the rise of Will as overshadowing her own supremacy, and she feared the loss of democracy, which was paradoxical. She wanted to see democracy come back to life in America but her ideas were oddly undemocratic — like using the hidden and not-so-hidden power broker tactics to gerrymander and restrict voting in any number of ways to favor the progressive liberals. *Shame on you!*

Dragon Lady also feared the failure of Outreach's many projects as democratic experiments. She worried about criticisms of socialism, dictatorships and the like — very interesting, especially coming from her. She'd spent all of her life fighting to be heard and appreciated. They tracked this one back to Dad's inability to recognize and support anything Leah set out to accomplish, be it a term paper or Medical School. She'd been run out of research science by the frigging patriarchs in her department, who found women threatening (or preferred them invisible), and had accepted a less combative career in family practice. Jane assured her she'd been at ease and fulfilled in that job, actually helping people on a daily basis. Dragon Lady was reminded that *she* wasn't the doctor. She could stay out of that department to simplify her life. Typically, doctors don't need to be warriors, though scientists do have that tendency. It was easy to see where that had led Dragon Lady.

She went on to point out that she'd been ridiculed, by Daryl, Dad and Eric, for choosing Waldorf Education for Nathan. That had stung, but she did stick with it. Thanks to Dragon Lady's obstinacy. When it came to the time in her life when she was faced with teaching things spiritual, she (Jane) had lacked the confidence to do it. It was Dragon Lady who put herself out there, even though she knew nothing about it. It turned out to be a rocky start. Okay, this was getting out of hand. Dragon Lady was really feeling sorry for herself and their walk was becoming an ongoing rant. Jane asked her how she felt about the Guardian at the Threshold. *No big deal* was the reply.

R-r-right. They began to meander down the path of anger — a long and winding road, to be sure. That path could be traced back to Dad and Eric and their conspiracy to deny her one single square inch of the limelight. *Ah-ha!* Now, they were getting somewhere, because that path of anger had a huge intersection with the path of jealousy/envy. She didn't envy Eric now and had made her peace with Dad. Come to find out Dragon Lady didn't like sharing the stage Leah currently stood on with Will, the millennials — even Joel, who was by far her biggest benefactor.

She'd been throwing off outer layers of clothing as the miles ticked off, tying them around her waist, and now felt like ripping her clothes off. How on earth could Dragon Lady sit in her cage and blow off the Guardian at the Threshold?

"The Guardian can only be approached in humility and honest accountability, you nincompoop!" the Bee Mistress screamed, to the heavens.

It seemed altogether hopeless. She'd made it to Sheldon, such as it was, and asked for a water bottle fill at the general, and only, store. After wolfing down her sandwich, Leah took up her notebook and began drawing the intersecting paths she'd defined. All roads led to fear, of course. She toyed with the cold hard fact that women's opinions and actions had not counted for Dragon Lady. Whereas those of men had mattered a great deal and had actually led to some of the worse parts of her life — the least satisfying paths on the picture. Why?

She could accept Dragon Lady as a male wannabe. Her experiences in lives past being male had power written all over them whereas those of oppression were female with male oppressors. She was living proof of the successful patriarchal model. What she needed was re-education. To accomplish that end, the Bee Mistress stepped in on the way home. She described Dragon Lady's stories as being oddly convoluted, much like her own before she saw the light. The Bee Mistress began challenging her with a situation and giving her two different paths to bring it to resolution. It was a clever tactic with dismal results. When she blithely made a choice that ignored the last three hundred years of evolution, the Bee Mistress was onto her. Dragon Lady was clinging to irrelevant, outdated and insane beliefs about how systems worked or could work. It could be concluded that the path of the Golden Queen versus the path of the Dark Queen were muddled together in a blur for her. She wasn't bound up in images. She was entangled in self-defeating beliefs. Of course, she didn't believe that, either. She felt she should be educating the rest of the personality package.

About what? They all wondered.

Leah had gradually put all her layers back on during the return trip. The low winter sun was sinking behind the mountains and a chill wind had risen as it often did in the afternoon. She remembered little of the return walk, having been riveted by the exercise the Bee Mistress was putting Dragon Lady through, and arrived back at the parking lot in shockingly good time. After arming herself with, yet another, loaf of bread and treating herself to a chai, she finished the walk home taking the back route. Chuck was stoking the boiler, doing his fair share. They had a good catch-up on the dysfunctional, filibustering, or shall we say fili*blustering* Senate. He had her in tears of laughter by the time he was finished. They made a date for a political discussion at the kitchen table the next morning.

Minutes later, Leah had stripped to stand in a hot shower — her therapist's office — eager to put together the big picture of Dragon Lady and how to free her from her past. Her water conservationist, Alice, turned the tap off five minutes later — and that was two-minutes into overtime. Chris found her wrapped in her blue robe and curled up in her favorite chair sound asleep. There was little time to spare to get to the movie before it started, so he nuzzled down in her neck to shower her with kisses. She opened one eye.

"I was hoping that was you, cowboy," she smiled.

"This is most unusual for you, lass. What have you been doing? We've minutes to get to the movie, you know?"

"Oh my," she said, with a start. "I'll explain on the way. Let me get some clothes on." She pushed herself out of the chair and hobbled to the bedroom. He noted her atypical physical condition but jumped in a quick shower and changed from his horse clothes while she dressed. When he offered to carry her to the movie, she burst out laughing and smacked is bum.

"I walked to Sheldon and back today, cowboy. I've got two stumps for feet but I reckon they'll make it there in time."

Chris liberated a couple bikkies from the cookie jar and they were out the door in minutes. She explained her struggle with Dragon Lady, and failure to come up with a solution before falling asleep in her chair — likely from the boring 'same old, same old'. Dragon Lady was ever so ho-hum, and, hey, life was humming along well without her. He reminded her that she was in a typical grace period with the Guardian, during which slackers were most often lost. *Gee, thanks for that, cowboy!* He further advised her to encourage Dragon Lady to pay attention to the movie. She was showing the movies for Dragon Lady, was she not?

He promised her discussion time that evening, knowing that Julie and Mandy were guests of Spence, Christina and Emily for dinner and play. Then he turned the conversation to the *Woodland Folk* before her brain could blank out about what to discuss. *Gosh Dragon Lady is clever at avoidance.*

He suggested she get the Trynel health report from Nick except to say that she was full of good cheer and looking healthier and younger each time over the ridge. The miracle of good food and loving care, she reckoned. Mandy had walked back, as far as the farmhouse, with Jürgen and Zenzi, who were showing her this, that and the other thing in the forest as they picked up edibles for their basket. She'd played with them most of the time whilst there but had a very moving meeting with Sissi when she first arrived. Chris reckoned it was past life related, since they both burst into tears when they met. Mandy had a noticeable effect on Trynel as well, though it wasn't so obvious as that with Sissi.

Zacker had been on his best behavior — such as it was. Julie seemed comfortable and pitched right in to prepare the comfrey for Nick, and then made a big pot of soup from what they'd brought over. Chris spent some time with Julie and Trynel interpreting a conversation about their heritages. He didn't learn much more than he already knew except to say that Trynel was a US citizen. She withdrew a cloth packet from under her lumpy pillow and showed them a social security card and citizenship papers. Obviously, both meant the world to her as remnants of the life she'd had. Leah's head was spinning by the time she sat down in the theater with her cowboy.

Viewing Episode II made her just as mad the second time as the first. Was Yoda the only one who could see what was going on with Anakin? Yes. Why? *The dark side clouds everything.* You can say that again. How could he witness the egomania taking over Anakin and not intervene? Well, that's life, isn't it? Because he saw the bigger picture, he didn't stand in the way of Anakin's soul expressions and karma. Great cycles of light and dark were at play. She'd let Dragon Lady dominate her ego for a good long time. If she could come to grips with the bigger picture there, she'd be ahead of the game. *The shroud of the dark side has fallen,* Yoda declares near the end. Everyone else thinks the war is over. Only wise Yoda knows it's just begun. Nothing is as it appears. What really annoyed her was the way in which the dark side was continually seducing Anakin through his fear, anger, hatred, jealousy and greed. Perhaps a little over-dramatized but obvious to the thickest of heads. The movie had a moral message directed at an impressionable age group. Our moral and emotional weaknesses are the dark side's portal. She couldn't argue with that.

Christmas leftovers had been split amongst the community and Joel was on vacation. That made for a simple dinner and early bedtime for Leah and Chris, but not before a good general, catch-up discussion. He poured the Zinfandel while she searched the bathroom drawers for a tube of foot rub that had been around for ages. In retrospect, it had been a little foolish to walk 10 miles when walking long distances wasn't even a periodic exercise activity. On the other hand, Chris had a way with his hands that made it all worthwhile. She spread a towel on the ottoman and positioned her chair for easy access to her resting feet. Ah, relief was on the way.

Interestingly, his foot massage seemed to loosen more of the memory than had the walk. Maybe she'd walked it down from her calves to her feet. Don Juan always spoke in abstract generalities — at least to her. She had her little sketch of the intersecting paths with fear at the center. They talked about those paths and the way a good bit of the emotional baggage had been transformed. She erased the road of greed first. Early on, she'd had a real enlightenment about wealth, and though she'd never suffered homelessness or even poverty and hunger, she'd volunteered to live amongst those who did, and lived it with them. Her empathy with the homeless was genuine.

The anger path was one of hills (hatred) and valleys (frustration) with long spans of flat road (steady-state anger). She'd lived this path with the patriarchy from her earliest memories of Dad and Eric. With time, and acquired knowledge, the path had flattened out and narrowed, but it still remained anchored in her judgments and opinions. The political and economic arena provided an endless pile of gravel to keep this road serviceable. Here, she reasoned, was where Yoda's privileged view of the great cycles of human existence could help her let go of her anger with acceptance. It wasn't like she couldn't see the shift in public opinion, the gradual awakening of the masses to oppression, and the slow, steady predictable nature of collapse. And, she was onto solutions and off ranting, even though Dragon Lady had been reluctant to let that ball bounce into Joel's court. She was hopeful about obliterating the path of anger.

Chris continued massaging, while she continued downloading. That brought her to the path of envy/jealousy. Here was a wily path if there ever was one. This was a circuitous road, fraught with hairpin curves, blind intersections and a good many side roads with unexpected dead ends. Judgment and criticism, mostly based on opinion rather than fact, fueled the vehicle driving on this road. This road got its start with the Dad-Eric conspiracy to leave her out. It drove her to succeed at any number of things that didn't interest her in the least. Once she entered the medical profession, the dominance of academia by patriarchs drove her out of research — and that stung. She wanted what they had. She wanted what men had, or seemed to have, which was power. The path ran into and merged with the anger/hatred path, making it nearly impossible to pull it all apart for a good assessment. So she'd avoided doing that, until now. And, wasn't it obvious that this life with Jane, the Bee Mistress and Alice was the perfect set-up to heal Dragon Lady's big, many-lifetimes, pattern? The were giving her no wiggle room.

When Demetri extracted the patriarchal implant from her field, a light illumined the path and most all of her work with Dragon Lady had ensued. Alice really enjoyed delegating responsibilities at the studio and within the community — Alice, who'd always been pressed for time, had time to spare now. Dragon Lady's reaction was to be possessive and controlling. Here was the jealousy of Will, of Paula, and of Joel. Dragon Lady felt Alice was trying to undermine her and she'd shown another ugly face — that of sabotage. Fortunately, the rest of Leah was strong enough to ignore her — so strong, in fact, that she didn't notice she'd escaped until it was nearly too late. Now was the time to love her back into the fold. The question was ... how? There was much unresolved on this road, though, lately, she'd noticed an absence of anger. Dragon Lady was currently into self-pity. Was that a sign that the two merged paths were free of each other? For Dragon Lady, beliefs needed to align with her mission. Priorities were shifting, she was aging, and younger people needed to be mentored. They were the future, not the enemy. So, *get with the program, darling.*

By this time, her feet were so relaxed she was unaware of them. Chris was sitting back into the sofa, eyes closed, listening to her. Leah looked down at her drawing. "I guess that brings us to fear, which served to blind Anakin, and, I reckon, most of us."

"True enough, lass. How does the fear bind your paths together there in the center of Sheldon?" he grinned.

"Well, that *is* the question isn't? Fear is at the heart of it all. I feel this self-pity Dragon Lady is feeling might be deceptive, which brings up the whole habit of self-deceit — and lying to others. I'll have to be watchful she doesn't try to sabotage Paula altogether. The rest of my 'tendencies' are enormously invested in the truth. So, Dragon Lady has something to hide that's worth lying about. If what she's after is power, obviously she doesn't feel she has enough or any. I could see her with an overriding fear of powerlessness. How humiliating would that be? But look, its been chasing her down on this jealousy path since the get go. A fear of powerlessness is a perfect fit with alternating lives of oppression and power. The former would have been terribly humiliating even with a good outcome like the freedom Jefferson gave his slave. The latter would have been fraught with Anakin's choice of how to use the power. That one wears a lot of masks but don't you think it boils down to selfishness versus selflessness?"

"That's a wee bit advanced," he suggested. "Look at Anakin. He wants the power because he fears he'll lose Padmé, just like he lost his own mother. She let him go out of her own fear and hopelessness. He took a load of guilt with him. He wasn't free and allowed his fear and anger to rule him. He can mouth the Jedi teachings but he isn't capable of following them."

"There's a similarity with the Ruby Order, isn't there, cowboy?" she asked, bringing her drawing over to cuddle on the sofa with him.

"Indeed. The more power you have, the greater the temptation of the dark side. The dark side has no use for weaklings. However, it relishes arrogance as the weakness easiest to penetrate in the powerful. The dark side, as it operates to control humanity right now, does so through the cultural "I". In a culture of violence, there's much opportunity to penetrate the arrogant, and infuse them with the lust for power. Their arrogance is often accompanied by keen intelligence. You would call it the loose cannon of the left hemisphere, if I'm not mistaken," he grinned.

"Right on. Go on, cowboy," she urged.

"I hardly need to describe it to someone who follows the culture. What I do want to point out is that the loss of the "I", which can only happen with the cultural "I", is the ultimate humiliation. It might look like their greatest triumph to the culture, but when they cross the Threshold, the truth of it cannot be denied."

"It would behoove us all to somehow become truly humble, consciously humble, before we approach the Threshold, then?"

"True, lass, but not the easiest thing to accomplish. True humility is to become conscious of being nothing, of being completely worthless."

"Before the eyes of God, a failure of creation by any human measure?" she whispered.

"That's the not-so-secret fear of every human being. That's your tree stump in front of the general store in Sheldon, California, lass," he said, tapping his finger on the central point, where all the paths crossed. "All other fears are secondary to those that hold self-judgment within our souls. If you can grasp that, all fear falls away, including that of the Guardian of the Threshold. Anything less is open to negotiation with him and few, if any, succeed."

"Chris, that sounds perfectly impossible!"

"Aye, but it's the only way to truly serve selflessly."

"Where might one encounter such humility, such lack of ego?"

"They're coming to your doorstep, lass. Your own longing for selfless service is drawing them to you. It's likely the greatest gift you will receive in this life, and that from a vision spawned within your own soul."

"The force is strong in your words, my magus. I do believe you, but the path is clouded," she smiled.

The dark side clouds everything. Impossible to see, the future is. Let's take those well-loved, sexy feet of yours to bed, Yoda."

The tour of Harmony Valley had been moved to Wednesday afternoon when the hikers decided on an overnight. Therefore, Leah and Mandy made a date to visit the bees on Tuesday, when the sun was as warm as it would get — around two in the afternoon. Chris would stand watch for bears, liberating them to get lost in bee consciousness. Mandy came by after Leah returned from a visit to the studio and the clinic. She was looking to play some games. Oma was a willing accomplice until Pops came home looking for lunch. They were just about to start a new game of Park and Shop, one of Leah's childhood treasures, when she excused herself to put some lunch together for all of them. In no time whatsoever, Mandy had recruited Pops to take her place.

"Parking and shopping isn't exactly my idea of a game, Little Dragon. I'm not much of a consumer, you know."

She rolled her eyes. "Oma, explain this game to him. He doesn't get it."

Leah tried to keep a straight face, while slicing a loaf of bread. "Well Pops, this game is more about building skill sets. This game trained my multi-tasker and efficiency expert — Alice."

"How so, Oma?" he asked, with an unabashed grin. Mandy was doling out the cars and cards.

"You've got to roll the dice and drive to the car park, get everything on your shopping list by visiting all the stores that sell them, walk back to your car, maybe stop at the car repair, the post office, or whatever chores you drew, on the way home and get there before Mandy gets back to her house."

"Do I sense competition here?"

"You could say that," she laughed, getting the point.

Mandy was ready to roll the dice. "Come on, Pops. Draw your cards," she pleaded.

"Oh," Leah added, "pay attention to what squares you land on, Pops. You could end up with a ticket, or a flat tire, or heaven knows what. I can't remember."

"I can!" Mandy called out, rolling her dice.

Leah stuck her head in the fridge looking for mustard to stop the giggles. Pops assumed a serious self-possessed posture at the table, though secretly amazed at Mandy's passionate game playing. His acting ability was evident to Oma allowing her to tune them out to finish preparing lunch, figuring the game would be over soon.

As they were both steaming home in their cars, Chris landed on a 'draw a yellow card' square. He drew the card and sat there staring at it.

"What's it say, Pops?" Mandy asked.

"Aye, the bloody car's crooked!" he wailed, dramatically, in rich country Australian.

Mandy was taken aback. "Pops, you talk funny!" she declared.

He looked her right in the eye, and gave her an Italian version of the situation.

"Huh?"

Then it was German, followed by Spanish, Portuguese, and French, all with authentic accents.

"Pops!" she yelled. "Just go to the gas station! Roll the dice!"

He countered with Hindi, then Arabic. Leah was beside herself laughing and slipped into the living room to get a grip.

When he came up with Farsi, Mandy couldn't bear it any longer. "Oma," she cried, "make him stop!"

Oma came back into the kitchen, wiping her eyes and clearing her throat. "You might try American, Pops," she suggested calmly.

"Oh!" he exclaimed. "Do you speak American?" he asked Mandy, with a perfect American accent.

Mandy rolled her eyes, then the dice, and made it back to her house before he could get another word out of his mouth. "I win!" she declared triumphantly, with a 'seize the day' arm pump.

"Wait a minute. What do I do about my crooked car?" he asked, seemingly bewildered.

"Ask Oma. I'm *starving*!"

Their trip to the bees was truly magical. About a hundred bees came out of Carmella's hive to swarm around Mandy's head. She was absolutely delighted. After they zoomed back into cluster, Oma took her around to the side and dropped the hinged panel to reveal the window. The bees had attached comb to the window glass, giving her a good look at how a cell was made. They were all in cluster in the box above but the roar of their beating wings, which kept the queen and cluster warm, filled Mandy's ears with a sound she would never forget. She looked up at her Oma and saw the Golden Queen instead, extending an invitation to walk down a golden path with her. Leah heard the Golden Queen's voice ring out within her soul. "If handled delicately, and with wisdom, this path can be guided without interference from the Dark Queen. This we ask of you, for the future of humanity."

Mandy fell into Leah's arm sobbing. She'd been frightened when she saw the huge bee, then was released from her fear by a tremendous outpouring of love. It took her heart by surprise. Oma and Pops both cuddled her for a long time in the apiary. And, unbeknownst to them, Archangel Michael took on the guardianship of the lineage through the coming times that would greatly challenge all that was good and true on the earth.

After Mandy returned to the guesthouse to be home when Nathan and David returned from their overnight, Leah and Chris collapsed on the bed to recover. After recounting and laughing as much as they needed to, the mood became serious.

"Cowboy, how on earth am I going to pull off apprenticing our free-spirited granddaughter? I don't want to break her spirit. Can you imagine her in other than a Waldorf School environment? They at least have an interest in children accessing higher consciousness. If she wakes up as late as I did, I'll have to live to 120."

"You've got a point there, lass, and I don't have an answer for you. I get the feeling her soul has sufficient gumption to make the path happen and she does know you're the one to mentor her, if in a child's way now. I say we take a day at a time and let her soul work it out with spirit."

"You certainly did push her buttons, cowboy. I assume it was deliberate, at least in part?"

"It was that ... and it was fun. She's an amazing kid. You'd want to watch her easy frustration and short fuse, I reckon, as well as *her* budding petty tyrant," he suggested. "I wouldn't have expected her to see the humor in my actions but when life gives her that maturity, it could lead further — to cynicism."

"Good advice, though hard to implement long distance. That part of her so reminds me of Dragon Lady."

"Hmmm, that's two young 'Padawan learners', lass."

"We've also got Joel and Will to mentor for the Order, Nick and Natalie ready to rise, and you have Demetri and yours truly to guide through initiation."

"Let's not forget, I've got to regain my own double, lass," he reminded her.

"True enough. *New Avalon* seems to be drawing together those strong with the force. I'd best complete my own apprenticeship before some true mastery is needed. Bloody good thing we've got you here, vortexing energy in the stable," she teased.

"Oma, you talk funny!" he exclaimed nuzzling into the warmth of her neck. "We're going to be late for Episode III, lass. Let's get moving."

The hikers returned, in one piece, from a great adventure. David came by to let Pops know he'd not found any arrowheads but did see a black bear close up and a lot of deer. The Marble Mountains were too high to climb on an overnight hike but they could easily see Mount Shasta from a distance, which reminded his dad of Mount Fuji when he'd visited Japan. And no one slept because the coyotes, or maybe wolves, howled all night ... or so it seemed.

Nathan and David could barely stay awake during dinner at Chris and Leah's table. They sent the whole family home early, after agreeing to start out for *Harmony Valley* right after lunch the next day, and sharing a Japanese dinner at the guesthouse around seven. David and Mandy had been invited to bike down valley with the older kids to play with Jürgen and Zenzi. Demetri would be there to supervise, feed them lunch, and make sure they got back before dark — well before Star Wars since he'd been front and center for the movie showings.

Though plenty tired themselves, Oma and Pops had a glass of wine each whilst cuddled together on the sofa. It wouldn't do to let the movie reviews back up on them. He wanted to hear about Episode III.

"Well, cowboy, there was a lot more of the same overacted ego and dark side taking Anakin over. We'll chalk that up to targeted story moral for the moment, since I would have enjoyed a subtler seduction myself."

"When you were fourteen?" he asked.

"When I was fourteen I probably still wouldn't have got it. Remember, I was preoccupied. Anyway, we had good depictions of the fear, anger and greedy desire making one vulnerable to the dark side and a surprisingly lucid moment when Anakin defends the Jedi as being selfless — in service only to others. His blind desire to prevent Padmé's foreseen death destroys the love they had for each other. On the other hand one could say that it lifted the veil for her long enough to be a warning. Although, to be honest, there'd been many she chose to ignore."

"She was a little clouded," he agreed. "Love can do that to you, lass," he added, tickling her knees.

Do you think we're asking too much of our community — to be in selfless service, darling? The master Jedi were obviously operating from their true "I."

"They were. I'll remind you that no one is being forced into it. Those who are ready are embracing it as a path they're walking, not as something they've mastered."

"Skipping to the end," she said, getting to the climax of the battle, "it's very painful to watch the Jedi being killed in the final battle and Yoda's sadness that they must retreat into exile. Of course he'd warned them all of Anakin's clouded future. It's also painful to watch Obi Wan destroy his friend, brother and apprentice — and leaving the job unfinished, at that. The ending was quite sad. Even though I know it takes up again, it's without the Jedi Council. So, in summary, it was a lot more of the same but with the final seduction to the dark side. Dragon Lady took note. Geez, the Senator turning Emperor is uglier *than*... after he fights the Jedi master."

He laughed. "You can't face him with any fear and survive, lass."

"He represents the Guardian at the Threshold, then? The ugliness in each of us?"

"He's actually a good representation — reeling in his apprentices to try to control the world. Everything the Emperor does is Ahriman's forte, lass."

"That should make for interesting dreams. Thanks, cowboy."

"Aye, no worries," he grinned, rubbing her back gently to loosen up the building tension between the shoulder blades. Then, moving up to her neck, he filled her with calming energy for an easy, deep sleep.

Leah woke up the next morning streaming. That hadn't happened for months. The stream had been preceded by a series of pre-waking dreams, each ending with a bowing iris, inviting her into the golden light. She was sure she'd deliberately ended the dreams escaping to find the flower in the next dream, and on, and on. She remembered thinking *not yet, not yet,* as she landed back in her body. And then, the stream began. She found herself in a little town standing in front of a butcher shop looking in the window at all the cuts of beef, which were distinctly labeled as grass–fed. It was a fancy window with old-fashioned gold scrolling framing the two plate glass windows. Overhead, hanging from a permanent awning or more like a roof over the sidewalk, was an oval sign indicating that the store was called 'Main Street Butchery'. Quaint. There were customers inside chatting with a butcher behind the counter. She walked to the next storefront, under the same roof along the attractively paved sidewalk. There were long flower boxes on the street side in front of the stores. The sign hanging in front of that store read, 'Max's Wine and Tapas Bar'. It wasn't open but looked like a great place to hang out.

On the other side of the butcher she found the 'High Country Sheepskin Clothier' with two bay windows of smart looking jackets, boots, hats and mitts for men, women and children. There were also stuffed sheep and bears for kids. She loved this place. It had such a good feel to it. All of the stores were beautifully designed in harmony with each other, and filled with useful quality goods and services. There was a coffeehouse across the street and, next to that, a café that was bustling. Further searching turned up a green grocery – all fruits and veggies – that made her think she was in Australia. Further on she found an herbal pharmacy, a hardware store, and more. The crossing roads met in a roundabout lending credence to it being an Aussie scene. It was beautifully landscaped with flowers, a park bench, and a meandering water feature with a natural looking rock waterfall.

She asked for an aerial view and was surprised that the village was so small. There weren't any other streets though there was plenty of parking beyond and behind the stores. And there were a good many cars parked there. Moving up higher she realized it was plunked down in the middle of gosh-darn no–where. Further down one road she homed in on a slaughterhouse with cattle in holding pens behind the building and a few trucks park along side. The signage on the front of the building said High Country Cooperative Abattoir. Up further in the air she saw a landscape of low mountains, rangeland and some traditional farmland. She begged her clairvoyance for a hint as to where she was – whether it existed as she saw it or not. She wanted a GPS readout before she got even more confused.

Soon Leah found her self flying back to town center then taking a left turn and flying out of town in that direction, which felt like west for some reason. She was soon flying over vineyards and zooming around the farmhouse belonging to her friends, Max and Julia Cummings. *Max's Wine and Tapas Bar, indeed!* She flew back to the roundabout, and drifted down to land near the waterfall. Looking above the porch roofs of the two-story corner buildings, she found the brass street signs bolted to the walls, just like they were in

France. On each corner building, on all four corners, in both directions, the sign all said the same thing 'Main Street USA'. She got chills, so much so that she reached for her blue robe to wrap around her as she sat there in bed. She looked over at the coffee shop where two flower boxes, instead of one long box, flanked a familiar looking tree stump. Sheldon, CA, USA? *What, the Sam Hill, am I supposed to do with this, Spirit?* Her soul cried out in frustration. *Was it a metaphor or mission?*

The vision faded. She sat there with chills still running up and down her spine and big tears welling up in her eyes. *How can we possibly take on one more project? And why? Out in the middle of nowhere. It makes no sense.* Chris woke up just as the tears started to spill and drew her down into his warmth to calm the trembling that was deepening within her. It would be hours before she could talk about it. When she did, Chris advised her to put it on her furthest back burner until it did make sense. There was no way Tommy and Will could even take on thinking about it at this point. In the future, it might make more sense after *Harmony Valley* was humming along.

Which is where they ended up with Nathan and Julie that afternoon. The kids were impressed with the size and scope of it all, the classy way in which the hotel had been remodeled, the farm surrounding town ... well, all of it. It moved Leah from a decidedly broody mood into her element — manifesting models of new systems. She'd brought small color copies of Tommy's big drawings, now in the studio newsroom.

"Mom, I had no idea you were doing something this complex, and vast. It'll be amazing if you can pull it off," Nathan said, while looking over the drawings.

"We've no problem with what's proposed there, Nat. We've done this before, admittedly on a smaller scale, in *New Avalon*, but it translates well to similar projects. What does concern me is the process of finding the homeless population to get it off on the right foot."

"All kinds, I imagine," he remarked.

"True. Natalie has taken the selection process on and now that we're a week away from the first round of interviews, she's admitting what we're up against. Amongst the homeless there are criminals, murderers, some who've murdered fellow homeless people desperate for a safe place to sleep. There are many, maybe a majority, who have given up and want to start a new life in another lifetime, and still others who actually take to the liberating aspect of the homeless lifestyle and know the ropes very well. Finding people with hope, skills that can be rekindled, reasonably good health, and souls intact, and who are not mentally ill, drug addicts, alcoholics or sex fiends is tricky. We've got good people in social services screening for us, but my guess is that it will be the most difficult part of this project. Second to that is the challenge of building community from the ashes of their lives."

"That's depressing," he admitted. "Does Natalie have the background?"

"None of us do. We're flying by the seat of our pants on this one. What we do have is good intentions. However, those, too, can be misconstrued."

"Can broken people be pieced back together?" Julie asked. "It seems daunting. On the other hand, this place feels nourishing and very comprehensive."

"We're asking a lot of them, in return for a legitimate second-chance, but it feels a fair exchange. They'll be in a good place to let go of the American Dream ladder to wealth and success if they haven't already left it in a gutter somewhere. They, more than any of us, know that's an outdated myth. Whether they can agree long-term to what seems socialistic is a good question. I try to put myself in their shoes, where this seems to me like a dream come true, but I know I'm not really in their shoes and have never been anywhere near their experience."

Chris chimed in with an interesting thought. "Have you considered that the experiences their souls have chosen for them have taught them one thing most people don't know?"

"What's that?" Nathan asked.

"How to survive. And to survive against all odds is to have an extraordinary will to live."

"Brilliant, cowboy. Natalie and I need to plaster that on our foreheads. That's exactly the kind of soul strength we need here."

"Aye, but there's the bugger of sorting that out, eh?" he grinned.

Chris shared his ideas about the sheepskin and wool industry proposal, which brought that gorgeous store in the Sheldon stream to mind for Leah. *Back burner, kiddo,* she reminded herself. As they were leaving, she realized that the road into old Felix from the southwest led to Sheldon, just slightly out of their way. She drove back that way and stopped in the middle of the future roundabout, explaining that she'd walked there on Monday and wanted to get the mileage round trip. The vision from the stream returned, to show her the actual future town. It was, as an oasis in the wilderness, completely outlandish.

Chris got out and stood in the middle of the intersection for a few minutes, shook his head and got back into the van. They were 5.2 miles from New Avalon and by her reckoning less than a mile to the Cummings' from the center of the intersection. An easy bike ride from *New Avalon* and maybe double that from *Harmony* Valley for what that was worth.

Later on, when Leah and Chris slid into their theater seats he put his arm around her and gave her a gentle squeeze. "Are you ready for this, lass?" he asked.

"Over–ready, cowboy. Hey, what had you shaking your head in the middle of Sheldon?" she asked.

"Aye, the force is strong there, lass," he winked.

"R-r-right," she drawled. Actually, he meant it!

They walked home with Natalie and Chuck, who invited them in for a glass of red. Chuck was leaving for San Francisco the next morning to meet political expectations with important donors. He felt it a miserable waste of energy but acknowledged that sitting back against Superpacs was a great way to lose an election. So he'd do it. His donors were progressives but no one gave money without an agenda. Natalie was going to devote the last two days of the week to *Harmony Valley* participant interview planning, and leave the news to Leah and Stu, doubting they really needed guidance from her. That was agreeable. Leah would be in her office on Friday to go over the news with Paula, and close out the business end of 2011.

As Leah and Chris prepared a salad to contribute to dinner with the kids, he questioned her about the movie.

"Princess Leah hasn't aged much since the 70s," she laughed.

"Doubtless she's matured though," he quipped.

"Right you are. She is a Jedi, after all. Okay, my mentor," she said, giving him a kiss before launching into her review. "Dragon Lady can relate to both Leah and Luke. He's waking up to who he is and she's not conscious of it at all. They're both warriors, like the masculine and feminine part of all of us. Obi Wan sees Luke's impatience as his weakness but joins him in the fight, which leads him to his destiny, his death, at the hands of Darth Vader. He evaporates before Luke's eyes. Now, that indicates a high level of mastery, cowboy. His voice leads Luke on, and, in the next film, to Yoda.

"I'm reminded that Yoda told Obi Wan he would teach him to communicate with his dead mentor when they went into exile at the end of Episode III. When Obi Wan disappears in death before Luke's eyes, it's obvious he's been working hard with Yoda to achieve the level of mastery that transcends physical death. Vader, no longer Anakin, has become the slave of Palpatine — the bionic arm of Ahriman.

"So, there were no wise sayings of Yoda, who is still in exile, but good Jedi teachings nonetheless. Through Obi Wan's instructions from the other side, Luke connects with the force and succeeds in destroying the death star — with some essential backup from returning Han Solo, who'd taken off when the going got rough. Of course, that sets Luke up to be continually hunted by unconscionable agents of the dark side for Episodes V and VI. I think the most powerful take home message for Dragon Lady was Obi Wan's advice to Luke — to embrace his destiny and be the Jedi, the force of good, he was meant to become."

"*Let the force move through you,* lass."

"A challenge I'll try to meet, cowboy," she replied, taking a big, replenishing in-breath. "Obviously, the force is the etheric energy, the cosmic Qi. I guess we're looking at etheric mastery in the Jedi, eh?"

"Aye, without the specifics. You're no master without complete control over that etheric center near your heart, lass — especially if you're going to transcend death. Plus, you've got to vaporize your body, which means it has been transformed from carbon-based to volatile salt-based structure. Now, that's mastery on a Christ order of magnitude."

"R-r-right. Well, that's another level of play to pay attention to in the last two episodes."

Mandy graciously instructed them in the fine points of eating Japanese food. She was feeding an ongoing inner hilarity that Oma and Pops were hard-pressed to contain. They managed by engaging both children in conversation about their day at Demetri's. For most of the morning, they'd been over in the forest, with Jürgen and Zenzi, learning to become invisible. Then after hot soup and sandwiches, Demetri introduced them to dragon games. Trying not to look alarmed, Leah caught Chris's eye, to convey grandmotherly concern. He was fascinated and casually questioned the children further. Though no clear description of what they were doing was forthcoming, it sounded like a fantastically fun and harmless day. Fair enough.

It had also been exhausting, what with the bike riding down there and all of the play. Mandy was begging to go to bed at eight and David was looking forward to the next chapter of the adventure book he'd been reading before the hiking trip. Chris and Leah kissed them both good night then cleaned up the dishes while Nathan and Julie got them ready for bed. They were hoping to have an uninterrupted adult chat with Oma and Pops that evening.

Julie came down the hall from the bedrooms first, since Nathan and David had a little bedtime ritual she called guy-time — the reviewing of David's day — to complete together. Leah smiled at the memory of having done something similar with Nathan from an early age. It was a great way to sort out and recapitulate the day and become comfortable sharing feelings with a parent, who could one day be a great friend.

Their adult conversation began around the dining table with a pot of tea. Nathan and Julie wanted to express their gratitude for the holiday and their generosity in all that had been provided for them. They went on, lovingly explaining to Chris the big gap that he'd filled in all of their lives. Nathan had little contact with Daryl and Julie's father had no knack for grandfathering at all. His strong suit was the discipline of the brain, which didn't exactly flow with the Waldorf curriculum. Lucky for the kids, he and Grandma Evelyn lived in Minneapolis where he taught at the University. Chris acknowledged their gratitude and turned it back on them. He, a childless man, was having the time of his life with their kids. They were all evened-up in his mind. He was already looking forward to the end of May.

Julie excused herself to check on the children while Nathan told them about his new book series. She came back indicating that both kids were sound asleep. Oma and Pops felt the mood change dramatically.

"What's up, you two?" Leah asked, sensing the need for a leading question and interview skills.

Nathan and Julie looked at each other, as Leah felt Chris move into space-holding mode. "You start Jules," Nathan urged.

"Yes. Well, I'm the one generating a family wobble. My job is being terminated as of the first of February," she told them, in her straightforward way.

"Any prospects?" Leah asked.

"I could work for nearly nothing. I'd be preaching to the choir trying to explain what's happening on the ground in this recession to you, Leah. I will say the publishing industry has been hit harder than many because upper level management wasn't behind the eight ball with digital publishing, Internet marketing, and now Print On Demand. That's no news. It was nice while it lasted but my position is one of hundreds being cut."

"No need to explain, darling," Leah, offered. "You actually managed to hang onto the position through what most would judge the worst of the job losses."

"I think we're going to see a secondary corporate purge, just like I don't think we've seen the end of the housing crisis."

"Tell me you're thoughts about that, both of you."

Nathan took the lead. "Foreclosing on millions of people who were bamboozled into thinking they could afford to own homes when the really couldn't is one thing. There are still many millions strapped with debt, either credit card or, as we are, from variable rate equity loans promoted by the banks at the height of the bubble. We're underwater, as are all of our friends in our age group. A second collapse will occur when interest rates rise if those loans and credit debt cannot be paid off, forgiven or reduced and rolled into new mortgages at low interest rates. It's not an opportune time to lose your job. At the same time any solution we think of seems futile."

"Did you get a severance package, Julie?" Leah asked.

"I hadn't been with the company long enough. I'll get a month's pay, accrued vacation and sick pay, and we do have some savings. I'm already looking for work."

"We've got my royalties and the advance on the new book, Mom, and we can make it if … if we let the Waldorf schooling go. It looks like we'll have to do that. We just don't have the assets and can't run the equity loan up any more," he admitted, looking grim.

"You're not alone, Nathan. It's important that neither of you feel that you've failed. It's the system that's failed and the 1% that have gained. Will you let us help? Seeing the kids through the end of the school year at the very least?"

"Do you think it's that important, Mom?" Nathan asked, feeling a bit sick to his stomach.

Leah looked at Chris who gave her an almost imperceptible nod.

"It's of the utmost importance, Nat. The children need stability in crisis. I have a personal rainy day fund for just this kind of an emergency. Your children are worth whatever it costs, and that's that."

Silence filled the room. "That will give you some time, no?" Leah asked.

"It will. Thank you so much," Julie sighed.

"What's the matter, darling? If I can ask?" Leah prodded.

"It just looks like a dark tunnel," Julie went on, with tears in her eyes. "It's not what either of us imagined would happen to us. We're bright enough, and creative, but we were really duped by consumerism and easy credit."

Nathan held Julie's hand and faced his mother. "It feels like bondage, Mom. We'll hold it together for the kids. If we were young and carefree we'd probably bolt."

Leah was silent, her heart aching. She looked at Chris who could read her heart and mind easily.

"Could I make a suggestion?" he interjected.

"Of course," they replied in unison.

"I suggest you finish the school year but put your house on the market early in the spring. No matter what your next move is, the house is more than a roof over your heads, it's a liability. The way everyone got bamboozled in the first place lies in the notion that home ownership means security and demonstrates success. Neither is true. Mortgages make the fat cats fatter. They feed the problem and ignore the solutions. When your mother dreamt up *Harmony Valley* I'm sure she wasn't imagining interviewing your family for residency."

Leah's heart felt like it was bleeding. She never expected Chris to be critical. Was that a judgment? She decided to love him for his brave heart instead, and wait to see where he was going. She heard Dragon Lady criticize her mothering of Nathan and told her, flat out, to shut up and listen.

Nathan spoke with care. "I hear you, Dad."

My God! Did I hear that? Leah's heart whispered within.

"I added up all the insurances, the taxes, the mortgage and equity payment, a year's worth of repair bills and utilities and came up with Julie's take home pay for the year. Then I researched what we ought to be paying at today's home value. I see why people are walking away from their homes. They want to be able to eat. I'm all for living simply. We've dumped the credit cards but now we're looking at no health insurance, which Jules' employer covered. Of course the school costs are outrageous, if well worth it, and there are no scholarships policies. It's hard to see a clear way out."

"I understand that, son," Chris, countered, flooring Leah a second time. "But, if *you* don't move the energy first, the banks will move it for you. It's your house to sell and we'll hold a space for you to break even, at least. If we have to help mop up the equity loan, I've no objections. Have you?" he asked, looking to Leah.

"No. Of course not," she said, unable to believe the way he'd given Nathan the prize of his life, a real on-the-job dad, at the same time he firmly set out a path of redemption. But where was that path headed, she wondered?

"And while you're here, have a good talk with Will Martin at the bank. He's our interface with the legal and economic world? Right, lass?"

"He's brilliant, Nat, and he'd love to help you two. You can consider him your uncle since he's a brother to me."

Pops invited Nathan and David to watch his Aikido practice with Will the next morning. It was a good way to meet Will outside the community events. Nathan assured him they'd be there. They'd discussed Aikido with David as part of his Japanese cultural heritage studies when he got interested in martial arts. Julie was second generation American-born Japanese but her mother and father had a wealth of stories from their immigrant parents who'd been force into detention camps during the war. She and Nathan had traveled to Japan before David was born — a pilgrimage her parents encouraged and funded.

On their walk home, Leah thanked Chris for stepping in and taking Nathan on as his own son. She could see Nathan visibly transforming during this visit. Old walls were falling down. And, Julie's job loss had back-handedly created greater access to her feelings. She was deeply concerned that their lives were in the process of unraveling — though who could be surprised by these stories anymore? If life was going to beat you up, the best you could do was gain from it spiritually. He agreed.

She also noted that with her nose to the grindstone she'd lost track of Chris' one-on-one interactions, like practice with Will and weight lifting at the bakery with Spence. Being home for the holiday break brought with it the awareness that he was out there touching everyone's life in personal ways, on a regular basis, like a gardener continually spreading rich compost.

Fortunately, Aikido practice was from eight-thirty until nine-thirty the next morning, giving David ample time to join the gang of kids barreling down valley again on their bikes at 10 o'clock. Chris had walked up to the exercise room with Will, filling him in on Nathan and Julie's situation and their concerns. Will was happy to make an exception to their *private* practice session for Light Beam's son and grandson and arranged a meeting with Nathan and Julie at the bank after lunch to talk about their situation and options.

Leah invited them to come over to the studio afterwards to see their new addition and documentary set-up. They were impressed. The studio had scaled up profoundly since their last visit. In fact they'd never even come to the studio when they'd visited in May. Now it seemed a hub of growth and activity for the community. Stu, known to them as Suzie and Celeste's dad, filled them in on the show's success, the collaboration with Joel Robertson, the burgeoning donor based initiatives, and the talents of his growing staff. They were particularly impressed with Rob who explained his work for his senior year project for Waldorf homeschooling.

Julie and Nathan spent their day walking around *New Avalon* discovering what the people they'd met at the community events did to earn their NADs, which Will had referenced often in their talk about economic freedom. When they wandered into the greenhouse on their way home from the warehouse, farm, and bakery, they found Leah and Ellia helping Sonia make pot blocks for the first seedlings of 2012. They were curious about the hydroponic fish farming operation, which was nourishing an upper level of watercress and other leafy greens in the dead of winter. Julie, a great fan of Sea Bass, wondered if such an operation could be used for saltwater fish. Sonia jotted down a website for a big commercial operation doing just that in the Bay Area.

Along their *New Avalon* discovery route, they'd picked up an invitation to dine with Spence, Christina and family. Mandy was already expected to go home with Emily after they'd biked back from play at Demetri's. Thus, Leah and Chris found themselves heading into an evening alone together. It was a great opportunity to eat leftovers, reorganize the game cupboard, and have a good chat about the kid's dilemma. Chris wasn't shy about moving energy. He'd suggested to Will that he broach the subject of life in *New Avalon*.

That had provoked the investigatory tour and one-on-one encounters that had filled Nathan and Julie's day. Leah was pleasantly shocked that he'd backhandedly initiated that possibility. He countered that the looming deadline for residency in the second community cut through the mustard of respectable boundaries. He clearly saw them in *New Avalon* at some point. Why not sooner, rather than later? She agreed it would simplify her work with Mandy and commented that present circumstances were serving to draw them all together in a most intimate way. The downside was the financial quagmire the kids found themselves in and what she knew would be their refusal to take a free ride — personal pile of gold in the vault, or not. On that note, they went on to review Episode V.

"Ah yes, we finally got to Luke's training with Yoda. That came about because Obi Wan appeared to him as he was close to freezing to death. It was a delusional vision but as the story continues we can be sure that Obi Wan is in his double, eh?"

"Aye, Obi Wan actually completed his work to be a Jedi."

"I loved the fun Yoda has leading Luke on a wild goose chase to recognize him, when they first meet. We note that he didn't use a show of power, which Luke was expecting. Obi Wan's voice has to step in to wake him up, and then there was the litany of good reasons for Yoda to refuse him as an apprentice. He learned much about his young Padawan in very little time. He admitted having watched Luke for years ... never with his mind on what he was doing and always hard to finish what he began.

"And then, the training begins by challenging his fearlessness, and on it goes. I did catch that a Jedi can know good from evil only when he's calm, and that the force is never used to hurt. That's the dark side use of it. His training begins, but so do the setbacks when he lets his attention, mind or vision stray from the present, and he fails. That leads him eventually to the big test. Yoda tells him he must go into a cave and meet what is there. Of course, Darth Vader is there. They battle with their light sabers and Luke defeats him, cuts off his head. We then find out that it's Luke's head inside the Vader mask. Unless I missed something, we don't find out right then that he failed the test in the cave, but he did. He's not a Jedi."

"What do you make of that, lass?"

"It's uncanny that I asked to see these movies. That's what I think. The Vader in the cave is the Guardian at the Threshold, the evil within Luke. Rather than owning it and transforming it, he doesn't recognize it and uses the force to harm himself. So what do I make of it? Properly completing all of the steps leading towards initiation is the *only* way to attain it — to become a Jedi. He'll need to do that in his actual encounters with Vader and the Emperor in Episode VI. He leaves Yoda guided by a healthy, but immature, ego, against the urging of both Yoda and Obi Wan, to complete his training. I'll say it was odd that he was pushed into the cave before he was anywhere near ready, but then Yoda knew his path, and a movie has it's time limitations. Yoda was 800 years into his life as a Jedi, after all."

"Aye, we can cut Lucas some slack there, lass. The lad was impressed when Yoda raised his ship out of the water but even that demonstration of power didn't sink in – in the moment."

"Luke was young," she reminded him, "although in the perfect scheme of our development, he'd have been ripe for higher consciousness. So, that really isn't a good excuse. For me, that does bring Mandy to mind and the advantage she would have maturing in this community. But, I digress.

"Back to the story … Yoda, having lifted the plane out of the water and gently placed it down on the land, takes Luke to task for his negativity. He doesn't believe in himself. He counters everything coming out of Luke. *Do, or do not – there is no try,* Yoda says. That's actually something Dragon Lady holds dear. She does have her good features. *My ally is the force. Luminous beings are we,* he says, and when Luke exclaims that he *doesn't believe* what Yoda has done, Yoda hits the nail on the head – *that is where you fail.* That's the end of that. Luke does promise to return but that will be with one hand and the knowledge that Vader is his father."

"And Obi Wan?" he asked.

"A master, cowboy. I assume that's where we're going with our little mystery school. By the end of the film it's clear he's appearing to Luke as his double, as a luminous being that survives death and, when you think about, he has amazing mobility but no ability to physically intervene in this reality. We don't find out whether he has been in and out of this reality for some time, ala Babaji, or, for that matter, if Yoda can do that as part of his training."

And, the big picture version of Episode V?" her mentor asked.

"Let me see," she said, taking a moment to gather her thoughts. "There's a price to be paid for pushing the river. As with all of these movies, nothing *is* as it appears, especially the dark side. Our beliefs limit us. To use the force to harm is black magic. And we can wrap this up by admitting that this initiation, which is the same one Demetri and I are preparing for, requires the complete conquest of self as well as the embodiment of the force. To imagine that you have the power of the force is proof that you don't."

"Beauty," he grinned.

She laughed. "Are you having these reviews with Demetri, cowboy?"

"Aye, lass – over the fish tank."

They made wild, sweet love that night – a true pleasure after having lived through weeks of scheduled, scarce lovemaking. The Bee Mistress had barely laid claim to her prize. She enjoyed it immensely but Leah's dreams were, once again, of wild storms and bending irises. She struggled to relax during yoga. Her muscles were tight and nerves fraught. She recounted the last week, noting there was one more Episode of Star Wars to absorb, one more sacrifice of Christ Jesus to try to understand and explain, and a very sober Dragon Lady crouched in the corner of her cage. On the back burner she now had Sheldon, California, two young Padawan learners and the Guardian at the Threshold. There were two days left in 2011.

Leah was due at the studio at some point, to go over the news of the week with Paula. Since the kids were all down valley *again,* she felt it might be the best day to go into her office and review and close out her working notebook. She would begin a new one with carry over, just like a new bank account, in January. She and Will would also go over the year-end financial stats, since it was the last banking day of the year. She moved through her shower and breakfast slowly, feeling herself seized by malaise. It was so out of character, she was prompted to take her temperature, feel her pulse and look at her stuck-out tongue in the mirror. That was when Chris walked into the bathroom to take his shower.

"Where are you going with that tongue of yours, lass? It bears some resemblance to the path of the bowing iris from this view," he said, resting his chin on the top of her head.

"I'm off, cowboy. It's nothing physical though. I might have some emotions stirring about Nathan's decision and their going home on Monday."

"Don't worry about it. He'll do what he must, and we still have to lick our way through a caramel sponge cake recipe. We can't afford to lose you now."

She turned around for a good cuddle and a welcomed pulse of energy — *the force* actually, into the back of her neck. That set her back on track. Chris and Nathan were riding down valley to Mr. B's farm to further clean out the small shed. He was bringing his drawings to help explain the barn conversion to the Performing Arts Center. If he noticed anything overtly devilish going on at Demetri's, he'd be sure to file a report with Oma ... expediently. Julie was getting together with Georgia and Leslie to talk about the school curriculum and plans for the future. The family would all reunite for dinner at Oma and Pops'. Leah had taken a plump chicken out of the freezer, with the accompaniments to be filled when the veggie box arrived.

Stu was at the studio when Leah got there around ten that morning, as were Rob, Matt and Paula. Natalie was at home, preparing for her trip the next day. Leslie had taken a much-needed vacation at home with her kids, and Jennifer was visiting her folks in Arizona. After going over the news with Paula and agreeing to meet at nine the next morning to finalize and tape it, Paula left to go horseback riding with Sam. It was downright balmy for the thirtieth of December.

Leah hit the notebooks, highlighting ideas or projects yet to be completed, along with all those back burner projects on hold indefinitely. The big one was the Restorative Justice model, which couldn't be addressed until the state legislature re-convened in January. Christina had been working the committee rooms and hallways before recess, gathering support for a hearing, at least. That would take some time yet.

In their faces, out of the starting gate in 2012, were the first rounds of interviews with potential *Harmony Valley* participants. Natalie was scheduled for the first go-round in Ashland on the fourth of January. Further interviews would be conducted in Redding, and finally Sacramento where a huge homeless encampment concentrated homeless people from many walks of life. If need be, they could resource San Francisco, Oakland and San José.

As she was copying the last of that carryover to her new notebook, Will appeared in her doorway, with a big smile on his ever so handsome face.

"Hey, what's up, Will?" she asked, dropping her pen and standing for their tradition kiss on the check.

"I remember your telling me to watch the donors for red flags, Light Beam," he began.

"You're right. I did. Although, I thought it was odd at the time. Have you got one to wrap up our year?" she asked with a smile, sitting back down in her chair.

"Maybe. Yesterday I had a call from a Wells Fargo agent wanting to direct deposit an Outreach donation instead of using the website."

"That's odd, unless it's big. What did Ali Cat do?"

"He sent the bank check ahead of time, remember?"

"Sorry bro, life's a blur this week," she smiled, weakly.

"The website isn't set up for donations over four figures."

"Right. So this one came directly into the account? What? Wire transfer?"

"Yeah. $30 Million, Light Beam," he said, taking the chair beside her desk.

Leah didn't bat an eye. She was recalling Yoda's warning that one must be calm to recognize the dark side. "Any notations?"

He smiled. "You're taking this like the President, Light Beam — Mrs. Joe Cool."

She smiled as he unfolded the paper he'd brought with him. "Maybe you can explain this to me. Our donor's preference is that this gift be used to support Main Street USA, if possible."

Leah remained stoic, a grin plastered on her face, while the maelstrom roared in her brain. The sound of its wind was deafening. "And who is our donor, my favorite banker?" she asked.

"I researched him — recently retired investment banker with CityBank, one E. Hegelman. Ring a bell?"

Her heart was pounding. *More like a tsunami siren.* "I'm sure it's bona fide, Will. That would be my brother, Eric. Main Street USA is a potential project — one I did not want to overwhelm Outreach with at this point. It's right here in my new notebook sitting on its back burner. Eric's knowledge of it is mind-boggling to say the least. I barely know of it myself."

"You've not talked about it with him?"

"We've had no contact since my mother's funeral and little before that, frankly. I doubt he'll try to contact us directly though I would like to know that it's clean money."

"I'll second that. Is he worth this?"

"Much more, I'd reckon. I didn't know he'd retired, but he was the chief investment officer worldwide, a real bankster. He would know I'd refuse anything that wasn't legitimate. Let's see what happens, mate. It's already in the bank."

"True enough. I'll finish up the stats then and leave them 'til Monday."

"Thanks, Will. That's soon enough to get organized for our board meeting on Thursday. Let's keep it between you and me for the moment."

"Good enough. Got plans for New Year's Eve, Light Beam?" he asked, getting up to go.

"Dinner at our house with the famed caramel sponge cake. You're welcome to join us if you two are free."

"I managed to get a slice of that on Sunday — don't ask me how. Your offer is very tempting, but we'll be at The Lodge with our families."

"Is everyone comfortable over there? I've been pretty wrapped up with the kids."

"The Lodge is one of our greatest assets — another of your winning ideas," he said, getting up to go. "You can spare me Main Street USA today, but I'm keen to hear about it when you're ready to share."

"I love you, Will. Thanks for all your support."

"Back at ya, Light Beam," he laughed, before heading back to the bank.

Leah's level of inner turmoil was dangerously close to panic attack. Her efforts to remain calm with Will were, in her estimation, heroic and possibly futile. It did avoid unnecessary drama but failed to provide insight. How the hell would Eric know about Main Street USA? Was he monitoring her thought field? That was frigging scary. What to do about it? What *could* she do about it? Nothing. She had no idea how to contact him. Moreover, she didn't want contact with him. However, his donation threw her into a moral dilemma. Which part of his life was he trying to download on her charitable organization? Did it have a big karmic tag on it or not?

She stepped out into the hall to pace back and forth. Most on her mind was a face off with the Dark Lord. She remembered Obi Wan, stopping to raise his light saber before allowing Vader to 'kill' him. She imagined a knight raising his sword directly in front of him pointed to the heavens — well, like Aragorn before the last stand against Mordor. Obi Wan looked invincible in that moment. Aragorn was the embodiment of valor. She stopped, closed her eyes, and ran as much energy as she could through her chakras searching for that magical energy center she was supposed to be building behind her heart. *R-r-right.* That was exactly the center of her panic. *Bring in the calming eye of the storm. Let the force flow through you.* She did calm, and felt a swirl of warmth behind her heart that seemed real. When she slowly opened her eyes, she was staring into Nick's.

"My God, Nick! Where did you come from?" she cried out, with a start, reaching out to touch his chest.

"O-o-o-h, sorry, doc," he crooned, trying to mellow her out. "There's a time and a place for Valium," he offered. She silently shook her head, trying to still her heart. "You looked like an angel just then ... by the way."

"That's a comfort, Nick. What's up?"

"We just got the mail and I thought you might be expecting these," he said, handing her two express mail envelopes — one of them addressed to Nathan and the other to her.

Leah felt the warmth behind her heart sink to her gut like a dump truck load of ice. "Thanks, Nick. I've a bit of family stuff going on."

He looked her over carefully, noting the angelic glow's diminishment. "Let me know if you need a session, doc."

"Thanks, Nick," she said, with a smile and hug. "I appreciate your love and concern. I *will* let you know."

"Good enough. I'm due at home to give Georgia a break right now. Later."

"Later, gorgeous boy," she whispered to herself, as he jogged out the front door.

Leah took the letters into her office, shutting the door behind her. She sat at her desk studying them. The return address was The Hilton Hotel in the San Francisco financial district. She took a deep breath and pulled the tab to open her envelope. On second thought, she decided to brew a pot of strong tea before looking at the contents. She took the time to have a full cup before returning to it, fully aware of Dragon Lady shaking the bars of her cage.

She withdrew the contents, a single sheet of hotel stationary, and read:

Sis, It's most urgent that you meet me at the Weed Airport, Saturday Dec 31, at noon. Come alone. Tell no one. Drive into the first hanger where my plane will be 'serviced'. Wait for me. I will arrive around 12:15. Thx, Eric
PS: Please wait to give Nathan his envelope until Sunday

As she drank her second cup of bracing tea, Leah tried to pick up on the truth behind Eric's note. He was flying his private jet to Weed rather than picking up a phone to talk, or showing up in person. He was either in a hurry or on the run, or both. To his credit he was trying to protect her identity by arriving after she'd be under cover. That was ludicrous, of course, since it wouldn't be that hard to link the two of them as siblings. His donation wasn't anonymous, though. *What have you done, Eric?* The truth was she would be spending 24 hours in limbo, period. Get on with the day. She locked the letters in her desk drawer, set her notebooks aside, and went home for the day.

Chris found her in the kitchen baking the sponge cake and topping up the cookie jar for kids of all ages. Nathan and Julie were going to share lunch together and have a financial disaster discussion while the kids were off playing. They'd be over for dinner at seven with the salad. Leah was brine-soaking the chicken and relying on Natalie to manage the initial roasting. Nat would join them for dinner, but leave right afterwards to get good rest before her big day and New Year's Eve with Chuck.

Leah tried her best to put Eric out of her mind but found him in there streaming around with the cast of Star Wars and the state of affairs in Greece, for some reason. When she and Chris sat down for a light lunch, he asked how she was holding up — perfectly aware of a huge dark storm in her astral body.

"I'm anticipating disaster, cowboy. It feels like the hurricane is unavoidable at this point, and close at hand."

"How do you plan to face it, lass?" he asked.

"I've been thinking about the way Obi Wan prepared for Vader's final attack — with calm, in the fullness of the force, except I'm having trouble allowing it to flow through me. I did have a moment today when I felt the etheric center behind my heart."

"Aye? Mission control. What did if feel like?"

"A swirling warmth, then I lost it."

"How did you manifest it in the first place?"

"By focusing on running *the force* through my chakras — right up from the base and down from the crown."

"It's a safe harbor in the storm, lass. Keep up the good work. Nathan is going to ride with the Rangers tomorrow. We're going out on patrol and to put together a plan for the Three Kings prep application on Friday next. We'll take a lunch. You're at the studio?"

"I am. We'll tape the news segment and Will's bit, and then stay to watch the whole thing play back. No devilish reports from the farmhouse for Oma?"

"Whatever they're doing, they're having a ball. Jürgen and Zenzi will be off over the ridge tomorrow though, so today will likely be it for the kids."

"They'll just move it up here, I reckon. They're playing as a tribe now," she laughed.

"Further thoughts about the Jedi?" he asked, with a grin.

"To be honest, cowboy, what runs through my mind, *a lot*, is the idea of power. I remember thinking everyone had it but me, as I was growing up. In fact I had a lot of power and yielded it ruthlessly at times. I wonder if power is abstract — something we see as a goal or necessity of survival. Otherwise, why would people get addicted to it? How much power do you need? How much money do you need? When is enough, enough? Who made it the prize at any price? And who made it look like money, right here and now? It irked me to see Vader kneel in subservience to the Emperor, who, for me at least, represents the fullness of the Ahrimanic, though not Ahriman embodied. I get that Ahriman wants to chain us to the earth — to challenge us in that way — but we have the choice to follow him or not."

"What's this really about, lass?" he asked, eyeing her over his sandwich.

"Sorry to rant, darling. I never found joy in controlling the lives of others. I found complexity, angst, and skewed responsibility. It feels consummately selfish to me now. Is our longing for power what keeps us from being happy?"

"I reckon. These are big issues to be working through, lass. If you stand well above the whole concept of Star Wars you're going to see the face of light and dark dancing through the ages. However, I might challenge the setting. Humanity's *Fall* is bound to the earth, as Lucifer's rebellion. I'm not so sure we can assume it exists in the rest of the galaxy, though for us the galaxy can only be apparent as part of our material world."

"Okay then, why do the power brokers want to control the world? At its core that desire seems to deny being human."

"Vader wasn't human. You did get that distinction from Obi Wan? Though Anakin had Jedi training, as Yoda rightfully predicted, he was unable to complete initiation. He hasn't faced the Guardian and he hasn't brought in his true "I" — yet. Vader was possessed, lass, but not beyond hope. He did pull it all together in the end."

"The Emperor was hopelessly possessed, then?"

"Aye."

chapter 12: redemption

A sizeable crowd gathered for Episode VI that afternoon and, right after the show, dispersed to homes and family for dinner. When Chris and Leah arrived home, Natalie had a perfect chicken roast nearly done in the oven. Leah had left potatoes ready to boil and fresh broccoli to steam. Julie brought a beautiful mix green salad with an Asian dressing. By seven they were all sitting around the table, hands joined, while Mandy and David sang grace. Harry was holding space right under the chicken platter. Natalie excused herself before the plate of cookies reached the table and asked them to show Harry home when he petered out.

Leah, grateful for the distraction the kids provided, became consumed with dread after everyone left that evening. She and Chris were set to wrap up the lessons learned in Episode VI. She felt strongly that, though it was just a news segment in the morning, she would adhere to her ritual download and tub soak to regain focus — with so much distraction going on (*excuses, excuses*).

Sensing her need for a good cuddle, Chris suggested they discuss Episode VI on the sofa together. He lit a fire, wiped up the kitchen and steeped some *Melissa* tea, while Leah fetched her sleeping bag and thick winter hat for the download right afterwards. She curled into his warmth and gave some thought to the conclusion of Star Wars.

"One thing I did notice, for the first time, was Yoda's reference to the dark side of *the force*. Of course, *the force* would be both light and dark. I always thought of it as the light, and the dark side somehow being of different substance."

"The difference is intent, lass — what you can do with *the force* is determine by how you intend that it flow through you."

"So Episode VI is about the abuse of power, cowboy, and that's all about choice — free will. Luke really gets put to the test in this final story. He goes back to Yoda to find him dying — *twilight is upon me* - and finds that the Jedi are not immortal. Even with the strength of *the force* in Yoda who is the highest of the masters, it isn't strong enough to prevent death. Okay, he's ready for a break after 800 years training Jedi," she laughed.

He gave her a squeeze. "The Jedi are etheric masters, not masters of the physical — yet. Of course, mastery of the physical is about immortality only in the sense that appearing in this reality is optional."

"Right. So, on his deathbed, Yoda reminds Luke that he isn't yet a Jedi. He must confront Darth Vader and kill him to be a Jedi. Then Yoda dies and his body disappears. Now, what he has told him seems contrary to the Jedi rule of doing no harm, but I see it as a metaphor. He must kill who Anakin became, the Ahrimanic being who possessed Anakin as the arm of the Emperor, as well as that representation within himself. Obi Wan appears, truly as his double now — maybe improved technology in filmmaking but a convincing double, in my opinion. Luke accuses Obi Wan of lying to him about his father and Obi Wan sits down to explain. When Anakin, his actual father, through his own journey to the dark side, became possessed, he left Anakin behind and was someone else. Yet, within that someone else was a remnant of his true self. That would be the white dot within the yang half of the Tao."

"Brilliant, lass."

"He must destroy the dark side — Vader — to release Anakin. He is warned not to allow his anger, hatred, fear and so forth, blind him to this mission. Of course, that's exactly what happens, and he must constantly pull himself back. And, even as Yoda has warned him not to underestimate the power of the Emperor, he does. And the Emperor takes him down. His humiliation is complete. He *isn't* a Jedi, and it's Vader who must save him by destroying the Emperor for him."

"What have you got for a big picture, here?"

"Redemption, of course, through the power of the yin within the yang. Luke believed his father to be an honorable Jedi and the power of his belief allowed it to happen for Anakin. I might add that a battle must be fought within and without to pass this initiation. We must face what we most fear, fearlessly, with hope and unwavering belief in the good and true."

"How was Luke rewarded for completing that initiation?"

"His life was saved through reawakened goodness, let's call it kindness, on Anakin's part. Darth Vader was no more. Anakin died looking into his son's eyes. That said; the real gift was his appearance at his cremation in his double with Yoda and Obi Wan, which proved that his act of destroying the Emperor completed his Jedi initiation. He did meet the Guardian and passed the test. They were gifted the return of the Jedi in Luke, who had completed his initiation as well. Another wonderful gift is the awakening of the Jedi lineage in Leah, and all women."

"I must add that I have never stopped loving the Ewoks since I first saw this movie. I consider them the most endearing of all the fantasy creatures portrayed on the big screen. They make me want to visit the Forest Moon of Endor."

"I have to agree. Well done, my Padawan learner. You did notice that c3po finally found his droid destiny as the storytelling god of the Ewoks?"

"That was absolutely priceless. Thank you for pointing that out, cowboy. Everyone found their purpose and got a healing in the process."

The download on the timber table felt decidedly different. It had nothing to do with the news and everything to do with opening that space behind her diamond heart. The energy flooding in felt like grace. She would try very hard to keep that heart open for her meeting with Eric. Dragon Lady would fight a fierce battle to gain control over the situation but she'd need to be a true magician to get out of her cage.

Leah was in her office at eight the next morning to meet with Paula, update the news and put it into the teleprompter. That was simple. Paula told her she'd forwarded a link to a story on NPR about a homeless man. It sounded interesting so she brought it up on her laptop for a quick listen, while waiting for Georgia and the makeup. The story provoked a colossal meltdown. Heroic efforts would be needed to calm her red puffy eyes. Paula had no idea she was in a fragile place and apologized profusely as she handed Leah tissues. Leah assured her that the story was incredible, and so timely, what with their *Harmony Valley* interviews coming up.

The man being interviewed had been a successful inventor — a multi-millionaire, in fact — who lost his money in the housing collapse through devalued real estate investments and a fraudulent Florida scam into which he'd been conned. He lost his own home, his wife and kids and ended up homeless — first living in his car until he lost that to repossession and found himself on the street. He lost his possessions to theft and carelessness as he wandered, but managed to hold onto his laptop, on which he kept his journals and invention ideas. He'd been chronicling his homeless journey on it as well.

His story demonstrated the rapid downward spiral of loss that many homeless people experienced. He was beat up for sleeping in wrong places within the homeless culture until he found himself a vacated dumpster. He realized he was nothing and that no one wanted him around or cared about him. He was shabby and he stunk. He was crushed. When he lost his dumpster, he found himself a place to sleep under a fountain hiding his laptop in a plastic bag. Some homeless thugs came along and beat him unconscious, destroying his prostate in the process; and they stole the computer. He felt more than alone. He felt an empty shell of a person who had given up on everything about this life, including the guilt and self-judgment that had been his companion throughout the journey. He felt completely empty — zilch. Leah realized that the state of mind he described was much like the state of mind needed to cross the threshold. His slate was clean. He carried his burdens no longer. Perhaps he, or rather life, had destroyed his shadow.

Painfully, he walked to the emergency room of the hospital, where he had to wait 19 hours for treatment of serious injuries. Homeless patients — parasites of the 'medical system' — were always the last to be treated. After finally being examined, he was assigned to a surgeon, an Asian man, who began to pull his story from him before operating on his prostate. He was a doctor concerned for his patient, not a robotic surgeon doing a routine job. He was familiar with and actually relied on some of the homeless man's medical inventions. This doctor gave the homeless man more than required surgery. He gave him back his life. He believed in him, and the long and short of it was that they were now in partnership together producing self-sufficient, secure, individual cubicles for homeless shelter — as inspired by his dumpster home. This story hit close to home — near Capital Square in Sacramento. The doctor was a true Good Samaritan, a doctor of the soul, as well as the body.

It was a heartwarming story that would make most people teary, but the kind of meltdown Leah had indicated a message in the story that touched her soul in a unique way. After clearing away the pile of tissues to the biomass waste, she closed her eyes to search for a clue. It was, overall, a story of redemption. A humble doctor extended loving kindness and respect to an absolutely destitute fellow human. He saw the goodness in him just as Luke saw the goodness in Darth Vader, who was also redeemed. The doctor was a well-integrated human being — a Jedi in the making.

More importantly, there could be no redemption without the clean slate, and no resurrection without the act of human kindness — Christ acting within us, coming directly from the heart. She would ask Natalie to find the two men for a future show — perhaps the poverty megatrends show. What *New Avalon* was trying to do for the homeless had to come from the heart of human kindness and not from notions like wealth redistribution or flat-out charity. It was important to recognize and honor each soul engaging the *Harmony Valley* experiment in self-sufficiency and human reclamation — it had to be redemptive.

Multiple applications of lemon juice toned down the puffy eyes and Georgia's makeup did its magic. The news was on tape, as was Will's segment, with plenty of wiggle room for Stu to tweak the show. Leah watched a bit of it and then excused herself to run an errand.

Leah backed her hybrid into the first hanger at the Weed airport at noon, to await Eric. Her stomach was churning — her dragon restless. She focused all of her intent on each breath, willing the free flow of *the force* within her. Eric's private jet, black with pin stripes no less, touched down not long after her arrival. His pilot brought it to a stop within the hanger and lowered the stairs for Leah to come onboard. The pilot went about his business tinkering with something outside the plane that supposedly needed adjusting before they could fly any further.

redemption

She was dressed in the navy print version of her wrap dress for the show, with sensible flats and her winter jacket. Eric was casually dressed in a black jersey crewneck and jeans. Though he had their mother's dark hair, she noted that he was balding just like Dad. Unlike Dad, he'd remained fit and trim. He took her coat, gave her a hug, shut the door to the front of the plane and asked her to sit in a lush beige leather swivel chair across from him. Between them there was a table with a tea set and brewed tea nearly ready to pour. That reminded her of Mother — and herself, of course.

"Thanks, for coming, Leah. How are you?"

"I'm curious, concerned, maybe shocked, but my health is good, if that's what you mean?" she smiled.

"Yes, well, I'm sorry about the secretive nature of this visit — best I can do. I think you'll understand before I let you go."

Dominator play. Take note but don't react to it, Dragon Lady warned. "Please, do explain about your donation as well, Eric. We're not at all sure what do about or with it … if you don't mind. I'll otherwise be unable to thank you for it. You know me."

"I do," he laughed. "I intend this to be a soul–baring experience for me, so you will hear about that. I don't blame you for cynicism and know you wouldn't trust any banker further than you could throw them."

"I do have a banker I can trust," she said, just to be ornery, "but go on, please."

She poured the tea as he began. She needed it. "I've just retired from my position at CityBank. While working there, I spent a great deal of time in Europe. I was required to collaborate with banks in London, Paris, Zurich and Frankfurt and others in the EU. I'm not telling you this to brag. It's part of the story. Of course, I was based on Wall Street when stateside. I actually lived for ten years of my training in Frankfurt and was in London when the banks went down here in '07 — '08. How I worked, was with my eyes wide open, sis. At near the highest levels of banking I saw crimes committed hundreds of times a day. I endeavored to be honest but I did play their game. I admit to that. I have a tidy fortune and a comfortable home in Zurich."

"Zurich? I thought you and Annie were in Scarsdale."

"Annie *is* in Scarsdale. We're divorced."

"Oh, sorry about that."

"We grew out of each other and I could leave her in good stead financially. We're still friends. What I'm really trying to say here is that there is, in the back of this plane, a safe full of documents that will, I hope, take the banksters down."

"Are you serious, Eric?" she said, aghast.

"Ever so serious. I had a good job surrounded by corruption. I like to think I earned my money honestly, but *in* all honestly, the money I was paid came, by one route or another, from the 99% — pure and simple. And, I was overpaid. I admit that. That's my motivation to fund your vision of local economies."

"Eric, It sounds like you're contemplating treason."

"Treason is political, this is whistle blowing. There are a good many people who should be in prison but the government covers for them. Too big to fail became too big to jail. Regulators are the kings of bribery, my dear."

"Well, I knew that. But I also assumed you were a true bankster and that you *all* needed to be in prison."

Eric laughed. "Believe me if I were to blow the whistle in New York I *would* be in prison and all the crooks would still be at large. Have you noticed it's the latest fashion to indict and prosecute the whistle blowers instead of the crooks their exposing?"

"I did, actually. So this is a dangerous game you're playing, Eric. I suppose that's why we're under cover having this discussion?"

"It is. I'm taking no chances at this point. Communicating with anyone over here could be incriminating for both parties."

"Why now?"

"I'll be in Zurich tomorrow. I'll be working as a Swiss citizen to clear their banks of corruption from the top down — for starters. It's an easier job than cleaning up Wall Street would be, but tricky, and it couldn't be initiated in the states. The Swiss government has hired me based on the information in that safe back there," he said, pointing, again, to the back of the plane. "I've been given citizenship and protection from deportation to the US to face criminal charges, if it should come to that. I intend blowing the whistle on all of them. I've taken care of Annie. I know you won't let me take care of you and doubt you need it actually, and so the donation yesterday is to your community's good works and, if you can accommodate me with it, forgiveness for the life I've led."

Dragon Lady wasn't satisfied. "Where did that $30 million come from, Eric?" she asked, bluntly.

"I invested my part of our inheritance when Mother died. I put half in gold and the other half in the stock of a company one of my friends started. Ever hear of Steve Jobs? It's honestly made money, Leah, not from Wall Street crime. I recognized his genius when we first met, and wanted to further back his launch of the smart-phone. The donation was mostly made from rocketing stock values after he revolutionized the world with the iphone but I was, personally, in from the get-go. I've been in San Francisco liquidating my assets. Now that he's gone, I don't think they'll be able to hold the stock value over the long haul."

"Are you not coming back?" she asked.

"Not with a bounty on my head, sis, and they could have frozen my assets. This is it. That's why I wanted to see you. I've just renounced citizenship here and I've learned to travel light," he said, pulling his phone out of his pocket. "We'll be in Canadian airspace in less than an hour and are scheduled to refuel in Nova Scotia."

"So what's the bit with Main Street USA? I'm curious as all get out."

"You shouldn't be surprised. I've heard you say that hundreds of times on your show."

"Our show? You watch *Light on the Crisis*?" She was shocked.

"And *Joel Robertson Live*. It's not a crime to do that here ... yet. I love both of your shows and both of you. I'll be watching from Germany expecting to see Main Street USA materialize."

"I was having just such a vision about a funky crossroads not far from home, but it's out here in the middle of no-where."

"Build it and they will come," he laughed. "I see you're remarried."

"It took long enough to find my match but better late than never. Chris is a wonderful man."

"I'm glad for you. I assume you invested the proceeds from the Carmel property to begin your community?"

"I invested it in gold at the advise of my trusted banker, and sold most of it this year. I had the house insurance to create the land trust. Our community is self-sufficient, the studio almost and we're pretty well set with donations for the Outreach programs. People have been very generous. You're a bit over the top in that regard."

"About time. That reminds me about the letter I sent for Nathan. You'll find it's about a gift from Dad, originally, but I was caretaker until Nathan was ready for it. Sorry it took so long for me to get out here to take care of it for him. He'll understand."

"He's visiting for a few more days with his family. I'll give it to him on Sunday as you instructed, Eric."

"If you can keep from telling anyone today, save maybe Chris, I'd be better off. Let me get to Zurich first."

"Fair enough."

"And look, I'm sorry if what I'm going to do causes you any harm. That's not my intention. You and Nathan should agree on how I sent it to him — in the mail, without personal contact. We've gone to great pains to make this a private meeting between the two of us. As far as the authorities are concerned, we've not crossed the line of our longstanding estrangement."

"Do you think it might come to that? What could they do to me? And who would that be?"

"I'll be exposing the regulators who do work for the government through the SEC. That will be an embarrassment, but might also end up going deeper into your exposure of government corruption. They could use the IRS to scrutinize your non-profits, the FCC since you're in broadcasting, and any number of agencies to intimidate. As soon as the tower of cards starts tumbling in Zurich, they'll be scrambling for cover over here, and they'll start digging up whatever they can on me."

"We've got impeccable credentials and are not mainstream television. We'll be audited regardless from a number of large donations. What you're doing is as important as what Joel and I do, Eric. Thanks for sticking your neck out. And you've not revealed anything to me that they could use. Right?"

"I've been careful, yes. I'm glad you're not upset. Since your show and Joel's inspired me, you two can take some of the credit — privately," he laughed.

"Listen if it came to that, I would ask Joel to interview me about it and we'd get the truth out before the media knew what hit them."

"Great. That's all I have to take care of to feel complete. Am I redeemed in your eyes? It's very important to me."

"You are, Eric. I'm the fool," she said, humbly, whilst staring into her teacup.

"How about you?" he asked, offering her a chance to clear the bad juju between them.

The can of worms popped open like a kid's jack in the box. "Would you mind helping me straighten out a few things from our childhood, Eric?" she asked, hesitantly.

"If I can. Shoot."

He sounded just like her dad. "I realize I was a bit of a precocious, even obnoxious child. I conclude that I was driven to anger, sabotage and even hatred because our father had no room in his life for me. I found it impossible to compete with you for his attention. No matter what I did, I wasn't able to share the limelight with you, Eric. So there's that to ask your opinion about. How did you see me as a kid sister? Honestly."

"Since this is likely our last chance to have a go, I'll honor you with honesty. You were all that and more, Leah. You were likely the fiercest competitor of my whole life and that's saying something. You were boot camp for work with the banksters. You seemed selfish to me then, and when you shut me out, along with Dad, it felt like we'd both failed you somehow. You did drama, really well."

"I just wanted Dad to love me. I realize now that he wasn't capable of it, but *then,* I felt I wasn't good enough. I was truly envious of you — of everything about you. I know it was irrational but it framed so much of my life afterwards. As I look back trying to heal those years, and there's plenty else to heal that you had no part in, I wondered if you wrote me off too. It seemed so."

"I think you demanded that of me. Listen, Leah, let me put you in my shoes back then. It might help. You saw me with all of the privileges. I was the 'chosen one' — the 'golden boy' —and you didn't count. Let me explain the life of a 'chosen one'. Dad decided everything for me. I had no choices in my life. He really was living vicariously through me and, for the most part, I had no interest in any of it. I would have preferred the freedom you had to run around playing, fantasizing, getting into mischief, being invisible, and being Mother's angel. I'm not a banker because I wanted to be. I'm a banker because he needed me to be in finance. "

"Are you kidding? What are you saying, Eric?" she said, shocked.

"Not kidding. Consider yourself lucky that you finally gave up and pulled up the wall. It's nice to see you again, now that it's down ... by the way," he smiled.

She had a sinking feeling about where the conversation was going, but poured another cup of tea and listened. She *had* asked for it.

"At my first investment firm job, I found out that dear old Dad was a crook."

Her tea spilled into the saucer. "*What?* What are you saying, Eric?" she whispered.

"If he were still alive today, I'd bring him down first. We thought he was a real estate agent, and he did sell real estate occasionally, but he also had a broker's license and wanted a son on the fast track for insider trading. If I have a talent for corruption and spotting it, darling, it's because of dear old Dad. I'd have been happy being a tennis pro, to tell you the truth."

Leah was stunned. "So Eric, in fact, you saved me from what could have been my worst nightmare? I doubt it was deliberate but I thank you, nonetheless. Our father was a crook. I can't believe it."

"That's because you didn't know him. You and Mother were tight."

"Oh well, I disappointed her in the long haul, I'm afraid. We had a lovely relationship in her elder years, though. Do you think she knew about Dad?"

"There was a lot she didn't know about Dad."

That brought to mind the playboy magazines and Leah's cheeks blushed. "Eric, I take full responsibility for being a competitive little shit of a sister but I do have one more question for this last chance to know the truth. Do you remember, our sexual encounters?"

He smiled. "Of course I do. You were a sexy little girl for your age, sis."

"That's appalling, Eric. I didn't ask you to stick your hands down my panties." Leah felt Dragon Lady ready to tear down the cage she was in to get at him.

"You didn't stop me. In fact, Leah, with everything we did do, I would describe you as engaged — complicit. Until you betrayed me."

"*I* betrayed *you?*" she sobbed, pulling tissues from her handbag.

"You might see that differently, sis, but think about it. At that age I had no sexual experience except what we both saw in Dad's playboys, and no idea that it wasn't something you did with your sister."

Leah was in tears. "Why did I know it was taboo?"

"I've no idea. Maybe Dad warned you about boys. Maybe Mom did. Maybe your friends did. I truthfully had no idea."

"I feel sick. I have carried shame and guilt for over 60 years about all of it and you claim innocence?"

"I *am* innocent — of guilt and shame. Leah, I loved you. I still do. I had, and have, a genuine affection for you — probably because I didn't have any taboos. Remember, I was the 'chosen one'," he mocked, puffing out his chest. "I could do no wrong, and got no moral education because of it. *Voila*, your friendly bankster."

It was a good thing she'd stuffed her purse with tissues. The tears would not stop.

"You'll figure it out, Leah. You're a frigging genius at figuring things out, always have been," he laughed. "I loved the way you presented the cotton pickers for private prisons, for example — step by methodical step, so people can figure it out themselves. Brilliant."

She nodded her head slightly, begrudgingly accepting his compliment.
"Are you finished asking questions?"

"Yes," she croaked, "I'm absolutely mortified."

"Don't be," he said, getting up. "Jeff is flashing me. We'll need to take off soon, sis. Shall I help you to your car? Do you need the washroom?"

She did use the washroom, which was luxurious but stuffy — or maybe she was the stuffy one. She looked terrible, but then she could barely see herself in the mirror through the tears. After splashing her face with cold water, she emerged to ask for her coat and take her leave.

"Don't forget Nathan's envelope, Leah. Greet him for me tomorrow. You'll be hearing from me through the Swiss economic cleansing and, hopefully, the fall of Wall Street. Who knows? They might be ready for *Threefolding* soon. Remember not to bail the banks out this time," he laughed.

"I didn't bail you out last time. The people didn't get to vote on that, remember?"

"Push for a transaction tax. It will help heal the karma," he said, with a charming smile while helping her with her coat.

She stood back and looked him over one last time. "You can count on me, Eric — and Joel. Good luck with all your big, risky endeavors. You're really going to come into your mission."

"What are you some kind of prophetess?" he asked, laughing.

"I'm a fool and a fraud, my brother. I've some serious work to do on myself."

"You want my advice?"

"No, but I know it won't stop you from giving it to me," she said, with the quiver of a smile.

"Be who you came to be — the amazing sister I love more than anyone in the world. That world needs what you have to give."

With that, he swooped her up in his strong arms and carried her down the stairs of the plane to her car. After a warm hug and kiss, she stood there staring at him as he bounded up the stairs and turned to wave goodbye.

"Eric," she called, "may *the force* be with you!"

"And with you, Yoda," he called back. Then he pulled up and locked the stairs as Jeff fired up the jets.

"Goodbye, Eric," she whispered. "I love you, too."

Leah sat in her car weeping until long after their takeoff. *He is not what he appears.* When she was able to drive, she stopped at the nearby rest area and vomited into the toilet until her ribs ached. She flushed the remains of Dragon Lady down into the earth, never to be seen again. She'd been exposed, diminished and redeemed by the one she'd most hated and feared — all in the space of an hour. He'd be damn good as a whistle blower.

She drove right by *New Avalon,* journeying on 5.2 miles to stop in Sheldon. After parking the car, Leah sat on the landmark stump in front of the convenience store, while *Main Street USA* came alive all around her. She saw its purpose, felt its vitality, smelled the roasting coffee, and heard the muffled sounds of the people who'd come. Build it and they will come, because *the force* is strong here. She reckoned the middle of the crossroads was sitting above a fortune in un-mined gold. She'd never tell. And neither would her magus of a husband, who would help design the future Aussie roundabout. On Monday, she'd call Max and Julia Cummings to see if they'd like to get together over a glass of Zinfandel, to talk about *Main Street USA*.

Later that afternoon, Chris found her curled up in her chair reading, Harry at her feet, along with a box of tissues and a small basket for the biomass bin. He circled around the living room a few times looking her over. "What are you reading, Yoda?" he asked with a big smile.

"Victor Hugo, my lad. *Les Miserables* — a magnificent tale of redemption."

"Aye, it is, and a wonderful musical as well." He sang a few bars of 'Who am I'" while coming in for a landing on her neck. "That reminds me to ask about your fourth sacrifice, which doubtless carries forth this theme of redemption. Shall we try for Monday night?"

"It's a date. Are you ready to explore the nuances of caramel sauce with me, cowboy?" she whispered in his ear, which he'd presented to her for a nibble.

"Aye. Let me get cleaned up first. Mandy and David will be beating the door down soon. Let's wait for them on the cake, eh?"

"Splendid," she said, as he pulled away. "I love you."

"I know," he replied — imitating, with good facial expression, Han Solo's ongoing dialogue with Princess Leah throughout the last three Episodes.

She laughed. "Were you ever cast as Jean Valjean, cowboy?"

"Not," he replied, heading towards the shower.

"Yet," she added, sticking her nose back into the book.

David helped Pops stoke the boiler while Mandy and Oma dotted the top of the leg of lamb with garlic slices then slathered it with Shelley's version of Dijon Mustard. It was placed in a very hot oven for 20 minutes to seal in the juices after which the oven was turned down to finish cooking. Then Oma guided the three 'kids' in the fine art of thick caramel sauce preparation. There were a lot of fingers testing the batch. Whipped cream followed with careful instructions not to over-whip it into butter, which wouldn't serve in this desert. Then the 'kids' gathered around the end of the table to put it all together, while Oma searched for her slivered almonds again — *funny how quickly things get buried in the baking cupboard.*

When the cake went into fridge storage (actually out on the timber table in the back garden with an Aussie fly umbrella over it) the real kids were then into the game cupboard, having nailed Pops down for couple rounds of *Sorry.* they heard Mandy warning David not to ask Pops to play Park & Shop. The two of them were cracking up in the kitchen washing up the potatoes.

"I sure will miss these two," Pops admitted, giving her a kiss on the top of her head.

"Maybe they'll be able to move here, cowboy. That would be the best of all worlds for all of us, I reckon."

"It would but you're right about Nathan, he has do it without the help. I was hoping he'd drop that old story but it didn't sound hopeful out there with him today."

"Maybe we can sit down with them and have a chat tomorrow. It's a New Year, you know," she said, on a positive note.

"Well, you never do know, lass."

That was all they got in before the game board was slammed down on the table and the pawns, four each, were distributed.

"Oh no, more bloody cards to draw," Pops moaned, dramatically.

"There's no dice in this game, Pops," David said, kindly.

"And the game is played in *American*," Mandy informed him, bombastically, but with a big smile.

Pops looked at Oma such that she had to leave the kitchen. The potatoes were ready and the peas would be simple. If she didn't lose herself in Victor Hugo again, her ribs would never heal. Harry decided to join her, curling up on the carpet in front of the fire for yet another nap.

Dinner was joyful and delicious. They toasted Chuck and Natalie who'd be at the pre-ball dinner right then, and a benevolent and prosperous New Year, upcoming. Saying goodbye to 2011 was remarkable. Firstly, they acknowledged the good health and prosperity of *New Avalon* with a toast. That was followed a toast for the transformation of *Light on the Crisis*. Next, they toasted the initiation of the many Outreach programs, and then the collaboration with Joel. Nathan and Julie added toasts to a good year in Colorado, all things considered, along with the good health and lively spirits of their family. Finally, they arrived at the gift of Chris' arrival at *New Avalon*, which they not only toasted with *"Yeah Pops!"* but with an added three *"hip-hip hoorays!"* for good measure.

They cleaned up together after dinner and played a few rounds of Yahtzee before dessert, which, needless to say, was relished bite by bite. There would be leftover caramel cake for snacking and for Chuck and Natalie's return.

Starting at four in the afternoon on New Year's Day, the community began a moveable feast around the commons. Each year, the house numbers moved up one notch in a list that began with drinks and hors d'oeuvres and ended with desserts. They traveled as a mob from house to house, first offering a blessing at the doorstep for the New Year on home and family, and then entering to share the next part of the feast. The guesthouses, if occupied, were included in the feast and, if unoccupied, were simply blessed.

Leah was explaining this to Chris after the kids had left for their guesthouse, where they would toast the New Year over sleeping children. Oma and Pops snuggle up on the sofa together with Harry, chatting about the richness of family life and their cooking duties for the moveable feast. This was the third year of the celebratory event, which had started at Tommy and Shelley's house when Georgia and Nick lived there. That meant Natalie and Chuck were assigned drinks and hors d'oeuvres, and their assignment was appetizers.

"What does that mean?" Chris queried, unsure of the difference between the two.

"In *New Avalon*, hors d'oeuvres are eaten with the fingers. Appetizers are most often served on a plate with cutlery."

"What have you got in mind, then?" he asked.

"We're going to make Tilapia *ceviche*. Ellia and Greg have appetizers too, so one dish should be plenty here and no drinks are needed. I'll make it early in the day to add flavor to the fish, then go help Julie with her main course. We end at Will and Sonia's with tea, coffee and dessert. I'm banking on her making a *Tres Leches* cake, but we'll see about that. Shelley and Tommy will offer a dessert as well. You'll be well fed tomorrow, cowboy!"

"I may have to drag the push-bike out again after the holidays, lass. I'm grateful not to have to face sticky pudding, though it does come with caramel sauce," he teased, tickling her ribs.

"Oh, watch the ribs, cowboy. They're quite tender," she begged.

"Do those ribs have a story to tell me?" he asked. "Your honeycomb etheric and astral bodies are looking like they received an upgrade today."

"You noticed," she laughed. "Well the rib cage is a metaphor for Dragon Lady's cage, which was vomited, along with her remains, into the ever-receptive Mother this afternoon."

"Do tell?" he grinned, pulling her in even closer.

She gave him the full accounting of the meeting with Eric, apologizing for the need to keep it a secret between the reception of the donation and letter and the right then and there. He assured her no apology was needed and applauded the way in which spirit presented her with the opportunity for mastery. What a coincidence it was to have paralleled that experience with the movies. To boggle his mind further, she told him the story of the homeless man and the doctor, getting teary-eyed all over again, in the process. He agreed with the redemptive potential of kindness or compassion when truly heart-felt.

They had one more duty to attend to over at the community garden that night. The initial stage of the Three Kings BD prep would be completed between eleven-thirty and twelve-thirty — the hour of power bringing in the New Year. They went off with Harry trailing behind, to meet Greg, Ellia, Will, and Sonia at her office. Together they ground the gold, frankincense and myrrh to a fine powder in Sonia's porcelain mortar and pestle. She emulsified it into vegetable glycerin for storage until the Epiphany — *alchemy and blessings for the New Year.*

David and Mandy were out the door early on New Year's Day to play with friends. Nick was leading a nature and tracking hike for the boys and Leslie was hosting the girls. That brought Nathan and Julie to the door of #4 West Commons to have a chat with Oma and Pops about their future. The fresh tilapia had already 'cooked' in lime juice and was now up-taking the savory fish and veggie broth, slivered red onion and jalapeños to make it true *ceviche*. She'd also made a double batch of potato *pierogi* for the children, which she'd sneak out and boil up fresh, while folks were visiting at Natalie' house.

Leah made a big pot of tea and arranged it on the tea table, within easy reach, as they made themselves comfortable in the living room. She curled up in her favorite chair facing Julie, who'd snuggled into the other chair. Nathan and Chris held down opposite ends of the sofa. After tea was poured and distributed, Leah asked them what they thought about life in *New Avalon*, now that the community was in its third year.

"There isn't any part of it that doesn't impress us, Mom," Nathan began. "We've always considered it an isolated community, and it is, but at the same time it isn't. You have all you need and everyone is joyful. When we think about our daily lives, it's with the admission of a lot of struggle just to get through the day with two kids, work and small city life."

"I don't think anyone misses that here, Nat," she replied. "The children are happy and secure because their parents are never far away and neighbors are extended family. You've done a great job being there for David and Mandy, both of you."

""We'd be an easy fit here," Julie admitted. "On the other hand there's so much to resolve back home before we can even think along those lines."

"Right Mom. I think we need to sell the house, like Dad suggests, and take our chances that we can find another good place to live if *New Avalon II* is filled up. It could take a long time to unload the house."

Leah looked pensive, as though she were turning something over in her mind. Then she looked up eyes wide, "My God, I almost forgot!" she exclaimed. "Give me a minute, darlings," she said, setting down her tea to go search the shallow top drawer of the secretaire. She found Nathan's large red, white and blue Express mail envelope from Eric, and returned to their circle to present it to him. "This came in yesterday's mail for you, Nathan." Leah announced, handing him the envelope.

Nathan pulled the tab opening the envelope and drew out a stack of papers. On the top was a letter, which he read silently, and then aloud.

Dear Nathan,

When you were a boy, and your granddad Hegelman was close to dying, he gave me $10, 000 to invest on your behalf, to be given to you as an adult, when I deemed it most advantageous to your future. I regret our estrangement these years and am now leaving the country, permanently. I expect this is the most advantageous time to fulfill my obligation. I invested the money in stocks in your name, with myself as your adult guardian, and opened an account at Wells Fargo bank in the name of the guardianship to accrue the dividends and pay all taxes. This is your legal inheritance as documented in these papers.

As I leave the country, I have closed the dividend account with full proceeds made into the attached cashier check in your name for the amount

redemption

of $354,673.00. I have also had the stock certificates reissued to your adult person 3135 shares, bought at $3.19/share now valued at $403.00/share. With Mr. Jobs' recent death, I would watch the stock over the next few months and sell if it hits $650.00. You can trust Daniel Schroeder Jr. in Denver or Jeremy Edwards in Palo Alto to look after your shares, broker the sale for you and re-invest when, and if, you choose. My advice, in that regard, is that you invest in people and their sustainable future.

We've done well, my nephew, save for the fact that we didn't share in each other's lives to any great extent. I hope this finds you ready for the responsibility of wealth management and not in too great a need.

With love and respect,
Your uncle, Eric Hegelman

On a separate sheet of paper he'd written a request that, should anyone ask, he could kindly state that the letter came to him anonymously, by mail, which, of course, it did.

Nathan looked to his mother, his face one big question. "Well darling, in the end, at least of this chapter, your uncle turned out to be a man of integrity, Nathan. Eric's life would be in danger if he stayed in the states," she explained. "He is going to be reorganizing the banking in Switzerland, while blowing the whistle on the banksters here, in the EU and in the UK. The Swiss government is giving him protection. He's renounced his US citizenship to do this, a sacrifice he hopes will benefit the 99%. We best keep this in the family, I might add. What else has he put in there?"

Nathan began sorting through the documents. "They're right here, Mom, mostly 100 share certificates and the check. This list indicates they're worth well over a million dollars." Nathan sucked in breath with those last words and began to weep. He reached out for Julie – also teary-eyed – to come cuddle with him. Leah tossed the tissue box to her surprised, but grinning, cowboy, who slid it down next to Julie. When he got control of himself Nathan looked from Chris to Leah. "I feel like I've been freed from prison by someone I hardly know."

Leah could relate to that for sure, and told him so. "Uncle Eric also liquidated the investments he'd made in Apple with his part of our inheritance. He donated them to Outreach for a new project called *Main Street USA*. He wants us to take it local and make it work – $30 million as it turns out. I trust he didn't drive your stock value down doing that."

"Did I just tell you we couldn't agree to be here until the house was sold?"

"Indeed, you did," she smiled. "Why don't the two of you take your booty home and talk it over. We'll come over to help with your part of the food around three o'clock. We're all set here, except for running up to the community center for sauce dishes and small forks. You'll need plates and cutlery, which we'll carry through the rest of the main dishes before washing them up."

359

"Nathan and I can take care of that while you and Julie do the cooking," Chris suggested.

"Sounds like a plan," she replied, agreeably.

"2012 is looking better by the minute!" Chris declared, slapping his knees as he rose to congratulate Nathan on his inheritance.

Chris and Leah stood in the doorway watching them walk down West Commons Lane kissing and hugging each other all the way home to the guesthouse. She had a good cry in her cowboy's arms as they curled up on the sofa again to talk about this latest gift from Eric. Nathan couldn't refuse an inheritance from his grandfather. Leah wasn't going to give any energy to wondering whether her dad had really done that or whether Eric had found an acceptable way to gift his nephew, the only grandchild in the family. Further she refused to judge her father's sources of wealth, but rather thanked him for his good intentions. None of it mattered. Energy had been moved, and with incredible timing.

After lunch, she and Chris cleared the dishes, washed up, and then sat back down at the table with a cuppa to compose the blessing for Ellia, Greg and their home. When they arrived at the guesthouse to help out with the main course, which was pork tenderloin with applesauce and dinosaur kale sautéed with onions and mushrooms, they were greeted with hugs and The Plan, which was that Nathan and Julie could pay off the mortgage and equity loan with the dividend check and rent their home easily, while it was on the market at a fair price. The check alone would make them debt-free and able to pay school fees with Julie's remaining pay. Her soon-to-be spare time could be used to get the house fixed up for a quality tenant — hopefully, a family from the school. As he had been for all those years, Eric would take care of income taxes on the dividends up to the date of transfer, but dividends earned from here on out would be Nathan's responsibility. Leah would let them know the outcome of the upcoming community meeting but she assured them of a place since there were still unassigned houses down valley. They would need to come out for the trainings with Natalie, who would advise them of the first date. If their house hadn't sold by the time they needed to move, he'd call one of the brokers to sell enough stock to cover their home price. Otherwise he'd watch it like a hawk to see if it hit $650.

Oma had been thinking about the options and wondered if they'd be happy living in the guesthouse where they were right now. It was a three bedroom, right next door to Spence and Christina's family, and a run across the commons from Oma and Pops. They might even be able to move in during the summer, if it were all approved. Otherwise, they would be down valley in a new community and a brand new three-bedroom house later in the summer. There were good points to each option.

They loved the house, the established community in which the kids already felt comfortable but if someone else was in line for it they'd step aside, no problem. Leah was meant to be figuring out the list and who would be where, when all was said and done. The community would let one guesthouse go to a family member, reserving the remaining house for family guests and do the same down valley. With The Lodge and its Annex rooms for guests of the community and the show, leaving more vacant room in the community was an extravagance. Whatever worked out would be perfect. Nathan and Julie wanted to start a dialogue about what they could do to contribute to *New Avalon*. Nathan wanted to be kept up to date on *Main Street USA* as a potential project to engage. He was qualified to teach English and creative writing, would continue to write his novels, and they were both keen to look into the publishing end of the studio work. Setting up Print on Demand as a hard- and soft-cover option to digital books was worth exploring. Many bookstores were installing the print–works to do that for customers on the spot. They were also wondering if the community needed a library. They'd be happy to take that on.

Leah brought up the issue of change for the children. They had friends at Shining Mountain they wouldn't want to leave, but they also had friends in *New Avalon* — a whole tribe within a stone's throw. Nathan and Julie thought it best to deal with that in Colorado, perhaps when the 'for sale' sign went up in front of the house and 'for rent or sale' signs went up at the school and in the bulletin. A good idea, it was agreed.

That was until the kids came home from play and Julie asked them to pack their bags to leave the next morning after breakfast. Nathan hung his head and dutifully said, "Yes, Mom."

Mandy, on the other hand stood frozen in the archway between the dining and living rooms — doll tucked under her arm — sporting an impressively pouted lower lip, and eyes welling up with tears. Pops was standing back in guarded amusement. Then she ran to Leah, tears flying like a lawn sprinkler out of her eyes, screaming, "I want to stay with Oma. I want to stay *here*." She grabbed Leah around the waist and wouldn't let go. *My God, she's a fierce and tenacious for a little girl!* Leah was shocked and tried to calm her down by stroking her head and back. She buried her head further into Leah's sweater until Chris came over to run energy into her neck.

"Must run in the family," he whispered to Oma with wink.

"R-r-right," she drawled, grateful to get her breath again.

Pops pulled a chair over and took Mandy onto his knee asking her why she had to stay with Oma and Pops. She was still sobbing but managed to blurt out, "I want to go to Demetri's magic school with everyone else."

Leah and Chris exchanged startled looks. "Really," Oma asked, "Demetri is going to be a magic teacher?"

"He *is* one, Oma, with Jürgen and Zenzi, and Sissi will be coming soon. It's *so* much fun."

"What about school, Mandy. You love school at Shining Mountain, and your teacher and friends would probably miss you, don't you think?"

"They'll get over it," she blurted out. All of the adults fought to maintain sobriety. Chris was certain she had real stage potential, although discipline might be an issue.

Nathan pulled up a chair across from them. "Well, we're not going to leave you behind, Mandy, so maybe we can strike a bargain, like Pops did with the caramel cake."

"Can we go home and get our toys and come back?" she asked. David let a little snicker sneak out, which instantly rebooted the lawn sprinkler.

Eventually, they were all gathered together in the living room where their parents explained the deal — so much for waiting until the 'for sale' sign went up. In the end Mandy agreed to go home and finish up school with the promise of a permanent return to New Avalon. She advised her parents that she would use the best of manners at school so as not to hurt the feelings of her teacher and friends — but that was it, she was out of there — no matter that it was one of the best Waldorf Schools in the country. When asked for his take on the move, David beamed a big smile at Pops, and gave it a definitive thumb's up.

Pops wondered if he should have a talk with Demetri. On their way back home with Harry, to ready the house for its blessing and community invasion, Oma reminded him that Demetri's training had started when he was a boy. Who better to foster magical Woodland Folk kids, and get the rest of the community children on board in the process? It could be just the ticket for Demetri to reclaim the upper astral for his retrograde subpersonality.

When they arrived at their gate, Harry padded across the front lawn to his house, sensing that Natalie and Chuck had arrived home. They were busy preparing to initiate the house blessings and moveable feast. Leah pitched in helping Nataliewith food preparations, while Chris and Chuck pilfered wine glasses from the community center. Glasses would be carried from house to house and bottles of beer, cider and kombucha were stashed in every fridge. Natalie had asked Jenny to order a case of magnum bottles of Zinfandel plus a couple bottles of Chardonnay from Max and Julia Cummings for the occasion. She quickly blended a fruit punch for the children from chilled apple juice and frozen strawberries and raspberries. There were cheese sticks from the bakery, and honeyed sweet and sour chicken wings in the oven. Her last act was to set out crackers and cheese, cheese-laden crostinis — a new hit in the community — and a plate of sushi that Julie had sent over with Leah.

The two women had time to catch up on the festivities in San Francisco, which were so far out of Natalie's norm it was laughable. And, she and Chuck had laughed a lot. He admitted being more comfortable riding a horse than socializing in a tux, while she tried hard to remember if she'd ever been to a ball before. They had a great time. Furthermore, she had pictures to prove it on her now-charging phone, which she would show Leah at the studio in the morning.

The men returned with the glasses, not five minutes before the community gathered outside their gate to sing in the New Year with a strong round of Wassail. The neighbors living in the house to the left (as one looked out the front door) gave the blessing on the house. Thus, Sonia and Will stepped forward for the blessing, while Natalie and Chuck stood in their open doorway. Sonia splashed Agua Florida water on the front step (scents of Peru and remembrances of Don Eduardo) while Will read a blessing they'd composed together for their neighbors. One of the children came forward offering Natalie a small wreath to hang on the door. The children had made them as a school craft project, from dried flowers, incense cedar bows, and golden dried wheat stems, heavy with seed. That complete, the community came over the doorstep to toast their neighbors for the New Year and sample their cooking of the land's bounty.

On it went around the commons for four hours, ending at Sonia and Will's house with tea, coffee, hot chocolate and *tres leches* cake. She'd also made *sopapillas* with honey, as a sweet and chewy option. There had been many toasts throughout the ritual for all the varied projects of Outreach, their generous donors, Demetri's house with the Woodland kids, (who'd made it back just in time for the festivities) and all that the future brought them in the way of service. A fond farewell with cheers went out to Mr. Brenner, whose gift, in passage, would seed *New Avalon II*.

Julie and Nathan stopped in to help Chris and Leah clean up and reorganize while the kids were saying their goodbyes to the other children. When they were tidied up, all of them went back to the guesthouse to do the same and get the children to bed for an early departure. Leah and Chris promised to be there when their car pulled out the next morning and they'd be waiting for them to return at the end of May, likely with a big moving truck. Of course, they might actually be back for the coursework before May. Nathan and Julie thanked them again for a life-changing visit in so many ways.

Leah was both happy and melancholic. With Eric, the good side of reconciliation was immense liberation, while the downside was mourning all of the lost years that could have been different. Chris reminded her that she and Eric had chosen that path for life lessons, and it wasn't like he was dead. He was actually collaborating with her and Joel — energetically. The kids would be back in the wink of an eye and they'd be strategizing ways to guide the little Padawan learner without any loss of her wildly extroverted personality. She'd more in common with her Oma than anyone else in her world. For his part, Chris found himself entertaining the notion of staging children's productions once the second community was established.

They journeyed to the stars in cosmic love that night. The plan was for Leah to practice finding her own way back through her tunnel. The way was clear and luminous. She slipped through her honeycomb tunnel to find her collected subpersonalities gathered together at the bridge. Little Alice, now a young adult, was sitting on the bridge with her arm around Yoda. She looked pleased as punch.

Still stuffed from the moveable feast, they pass on the Anzac bikkies when they returned to earth, but did share a small pot of Chamomile tea and the joyful news of subpersonality reunion. The work of personality integration could now begin. Chris vowed to assist with that and gently reminded her to be most careful during the coming months, as Yoda would surely be put to the test. She'd Demetri's experience to affirm that truth. *A paradox life is.*

They kissed, hugged and waved the kids off at eight the next morning. Mandy, clutching her doll and trying to smile, was madly waving goodbye through the car window with tears streaming down her face. *Bye, for now, little Bee Mistress.* They walked back home by way of the stable to clear the 'air', and arrived at their door in time to send Chuck off to Washington. When she finally got to the studio, Leah called Julia Cummings to arrange a dinner date. Julia laughed, and told her that she and Max had been talking about just that, last evening. They were eager to give them a tour of the winery as well. They made a date for Saturday night at six. Julia's mother was visiting and able to help with the little ones. If Leah were to bring along a salad, it would be perfect.

With that settled, she turned to the outline for the show. They were looking for everyday ways in which viewers could help provide solutions to pressing problems — aside from the obvious power of their vote. The aim of the show was to turn around the mindset of helplessness that fueled American complacency by empowering individuals with affirmative actions. The millennials were coming up with lists of ideas, and there were great stories out there about people who'd vowed to live without buying imports, especially from Asia, those who were living locally, boycotting unethical businesses, biking to work instead of driving, cutting there carbon footprint to zero, and actively engaging in peaceful protest. They could highlight community gardens, neighborhood tool sharing, backyard gardening, food–sharing groups, swap get-togethers for clothing and household and garage items. Then there were big ways to back legislative movements to amend the constitution to exclude corporate personhood and money in politics. There were boycotts to be supported, which brought to the fore the real power conscious people had to make a difference with every dollar of their spending.

There was also the *Occupy*-inspired movement to move banking to local credit unions and recent talk about an apartheid movement to rid the portfolios of public institutions of investments with companies that contributed to or ignored climate change. Since the topics were short and varied, their key guests would appear via Skype and several through audio transmission. Leah's task was to know each guest through the staff's research and use her interviewing expertise to draw their stories and inner thoughts from them. There would be plenty of references to websites and organizations involved in pro-active projects — all to be posted on the website with links for their viewers.

Joel was back on the job looking tanned and feeling well rested. Their Skype session had nothing to do with work and everything to do with family holidays. They would deal with politics on Friday. Kim would soon be in touch with Natalie to finalize plans for her visit to DC in February. Leah then met with Paula for a news update. Paula expressed her gratitude for the whole experience of community over Christmas and was genuinely taken with the idea of having Mandy and family joining *New Avalon*, with consensus approval, of course. She and Sam were on that list as well. They'd returned from a week in Montana with her family on New Years Day, with reports that winter was actually happening in Montana.

After two weeks of toned down workloads and vacations, they decided to call a staff meeting that afternoon to kick off the year well-organized, and ready to meet their goals. For the show, the biggest shift would be a daily show in just a few months. Joel was going to suggest it to *freedomofspeech.org* soon. It would put them on the regular evening news menu rather than being a hit-and-miss Saturday mid-day choice. They were ready for the increased costs of broadcasting five times a week rather than one, and spent some quality time during the meeting imagining a variety of formats with one high-level panel discussion on Wednesdays and another panel format of the week's news in review on Friday. The other days could focus on specific topics with interviews, economic reports, environmental updates, Willow's *Occupy 2012* stories, exemplary success stories of change and so forth, with a short news round up at the beginning. Leah was pleased with the staff input, which was creative and often brilliant.

One thing she thought worth exploring, politically, was the long-term, hidden agendas of the power brokers to destabilize democracy. They'd already explored the elite's tireless and well-funded efforts to privatize prisons, the post office and other domains of the commons. Leah was picking up the same game plan on a big scale with countries like Greece. Although sabotaged by their citizens, Iceland may have been the first attempt by the power elite to privatize — corporatize — an entire country. Greece was in process, with all of the hallmarks present. It would be relatively easy to document the long sad story of their ongoing collapse; the technocratic leadership change, the role of the credit rating agencies who'd given Greece a grossly undeserved AAA rating to encourage borrowing, and the actions of the ECB and IMF and other big banks to debt-cripple the country. Then there was door-opening complicity and corruption at high levels of government, and the insidious advent of the corporate investors to take over Greece through privatization.

Leah thought it would make a great story over, say, a series of Monday daily shows. Further, it was a story they could revisit periodically to hammer the truth into the sleeping American psyche — that Greece was a deliberate model of corporate takeover, which was already being implemented in America and Europe. They would also need to follow Italy, Spain and Portugal as the model continued to unfold there, and re-look at Iceland and Ireland to see how all those stories lined up. She was absolutely certain that Joel and his staff would collaborate on this project to get the truth out and Will was agreeable to advise and contribute to a much needed exposé. When that sunk into the minds and hearts of their viewers, they'd need to be ready with solutions for reclaiming democracy at various stages of the unfolding agenda. That was where *Social Threefolding* needed to be understood and implemented.

The millennials were excitedly writing it all down, suggesting they put together a documentary about it as well. They thought it would be good to draw parallels with the USA as the story unfolded, like the number of millionaires and billionaires in congress — an exclusive club in the senate and alarming trend in the house. Stu was all for it — *after* they had a case. If Joel had a couple of sharpshooters to put on the project they could do it without another hire. If not, they'd need to have a second news analyst. Natalie would interview potential assistants that week but with her schedule, her staffer would be fulltime helping her out. They'd see what Joel could do first. If they could come up with staged, hypothetical solutions for Greece, they could be applied anywhere *We the People* rose up to reclaim power.

Stu gave an update of the documentary progress, reporting that the first, about *New Avalon,* was on schedule. It was a good pilot to hone their skills, but also to identify missing equipment, missing interviews to clarify a point, and the efficacy of the whole production set up, which they hadn't touched yet. He'd be filming the seed-planting in the greenhouse starting that week, garden planting, and the arrival of the WWOOFers to wrap it up. His new hire, Pavak Kapoor (Pavi for short), was arriving on Wednesday to settle into The Annex and start work on Thursday. Although unemployed, he was experienced in production as well as film editing — another millennial committed to a different future than the one unfolding out there in the culture. Stu would go down to the bay area periodically to film the Inner City project and send a camera with Rob when he went to visit his dad. He was ready for the entry of homeless participants in *Harmony Valley* and hoped he'd be able to interview some of them once they were settled in.

They went through the show themes for the next month and a half, which were climate change, then Megatrends followed, weekly, by the quartet of individual Megatrends (economy, violence, depletion of resources and poverty) inspected more closely, to provide a heads up for journalistic ideas. Jennifer gave a summary of the Canary Project, which was picking up steam and ready for oversight, and then Paula gave a report on her '*Oh Really?!*' project, which would premier that coming Saturday. She was set to audition with a teleprompter right after the live interview between Leah and Joel on Thursday afternoon. Leah wanted to incorporate the report into the news segment of the show. When they went daily, that might be expanded to a weekly summary on Fridays.

Since Eric's donation had not come through the website, there was no need to discuss his phenomenal generosity at that time. It *would* be necessary at the board meeting on Thursday and community meeting the following Tuesday. That gave Leah time to consider *Main Street USA* as an Outreach proposal in its conceptual stage. To that end, she'd set aside a chunk of time on Tuesday afternoon to work something up for the Outreach board at the kitchen table, hopefully, with the Golden Queen's portal of vision. Wednesday would see her over the ridge with Chris to check on Trynel.

By the time she and Chris settled into their discussion positions that evening, it felt, to Leah, like the end of a long journey. So many parallel events had woven their way through the story of the four sacrifices, especially since she'd finished the summaries and put them in the secretaire before Christmas. She had them lovingly spread out on the tea table to the side of her chair. Chris had a nice fire going and was pouring them each a glass of Zinfandel for the discussion. When settled into his sofa nest, he waved her on to the finish line.

redemption

"This sacrifice took place in 33 AD, as we're well aware, during the age of Greece and Rome at the midpoint of our post-Atlantean epoch. There are a number of stories within this story that contribute to the sacrifice on Golgotha, but first there's the human condition at the time, which necessitated the sacrifice. What was being threatened was the human "I", the gift of the clear light of day consciousness that the angels went through during the 'Old Moon' stage of consciousness, the Archangels during 'Old Sun' stage consciousness, and the Archai during 'Saturn' stage consciousness. That's as far back as we can take this creation story using clairvoyance, according to Steiner. Apparently, the gift of the "I" came to each hierarchy during the mid-fourth to mid-fifth epochs of each stage of consciousness.

"That means the mid-Atlantean to the mid-post-Atlantean epoch of the earth stage of consciousness for humanity — our present epoch being the post-Atlantean, the mid-point of which was punctuated by the fourth sacrifice. I assume the "I" was received on a gradient as the human bell curve progressed through the window of reception. We've moved beyond the mid-fourth to mid-fifth window of time, if I've calculated it correctly. It's possible there are some within our hierarchy who did not receive the "I" and still others who might have followed Lucifer's rebellious example to fall between the cracks, but that's pure conjecture.

"At the same time, the "I" was being fully integrated and mastered by the leading edge. There were likely those at the leading edge, Zarathustra, for example, who were making good use of their "I" early on and at the time of Christ Jesus' earthly sojourn. Some have since ascended. A few, like Buddha, ascended well ahead of the sacrifice. Most were probably wobbling around with it, and some were still in the process of receiving it. Do you agree?"

"I do, lass. Like all of the gifts of the hierarchies, it's progressive, not like a parcel falling out of the heavens all at once. And, each of them will have worked with us in turn to prepare us to work with it ourselves."

"Which would be during this post-Atlantean epoch. And, it was during that very window on 'Old Moon' that the Luciferic angels fell, turning away from their true "I", and likely making this a far more difficult passage for humanity as our turn came. I should also remind us that Earth Consciousness had already been through the Polarean, Hyperborean, Lemurian, and Atlantean epochs — meaning energetic repeats of Saturn, Sun and Moon had already upgraded our rainbow bodies to begin receiving the "I" during Atlantean times. Given the bell curve and the wobbles, I conjecture, again, that what happened to call forth the fourth sacrifice was a serious attempt, by the Ahrimanic legions, to inhabit the human "I".

"In fact, Steiner referenced the fact that there were those wandering around in his time, likely more so now, who had no "I" but rather an Ahrimanic presence. Eliot referred to these Ahrimanic possessions as subhuman beings, maybe souls caught between our world and the astral animal world. The Luciferic legions were contentedly interfering with our thinking since seizing our intellectual-mental bodies. I also need to state that Lucifer had come into the body of the Yellow Emperor around 3000 BC for 3+ years — the same

367

amount of time that the Christ would later embody in Jesus. We're to expect Ahriman to do the same in our era. Although, reflecting on that quote from Steiner about people with no "I", he is already expressing himself in the culture.

"The way the attack on the "I" is described is quite interesting. At that time, noted in ancient Greek and Hebrew documents, there were many prophets. People relied on Oracles for advice right up to the highest of leaders. Just as the "I" was ready to steer Greece forward, a distortion in thought came through their Oracles that was called "Sibylline". There are mythic tales of the Sibyls that speak of confused thinking, misdirection and crazy-making distortion of the "I". Sometimes they brought forth wisdom but at other times insanity, deceit, and confusion.

"What happened to them was an example of what might have happened to everyone. The pure channels used by the hierarchies to guide humanity had been polluted by 'you know who'. I guess I should point out that this fourth sacrifice was to salvage the fourth functional part of man. Previously, Christ Jesus had sacrificed in the spiritual world to save the physical, the etheric and astral bodies. This last part of man was gifted during Earth Consciousness, making it necessary for Christ Jesus to come *to* earth to redeem the "I". It couldn't be done from the spirit world. This part of the story suggests that our "I" has the capacity for wisdom and would have come in to take the place of the guidance coming in from the hierarchies. Eh?"

"Correct. And, someday it will, but not if Ahriman is roaming around there."

"Back to that later, when we talk about the rainbow body. First, the hierarchies faced a much more complex sacrifice to make this correction. The Son of God, the Christ, could not be born a human. However, he could come in to inhabit the "I" of a human prepared to take on such an enormous Divine Presence. That would be our staunchest ally in spirit world, Jesus, who was a composite rainbow body with the archangelic (or higher) consciousness of the being who'd sacrificed three times in the spirit world on our behalf. Even so, it was an impossible task for one human being to pull off — and, of course, he'd never been human. To have the proper physical, etheric and astral body required that a parallel human life carry a powerful "I" until the lower bodies of Jesus were properly mature. Thus, we have the story of the two Jesus boys and their parents. At Christmas, in the apiary, we heard the first story, from the Gospel of Luke, of the birth of this boy, who was the being who'd sacrificed for us previously. He came into the Nathan lineage of the house of David, but taken all the way back to Adam. His impending arrival was announced to his mother, Mary by Archangel Gabriel. She'd also come into this human life for the first time to conceive him.

"Like his mother, Jesus, came in with a perfected human physical and etheric body. These were the bodies sequestered by the Elohim in a hidden mountain sanctuary for just such a situation. It was, perhaps, foreseen. His was the physical body of Adam *pre-Fall*, with a perfected phantom, which, I have to assume wasn't carbon-based but volatile salt-based, in composition.

redemption

That does bring up thousands of questions for the years ahead, mind you," she said, as an aside. "His mother's body was modeled on the perfected phantom from Eve. This was the meaning of 'virgin birth'. He was born in a stable in Bethlehem where his parents had gone to be counted in the census. They were poor and those who came to pay him homage were shepherds to whom Gabriel had appeared. He had a two-part soul, or astral body, of Adam and Buddha — one part as pure as the first *pre-Fall* human and the other purified through exemplary human existence. After the birth, the family returned to their simple life in Nazareth where Jesus would grow up to become a joiner by trade, after apprenticing with his father, Joseph.

"The second boy, described in the Gospel of Matthew, was born in Bethlehem a little later in time, to wealthy parents in direct descent from Abraham, David and Solomon. This boy would have been the heir to the throne if the Jews had been in control of their own destiny. The family fled to Egypt with the child when Herod decreed the killing of all boy children who might threaten his rule. When it was deemed safe, they returned to settle in Nazareth near to the family of the Nathan Jesus. This royal family boy was carrying the soul and "I" of Zarathustra, a great soul, carrying alchemical and cosmic wisdom. His birth was honored by the visitation of the Three Kings, the Brotherhood of the Magi, which we honor this Friday as the Epiphany.

"The two boys, whose lives were guided by the hierarchies through their parents, grew up in the same community of Nazareth but of different classes. The poor Nathan Jesus boy worked with his father as a joiner, and we must remember he didn't have a human "I" so would have appeared simple. Although, he might have accessed his Archangelic "I", now that I think about it," she added, penciling a note in the margin of her papers. "In contrast, the wealthy boy Jesus was educated by the best tutors and, as he matured, was frequently in the temples learning from and teaching the elders. It was during one such temple visit, at the age of 12, that the hierarchies intervened to complete the maturation of the loving and compassionate Nathan Jesus child. Whilst in the temple together one day, the human "I" of the brilliant boy was transferred to the simple, loving Nathan Jesus boy. He was then capable of teaching the elders with Zarathustra's wisdom but from a space of the pure and compassionate soul of Adam and Buddha. The Jesus who would one day become the receptacle for the Christ was complete in his rainbow body. The wealthy boy withered and died, his enormous mission complete, and his kingly father also passed. The mother of Nathan Jesus, her Eve mission complete, left the physical world and the two remaining parents married and raised our legendary Jesus to manhood.

Leah stopped to blow her nose. She'd been quite choked up through this part of the story. Chris smiled, maintaining his meditative state.

"Throughout his life, Jesus experienced the temptations of Lucifer and Ahriman as triplet reflections of his three previous sacrifices in Lemuria, early Atlantis and later Atlantis. He saw these reflections in the loss of spirit both amongst the Hebrew people, but also the pagans, and even the Essenes, whom he visited frequently at their compound outside Nazareth. He saw them again as three encounters on his way to be baptized by John, and again as the three temptations in the desert. The last of those, Ahriman demanding that he turn stones to loaves, he could not challenge, as he knew humanity would be traveling with Ahriman until the end of the Earth Stage of Consciousness and physical body mastery. It turns out these temptations demonstrate to us the fragility of the "I" and, in his case, the two of them occurred when he had no "I" at all — times of very high risk, I'd imagine.

"Before he was to be baptized, he had an intimate conversation with his step-mother for whom he had the greatest respect, and with whom he regularly took counsel. She facilitate the flight of the Zarathustra "I", which he'd ensouled to properly prepared him for his destiny, and he went to his baptism, once again with no "I". During the baptism, at the age of 30, the Christ descended into his greatly advanced consciousness soul space, so recently vacated by the Zarathustra "I". The heavens opened and His Father spoke.

"We know what his life might have been like from history, and because it was, in part, remembered orally, but what wasn't recorded accurately was the struggle to embody the Christ. This wasn't in completion, actually, until the end when his life hung by a thread through betrayal and torture. We might all wish for a slate as clean as his, by the way. When he died on the cross, it was both the Christ and Jesus who died, who sacrificed the fourth time, through the ensoulment of Jesus by Christ. Jesus' consciousness was once Angelic or Archangelic — close enough to humanity to facilitate these sacrifices (and who's to say he hadn't once been a Moon God, of our own pre-Earthly lineage). Now, unless I'm mistaken, he is clearly of the Powers, the Elohim, as Sananda Kumara, in continuing service to humanity.

"So, Christ has no body. God cannot have flesh. It was the flesh of Adam sacrificed that day and his blood that redeemed us as it soaked into the earth infusing Our Mother with the Christ Spirit — which will remain with us until the end of days. And, I might add, our ability to regain our phantom was returned to us. Jesus appeared in his double at the Resurrection, and until the full ascension, would still embody the Christ to teach his apostles. Now the Christ appears, to those who can see, using the countenance of Archangel Michael. I've, thus far, gleaned that much from reading the Michael book.

"What I believe, but actually haven't found in print yet, is that the etheric body of Adam, which blueprinted the perfected phantom/physical body of Jesus, experienced the same death and would have been the etheric double risen again. This etheric body would have to have been complete when incarnating. What I'm suggesting is that the highest part of our etheric body, which was sequestered in spirit world for us at *The Fall*, was present in Jesus' Adam etheric body. It would *have* to have been to complete the blueprint/ template of the perfected phantom. Thus, this sacrifice also returned to us the possibility of regaining that highest part of the etheric body, which the Elohim have sequestered in spirit for us. That's why we can master the double and one day reclaim the phantom. It would not have been possible prior to the return of that sequestered highest frequency part, though, somehow Buddha made that happen for himself prior to this sacrifice. I imagine it was always available to those who earned it, but that this sacrifice brought it into range for all of humanity."

"That makes sense. We do have that potential, and mandate, now. Go on, lass. This is beautifully complex," he grinned.

"I found a great deal of wisdom about the rainbow body in this story of Jesus. First, we found out that the sequestered physical and etheric bodies of pre-*Fall* Adam and Eve are no longer sequestered but available to us in mastery. That harkens back to the story of their creation by the Elohim as the first humans of the third root race in Lemurian times. Their offspring, Abel and Seth, were of a purely human lineage whilst Cain was half-divine because an Elohim came down to earth to impregnate Eve who birthed him. Because Jesus' mother had the pre-*Fall* Eve physical and etheric bodies and her son came in with that of Adam, these two original lines would be united in Nathan Jesus, as I see it. This would be a healing of the Elohim's Cain–Able/Seth fracture that has come down humanities two lines since *The Fall*. He truly *was* the Fisher-King, which is symbolic of that union.

"We also learn that historic etheric bodies, astral bodies and "I"s can appear again as composites, as needed, in evolution. So, our Nathan Jesus was a composite human with an astral body of Adam and Buddha. I'm not sure if his astral body, which would have been all three layers, given Buddha's state of enlightenment, was divided between these two souls or if they cohabitated. To be honest, most of this will take me ages to understand and may or may not have an impact on the outcome. Suffice to say that the average human wasn't yet operating in consciousness soul with their "I", but Jesus would have been.

"As far as I know, the astral body of Adam wasn't sequestered in the mountains of Asia but was used as soul in that first man prototype created by the Elohim at *The Fall*. The same would be true for Eve. I could be way off on that one, though it seems logical. Zarathustra's astral body or soul, with his fully integrated personality and true "I" were born into the kingly Jesus with the true "I" maturing/descending fully into consciousness soul at a younger age than it would have in most humans. Both boys were fully conscious in the third layer of the astral body, whereas most of humanity was likely trying to stabilize the third astral body at that time. That the Zarathustra "I" could be transferred to the Nathan Jesus, and later be returned to spirit world so that Jesus might accept the Christ "I" is mind-boggling at best. Zarathustra, who agreed to the use of his soul and "I", thusly, would have gained immeasurably in the light of his selfless service. It would have been Zarathustra's soul and "I" that brought forth the wisdom of Jesus' teachings that still guide many people through daily life. Zarathustra's "I", coming in with the knowledge of the mysteries, would also have taken him through the Egyptian Therapeutae training to its highest level as well. Within those teachings were keys to what we gained with this sacrifice, which was a capacity for truth, a deepening of the soul's experience, and moral imagination.

"Obviously, Zarathustra's "I" was at the level of consciousness soul — well advanced on humanity's bell curve — and likely had bridged to *manas* in his second Zarathustra life. The spirit-filled wisdom he'd previously acquired would have given him enormous respect amongst the temple wisdom-keepers and Therapeutae masters. Now, this assumes that Zarathustra and Buddha, for examples, were gifted back the sequestered part of their etheric bodies when they reached the level of etheric mastery. I don't know how else to fill in the puzzle pieces on this one, cowboy. Perhaps that's when we all receive it back. It makes sense that we wouldn't be able to manage it before that level of mastery, making it a high risk to give it to everyone before they're ready." When Chris didn't offer any help or objection, she took a sip of wine and continued.

"That brings me back to the rainbow body and the presence of the consciousness soul. Thus far, there's no mention in my reading of the creation of this third layer of the rainbow body, but I have to believe it began to show up as the prefrontal lobes were developed and explored by the leading edge of our bell curve over the 30,000 years since their inception. Because this is tied in with brain development, let me go there next. In late Atlantis, I hypothesize, we mastered the right hemisphere, subjugating the lower brains to it, and we finished maturing the left hemisphere. The prefrontal lobes were just coming into existence near the end of Atlantis. I suggest that in the late-Atlantean and early post-Atlantean epochs, we mastered the left-hemisphere, bridging it to the right hemisphere with the corpus callosum, and subjugated the lower brains to the combined neocortex. Now we're in the process of maturing the prefrontal lobes, which are meant to subjugate all the other brains and act as the master brain. They mature for us between 15 and 28 years of age, reflecting the stage of evolution we're in right now. These are the lobes I would associate with consciousness soul, the enlightened brain and the true "I". Right now, they don't appear in fetal development, but rather begin to grow right after birth. Comparatively speaking, this is a very new brain accompanying the gift of our true "I". Apparently, humanity will really anchor the "I" in the sixth post-Atlantean epoch, which follows the current epoch around 3573 AD.

"Now we come to a real twist in the story. Enter the consequences of this redemption. There have been, you'll remember, some remnants of the original disordering in all the sacrifices, and the fourth is no exception. They're coupled with our gifts, some of which I mention above, so I'll speak of them together. We were gifted the true "I" and a sacred space within consciousness soul or the spiritual-mental body, to sequester it after it descends at age 21. This space within the upper astral body is sacrosanct — protected from Ahrimanic and Luciferic influences, but very much desired by the Asuras, who are renegade Archai. That tells me we have a way to go in maturation before it's stabilized. We must earn consciousness soul through our ascension process and must build the temple there to house the "I", where it will be safe from all intervention before the time of its true descent. We earn this by raising consciousness to that frequency through personality transformation and astral mastery.

redemption

As a consequence of that gift, an inauthentic cultural "I", became established in the lower astral, which is easily accessed by the Luciferic and Ahrimanic beings. In this sense it recreates the distortion of the Sibylline prophets, as is especially prevalent in channeling of questionable integrity. Nothing elevated is coming through the cultural "I" consciousness — mired in the maya as it is — though it can be cloaked in such a way as to be pretty convincing. In the best of worlds, we're educated as to the difference between the cultural "I" and the true "I". To properly ensoul the true "I", we need to leave behind the cultural "I" to engage that of the true "I" at 15 years-of-age. This is simultaneous with neural tracking to the prefrontal lobes in brain development. If we cannot see that choice or are not aware of it, we stay on the cultural "I" road and digest the neural tracts, which leaves us with minimal prefrontal lobe function instead of its highest potential. This is the evolutionary dualism of potential and disaster we're living through right now.

"The culture of violence leaves most young people no alternative to the cultural "I". They're captured by Lucifer's distraction and Ahriman's deceit. We receive the gift of the true "I", *if* we can claim the consciousness level of the upper astral, and *if* we're able to build the bridge to spirit world. Here, again, we have the Luciferic impulse of free will and its Catch-22. We can choose the road of the Jedi, or that of Mr. Smith — at any age. The Mr. Smith route reminds me that Steiner predicted Ahriman's incarnation in this time period, and that, like Christ, he has the powerful magic of numbers. I imagine most would envision him as the ultimate power broker and enslaver of mankind. And, that could be true, but I see it as Mr. Smith taking over humanity, pulling us, one soul at a time, off the trailing edge of the bell curve. That scenario would be far more devious.

"To wrap this up, from the perspective of selfishness, Ahriman's dive into our "I" is as selfish as it comes. And, we can assume that those walking around amongst us with his subhuman "I" have surrendered their cultural "I" to ensoul his "I", which is end stage seduction by predatory energy in my book — possession. The inauthentic, Ahrimanic cultural "I" is seductive and extremely self-absorbed, as you would expect.

"That brings me to our true redemption through the mystery of the fourth sacrifice. That's the return of the phantom. The phantom is held within the earth for our eventual physical body mastery, which must be completed before the end of the Earth stage of consciousness. With the potential reunion of the sequestered, highest frequency part of the etheric body, I assume we gain the potential mastery of the double as Christ Jesus modeled through his life and in his Resurrection. Christ, we're told, is now present within the etheric body of the earth as an angelic Presence, and, through his magic of numbers, we can embody him in our own etheric body, after, I assume, we have claimed that missing part necessary for mastery. The choice is whether to embody the cultural "I" or abandon it to quest the true "I", which, as we know, is a lot of hard personal work. The good news is; we can be *in* the world and not *of* it. With these gifts, is the obvious ability to build the bridge to *manas* and consciously access our spirit.

"Earth stage consciousness is about death and separation from our cosmic purpose. Our task is to remember the pearl and return to our heavenly home, with it in our grasp. Death occurs only on earth and only to humans. Thus, only for humans is victory over death possible. For that reason Christ had to come to earth and experience human death. We must achieve "I" consciousness in physicality, and death is necessary to that end. Christ came to show us victory over death in Resurrection. Because Christ now inhabits the earth's etheric body, we can prepare for and experience Christ at the moment of death, taking that blessing into our afterlife to support further growth. Furthermore, Earth is the only place where we can learn to love.

"Granting that I've only touched the tip of the iceberg with this preliminary research, my conclusion is that we live at a time of great opportunity as well as great peril. We could be moving towards a huge split in the bell curve or a massive awakening and ascension — or both! It occurs to me that the cultural "I" is unaware of the meaning of this sacrifice — is quite stuck in the 'Old Moon' third sacrifice prison of relentless images, in fact. The fourth sacrifice is meant to awaken us to that peril, and through the renunciation of the cultural "I" and embodiment of the true "I", lead us beyond death in resurrection."

"Beauty. And, the big picture of the fourth sacrifice is?" Chris asked, sitting up to have a drink of wine.

"Redemption, cowboy — driven by unconditional love. It is an exemplary model of selfless service to humanity. That's the big gift from this sacrifice. We have been delivered from Ahriman's attempt to selfishly possess our "I" and are capable, therefore, of absolute selflessness and the fulfillment of consciousness soul that reconnects us to our spirit self. What's more we have the Son of God and Lord of the Sun, to guide us on our journey home."

"If you knew nothing of the rainbow body, lass, would you believe the true story of the two Jesus boys?"

She thought a moment. "It resonates with my soul. I suppose I could accept it on faith as I did many church beliefs when I was young. But that doesn't make it my truth. Knowing what I do of the rainbow body allows me to anchor this in my assemblage point, as my owned/claimed truth. I'm so grateful to Christ Jesus for all four sacrifices and his unending love for humanity. It makes me feel we have a chance at redemption. I'm also grateful to Dr. Steiner's for his courage in bringing it into the clear light of day, and for leaving a legacy in print to inspire my continued research. And then, there's Elliot to thank — my reluctant mentor in that regard — and you, dear cowboy, my fully present sounding board."

"Are you going to do a show on it?" he grinned.

"*Never!* If people are meant to know this truth, their souls will lead them to it."

"That's why it was hidden in the mystery schools before he brought it out into the clear light of day, lass."

"Indeed. Let's imagine, as he likely did, that the veils masking the mystery schools become less opaque as our bell curve shifts to consciousness soul. This truth still remains a mystery — known only to those with 'eyes to see'."

part five: first light 2012

chapter 13: epiphany

Chris saw the four presentations, complete or not, as Yoda's rite of passage into the circle at the bridge. Jane was the bearer of love and compassion. The Bee Mistress held a space that was all about magic and moving energy. Alice bore the imagination and creative energy. And, now, Yoda was keeper of wisdom. Her next task was to blend them into one personality without the loss of power. In fact, there would be a synergistic increase in power. From Chris' perspective, this would play out through Eric's gift to the future Outreach initiative of *Main Street USA*. Of course, he would meet regularly with Leah and Demetri, but mastery didn't happen in meeting rooms. It happened on the ground, serving human evolution. This needed to be the organizing principle for every Outreach project and, in particular, for that one. In addition to their selfless service to humanity, humanity needed to gain spiritually from each initiative. That much, he shared with her the next morning at breakfast.

"We'll be challenged with that one, cowboy," she admitted. "This project will recreate a local economy without the egalitarian concepts of equal pay. I see a non-profit umbrella but within it worker–owned cooperatives with suppliers who expect profits. It's meant to provide a market for local businesses where the majority of the profits stay in the community."

"It'll be interesting to see what Max and Julia think about the idea. Are you going to have a plan to show them?"

"I need a plan for the board meeting on Thursday. I'll be back here this afternoon trying to get a grip on it and add to that whatever free time remains tomorrow after our visit to Trynel. Maybe I can run it by you tomorrow night?"

"Should do. We've a choir practice on Thursday and the Rangers Friday. You've got the women's group tonight, right?

"I do. We'll be back to our clearing work but I also wanted to begin explaining the first sacrifice. What do you think about that?"

"I reckon it will look different to you now ... maybe make more sense. There's much to be gained for all of you. We'll need to set something up with Demetri as well."

"Sunday's all we have, sport. Next week is busy though some time could be spared on Thursday. I'm meant to start up in the greenhouses again planting seeds next Wednesday. I love the return of the light and start of the garden season."

"Let's take a day at a time, lass. Nick and I are going out this morning to place markers for the BD application on Friday. We'll use the horse trail as far as we've taken it, then drop down to the road to the end of the Taylor's farm."

"We need to wait on Mr. B's?" she asked.

"We do. Sonia has read up on the prep. The land needs to be in transition to biodynamics, already receiving the 500 and 501 preps and compost. That gives the Nature Spirits confidence that they'll be nourished in the bubble we create for them."

"Great. That means next year the whole valley can be included. Are we splitting up the application to spread the work around?"

"All the Rangers want to saddle up and help out," he smiled. "We thought we would ask you to start it off and Sonia to finish it. How's that for a plan."

"Splendid, cowboy. Holly and I want to get our bit in, for sure. We need a get together on the commons as well, maybe with a fire, where the children can tell part II of the story of Jesus, and the choir can lift their voices in song."

"All in good hands, lass, no worries."

Leah got dressed and headed off to start a bigger than average workday. She would need to complete the show outline and have it ready to fill in Thursday with the staff's research. A presentation had to be assembled for the board on Thursday, and it would help to have a bit of time to review the first sacrifice for the women's group. This would not be as simple as presenting it to Chris for comment. Instead there would be huge chunks to explain and mystery teachings to authentically transmit.

After lunch that afternoon, she brought home some checkered paper and, after lighting a candle in the niche for the Golden Queen, spread it out on the dining table. There was no need to sit on the stump, since there was little to note in Sheldon beyond the stump and the convenience store, which she knew would be replaced by a coffee shop. She'd a start on each part of the intersection but admitted to having skimmed over a good many essentials. That's where she would ask the Bee Mistress to bring in vision. The hours slipped by and the picture of a vibrant local wholesale/retail economic community emerged, with links to *Harmony Valley*, *New Avalon* and nearby farms. Patrons came from as far away as the 150-mile radial limit of their definition of local (though that could be up to 200 miles by some definition.

In time, it would become a hub of activity for a new breed of eco-tourists wanting to see first-hand what could be done by, and for, community. Although the land would be held in trust and the businesses would, initially, be funded by the non-profit *Main Street USA*, in time, the employee owners would buy the businesses back, even the buildings in which they lived and worked, so long as the original intent wasn't corrupted. Within the co-ops, wages would vary with responsibility, skill and longevity in the work. However, profits within each business would be shared equally. They would buy wholesale from the local farmers and growers, including *Harmony Valley*, and bigger businesses outlying town center, like the abattoir, tannery, farm co-op and dairy, all of which would be worker-owned co-ops. Any organic farmer could process his stock through the abattoir and sell his meat wholesale to the local butcher, other butchers, or retail it by mail order as some already did.

There were currently no licensed public slaughterhouses in the area, which meant that farmers had to take their stock five hours up the highway in Oregon for slaughter and transport the hanging meat, refrigerated, back five hours on the highway. There were an increasing number of organic, grass-fed operations in the area that could benefit from the slaughterhouse and sell their animals skins to the tannery. Leah was well aware that establishing certified dairies, slaughterhouses, tanneries, etc., could run into the millions given all of the federal, state and local regulations. If that was the only way to start a trend back to *small is beautiful* so be it. It would put people back to work locally and pay for itself long haul. It might also inspire less oversight — at the federal level, at least. Corruption traveled in top down economics, not bottom up.

When Chris came home from the stable, he leaned over to have a look at the drawing.

"It's filling in nicely, Lass — reminds me of *Harmony Valley*."

"I suppose it does, from the center of town. It would be set up a lot differently, though."

"How so?" he asked, sitting down next to her.

"This is like small shopping district America, a village we'll call it, with no houses as yet, but people living above the stores, if that works for them. Some would come in to work from nearby farms or small towns. Their wages are not based on equal pay for equal time like our community or *Harmony Valley*, but rather on merit, and level of responsibility like you'd find most anywhere. They would have supervisors but not a business owner. The workers own the business. It's small-scale Mondragon. They make decisions cooperatively; agreeing on expansion, pay raises and decreases, hiring, promotions and dismissal, or investments, the buying out of their loans or real estate — plus they share profits equally. Every business will be set up that way, including the services outside town. This is a co-op community."

"Take me through it, if you have the time, lass. It's fascinating to me."

"That's great. It's darn confusing to me. Okay, let's take one block at a time, starting with the SE corner. There we find a green grocer selling fruits, veggies,and nuts, like in OZ. Just south on that block is a food-co-op that will take care of dry food needs, like grains, dish soap, paper products, and all you might find in the center aisles of the grocery store. It won't be huge because we've got the rest of the food, the outer ring of the store, covered by small businesses. There's room for more down that way but let's go back to the Green Grocer, who by the way buys wholesale from locals, including *Harmony Valley*. On the east side of that block, next to the Grocer, is Max's Wine & Tapas Bar — that's our friend Max, but he doesn't know this yet," she giggled.

"Next to Max's Bar we have the meat market and finally the High Country Sheepskin Clothier where *Harmony Valley's* sheepskin products will be bought wholesale and sold retail. We're creating markets at the same time we're assisting established markets. Across the street from the clothier I've got a dairy. This is a retail outlet of the creamery at the north end of the village. Here you'll find milk products, ice cream and cheeses. In addition to the cheese from their creamery, they'll carry other local cheeses — maybe some of Shelley's. Next to them is the Spence-like Old World bakery, then the coffee shop where they also roast beans and sell teas. This is an exception to locally grown food, which we'll also see in some restaurant fare. They'll use milk from the creamery and sell baked goods from the bakery to make up for the imports. A small breakfast and lunch café is next. On the round-a-bout corner I've put a hotel."

"Really. Who's going to stay there?"

"Tourists coming to see the model, but also folks coming for an overnight, a great meal and small town boutique shopping. The street heading north from the round–a–bout will have local artist galleries on one side and a row of stores with local crafts, like felting, dressmaking, knit sweaters and baby gear, and beyond that's the cooperative creamery, hopefully with certified raw milk from local green pasture dairy farmers that we'll have to attract to the area. There's no certified dairy — raw or otherwise — in the region now. It might offer raw milk along with conventional milk and milk products including some from goat milk. The hitch is pasture irrigation in the summer months. That's why most of the big dairies are over on the coast where it's wet year–round. Dairies are outrageously expensive to establish in this highly regulated culture of ours, but it's important to have local access to dairy products — both cow and goat. Across from the dairy on the edge of the village is the Farmer's Co-op where they can save and exchange seed, buy feed that fellow farmers have grown locally, and likely organic fertilizers and pest control. That's really out of my league but I think it would be a good business.

"Now go back to the center after passing the craft shops and you find on the round–a–bout a very popular five-star restaurant with a top chef and mostly local food including the butcher's meat. My vision of the future saw this place drawing people from Ashland/Medford as regular customers for the best restaurant in the district. And, they have some wonderful eateries in Ashland. Turning right toward the Cummings' we would find a pub that's part of the restaurant, a civic center for get-togethers, council meetings, and co-op meetings. And then a nursery with garden supplies.

"Across the street coming back to center I saw a boot and shoe store across from the nursery. They could buy from a local source, like *Harmony Valley* or the Restorative Justice community, or a manufacturing business could start here, using leather from the tannery. Next to them a big hardware and dry good store with the barrel nails and other old fashioned sales features. Then we have an herbal pharmacy/health food store. They might have an herbalist or naturopath on site. That's next to the People's Bank credit union on the last corner at the round-a-bout. To ease the business models for everyone, since they're all based on the workers co-op model, we can have a central management office, also a co-op, next to the bank on the south road, with professionals who can process all the business paperwork, receivables and payables, pay taxes, rent, insurance, salaries, benefits and profit sharing for the village, as well as their share of power, water and sewage. We can look at wind power and solar for this project and will have to ask Tommy what he thinks about heating.

So this leaves the customer relations of buying and selling and the creative aspects of business to those working at the businesses. The management service will advise each business about investment, inventory levels, and hiring. Remember, there aren't owners to make these decisions. All the day's sales go to the credit union in one form or another and the management service uses that money to pay the bills, the employees, and at the end of the year disperses profits after an employee meeting agrees by consensus on what to bring forward, and what investments to make for the coming year — for example, buying new equipment, upping inventory levels, or buying the business from the non-profit. Everyone would subscribe to this central service for separate businesses, which could be run online quite efficiently. I see all of our local currencies and US dollars being interchangeable, but that would be Will's task to figure out, along with all the legalities.

"We can fill in the rest of the businesses going south down that street as needs are defined and bright entrepreneurs show up. The village ends with a co-op tannery, which would process leather and sheepskins from across the road at the abattoir. *Harmony Valley* and *New Avalon* sheep can be slaughtered at the abattoir, for example, their hides tanned and returned to the sheepskin wholesale business and the hanging meat returned to the communities or sold to the butchers. A lot of commerce circulates right in the village and though the hardware, for example, would be supplied from outside the region it would not be a franchise of a huge chain. It would be local. Over the stores we can have co-op rental apartments for workers."

"Aye, let's put those millennials to work, lass. I love this idea. Are we taking this to dinner on Saturday night?"

"Indeed, cowboy. I'll give it a go at the board meeting first. We'll establish the ground rules to get them going, but these folks should take off on their own, whilst *Harmony Valley* will need oversight for some time to come. Now, how about I get dinner while you study this to see if I've neglected anything. Remember, it will have to birth a commons, will abide by local laws and regulations, have something like a village council and charter, but will follow *Social Threefolding* economic sphere guidelines to a tee."

"They don't need a petrol station?" he asked.

"Petrol is definitely not local, cowboy, and represents what we're up against. I'd wager someone would build a station nearby once this village gets going. Alternatively, someone might be interested in starting a bio-diesel plant given the presence fuel resources."

He fell silent, carerully studying the picture map, while she put together a simple meal. They were still in recovery from the holidays.

"How about housing as the town grows, or don't you think it will?" he asked, looking her way.

"I do think it will. The land in trust cannot be owned but long-term leases could be made for the building of co-operative housing. For this town to work, it all has to be profit and cost sharing. Managerial jobs could pay enough to support a mortgage on a condo, for example, where co-operative ownership of the Commons prevails. Houses could be built by a cooperative building company, which we might initiate to build the town. The credit union could offer such mortgages as local investments. You would expect that home values would rise as businesses succeeded, along with raises in wages and/or profits. Prosperity would touch everyone, including the local suppliers who are not part of the village per se. On the other hand, because it's all local, with local currencies to fall back on, it could be somewhat sheltered from runaway inflation and recession in the greater economy."

"You would want people to come into this project that believed in a prosperous future then. And the young people living in the co-op apartments and working the lower paying jobs would work up to those managerial positions at that business or another one, and possibly own a condo or live outside the community if they prefer."

"Yep. That's how small towns use to prosper, cowboy. It can happen again if we keep the money circulating within the town, as much as possible. I reckon this project will attract people who will apprentice not only the job but the system, and take this solution far and wide."

"Beauty. So the idea is that it's cooperative, community, every step of the way, and profit sharing puts a cap on wealth accumulation by a few, dispersing it to the many."

"Right. So a butcher, for example, is a credit union member, a housing co-op member, and a co-op owner of the meat market. He gets paid butcher wages, would have butcher colleagues, and they would have young apprentices who get paid fair wages for their work. But at the end of the year, the profits are split equally amongst them. Everyone puts in their best efforts to share in the profits, or they're dismissed by an agreed upon majority vote of all employees. Decisions about the market are made by consensus of all worker-owners at the market, with the guidance of the management center. This educates the apprentices as business members, promotes improvements, better work ethics, and the making of decisions that advance the business — maybe adding assets by sacrificing immediate profits, for the sake of future profits. It teaches a good economic model to young people who will carry it forward. *And*, they learn to care for each other in community — very much a hallmark of this generation."

"It looks good to me, lass, but I would suggest you beef up the community center with a good dance and exercise floor and a room with workout equipment. They'll need to work off their excess energy and stay in shape, plus the social benefits will pay off for community."

"Write it in there, cowboy. You're absolutely right about the building, but it would need to be commons, unless someone turns it into a business. Then we can support their effort to have a workout center," she said.

"So fire and police are commons and not included?"

"Right. On the other hand they could decide to establish a cooperative security business for local protection, and they could build a water tank for immediate water deployment in case of fire."

""I'm getting it, lass. So a library would also be commons."

"It would. They'll build the commons themselves and have to tax themselves to pay for it. They *are* the commons, after all. If they want parks and community gardens, it will happen on their own — and I assure you, it will. We can dedicate some land to the commons and they can rent or buy buildings for their activities. We'll also give them a unique town charter to protect the experiment from opportunists."

"If I were you, I'd change the pub to a microbrewery. We went to one in San Francisco that was amazing, and filled to the brim with loyal customers."

"Excellent idea, lad! Would you mind changing that for me? We can entice someone to come up here from Chico to undertake it. They'd know what their doing in the beer department down there."

"Done" he grinned. "When the town grows, what will you do to attract doctors and lawyers, for example?"

"They can work in cooperatives. Wages are not set, darling. They can charge what they want for their own salary but profits will be shared with their nurses, assistants, receptionists and other help. They could be part of the community's health care co-op too. I expect owned businesses to be established nearby the town that community members can support or not support — their choice. Remember the local farmers own their businesses and can sell to *Main Street USA* or to *Harmony Valley* or *New Avalon* as well as to their regular channels."

"Do you think the folks at *Harmony Valley* are going to see this as a better deal than what they have going?" he asked.

"A good question — for Will. We're going to have a number of models working themselves out in the same neck of the woods. It could be a challenge but at their core, they're all very different. *Harmony Valley* will be set up with *Social Threefolding* where as *Main Street USA* will begin with one third of that ideal and the challenge of building the commons and the judicial as time goes on. Harmony Valley may become *their* template."

"I think it's a timely and inventive experiment, lass. Eric's done himself proud launching this one!" With that, he accept a warn kiss on the neck and a shoulder rub before heading off to the shower.

On his way down the hall he declared, "I reckon I know why mission feeds these streams to you, lass — now that I've played Park & Shop." "Ha-ha," she laughed. "You rascal!"

Leah set their places at the opposite end of the table, with place mats, cutlery and salads, then went back to finish the steaming veggies and sear the fish. Over dinner, she cautioned that what she had on paper was a bold plan that may or may not work. Will would not have quality time to look at the business end of it for weeks and Tommy was tied up for months in the Bay Area. So, for now, it was a big imagination to plant in the minds and hearts of the community, requesting feedback and suggestions from everyone. She was sure the non-profits engaged in the Evergreen Project in Cleveland would be eager to help them out, when the time came. The Schumacher Institute crossed her mind as well.

Chris informed her that Tommy and Will would be stoking the sauna for the end of the women's circle that night. He thought he might crawl into bed early and meet up with her in dreamtime.

The whole evening went beautifully. The women were making progress shooting down images of sexual fantasy and were especially receptive to the teachings of the first sacrifice. The sauna was both ceremonial and social, with a good many songs sung and stories shared in the flickering shadow–light of the fire.

She curled up with her cowboy in bed that night, and immediately fell into a deep sleep. When she found herself in Master Mukda's ashram garden, she didn't bother trying to get in the ashram door. Instead she went to the flowers, looking for the bowing Iris. When she found it, with its glowing golden path of light dipping down to meet her, she knelt and said a prayer. She asked for the protection and blessing of Archangel Michael and the Christ Spirit as she made a first attempt to enter the elemental world and to face her own dark side.

Leah was conscious in the dream, deliberately directing her actions and intent. She asked for the treasure of humility, while wishing to see all that remained to be shed from this life to truly serve selflessly. She asked for ease and grace, and the gift of vision to proceed with her personal work while in steadfast service to and with her community.

When she felt the reception of her prayer and the protection of its blessings, she merged with the golden light, allowing it to lead her to the threshold. For Leah, it became a tunnel of golden honeycomb just like the bridge to spirit in her cosmic loving with Chris, except that there was no bridge. It was more akin to the tunnel awaiting Mr. B. when he died. At the end of the tunnel an image of herself, aged, withered and dressed in black, awaited her. That was her first frightening experience. They were in a landscape not unlike the earth but with luminosity ordinarily reserved for visionary experiences — perhaps the landscape experienced with the Ayahuasca medicine. It seemed the elemental world.

epiphany

Her dark self traveled as a shadow in the elemental world, while her dreaming self traveled with conscious trepidation. In fact she felt more fear than she could remember in her present life. And that fear began manifesting fearsome images of monsters, serpents, and predatory animals. She recognized she wasn't without fear but consciously refrained from running away or lashing out defensively (*thank you, Luke Skywalker*), trusting that her intent to learn from the experience would protect her instead. Typically a dream would end with the appearance of something scary. In this experience the fear needed to be faced and overcome, not because one wished invincibility but because one wished to serve without the impediment of fear.

The entire dream was spent meeting fears of every kind. After the scary animals, came scenes of harm to loved ones, followed by witnessing the power of the dark side against mankind, and then came the trials of judgment against her own life. She did not try to rescue others. She did not run from the dark side of humanity. She did not try to defend her own actions in life. At the end of her trial, wherein her shadow self was the judge and jury, and during which she owned each and every action in her life caused by fear and its consequences, her shadow self returned her to the honeycomb tunnel, telling her they'd meet again. Her trials had barely begun.

Leah returned to the ashram garden to meditate at the pool. Looking in the pool, Leah saw her shadow self instead of her conscious self. In that instant she knew this shadow of death would be chasing her down the long road of mastery. She awoke in a pool of sweat so profuse she had to get up to take a shower. While under the running water, she reviewed the dream meticulously. It would be recorded in her notebook and shared with her mentor. *Wow! I can have a full plate in both realities. What a comfort.* The good news was that what she'd seen of her life were subconscious memories, not those she'd already consciously recapitulated. The surprise? ... *So many.*

Leah and Chris planned an early start for their visit over the ridge. The bed was stripped and linens washed and in the dryer before they left for the stable. She'd written the dream in her personal notebook but wasn't ready to discuss it yet, so sweetly smiled at the inquiring eyes of her cowboy, when he discovered the puddle she'd left behind in bed. He'd missed menopause.

The early start would give her more afternoon time to go over the *Main Street USA* plan before the board meeting and to check in with Paula before she went home. Natalie was conducting homeless interviews in Ashland that afternoon and promised to track her down in the evening to give her a report.

They mounted their horses, with saddlebags stuffed, shortly after nine. It felt to Leah like her last trip over before the winter really hit them, but who knew anymore about the weather. It was positively balmy for the first week in January. Holly and Thunder knew where they were headed and led the way handily, while she and Chris chatted about the evolving Epiphany plans. She recapped the wonderful sauna as well, and the receptivity of the women to the teachings. Their work with image clearing stayed within the women's circle.

385

When they arrived at the *Woodland Folk's* cabin, Sissi ran out to greet them. She also felt the imminence of snow, and her journey to *New Avalon,* but would not talk about that in front of her mother. Trynel was looking very good. She was strong enough to use her arms to shift around in the bed with ease. Her flesh was filling out nicely and there was a healthy bloom in her cheeks. Zacker was in the house but busy with the fire and something in the kitchen area while Leah worked with Trynel. There was no need to remove the full cast, which kept the leg immobilized from above the knee to the middle of the foot. The superficial wounds had healed before the cast was put in place. She was interested in the bone knitting. Sissi had seen to comfrey tea every day and there had been no need for the painkillers she returned to Leah. The biggest problems were boredom and frustrating immobility — both good signs of recovery.

The tibia fracture looked well-knitted to her visionary eyes. It needed time to stabilize but function could be fully restored. When she lay across the bed to observe the fibula, she found it healing more rapidly than the tibia. She put in a quick but sincere request to the Archangels to attend to both bones thereafter. Leah had to admit that the fibula looked capable of full recovery as well and with the cast in place, felt Trynel could try to use crutches soon. She would send them with Nick when he and Chris came over on the 13th.

Sissi and Trynel were both very pleased with her progress. Even Zacker stood back with a smile on his face. They talked about the possibility of weather, which was forecasted as clear up to the 13th, at least. Winter temperatures were typically at their lowest in December but precipitation could be heaviest in March. Usually, the pass over the ridge would be melted for walking, or at least for the horses in April. Leah laid out a plan for physical therapy, which Sissi wrote down in German for her mother. She felt the cast should best stay in place until spring. She would send a boot with Nick to fit over the foot end with a solid support on the bottom. Trynel was to rely on the crutches completely for four weeks from Nick's visit. Then she could begin to apply weight to the leg a bit at a time. The good news was that after Nick's visit she could practice getting around the cabin with Sissi and Zacker's help. It wouldn't take her long to become independent again, but outdoor activity was out of the question. Those arm lifts in bed were going to make the crutches more tolerable, so it wouldn't hurt to increase them.

Chris had loaded the saddlebags with fresh bread, cheese, greens, a bag with a couple frozen Tilapia filets, more comfrey tea and sandwiches they'd put together that morning. They enjoyed lunch together, especially since everyone's spirits were high from the checkup. When they were about to go, Chris presented Trynel with two books written in German that Tommy and the boys were willing to loan her until spring. They would help reduce the boredom and entertain the two of them.

Zacker was reserved but very cordial with Leah, thanking her sincerely for restoring the health of his wife … or so Chris translated. On their way back over the ridge, she asked him what sort of miracle he'd worked on Zacker to salvage him from the tail of the bell curve. He just smiled at her and tipped his hat. She reckoned it wasn't something she wanted to know, so let is slide.

Holly got a thorough currying and massage to make up for Leah's absence over the holidays. Although er sitting bones were tender, she was otherwise unaffected by the ride, and really pleased with Trynel's progress.

The day was decidedly upbeat until Natalie had a meltdown on their doorstep, soon after she returned from Ashland. It looked like she'd been crying most the way home. Harry was at a loss to calm her down. Leah took her in her arms and led her to the sofa where she could have a good cry on her shoulder — with tissues. Chris poured them each a glass of Zinfandel for post-recovery then stepped in where Leah had dropped the dinner preparation, setting a third place at the table.

"I don't think I can do it, girlfriend," Natalie sobbed.

"Why don't you tell me what you experienced, Nat. Give me a feel for the process," Leah suggested, as Harry curled up between them.

"I feel like ground meat must feel when it ends up in hamburger after starting as a cow. I've been through every emotion possible and then some, Leah. And that was with astute pre-screening. Some people made my heart ache with their stories, others were aggressive and angry, still others interrogated *me* about *our* intentions — like, what were we getting out of this? I felt glued to the hot seat, almost like their homelessness was my fault. I was never cut out to be a therapist, darling," she admitted, reaching for a sip of wine. "I don't think they got it."

"I doubt many therapist would survive what you're doing, Nat. Did you find anyone who actually wanted to engage the project?"

"Amazingly enough, I did. That's because the farmer we had on the homeless show came in for an interview. In fact, he was trying to give *me* therapy by the end of the day. I'll remind you that he lost his farm a year after the 2008 crash and hit the road trying to find work shortly after, leaving his wife and kids with her parents in Eugene. He's not sure they'd come back to him now, but he'd like to try the community on his own, at first, and work on the farm. He's a Buddhist, if you can imagine that."

"I can, and it bodes well for the kind of farmer he was, and will be again. Anyone else?" she asked.

"One of the heartbreakers was a fairly young Hispanic man who'd been years picking fruit for a Medford company and sending all his spare cask back to Mexico for his family. Those left back in Mexico got caught in the middle of a cartel battle and were gunned down en masse. Unable to deal with his grief, he lost his will to work and ended up on the streets. He's got skills from planting the trees, through pruning, picking and cold storage. He could probably take on the orchards for us. He'll need to find a partner, that one," she sighed, "and get some non-medicated mental health care."

"More?"

"Actually the guy that practically attacked me, wanting me to be clear about our intent, turned out to be reasonable in the end. It just sounded way to good to be true for him. Maybe he should work in law enforcement. He sure did rattle my cage," she said, her heart lightening.

"So what's his gig?" she asked, reaching for the wine. She could smell the Basmati rice cooking and hear Chris throwing veggies in the sizzling wok. "You're staying for dinner, by the way."

"Thanks. I probably won't need much, the way I feel. This fellow could work at the production gardens. He's had greenhouse experience, not organic, and a lot of nursery work. He found himself unemployed — now, long term with no more benefits. He had a girlfriend but she hit the road when the money ran out. He lived in his car and ended up in Ashland, still living in his car but going nowhere in it."

"That's not a bad haul for an afternoon of interviewing, girlfriend. Sorry about the collateral damage, though. How can we change this for you?"

"You can do it. That would be good," she laughed.

"How about we do it together next week. I doubt it's my calling either but you might catch some tactics you hadn't thought about. I do have a knack for interviews, though they haven't been with destitute people, I will admit."

"That sounds like a good plan. It's all the way down in Sacramento, though," she reminded her.

"I'll tell Sonia I can't make the greenhouse on Wednesday and it shouldn't affect the show. I was gone most of the day today. We'll be able to sort out the experience on the way home, too. Have them set up the interviews from eleven until four in the afternoon, starting with a group meeting. I think we need to explain ourselves and have a group discussion up front, and then the interviews will be pretty straightforward. We'll get home in four-plus hours and could maybe fit in a pickup at the specialty stores down there for Jenny."

"Okay, doll. You're on. I should have thought of the group meeting. We have a long way to go to fill up that hotel," she sighed.

"Hmmm, I reckon there will be more to chose from in Sac and if not, you could include San Francisco when you're there for the Inner City project or the community work with Elliot. Don't beat yourself up over it, darling. It's all a learning experience — all part of your path."

"Dinner's served, ladies," came the call from the kitchen.

Natalie's spirits had been lifted enough to eat a good meal and take Harry home for an early night.

Pavi, Stu's new hire, showed up for work at nine the next morning with the millennial gang from The Lodge Annex. They were getting along famously and fast becoming a collective 'force to be reckoned with' as a youthful surge in community, especially at the studio. Pavi who'd been an Oakland *Occupier* during the violent outbreaks, was glad to engage a path of change in the film room. In addition to taking charge of production once the finish products were ready to be produced, he was a wiz at web-mastery and took on both websites for overhaul. Where he shone was infrastructure, making everything work more efficiently and creatively, without loss of intent or content. *Go Pavi!* He was a great kid, first generation American with a lot of Hindi accent, reminding all of them of the young fellow who starred in *The Best Exotic Marigold Hotel*. It was just another melodic overlay to integrate into life at *New Avalon*. He came with a passion for cycling that would catch on with the millennials as well.

Leah, Stu and Natalie went off to the board meeting the next afternoon, right after an uplifting live interview with Joel about how austerity, brought on through budget cuts had further crippled the economy and miraculously spared the 1%, who weren't at all trapped in the ruined economic system they'd created. They lived in a different reality entirely where money flowed freely and abundantly — thanks to the Federal Reserve's current policies of printing new money (for the 1%) like it was going out of style. It soon *would* go out of style and become a trap of unimagined proportions, according to Joel. Theirs was a palatable blend of truth and humor that hit home for progressive viewers globally.

Paula then received a round of applause for her live audition of *'Oh Really?!'*, which Stu taped for them to critique. She and Leah would find the right moment to include it within the news report. Paula would present it live, sitting in the first panel position across from Leah at the news desk. Again, truth and humor combined to get the message across. She was bi-partisan (though the right tended towards more guffaws given their private-logic view of reality), and non-judgmental. She presented the politicians, their spokesmen, their ads and those of supporting Superpacs on video or in quote of written words, and followed with the documented proof of the lies. Hers was a simple and straightforward correction of mind-control political advertising and mainstream media so-called news.

The board meeting got underway with a *Harmony Valley* update that held no surprises. They were on target and, as Natalie soberly reported, looking for their residents. Tommy updated on his end of the Inner City project and his plan to move down to Marin after the community meeting the next week. Infrastructure was advancing with city help and they would be ready to build this month. Remodeling was already underway.

Will had some welcomed news. He'd found a farm property to look at with Greg, and possibly take as a hybrid purchase/donation from the retiring owner. It was well situated to supply San Francisco and Oakland. He now expected the third city to complete the first tier of the Inner City project gift pyramid (along with LA and Oakland) to be Seattle, and was scheduled to present it to their city council later in the month. There was a strong group of benefactors ready to take it on at the same time they took on their own initiation of the community program with Natalie. This looked like the best of all worlds. He confirmed that Ali Cat had made a huge donation at the end of the year and would donate his mansion and property in the LA hills to be the farm for the LA Inner City project, where he would be the first resident. It felt like the Inner City Outreach model was really going to take off. Caring people were on the ground raising money and garnering citizen and city support. Apprenticing in San Francisco was being set up for the first tier as was their first Founders Circle community workshop with the presently committed residents. Natalie was streamlining the community program for the city project. She reported having an assistant hired and coming in on January 16th to start work. Sonia, Georgia, Will and Nick were going to take on the intensives, while Natalie filled in the spiritual work.

Natalie updated on the various community programs and apprenticeships as they currently stood. Though running behind the Inner City effort, which had city support, the community programs were nonetheless forming their own gift pyramid which she expect to blossom fully in 2013-14. There was a long list of groups gathering initial community members together, in addition to those ready to go for it, which included Kim's group in Virginia, Ukiah, and the Seattle group. This would be her first tier under Ashland, and getting that up and running with apprenticeship was her major goal and challenge at the moment ... well, one of many.

The homeless pyramid was the slowest forming, though Kim's group was in on the first tier to apprentice *Harmony Valley*. Natalie felt it would all fall into place as soon as *Harmony Valley* began functioning as a viable community. In addition to Kim's group in Baltimore, Sacramento had inquired, as had San Francisco. She noted suggestions to include an influx of unemployed millennials at *Harmony Valley*, even though they might not be homeless, but relying on parents to support them. Their energy would be a boost to the project and their generation was needed to avoid a community that aged and disappeared. They could call it homelessness prevention and put it to the community for a vote. Tommy added that the community ought to vote on the next phases of Harmony Valley now since aspects of these phases dovetailed nicely with the end stages of Phase II.

It was in Will's presentation of the donation tallies and bank balances for Outreach and the Studio, which had separate coffers, that, with Leah's approval, he mentioned the monstrous donation from one Eric Hegelman. *"Who's Eric Hegelman?"* they asked, in unison. That was when Leah, laying out her work-in-progress map on the table, took the floor and kept it until the whole of *Main Street USA* was proposed as a future project. Eric's donation would kick start it but they would have to rely on the generosity and good sense of their donor base to believe in and support it. They were flabbergasted, stunned, overwhelmed and wildly enthusiastic. Will, keen to try it as an economic sphere model, would look at land purchase to get the ball rolling and see what they were up against. Leah and Chris would feel out Max and Julia about the farming community to which they belonged, and everyone else would don their thinking caps to put the idea to the test. They all felt it a good idea to work with the model within Outreach, before staggering the community with a very complex project. There was, at this point, nothing to approve anyway.

That brought them to the concluding report on *New Avalon II*, which would be up for consensus voting at the community meeting. Leah's resident list was nearly full with a few possible alternates should anyone fail to get consensus approval or drop out. Natalie felt it advisable to proceed as with any Community Program — by initiating the workshops and intensives, to arrive at a Founder's Circle and a second wave. They all agreed. With half the village established when the other half came in, integration would be a breeze. Especially since they'll have been through the initial programs together.

Leah proposed a slight rearrangement to put before the community on Tuesday. They'd agreed that two guesthouses in *New Avalon I* was overkill and that one could house an addition to the community. Secondly, with Katia expecting in late spring, she and Mitch needed a bigger house for their growing family and wanted to be near her incoming brother and sister-in-law. Leah wanted to suggest to the community that Georgia's parents take Mitch and Katia's house, which was right next door to Nick and Georgia, while Mitch and Katia moved down valley to establish a larger dairy operation supported by the addition of two more farms to the community.

Tommy wondered at the difficulty a new family might have fitting into the *New Avalon I* community in the spare guesthouse. Leah agreed but argued that they had two families coming in who were children of existing members and well known to everyone. They all knew that Greg and Ellia's son and family were on the list. Greg mentioned that Pete was planning on the community down valley since he'd likely be running the market gardens, as was his forte. It was then that she announced the addition of Nathan, Julie, David and Mandy to the list. *Cheers!* That was settled as far as the board was concerned.

Nick was rapt with the idea of Adelle and George living next door. They could keep an eye on them as they continued to age, and have ready helpers with the kids when they were in a pinch. Adelle would likely be working with Georgia at the school. For his part, Greg thought it a positive move to separate the dairy cows and goats from the cattle and the buffalo, and thought that could be worked out between Mr. B's farm and the Taylors'. He laughingly proposed light rail along side the valley road. Tommy actually thought it a possibility — not high speed, of course. The meeting adjourned on that humorous note.

During their Friday morning Skype session, Leah put her power broker hidden agenda hypothesis to Joel. He was, at least for a moment, speechless. Being able to see him process the idea was priceless.

"I admit it's premature, undocumented, and a bit far-fetch, at least for mainstream media, but do you think it warrants investigation?" she asked.

"You bet your boots it warrants good, solid journalistic investigation. I'd suggest going back decades to track the subtle underpinnings of sabotage, changes in laws and who lobbied them, political propaganda, manipulation of markets, political appointments, national debt and relationships between the government and banking both here and in Europe. And, in Greece, particularly, the rise and fall of political parties and factions."

"By the time we get that done, Greece will be corporate-owned, Joel," she warned.

"Would you mind collaborating?"

"I'd love collaborating and so would my tiny staff. I was thinking we could launch our back-to-back daily shows with a once-a-week look at Greece."

"I so admire your ability to see the patterns in the big picture, Leah, but broadcasting is my department. If we don't hit it hard day after day until it's hammered in, even *our* viewers will loose the thread."

"So we need to have the whole story before we open our mouths?"

"If we don't, we won't get to open them because the elite you want to expose will discredit our efforts, or worse. No, Leah, if this is major, it needs to take the world by storm. And, we've got to take it right down to the personal level, right into personal debt and despair."

"So from the get-go we're drawing parallels between the Greek unraveling and the rest of the EU, the UK, and here in the USA. Austerity destroys the commons hitting the homes, families, bank accounts, businesses and retirement funds of *We the People*."

"Sure. That's the easiest way to privatize the profitable and eliminate the humane."

"R-r-right. *Privatize the gain. Socialize the pain.* We need to get inside the heads of the right wing — their lobbying and legislation–writing organizations."

"If you can figure out how their brains work, we'd all be grateful," Joel laughed. "It will be easier to get information about what they're doing than why."

"They're a generation of bottle–fed loose cannons, Joel. Like the banksters, their reality is self-absorbed to the extreme. Their accumulated wealth and privilege puts them in a bubble world that denies the rest of the world and bestows upon them a private logic. That suggests intellect, or shall we say cleverness, without morals, no checks and balances in the brain, and certainly no inroads into our most conscious brain, where empathy informs actions. I believe it will one day be categorized as a mental illness. Would you like to suggest our strategy, darling?"

"It's time to apply the 'Art of War'. Let's start with the in-house ground forces," he laughed. "Gavin would be in for sure," he said, referring to his producer. "And, I could put one other person on it full-time. Who can you spare?"

"Paula is in for sure but she'd be adding that on to other projects. I think Matt would help out and maybe our new hire, Pavi, since he'll be multi-tasking full time. Will can add financial and political oversight. We've got a growing number of our Canary troops on the ground out there, with their eyes wide open."

"Swell idea. I think we're assembling a group who can get along together and dig deep. We both need to put our own minds to strategies and make it a high priority. I, for one, will make sure that the Greek economy stays in the news. We may need to send someone over to Athens or find a credible collaborator on the ground over there."

"I'll ask Demetri about like-minded investigative journalists in Greece. What about security, Joel? We don't want anyone investigating us!"

"Our collaborating staff can use our studio-to-studio video transmitting to have meetings. I should think that to be the most secure, but we'll monitor it, maybe encrypt the audio. We'll have to scrap the topic from future Skype session, phone, text and so forth and any assignments to your canaries will have to be vague or abstract."

"We might have to resort to a secure delivery service with written documents and, perhaps, some in-person round table discussions. Is there a way to encrypt emails and translate them at the other end?"

"Gavin can look into that for us. He's got contacts in the cyber security industry. Anything else coming through your vision, sister?" he laughed.

"I'm not talking about it yet, but another seed of change is germinating."

Gotcha. I'll wait for the flower. Time to go now."

"Love you, Joel. Keep up the good work."

"Back at ya, Light Beam," he laughed, doing a good imitation of Will's most reliable response.

"Leah organized her desk, while contemplating the session with Joel. Security was a legitimate issue for the Greek Caper, but at the root of it was a knowing that she'd be scrutinized, and likely attacked by the right, when Eric blew the whistle. It might not be immediate fallout, but it was inevitable. As a precaution, she decided to give Pavi some to time working with the crew before involving him in the caper. She'd meet with Will, Paula, Matt and maybe Sam to go over the plans, but she'd first lay it all out for her favorite banker, who'd not been at the staff meeting when she'd brought it up.

Leah, Sonia, Greg and Chris met in Sonia's office on Friday afternoon, at one-thirty, to stir the Three Kings BD prep. Sonia added the right amount of the Three Kings prep glycerin emulsion they'd made on New Years Eve. At four in the afternoon, Leah, Sonia and the Rangers would apply it to the perimeter of the valley, to include all but Mr. B's farm where biodynamics weren't yet established. They'd be on horseback with a sprayer and containers with refill — each one passing on the task to the awaiting Ranger after their segment of the perimeter had been sprayed. When Sonia, with Will as her partner, returned, in darkness, from the last leg of the application, a bonfire would be lit for the community gathering on the commons.

They pulled it off without a hitch, though Sonia and Will were ten minutes early returning to the commons. It gave them time to return Myrtle and Magic to Alex at the stable before joining the community around the fire. The energized riders joined family members to form the choir, again embracing the children who stood before the fire facing the adults. They had just one song to sing — We Three Kings of Orient Are. Chris explained that the three kings were actually three magi or wise men. Two weren't kings at all, but the magus from India was a maharaja — an Indian king. Their song of the magi's journey to honor a great master of their lineage, with Tommy's simple accompaniment on guitar, was gorgeous.

When they'd finished singing, the children told the Matthew gospel story of Jesus' birth, with the angel's annunciation to his father, the kingly heir to the House of David, and the visitation of the Magi to honor the soul incarnation of a great magus of the brotherhood, Zarathustra. They charted their course with the stars, based on the prophetic astronomical records kept within the

Brotherhood of Magi. The wise men brought the babe kingly gifts of gold, frankincense and myrrh. The children told of the family's flight to Egypt and return to live in a new town, Nazareth, where the first baby Jesus lived with his parents.

Leah finished the story, with the great mystery of the rainbow bodies of these two Jesus boys and how they combined to bring forth the chalice, the Holy Grail, into which the Christ Consciousness would be poured at the baptism of Jesus. She didn't complicate the story with the first three sacrifices. Those could be passed on by the women's circle in due time. She emphasized the extraordinary sacrifice made by the soul and ego of Zarathustra to help prepare the rainbow body of Jesus, who gave us the teachings of love and brotherhood as well as the greatest service and sacrifice of all. They would take that story up at Easter.

It was then Sonia's turn to come forward and tell the story of the Nature Spirits and their need for safe haven on the land. They were feeling the pain of man's destruction of the environment and were actively participating in climate change in retaliation. Nature Spirits could get angry and distraught and cause some terrible storms in the heavens and droughts upon the earth. The community vowed to remain conscious of their needs and participate in this yearly gifting of gold, frankincense and myrrh to provide the Nature Spirits with a biodynamic safe haven. Next year they could include *New Avalon II* participants and planned to protect the land in *Harmony Valley*. The ceremony ended with the chorus of the song ... *O, star of wonder, star of light, star of royal beauty bright. Westward leading still proceeding, guide us to thy perfect light.*

After quick dinners, the Rangers were off to meet at the community center. They'd previously arranged to have Jenny and Ellia stoke the sauna fire for a ten o'clock Ranger invasion. Leah was still working her way through the Archangel Michael book whilst multitasking a list of investigatory points for the Greek Caper. She'd talked briefly with Demetri at the fire. He would call his brother to see whom he might recommend as an Athens contact. She advised he write a letter instead. She put her book down at nine to begin her pre-show ritual under the stars — *hmmm, nice continuity with the Three Kings.*

The Saturday show was a bit challenging for Stu and Rob, who had the cameras on the panel in addition to a number of Skype interviews on LCD screens — some simultaneous, with innovative everyday people who were making a difference. Paula's *'Oh Really?!'* segment was stunning for a first run, despite her level of nervous tension. She'd been heavily into oat straw tea trying to calm her nerves that morning. Matt had helped her put together the film clips to go with her report such that they'd have had a good many people smiling, even laughing, along with her. While Paula admitted to a satirical streak, she was nonetheless astounded at how regularly the Republican presidential primary candidates put foot to mouth. It was going to be an astronomically expensive, ruthless and entertaining political year. The public would likely waste a lot of time imagining what Americans could have done with all the money spent trying to brainwash them, had it been put into public programs or directly into their pockets. *Sigh.*

That afternoon, Leah laid out the *Main Street USA* plans again, this time to consider the interactions with local growers like Max and Julia. She considered the savings to a grass-fed beef farmer who could process his meat, with proper inspection, locally. He'd be able to reduce the wholesale price of his meat to local butchers who, in turn, could keep prices reasonable for their own customers, including local restaurants. The abattoir or farmer would sell the skins to the tannery, which would, in turn, sell the leather, suede and sheepskins to local manufacturing enterprises.

Harmony Valley could be considered a local farm but also a local manufacturing center that helped Main Street become prosperous through using the abattoir, the tannery, and the retail outlets for produce and sheepskin products. *Harmony Valley* would keep their dairy operation within the community and feed the community first, before selling produce and meat, but it did make sense to use the local abattoir over maintaining their own slaughterhouse. It would mean that their meat could be sold outside *Harmony Valley* as well.

Included in the local farmers' on-the-hoof price for livestock processing would be a fee to offset regulatory fees and inspection-ready maintenance of the slaughterhouse. All meat thus processed had to be certified grass-fed, organically raised, and would be humanely slaughtered. Feeder-lot farmers were out of luck, in that regard, but big operations routinely trucked their animals a good distance for slaughter and impersonal mass distribution anyway. Though she seemed way out of her depth, her interest in making local economy work had brought Leah to the inevitable endpoint and new beginning called 'meet the farmer'. That began later that evening at the vineyards of Max and Julia Cummings.

After an introduction to Julia's mother, Sophie, Max led Chris and Leah on a tour of the winery, giving Julia the time and space to put the finishing touches on dinner. Max was maybe forty-five years old, lean and quite handsome, with spirited eyes and an easy smile. They began in the tasting room where people could stop to sample the wines and purchase what they liked, directly from the vintners. Knowing their preference, Max pulled four bottles of red up from under the counter, and placed three glasses on the bar. He felt there was no need to offer them a sample of their 2009 Zinfandel since *New Avalon* was their most reliable customer for that particular product. Instead he pulled a Zinfandel from 2007, which he considered to be their best year yet.

"Max, this is divine. We'll order a truckload," Leah laughed.

Max had an engaging smile. "We'll take this bottle in with us for dinner, along with one of its sisters. Unfortunately, we haven't much left of this one. Zin doesn't age well, so this 2007 could be on the edge. We'd best make the most of it."

"Aye, a splendid idea," Chris agreed, amiably, draining his sample.

"So what else have you to sample?" Leah asked. "I assumed Zinfandel was it."

"Our initial planting was with Zin — a blend of vines from the old world and those developed here in California. But, we've continued adding a new vineyard each year, working with other grapes that do well at our elevation. Actually, the climate right here isn't terribly different from Napa and Sonoma except for the shorter season and harsher winters. This next one is a Pinot Noir. Tell me what you think? We've not commercially bottled any of it yet."

Chris and Leah went through the ritual of swirling, checking the legs, color and smell, before sipping.

And so it went, moving onward to a Merlot and ending with a Cabernet Sauvignon. Leah loved the Merlot, Chris favored the Cab, but both of them still loved the Zin for its peppery aftertaste. Max offered them crackers and cheese to balance the alcohol intake. Tasting rooms were notorious places to get your head spinning on very little wine. They moved on to the aging room, where three levels of huge oak barrels were stack in steel racks. Aging for each wine was monitored from casks set on wooden floor racks in front of the stacks. Max showed them how he drew out a sample into a glass to gauge fermentation initially and the aging process over time. He drew out a sample of their 2011 Merlot to share with them. It was fizzy and yeasty, early in its process. He advised that one could get drunk on this ferment in a heartbeat, and terribly hung-over, though it *was* fun to drink — like carbonated grape juice with a huge kick. They explored the bottling room and then the grape cleaning, de-stemming, crushing operation with the big, shiny, stainless–steel tanks for initial fermentation of the *must*, with twice daily hand–mashing.

Thus far, they'd planted vineyards on 120 acres of the 500+ acre farm, were reserving 30 acres for their own food farming, and expected to increase the scope of the vineyards as their wines proved themselves to the public. It was best to take it slow and sure.

Leah asked Max about their distributing system and profitability. They sold locally and delivered within 150 miles for orders over $500. In addition, there was a small distributor in Medford and a large one in Sacramento who handled their wines on consignment. Distribution costs were higher than if they were in the Sierra foothills, due to their isolation, but they were marketing boutique wines at higher prices than mass produced wines, so it sort of evened out in the end. They were making ends meet while steadily improving their business.

When the threesome made it back to the house to join Julia, Sophie and the children, she had the breakfast bar between the kitchen and dining room filled with appetizers — *tapas*, as she explained. Leah, already a bit giddy from the wine tasting, got such a case of the giggles she needed a shot of energy in the back of the neck to get back on track. Julia and Max were more than curious about her funny relationship with *tapas*. She took that as the lead-in to *Main Street USA*, which became a vibrant discussion over dinner, desert and after dinner drinks. Leah was taking notes *(why not?)* and asking the kind of rare questions that inspired Max and Julia to new levels of sustainable vision.

After the dishes were cleared away, she laid her map on the table for an open discussion.

Needless to say, they were shocked to find out they would have a wine and *tapas* bar on *Main Street USA*, but were enthusiastic about imagining that down the road. Chris reviewed her *tapas* as 5-star, fantastic, and worthy of sharing with the public. In fact you'd have to search the small villages of Spain to find their equal. Julia, still breastfeeding her youngest child, Greta, blushed beautifully with the compliment. She was a lively blue-eyed blonde compliment to Max's dark good looks.

One of the reasons Julia and Max had wanted to get together with Chris and Leah was to talk about the grassroots movement of local organic farmers that was casually forming in the area. She thought they'd be overjoyed with her proposal and eager to be part of it. They were working together to rotate the Farmer's Markets, selling each other's produce. That way they might need to show up at one or two of them each week rather than four, but their produce would make it there without them. It sounded like the beginning of a cooperative, amongst the market farmers at least. Awareness of what everyone was growing also spawned diversity and staggered planting to avoid competition and provide a steady supply of food to the region.

That sort of thing was exactly what Leah had hoped to hear. Max also reported that farms were being bought up by young families wanting to get into or back to farming organically. They were also encouraging more wine growers to come to the area for good land prices and an acceptable climate for grape growing. The grass-fed beef movement had hit the area around the same time they established their first vineyard, and continued to grow right up to Yreka in the North and into the foothills to the east and west. It was an exciting time to be a sustainable farmer, especially when the obvious hitch of marketing and distribution could be alleviated through the *Main Street USA* initiative. Max suggested that Leah add a distribution center to the outskirts of the village to handle mail orders and shipments to distant distributors. Leah wondered if the center planned for *Harmony Valley* might suffice and got a thumb's up from Max, who had no idea what *Harmony Valley* was all about, except that it was for homeless people.

Chris and Leah left for home with a promise, from Julia, that she would organize a talk for Leah with local growers about some basic concepts, including workers cooperatives, or cooperation in general, and the big picture of *Harmony Valley* — or maybe the mid-sized picture, especially addressing local interactions, benefits and any foreseen drawbacks. She felt such a talk would be timely and well-received. After that introduction to the local farmers, *Main Street USA* could follow in a timely manner. They also left with three bottles of the 2007 Zinfandel to love, cherish and consume sooner rather than later.

On their ten-minute ride back to *New Avalon*, Chris and Leah talked about the need to reach out to the larger community. *Harmony Valley* and *New Avalon* could easily remain isolated, perhaps feared, experiments in self-sufficiency without weaving the same filaments of prosperity through the greater community. Talking to the organic farmers was an excellent idea. When he asked her about the prison project, thinking it likely to be the most feared of their endeavors, she shook her head. "Not here — at least for now, cowboy. I reckon Ali Cat's deep desire to help will magnetize the pilot project to Southern California for starters ... and soon." She figured they'd be making the desert bloom somewhere east of LA.

They got caught up with each other on a deeper, feeling level, the next morning — the first Sunday morning without a schedule since before the holidays. There would be the *Threefolding* get-together after the community dinner, but the rest of the day was theirs, including lunch with Demetri followed by the next meeting of the wee Mystery School. As they languished in bed together with morning tea, there was more talk about *Main Street*, a review of the show, and the sharing of the Greek Caper. It called for diligence — not only in the investigatory work but also with the solutions Outreach was putting in place ahead of collapse. Greece was the biggest 'Canary in the Coalmine', *ever ... so far.*

Leah speculated on the reactions of the economic sector and its corporate-owned media, regulators and government to Eric's upcoming revelations. The Department of Justice had made no moves to prosecute any bankers for their crimes, but had fined them and accepted huge settlements, which they doled out to cover some investor loss. The whole legal system was operating on the level of the 1%. In the old days, the crooks would be hanging from trees. Now they were beyond reproach. And, she was certain she'd be targeted with an investigation. Will felt certain they'd be audited in a major way by the IRS. Early spring would be littered with distractions. Furthermore, Leah felt it was probably a good idea to assist with Natalie's interviews of the homeless applicants, to prevent sabotage. A great deal was riding on *Harmony Valley's* success. They couldn't afford delays to its completion or even the smallest non-compliance with the law. And, Will would have to be extremely careful of the law when *Harmony Valley* collaborated with *Main Street* and the outside world, in general. Leah actually saw the audits as the best way to affirm their compassionate intent.

Chris wasn't concerned about her preparations for battle. He detected no fear there. Her plan to be up front about Eric in a Joel interview was both courageous and brilliant. Leah would chop off the talking heads before they got started. Clairvoyance was a valued skill in the 'Art of War', after all. He saw the analogy between Greece and the rest of the crumbling economies of the West and thought that whole project to be part of mission. They knew what they were up against — the most powerful aspects of the status quo — but could likely get the truth out there to the public in spite of massive propaganda to the contrary. He supported her fully and was really pleased to see Yoda sitting in the drivers seat on all of these issues. *Wisdom is the better part of valor,* he reminded her, with a kiss to the forehead. *Yoda has the wisdom, now he'll need the training to use it impeccably.*

chapter 14: a threefold republic

Demetri had been thinking about Leah's project on the Greek economy — a topic they took up over Greek salad and *spanakopita* triangles. She filled him in on the guarded nature of the work and the need for a source in Greece willing to commit to secrecy until the story broke. Then, they'd get their proper kudos.

"This isn't a problem, Leah. There are many people of integrity in Greece."

Demetri, you're Greek, what's your take on the way this crisis unfolded?" she asked.

"You'll recall I was with Chris the 10 years leading up to it, and during the actual crisis. I've no first-hand experience with it, other than the week I spent in Athens with family, which was very sad, even before my brother's death. In Cypress the economy exists because our banks are tax havens for the wealthy (Russians mostly), like the Cayman Islands and Bermuda. That could become problematic as we're affected by the crises in southern Europe. We *are* in the European Union. On the other hand the great distraction for Cypriots is the eternal Cypriot-Turkish conflict, which seems irresolvable."

"I see. So, tell me about the Greek people. You're family is Greek. Why is it that many people say the Greeks are lazy, so no wonder this happened to them? I know this isn't necessarily true, but how do you respond to that accusation?"

Demetri gave that some thought before answering. "I would hope to give you useful insight, Leah. That requires me to point out that they say the same thing about the Italians, Spaniards and Portuguese and all of these countries are in trouble. The Greeks are, perhaps, the most passionately embracing of the enjoyment of life, philosophically. This crisis is tragic because they're as far from that passion as can be imagined now. Perhaps these southern nations are important to the rest of the EU because of their ports and shipping capabilities, or perhaps their leaders are not at all like their people. I don't pretend to know. What I can tell you is that there exists a fundamental difference between these nations, north and south, with France a hybrid of the two. If you look to America, the difference is even more striking."

"And, it's lifestyle?" she asked.

"Indeed. It's what you call 'work ethic' that divides the EU. America has an extreme work ethic, probably Germany next in line with the rest of the northern EU and UK in that general mindset. In the south we value the enjoyment of life more than working for financial gain. I think it's as simple as that. So in crisis, it appears the Greeks are lazy. In actuality, they were doing what they've always done, which didn't include being slaves to bankers. But, when easy credit came along with the enticement of accumulated wealth and property, it was, for them, like your game of monopoly — like fantasy. It seemed something for nothing, and the government approved it. We can see, now, the weight it carried with it. We have been taken for a ride, as you say."

Leah nodded agreeably. "We have the experiences of Iceland and Ireland to reflect back on as well. The crafty bit is the way in which the economic institutions have rubbed elbows with the governments, influencing policy and encouraging unregulated free-market capitalism. The people know easy credit, quickly accumulated debt, and austerity as the sweet and bitter medicine to swallow for their gullibility. They've been taken on a real roller coast ride."

"And in the states, it's the same?" he asked.

"You're right that most Americans are work-oriented, but to balance that, most are distracted, well-entertained, politically complacent and economically ill-informed or ignorant — a generalization, of course. In a way, the situation is similar to Greece. We just have different concepts about the enjoyment of life. Greek concepts make them look like their having too much fun, while ours make us look like we're anesthetized. The anesthesia is cortisol from constant over-stimulation, most often with violence." she offered. "Most of the country has been sound asleep, but it's time to wake up and save democracy, while we still have a constitution to represent us."

"I wish you the most success of your career, Leah. I can tell your passion is high for this project," he smiled.

"It is. And I wish for the future stabilization of Greece and a return to democracy. Greece is where the concepts of democracy were birthed. I surely hope we can make a difference," she added, drawing their conversation to closure. "What's on your mind, cowboy?"

"Not to change the topic but I'm curious about something, Demetri. Our Mandy tells us she wants to attend your magic school," he said, with grin.

"Ha-ha," Demetri laughed, heartily, "I've been found out. What am I to do, brother? I've taken on your little orphans who turn out to be amazingly transparent to the other worlds. It doesn't seem to matter to the other children that their English is minimal. They see what they have and they want it. I'm like the ringmaster at the circus, my friend. It's quite extraordinary. I have some gifts to share from my training and these two elves have many more. And soon their sister will join us. Who knows what that will bring?"

"Sissi has the sight, for one thing. Are the children mostly out in nature when they're down here?" Leah asked.

"They are. Jürgen and Zenzi have tremendous resiliency in the outdoors, especially in the forest. They could likely care for themselves if needed."

"I reckon their parents made sure of that, given where they live and how little they have of their own food. They forage incessantly."

"And well. I'm told to look forward to a very green pesto sauce when the pine tips start to grow! I'll have to make some Greek noodles. Actually, they're doing well with their English lessons because Mike is so interested in their skills. Rob comes when he can but Mike is committed to them in a brotherly way."

"He'd be getting some nice low-German lessons for himself in exchange," Leah added. "It sounds like a lot of fun, Demetri. Mandy will truly enjoy it."

"When will she come to visit again," he asked.

"They're coming to live here, but don't say anything until community approves it on Tuesday evening."

"Wonderful news. You know, Mandy reminds me of you, Leah, in so many ways. It makes me think of the day in Peru when I came to greet you for the first time — with Ramandi and Sheik Fakoum," he sighed. "Our Lady of the Ruby Order, I salute you," he said, lifting his kombucha.

Leah was blushing beautifully. "Oh yes, I remembered the wild-eyed Cypriot with the Raj and the Sufi Master. Your stories were priceless and the joining of the sword of the master a miracle, my brother. I salute you as well," she said, raising her glass.

"That really does bring us around to our discussion of the mysteries today," Chris interjected, with a broad smile, recalling that meeting well. "Shall we?"

"Absolutely, my brother," Demetri agreed. "Let's clear away the dishes and brew some tea."

When they reconvened, Chris asked them to recapitulate what they'd experienced, reflected upon, and realized since their last meeting on December 18th. Demetri was to begin with his story.

"This part of me that slipped back down from consciousness soul was a part that has a great love for family. I supposed that's why my brother's death was traumatic enough to cause the descent. The path I walked to elevate that part of me was one of the reconciliation of my desire for partner and family with the reality of my life. I can say that these children have been a gift in that regard, healing the loss of family that was a consequence of my training and my service to the Order. The overbearing rebel whose behavior took me to my teacher in the first place was the easiest part of me to elevate. The concept of spiritual warrior was both enchanting and soul–stirring for me. I worked very hard at that aspect of self and with my magician and my inner teacher, but felt self-pity in this part of myself I call the unrealized family man.

"It makes sense that I find so much solace with the fish," he laughed. "They've sufficed as children, in the moment. Jürgen and Zenzi have obliterated the self-pity. No — that is not true. They exposed it in a very conscious way for examination, and I obliterated it — to be truthful. My ten years in service with Chris, Ian and Peter gave me many opportunities to elevate all of the aspects of self. Chris, you were an amazing teacher, but also an awesome example of the Order's high standards. I took that home to work with the leftover part of myself, who was still bound to the culture. So that's healing and elevating here in *New Avalon*. I thank you both for that, as well as the powers that be, for the magic that can happen in everyday life.

"I met the Guardian once, and I'll meet him again, and he is me. I'm most grateful for the Star Wars movie showings to remind me about the way one approaches mission. I'm using this time and space to recapitulate my life once again as the new and varied circumstances bring forth more memories to heal. There you have it," he concluded, spreading his hands out before them.

Leah poured the tea, and then shared what she could of her journey. "By contrast to Demetri's life of contemplation, my life has been full of experience and the awareness that can come with that. I was struggling with a part of me called Dragon Lady, which you both know well from the implant removal. I chose to discipline her with a kind of exile, because she wasn't projecting what was to be expected of her. I nearly lost her in the process as she escaped from my field through an unguarded portal from previous trauma. I reeled her back in, but found her in a cage — bamboo, as it turned out, with no exit. So I really had imprisoned her. I found her easier to communicate with in that cage, and really had no need for her contribution to my life over the holidays. That part wasn't so difficult. She sat in her cage watching Star Wars and getting similar messages to yours Demetri. She really heard Yoda's wisdom and saw the consequences of impetuousness. She also saw the power of clarity — the kind that comes with mastery. I guess if we needed a good affirmation of the double, we got that too.

"Because she'd no way to get out of her cage, it took an even bigger trauma to bust her out — not as a freed Dragon Lady but a reformed and elevated character we shall call Yoda. When I came face to face with my supreme dragon nemesis in this life, and was free and able to confront that dragon, I found out that I was the dragon. Like Luke in the cave with the adversary he imagined was Darth Vader. My humiliation was debilitating. My nemesis gifted me kindness in that moment and Dragon Lady was released from her cage ready to play a different role in this life. I know she'll be tested ... many times in many ways. I look forward to those tests and her conscious winning of hearts and minds on behalf of the mission. This is a process.

"Lastly, I had a dream in which I believe I was conscious. I followed a path of light through a flower into the elemental world. I was accompanied by my shadow self. The test was fear. I was able to overcome all of the fear except the fear of what comes next for me — the unknown — in that world. The dream likely sprang from a conversation Chris and I were having about the crossing roads in life. It seems the biggest road is fear, but it's crossed over, for me, with hatred, anger, greed and envy. Sometimes the roads merge for a bit in life. Our job is to clear those roads, making them transparent thoroughfares of virtue. I'm thinking, on that roadmap, that the road originates in a village called prudence. That's the best place to begin exercising consciousness with wisdom and sound judgment. That really is a Yoda quality. It does not support impetuousness. It demands forethought and accountability. It sees through the veil of the dark side. Enough said."

Chris looked from Leah to Demetri and back again. "Anything else?" he asked.

"Was that shadow of me a tour guide or a metaphorical guardian of the threshold?" Leah asked.

"Your experience was real, though I feel it could have been preliminary and not actually the threshold. So you might be right about the tour guide giving you a taste of things to come. On the other hand you might have many such conscious excursion into the elemental world and end up meeting the guardian in this reality. You've still got personality/higher self–integration to work on," he replied.

"Why would I be able to *do* that then?" she asked, a bit baffled.

"Gifted clairvoyants can access the elemental world without ever experiencing initiation. Remember, you'd taken the wrong route before. You were already aware of some elementals with the bees. It's a world worth exploring for one as enamored with the plant world as you seem to be. Since you are starting in with the greenhouse work for Sonia soon, why not apply your gift to the plants, starting with the seed, which holds the lion's share of life force within the plant's life cycle."

"Right — enough to power the Atlanteans ships," she recollected, with a wink his way. "Fair enough, I shall give it my best, cowboy. Thanks."

"No worries. Then try to visualize the plant's etheric field such that you know it's there prior to the plants growth and the plant grows into it."

"Like our own etheric body, it acts as the blueprint for the physical."

"Aye, and that etheric memory falls into the soil with the dying plant and its seed to rise again with the return of light, warmth, and water." Leah was making joyful notes in her book, along with one note to investigate how that applied to extinction, as Chris turned to their brother. "Demetri?"

Perhaps," he smiled. "Maybe you can help me with my 'fallen angel', brother. When I succeeded with this step before, it was after our service together and with an influx of what I would call grace that came to me when I returned home. I felt assisted from outside myself, and if I hadn't gone to Athens, it might have been enough but, who knows, maybe not. Maybe it must come fully from within the personality itself. Leah, what shattered the cage for Dragon Lady, if I might ask?"

"Demetri, I would have to guess that it was a feeling of being less than trash — emptied of all pretense. I was mortified to find that I'd lived most of my life in denial of truth — up front and in person, mind you. I was a phony baloney, inauthentic fraud. With the realization of that truth, which was a shocking humiliation, I do believe Dragon Lady was able to free herself from the cage — maybe slithering like a snake instead of blowing it apart like superwoman, now that I think about it. However, the blow to the ego isn't enough for ascension. I believe in the power of redemption. My life was redeemed by the loving kindness of my assailant. It surely is an interesting paradox."

"I see," Demetri pondered. "In retrospect, I think I was uplifted by grace, perhaps by the angels. I was definitely tested by Ahriman in Iran. I had courage but I did feel fear — plenty of fear. I acted in service to my brother," Demetri said, glancing at Chris, "but I didn't feel as less than trash until depression hit me at home. And that was healed by the grace. When my brother killed himself in Athens, I was thrown back into the depression. That's my cage. How that fits this personality part that faltered, is that longing it has for love. Of course, the lesson is to love one's self. That's my task. It was easy in grace. Now it's work. And. it has played out that I was so low as to be leaving the planet when my brothers and sister healed me in the apiary with their selfless service, in loving kindness. I think you do have a point there, Leah. It has been uphill since then."

"Demetri, you can thank Archangel Michael, Lord Sananda and even Lucifer for the healing. You are blessed in many ways, my brother. I honor the mission that must await you, for you too have been given a second chance in this life. And I would not shut the door on love, if I were you. Acquiring self-love could open doors you can't imagine at this moment."

"Thank you, Leah," he said, his eyes glistening with tears.

Chris sighed. "Well done, both of you. I really mean that. If we can move through this with insight, there's far more to be gained. Leah, have you thought about this blow to Dragon Lady having come as the devastating exposure of self-deceit, to one who has been so bloody dedicated to the truth?"

"Nothing is as it appears when the dark side clouds everything," she laughed. "It's time to use the fire initiation transparency to look within."

"And, what is within?"

"Water — abandoning illusion along with the baggage. I must lift the dark side's cloud, using all the filters available to me to discern the truth. It fits met to a tee, cowboy. Look at all the projects we've engaged of late. They're all stalking truth in a culture of lies."

"Now that you've attained consciousness soul, lass, it's time to start dissolving the boundaries between these aspects of self. This comes with their attunement to the good and true within the tendency they carry, and their willingness to use their gifts in selfless service. You're right. It's a process with some tendencies more apt to combine than others, for example the Bee Mistress and Alice, who have likely served together in the past."

"I get the picture of initially needing to remind Yoda that he's not acting alone," she replied. "Jane is all inclusive and may be the one to manage the weaving then disappear within it."

"That's a good start. Learning to train our quick thinker to rely on consensus amongst our tendencies isn't easy. In our culture, we're schooled to shoot answers out like bullets. In mastery, we have the deliberate thinker, the wise one, whose wisdom isn't available to the impetuous amongst us."

Leah was writing in her notebook, loving the dialogue. "Right. We're the last to say 'let me consider that' because we don't like to be told that ourselves. We want the information yesterday," she laughed. "This will be a challenging exercise for me. That's great."

Chris turned to Demetri. "My brother, continue to let the children draw you outside yourself. We cannot approach egoless self-love without personal relationships. In your service to Jürgen and Zenzi, and soon Sissi, observe the qualities they seek out in you. Seeing the truth of what we bring to others, without attachment to it, is as important as the empathy we feel for them. A next step is the discernment to know when and if our gifts are needed.

"The other piece for you lies in healing your own childhood. You began learning from your teacher, Vladimir, at a young age and went to live with him in early adolescence. He did manage to tame the undisciplined boy within you while preserving the wildness in your nature. Otherwise, you would never have opened your gifts of magic. What you experienced was a monastic sort of adolescence and the channeling of that energy and your hormones into disciplined tasks, education, and the gradual opening of your gifts. I suggest that you've a great deal to learn about adolescence from the boys here — Rob on down — and a great deal to give them at the same time. It's a good time to drop your teacher and, instead, engage them in their activities like a truly dedicated father. I think you'll pick up, for yourself, a piece missing from your childhood that belongs to this fallen aspect of yourself."

"Soul retrieval," Leah whispered. "Claiming the part under-nurtured by life's circumstances."

"Ah-h-h," Demetri sighed. "I get it. I get it all. This is why I'm here and not in Cypress. This part of me needs to collect some missing experience and, shall we say, all the paradoxes, challenges and fun that comes to a boy that age. This is an excellent way to approach my interactions with the children. I've been thinking of re-engaging the building project you started with them up at the springs."

"Excellent. Mike knows where the scrap materials can be had and there are plenty of tools in the community shed. The snow will fly soon, mind you. It would be nice to have it roofed before then."

"Yes! We'll get on the project next weekend. Mike and I can look it over during the week when he comes down for English lessons. I hear what you mean, brother. I'll keep careful records of my activities and learn what I can from them. Thank you, both."

"Aye. Now let me address something that might shed light on Leah's dream and other experiences with the elemental world. We know that we have an etheric body living within and delivering life force to our physical body. These two bodies don't experience the same parameters of existence even though they share experience, consciously or not. Here we assume individuation as part of our evolutionary plan. Our souls embrace this to varying degrees as we evolve. There are weak souls and strong souls, in this regard. In the elemental realm, where our etheric being exist, there's a unique form of individuation.

Whereas here, we experience a thought as our own, in that world the thought is more like a being that merges with us. And we're beings woven into a greater whole, which is the etheric body of the earth. Navigation in that realm requires that the *soul* be especially strong in its sense of individuation. That's why we master the astral before the etheric realm. We sort out the culture and arrive at our true "I", which is capable in both worlds.

"Without that mastery, we live in dread of that world. We haven't the courage to navigate there. Without the astral mastery we've no chance at etheric mastery. We'll always exist as an etheric being but may never be conscious of ourselves in that world. I take Leah's dream to be a gradual immersion in the elemental realm, which cannot be perceived with dread or fear. I know you have a great love for ease and grace, lass, and think you have called this experience to you as a gentle way to become conscious in that realm. We all have different tendencies in that regard."

"That does make sense, cowboy. I'll take some time with this to integrate it and call in more experience in that realm. Is it possible, then, to perceive in both worlds at once, when something is confronting us here? Is that what you meant at our last meeting?"

"It is, but without that strong and courageous soul, it could look like insanity."

"R-r-right. Well, we'll look out for that now, won't we Demetri," she said with a wink.

"Is that a reference to my healing?" he asked. "You said my etheric body was too tightly bound to the physical body, as I recall."

"Yes. It's referred to as possession since the shadow gets deliciously into this realm — Ahriman's ultimate achievement if he can pull it off. It appears more as a soul loss or disconnect with an imploding personality. Of course, he can't succeed because we die before that can happen, as you nearly did, but that doesn't stop him from trying. If it were the other way around, and Lucifer's grip was the tighter — drawing the etheric body into the astral — it could also result in mental illness that disconnects from reality. There's lots of that with drugs. Sorry to diverge from the agenda here. You taught me so much through your experience, my brother."

"Not a divergence at all, lass," Chris said, pleased with her assessment. "This is important to understand if we're to capture our own double one day, and in the meantime, to understand mental illness for what it is. The soul is capable of love, compassion and empathy, but also hatred, immorality, and brutality. Here we have the two-edged sword and the bottom line when it comes to our exploration of the supersensory worlds.

"If I'm not mistaken, compassion, love and empathy are qualities of our highest brain, the prefrontal lobes. According to our brainy lady here, this brain is the operating principle within the realms of consciousness soul, where the true "I" situates itself in the Inner Sanctum as higher self. This is the rationale behind waiting until the lower astral is mastered and the soul strengthened, before entering worlds where both edges of the sword are apparent.

"Well, that should do for today. Remember that power center behind the heart. Any questions?"

"Later, mate. My cup is full," Leah laughed.

"I'm full too, Chris. I'm very grateful for these insights," Demetri said, tapping his pencil on his notepad.

"Let's cleanup then, and meet again at the community dinner," Leah suggested, gathering up the teacups.

After a joint trip to the apiary to refill water containers, she got on task at home with the wash, while Chris checked in with the horses and Alex. He found her at the table with her *Main Street USA* drawings and notes, adding ideas and corrections that had filtered through after their dinner with the Cummings'.

"Hi Cowboy, how are the ponies?" she asked as he bent to kiss her neck.

"Aye, they're looking for rain, though I know I'm not to mention it publicly. I don't want to jinx the possibility. "How's your project coming?"

"The whole concept was so in keeping with Eric's advice to Nathan to invest in people, cowboy. The project will have to start with education though. If people don't have the big picture, their personal ideologies could easily cause conflict. They would have to believe in the outcome, success in a cooperative environment, and the need to look out for the collective as well as self-interest."

"And, what do you think the odds are of finding such people?" he asked.

"It wouldn't be for everyone out there, at least not right now, but it would establish a local economic model that the conscious amongst the younger generations, whose primary concern is the future of the planet, could and would embrace. I think a philosophy of *enough* will win out over the scarcity model, which will be in full operation as the climate changes and resources run out. Yesterday's show was very much about getting it down to the minimum without feeling pinched."

"Shall I get on the salad, then?" he asked, checking the time.

"Take your shower, my lad. The salad is under control," she replied. "I do want to talk to you about an insight that came home with me from the apiary, but that can wait until you're ready for it."

As they were walking up to the community center, Leah shared a little journey back to the fourth mystery of Christ Jesus with Chris. "It's about the rainbow body, cowboy. I think often of the way in which the second Jesus child carried the "I" of Zarathustra for the Nathan Jesus child. That allowed the Nathan child to live in a space of love and purity until the time of puberty. In developmental terms, his reptilian and limbic brains would have been fully developed without the interference of an "I". If he had no "I" as it's stated, I doubt he would have had a cultural "I" either — what Don Juan called the *foreign installation*. And he was Ahriman-free due to his virginal physical and etheric bodies. Surely he was protected from Luciferic influence because his intellect would have held the Adam-Buddha soul. Adam never knew Lucifer, and Buddha personally redeemed him.

"So right there, he is modeling to us the perfected human in body and soul, returning that possibility to us because no one had ever been born without the influences of *The Fall* since before *The Fall*.

"You follow?" she asked.

"Aye, go on, lass," he replied, curious to see where this was going.

"So the other boy lived fully in the Zarathustra "I". Assuming Zarathustra to have been a fully realized human, his "I" would have afforded that boy all the gifts of consciousness soul, including an integrated personality and a solid connection to higher self. When the Zarathustra soul and "I" came to live in the pure and loving Nathan child, he was transformed into a perfected human with a cosmically oriented true "I". But that "I" was fully human, having lived in the soul of someone who'd worked hard to become realized — like us. And Buddha had followed the same path to enlightenment as Zarathustra, though he went a step further. After his service as a Bodhisattva he attain Buddhic consciousness — the level of the second spirit body. So, we have two elements of Jesus' composite rainbow body that came through fallen humanity. In this reality we would regard him as a fully enlightened human with a perfected physical and etheric body and consciousness at the Buddhic of spirit world.

"Then before the baptism, Zarathustra took his leave — his soul and "I" returning to the spiritual world. I believe that the Zarathustra child, through the good nurturing of his parents, provided Nathan Jesus with the essence needed for his brain to absorbed the cosmic mind of a truly realized man along with a blueprint for the development of fully functional prefrontal lobes infused with wisdom, empathy love, and compassion. With this new capacity, the adolescent Nathan Jesus would have been guided along the high road of development to arrive at a point, after his twenty-eighth year, of having built his own sturdy bridge to spirit. This could well have been his gift to Zarathustra's soul and "I" for its selfless service."

"I like that, lass," he grinned, as they climbed the hill to the community center, "and then?"

"When he out-breathes the soul and "I" of Zarathustra to spirit, he makes the connection between *heart* and brain that is our future brain, creating a worthy receptacle for the Christ, which, of course, he had to grow into at the expense of his earthly body. Well, that's the metaphor, cowboy. If we lived in a perfect world — and I do understand we wouldn't be here if it was so — our true "I" would descend when we turn twenty-one, and we would draw in our archangelic consciousness at twenty-eight years of age, fully connected to the *manas*.

"That means the bridge to spirit would be built and we would be bringing spirit-filled thought into this reality. Across that bridge is the fifth dimension, and the call to Christ Consciousness — embodying the Christ and walking in this world as a Bodhisattva. Cowboy, he really did show us the whole big picture of the way back home. and Steiner got it. That's the core purpose of Waldorf Education, when it's really done right. We *really* have to do it right, cowboy," she concluded, with tearful passion.

a threefold republic

Chris stopped her in the entry hall, setting the salad bowl down on a bench there. He wiped her tears way and took her fully into his loving arms. "And, we will, lass. Everything we do is for the children. I know that, and I know why. I'm with you all the way." What he didn't tell her was that her insight was a sure sign to him that she was already accessing wisdom directly from spirit.

The plan was to mix the members of the three spheres during dinner, and afterward to hear amendments to the duties, rules and regulations of the spheres and organization of them, in general. There would be time to challenge the sphere members regarding their rights, as well as overreaches needing exposure and corrective solutions. Finally, they would argue feasibility of the system they'd mapped out at the last *Threefolding* session for *Harmony Valley*.

One disparity to be hammered out was the placement of the farms, orchards and food production greenhouses. Were they in the cultural sphere or the economic sphere? They first provided food to the community, which would be purchase with local currency. Surplus would be distributed to the outside economic sphere in return for US dollars. It was agreed, after some discussion, that the farms, orchards and gardens, as property, were part of the commons, whereas the production and distribution of farm products, including those reaching the outside world, would be an economic arm of the community that should benefit the commons – particularly the farms and gardens. A committee was formed, with members representing each sphere, to iron out the details of applying these principles to reality.

A second discussion ensued about infrastructure and utilities. The infrastructure was being provided by the Outreach funding of *Harmony Valley*. Maintenance of the infrastructure needed to be part of the cultural sphere outlay for repair, expansion, and labor. The influx of building trades homeless residents in Phase II would provide electricians and plumbers sufficient to maintain and repair solar and wind installations, residential needs, and service to the economic sphere businesses as needed. These laborers would be freelance contractors with pay coming from both the cultural and economic spheres. There was a need for labor in the biomass operation, but Tommy thought anyone willing to take it on could be trained without too much fuss. The plant construction was nearly complete and would provide bio-fuel for vehicles, industrial use, home heat and cooking, whilst using all the bio-available waste of the community, businesses and farm excess. Tommy had designed the plant to produce liquid fuel or back-up electricity, as needed. Leah suggested the additional space in the valley reserved for the prison could probably be planted to bio-fuel crops and perhaps house the hog farm since no one had yet imagined a good space for the pigs. She indicated that the prison project would likely be initiated in the southern part of the state.

That brought the discussion around to payment for usage of utilities. This would require metering of businesses and setting amperage limits on residences. Cultural sphere usage for schools, the bank, chapel, security, community center and so forth would be free but conservatively used and monitored. They would establish a flat fee for residential use, taken from the HAD accounts of a householder monthly, along with a flat fee payment for rent, part of which would be held in trust as equity. This fee would begin with two week's pay, averaging 1600 HADs. During their first five years, 10% would be put into equity and after that period, 25%. This encouraged long-term residency and stability. The non-equity part would be used to maintain the *fixed fund* for *Harmony Valley* retirement, insurances, universal health care and taxes.

That left 1600 HADs per month of full-time work for living expenses, out of which they estimated half would be put back into the community and emergency funds during quarterly demurrage cleansings to cover the cultural sphere costs and unforeseen emergencies. One necessary oversight needed for the homeless project was monitoring hoarding and alcohol consumption. It wouldn't be necessary forever and would be offset by good counseling programs. They'd no idea what the outcome would be when those who'd lived near starvation were suddenly thrust into food abundance. A stabilization period ought to be anticipated.

Everyone was pleased with the outcome of the discussions, though little time remained for the challenges. It was agreed to study the plans further, send out the updates from the discussions that night, and take on the mini-dramas the following Sunday.

Leah's Monday morning included a good long chat with her favorite banker about the genesis of *Main Street USA* in her mind. Then she had the delightful task of taping two interviews with Joel for the next two Saturday shows on 'climate change' and 'megatrends — an overview'. These were preceded by their Skype session, which was focused on the interview topics. Natalie had assembled a good panel of scientists and activists to talk about climate change, and printouts of the latest predictions and conditions were due to land on Leah's desk all week long from Paula. Natalie was already nailing down participants for the megatrends show covering the economy, violence/terrorism, poverty, and depletion of resources. They had a short 'welcome onboard' staff meeting for Pavi, who liked everything he saw thus far — including Jennifer. It looked as if the interest was mutual. Life was happening at *Light on the Crisis.*

Leah asked Natalie in for one of their desk-side chats about the homeless interviews.

"Hey, girlfriend, what can I do for you," Natalie began, sliding her chair alongside Leah's desk.

"Well, Nat, I've been giving these interviews some thought, and that thought is to assist you with all of them. I think we'll be a great team and my reformed warrior will get some good training in discernment."

"As if you need it," she laughed. "I do appreciate the help, though. Trust me."

"Good. The meeting last night really lit a fire for folks. The reality is, we're ready to move and need to find enthusiastic people to fill projected needs for

Phase I and II. So, what's the schedule?"

"I've made them all on Wednesdays. Sorry about that with the community garden."

"No problem. I'm a Thursday mid-day helper for the time being. It doesn't matter to Sonia, or the plants."

"Great. As you know, this week is Sacramento. They have a full day of interviews for us from gardeners to electricians, so that should be good. Then the following week we have them set up in Redding, where there isn't as much to choose from, except that building tradesmen seem to dominate thus far. Then we're open to what we do next."

"Okay. Let me suggest that we go back to Ashland for second interviews. You can ask if they have anyone else beside the three you describe — and we want them to come for a second interview if they're still interested. Then, set up what we can in Yreka on the way home, maybe these should be next Tuesday before Redding. We start with a talk and discussion in all cases. It won't be long, but it will help them sort things out up front. I can work over the weekend on the megatrends show. We've nothing on. Then, try to arrange interviews in Eugene and Portland the following Tuesday and Wednesday. It will be an overnight for us, but I'm guessing it will be very productive. I reckon we'll have the hotel filled by then. Tommy would prefer that the builders be housed in the WWOOFer space for the time being."

"That would be great, and we can be side-cataloging folks for Phase III."

"Exactly. This should get easier not more difficult. Make sure your phone is set up to record the talks, their questions, and interviews, so we can go over the gist of the questioning and learn something about these people we're trying to help. At some point, you'll be looking at a manual for homeless projects and need the data."

"Gads, Yes!" she agreed, "I hadn't even thought of that."

"No worries," Leah laughed. Natalie was far too busy managing the present to be fixated on the future. "So we'd best take off at six-thirty, Wednesday morning, Nat. Let's pack up a couple of meals and beverages and see if Jenny wants us to pick anything up for the warehouse. Christina isn't coming back up for awhile. She's making good progress with the Restorative Justice model instead."

"Good for her. Chuck has done what he can to influence some players, including the governor, and is playing it low key in DC."

"Smart. I think California is the place, and Ali Cat and company will be the motivators."

"It's exciting. And Tommy is off to San Francisco on Wednesday to add rocket fire to the Inner City Project for Will."

"Timely, I'd say. He, Greg and Will are planning to look over the potential farm in a couple weeks. It's looking like 2012 will have a theme of expansion."

"With ease and grace," Natalie added.

"If you say so, darling," she replied, raising an eyebrow.

The next bridge to cross for the community was a really full-on community meeting on Tuesday night. The community's kids were having a sleep over at Nick and Georgia's with Mike in charge since Rob wanted to be in on the meeting.

Jenny gaveled the group to attention. She asked for any simple notice or requests to start off the meeting. Nick came to the podium with the first order of business. "Hi Everyone. Chris and I would like a vote of approval to tap the sugar maple trees in the commons and down valley past Mr. B's to make our first batch of *New Avalon* syrup this spring."

Leah got the giggles and an elbow in her ribs. No one was opposed to maple syrup. "Good grief, do you think we're nuts?" Bernie shouted out, laughing. "Well great," Nick said. "We'll be engaging the Rangers for this one."

Chris actually came up next to ask if they'd approve the Rangers helping him begin the interior of the Performing Arts Center over the winter. They could get a leg on the classrooms, stage and balcony and save some money for the community. He got a consensus vote with no argument.

Leah had a simple request to put to community for *Harmony Valley*, and that was that they include unemployed millennials in the resident population as well as the homeless. The community would need young blood to be ongoing, and jobs weren't going to show up anytime soon for these kids. Perhaps they could live in the planned apartment building. She also wondered if they could look at a way to help them repay their student loans, perhaps working extra hours and allotting their 10% equity to repayment along with what they could spare of their pay. This meant US dollar conversion. Some feedback would be helpful.

A short discussion ensued in which Will took the lead. It ended in a consensus vote backing their inclusion, and whatever Outreach worked out for the loan payments based on Will's assurance that no financial risks would be taken and repayment would come out of their earnings. Further, they'd be paying taxes on that part of their income. In the meantime, they would continue to hold a space for a Jubilee that released everyone from debt at the expense of the banksters. *Yeah!*

Next up were Will and Jim Taylor, who went over an agreement they'd worked out to trade Jim and Gayle's farm for residency. It was a simple trade of equity with Jim's donation to the non-profit at the heart of it. His equity would look like everyone else's investment in their homes — meaning that Jim and Gayle would be getting their donation back if they chose to leave at some point in the future and would need to pay any capital gains taxes on the real estate at that point. A one-bedroom home in *New Avalon II* was a fair trade for their farm acreage and home and outbuildings at current market value. Jim would run the down–valley farm. A new barn would be built for the dairy cows and goats, and the rest would be grazing sheep and buffalo, pasture and crops with appropriate outbuildings.

a threefold republic

They were applying the BD preps to the Taylors and Mr. B's land again in the spring, ending the use of any mineral supplements — the only non-organic application in years to Mr. B's. Still, it would be some time before they were certified organic and then Demeter certified on those farms. Buffalo, it seemed, were able to accelerate the detoxification of the land. They would be put to graze on the fields where minerals had been applied by the hay farmers in the next valley. There was plenty of good, clean pasture for the dairy cows and goats, and most of the sheep would be grazed on the Taylor farm, which was organic and could be certified during the coming year. The leases with the hay farmers from the next valley ended with Mr. B's death. However, Greg and Jim had, mindfully, gone down river to speak with each of them personally about the change in property ownership.

All of that seemed logical and received easy consensus and congratulations to Jim and Gayle on their admission to community. That was a good lead-in to the biggest topic of the night, *New Avalon II*, since Jim and Gayle would be doing the community training program with the incoming community. Leah approached the podium with her notes on the roster for *New Avalon II*.

"This is it, folks," she began with a big smile. "We have enough interest to fill the new community in two stages, which will make it easier on Tommy and company with the building projects. He'll be up here right after me to show you the drawings and go over the specs for the dwellings and commons. We'll be discussing additional community food projects, business ideas and additions to the commons at a future meeting. Tonight we want to vote on the residents. I have talked to all of these applicants to assess their readiness, both with the investment and the timing, and, of course, their desire to be part of the expansion.

"On our Phase I list we have our own relatives at the top of the list. Adelle and George Parrish are in the first position on the list. I have spoken with them recently to ask if they'd be able to wait until the completion of Phase I for reasons I'll explain momentarily, and they're fine with that.

Second on the list we have Peter and Lisa Thieren and their children, Mitzy and Mark. Pete is taking on the community gardens and greenhouses down valley and has a preference for a Phase I, three-bedroom unit there. Third and new to the list, and it makes my heart skip a beat to say this, are Nathan and Julie Erickson with David and Mandy. *Applause*. Thanks everybody. Now I have an idea about these folks. They would love living in the three-bedroom guesthouse next to Christina and Spence's family. That would bring us down to one guesthouse, which was a goal. So we'll need a vote on them and that house assignment. Let me go on for a moment to finish the relatives before we have a round of voting.

"Next we have Christina's sister, Elizabeth, her husband, Jerry Northrup, and their daughter, Stacy. They're in for a two-bedroom and are fine waiting for Phase II. Our last family members are Kazmir and Suzie Novakova, Katia's brother and his wife. They would like a two-bedroom with the possibility of a third bedroom depending on the distribution of their offspring. She is also pregnant and expecting before Katia. They would love to be part of Phase

I down valley and Katia and Mitch would like to move down next to them to be able to run the expanded dairy together. Mitch and Katia would also like a two-bedroom with expansion possibilities. Both families are going to be working off their investments over time with some equity already invested for Mitch and Katia and a good deposit forthcoming from Kazmir and Suzie. *Applause.*

"I should add that Adelle and George, Pete and Lisa, and Nathan and Julie are able to make the full investment. It makes sense to me, and we'll see about all of you, to assign Mitch and Katia's one-bedroom home in our community to Adelle and George Parrish, who are very much in favor of this option. So let's take time to vote on family members." They were all shoo-ins, of course. The house swapping was easily approved as well as the dairy work-off. *Bring on the butter!*

"Moving on," Leah continued, "we turn to our most immediate neighbors, Jim and Gayle who will take a Phase I one-bedroom. Jim will run the farm and Gayle has ideas aplenty," she laughed. "She is already our political voice in the district. To top off Phase I, leaving one guesthouse with two-bedrooms, I've moved up Blake and Patricia Cary who would like to be here for Emily's senior year project, which will probably have something to do with the Performing Arts Center."

"Aye," Chris affirmed.

"Okay, let's complete the vote on Phase I."

They all asked for a quick break after having approved the last of Phase I. Fifteen-minutes later, they reconvened to polish off the Phase II process.

"On to Phase II," Leah said, turning to a new page in her notebook. "We have Jerry and Elizabeth Northrup at the top of this roster with a two-bedroom home, fully funded. Then we have Liu Chow and Tip Richards with their boy, Jasper. They would like a two-bedroom as well, and can buy in with the sale of their home in Vancouver, BC. In fact most of these people will need to sell up to do this so we'll have to be flexible with timing and may have to wait for some of them. I think that's to be expected.

"Next we have the Osterholm family who have already put their fruit farm in New York on the market but expect it to be a slow transfer, making Phase II best for them. They'll need a three-bedroom home. Fourth on this list, I have put Sam Cohen and Paula Wilcox, who have made themselves undeniably indispensable in a very short time at both the bank and the studio. I can attest to Paula's character and Will is happy to stand up for Sam. They'll be rustling up a deposit but will need to work off the balance for a two-bedroom home with possibilities of expansion. I feel they'd make a smashing addition to the community. They've not come tonight because we're making these decisions, by the way. They've observed our process, come to all the Sunday night dinners, have participated in the *Threefolding* work, and have been wonderful helping out at The Lodge.

"Last on the list is Amy Donnelly. Some of you may not be familiar with Amy. She has been on one of our shows about health care systems and runs a non-profit health care center in the bay area. Amy was quite taken with our community. She is nearing retirement age, wants to take her retirement, but devote her time to helping establish the future non-profit medical co-operative in *Harmony Valley*. I consider her a Godsend in that regard and recommend her for the community. She has a long time partner, Melissa or Missy Hendricks, who's a bit younger than Amy, a gallery-consigned fine artist, teacher of art, and beekeeper. She could establish a second apiary at valley end. Perhaps we can make their approval contingent upon their visit up here for the program, or we could have them up any time to get to know them better. They'd be a nice elder addition to the down valley younger families. Amy, as you'll recall, is a hospital administrator and CEO, not a doctor or nurse. I actually don't have a sixth applicant for Phase II, but have a strong feeling that someone is coming along quite soon. For now, I think it might be nice to leave the space open while Phase I gets started. We do have the option to bring an additional family into the guesthouse planned for Phase I, though it will likely be handy as a guesthouse while the community establishes itself.

"Can we vote on these last applicants now?" she asked. When approved, with the contingency for Amy and Missy, she added that all of the applicants were planning to take the community program at The Lodge with Natalie as soon as she scheduled it. Natalie stood up, indicating that March 12-16 was her first choice for the initial workshop. She was leaning towards making all four meetings five-day intensives, because everyone was coming a good distance to engage the process, they didn't have the advantage of community back at home like the Ashland or Ukiah groups, and it would likely ease their integration into the larger community. Natalie would put that out to the present list by email and see what response came back. She was flexible as long as The Lodge was available, and there was plenty of overflow lodging in The Annex.

"In closing," Leah went on, "one item that we should be working on in small groups, before our next meeting, is education. With an influx of children, of all ages, we need to come up with a plan for the school at Jim and Gayle's farmhouse. Keep in mind that Adelle is a Waldorf teacher, and that Patricia Cary is a Waldorf school administrator and teacher. Nathan is qualified and interested in teaching English and creative writing to the older children. Jerry Northrup is a high school science teacher, Lisa Thieren is a music teacher specializing in stringed instruments and Missy is an art instructor. That actually begs the question of housing the music, voice and theater parts of the school curriculum at the Performing Arts Center. We could form discussion groups for curriculum, transportation, the physical structure of the school, and logistics of remodeling, infrastructure, safety laws, etc, and perhaps a study group looking at the need for newly trained Waldorf teachers or apprentice teachers, who could live in The Annex. Georgia, could you write these up and make sign-up sheets for next Sunday's dinner?"

"My pleasure," she beamed. "This is so-o-o gosh-darn exciting."

Leah blew her a kiss. "The other project that's up for some small group discussion is the apprenticeship program facilities somewhere on the property at the second farmhouse where Demetri and the Woodland children are living.

The Ashland group is ready to start this spring, so perhaps a barn conversion to provide them with a four-night-a-week hostel might suffice. Natalie, would you create sign up sheets to cover several aspects of this project?"

"Delighted to do so," she affirmed.

"Thank you, everyone. This has been quite a process for all of us and, of course, the building of this community is yet before us. We're going to be abundantly enriched by these beautiful people and, remember, in addition to the homes filled down valley, we're filling a guesthouse up here. I'm done with this task for the moment and gratefully turn over the financial arm of the housing investments to Will and Sam, and the building to Tommy. I'll keep my eyes and ears open for the last occupant down valley, but now this project is in the hands of community. We're birthing our own twin! I'll be very happy to call Nathan tomorrow to let them know and Nat, Leslie, Stu, Will and I might convene a circle with Sam and Paula to give them the good news. Greg, Georgia, Katia, and Christina should call their siblings or kids to deliver the approval, personally. I'll notify everyone else. Amen, and God bless *New Avalon II*."

Leah received a round of applause and a lot of gratitude for having taken on the task for the community. It had been a labor of love, which now left the door open for something new — or she could take a plate off the table. *Hmmm?*

Tommy came up briefly to give a timeline on the project with completion of Phase I scheduled for September or October. Hopefully, the dairy barn, though costly, wouldn't be overly complex and could be up and in use by the same time. Equipment would be salvaged from the present dairy and expanded upon. He also had the first neighborhood construction beginning in *Harmony Valley* soon. Completion of that project would allow the first group coming in February to go to housing later in the spring, while additional tradesmen occupy the hotel to build the apartments, the town center and neighborhoods where they would, eventually, live, and so on. He'd have local crews working as well homeless tradesmen. The WWOOFer and apprentice complex was near completion and the hotel ready for occupancy. He was off to get a good three-month leg on in San Francisco before things really got busy at home. *Amazing.*

Will gave a report on the Inner City Project in San Francisco, and the second-tier participants in the gift pyramid. He then delivered the year-end financial report for community, which would also be emailed to each community member. Sonia and Jenny followed Will with the year-end garden and warehouse reports. For the record, Nick asked for consensus from the community affirming their participation in baseline studies for a new branch of medicine meant to treat the whole rainbow body. Everyone thought that very exciting, and wholeheartedly agreed to being Guinea Pigs for him and Leah.

The last person to take the podium was Greg. He was there to organize their requests for WWOOFers for 2013 for both *New Avalon* and *Harmony Valley*. All those who didn't need WWOOFers were free to go home, whilst those in need were to stay and map out their strategy. Alex claimed to have a two-year visa, so Chris was good at the stable and he couldn't think of a reason to have a WWOOFer at the Performing Arts project, though he'd eventually put in for some HOOFers. He went home with Leah, Natalie, Nick, Georgia and Will. Everyone else wanted help, including Spence, who'd be trying to train someone for Phase III at *Harmony Valley* and keep the bakery running and expanding at home.

Demetri was interested in having his Spanish apprentice in Cyprus apply for WWOOFing, so stayed to find out where he might fit in — maybe with Sonia and the fish. They'd all done their homework and didn't actually have to stay that much longer than those who'd left. Their listings would be grouped together under *New Avalon* on the WWOOFer website, with Jenny and Katia agreeing to edit and list the postings and sort through the applicants. It was up to everyone to select and secure their own help while arranging transportation as a group to save on fetching them all from airports or bus stations. After Greg agreed to be the hub of the wheel on that one, they were done. They'd be looking at 45 WWOOFers between *New Avalon* and *Harmony Valley*. Hopefully there'd be a good enough soccer coach amongst the new homeless residents to organize their home team.

By the time Leah and Natalie arrived at the interview site in Sacramento, which was within walking distance of the homeless tent city, the two women were thoroughly caught up with each other. Leah wouldn't burden her best friend with the truth of Eric's visit, in case she should ever be questioned. Will knew of the donation. Nick delivered the letters but didn't know who'd sent them. Nathan had one perspective and Chris had the whole story. He would know how to handle snoops if they came around. Mostly, they'd talked about Chuck, their deepening relationship and what the future might bring — all in the realm of grounded speculation.

When the organizers had the homeless applicants assembled in a large room with plenty of chairs, Leah and Natalie took their places at a table in front of the group. They had access to a white board if they needed it, and a staff member sat at the door as token security. A quick scan of the room gave an approximate total of 30 people, mostly men. A quick scan of Natalie and Leah found them in jeans, flannel shirts, and cardigan sweaters. Natalie had worn a dress to her first interviews in Ashland. Natalie introduced Leah, as the person who had the inspiration for the *Harmony Valley* project. She assumed that everyone in attendance had, at least, some interest in the project concept, and that Leah would precede the interview process with a brief talk about *Harmony Valley*. A discussion period would follow.

"Good morning, everyone," Leah began, standing up behind the desk. She liked to move around as she talked and had plenty of space at the front of the room to do that. "I'd like to welcome you to this interview process. I'm glad for your interest in our project and want to explain who we are, why we are inspired to help the homeless, and what can be expected should we mutually agree upon your residency.

"I'm the anchor of a progressive internet television program called *Light on the Crisis*. Natalie is the producer of the show, and we have a staff and studio not far from *Harmony Valley*. Every week we have a panel discussion about problems in our society that need to be addressed with sustainable solutions. One of those topics has been the economic catastrophe of 2008 and the fallout from that crisis, which, amongst many side effects, included massive job loss, foreclosures and, as a consequence, a constant rise in homelessness.

"It isn't enough to talk about these scars on our society. In fact, I don't believe we have any right to talk about them at all if we can't come up with workable solutions. I'm also a medical doctor who believes in cures. And so, *Harmony Valley* is one cure, one solution, for homelessness. It isn't a handout. It comes with criteria and commitments, which I'll attempt to help you understand but, first, let me tell you who we are and what we're about. We live in an eco-village community called *New Avalon* not far from the *Harmony Valley* site. We're a non-profit community. Much of *Harmony Valley* will be modeled after out self-sustaining community because the model works. We can exist in the midst of crisis and thrive. And, we've done that because we believe that people need to begin taking care of themselves locally to safeguard against collapsing systems.

"That's what we want for you. We're not a religious cult. Nor are we fanatical anti-government anarchists (a few laughs). We are spiritual people though, and believe that the easiest way to live in a community together is for each of us to get past the drama and limiting beliefs of our life. We all did that work together and, because of it, we get along, arrive at consensus decisions, and have a lot of fun. Also, because of it and our success, we feel, in our hearts, the desire to share it with others.

"Natalie leads that work in circle for our community, for many communities in the area that are forming to be similar to ours, for some projects we have in the inner cities, and, with help, she'll be guiding the participants in *Harmony Valley* as well — and soon. We're ready for those in our first two phases of development to engage the project. Phase I is meant to get food production up and moving towards sustainability and Phase II is further construction, which will put carpenters, plumbers, electricians and other trades people back to work. So, think about it. One of the people we need to make that happen could be the person sitting in *your* chair.

"Another thing I want to make clear to you is that *New Avalon* Outreach is one branch of our non-profit that funds and fulfills these charitable projects. Our aim is to empower people to help themselves. It's to get folks like you back on your feet, feeling fulfilled in life again or maybe for the very first time. The funds to fulfill the vision of *Harmony Valley* and all of our other projects have come from generous people all over the world who contribute through our website. The land and a good deal of the construction costs thus far have been donated by generous local folks who care about those who've suffered the loss of their productive lives, usually through no fault of their own.

"That brings me to the project and your potential role in it. *Harmony Valley* will, in the not too distant future, be a fully functioning eco-village.

a threefold republic

You could call it a republic, actually. It will have three independent sectors, an economic, a cultural and a judicial sphere. There will be businesses and cultural sphere projects, like clinics, schools, and so forth, run cooperatively by the workers — you. The republic has its own bank and currency, which circulates within the community. Everyone earns the same amount per hour whether they're supervising a greenhouse or schlepping garbage (laughter). Initially, incoming Phase I participants will be housed in a three-story hotel that has been remodeled to provide 2-bed, comfortable sleeping quarters with shared baths, one laundry room per six bedrooms, a dining room and professional kitchen. First Phase residents will be needed as cooks, market gardeners for greenhouse operations already underway, farmers, and technical people to run infrastructure facilities like the solar farm, wind farms and the biomass fuel plant. *Harmony Valley* is to be energy independent, self-sufficient and, eventually, food independent.

"Phase II participants will live, temporarily, in a compound that will house volunteers from all over the world who come to help farm, garden and so forth, in the late spring. Until they come, the building trades folks will be housed there, while they complete construction of the first neighborhood and an apartment complex. When those projects are completed, the Phase I residents will be moved into family or shared homes in the first neighborhood or into an apartment complex downtown. At that point, the hotel can house the building trades people, who've helped to build that neighborhood, and the incoming volunteers will be housed in the compound they've vacated. The building trades people will then work on the business and social service quarters in town center, and a second neighborhood, where they can have homes.

From the get-go, the construction teams will include trades people from the local population who won't be living at *Harmony Valley*. They're already working on several parts of the project. That's to say that the building of the whole community, which seems like a massive undertaking, will not be left soley to those of you who join this effort. There's an engineering team overseeing all of it. We're keeping files on people with Phase III skills now, so please interview with us now if you are interested in town business and service jobs, and tell others in the homeless community that we'll be looking for those skills when we come back to interview in the spring.

"So the community will progressively fill up with good people working cooperatively — not competitively. They'll have access to good healthy homegrown food and comfortable dwellings. During the months of high food production, those young people from around the world, who volunteer for the opportunity to learn about this new system, will join the residents of *Harmony Valley* in their work. There will also be apprentices helping out, who are planning to initiate a *Harmony Valley* in their community. All jobs (and everyone will have a job) come with universal health care and retirement benefits within the community. We're looking for long-term commitment to a new model of the future. I should add that we're also going to be looking for residents who are jobless college graduates with no jobs in sight and student loan debt they cannot repay. They would all be homeless, and some of them are, if their parents had not taken them back into their homes. That will bring generational diversity to the population and, some speculate, winning soccer and basketball teams." That comment got a lot of laughs and a round of applause.

"There are a good many details to be absorbed once you are committed as a resident. This is just an overview. I think anything else that needs to be said might best come from your questions, so let's open the floor to hear them."

Leah sat down behind the desk, allowing Natalie to field the questions. The first came from a bearded man in the rear who wanted to know what kind of farming was planned.

"Good question, thank you, sir," Natalie responded. "We've already fenced and seeded acres of pastures, which we're irrigating. We're waiting to bring in sheep and cattle to graze there until we get assurance of rainfall. It should be soon. So there will be grazing animals, dairy cows and probably goats, pigs, and chickens for meat and eggs. We need farmers who can care for and breed animals, but also milk, shear sheep, and cull chickens. Those with some skill and an inclination to that, or any specific work I mention, will be trained in it. Greg Thieren, our farming expert, will apprentice all farmers to fully organic, self-sufficiency. The farms usually have a lot of volunteer help. We need farmers who can grow the crops to feed the animals and the residents. All of our land is organic and all of the meat is hay/grass fed. The chickens free range and eat some grains and lots of greens, garbage, and bugs. We spread manure and compost and do not use pesticides. If the land is healthy, the soil vital, so are the crops. Meat that's beyond the needs of the community will be sold to profit the community. The specifics of how the community funds itself, I reserve for orientation once you are in residence. It's complex but thoroughly democratic.

"One of the installations in *Harmony Valley* is a warehouse, where community food is preserved, processed, and stored. People are needed to work there as part of Phase III. Those who could manage such an operation are needed now. Those in the first wave will be taken care of, food-wise, at the hotel and the compound by Outreach and our community, until you are self-sufficient and in your own homes. There will be more of you than there are of us. I reckon we'll be purchasing some good organic food for you from local farmers and market gardeners. Does that help you out, sir?"

"Sounds more than sufficient, thanks," he affirmed.

The next question came from a younger fellow sitting up front. "What kind of future do you see for someone like me, my age, single, high school graduate?"

"What do you like to do for work, if I might ask?"

"I can do a lot of things, but what I love is to be outdoors. It doesn't much matter what I do, as long as I'm not shut up in a building."

"There are many opportunities on the farm, in the gardens, and at the power installations where you could be trained to work. I should mention that there's a plan for a technical institute to job train for specific work. So there might be an opportunity to switch jobs in time and gain more experience. Heck, if you want an outdoor job, you can collect recycling for the biomass plant.

"Now, that brings up the fact that aside from farm and garden vehicles, *Harmony Valley* is a walking and bicycling community. There will be electric vehicles for the trash pickup and produce transports, but there will be no big trucks coming by your home and no fumes to pollute your lungs. Does that take care of your question?" she asked him.

"And then some. Thanks, Ms. Baylor."

"You're welcome."

" Who's next?" Natalie asked.

"I'll go," said a crusty-looking fellow to the right. "So is this just labor exchange for food and shelter, or is there more to it than that?"

Natalie tossed that one to Leah. "Excellent question, sir. Obviously from my introduction, there's quite a bit more to it than can be explained right here and now, but it isn't just a barter to pick you up out of the tent city and use you. You'll be building your future community and if you don't want to live in one, I wouldn't bother. It's not a way to get a little pile of cash and bolt. It's a way to invest in your own future and that of the community. Those who adapt to it and stick it out will be rewarded with equity over time, retirement in a nice adjoining village and a second chance at life. I'd look to other charitable sources for a rescue. If you need to be in a big city, forget it. This place is in a large valley surrounded by fir-forested mountains. We're looking for game-changers — builders of a new way of life. We'll be your neighbors in an ever-expanding community that can take care of itself. How's that?"

"Ah-ho! That actually gives me hope. I'm looking forward to the interview," he laughed.

Leah realized then that he was a Native American man, who'd likely seen a good many years on the streets. She was looking forward to that interview.

Natalie stood up again. "Anyone else, or shall we get on with the interviews?" When no one responded she wrapped it up. "You are all assigned an interview time. If you would like to cancel that please do it now, so that others can be moved forward. With the turnout today we're going to have to be concise and spill it all out there in about fifteen minutes, so think about that as you wait. If you are down the list you can wander off and come back at your assigned time. If you really aren't interested, please make sure you are crossed off the schedule before you leave the building. However, let me remind those of you who are not farmers, gardeners, trades people or cooks, and do want to engage this project, stay for your interview so we can add your file to our future interviews. It won't be like waiting a lifetime. This project is moving quickly. Thanks very much, all of you, for coming in today. I hope to meet you personally before the day is done.

Leah added. "We're going to take a short break to get organized in the interview room. I brought some drawings of *Harmony Valley* with me and will tape them up on the white board for you to examine as you're waiting your turn."

Leah got an unexpected round of applause. Natalie was darn impressed herself and joined in. She turned off her phone recorder and pulled out some masking tape and copies of Tommy's drawings that hung in the studio newsroom. After taping them up on the white board, they left the group with the social service employee, hit the restroom, and set up shop in an adjacent room reserved for interviews.

Two hours over their assigned time, and after picking up a load of cartons containing tea, coffee, chocolate, sugar, avocados and citrus for Jenny, they started home, with Leah at the wheel of her hybrid. Natalie was using that first bit of free time since they arrived to tally what they'd come away with. They'd eaten lunch a bite at a time and would do the same for dinner as they were driving home.

When she concluded the tally, Natalie reported that they had, for Phase I, two farmers, an orchard helper, six market garden or community garden workers, one with a degree in horticulture and permaculture experience, and a second with experience in food storage and distribution, one mechanical mister fix-it, an electrician, a plumber and two female cooks, one with a two-year old girl. Of those people, two were black men, two were Hispanic, one of those a woman for orchard help, and the Washoe Indian who could take care of the fish farming.

Two of the other gardeners were women bringing the gender diversity totals to five women (plus a child) and ten men. For Phase II, there were four carpenters with homebuilding experience and a fifth who was actually a laid-off structural and civil engineer. Tommy would be rapt. Natalie wondered whether they needed to go up to Portland and Eugene yet. Leah was adamant. There were people there that were key to the markets in town and maybe light industry in the future, though she didn't know where exactly they'd fit in. That was the reason for going. In addition, it might motivate Portland or Eugene or both, to get on board with their own project.

In her mind, Natalie was going over some of the interviews recalling how Leah had used compassion when it was needed, empathy at other times, hard love once, and always gave everyone a wide berth within which to unfold before their eyes. She'd started every interview with two questions. The first was: Do you want to build a new life for yourself within this experimental model of community? If the answer was no, the interview was over. Period. If the answer was yes she asked the second question: Do you believe we want to and can help you find that new life? She needed a yes to continue the interview. If they hadn't been listening to the talk, they wouldn't 'hear' community either.

Natalie was challenged to wonder how she could absorb that technique for her interviewing skill. Leah wanted her to conduct either the Portland or Eugene interviews, while Leah observed. She'd do her best to be a sponge and listen to the recordings in the meantime. She also had some story for each incoming participant along with core issues they'd need to address in circle. For some reason, their stories weren't as overwhelmingly full of victim as those in Ashland had been. *Did she draw that experience to her up there? Good question. Find the answer.*

Exhausted, Leah fell into her cowboy's arms that night and slept like a newborn babe. Just after dawn, she found herself in a dream, in the Ashram garden, where she met Chris as she had many times in the past. He took her into the Ashram to the sparring room and engaged her in energetic sparring. She felt much more centered than she ever had before and approached the use of energy with a more focused intent, which resulted in greater power. It was a subtle form of training, wherein yielding opened energetic doors previously closed for her. She was energized and conscious of the shower of kundalini they created around them. The session ended with a lovingly sexual embrace and kiss, which awakened her to the earthly Chris who was engaging her in precisely that way, in the pre-dawn light.

"Good morning, lass," he whispered.

"Good morning, cowboy. Thank you for that. I'd been longing to go back inside the Ashram rather than into the flowers," she smiled.

"A small recognition of mission well done yesterday. You never said a word about it but it was written all over you."

"I was possessed by some force, cowboy. Is that what mission really feels like?" she asked.

"That's what higher self feels like. Get used to it. And I thought you were a formidable opponent before," he grinned.

"R-r-right. Well we've got cooks, farmers, gardeners, fruit growers, some good infrastructure support and builders. I'm not sure what sort of attrition rate to expect but we'll work within the confines of the hotel and WWOOFer compound for starters. I think I'll need to sit in on the first few circle with Natalie to watch for any troublemakers. I expect we'll have the hotel three-quarters full in a few weeks, and then start in on the Phase III-IV enlistment, which will include shopkeepers, bakers, butchers, and light industry laborers. We asked them to spread the word around the tent city for those upcoming interviews. We do have ourselves a sheepshearer, by the way. How bizarre is that! He was the first fellow to ask a question, in fact. He can probably take on the sheep farming with one or two helpers. As you have pointed out, we have a lot of sheep."

"I'm excited to get *Harmony Valley* up and running so you can make the link with *Main Street USA*. That co-creative piece will be a beauty."

"One day at a time, cowboy. Hey, guess what? I'm in the greenhouse from eleven to two today, where I'll be focusing my 'sight' on the etheric nature of the seeds. You could bring lunch over to share with me. I've got to be to makeup for *Joel* at two-thirty."

"Will do. And, tonight, we're teaching the tango," he added.

"*What?* Cowboy, I'm in no way ready to teach the tango — not even to these very forgiving people, whom I love with all my heart," she insisted.

"Then consider yourself a prop, which I'll be using to teach the tango. Sonia will pick it up in a flash, if you need a stand-in later on. Nice and easy, no worries, lass."

"Let's go back to sleep. It's barely dawn," she groaned.

When she woke up the second time, it was with the blessed knowing that *Harmony Valley* was going to be a real game-changer for the homeless. Word was going to get around through their underground network with lightening speed. Sorting them out would be the hardest part of their work.

She went into the studio early on Thursday to fill in the core of the climate change show using summaries of their guests' expertise and beliefs regarding global warming. The hour could be cut into four segments: old norms, signs of crisis, new norms, and solutions. Paula had done her homework, along with the news reports, her *'Oh Really?!'* research, and Canary monitoring. Talk about indispensable. The plan afoot was to gather Will and Sam together with Leslie, Natalie, Leah and Stu, after the *Joel* live transmission, to toast their place in the new community. Until then, there was no mention of it — as if they'd forgotten or were holding back bad news. Leah could feel the tension rising as the morning wore on. She excused herself a bit before eleven to help Sonia, promising to return by two.

In the greenhouse, she came face to face with around 1000 pot blocks in open trays awaiting lettuce seed. Sonia gave her packets of saved seed from 2011 and a few from 2010 and instructions about labeling and numbers of pot blocks of each. She suggested two to three seeds in each block and 100 blocks of each of the ten varieties of romaine, butterhead, bib, and leaf lettuces of green and red variations. When she finished, she could arrange them all on the empty bench and give them a misting with the hose. Sonia gave her a small hand-held seeder, which allowed her to drop one seed at a time with each finger tap. She sowed three seeds to a pot, as a triangle, in an impression in the pot block. Before Leah started, she labeled the trays and lined them up on the bench where they'd stay until transplantation.

Her attempts to define the etheric force field of the seed weren't especially successful — beyond feeling it, when she held the seeds in her hand. Later on, when she'd finished, she wandered over to the last batch of seedlings, planted just after New Years, and could make out a white light permeating and surrounding the sprouts. Chris, with lunch in hand, found her there and proceeded to rig up a backdrop for the plants covered with a peach colored T-shirt from the ragbag. The etheric field of the plants sprang out at her. *What the?* Chris didn't know the physics of it but it worked for the human etheric body as well. She had to laugh because she'd insisted on painting her treatment room a light peachy color and both Chris' and Demetri's etheric fields had been easy to see in there. Chris did point out the ease with which anyone could see the etheric force field hovering over the trees at twilight. *Of course!*

Time flew by, and she was soon hoofing it around the commons to pick up her dress and get back to the studio for makeup and filming. Joel was switched on about climate change due to a big snowstorm that had hit New England earlier that day. It was still coming down, and was being cheered for ending a two-month long dry streak. Wasn't this erratic weather a perfect example of climate change? They were off and running. Fifteen-minutes didn't seem sufficient, but they said their goodbyes at three twenty-eight, ending with a promo for her show. Minutes later amidst the flurry of activity that occurred after transmitting, the cork popped on a bottle of champagne in the studio lobby, just as Sam and Will entered the building. It was a jubilant end to the day, and such a happy moment for Paula and Sam.

That spirited party mood carried right over into dance night. Leah had refused to wear the long red dress — knowing in her heart that Chris was teasing her — but did concede to wear the red wrap dress, which was more apropos anyway. They put their all into a tango demonstration, still relying on the one song from Sonia's CD. There were giggles, sighs and grabbing of partners as the dance concluded. Everyone who came was in. Natalie had stayed home wanting to save it as something to do together during Chuck's next visit and Nick and Georgia had stayed home with the kids, having just imposed on Mike for the sleepover. Pavi and Jennifer came together and Alex showed up with Megan Prescott. The group didn't get very far with the practice but the idea was imbued, and they did beautifully with what Chris taught them. Chris was right. Sonia picked it up in a heartbeat, as did Alex — as one might expect. "Same time — same place, in two weeks, but keep practicing what we've done," Chris announced. "Next week is choir. We'll be working on our Alleluias."

Chris and Nick were off over the ridge the next morning with more supplies, a few repair task materials with tools, a foot boot and a pair of well-padded crutches for Trynel. Leah and Nick had a good coaching session on how to use the boot. He knew the crutch bit from his own reckless youth. Leah sent her love along to Trynel and Sissi, and hope for Zacker, when they departed from the clinic that morning.

Leah had a full morning pulling the show together and rehearsing with Georgia. She reviewed Paula's film clips and script for her 'Oh Really?!' segment. They were both laughing to the point of tears. Leah was really pleased to have a regular spot of humor to offer their viewers. The feedback on facebook and twitter confirmed that viewers found it smart, sassy and funny as all get out. *Go, Paula.*

After rehearsal, Leah and Natalie had lunch together at the greenhouse. It was an inspiring bit of landscape on an otherwise chilly winter day. She stopped home to slap sandwiches together then continued on with a filled picnic basket. Natalie was bringing hot drinks. Her best friend was still in a pensive space — the after affects of the homeless interviews. Leah wanted to get to the bottom of it with her. They balanced the basket on an empty bench to keep it out of Harry's reach and pulled over a couple of high stools.

"Okay, sister," Leah began, "tell me what you're up against."

"I'm up against a formidable role model — you. Always have been though," she laughed. "I just can't figure out what you did to those people.

They had the hostility charmed right out of them. I know for a fact, I would have agitated them, so please share."

"Don't forget, I took the Hippocratic oath, Nat — do no harm. You get in the habit of living your life that way, if you really believe it, and I do — though it doesn't stop me from beating up on myself." She added with smile. Leah looked her best buddy in the eyes to lock their souls together, reminding her of young girls walking arm and arm in comfortable friendship.

"So, here's the deal, sister. When I first looked out into the room of 30 or so people, mostly men, I scanned them, clairvoyantly. I saw a lot of skepticism, cynicism, depression, the long path downhill, strewn with all manner of charitable efforts that don't really change much at all. So, we start by telling them a story. We engage them in this story such that they could imagine being players in it. The story is full of hope, interspersed with some strangely progressive concepts that might take some getting used to. What we need to override is their mindset that nothing works, that their situation is hopelessly permanent, and that no one really, really cares. Most people, they feel, would like them to be picked up and carried off with the garbage.

"So what we build into our initial talk is respect for them. We dress down. We're real. We assure them we have no agenda beyond building workable systems for a future that needs to survive collapse — a concept they're more familiar with than we are, frankly. We address them formally when they ask questions. We put ourselves in their shoes to understand what they're feeling in that moment. That's empathy. They've had their fill of enduring fundamentalist preaching in return for a meal, and have come to believe that everyone has an agenda when it comes to the homeless. What we ask them in interviews, to override this, is what their agenda is for their own life. Those two questions we ask to each individual are perhaps the biggest challenges their souls have faced since they hit bottom. Now it's in their court. They have to heal themselves, learn to survive from their own work again, and allow themselves to feel respected. If they cannot answer those two questions, we'll keep them on file until they can, just like I told the one's we sent away. They've got some motivation to stir their souls. No one has gone away empty-handed.

"What the initial talk took care of were the ten or so people who were there looking for handouts or a way to milk the system. They were out the door after the talk. If we keep track of the stats on these interviews, we might find a 30% attrition rate right off the bat as being normal. What we can't do is feel it had anything to do with us, or our project. We turn to the remaining 70% and start sorting them out on the strength of their souls. We wound up with 14 on the roster, 4 on hold for Phase III, and sent only 3 away to reflect and either bloom or fade — their choice. Even though we had pre-screening, those stats are remarkable.

"You are right to want to map this out and get a handle on it, Nat. We'll need to apprentice this to a couple people from Kim's group, and in two other groups to complete our gift pyramid for the homeless."

"I know, Leah. So I see there's the passionate dream of the system change for one, the passionate dream that the homeless can be redeemed and enter that system or actually help create it, and the ability to hold the group in that high statistical state of hope. Can this be learned?"

"Why not? If you lack the passion, you don't believe in what we're doing. Go in and look at the beliefs standing in your way and change them. Allow vision to open. It's *the work*, Nat. Bundle up and go on over to *Harmony Valley*. Sit there, in the center of town, until you get it. Let your mind imagine it's filled with people going about their day. *Spiritually? ... They're already there.* We just need to find them. Tommy got it. Will got it. Greg and Sonia are getting it. You've relied too much on my passion. It's time to find your own. You're ready to make a leap into those prefrontal lobes of yours, sister. Your cynic is ready to ascend."

Natalie had to laugh at that one — too true. "Perhaps. I feel like I'm in a rut that began when I first embraced the spiritual work with you. It was a great rut, but it was a rerun of your genius. You busted out of it and continue to break every rule in my book making things happen for people. So, yes, I need to take a good look within ... and, I will. Who am I, really, and what do I bring to the table from my own soul."

"You are one of the most talented women I know, Nat. Don't be afraid to break the mold. Perfect timing, with Chuck in your life, I might add. He's a real system buster for you."

"As are you. I've got this all on my phone by the way," she laughed, pulling it out of her pocket. "I'm already writing out guidelines to approach the homeless, from the recordings in Sacramento."

"Good. We're going to spend three weeks immersed in this interview process for Phase I & II. As far as I'm concerned, it's time well spent, so I'll hear nothing about what I might be sacrificing to be there with you. Let's make every minute of it count. Please, keep asking me, as *in* the moment as possible, why I do this, that, or the other thing. I'm assisted with that accountability, not put off by it. When we go out there for Phase III and IV, the story changes. We can demonstrate with more than drawings. We can show them interviews with Phase I & II participants, film clips of the farm and market gardens, and the town as it unfolds. And, eventually, we'll have Stu's full documentary to show interviewees in the gift pyramid — in addition to the passionate talks your apprentices will be giving. They may make mistakes that I'm able to avoid with clairvoyance, but that's how you gather insights that lead to vision and discernment. Life is trial and error, and try again."

Natalie sighed. "This really is happening, sister. I can feel a stirring in my soul. I'll truck on over to *Harmony Valley* after the show tomorrow. Thank you, so much."

"All we have to do is succeed mightily in *Harmony Valley*. Then the pyramid will start to stack itself. Let's set our first goal as being able to trade spaces. Then you can start grilling me on how to hold space for someone else. This is upper astral work, sweetie. Welcome to consciousness soul. You might find yourself move to tears quite often as you settle in."

"How about a hot chai?" she grinned, setting her thermos on the bench. She'd stopped at the coffee house for a fill on her way home.

"Are you reading my mind?" Leah laughed, digging the cups out of her basket. "I'd adore it."

chapter 15: luminous beings we are

Chris slid in next to Leah for Joel's Friday show. He looked tired, but perked up when Joel appeared, full of good cheer and another massive fraud in the banking industry. How odd that banking had become an industry, but so it had. And like all the moguls of business the banking kings were untouchable. Money actually did move mountains when it came to the avoidance of the law. Leah and Joel had agreed that he would begin setting up their exposé by including regular updates of the Greek crisis along with some historic reminders of the stages of collapse. His intent was to keep Greece in the news and on the minds of his viewers so they really would get it when the time came. Joel was masterful in that regard. He held his cards close to his chest until he was ready to play. In the meantime, he'd fill in the details on the map of Greece's collapse.

After Joel said 'goodnight and have a great weekend', Chris wanted to look at the weather. She brought it up and asked for a 10-day forecast.

"So, are we meant to believe this, lass? It shows snow coming in next Thursday, light, and then increasing. If this is true, what can we expect of this storm?"

"If it doesn't disappear in the next week — believe me, it could, so keep an eye on it — a typical winter storm trickles in, worsens, then really dumps on you before backing out with patchy blue skies. Often they cycle around a few times like that with some sun in between. This doesn't indicate really heavy snow and they usually can predict snow depth by altitude. Look at it again on Tuesday."

"Fair enough. I'll need to go after Sissi when the first flakes start falling. I want you to come with me, lass."

"Why? What happened today?" she asked, as they shut down the computer and got their coats on to go home.

"Nothing notable. Nick reported that the boot worked well and she'll practice with the crutches as much as possible. It was exhausting for her."

"Of, course. Her leg muscles will have atrophied with lack of use, and the broken leg will be worse than the good one. That's why she mustn't put weight on it yet. Her muscles are not strong enough to support the healed fracture and it could recur. It will be a slow process at best."

"She'll be careful, lass. Trynel has a very strong will," he went on, as she set the alarm and locked up the studio.

"Then why should I go? And, why are you so tired, my lad?"

"Zacker and I had to secure the chickens. There'd been a minor breach and a bit of bloodshed. It was just a lot of work in the cold but I'll get to bed early. Your into your ritual right?"

"Oh yes. Climate change needs all the help it can get from the cosmic beings. So why must I go?" she asked again.

"You just need to be there, lass. I can't say exactly why. It's there in my heart."

Leah fell silent, while they walked down the hill to the commons. As they were passing Will and Sonia's house, she, outwardly, came to grips with his request. "I see, cowboy. I'll go with you, of course." Then she turned inward, searching her soul:

A disturbance in the force, I see.
Shifted their lives will be.
Veiled from me, it is.
But changed, it can be.

She gave his hand a squeezed as they reached their gate and met his glance with sparkling eyes and a warm smile.

A broad, crooked grin spread across his face, in acknowledgement of the peace she'd found within. "Aye, it will be wonderful to have some moisture at last."

"And another bright young wizard for Demetri's magic school."

"Aye. Sissi is full of wonder and wild expectations — a good addition to the mad Cypriot's house of borrowed children."

Chris hit the pillow after a brief post-dinner discussion about the homeless interviews and Natalie's struggle. She let him know they'd be in Ashland and Yreka on Tuesday and Redding on Wednesday, Eugene and Portland the following week with an overnight. "That frees you up to have lunch with Thunder, cowboy, and dinner wherever you choose."

"He and I will probably be down valley drilling maple trees. They won't be running until the spring sun hits them but the spigots will be in. When we see the first drip up here, we'll run the buckets down there. Nick and I are on this one, lass, no worries."

"Well, that's a comfort. Wisconsin is definitely not in our locavore radius," she laughed. "When will you start building in the barn?"

"We'll wait. I've been given the tour of the *Harmony Valley* recycling yard and am free to take whatever I can use. There isn't that much good wood since the place was a bloody disaster to begin with, but there's a bit. Mr. B's house is coming down, which will give us more recycled materials."

"Just like that? Gone?" she asked, sadly.

"Aye. Now, remember lass, Mr. B isn't gone, just his house, and he did want a community center built there."

"Yes, yes. I know. Go for it, cowboy. It will be a great honor for him. How are you going to salvage anything from bulldozing, though?"

"Nay. We're taking the house and outbuildings apart one board at a time to save the wood. There's some great timber in the roof. The Wilson's will come in to bulldoze the remains, dig out the foundation and take away the rotting shingles, plaster and all that. The Rangers are already on it, but the snow will get in the way."

"Hmmm. It often melts in a hurry when the sun comes out. You'll get it done. I love the idea of the Rangers initiating *New Avalon II* and working magic on what's left of Mr. B."

"We all feel good about it, lass. The community is plenty ready for the project to get underway. What's the plan for resident occupation?"

"Hopefully, by the end of summer, but, honestly, I think Tommy plans to work down the first half of the homes finishing them off like an assembly line. People could probably move into the first units before the last are done. He'll have a crew getting the dairy barn built and operable too, since Greg needs to farm out the heifers he's been saving for the last couple years to add to the herd. They're outgrowing the operation up here. It could be the Taylor's, Pete's family, Kazmir and Suzie and then Katia and Mitch moving in earlier in the summer."

"I had a thought about that last house in the second phase being left for visiting artists. They'd be long term, like a year at a time. I have a hunch we could get grant support for them to cover the rent."

"They ought to write the grants to support their scholarship," she suggested.

"That depends, lass. If they're teaching us, we ought to find the funds or fund it ourselves. If we're teaching them, I agree with you."

"Ah-h, either way, it seems a great idea. We can suggest it next meeting."

"And *Harmony Valley*?"

"That'll be ongoing for years, of course, but as soon as the WWOOFer village is done, we can bring in the phase II building trades homeless folks. As we conduct these interviews, we're compiling a file of those who could fill those positions. I expect they'll work in with the local crews until they're solid. They've got to build the downtown and the first neighborhood, which, as I understand it, is foundation- and infrastructure-ready."

"Has Outreach set a limit on the population?" he asked, wondering where it would level off.

"We did. We picked 150 adult residents. That's Dunbar's number — based on the average number of people someone can interact with personally — a village, really. That won't include the retirement village, which might follow the same criteria."

"On that hopeful note, I'll leave you to your ritual and hit the sack, lass. I'm fading fast."

"I'll get my sleeping bag out of the closet then," she said, getting up to give him a proper send off.

He wasn't meager with his affection.

"Pancakes in the morning, cowboy?" she asked, suggesting a breakfast of sexual mischief.

"Beauty, lass — with maple syrup. Let's do it up proper."

Natalie had requisitioned a slate chalkboard for her office. It was handmade by a local craftsman with more-or-less local slate — to be on mission. On it, she'd diagrammed the upcoming megatrends booking challenge for the next five shows. Climate change was behind her, but right in front of Leah, who had her head together with Paula's early on Saturday morning. Looking ahead, Natalie had half the guests coming via Skype from distant sites in America and Australia, but the man who'd written the book on megatrends, Cliff Ashford, would be present in the studio to tell his story along with a climate scientist from Stanford, Emory Dratzkoff. Natalie had worked with Cliff to arrange the Skype interviews with some of his respected sources of data for the book. Some of those people would be reappearing on the subsequent shows that showcased each of the four trends separately — economy, violence, resource depletion and poverty.

Leah, Natalie, Will and Paula had read Cliff's book, *Megatrend Alert!*, as had Joel, who had him on his show, periodically. Still, this would be a learning experience for them, as well as their viewers. Natalie was filling in the rest of her diagram with futurists, trends analysts from the four subtopics, and experts on homegrown, foreign, police, corporate and cyber terrorism, currency wars, bond bubbles, dysfunctional economics in general, poverty, starvation, fossil fuel depletion, food and water shortages and commodities' market manipulation. It would be a full month of eye-opening future predictions that were, frankly, undeniable — not fantastic.

Their job was to be ready for the last fifteen minutes of each show — solutions. After the show that day, Leah devoted the weekend to megatrends, researching everything she could get her hands on *and* researching clairvoyantly. Because of the time committed during the week to homeless interviews, this was the look of the weekends to come — each one topped off with a community dinner and *Threefolding* exercise intensive. Chris was content ripping apart Mr. B's house with the Rangers — snow or no. The fellows loved teamwork, with or without the whole crew, when some were busy. Tommy had disconnected the power and water giving them free rein to be the destroyers their little boys had always wanted to be. It turned out to be good, dirty fun. Mr. B's walls and ceiling held the dust of 80 years.

Chris was rapt to see the timber of all sizes filling up the barn floor. He planned to start building the first floor classrooms, then their second floor counterpart on top of them, while allowing Tommy's new foreman, Jess Lovett, to hire a construction crew to cut back and reinforce the hayloft balcony and build a code approved fireproof stairwell for second floor access. Tommy's hire in the office, Billie Holmes, had taken the time to put Chris' drawing to functional blueprints, and had them approved by the building codes department in Yreka. Inspections would be called for as required.

After the Sunday community dinner, the three groups imagined themselves to be the councils for three spheres of the *Harmony Valley Democratic Republic*. Since the whole region, from Southern Oregon all the way down to Redding, was wishfully thought of as the 'State of Jefferson' by the locals, the idea of a republic was more than appropriate. *Might as well live up to our adopted homeland's true nature,* they all agreed. Each council would hear the complaint, concern or accusations from individuals or another council and explore the ways to deal with them. Some of them were resolved on the spot, while other would be deliberated upon during the week. Gradually, they hoped to build a working constitution with a Bill of Rights for the Republic that would hold the community in good stead long-term. They felt a timeline of five years to self-sufficient government would be required, meaning that their oversight/ governance would continue until certain criteria were met, even if it surpassed five years. That was built right into the law. *Social Threefolding* was turning out to be a course in civic mastery. Will was awesomely in his element. Gayle Taylor was beginning to find her mission too. She was politically dynamic, in every sense of the word, and had taken to *Social Threefolding* like a duck to water.

Natalie had also requisitioned an assistant who arrived that Monday morning, brimming with enthusiasm and organizing skills. Her name was Rachel Brooks. She came with a combined degree in business admin and media from Southern Oregon University in Ashland where she'd stayed on after school, working at a green building products store in the next town. One of the Ashland community members tipped her off about Natalie's need for an assistant and she'd called the studio looking for the job. How easy was that? And, she was perfect. She would stay in the Annex and make it up to Ashland to see her friends on Sundays.

Rachel was an avid skier who watched the weather like a hawk. She agreed to be their in-house meteorologist, at least for the winter. She was, in addition, a brown-eyed, raven-haired, beauty with flawlessly radiant skin. Leah was beginning to delight in the millennial milieu stirring up fun and young emotions in the studio. *About time we had something to work with here,* she declared — to herself. Pavi seemed immediately able to spread himself around, however, she saw the dawning of light in shy, brilliant (and handsome) Matt. What could she do but hold a space of magic for the future of these bright young adults. In her book, this was as good for her as Jacques' Elixir of Immortality. Although, she wouldn't turn it down if Jacques offered it to her again. Chris was still waiting to hear back from Jacques about meeting up in

DC for a visit to Joel in the spring. He was likely on mission for the Order of the Ruby or his mentor, St. Germain.

Leah had a lively Skype session with Joel on Monday morning during which he reviewed her show — first rate, as usual, and, by the way, could he *buy* Paula from her ... please? *Fat chance, brother,* she'd assured him. She did concede that if Paula were found to be spilling over with show-stopping film clips and truth-speaks before they went daily, she'd allow it to spill in his direction. At the rate the primary presidential race was gaffing and lying itself along, the stats were stacking up in his favor.

After signing off with Joel, she and Natalie got together to formulate a website post for out-of-work, indebted, millennial college grads who wanted to do something to make their country more sustainable — both in terms of the environment and grassroots local living. They would be participating in an experimental self-sufficient community (with a link to the *Harmony Valley* webpage for the curious) that would model one alternative to the mess made of American values. Natalie and Rachel would work it over and show it to the staff for comments at their afternoon meeting, while Leah went back into megatrends–mode over lunch at home.

They were hauling in chairs from their offices for the staff meetings now that they were officially a crew of eleven, including Will. He'd recently hired another assistant to handle the banking, as his time and interest were consumed by the application of *Social Threefolding* to their many projects. He'd hit his stride with it at the community dinners and was officially lit up and shining his light freely. Will was into full-on Constitution writing, a task he'd missed out on as Jefferson, when smart phones didn't exist for transatlantic consultations — though he'd greatly influenced and mentored Madison, who 'fathered' it and wrote the original Bill of Rights.

Leah held onto the truth of Will, like a coveted slice of caramel cake. She would savor it privately and not give it away until Will 'got' it. He'd borrowed Pavi part–time to help him write a computer program that would guide community members, from any Outreach project, on the letter and interpretation of the constitutional law. If each Inner City resident, for example, used the program to familiarize himself or herself with the *Threefolding System,* and the governance he was spelling out in their constitution and Bill of Rights, they could ratify the law in good conscience. When he visited the sites to participate in the intensive modules Natalie was organizing, he would do a new module on *Threefolding* as well as his usual banking module. Those participating in the community programs, like the Ukiah group and Kim's upcoming group, could opt to learn about that as well. He wasn't writing constitutions for them. However, they could use what he'd done as a model. *Thataboy, Will. Gift it forward.*

During the staff meeting, the millennials applied their talents, with gusto, to editing the proposed web post. They arrived at an offer no conscious out-of-work millennial could refuse. What could be better than abandoning your childhood bedroom, or the streets, in favor of a game-changing democratic republic experiment? That and an opportunity to settle down there, get your loans paid off and work at something you love? Come on? Since, they expected an onslaught of inquiries, they asked that people consider that it wasn't near a big city, and that those wanting to build a community worth staying in would be favored. A tweak here and there and it was posted. They ordered in lattes, chai, and some baked goods from the courtyard to celebrate the arrival of Rachel, and the flood of great reviews for *'Oh Really!?'*, before getting back to work.

Leah had been tracking Will from a distance. He was discovering a part of himself he'd stuffed after his earlier life experiences in DC, trying to get anyone to behave like an adult. She could hold off on *Main Street* until he'd finished 'channeling in' new government. Give him the soil (*Harmony Valley*), the seed (*Social Threefolding*), the rain (their viewers unending support) and the sun (*New Avalon's* spirited community) and watch his mission bloom. She was hoping this would happen to everyone in time. For Will, the timing was divinely present.

In Ashland the next morning, social services gathered together the three people Natalie had not rejected on her first round and eight others who'd heard about the interviews in the meantime. Leah gave a similar talk, put Mr. Aggression in his place with some tough love, and answered some good questions before the interviews. They came away with the Buddhist farmer who would love to work growing and harvesting crops and maintaining pasture, the Hispanic orchardist, who'd the courage to return a second time, and a woman who could clean the hotel and work at the desk. She could help get food to the tables and wash dishes as well. She'd be coming with a four-year old boy. Oddly enough, they found a college history teacher who'd been caught in the middle of a political struggle that cost him his job. He was helping counsel at the shelter, so could wait to be called. They would save his file for Phase III or IV. Mr. Aggression was rejected on the basis of a looming darkness in his etheric body (shared only with Natalie).

Five people showed up in Yreka for the same routine. They came away with another woman who would clean and help out in the kitchen and another gardener who favored the community gardens but would work greenhouse if needed. He was a younger man, who was fascinated with composting and keen to be outdoors. On the short drive home, Natalie wanted to hear more about Mr. Aggression, wondering if she'd had a niggling feeling about something Leah had seen clearly. "Yes! Natalie. Trust your feelings. You don't have to *see* it." It had been a worthwhile day. *Geez – a really lovely college history professor?* What was this world coming to?

Leah led a thoughtful discussion about the first sacrifice of Christ Jesus with the women's group that night. They'd taken the story home from the last meeting and allowed it to permeate their souls. It all made sense. They didn't necessarily understand the Saturn incarnation of the Earth but that would come in time. They were eager to learn more about the Lemurian times, when she felt up to it. She promised the second sacrifice when they met on the last evening of January.

Chris was stretched out on the sofa reading her book on Archangel Michael, when she got home. They shared a glass of Zinfandel before bed, recounting, in detail, the interview processes that day and Natalie's gain from listening and recording. Chris felt, as she did, that they were mining gold from the thoughts and feelings of homeless people that would make everyone's homeless projects easier and more fulfilling for the participants. Natalie was fully aware of the importance of the data she was gathering and could hand pick a few of their choices to share their stories in the documentary, if they were willing. Leah thought their stories ought to be written up or orally archived for posterity. Some of them, like the story of the inventor Paula had shared with Leah, were unbelievable. Most were candidates for redemption. In fact, she could see a kind of collective oral library linking all of the homeless projects across the country. "We ought not to forget this blot on our history, cowboy. It's absolutely shameful."

"And, tomorrow?"

"Redding. They're expecting ten to twelve shows. Eugene and Portland are going to be big groups and we have arranged for Eugene to be Tuesday afternoon and Portland Wednesday morning. We can get up to Eugene in three hours and back from Portland in five. We'll stay over in Portland Tuesday night — FYI."

"It's good you're not going to push it, lass. With what you are putting out and trying to teach Natalie at the same time, I recommend you pace yourself and seek out a little distraction and good food while you're there. Can you stock up on your creams and lotions, shop for things you need? Natalie had all of a half-day in San Francisco with Chuck as her escort. She might need some girl time in the shops herself," he laughed.

"Good idea. There are some good organic restaurants to check out and I've been asked to give a talk to the combined staff of the homeless projects in Eugene. Maybe they'll be inspired to get on our Gift Pyramid."

"What does that mean? Do you fund them for the project?"

"Oh no. They have to raise their own funds. We provide the model right down to the Constitution and Bill of Rights," she smiled. "We'll certainly help out 'on the air' and on our website to direct people to their project, along with the apprenticeship and spiritual training that comes with the pyramid and needs to be covered by the fundraising. Kim and her friends are organized, have the non-profit approved in Baltimore, and are fund-raising already. Eugene needs folks like Kim's friends to show up for the talk, along with those who volunteer at the shelters. Those networks run true blue in communities. If the word gets out, they'll be there. I can't tell you what a difference the documentary will make when it comes out. I think this solution will really take off."

"Can you film any of the interviews — with permission, of course? And will Stu have the liberty to catch them getting off the bus, or arriving at the hotel?"

"Before and after, eh? Well they know they're part of an experiment. I think they'll cooperate when they arrive and when they're on the job, as he gets footage. I'd like a group photo in front of the hotel when they get there. We can blow it up for the dining room wall. So far, we have an amiable and grateful group of people. Most of those looking for handouts, and the cunning thieves, are out the door after the talk."

They hashed over the new staff, Will's rising star and the staff meteorologist's report — still snow starting on Thursday. She'd need to give all of her efforts to the show on Thursday, when they got home from the *Woodland Folks*, and all day Friday. She'd skip choir this round and catch up with them in two weeks. That reminded her to let Sonia know she'd be unable to sow seeds at all that week. Hopefully, Ellia could help out in her stead. *Sigh*. Bedtime.

The two crusaders arrived at the social service center in Redding just before ten the next morning. The staff had gathered up ten interested homeless people to listen to the story and stay for an interview, or not. The story hadn't varied much, except to incorporate the answers to typical questions into the talk, giving a wider berth for more imaginative inquiries. As the talks piled up they got richer and closer to home for the listeners than they'd been when it had all started in Sacramento. They were lucky to find someone experienced at helping in a dairy operation, although they still needed an experienced dairy farmer. This fellow wandered up the pike from Modesto where he'd lost his job, house and family in a job-slashing corporate cost–efficiency program. He liked the idea of a small community and a small dairy with healthy cows — though goats were fine, too. There was also a woman who had a lot of experience as a receptionist. She'd been another corporate fatality who applied for over 500 jobs without so much as a reply. She figured she was too close to retirement age, but not close enough to get social security, so lost her house and then her car, and, as was usually the case, her friends, loose relations and self-esteem. Leah saw a perfectly lovely lady in her — pictured her at a desk in the health care center, in fact, and told her to be ready for action soon — at the hotel front desk, for starters. She would also find a lot of love and joy caring for the few children coming to *Harmony Valley*.

For Phase II, they added two carpenters to the list, a shop teacher who could also build just about anything, and *(hip, hip hurray!)* a stonemason. Redding was eclipsing the statistics with the addition of a master gardener who would love to run a nursery, but not without help. That sounded doable. Leah suggested the woman start in the greenhouses and take on the nursery when it was established during Phase IV. The last find was a plumber who could probably help with the bio-diesel plant on the sewage end of things. He'd been in the pipe-fitters union before commercial construction jobs were slashed. The job market was flooded with construction workers. The problem was that there were no construction jobs to market. His was another downhill slide of a story.

On the way home, from a tiring day, Leah and Natalie talked about accelerating Phase III so these people didn't have to wait very long to come onboard. It was the lodging issue and finding some cooks to feed everyone staying at the WWOOFer hostel that had to be worked out. Leah would call Ed Driscoll in the morning to see how that project was going. The unemployed cooks ought to be easy to find in Portland, unless people were really eating out there. Natalie would apply herself to filling in her new slate chalkboard for the month of shows and see if Rob or Matt could download the talk and interviews from her phone as mp3s, which she would ask Rachel to transcribe. That ought to help Rachel get aligned with the spirit of their work and give Natalie time to think about it all. Leah had indicated that Natalie would be the one *lecturing* in Eugene. Then they'd flip and she'd conduct the *interviews* in Portland.

Leah checked in at the studio the next morning to let everyone know they'd be over the ridge to get Sissi, and back before dark. She called Ed Driscoll to get some dates for occupation of *Harmony Valley*. Ed was optimistic. The hotel had passed inspection and was ready for occupancy. The building crews had just finished the roofing and moved inside to do finish carpentry on the WWOOFer hostel. He thought Leah could bring people in the first of February, but that was contingent upon inspection and the arrival of furnishings for both the WWOOFer and apprenticeship compounds and installation of the restaurant size gas stovetop/oven, which was due any day, at the hostel. The rooms were done, with bathrooms and showers all in working order. What remained was laying the flooring, baseboard, window and door trim and a test run of the kitchen — oh, and final inspection. They'd built cupboards into the closets eliminating the need for dressers and Shelley had ordered the beds, night tables, chairs and furniture for the dining hall and commons rooms.

The hotel room furnishings were due to arrive the first of the week but the kitchen, baths and laundries were complete and functional and the old dining room tables and chairs had been salvaged. Shelley had ordered the bedding, towels, and dining room and kitchen gear for both places. Ed would give Leah a heads up when it all arrived and inspection was passed. Leah would talk to Shelley and Jenny about filling the pantries, stocking toiletries, haircut days and cooking lessons for the hotel and WWOOFer hostel.

In addition to a spread by the Yreka second-hand shop, the western clothing store in Yreka, where work clothes predominated, was going to bring over jeans, flannel, fleece and wool shirts, winter jackets, under garments, socks, belts and work boots in various sizes for fittings. Outreach would foot the bill for a warm coat or jacket, two sets of clothing, seven of socks and undergarments and a pair of boots to launch them. Anyone could opt for sneakers or Crocs if they weren't working around animals or machinery. Further clothing purchases would be made with earned HAVs at their own clothing store — down the road when town center was finished. The same would be true for toiletries, haircuts, etc. — all in good time.

Ed indicated that they would move over to finish the apprentice quarter roof the next morning, just before snow was forecast. It would be a bit muddy from construction, but they could put walkway boards down and he didn't think anyone would mind. She updated him on her cache of construction workers coming in to live there, along with the stonemason, plumbers, electrician and all those who'd be waiting for work in the shops as they were built. If need be, Outreach would take care of people before they were needed, just to get them off the streets in the dead of winter, but Ed planned to get going on the first neighborhood straightaway. Tommy had given him a master plan and he'd put the homeless trades people to work as soon as they were able.

Ed had lightened her heart. Maybe she'd be able to stop dreaming about being homeless. True, she was working through their stories, maybe on their behalf, but she was, oddly, looking forward to sliding into a bowing Iris instead. She packed up her notes on megatrends for work later in the day and that evening, made an early date with Paula for Friday morning, and left to put on warm riding clothes for their last trip over the ridge.

Leah stopped by the clinic to pick up a gift for Trynel that she'd ordered from the Yreka rehab shop. Chris could secure it on the extra horse they were taking for Sissi to ride to *New Avalon*. By the time she packed a big lunch and met Chris at the stable, flurries of snow were in the air and the dark clouds were moving in. They would probably hang there for a day or two, retreat, then hang around, and finally spill on Saturday, as predicted. He had Thunder, Holly and Cinnamon saddled up for the journey. They were off down the tractor trail in short order. Leah had wrapped herself up in waterproof expedition outerwear with a wool hat, scarf and gloves. Chris was snug in his shearling coat, leather hat and gloves with a warm wool scarf tucked in around his neck. He looked every bit the Aussie drover.

At the top of the ridge, the snow had begun to stick, making the trail mucky for the horses, although they were unperturbed by it. These were three very sure-footed steeds, Chris assured her. Sissi flew out of the house to greet them, declaring that she knew both of them would come that day. After warm hugs around, they brought the lunch inside and found Trynel on her crutches at the water tap in the kitchen. She was filling the kettle with her injured leg propped on the boot out to her side. Sissi took the kettle from her to put it on the grill over the fire and Trynel had her first hug with Leah whilst on her feet — or foot, actually. That alone made the trip worthwhile for Leah. The two of them had a few tears together before Zacker came in the back door with a big load of firewood in his arms. He laid it next to the fireplace, gave Chris a 'guy' greeting and came to greet Leah with a firm handshake and big, actually very engaging, smile. She was cordial without displaying her astonishment.

Sissi had her gear packed up. Like her siblings, she traveled very light but brought a few pieces of warm clothing in her gathering basket, along with a homemade rag doll she'd dragged around for years. *New Avalon* would be seeing to a small practical wardrobe for her time in the community.

Trynel was sad that she wouldn't be seeing Jürgen and Zenzi for some time to come. Leah reminded her that it was an odd year thus far, so anything might happen with the weather and she had a lot of practicing to do with the crutches without little ones underfoot. They went through the rehab program she'd outlined on the last visit to make sure it was understood, and then Leah had her lie on the bed to get a good look at the bones. *Amazing.*

Zacker had come to sit next to her as Chris interpreted the rehab schedule. Trynel's big blue eyes were shining with light and her golden braids, curled up around her head, made her look downright angelic. Zacker's eyes were full of love for Trynel, such that Leah felt the two of them were bound for a complete, respectful reconciliation. Well, that wasn't the right word for it. Perhaps, it would actually be the beginning of the marriage they should have had if life had favored it when they were young. Time would tell.

They had plenty of food stores, firewood, water and books to while away the winter, plus the outdoor chores to keep Zacker fit and energized. He and Chris gave all their stock, chickens and outbuildings one more inspection together, while Leah, Sissi and Trynel had a womanly chat about what the spring might bring. One thing it wouldn't bring was a pregnancy, because Trynel, currently incapable of having sex, was stocked with 'morning after' pills for the time when she would be physically capable.

Leah had Trynel open her gift, which funnily enough, was a folding frame with bedpan — her own 'in-house' outhouse. They all had a good laugh over it but could not imagine anything more practical to the present situation. In Leah's mind, she was reinforcing the firm command to stay indoors, on the crutches, until spring.

After the men returned, they all sat down to a hearty lunch. Leah had stopped at the café to pick up several loaves of fresh bread. They had a stash frozen in the tool shed and Sissi had been keeping the sourdough culture alive for the time when Trynel needed to make their own bread again.

While Trynel and Sissi had a tearful/joyful parting, Zacker approached Leah, bowing his head, and in good English asked for her forgiveness for his previous lack of respect. He thought her a beautiful woman, a miraculous doctor and, hopefully, a good friend. The tears rolled down her face as she gave Zacker a big hug. It was a bittersweet parting all the way around.

When they finally mounted the horses and started off into the forest, she looked at Chris with the hugest smile ever. "You're the miracle-worker, cowboy. I stand in awe of your generous and beautiful heart."

He tipped his hat to her and, wearing that endearing crooked grin of his, gave Thunder a nudge to hasten the trip back home. As the trail narrowed and began to rise to the ridge, they strung out with Sissi and Cinnamon between them, Leah in the rear. Looking up the hill at her drover husband, so willing and able to play his role in the divine plan, and behind him, the wool-wrapped, angelic teenager who was riding into the hearts of *New Avalon*, her mind journeyed back to Episode V just after Yoda had stunned Luke by raising his ship from the swamp — *luminous beings are we.*

The snow fell all day and night on Saturday, piling up a good foot by the time it stopped. Sunday saw all of the children with Nick, Georgia and Leslie sledding down the hill behind the credit union on anything they could find that would slide. There were old fashion wooden sleds with red runners saved from their grandparent's childhoods, a toboggan, garbage can lids, scrap metal, and bellies facilitating the fun.

After getting the joyful mob on film, Stu went out plowing in the parking lot, on the outer rim road behind the houses and the farm road, and then far enough down the valley road to dig out Demetri and the kids and give them a ride up to join the fun. The county could finish the rest of it ... in due time. Alex thought snow–blowing to be more fun than sledding and was having a ball with the commons circle, while all the residents were passing shovels door-to-door and clearing their own walks.

Chris, a warm-climate Aussie who'd been in miserable snowstorms in Pakistan, thought this one good fun — as did the horses, who galloped around the paddocks kicking up snow in white clouds around them. In the quiet of the dairy, on the hill behind the barn, and in the community garden office, Mitch, Katia, Greg, Ellia and Sonia lit sage and sweet grass offerings and prayers of thanksgiving on the community's behalf for Mother Earth's long-awaited gift of moisture.

Leah and Chris put on snowshoes and grabbed shovels to journey across the field, through the oak grove and down the hill to the apiary. They cleared the gate, dug out the hives and made sure the bees had water. The singing of the river and roar of the bees in cluster broke the hushed silence of a pristine winter day.

The Saturday show had been perfect in spite of the fact that Leah had chopped up her workweek but good. The community, very interested in megatrends, watched the rerun on Sunday afternoon *en masse*. They went on to have an especially nurturing community dinner, officially welcomed Sissi to the fold, and continued on exploring the nuances of *Threefolding* with their intrepid, inspiring leader, Will Martin. The following week they were scheduled to discuss and come to consensus about the Constitution and Bill of Rights that he'd put in each of their amazed hands.

Leah had used the weekend wisely, laying the groundwork for the 'megatrends in economics' theme for the coming Saturday show — January 28th. Will would co-host with her and, with Paula, was organizing the core of it, whilst she and Natalie traveled north for interviews. The show would touch on the good, the bad, and the ugly in the economic world, with ideas to rebuild economies for all the people. Monday found her taping two more interviews with Joel and filling in the gaps in the show outline with Paula.

To prepare for the trip, Leah and Natalie composed a wish list of missing skills for Phase I & II at *Harmony Valley*. The dairy farmer was on the top of the list followed by one more gardener and another plumber — requested by Ed. Looking ahead to Phase III, they asked for help with small businesses, warehousing, a baker, butcher, someone for the bank, nursery, and a lead-in for light industry, leaving exactly what that looked like to the Divine Plan. They built a crystal grid in the newsroom under Tommy's framed drawings, and set it with the intent for *Harmony Valley's* highest good.

The girls were on the road again before seven o'clock on Tuesday morning, this time in Natalie's four-wheel drive wagon — ready for possible snow on the mountain passes. Leah had her laptop with the *Harmony Valley* presentation sporting updated photos of the hotel, construction on the hostels, town center, and the foundation of the first neighborhood plus a slide with current stats on their growing homeless participants. Stu and Matt had worked like beavers to polish it up on Monday. She and Natalie both had cost projections on their phones from Will, should fundraisers show up at her talk that evening.

Natalie could feel Leah holding the space for her as she got up to give the Eugene introductory talk to a group of twelve homeless people, two of whom were women. Natalie was certain she hadn't missed anything when it came time for Leah to field questions. The talk now ventured into small business and trades involving food and its distribution, as well as building trades. Their coordinators at social services had expanded the list when putting it out to the homeless community as well. The questions ranged from living quarter specifics, what kinds of people were participating, and what sort of medical care was planned, to whether job training was included for diversifying skills. The energy was definitely rising.

Everyone stayed for interviews, curious to see if they could find a place for themselves at *Harmony Valley*. And, many of them did. Over dinner at a cooperative café in downtown Eugene, she and Natalie tallied up the long-awaited dairy farmer who came with a wife eager to help with the goats, and a boy of fourteen who knew his way around a barn. They'd also added another plumber to the trades and a green grocer who would start in the greenhouses and move to run the food market in town, when it was finished.

For Phase III, they'd a young fellow whose whole life revolved around bike repair (*why not?*), and a nurse who'd — sadly for her community — lost her job to state budget cuts at an early childhood health project. Leah was shocked to see a medical professional amongst the homeless, though glad that she'd come forward. She was suffering from manageable depression. A second woman had the experience to help run the nursery and landscaping operation with the woman from Redding. The real bonanza came with a pair of butchers. They actually knew each other and had both been laid off from different stores in a grocery chain bankruptcy — the result of a huge money absconding scandal in the front office. One of them had experience with smoking and curing meat. Counting the teenager, that was ten out of twelve — a lucky day, indeed.

Returning for the talk about the homeless model, they found a good crowd waiting, including people from Portland who'd driven down to hear it. It wasn't a long talk but the questions filled out the evening. Leah was quite taken with a bright young couple standing against the back wall, holding hands. They came up to talk to her after the crowd had thinned out. The young woman stirred something deep within Leah's heart.

"Glad you two came tonight," she said, reaching out to shake their hands. "Do I know you?" she asked the woman. "You look and feel so familiar." The young, red-head smiled, and magically beautiful dimples showed up on her freckled-face. Her green eyes sparkled.

"You'd know my mother, Ms. Erickson. Both of our mothers worked with you in Seattle years ago. It's because of you that Jake and I know and love each other, and that we both went to the same Waldorf School growing up. Thank you for that. I'm Abby McPherson, my mother's name is Suzie."

"I do remember her. Bless your souls." Leah was taken aback at the reference to Waldorf education. It had been years ago ... yet she'd had, at least, her little toe in the Steiner stream back then. *Remarkable.* "And what is your story?" she asked turning to her partner.

"I'm Jake Lawson, and my mom is Mary Edwards. Pleased to meet you."

"I remember both of your mothers. They came to an intro workshop as I recall, but they didn't continued on with the course. I actually recollect feeling sad that they hadn't returned at our second meeting — such bright lights."

"They didn't need to," Abby laughed, eyes sparkling. "You changed their lives in one weekend. We're living proof of that."

"That you are. Now, tell me what you're doing here. Have you an interest in helping the homeless? Do you work in social services?" she asked, as Natalie came up to join them.

"We were both raised to serve and care deeply about the homeless," she began. "We're also an unemployment check away from being on the streets ourselves, unless we're to go home. My mom watches your show and keeps pretty good track of your projects. She saw the web post for millennials to be part of *Harmony Valley* and called the studio. She spoke with someone named Jennifer, who told her about your interviews and this talk. Mom then told me to *shag my ass down here,* to use her exact words," she laughed.

"Where do you live and what were you doing before unemployment?" Leah asked, fascinated with the way their story was unfolding.

Jake spoke up for them. He was a lovely looking fellow with thick dark hair, pushed straight up off his forehead, kind blue eyes and cheeks blushing with health. "We had a dream of our own restaurant, all organic and biodynamic, with a really folksy atmosphere. Of course, Portland is full of good restaurants and startup costs are as daunting as the competition. We both graduated from the Culinary Academy in Portland, had jobs for a year or so, but eating out is way down in this recession and the newer you are the harder it is to hold a job. We have sizeable student loans, to be honest, and really want to establish ourselves in a nice place to raise kids someday."

"I see. Chefs, are you?"

"Oh yes. We've got our diplomas and our knives to prove it," she chimed in, "just no work. We both feel strongly about service and think your community has the right idea with all of your projects. I'm not sure *Harmony Valley* is the right place for us, but the offer sounds interesting and we can pack up and be there in a heartbeat. Would you give us a try?" she asked.

Leah's eyes had glazed over listening to her. She actually saw them with a very popular restaurant at the round-a-bout on *Main Street USA* — *Well, wonders never cease!* "Listen, you two, call your mothers and tell them how very grateful I am that we've made this connection. I'd be honored if you'd bring your talents to *Harmony Valley* to help us train cooks and do some cooking yourselves. We have two kitchens to staff and an idea for a light industry in food preparation — like lacto-fermented foods, biodynamic fruit products and so forth. Does that appeal?"

They both nodded, with broad smiles. "Are you sure you want to mingle with those we're taking up off the street?" she asked.

"We're *so* sure we're going to come mingle with them in the morning, when you interview in Portland," Jake laughed. "We want to hear more and see what kind of questions the homeless people ask. Is that okay?"

"It's fabulous. We'll see you there, then?"

"You bet," they replied together. They shook hands with Natalie and Leah, and then walked out of the room hugging each other.

When they got to their hotel in Portland, Natalie and Leah had a glass of red together in the bar to celebrate the serendipitous magic of life.

Chris checked in with Leah early the next morning. He loved the story and wished them as much or greater success with the Portland interviews. Portland was very well organized in terms of homeless shelters, soup kitchens and rehab programs. For that reason the group was streamlined to their needs. Natalie conducted the interviews with great compassion and discernment. With the Phase I quota already filled, the only people they let go would have been best in some of those positions. They would keep their files in case of attrition, and, otherwise, nearly filled up Phase II; adding two more carpenters, a married couple with experience appropriate to the warehouse, and a baker (*by golly*). Also in the tally were a bank manager and teller, from a swallowed-up regional bank. They'd been on the streets for three years. And, lastly, they found a younger man who worked leather into beautiful art that just wasn't selling. He reckoned he could figure out shoe and boot repair then expand into belts, jackets and, well, whatever — maybe even learn the true, vanishing art of cobbling. Leah's *Main Street* vision was touched once again.

Jake and Abby had come for the talk, stayed for the questions, and had left Leah and Natalie with the best lunch in either of their memories — compliments of the chefs. Jennifer had their contact details and they'd come when they were called, bringing their knives with them.

Jubilation ruled on the ride home. Phase III was sold out, and Phase IV too far in the future to think about presently. They began the journey home at three o'clock that afternoon, stopped briefly at an outlet shopping mall, and took turns driving and checking in at the studio. One of Saturday's Skype interviews had to bow out with the flu, causing Natalie an hour or so of work on the phone to nail down an alternate. Joel had sent Leah an email with the live interview questions for Thursday and the weather cam on Siskiyou Pass indicated an all clear passage out of Oregon and into California. As they came over that pass and around the bend, the moonlit peaks of Mount Shasta took their breath away. They clasped hands with the certainty that there was no turning back from destiny now. Every day would be a challenge in *Harmony Valley*, until the day it wasn't. And then it would be self-sustaining magic.

On February 5th, 2012, at three in the afternoon, a social services bus originating in Portland, Oregon pulled up to the edge of the paved walking mall in *Harmony Valley* delivering the Phase I, Phase II, and a few Phase III homeless people from Yreka, Ashland, Eugene and Portland to their new home for orientation. They took their last walk as homeless Americans down a short stretch of street that would soon be filled with businesses and services to support and, possibly, employ them. They came with very little, besides hope, and respectfully gathered together in front of the hotel for an arrival photo, before stepping into the hotel. Jake and Abby, who'd hopped off the bus first, and those in the building trades, would be shuttled down the service road to their rooms in the WWOOFer hostel after everyone got their bearings, heard an intro talk and picked up needed new clothes.

In addition to the stuffed chairs and sofas, the parlor had been filled with rows of dining room chairs where they sat down to listen to some instructions about the rest of the first day of their new lives. Leah and Natalie were there to welcome them, and introduce them to Shelley, Stu, Ellia, Nick and Chris who'd come to help out. The dining room tables were stacked with new and secondhand blue jeans, shirts, heavy sweaters warm vests, and parkas, as well as undergarments, socks, boots and a nondescript, zippered case filled with personal items. The idea was to find the right size for all the clothes they needed, and if there weren't enough to go around, or their size wasn't there at all, the store and op-shop personnel would see that something was delivered to the hotel within several days.

Natalie began with logistics — like the location of the two toilets off the hall in the lobby. She had building rosters of roommates and informed them that the bus from Sacramento would be bringing the rest of the initial participants, from the southern locations, the next day. Orientation would be repeated for that group. Some of their roommates would arrive then. Roommates could be swapped by mutual agreement after they got to know each other better, but the staff needed to have changes on the record books to be able to locate people. So, please inform. For the next three or four days, they were to get comfortable, rest and eat well, get to know each other, and explore the town — allowing for vision in that regard. The first neighborhood, rising around a commons adjacent to the back of the hotel, was being framed in right now. With the arrival of a good many tradesmen, it wouldn't take long to finish. Then they would begin the apartment building and second neighborhood followed by the food warehouse and the businesses at town center.

When their discarded clothes were ready for the trash, they could be stuffed in the barrel down the hall beyond the toilets, *please*. After orientation, they would be taken upstairs or down the road to their rooms. They'd be shown the laundry on their floor where there was a spare toilet room attached. They were expected at dinner in their respective dining rooms at six sharp, all cleaned up. Shared bathroom arrangements in the hotel could be discussed with those in the adjacent room. They were asked to respect the brand new bedding and towels by using the soap provided, lavishly. Shelley would show up every day at nine in the morning to begin giving haircuts to those who signed up for them. They needed to have their hair washed and combed out for her. They could sign the sheet on the lobby desk to make an appointment. If they wanted to cut their beard or had a lot to shave off trimming them, Shelley would do that for them to avoid clogging the sink drains. If they had lice, she recommended shaving their heads over the medical treatment. Shelley would take care of head infestations behind the hotel as soon as the talk was over. Everyone had a safety razor in their personal zipper bag to get them going, along with shaving cream, hair and hand brushes, combs, lotion, after shave, toothbrushes and toothpaste. All sinks and showers had soap and shampoo dispensers and on-demand hot water systems to avoid cold showers at peak hours — like now. After everyone was settled in, they would establish a person at the desk, who could call *New Avalon* for assistance, and rotating in-house floor monitors from amongst them, who could make sure everything was going well.

Natalie asked for a show of hands from meat-eaters and vegetarians. They thought that was funny since they'd all been in some dodgy situations with food. "No tin cans here," she cheerfully announced. "All the food you'll be given is fresh, cooked just for you, locally grown, healthy as all get out, and nourishing to the max. The meat is all grass-fed and homegrown or local. Your most important task is to rebuild your body so that you can put it to useful work in community. The best way to do that is with adequate rest, exercise and good food, along with drinking at least a gallon of water a day to flush out the past and prevent dehydration. Make sure you leave a little extra room in the jeans you pick out for a few extra pounds."

She explained that after the three days of energy restoration from physical hardship, work would be gradually introduced until they were fully functional. If they weren't ready for their skill, they'd be put to work somewhere. She would be back with Ellia to begin their sharing circle later in the week. Some of the *New Avalon* women would work alongside the cooks and assistants in both kitchens, sharing spiritual insights and helping them with their stories. In a few weeks, the men would meet in a separate circle with the *New Avalon Rangers*. She introduced Chris as the men's group leader, Nick as a natural doctor and chiropractor on call for them, and Stu as the one who would be documenting their story to help other homeless people across the country find community and meaning in life again. She explained that Stu might like to interview individuals who were willing to share their story on film. Some residents would be riding a shuttle bus over to *New Avalon* to apprentice work. Likewise, people from *New Avalon* would be coming to *Harmony Valley* on a regular basis to help out, answer questions, and see that they had what they needed. Those in need of chiropractic or medical care would take a regular shuttle bus to the *New Avalon* courtyard for their clinic appointments.

If such a time came that they wanted to contact family or friends to say hello, or to let them know they were okay, or to inquire about the wellbeing of others, they were to ask to use a phone. Otherwise it was best to form community here and to be here for each other. As the building of the town progressed, there would be a community center right across the street for gatherings, movie nights, and dinners with the whole community. For now, they'd make do with the two dwelling spaces, the farms, and market gardens, which any of them could wander down and tour whenever their curiosity got the better of them. On that light note, Natalie assigned Chris to the third floor occupants, Nick to the second floor occupants and Stu, who had the van, to those living in the hostel down the service road. The cook with the two-year old and the cleaning woman with the four-year old would be taking the room with the bunk beds, next to the kitchen and at the end of the lobby hall.

While the homeless were selecting clothing, Stu ran Jake and Abby, and their backpacks, down to the hostel where Jenny was waiting to show them their rooms, the commons, baths and the kitchen. They would start cooking there, so as not to split them up right away. Then as they became comfortable with the situation, they'd pair up with one of the hotel cooks to upgrade their short order skills. In the meanwhile, Shelley would be in the hotel kitchen helping the cooks make the meals. Both kitchens had female assistants, from the homeless participants, who doubled as servers/dishwashers and cleaning crew.

It was a chaotic, noisy scene while the clothes were requisitioned. The personnel from the Yreka Mercantile and the Yreka second-hand shop— their stores closed on Sundays — had brought all of their stock and pretty much had everyone clothed — save for a few boots of common sizes that would be forthcoming. Then the newcomers found themselves on the room rosters and waited for the others on their floor before they were led up to tour the facilities and claim their room. If they hadn't a roommate that night, they would the next night. The hotel was fully booked.

At dinner, the food was laid out buffet style in the dining room where the tables and chairs had been returned to service. Likewise, the dinner was served from a sideboard in the community dining room down the road. Everyone (a good many bald) went to bed with full bellies, clean sheets and blankets, adequate heat, peace and quiet, a private toilet nearby, and an imperceptible stirring in their souls.

Over in *New Avalon* the community dinner had been cancelled since many in the community were in service to the homeless. Stu dropped Ellia, Chris, Leah, Natalie and Shelley at their back gates, and he and Nick walked home together from the parking garage. Natalie and Leah had a really long hug, while Chris stoked the boiler. Then, they went their respective ways to enjoy dinners prepared by those who'd stayed behind — and a much–deserved rest. Leah and Chris unwound after dinner with a glass of their very special

Zinfandel, which did remind one of the nectar of the gods. She was near to a stupor — sitting there staring at the glass.

"A job well done, lass. We've a nice group of men and women to work with over there."

"I'm filled to the brim with their stories, cowboy. I've got to clean my slate while they do the same," she said, her fatigue palpable.

"I expect you will, after tomorrow's group is settled. These are their days of redemption. Your vision called it in for them, now you've got to hold it until they rise again."

"You're right, of course," she sighed. "How did they react to their rooms?"

"A few teary eyes, a backslap or two, but not a question asked. I guess you'd call that gratitude. I think most will be out exploring in the morning. They're eager for a new life, not handouts with dead ends."

"It sure was good to see the WWOOFer hostel and apprentice lodge done and the housing going up. That does give me hope. In fact, it's been miraculously fast. I'll ask Alice and Burt to come over to see their old hotel holding ground zero for the whole effort. What did you think of Jake and Abby?"

"Aye, great kids, those two. I hope to sit regularly with you in their restaurant one day, looking out on the bustle of *Main Street USA* — could be a nice Saturday night ritual for us."

Leah smiled, raising her glass of Zinfandel ... ready, at last, to imbibe the god's nectar. "I'll drink to that, cowboy. Cheers!"

Though the Mercantile had pulled some stock back onto their store floor, the next day was a duplicate of the day before. By the end of the day, all the hostel and hotel rooms were full and all the new residents were fed, clean and soundly asleep. A few from the first wave admitted it was difficult to let go of the watchfulness one needed on the street, or in shelters, when trying to sleep, but had quit struggling in the middle of the night to sleep well beyond breakfast.

On Monday a shuttle bus began operating between the two communities. To begin with, most of the *Harmony Valley* bus riders were seeking medical or chiropractic attention. Leah knew what to expect from their interviews, and had stocked needed sundries and medications to take care of immediate needs. Nick was the busy one, trying to iron out the kinks in bodies that had slept on the street. He'd be busy for some time to come as word got around and folks returned for second, third and further treatments. He wanted every one of them colon cleansing by the following week and that was just a start.

Nick used natural herbal meds and consulted with Leah as to how they could favor those over pharmaceuticals. She was all for it, but had needed to address some sorely unattended infections with a wallop. They teamed up to begin filling in whole rainbow body medical charts for their patients as they continued getting baseline data from their community. Leah brought Sissi in to observe, and assist the formerly homeless nurse, a black woman, fortuitously named Patience, who was working mornings in the clinic and afternoons at the hotel. Before long, Patience would be handling intakes, and a good many minor and triage appointments on her own. It was a researcher's dream-come-true, in that regard.

Soon the shuttle bus was carrying over those who would learn their jobs in *New Avalon*. That included Sid and Grace who would run the warehouse and learn the ropes helping Jenny and Bernie. The bank manager, Nel Freeman, was coming over to learn the local currency banking from Will and Jess, his new hire. Once Nel learned the program they'd been creating for HAVs on the *New Avalon* model, Will, Jess and Nel would train the residents about their personal accounting in the hotel parlor and dining room and Will would give them an overview of how local currency could served them. Until they got everyone stabilized, mornings would be intense for all of those training the *Harmony Valley* apprentices.

Also coming over was Ken Jones, the Washoe Indian, who was being tutored in the fine art of happy fish farming by Demetri. They took an immediate liking to each other — having serious fun from the get-go. Greg had the stock farmers over to work with him, since he wasn't going to buy cattle or shift sheep or pigs until they had bone fide green pastures from rain to graze on at *Harmony Valley*. The Buddhist crop farmer, Virgil Prest, was getting the lay of the land in *Harmony Valley*, checking fences, irrigating pasture as needed and sorting through the seed and feed rooms in the barn. Greg paid a visit three times a week to go over plans with him and assign some tasks in a gradual shift of responsibilities.

Their sheep farmer/shearer, Rick Crystal, who'd be taking care of the chickens as well, was over to see the *New Avalon* operation. Ellia was doubtful they'd need the electrical fortress chicken yard, since bears and mountain lions rarely trekked across open land from the mountains. They were setup for protection against small night predators like foxes, raccoons and wild dogs. She and Greg both cautioned Rick about poaching, and the odd mountain lion picking off young lambs on the periphery. In addition to the alpacas in with the flock, he'd want to rotate paddocks for ewes with nursing lambs closer to the community and watch his stock counts like a hawk.

John and Bernice Huffman, the dairy farmers, were over early everyday to work with Mitch. Katia was supervising from the sidelines — good timing for baby and for the calving and kidding season, which was in full swing. This couple was delighted to be back in a dairy barn again, she with the Nubian goats, and he with the Jerseys, which is what they'd be herding over in *Harmony Valley*. Joe, their serious-minded, 14-year-old who'd missed a few years of schooling, was sitting in with the older boys at Georgia's Waldorf homeschool, and helping out on weekends. Because there were few children with the homeless, they would almost certainly be brought into the growing *New Avalon* School, and shuttled back and forth with other residents, for the time being.

Sonia split her time between the two communities guiding the building of soil, sowing of seed, and transplanting of veggies in the greenhouses and community gardens. Brassicas she'd seeded in both community gardens were up and leafing out — loving the cool weather, and both greenhouse operations were full of leafy greens and starts for a good many other veggies. There was a lot less snow in *Harmony Valley* and *New Avalon's* snow melted quickly. In fact, it could be said that spring was in the air with all the force of rebirth it engendered.

For Leah, the clinic duty meant short lunches, heavy afternoon work at the studio, and additional work at night on the show. Interruptions were nonstop as *Harmony Valley* settled in, but they agreed to share that responsibility between the bank, clinic and studio and call on Leah only when it was a medical issue or ideation beyond the stretch of Natalie's blossoming imagination. One of the offices in the courtyard was turned into a shuttle drop-off and pickup station, with a coffee and biscuit table that was continually serviced by the coffee shop. Over the first two weeks of their occupancy, they noticed the residents beginning to smile — hearts were lifting.

This was Natalie and Ellia's cue to get the sharing circles going. They would take as long as was needed to work through the life stories of these people in two circles — one at each residence, one half-day at a time. In time, they would bring them together into one circle and step up the work of clearing the past — conscious of the gifts it had given. The *Harmony Valley* version of the first intensive with modules wouldn't take place until they were emotionally and mentally stabilized.

On the other end of what was turning into the busiest winter yet, the millennial staffers were working hard, filling in the gaps, coming up with great ideas, and compiling Skype interview lists for their out-of-work compatriots, who were answering the call posted on the website. They wouldn't be able to join community until the apartments were finished, but the way construction was going, it wouldn't be long. Kim's homeless project apprentice group was expected in their compound by March 1st. It would be ready well ahead of that time, cleared out of temporary residents. Of course, they'd need the hostel for incoming WWOOFers in April, so Tommy split the crews with the new resident tradesmen fitting in nicely, hired on more locals, and started on the three-story apartment complex, which would fill the second block NW on the N-S street of the walking mall. There would be businesses, storage and bike space, on street level and one and two-bedroom apartments above for as many as 50 people.

The second neighborhood (behind the *Harmony Valley* SW block in relationship to the town center fountain and town center businesses) was currently being excavated for foundations and infrastructure. It would be ready for the building crews in April. The two neighborhoods were needed to house those already brought in and those waiting and on file. That occupancy would signal the initiation of Phase IV Outreach spanning a year or so of time, to staff light industry, more small businesses and services in town center, and round out the community with the last two neighborhoods.

Tommy had designed each of four neighborhoods to circle their tree-lined, green grass commons in four curved complexes of three homes each. The Mission-style homes had a similar floor plan to a *New Avalon* two-bedroom home with a common laundry on one end of each complex. There were front porches and paths on the commons and a service path in back of the homes with linking paths between the service path and commons circle. Every house had an attached shed on the outer ring for bikes and outdoor gear. In the first neighborhood, there was a community garden and common tool shed on the NW corner of the block with picnic space, playground and barbeques. The back paths of the first neighborhood also serviced the N-W town center businesses that corner-framed the neighborhood, including the hotel and the rear of the up and coming apartment building. A similar plan would unfold in each neighborhood. From the air, they looked like the old wagon train circles of protection from Americas' era of *Westward Ho!*

From her desk in the office she shared with Paula, Rachel was lining up Skype interviews for young people having interesting indebted educations, who'd answered the web post for millennials at *Harmony Valley*. Their training ranged from hair-styling and fashion design to business admin, finance, social services and retail management. Leah and Chris immediately imagined the High Country Sheepskin business getting a start with these creative young adults, providing another link to *Main Street USA*. That opened Leah's vision to imagine some living in *Harmony Valley* and working at the store in Sheldon for HAVs, or moving to Sheldon to work in that economy, opening *Harmony Valley* up for more homeless participants. Everyday, *Main Street USA* was making more sense to her, as a next step. She had a talk scheduled with the local farmers in March, and Will was looking into land prices and possible acquisitions.

Stu was getting it all on film and trying to decide when to call it a day with the filming for the homeless documentary. Leah suggested he wait until the millennials showed up in the spring, along with the farm stock, growing gardens, busy workers and a convincing finale, showing that the model *did* work. In the meantime, they kept the Outreach Homeless Community Model website fully charged with photos, interviews, inspiring updates and a very attractive donation button under which they'd posted a timely reminder — "What a great way to work off *karma*."

Kim's group would have a website up and running for the Baltimore project in March, followed shortly after by Sacramento and the good people of Portland, who were keen to sponsor their own community for the homeless now. Stu would rig up the website links in a pyramid diagram and just keep filling them in as the second tier paid it forward to nine more communities. The same thing was happening with the Inner City Project Model webpage, which had links to upcoming second tier projects in LA, Seattle, and Oakland. Ali Cat was out there with his message and already had a third tier for LA from Phoenix, San Diego and Denver. Maybe expansive 2012 would also be the year of the apprentice — *gifting it forward*.

"Thank God, Paula is paying attention to the news," Leah remarked to Chris as they shared a hasty dinner on the evening of the 25th of February. Natalie had returned from a weekend in DC on Tuesday afternoon to help pull the show together. She'd stayed with Chuck and facilitated the first workshop with Kim's group for their community project in the Virginia foothills. *Light on the Crisis* had just put on a stunning show having the theme of 'redemption', which would end up earning them journalistic awards — that after a compelling quartet of shows on the individual megatrends. To ice the cake, the program director at *Freedomofspeech.org* had called on Wednesday, after Leah's Skype session with Joel, to offer them a daily show back to back with *Joel Robertson Live* to be transmitted at three o'clock Pacific Time beginning on April second. The tandem shows would be repeated three hours later to service prime time on the west coast with *Light on the Crisis* at six o'clock. The millennials took care of the champagne to celebrate a victory over all odds.

"Pretty big week, lass. How do you feel?" Chris asked, plunging his fork into a good looking, fresher–than–fresh salad. His eyes were filled with mirth and that crocked grin of his began stealing across his face.

"I feel like I'm standing on the abyss that Steiner writes about, in his books about the initiates' path. All of life is noisily coming to fruition behind me, and before me there's the dark, silent sea of creative potential," she said, wistfully. "And, there's the opportunity to plunge into it."

"I can think of no place that suits you better, lass."

"It's enticing. I will say that. Of course, I wonder what Eric is up to, how Zacker and Trynel are getting on, what our medical model will look like, and imagine the magic of having the kids across the commons soon. Oh, and the public reaction to *Main Street USA*. Well, all that and much more, to be honest. What's on your mind, cowboy?"

"Aye, I wonder how were going to manage all the soccer matches," he said, perfectly deadpan. "Nick needs to catch up on his patients and pay attention to what's looming on the horizon."

"R-r-right."

appendices

Appendix A
Harmony Valley

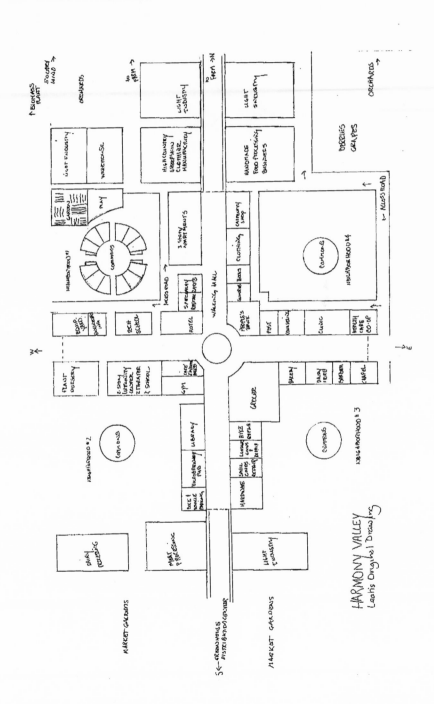

HARMONY VALLEY
Leah's Draughal Drawing

Appendix B
Social Threefolding Chart

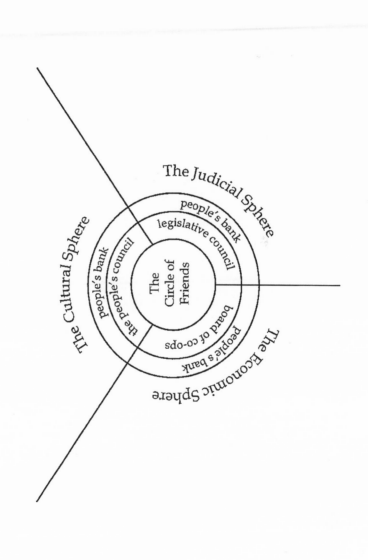

The Cultural Sphere

The Judicial Sphere

The Economic Sphere

people's bank

the people's council

legislative council

people's bank

The
Circle of
Friends

board of co-ops

people's bank

21498881R00267

Made in the USA
Charleston, SC
20 August 2013